ECCENTRIC
NEIGHBORHOODS

ECCENTRIC NEIGHBORHOODS

ROSARIO FERRÉ

FARRAR • STRAUS • GIROUX

NEW YORK

Farrar, Straus and Giroux
19 Union Square West, New York 10003

Copyright © 1998 by Rosario Ferré
Distributed in Canada by Douglas & McIntyre Ltd.
Printed in the United States of America
Designed by Jonathan D. Lippincott
First edition, 1998

Library of Congress Cataloging-in-Publication Data
Ferré, Rosario.
    Eccentric neighborhoods / Rosario Ferré. — 1st ed.
    p.   cm.
    ISBN 0-374-14638-1 (cloth : alk. paper)
    I. Title.
PS3556.E7256E27   1998
813'.54—dc21   97-26689

Grateful acknowledgment is made for permission to reprint chapter-opening photographs from the following sources:
For chapters 1, 4, 6, 8, 23, 25, 29, from *Our Islands and Their Peoples, as Seen with Camera and Pencil*, edited by William S. Bryan (N. D. Publishing Company, 1898). For frontispiece and chapters 3, 10, 11, 12, 13, 18, 19, 31, 32, 40, 41, 48, 54, 55, from *Puerto Rico Mío*, by Jack Delano (Smithsonian Press, 1990). Photos courtesy of Pablo Delano. For chapters 5, 14, 15, 28, 38, 39, 51, 52, 58, courtesy of the Library of Congress. For chapters 16, 33, 50, photos by Rodriguez Serra, courtesy of the Library of Congress. For chapters 17, 45, 53, 57, photos by Jack Delano, courtesy of the Library of Congress. For chapters 20, 21, 35, 36, 49, photos by Edwin Rosskam, courtesy of the Library of Congress. For chapters 9, 27, 30, 34, 37, 56, courtesy Corbis/ Bettmann. For chapter 42, from *Puerto Rico 1900: Turn of the Century Architecture in the Hispanic Caribbean, 1890–1930*, by Jorge Rigau (Rizzoli, 1992). Photo courtesy of Jorge Rigau. For chapter 43, from *El Album de Oro de Puerto Rico*, 1939. For chapter 46, from *The Venice I Love*, photo by Jean Imbert (Tudor Publishing Company, 1957). For chapter 47, photo by Valeria Shaff.

To the ghosts who lent me their voices

My heartfelt thanks to my agent, Susan Bergholz; my editor, John Glusman; and my husband, Agustín Costa, whose faithful support and understanding made this book possible.

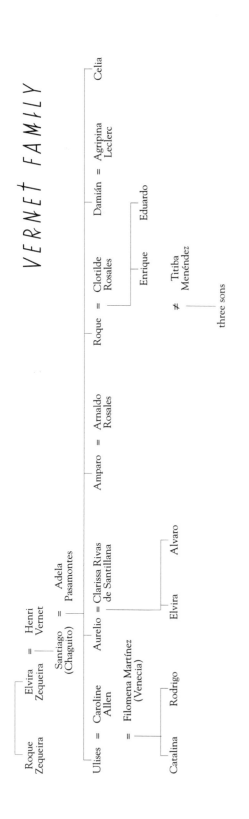

VERNET FAMILY

Roque Zequeira

Elvira Zequeira = Henri Vernet

Santiago (Chaguito) = Adela Pasamontes

Ulises = Caroline Allen
= Filomena Martínez (Venecia)

Catalina   Rodrigo

Aurelio = Clarissa Rivas de Santillana

Elvira   Alvaro

Amparo = Arnaldo Rosales

Roque = Clotilde Rosales

Enrique   Eduardo

≠ Titiba Menéndez

three sons

Damián = Agripina Leclerc

Celia

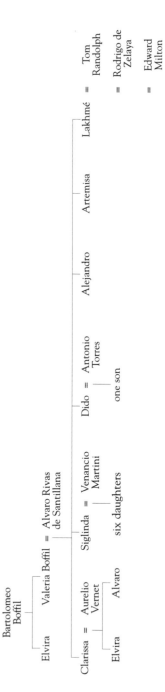

RIVAS DE SANTILLANA FAMILY

Bartolomeo Boffil

Valeria Boffil = Alvaro Rivas de Santillana

Elvira

Clarissa = Aurelio Vernet

Elvira   Alvaro

Siglinda = Venancio Martini

six daughters

Dido = Antonio Torres

one son

Alejandro   Artemisa

Lakhmé = Tom Randolph
= Rodrigo de Zelaya
= Edward Milton

PART I

EMAJAGUAS'S LOST PARADISE

Geographies can be symbolic; physical spaces determine the archetype and become forms that emit symbols.

—OCTAVIO PAZ, *Postdata*

ONE

FORDING RÍO LOCO

Río Loco got its name because it was so temperamental. When it rained in the valley and the other rivers stampeded toward the sea like runaway horses, Río Loco was dry. But when the sun was nailed to the sky like a hot coal, charring the cane fields and forcing the scorpions out of their burrows to look for water, it reared up like a muddy demon and tumbled this way and that over the dusty plain, enraged at everything that stood in its way. The river's source was far away in the mountains, and when it rained the floods rose, even when there was fair weather in the valley.

Río Loco always reminded me of my mother, Clarissa. We would be sitting peacefully in the pantry having breakfast—Aurelio, my father, would be reading the paper, Alvaro and I would be reviewing our homework before leaving for school—when Clarissa would suddenly rise and run to her room. Aurelio would follow hurriedly behind her. As I left for school in the family's Pontiac, I could hear Clarissa's sobs behind closed doors, mingled with the apologetic murmur of Father's voice.

She never explained to me why she cried, and if I insisted on asking, I risked putting myself at the mercy of one of her sharp pinches or an angry yank at a tuft of my hair. It was as if it were raining in her mind, when all around her the sun was shining.

Once a month Clarissa and my aunts journeyed to Emajaguas from different parts of the island to visit Abuela Valeria. I used to accompany Mother on these trips. Family was very important then.

I always knew when we were driving to Emajaguas because Cristóbal Bocanegra, our black chauffeur, would start whistling softly as soon as he was told of the trip. Cristóbal had a good-looking girlfriend in Guayamés, and when we traveled there he always spent the night with her, happy to get away from his wife.

Crossing Río Loco was one of the high points of our journey to Emajaguas. The old winding road from La Concordia to Guayamés had been built by the Spaniards, and although the towns were really not that far apart—twenty miles at most—the journey took two and a half hours, much longer than it should have. Father always joked about it with Mother and said the Spaniards had used the "burro method" when they built the road: they took a burro from La Concordia to Guayamés, let it loose, and followed it as it ran home down the shortest path.

Río Loco remained without a bridge through the 1940s; it was the last important river on the island to be spanned by one. The government was too impoverished to build one until the 1950s, when a human wave rose from the island and thousands of immigrants crashed into New York. They were desperately poor, and in the Bronx and in Harlem they'd still be poor, but a little less so. The bridge was good for the local economy, and soon the government began to invest in public works.

Río Loco was shallow, and most of the time we could drive across its dry gully without any problem, skirting the huge boulders that lay on the bottom like dinosaur eggs and the massive tree trunks left by intermittent floods. Come September, however, Río Loco was often flooded, and its waters pulled along everything that clung to its banks. Most of the poor peasants who worked the *central* Eureka cane fields lived in barracks; they cooked outside on coal stoves and shat in the latrines the owners had built for them. The company store was nearby, and there they could buy food on credit when they ran out of money and obtain medical supplies and services. But workers living in the barracks were closely supervised by the overseer, who would keep a tally on their debts. For this reason, some preferred the dangerous freedom of the riverbank, where they built their own shacks, to the convenience of living at the *central*. Riverbanks, like beaches, are all public property on the island.

The earth was black and fertile along the banks, and the peasants grew splendid plantains, manioc roots, and cane stalks there. But when the river flooded, it reclaimed with a vengeance the terrain it had temporarily ceded to the squatters. You could see doors, corrugated tin roofs, rocking chairs, tables, cooking pots, mattresses, all floating slowly toward the sea, as well as dogs, pigs, goats, and even cows, already swollen, pulled along, legs up, by the brown, toffee-like mass of water.

I loved crossing Río Loco when it was flooded, and as the family car set out for Emajaguas I always prayed for a *crecida*, never thinking about the havoc the river created for the peasants. It broke the monotony of the trip, the silence that inevitably sat like a block of ice between Mother and me. As we neared the river, my heart would begin to pound faster and faster. We never knew whether the current would be high or not, and if the river couldn't be crossed, we would inevitably have to turn back toward La Concordia, with Mother in tears.

As soon as we neared Río Loco's banks, Mother would instruct Cristóbal to drive the blue-and-white Pontiac to the river's edge, and I would stick my head out the window to see what was going on. If the current was high, Mother would order him to pull up close to the water and we would wait in silence under a mango tree to see if it would recede. Mother could never wait very long, however. Without a quiver of fear in her voice, she would command Cristóbal to drive the Pontiac into the murky current. The car would soon be bobbing and half floating over the riverbed, maneuvering its way across the now-invisible boulders. By the middle of the river, Cristóbal would hardly be touching the accelerator; with the dangerous current flowing by on each side, we would be stranded, unable to get out.

This is precisely what happened one day. Cristóbal was following in the wake of some hardy soul who had plunged his car into the murky water ahead of us, when all of a sudden the Pontiac had an attack of delirium tremens and died midstream. Clarissa ordered us to roll up our windows, and for twenty minutes the three of us sat there in silence watching the brown water rise inch by inch until it was licking the windows, carrying with it the debris from upstream. The car was full of good things to eat that our cook at La Concordia had prepared—a leg of lamb, a roast turkey, a cauldron of *arroz con gandules*—and soon the delicious odors were all but stifling. A basket of oranges, pineapples, and breadfruit picked that morning from the garden lay on the seat between Mother and me. It was like sitting inside a watertight paradise dressed in our Sunday best—Clarissa in a printed silk georgette gown and high-heeled Saks Fifth Avenue shoes and me in my white organdy dress with a satin bow on my head—watching all hell break loose around us.

Clarissa looked at her diamond Cartier wristwatch on its black grosgrain band and saw that it was already half past eleven. If we didn't hurry, we would be late for lunch at Emajaguas and wouldn't be able to sit down at the table with Abuela Valeria and my aunts. Mother ordered Cristóbal to start the engine. He turned the ignition key; the car gave a couple of lurches and died on us again. Clarissa then commanded him to honk the horn. Soon four barefoot peasants dressed in faded khakis and scraggly straw hats, who had been standing on the shore with their oxen watching our predicament, waded silently into the river.

With rushing water up to their waists, they approached the car, yoked animals in tow. Clarissa opened her handbag, took out a dollar, and waved it at them from inside the window. The peasants tied the beasts to the Pontiac's front bumper with a thick hemp rope, and slowly the car began to move forward. The smell of mud grew stronger, and I stared in horror as a thin line of water began to seep in through the bottom of the door. Clarissa signaled emphatically to the men to poke the oxen more sharply with their long poles. Once on shore, she slipped the dollar bill to the peasants through a crack at the top of the window and ordered Cristóbal to start the car. The Pontiac jumped forward, its shiny blue-and-white surface dripping with mud, and took off at full speed, an anxious Pegasus flying down the road toward Emajaguas.

TWO

BÓFFIL AND RIVAS DE SANTILLANA

Mother was born in Guayamés on January 6, 1901. Her father, Alvaro Rivas de Santillana, believed she was a present from the Three Kings, but Valeria Boffil, my grandmother, didn't agree at all. She was sure Clarissa was born because of the rains.

In Guayamés it rains a lot from July to November; gray clouds are always rubbing their bellies against the roofs of houses, shutting out the sun. The rains influenced Mother's life from the start. During the rainy season people stay inside much of the time. Anything can happen then: a sudden gust of wind may bring a tree branch down on your head like a punishment from God, or a wave of mud from the nearby Emajaguas River may roll down the street and whisk you away.

Every year, from July to November, Abuelo Alvaro moved into Guayamés with his family instead of staying in Emajaguas, where he could easily supervise his cane fields and his sugar mill, the *central*

Plata. He was always bored in town, and for that reason Abuela Valeria usually got pregnant at the end of each July and gave birth at the end of each April. Mother was the first of their six children. As an infant she was bitten by a mosquito bred in a pool of stagnant rainwater; she developed rheumatic fever, which caused a *soplo*, a murmur, in her heart. So you could say that she was born because of the rains of Guayamés and also that she died because of them.

The house in Guayamés had a balcony that opened out over the main plaza, from which Clarissa watched the Lenten procession every year with her three sisters—Siglinda, Artemisa, Dido—and her only brother, Alejandro. Wearing white lace mantillas, the girls would lean their elbows on the rail to get a good view. Lakhmé, the baby, would peek between the balusters and admire the purple silk platform where Jesus carried the cross on his back and the black velvet one on which La Verónica, with her tear-streaked face, swayed to and fro over a sea of heads. But the Lenten procession didn't elicit any special feelings of piety; for the Rivas de Santillanas, religious excitement and pagan celebration were all part of the same play.

Around the middle of December, when the rains had stopped and the canes ripened in the fields, the family moved to Emajaguas, three miles down the coast. Abuelo Alvaro had been born there in 1880. Both his parents had died young, so he had been brought up by two maiden aunts, Alicia and Elisa Rivas de Santillana. When he was eighteen, his aunts had bought a house in town. With the arrival of the Americans on the island, the quality of life in Guayamés had improved greatly: streets were paved, there was running water, a sewage system and storm drains had been installed.

Abuelo Alvaro's aunts had always pampered him, and even though they were only moderately well-off, they spared no expense in his education. He was taught French by private tutors and could do his arithmetic competently enough. But he didn't like to read and was wary of people who read a lot, because they seemed to think they were above the rest.

Abuelo learned firsthand everything there was to know about the sugar industry by struggling to keep his cane fields well tended. His aunts trusted him and put everything in his hands; with their combined fortunes, Alvaro was able to keep Emajaguas in working order. But Alicia and Elisa died during the typhus epidemic that ravaged Guayamés in 1900. Alvaro and Valeria were married that same year

—she was sixteen and he was twenty—so when they moved to Emajaguas, they had the whole house to themselves. Although Abuelo
Alvaro was saddened by his aunts' demise, he had been so spoiled
that he thought it only natural that they should pass away. They were
merely being considerate of his need for housing in his newly married
state.

Abuelo remained a man of simple tastes; he was used to country
life and mistrusted city ways. After he married Abuela Valeria, the
only time he traveled to Europe was in 1920, and only because Valeria
dragged him there by the hair. In Paris he moped around the whole
time because at the Café Procope he couldn't order *ropa vieja*—his
beloved string beef stewed with onions—and *tostones*, the luscious
crumbly plantains fried in oil. Abuela Valeria, on the other hand,
loved to travel and took her children to Europe several times. She
would spend a month in Paris, a month in Rome, or a month in
Madrid, installing herself in the best hotels with her six children, a
nanny, and her personal maid. She would go to the opera almost
every night, as well as to concerts and museums, and would always
insist that a trip to a foreign country was as valuable as a college
degree.

Valeria was the youngest daughter of Bartolomeo Boffil, a Corsican
merchant nicknamed Mano Negra, who had made a fortune at the
end of the nineteenth century smuggling merchandise from Saint
Thomas and Curaçao. Both these islands belonged to the Dutch at
the time and had a long tradition of illegal trading. They were very
prosperous commercial centers. There one could buy perfumes, shoes,
fine linens and laces from France, and all sorts of farming tools. Machinery for the sugar haciendas was not manufactured on the island.
It was smuggled in from England and Scotland.

Bartolomeo Boffil was a rough man with no education, but he was
proud of his business and considered it in keeping with the rebellious
nature of his ancestors. The word *corsair* comes from *Corsican*, he
would tell his friends. "If we Corsicans hadn't managed to dodge the
embargo the Spanish authorities smacked on the island for three hundred years, these people would be so poor they wouldn't have shoes
to put on their feet." Commerce with the rest of the world was
banned by Spain, which wanted to benefit from it exclusively. The
island had no choice but to depend for all its imports on Spanish
ships coming in through San Juan.

Bartolomeo was born on Cap Corse, Corsica's most inhospitable peninsula—a veritable tongue of rock where only billy goats prospered. He was a small, evil-tempered man who lived alone with his daughters Elvira and Valeria. His wife had died giving birth to his youngest daughter, and for that reason he was often cruel to Valeria, as if wanting her to pay for her mother's untimely passing. He loved her dearly but couldn't help thinking that if she hadn't been born, his wife would still be alive and he wouldn't be alone.

Bartolomeo's farm was on the outskirts of Guayamés and he tended it himself. He grew ginger, tobacco, cotton, coconuts, and cacao, but his real profession was smuggling. His farm had several protected coves where fishing sloops came in from Saint Thomas and Curaçao and dropped anchor at night. A half dozen rowboats would silently skim over the waters and unload the crushing mills, iron winches, and centrifugal steel pumps for which the Puerto Rican sugar hacienda owners paid a handsome price.

Bartolomeo loved to go up into the mountains to hunt blackbirds with his dog, Botafogo. Blackbird pâté was his favorite dish; he was sure it had magical qualities and he made Valeria eat some every day. As in the story of the Chinese emperor who feeds his daughter nightingale tongues so that she will sing more sweetly, Bartolomeo was convinced that blackbird pâté would refine his daughter's voice, as well as make her more delicate and beautiful. Valeria felt terribly sorry for the birds, but she was an obedient daughter and dutifully ate what her father served her.

She was brought up practically a prisoner, never permitted to go out of the house by herself to visit the neighbors and always accompanied by a chaperon. At home she was taught the arts of embroidery and music by a governess; she could sing in French, English, and Italian and play the piano beautifully, but she couldn't read or write. Her father had forbidden the governess to teach her how, so when Valeria turned sixteen she was still illiterate. This way, Bartolomeo hoped, Valeria would have no alternative but to stay at home and take care of him in his old age.

Valeria sometimes went to Guayamés to visit her sister Antonia, who had married a man of means and lived in a beautiful house at the entrance to town. Bartolomeo had had no misgivings in letting Antonia leave; it meant one mouth less to feed. The youngest daughter was the one who was supposed to stay home and take care of the widowed father.

Abuelo Alvaro met Abuela Valeria during one of her visits to her sister. When he heard her sing and play the piano, Alvaro immediately fell in love and asked her to marry him. But she refused. "I can't get married, because I can't read or write," she said tearfully. "What will you do when I sign the marriage license in front of the judge with an X? You'll be so ashamed of me you'll change your mind."

Alvaro answered, laughing, "That won't make any difference to me at all. If you can cook as well as you can sing, everything will turn out all right." And that very afternoon they eloped, asking a judge in Guayamés to marry them.

Bartolomeo found out the next day. Rumor has it he ran to his son-in-law's house and tried to batter down the door with the butt of his rifle. When Antonia and her husband refused to open it, he began to hurl insults at them, calling them scoundrels and panderers until he was so beside himself he suffered a heart attack and died. Clarissa didn't believe the story at all, and she found out what really happened. Bartolomeo was caught in a shoot-out with the American coastal patrol, which kept a stricter eye on his coconut groves than the Spanish Guardia Civil. When Bartolomeo died, Valeria came into a third of his fortune, and her inheritance made it possible for Alvaro to consolidate his economic situation.

The first thing Valeria did when she could afford it was to have the schoolmaster from Guayamés's public school come to her house and teach her to read and write. Soon she became a passionate reader. She practically devoured the best Latin American novels of her time, Jorge Isaac's *María*; Getrudis Gómez de Avellaneda's *Sab*; José Marmol's *Amalia*. Sometimes she read them out loud at dinnertime for the family's benefit. Alvaro, by contrast, didn't care for literature at all; novels bored him, and he preferred books that dealt with life as it really was. After their wedding, Valeria refused to make love if he didn't read at least one novel a week, and in this way she managed to educate him.

Guayamés is surrounded by lush green hills where the last of the Taíno Indians lived before they were wiped out by the Spaniards in the sixteenth century. Its houses spill into one another without order or logic, as if huddled together for protection. The streets are narrow and cleave to the uneven terrain like ribbons of red mud; many are named for the Taíno Indians: Calle Guajira, Calle Urayoán, Calle Guaquiminí. On top of a nearby hill, overlooking the town like a huge white fowl spreading its wings, sits the cathedral, one of the oldest buildings in Guayamés.

The climate is unusually humid and rain falls in pellets that melt before they reach the ground. The frequent rains, as well as the tranquil atmosphere, bring out the vivid colors of the landscape: the limpid blue of the sky, the soft moss-green of the hills, the hard beveled green of the sugarcane fields. Perhaps for this reason a romantic imagination, an acute aesthetic sensibility, and a deep love of nature are common among the inhabitants of Guayamés.

During the rainy season, the town was relatively safe from the storms that uprooted trees and left the hills strewn with gabled tin roofs that had whirled away from outlying houses like saws in the wind. December meant the family's return to Emajaguas for the *zafra*—the Plata's sugarcane harvest—and over the next six months the rains were sparse and the breezes cool. April brought scattered showers (*"Las lluvias de abril caben en un barril,"* as Abuelo Alvaro used to say), May brought thunderstorms (*"Las lluvias de mayo se las bebe un caballo"*), and June, July, and August were dry as cane husks (*"Junio, julio, y agosto, marota seca para los cerdos"*).

The children began to arrive in quick succession, Clarissa in 1901, Siglinda in 1902, Artemisa in 1903, Alejandro in 1904, Dido in 1905, then Lakhmé in 1923, when Abuela Valeria was thirty-nine years old. Lakhmé was the baby of the family, and Abuela spoiled her because of it.

As the children were born and as Abuelo Alvaro prospered, he added several rooms to Emajaguas and modernized the kitchen and bathrooms. The children didn't go to public school, as they did in Guayamés; they took lessons with a tutor, a skinny, bald rural teacher who drove from town every day in his horse and buggy. This meant they could spend the afternoons horseback riding or swimming in the river; they didn't have to wear uniforms or even shoes. I suppose that's why, when Mother talked to me about her childhood at Emajaguas, it was as if she remembered a lost paradise, a timeless place where days and nights chased each other merrily around on the tin sphere of the grandfather clock that stood against the dining room wall.

Emajaguas was built on stilts, and the living quarters were entirely on the second level. The first level was used as Abuelo Alvaro's office and also served as a garage. Fresh straw rugs gave it a grassy country smell. All the windows were louvered and painted turquoise-blue, so that when one looked out, the waters of the Guayamés bay seemed to flow into the rooms. A wide granite stairway led from the front of the house to the palm-lined driveway, which descended to the main road bordering the seashore. At the back, a narrow balustered stairway painted white led from the kitchen to the garden and the fruit orchards.

A steep wall circled the ten-acre property, which included mango, soursop, and grapefruit trees, a tennis court, and a pond with goldfish. A half dozen geese patrolled the garden like a row of noisy midget soldiers. There was a well-stocked library (the pride of Abuela Valeria), a grand piano in the living room, a record player, and all kinds of table games for rainy days. There were so many things to do at Emajaguas that one rarely went into town. It was only a fifteen-minute walk to Guayamés following the road by the sea, but hardly anyone ever took it.

The house had two natural boundaries that separated it from the outside world: the Emajaguas River on the right (more a creek than a river except when the heavy rain turned it into a dragon's tail of mud) and the public road. Four feet beyond the highway, the land fell away abruptly and the sea battered the rocks that had been placed there as a barrier. In spite of them, the waves ate away an inch or two of the highway's foundation each year.

When my brother, Alvaro, and I were children and we used to visit Emajaguas with our parents, our car had to draw up as close to the cliff as possible in order to turn into the driveway. I was always afraid we would fall into the water, and I'd shut my eyes in terror. At night I had nightmares that the sea was creeping closer and closer and that one night it would reach up to grab Emajaguas by the roof and drag us down to its depths.

There were four bedrooms and three bathrooms in the house. One bedroom had been Abuelo Alvaro and Abuela Valeria's and was connected to the bathroom by a narrow inner hallway that always smelled of Hamamelis water, an astringent made of witch hazel that Abuela Valeria dabbed on her face with cotton every night before going to bed. Everything was white in this bathroom, and it was so large that as a child I used to get the words *bathroom* and *ballroom* mixed up.

There was a cast-iron tub with griffin's feet, a shower with a halolike nozzle, and a cylinder with rings that sprayed at you from every direction when you stepped inside naked. The shower had American Standard star-shaped spigots of stainless steel. These must have been mixed up in the installation, being labeled (logically in Spanish, but incorrectly in English) C for hot water and H for cold. Abuela Valeria, who didn't speak English, assumed that C was for *caliente* (hot) and H for *helada* (freezing), because in the States cold water was always ice-cold. A squat square tub, a *baño de asiento*, sat in the corner. It was ideal for reading, and it was there that Abuelo Alvaro devoured from *María*, *Sab*, and *Amalia* the morsels Valeria fed him to whet his appetite every night before making love.

Tío Alejandro's bedroom was next door to my grandparents', in the right wing of the house. It was spacious and had a four-poster canopied bed, its own private bathroom, and a bay window that opened onto the garden.

The other two bedrooms were in the left wing of the house. There my aunts and my mother had slept long ago. These rooms shared a bathroom, a small, low-ceilinged cabinet that Abuelo had built under one of the gables. Later, when the grandchildren came to visit at Christmas, they slept in this wing of the house. Since the bathroom could hold only one person at a time, there was often a cramped line of little boys and girls in front of the door nervously crossing and uncrossing their legs.

Almost every room at Emajaguas had its own skylight. Skylights were a way of saving money: one didn't have to turn on a light except when it began to get dark. But they also gave the rooms a special atmosphere. There is a dreamlike quality to a room with a skylight; it eliminates the passing shadows of the world outside, the swish of headlights on the road, the streetlights coming on at dusk. A room with a skylight gives one a sense of security. Nothing bad can happen there; there's no reason to be afraid of what the future might bring.

The skylights of Emajaguas were always located in strategic places: over the dining room table, for example, or above the bathtub, where sunlight fell directly on the naked body. At the Sacred Heart in La Concordia the nuns taught us that looking at yourself in the mirror without clothes on was a cardinal sin. Girls were supposed to be ignorant of their bodies—the little bushes of hair beginning to sprout in unexpected nooks, the bulbs pushing out in flat places, and all kinds of fluids beginning to run—and modesty was an important part of being a decent person. Thanks to Emajaguas I always laughed at all that. I loved to stand in the bathtub under the skylight without a stitch on. By the time I turned twelve I knew my body's secret places by heart: a nest of downy fleece growing here, a delicate pink halo appearing there. I grew up liking the way the creamy curve of my breast melted into my belly and, when I bent my elbow, how the hidden part of my underarm resembled a freshly baked loaf of bread. At Emajaguas I could caress and touch myself at will. Exposed to the light of day, my body was innocent and had a life of its own; shame and sin meant nothing to me.

I was thirteen when I discovered the answer to the age-old enigma of how we arrive in this world. One morning at recess one of my girlfriends, María Concepción, came over excitedly to where I was sitting with a group of other students. She said she wanted to tell us a secret, so we rallied around her in the school yard, as far as possible from the *vigilanta*, the lookout sister. "I found out where babies really come from!" María Concepción said. "They don't come from Paris on the wings of Jesusito at all, like the nuns say!" Then she proceeded to describe the biological process of copulation and birth, leaving out none of the details. A naked man and a naked woman in bed, kissing and caressing, the man putting his penis into the woman's third hole. (Was there a third hole? I wasn't aware there was one until then. "It's between the ass hole and the piss hole, you nitwit!" María Concepción whispered, pinching my arm.) And that was the hole the baby came out of nine months later. I was shocked.

It was Friday and that afternoon we left for Emajaguas, where we would spend the weekend. As soon as we arrived, I went to Mother's room to ask if what María Concepción had said was true. Mother was taking a shower, and I knocked on the bathroom door. She didn't turn off the water but over the shower's din asked me what I wanted. I opened the door a crack and poked my head in. I could see Mother's shadow: she was standing naked behind the shower curtain—the skylight a rectangle of light above her head—and steam was coming out from the top.

"Mother, is it true that babies are born only after a man puts his penis inside a woman and pisses on her, and nine months later the baby comes out a third hole that only women have?" I shouted. A silence followed, during which the shower's din became a roar. "Yes, it's true," Mother answered. "And please close the bathroom door, because I'm getting a draft."

A few months later I got my first period, and I went back to Mother's room. I showed her my panties and she didn't say a word. She went to the closet and took out a box of Kotex and a little pink elastic belt. "Here, put one of these on. And don't change it unless you have to, so you make the box last." That was the last time she ever talked to me about sex or babies.

There was only one room in Emajaguas that didn't have a skylight: the toilet. One relieved oneself in total darkness, hidden from the eyes of the world as well as from one's own. Shitting and pissing had to be performed in secret, so as not to offend the aesthetic sensibilities that prevailed in the Rivas de Santillana family.

THREE

ThE SUGAR SULTAN

Abuelo Alvaro was tall and very good-looking. He reminded you of a Moorish sheikh, with his love for *paso fino* horses, his well-tended cane fields, and his house that resembled a harem with Abuela Valeria, Clarissa, and my four aunts all bustling about like partridges. The female sex also prevailed in the third generation: there were seven girls and only two boys among the Rivas de Santillana grandchildren.

Sugar planting was Abuelo Alvaro's passion. "Sugar," he would say, "was a gift from the Arabs, who brought the first cane stalks to Europe from faraway Malaysia. For a long time it was a luxury as rare as musk or pearls, but the Moors had a sweet tooth like you, and they became expert sugar planters. Once sugar spread to the south of Spain, the Moors took it with them to the Canary Islands, and from there Cristóbal Colón brought some stalks to America aboard one of his ships.

When he arrived on our island, the first thing he did was plant a stub of cane at the mouth of the Emajaguas River, just around the bend from our house. It's because Cristóbal Colón planted our first cane stalk that the sugar from the *central* Plata is the sweetest in the world." No one believed him when he said things like that, but they loved to hear his stories.

Abuelo Alvaro had other exciting tales. "Long ago," he'd say, "our island was a peak as high as the Aconcagua, a mountain in the Andes, part of a very rich country that sank to the bottom of the ocean during a formidable earthquake. We were the only speck of land left from that magnificent El Dorado, and for that reason the Spaniards named us Puerto Rico, 'rich port,' although our island is actually very poor."

Alejandro loved to hear about Miguel Enríquez, a black shoemaker turned pirate who almost became governor in the eighteenth century. The girls preferred José Almeida, the Portuguese corsair, who sheathed his galleon with copper plates inside and out to protect his beloved Alida Blanca from cannonball fire after she decided to join him at sea. When she died he buried her in a glass casket on the island of Caja de Muertos and would visit her there every year. The girls cried on hearing this, and Abuelo Alvaro gave them his huge linen handkerchief, smelling of orange blossoms, to dry their tears.

Abuelo Alvaro and Abuela Valeria had been reared in a subsistence economy. The arrival of the Americans on the island triggered an economic crisis. The new American banks didn't trust the local hacendados and denied them credit. The local planters had no money to replant the cane fields, and the banks refused to issue them loans. The only way they could raise money was by selling a part of their farms to finance their harvests, so that each year they had less land to plant and produced less sugar, until they finally had to close down their mills. This happened to many hacienda owners in the Guayamés valley.

Abuelo Alvaro was deeply nationalistic. He always thought of himself as Puerto Rican, in contrast to many of the island's other hacendados, who retained their Spanish, French, or British citizenship even after the Americans arrived. At the end of the nineteenth century, in the heyday of sugar production, many of the rich criollos had moved to Paris, Barcelona, or Madrid, where they lived a princely life. They usually left their mills in the hands of a nephew or a son, who would send the income on to Europe. This was never true, however, of Abuelo Alvaro, who reinvested every penny he had in the *central* Plata and owned five thousand acres of the most fertile land in the valley.

When the criollo hacendados began to sell their farms, Abuelo Alvaro wouldn't part with a single acre. Instead, he was always on the lookout for more land, either purchasing it from those neighbors who were in a tight situation or renting it from those who had already sold their mills. Another way of acquiring land was by marriage, and Abuelo Alvaro had hopes that one day Alejandro would marry the daughter of a rich hacienda owner from Guayamés. His daughters should marry into landowning families also, because those families would be his allies; but this wasn't as important as Alejandro's making a good marriage.

On one rule, however, Abuelo Alvaro was adamant: both Alejandro and his sisters had to "marry white." Marrying mixed blood was the one sure way of losing one's foothold on the already shaky social and economic ladder of Guayamés's plantation society. Even recent immigrants, therefore, were looked on more kindly than many of the local suitors who courted the hacendados' daughters. Modern urban life permitted a great deal of socializing between peoples of different backgrounds, and the inevitable liaisons that resulted were regarded by the hacendados as highly undesirable. "Peninsular, penniless, but white" was the proud motto many of them adopted when they described their daughters' fiancés. And these young men had one advantage over the pampered sons of the hacendados: they were used to hard work and willing to do whatever was necessary to get ahead. They were welcomed in the best social circles on the island and were soon whispering niceties in the ears of the hacendados' daughters.

Abuelo Alvaro managed to solve his cash problem when it was time to plant his new harvest by leasing small parcels of farmland to the U.S. naval base at La Guajira. But Abuela Valeria, like many of her landowning friends from Guayamés, never got over her terror of falling into bankruptcy. This was why she was so frugal. In her kitchen, for example, nothing was ever thrown out. The squeezed grapefruits were boiled with sugar and made into compote, the water from the boiled grapefruits was made into *refresco de toronja*, the beef bones were dropped into the bean stew, and the chickens were cooked whole, yellow claws sticking out nonchalantly from the elegant china soup tureen when the maid brought it to the table.

Abuelo Alvaro liked to drink wine with his meals, and at the back of the house there was a huge pyramid of empty bottles stacked in perfect order, neck-to-neck and back-to-back. Every single bottle that was drunk at Emajaguas found its way there: Liebfraumilch, Bolla, Saint Emilion, Riesling, Veuve Cliquot, Dom Pérignon. Some of the labels must have dated from at least twenty years before. Abuela Valeria simply couldn't bring herself to throw them out when she learned that Abuelo Alvaro had paid for one of them what one of his workers made in a month.

Abuelo Alvaro didn't believe in buying anything on credit. He looked down on people who owed the bank money and saw them as weak and unscrupulous. A man should be able to tighten his belt and do without for a month rather than take a loan from the bank. Each time Abuelo bought a new car he paid for it in cash and put the old one away instead of trading it in. The carriage house at Emajaguas looked like a transportation museum: there was a horse-drawn carriage with patent-leather mudguards, a two-wheeled chaise, a black Packard from the twenties with gray cartouche seats, a navy-blue Lincoln Continental from the fifties, and a silver-gray Cadillac from the sixties, Abuela Valeria's last car before she passed away.

Whenever Clarissa talked to me about Abuelo Alvaro, three things came to her mind: the small key with which he wound the grandfather clock in the dining room every morning, the gold wedding band he used to twirl on the dining room table, and an impressive switchblade knife with a mother-of-pearl handle he showed her once in the privacy of his wardrobe. The blade had something written on it—a mysterious series of numbers that read something like: R 4–24 L 6–32 R 3–22. She could never remember exactly what they were.

For a long time Mother wondered why Abuelo had shown the folding knife to her. The first time she was ten years old, and she thought he had wanted to amuse her. She had probably been pestering him, asking him questions about pirates and lost treasures. But once in a while he would take it out of his own accord, push the secret knob, and make the blade spring before her like a silver tongue. "When you grow up, I want you to have it," he told her when she was fifteen. "I always carry it with me when I ride out to oversee the farms, and if anyone attacks me, I'll slice his jugular vein in two." Clarissa had no idea what "jugular vein" meant, but she knew it must be something very serious. When she asked Abuelo, he said: "It's a vein in our necks and it goes straight to the heart. If it's cut, life floods out of you and cannot be stopped." Clarissa was horrified. It amazed her that her father should have enemies who wanted to kill him.

Clarissa knew the switchblade had a secret meaning for Abuelo Alvaro, but when she finally realized what it was, it was already too late to do anything about it.

FOUR

†HE PƗSS PÖ† ÖF †HE ƗSLAИD

Abuelo Alvaro was very conscious of his ancestors, and once Clarissa told me the story of what had happened the first time Father stayed for dinner at Emajaguas. Aurelio was courting Clarissa and had managed to make a good impression, until the moment Abuelo began to talk about family trees. He told Aurelio how he had traveled to Spain and visited an old Jew in Córdoba, whom he had paid a few hundred pesetas to trace the Rivas de Santillanas' ancestral line. The Jew was an expert at genealogy and had combed the cathedral records in Figueras, where Abuelo's family originated, for information. A few months later he mailed Alvaro a thick leather-bound folder with an intricate oak tree drawn in green, blue, and red ink from whose branches dozens of armored *caballeros* sprang. Abuelo got up from the table to look for it and proudly showed it to Aurelio.

"As you can see," Abuelo said, "the roots of our family tree date from the twelfth century, when King Alfonso the Wise married Doña Violante, one of the granddaughters of Don Rodrigo Díaz de Vivar, El Cid Campeador. Our branch is this one on the right, drawn in red ink. The Rivas de Santillanas had a castle in Figueras at the time. Do you know what town in France your family originated in, Mr. Vernet, before they emigrated to America? I require this information before I give my daughters away in marriage."

Aurelio sat there dumbfounded. He wasn't even aware family trees existed, but he promised to ask his mother and father about it when he got back to La Concordia. The next day, when Santiago Vernet, his father, heard what Abuelo Alvaro had said, he was incensed. "Henri Vernet, your grandfather," he told Aurelio, "was a Freemason, and when he died in Santiago, they buried him in the Chinese cemetery. This eliminated any possibility of family records because Masons are never inscribed in Catholic parishes. And in any case, who cares! Tell your pompous Mr. Rivas de Santillana that the Vernets don't give a damn where they came from, but they sure as hell know where they're going."

Fortunately, Father did not relay Abuelo Santiago's message to Abuelo Alvaro but instead laughed the whole thing off.

Emajaguas was almost totally self-sufficient: it had a vegetable garden, an orange and grapefruit orchard, a plantain patch, several milk cows, a chicken coop, ducks, pigs, and a fishpond. But these didn't make the house a farm, because, with the exception of the cows, the animals were simply waiting to be consumed and were never commercially reared. Family diversions included walks through the woods, sailing expeditions on the bay, and picnics almost every weekend at the beach, with an army of servants carrying practically the whole kitchen with them.

An ascetic sensibility was an important part of the family's ethos and very much in tune with its rural austerity. Even though dinners were carefully prepared, the serving dishes brought out from the kitchen were filled not to the brim but only halfway. One time Antonio Torres—Tía Dido's husband—newly emigrated from Spain, was so dismayed to see that the platter of chicken with rice was almost empty by the time it reached him that he didn't dare serve himself.

When Abuela Valeria chided him for his shyness he turned bright red, certain she was making fun of him. Antonio was convinced that our family was just stingy and that niggardliness had nothing to do with an "ascetic way of life," as Valeria liked to put it. For Spaniards like Antonio, the most convincing proof of one's success in the world was to sit down to a well-stocked table steaming with pork sausages, spicy stews, and all kinds of fish and fowl to satisfy a healthy appetite.

At Emajaguas the smell and appearance of "viands" was much more important than the amount of food served at the table. Lobster claws were split open in the kitchen so guests wouldn't have to go through the barbaric process of cracking them, and the meat was artistically arranged on a platter. *Pasteles*, Caribbean tamales of mashed green plantains and spiced ground pork, were always served open, since it was considered vulgar to unwrap the greasy leaves with one's fingers at the lace-covered table. Roast pig, baked snapper, and stewed chicken all came to the table decorated with laurel leaves strongly enough perfumed to "revive a corpse," as Abuelo used to say. Wine was served—*rationed* would be a better word—in small red glasses with golden halos around the rims, in quantities that made one jovial but never drunk, and at Christmas, eggnog was poured in such moderate amounts that what I remember most vividly about it is not its taste or its potency but the tickling sensation of nutmeg on my nose.

The family was equally frugal when it came to rainwater. Abuelo Alvaro had a tank built on the roof of the house because the municipal plumbing system on the outskirts of town was not always reliable. In Guayamés it rains punctually at three o'clock every afternoon. "Guayamés is the piss pot of our island," Abuelo Alvaro would say smugly as the family sat down to dinner, "and rain is God's urine. He waters our cane fields every day free of charge."

But rain was also cosmetic at Emajaguas, as Abuela Valeria insisted that it made one's hair shinier and silkier than any cream rinse could. She practiced what she preached, and every September, when the heaviest rains fell, she would make all her daughters and granddaughters troop down to the garden in their underwear and bathe half-naked in the icy jet that poured from the gutter spout at a corner of the house.

I loved the idea of bathing in the rain, but when I was in third grade something very frightening happened. One of my classmates at the Sacred Heart in La Concordia was hit by lightning, and after that

I was terrified of thunderstorms. My friend had been riding a bicycle in the street and as she went near a telephone pole a sudden bolt struck her down. The nuns sent the whole class to the wake, and for weeks afterwards I couldn't sleep. I kept seeing Monsita's chalk-white face in the satin-lined coffin, with purple rings around her eyes, her jaws clamped shut.

A few days after the funeral Clarissa took me to Emajaguas. A rainstorm was brewing, and as soon as it started to pour, Clarissa told me to go to my bedroom and take off my good clothes because we were all going down to the garden together. White light was flashing intermittently at the window, and instead, I hid under my bed.

Clarissa hadn't heard the story of my dead classmate and had no inkling of my horror of thunder. Angry at my rebellious attitude, she got a broom from the kitchen and began to poke under the furniture. But she couldn't find me anywhere.

"Get Elvirita and bring her here immediately," she ordered Miña, the maid.

"I don't know where she is, Doña Clari. She's nowhere in the house. Maybe she went out with her father before it began to rain."

Clarissa went on poking under beds and bureaus, and I soon realized there was no escape. Slowly I stuck a leg out from under the bed skirt and Clarissa pulled me out by the ankle. I began to cry and to blow my nose, pretending I was coming down with a cold. But Clarissa wouldn't relent: I had to learn to obey. And then Mother did something terrible. She ordered Urbano and Confesor, Valeria's chauffeur and gardener, to grab me by the arms and carry me downstairs kicking and yelling. Since I wouldn't let Miña undress me, Clarissa ordered that I be pushed, fully clothed—shoes, socks, cotton smock, and all —under the icy stream that gushed from the pipe. For a few seconds I gasped, sure I was going to drown. And then, when lightning bolts began to crackle in the palm grove nearby, I fainted at Clarissa's feet.

FIVE

CHRISTMAS EVE AT EMAJAGUAS

Christmas dinner was always a big occasion at Emajaguas. The cars arrived at the house in the early afternoon full of good things to eat: roast leg of pork enveloped in crispy golden skin, turkey stuffed with chestnuts, ripe plantains stewed in red wine seasoned with cinnamon, rice with coconut milk, pineapple custard, nougat and almond pastes, all cooked especially for the occasion. We arrived dizzy from the winding roads that crisscrossed the island, our mouths watering from the delicious odors.

I remember one Christmas Eve especially. It was in 1945 and Abuela Valeria had asked Mother to bring the dessert. Clarissa had cooked an angel-cloud meringue with caramel glaze on top and a pool of heavy cream swirling at the bottom. Before we left La Concordia Clarissa had placed it on her best Limoges platter, wrapped it carefully in cellophane, and wedged it on the floor in the back of our blue-

and-white Pontiac, where it would be safe and the cream wouldn't spill and ruin the upholstery. Alvaro and I were to keep an eye on it from the backseat while Mother and Father rode in front.

As usual, I couldn't keep still thinking about getting together with my cousins, whom I hadn't seen for months. During the two-and-a-half-hour ride from La Concordia I leaned out the open window and watched the towns fly by—Saramá, Valverde, Vega Llana—each with its white-domed bell tower pealing in the distance, the plazas dotted here and there with mushroom-shaped laurel trees decorated with yellow, red, and blue lights. There were many people on the road that day, as everyone was traveling somewhere to visit relatives, dressed in their Sunday best. Many women wore yellow, which was supposed to bring good luck at Christmas. Little boys were dressed as shepherds, with red satin sashes around their waists and canes in their hands, and little girls as shepherdesses, with red-and-black-striped skirts, or as angels with marabou wings and blue satin smocks tied with silver cords. Each town had its own Christmas pageant that evening, and people walked for miles to reach it.

By the time we arrived at Emajaguas, I was so excited I completely forgot about the dessert. The minute Aurelio parked the car in the driveway, I opened the door and jumped out, stepping squarely on Clarissa's angel-cloud meringue as I went.

"What did you bake for Christmas dinner, Artemisa?"

"I brought a stuffed turkey basted in sherry sauce," Artemisa answered.

"And I brought a ham glazed with cloves, cherries, and pineapples," Dido added.

"And what did you bring, Clarissa?" Artemisa asked my mother.

"Angel-cloud meringue, with Elvira's footprint on it!"

Alvaro was eight and I was seven and we both believed in Santa Claus, but several of our cousins believed in the Three Kings. Our parents were fervent statehooders, so they gave Santa Claus more importance. Tía Dido had Independentista sympathies, and her son believed in the Three Kings. He always got his presents on the sixth of January, which was sad because school started on the seventh, and it left him only a short time to play with his new toys. So when Alvaro and I opened our presents on Christmas morning, Tía Dido's son always stared at us with melancholy eyes.

Most of the nuns at the Sacred Heart were Independentista sympathizers, and they'd recently begun a campaign to undermine Santa Claus's credibility. The Three Kings existed, the nuns told the students, because little Jesus, to whom the kings had brought their presents, as well as the Virgin Mary and Saint Joseph, also existed; they were all in the Bible and were holy. Santa Claus was just a gimmick that Sears, Roebuck and Woolworth's had thought up.

To keep the nuns happy, I wrote a letter that year addressed to both Santa Claus and the Three Kings and gave it to Clarissa to mail. Mother had addressed it, diplomatically, "To the Heavenly Couriers." But what happened a few days later precipitated a religious crisis for me.

The letter was in both Spanish and English. I asked Santa and the Three Kings for a "fairy godmother costume"—*un traje de hada madrina*—I had seen advertised in the Macy's toy catalog: a tutu with pink feather wings, a glittering star as a headdress, and a plastic magic wand. Clarissa had taken the catalog to Monserrate Cobián, our seamstress in La Concordia, and "La Monserrate" had faithfully copied the costume in my size. Aurelio had ordered the magic wand from Macy's and it had arrived just in time.

That evening, after Christmas dinner, we were all put to bed by our nannies. I placed two shoe boxes full of freshly cut grass under my bed, one for the Three Kings' camels and the other for Santa's reindeer. After Father and Mother came in to kiss me good night, I stared into the dark for a while, listening to the noises of the house die down—the clatter of dishes in the kitchen, the tapping of high heels across the living room floor, Abuela Valeria's rocking chair softly nudging at the darkness in her room.

My aunts and uncles all began to leave for Midnight Mass, and Mother went with them. I heard the cars start up and the doors slam. Then I watched the headlights swish silently over the bedroom walls. The rest of the children in the room were asleep, but I still hung on to consciousness. The grandfather clock slowed, as if the house itself were synchronizing its heartbeats to mine. Finally, sleep enveloped me like a soft blanket.

All of a sudden I sat up in bed. A light breeze drifted in through the window, and the mosquito netting began to billow in formless shadows around me. I heard the door close softly, and I was sure Santa had just left the room. I got out from under the covers and quietly climbed out of bed. Sure enough, a huge pink box sat under the bed.

I opened it, took out the fairy godmother costume, and put it on. Then I turned on the lights and began to jump up and down, waking all my cousins to show them what Santa had brought me.

A few minutes later Aurelio, who hadn't gone to Midnight Mass but had stayed behind to "do the presents," came running into the room. Extremely annoyed, he ordered everyone back to bed again. I began to protest, but he told me to be quiet. "Take off that dress! Santa Claus hasn't come yet!" he shouted. I took off my tutu, pulled my pajamas back on, and Aurelio put everything back in the box and stomped out of the room with it.

I lay in the dark, tears streaming down my cheeks. And that was the last time I ever believed in Santa Claus, the Three Kings, little Jesus, Mary, or Joseph.

SIX

THE ZEUS OF EMAJAGUAS

Emajaguas was a place where one could find peace simply by admiring the geometric perfection of a red poinsettia or by glorying in the bougainvillea vines that hung from the palm trees like purple mantles. At Emajaguas, nature gave you back the guilelessness of innocence in spite of the fact that a sugarcane worker's life expectancy was forty years, that his salary was less than a hundred and fifty dollars a year, and that during the *tiempo muerto*—between harvests —he often starved to death. The human misery that raged outside Emajaguas's ten-foot wall had no relevance within. Justice and beauty were never at odds with each other there.

The house had a large veranda where the family used to sit in the afternoon before the sun went down and a cloud of gnats descended on us, making us feel like pincushions. The veranda faced seaward, and the floor was made of colorful *losa nativa*, a locally made glazed cement tile decorated with arabesques of fruits and flowers. It was like a magic carpet on which one could fly away to Europe or to the United States. Planters full of ferns encircled the veranda, the curly green leaves melting into the blue of the sea as if the house itself were about to set forth on a voyage. At night the house's lighted windows glimmered on the water like those of a ship, and the murmur of the waves drifted in and out of the rooms like the very essence of sleep.

The dining room was the most important room at Emajaguas. As you entered the house you walked down a corridor that opened directly onto it, as if it were a stage where the family's dramas were enacted. The table was Spanish-colonial style and seated fourteen people. The ceiling was higher than those in the rest of the house. It rose like a magnificent hat, with pastel-tinted windowpanes all around. As you ate, you could count the clouds as they slid by.

Clarissa, Siglinda, Dido, Artemisa, and Lakhmé all resembled one another. They had the same swan's neck, milk-white skin, and delicate nose, and for that reason Abuelo Alvaro was known in Guayamés as the Zeus of Emajaguas, father of the five Ledas of Mount Olympus. The swans had their humorous counterpart in the five geese who noisily patrolled the grounds, running after unwary visitors—orange beaks wide open and red gullets bared—ready to swallow them whole. In Guayamés, the geese were said to resemble my aunts running after their suitors.

On the right wall of the dining room were the wedding portraits: the sisters in their bridal finery, standing next to their tuxedoed husbands. Each photograph was a kind of trophy, the result of years of effort directed toward achieving that respectability and peace of mind which only marriage vows conferred. It permitted each of my aunts to be photographed next to her hard-won prize, the young man she had brought into the family's bosom.

The left wall was also covered with pictures: a seedbed of grandchildren of all ages and sizes, the progeny of the unions displayed on the other side. There were Tía Siglinda's six daughters; Tía Dido's son; Alvaro, and me at different stages of our lives. The pictures overflowed the wall and hung helter-skelter over the doorways. Caught in the midst of graduations, First Communions, picnics, horse shows, and senior proms, we smiled at the camera without a care in the world, vying with one another for attention.

Several of Valeria's granddaughters had inherited the Rivas de Santillana looks and these girls she always treated with a shade of distinction. Beauty would undoubtedly help them succeed in the world, enabling them to get away with gaffes and blunders unforgivable in the less fortunate. Those born like me with a pug nose and a thick neck would have to learn to be a lot smarter if they wanted to get ahead.

Grandchildren under twelve were not allowed to sit at the dining room table during Christmas dinner. We were exiled to the pantry, where we could eat drumsticks with our hands, lick the custard bowl clean, and stick our little fingers in the coquilles Saint Jacques. Once we were old enough to join the grown-ups at the table, discipline was strict: we were not permitted to wipe the sauce from our plates with a piece of bread or to push our food around with our thumbs—something only the Americans did. We had to chase each morsel of food patiently around the plate, hoping that the china slope of the rim would somehow make the last grains of rice and beans fall strategically onto the fork instead of into our laps. If perchance the last bit of food was an okra pod or a slippery pig's knuckle, it was best to renounce it in advance rather than risk the pinch of one of our aunts' long, Elizabeth Ardened nails.

Abuela Valeria's relationship with nature was almost mystical; her bedroom opened onto the veranda, and at night she slept with the doors wide open so she could hear the waves breaking softly on the sand and the palm trees swaying in the wind. One Christmas Eve something extraordinary happened. Abuela Valeria consented to have a pine tree brought into the living room.

The family should have kept her eccentric beliefs in mind when it decided to put up a Christmas tree at Emajaguas. Since the Americans had arrived on the island, Christmas trees had become very popular, much more so than the *nacimientos*, with their shepherds and Holy Family carved in wood or in painted gesso, kneeling in front of Jesusito. Pine trees were shipped to the island all the way from Canada and New Hampshire. That year my aunts insisted that Valeria buy one, so a twelve-foot Canadian spruce was brought into the house on Christmas Eve. At first Valeria thought the whole thing was silly. She had never traveled to the United States, as several of her children had, and a Christmas tree struck no sentimental chord within her.

When the tree was set up in the middle of the living room, Abuela Valeria sat before it entranced. It shone like a soft emerald torn out of the forest, and it filled the house with its perfume. But then Valeria inexplicably began to feel sad. She had a vivid imagination, and as she looked at the tree her mind went flying off in an unexpected direction. Tall and elegant, the tree had stood guard for years over acres of virgin forest, before perishing under the woodsman's ax. The soft, damp moss, the murmuring rivers, the rustling wild deer all came into her living room in the wake of the scent that wafted from its branches. She felt like singing one of Mahler's songs, to console it for its impending death, the doom that was already hovering around it.

Oblivious to Abuela Valeria's distress, we all began to decorate the spruce, and soon it was decked out with shiny glass balls, tinsel, twinkling electric lights, and Ivory soap flakes. When Abuela saw what we were doing, she grew even sadder. In a matter of hours the tree had become a yellowish brown because of the heat and had begun to shed its needles. Loaded down with heavy ornaments, its boughs drooped like the wings of a dying bird. Abuela began to cry and locked herself in her room. Behind the locked door she told her family in no uncertain terms that they would have to get rid of the tree if they wanted her to come out. Her children had no alternative but to call the mayor of Guayamés and offer him the tree as a gift. The mayor immediately sent a truck and his workers removed the tree, which shone that night, with all our elaborate decorations, in the middle of the town square.

Once the tree was taken care of, preparations for Christmas dinner proceeded as usual. Abuela became her old energetic self, summoning all the servants together to organize the details of the feast. Urbano the chauffeur, Confesor the gardener, Gela the cook, and Miña the housemaid all followed her around, sweeping, shining, dusting, and decorating the house with fresh poinsettias brought in from the garden, until Emajaguas looked like a tropical Currier and Ives print.

SEVEN

ABUELA VALERIA'S STANDOFF

The day Abuela Valeria died was the first and only time I ever saw a Catholic priest at Emajaguas. Abuela Valeria was a Rosicrucian and a staunch believer in *espiritismo*, which she blended with her belief in the "positive currents of the universe." She read *The Christian Science Monitor* in Spanish, but she liked to think of herself as "an independent." Through the mail she received a constant stream of leaflets that she read to her children, insisting that the body could be healed through the power of the mind. When all her daughters except Tía Lakhmé had left Emajaguas and gone to live in distant towns, she'd travel to their sides with her handbag full of little Rosicrucian and Christian Science prayer books the minute she heard one of them was sick. She'd come into the sickroom, stand near the bed, and ask her daughter what was making her sad.

"It's the soul that makes the body sick," she'd say. "Close your eyes and tell me about your troubles. I'll take them away with me." My aunts would tell her what was worrying them and let her rub their temples with malagueta leaves and camphor oil, so that they felt better immediately. When Mother became ill because of her *soplo*, Abuela came to our house also and stood next to her oxygen tent for hours, praying.

Valeria believed in her own kind of afterlife, and when Abuelo Alvaro and Tío Alejandro died she communicated with them at least once a week through a Ouija board. She'd sit in her room in front of the open window, the board on her knees, close her eyes, and listen to the waves breaking on the sand below. Then she'd let the little wooden wedge point this way and that toward the letters of the alphabet, making words and phrases that she swore were messages from the other world. My aunts tended to look on her eccentric behavior as a symptom of approaching senility. But I loved to be with Abuela when she played with the Ouija board. I knew it was her way of denying death and asserting her faith in the positive currents of the universe. "Everything is interconnected and interdependent," she'd say. "The positive currents of the universe make you see the unity, not the differences. Believe in unity and you will see God."

Abuela revered the sun and prayed to it every morning at dawn. She had a deck built next to her bedroom, facing east. She took sunbaths there well into her eightieth year and would lie naked for an hour on a chaise longue behind a canvas screen, her flesh hanging from her bones in soft brown folds and her breasts completely bare. She didn't mind it when we grandchildren peeked at her, giggling through the rose trellis. She had a beautiful body; she walked as gracefully as a ballerina, her wide shoulders fanning out elegantly and her neck a delicate vase that carried the faded flower of her face.

Valeria never went to church. She believed people should pray silently and in private, not loudly and in public. Neither Abuelo Alvaro nor any other man had ever dared order her about, and she insisted that she'd rather go to hell than to Mass if it meant she had to kneel when the priest told her to. But she was sure she could still manage to get to heaven by doing things her own way.

By way of explanation she enjoyed telling her family the story of *"Corso ni vivo ni morto"*:

"Long ago," she said, "when my father still lived in Corsica, my uncle Basilio Boffil had a fierce argument with a neighbor. The boundary between their farms was a creek that changed course every time it rained. One day the man who owned the farm next to Basilio's insisted that the land that the creek passed over now belonged to him, and he proceeded to move his fence to include the adjacent piece of property. Basilio was enraged; he went to his neighbor's house, called him a crook and a liar in front of everybody, and then went out into the field to put the fence back where it belonged. In the morning his neighbor's knife turned up buried in Basilio's front door and he immediately knew what it meant: he would have to fight the man to the death the next day.

"The priest of the nearby town came to visit Basilio. 'You have to patch things up,' he told him. 'If you kill your neighbor you'll go to hell, and that forlorn piece of land you're fighting for isn't worth it.' Basilio answered that he didn't care. If he didn't do anything and let his neighbor kill him he would go to heaven, but it would mean a dishonorable death. He preferred going to hell. The next morning Basilio got up before dawn, walked to a mountain pass that overlooked the road his neighbor had to travel, and lay down on high ground. He loaded and cocked his rifle and propped it up carefully before him. He waited almost all day, but his neighbor didn't come. As the sun went down it got colder and Basilio fell asleep. Soon it began to snow and Basilio froze to death. But he still lay there, covered with powdered snow, his rifle cocked in his hands. The sun had almost gone down when his neighbor finally came walking along the road. He carried a loaded rifle and warily looked up at the hills as he approached the mountain pass. He suddenly saw something glint in the distance, lit by the sun's last rays. He cocked his rifle and fired. The bullet hit Tío Basilio's body, his frozen finger jerked the trigger, and he shot his neighbor to death. Basilio managed to go to heaven, and he also had an honorable death."

When she finished telling her story, Valeria would look at Abuelo Alvaro and her children, head held high, and add defiantly: "That's how stubborn the Boffils can be."

I loved Abuela Valeria and couldn't understand why Mother had a grudge against her. When Abuela Valeria grew seriously ill, it was as if her sickness followed a trail of gunpowder. The family was told she was dying, and we all traveled to Emajaguas from different parts of the island, prepared to spend the night there. The next morning my aunts stood sadly around her bed waiting for the end—the doctor had assured them Valeria wouldn't last more than a few hours. Everybody was depressed but we maintained nonchalant expressions; we knew Abuela Valeria wouldn't like to see us cry. She had always insisted death wasn't a tragedy, simply a transformation, a passage from one natural state to the next.

Tía Dido sat by Abuela Valeria's bed reading her a poem, something about the moon lighting up the road like a silver guitar. Tía Lakhmé opened the doors to the terrace so Abuela could hear the waves breaking on the beach and periodically dabbed her forehead with a handkerchief soaked with eau de cologne. Tía Artemisa put a yellow rose next to her bed and tried to cool her with a fan. Tía Siglinda hummed her a song and held her hand. But Mother stood in front of Valeria's bed stone-faced and dry-eyed, not saying a word.

My cousins and I stood at the back of the room gaping at Abuela's livid face, terrified by the strange sound that was coming from deep inside her throat. She was the first dying person we had ever seen.

Abuela was propped up on her pillows with her eyes closed, and after a while she seemed to fall into a deep sleep. Dido, Lakhmé, and Siglinda talked to one another in whispers, thankful that she had been given morphine; that way she would pass away in peace. All of a sudden, however, a priest walked into the room. He was wearing a black cassock buttoned to the neck and was followed by three attendant nuns. Artemisa had brought them; she wanted the priest to give Abuela absolution and the sacrament of extreme unction. The four of them pushed their way into the room unceremoniously and made everyone stand back. It was hot, and a sour odor of perspiration wafted from their rustling black robes.

As soon as the priest approached the bed with his little jar of holy oil, his salts, and a sprinkler of *agua bendita* in his hand, Valeria became conscious and looked up at him wide-eyed. Everybody was surprised.

"Valeria Boffil, in the name of God, can you hear me?" the priest asked in a loud voice, standing before her, ready to asperse holy water on her body. I began to tremble.

"Yes," Abuela Valeria answered clearly.

"Do you know you're dying? Do you accept the will of God?"

"Yes," Valeria answered. "I'm dying. And I accept His will."

"And do you repent of all your sins before you go unto His presence?"

Abuela Valeria stared at the priest without blinking. "What sins?" she asked defiantly. And before the priest could give her absolution, she gave up the ghost.

PART II

THE SWANS OF EMAJAGUAS

Writing a memoir is the same as making an appointment with the dead. A meeting of ghosts takes place, a series of familiar décors passes by, where those absent repeat the same gestures over and over, as they patiently await their turn to be explained.

—JUAN GOYTISOLO, *Coto Vedado*

EIGHT

†HE REPENTANT MUSE

Tía Dido was shy and unassuming, and Mother always teased her, telling her she had a violet's timid soul. When she was in elementary school she often forgot her own name, and when the teacher called on her she got so nervous she left a little pool of water wherever she was standing. The teacher, sure that Dido had peed on purpose, pulled her by the ear and ordered her to write her name on the blackboard a dozen times. Dido obeyed but she continued to be painfully shy. That's why everyone at Emajaguas was surprised at the change that came over her when she met Antonio Torres.

They met in 1925, when Dido was a junior at the University of Puerto Rico in Río Piedras, during the Fiesta de la Lengua, the annual celebration honoring the Spanish language. The most promising young poets studying at the university were invited to recite their poems in the auditorium, and, after much hesitating, Tía Dido decided to take part. Her literature professor was enthusiastic about her talent. If she went on writing, he told her, she might become an accomplished poet.

Tía Dido wrote every night until dawn; she believed literature was two percent talent and ninety-eight percent hard work. During the day she was always scribbling poetry—on used envelopes, parking tickets, even on the backs of blank checks. She would be sitting in her car waiting for the light to change when a poem would come drifting in through the window. The cars behind would start to honk, their drivers shaking their fists at her, doors slamming, but Dido wouldn't budge until she had written it down.

Tía Dido's poems were as fragile and delicate as she herself was. Abuelo Alvaro had some of them published in a slender volume bound in elegant antelope skin. He chose an esoteric publishing house in Antofagasta, Chile, because his daughter's anonymity was very precious to him. The fifteen copies that were printed were distributed strictly among family members. But Clarissa secretly mailed a copy to the jury just before the Fiesta de la Lengua, and the book won first prize.

Tía Dido was ecstatic. She went to the festival wearing a flounced yellow skirt with a black lace mantilla held high over her head with a tortoiseshell comb. Clarissa went with her—they were both studying at the university at the time—and Dido was wonderful. She appeared on stage and recited her poem, which was in the style of Juan Ramón Jiménez, her favorite Spanish poet; it began: "The moon trembled against my window, begging to be let in, pursued by a thousand dogs that licked at its golden sheen."

Antonio Torres sat in the audience. He had gone to the festival because he felt homesick and thought he might meet other Spaniards there. When he saw Dido dressed like a Spanish *maja*, he waited until she came down from the stage and approached her. He took his Montecristo cigar out of his mouth and bent to kiss her hand. "Antonio Torres Moreno, *para servirle*," he said politely. "Your poem was very beautiful, Miss Santillana. Someday I'll have to introduce you to Juan Ramón Jiménez. He's a childhood friend of mine. We're both from Moguer, a little town in the south of Spain." Dido forgot all about Clarissa and went off with Antonio. Mother returned to her dormitory alone.

Antonio Torres was shorter than Tía Dido and bald, but she was taken with him from the start, mesmerized by his beautiful Spanish. He spoke perfect Castilian, and Tía Dido found listening to him a delight. She couldn't detect a single mistake. He spoke as if he tasted every word, savoring it to its very marrow. When she listened to Antonio, Dido wanted to become a Spanish word, caressed and licked by his tongue.

He didn't swallow his final ss or garble his rs, as Puerto Ricans did. He pronounced his cs as precisely as castanets, curling the tip of his tongue against his teeth. Clarissa couldn't see what Dido found so attractive in Antonio. She looked for other things in men, like good manners.

The day after the reading Antonio went by the Pensionado Católico, the dormitory for out-of-town girls, and asked for Dido. She came down from her room to the reception hall, and he invited her to go for a ride on the trolley to El Morro, the Spanish fort in Old San Juan. The trolley had all its windows open and a soft breeze blew in from the sea as they traveled down Ponce de León Avenue. It was old and uncomfortable, and the seats were made of wooden slats, but neither of them noticed, so entranced were they by each other's company.

After three months of courting, Antonio knew he should propose marriage to Dido. But he couldn't bring himself to. In his opinion, Dido had one defect: when she was with other people she was painfully shy; she hardly spoke at all. But when she was with him she couldn't stop talking, and it was always about poetry. It bored him no end.

Antonio didn't have anything against poets. In Moguer, he told Dido during one of his visits to Emajaguas, he had many writer friends. But in Spain wives stayed home taking care of their children, and husbands didn't like their women traipsing about giving poetry readings or publishing poems in which they bared their intimate feelings to the world. What would Antonio's friends in Moguer say when they heard his wife was a poet? Gossip would roll in waves all the way from the island to the mother country.

Tía Dido was never as liberated as Tía Siglinda, but she was fairly outspoken. One afternoon she told Antonio: "We love each other; why don't we get married? I'm sure Mother will like you because she likes Spaniards. Even if you have no money you're bound to make some one day because you're white and hardworking."

Antonio hedged. "Let's get to know each other better before we take that step," he answered diplomatically. Tía Dido was downcast, but she didn't let Antonio's temporizing quench her enthusiasm. Every day she wrote a new poem and added it to her manuscript as the vine adds a grape. Unaware of the negative effect her poetry was having on her sweetheart, she was keener than ever to become a poet.

Six months went by and it was already spring; school was over before the lovers realized it. Dido finished her junior year at the university and came back to Emajaguas. Antonio traveled from San Juan to Guayamés every weekend to see her. But he still hadn't asked Tía Dido for her hand. Every time he came to visit, Dido would sit with him on the terrace and read him a new poem. But as soon as she began to read, Antonio closed his eyes, and before she was finished he'd be snoring loudly. Clarissa spied on them from the window that opened onto the terrace and had to admit the situation did not look good.

During summer vacation Tía Dido told Valeria, "I'm not going back to the university next semester, Mother. I'm tired of so much studying; I want to take a year off." Abuela was upset, but Dido was twenty years old; she couldn't force her to go back. Dido had decided to intensify her marriage campaign. She asked Gela to teach her how to cook and Miña how to wash and iron men's shirts. She spent hours in the kitchen learning to make chicken with rice, guinea hen stewed in red wine, and *piononos*, ripe plantain pies fried in batter; and every time she ironed one of Tío Alejandro's shirts, she went around the house showing it to everybody, proudly holding it up on a hanger.

One day Antonio announced that Juan Ramón Jiménez, his poet friend, had come to the island on a visit and that he was bringing him to lunch at Emajaguas the following week. Everybody was terribly excited. He and Juan Ramón would drive from San Juan to Guayamés in the morning, Antonio said, and return to the capital that same day. Tía Dido almost fainted when she heard the news. Juan Ramón was like a god to her; the tiles of Emajaguas's floor weren't good enough for him to step on.

Dido had the furniture in the sitting room polished and fresh flowers put in vases; she spent a whole week planning the menu. Having heard that Juan Ramón loved seafood, she asked Urbano to have his father-in-law, Triburcio Besosa, bring his best catch to the house.

Triburcio brought a basket full of the most exotic shellfish: river prawns, crayfish, lobster. This wasn't going to be one of Valeria's spartan meals. Dido was going to prepare a bouillabaisse that would have made even Lady Lent's face turn purple.

When Juan Ramón Jiménez and Antonio arrived at Emajaguas in Antonio's blue roadster, the whole family was waiting for them at the door. Aurelio was already Mother's beau, and he drove up from La Concordia for the occasion; Tía Siglinda and Tío Venancio came from Guayamés. Artemisa, who was still unmarried and living at the house, and two-year-old Lakhmé were also present. Abuelo Alvaro and Abuela Valeria gave the visitors a warm welcome.

Juan Ramón was very aristocratic-looking: he had large, soulful eyes and a high-domed brow. He had very little hair on his head, but he made up for it with a jet-black goatee so meticulously groomed it shone as if it were carved in onyx. He looked like a modern version of one of El Greco's apostles, and it was easy to imagine the Holy Spirit's gift of language hovering above his head in a tiny flame. Everyone at Emajaguas had read Juan Ramón's poems, and the sisters all brought him copies of his books so he could autograph them. His poems were full of the romantic mysticism of Castile, with windswept towns and black-clad women whispering behind latticed windows.

When lunch was finally announced, the poet presided at the head of the table, with the family reverently seated around him. Tía Dido herself brought in the trays of food, helped by Artemisa. When Miña protested, Dido explained that in Spain, when an important guest came for dinner, he was served by the daughters of the house and no servants were allowed into the dining room. In any case, Dido didn't want Miña to carry the soup tureen to the table. She was afraid Miña might drop it in Juan Ramón Jiménez's lap, so angry was she at Dido's leaving the university because of Antonio Torres.

When the steaming tureen was passed around the table and Juan Ramón lifted its lid, he almost swooned from the delicious aroma that wafted out. Juan Ramón served himself a generous portion and then passed the tureen around.

Tía Dido hardly dared look at her idol, who had tucked a napkin around his neck and was attacking the bouillabaisse with gusto, noisily sucking on the prawns and prying the mussels open with his long, almond-shaped nails, then washing it all down with wine. She sat next to Antonio, her head lowered shyly, and delicately sipped at the broth.

Juan Ramón loved oysters, and a veritable duel of shell sucking broke out between Antonio and his friend. Antonio would squirt fresh lemon juice on the live oyster, which curled up the little black flounce of its edge when it sensed the acid, then throw his head back to let the oyster slide down his throat. Juan Ramón would laugh uproariously and immediately do the same. In less than ten minutes, they had downed a dozen oysters each.

The family watched in amazement. They couldn't believe that such a glutton could be the author of such spiritual poems as "Mariposa de luz" or that he could write about the burning cinders of the soul hovering around the heart of the rose.

When lunch was over, Juan Ramón sat back in his chair, a satisfied look on his face. "My friend Antonio here tells me you're a poet," he said to Tía Dido with a condescending smile. "I'd be more than glad to read some of your poems. Would you have a copy of them I could look at?" He really hated to read the work of other writers, but the lunch had been so good he felt it was the least he could do to repay his hosts. Poor Dido got up from the table and, with trembling hands and knees, went to her room to get her poems.

Juan Ramón retired to one of the guest rooms for a nap, taking Dido's manuscript with him. When he came out an hour later, looking refreshed and ready for the long drive back to San Juan, he returned the poems to Dido. "I've written a little something on the last page, to let you know what I think. But please don't read it until I'm gone," he told her as he warmly said his good-byes.

Tía Dido took the manuscript from him reverently and didn't look at it until she went to bed that night. "Your voice is as sweet as a nightingale's," Juan Ramón had written on the last page. "But the best nightingales—the true *rui-señoras* of this world—sing their love songs in secret. I'm sure my friend Antonio will marry you if you do the same." Tía Dido read Juan Ramón's advice and cried herself to sleep that night.

"You're a nincompoop and a loser!" Clarissa told Tía Dido angrily the next morning when she read what the poet had written. "At least your namesake got to be queen of Carthage before she committed suicide over that thickhead Aeneas. But you'll never be anything other than an excellent cook."

Tía Dido took Juan Ramón Jiménez's suggestion and kept her love songs a secret from that day on; she put her literature books away and never wrote another poem. Antonio married her in the Guayamés cathedral the following month and took her to live with him in San Juan.

NINE

THE SNOW ROSE

Tía Artemisa was the tallest of all the aunts. She was so tall my cousins and I teased her that she had her feet firmly planted on the ground but was always bumping her head against the clouds. Tía Artemisa, like Tía Dido, lived for the imagination, but of a different kind. She was always dreaming of Jesusito, who lived in her heart.

She was a keen businesswoman, and she was also very religious. Thanks to her unusual combination of financial savvy and religious devotion, she almost landed one of the richest men in Guayamés, Don Esteban de la Rosa, the owner of the *central* Santa Rosa. The story of their romance was one of the most picturesque I'd ever heard.

Tía Artemisa fell madly in love with Don Esteban de la Rosa in 1947, when she was forty-four and regarded by everybody as a spinster. In contrast to my other aunts, who loved beautiful things and were always buying expensive baubles to adorn themselves, Artemisa dressed in black from head to toe and never wore any jewelry except for a perfect three-carat solitaire that shone, night and day, on her finger.

Tía Artemisa was as intelligent as Tía Dido, but she didn't finish her studies at the University of Puerto Rico either. She only went as far as her junior year. She was beautiful and charming, but she had one flaw, her religious fanaticism.

Swearing in front of Tía Artemisa was absolutely out of the question because she would immediately pull a long face and make you feel ashamed. Once, during Christmas dinner at Emajaguas, little Lakhmé made a joke. Saint Tecla, she said, was at death's door and Saint Peter and her friends were kneeling around a hole in the clouds looking down, waiting for her soul to come out of her body and begin to rise toward heaven. Saint Tecla's spirit finally went forth and began its ascent through the clouds, but she had been so saintly in life that she rose higher and higher and soon passed Saint Peter and kept on going. When Saint Peter saw this he called out: "Saint Tecla, please! Say a couple of *carajos* so you'll stop soaring and stay down here with us!" Saint Tecla did and came tumbling back to Earth. Artemisa was furious and made Abuela Valeria take Tía Lakhmé to the bathroom to wash her mouth out with soap and water.

Everybody in the family liked Don Esteban and hopes were high that he would marry Artemisa. He was a widower and had had a tragic life. His wife had died of breast cancer when she was still relatively young, and his only son, Valentín, had been killed at Saint Laurent, during the invasion of Normandy. Valentín's remains had been buried in a cemetery in Calvados, and Don Esteban wasn't able to visit his grave until two years later.

Don Esteban's sixteen-year-old granddaughter, Blanca Rosa, was the apple of his eye. Blanca, Valentín's only daughter, was one of the beauties of Guayamés. She was blond and blue-eyed, and her skin was so white her friends called her the Snow Rose. Don Esteban didn't want Blanca Rosa to marry any of the local young Turks, so in 1946—a year after the war was over—he decided to travel with her to Europe and introduce her to some young men of good standing. They flew on a Pan American Clipper from San Juan to New York. There they boarded the *Gloucester*, a luxury steamship of the Grace Line, and landed in Le Havre at the end of November.

Don Esteban rented a limousine with a chauffeur, and he drove south with his granddaughter down the Normandy coast to visit the cemetery where Valentín was buried. The weather was misty and cold, but the landscape was beautiful. Trouville-sur-Mer; Deauville; Fleurie: the towns that Don Esteban had read so much about in *A la Recherche du Temps Perdu* and that the Impressionists had painted so many times went flying by before his eyes. Many were being reconstructed after the terrible damage the war had inflicted. Debris littered the dunes on the beach and signs were posted everywhere warning of land mines and forbidding people to walk along the shore. They finally reached Omaha Beach. Don Esteban hadn't said a single word the whole time, but he felt in control of himself. His son had died a hero's death defending his country, the United States. Valentín was thirty-five, in the flower of his youth. Now he would never grow old, would never experience sickness or grief. When Don Esteban thought about it that way, he was almost glad a piece of German mortar shell had flown through the air and embedded itself in Valentín's brain.

They passed the cemetery's gate and the marble sculpture of an angel carrying a fallen soldier in his arms. Ten thousand limestone crosses stood on the rolling green meadow like gulls poised for flight, several Stars of David interspersed among them. The steel-gray waters of the English Channel glinted restlessly in the distance. Don Esteban took a deep breath and got out of the car. In his pocket he carried the small map the army had sent him with the exact location of his son's grave. He took Blanca Rosa's arm and together they began the long walk to where Valentín's cross stood.

They reached Paris that evening and drove to the Hôtel Crillon. Soon they were installed in a beautiful suite with a view of the Place de la Concorde. Blanca Rosa was to attend the Christmas ball at Versailles in a few days—the first such ball since before the war. She had brought a trunk full of clothes with her, and Guayamés's best dressmaker had designed her a beautiful evening gown for the ball. But Blanca Rosa needed a winter coat, and since it was always warm in Guayamés, winter evening coats were not for sale. So Don Esteban asked the dressmaker to sew Blanca Rosa a coat made of marabou feathers, which were very fashionable at the time. "I would like to buy you an ermine cape with a hood," he joked the day he gave her the feather coat, "but I would have to sell my best farm to pay for it. Marabou will have to do. The feathers are very fine; they come from

Africa and only brides wear them." Blanca loved the coat. She didn't know what ermine looked like, but it couldn't be as soft and beautiful as marabou.

The night of the Versailles ball Blanca met a French count, Jean-Baptiste de l'Abbaye Richey, great-grandson of one of France's *grands maréchals*. Jean-Baptiste asked her to dance, and they sailed together across the parquet floor. The air around them swirled with laughter; champagne flowed from dark green bottles like liquid happiness; the chandeliers were hives ablaze with excitement above their heads. But they didn't notice a thing, because they had fallen in love.

By the time the orchestra began to play "La Vie en Rose," they had decided to elope. They would drive from Versailles to Nice that very night. It was the middle of December, and although Blanca Rosa knew she looked very attractive in her silk chiffon dress, she was amazed that, with so many beautiful girls at the ball, Jean-Baptiste should have eyes only for her. "You look like a Venus draped in alabaster folds, and I love you more than my life," he whispered, drawing her close. Blanca Rosa believed him.

At midnight Jean-Baptiste took her by the hand and they slipped away unnoticed. Blanca Rosa threw her marabou coat over her shoulders and ran with Jean-Baptiste down the hall of mirrors, crossed the military court in front of the palace, silver heels flying over the stone slab floor, and got into Jean-Baptiste's red convertible Alfa Romeo.

"Is that coat warm enough?" Jean-Baptiste asked her dubiously as they got in the car.

"Of course it is," Blanca answered, smiling, not wanting him to think she was a small-town girl. "It's tropical ermine. Father gave it to me as a present to wear at Versailles."

The car took off like a bullet in the night. Soon Blanca Rosa felt the knife of the wind fly by, but Jean-Baptiste put his arm around her shoulders and pointed to the dome full of stars. "There must be thousands, but you're more beautiful than all of them, because you fell from a tropical sky," Jean-Baptiste said. Blanca snuggled close to him. Orion was flying above their heads, arms and legs spread wide against the sky, wearing four stars on his belt and three on his dagger, as he always did. Orion made Blanca Rosa think of Don Esteban. All of a sudden she missed him and was sad to think how distressed he must be, not knowing where she was.

"Can we stop at the next gasoline station, so I can call my grandfather?" she asked Jean-Baptiste. "He must be terribly worried." But at that hour of the night all the gasoline pumps were closed. Around four in the morning, as they were nearing Nevers, Blanca tried again, but Jean-Baptiste didn't think it was a good idea to call. "We still have too many hours to go before we get to Nice," he said. "Your grandfather could warn the police, and they'll send a patrol to stop us before we reach the hotel. Let's wait until tomorrow, so we can spend the night in each other's arms." Blanca looked up at Orion and sighed. It made her feel better that he was looking after her from up there.

Soon the sky was shrouded with a mantle of clouds, and tiny featherlike snowflakes began to caress Blanca's cheeks. "You look even more beautiful under the snow than under the stars," Jean-Baptiste whispered in her ear as they flew past Lyon at a hundred kilometers an hour. *"Ma rose de neige."* And Blanca was so much in love and at the same time so afraid of what Jean-Baptiste might think if he found out her coat was made not of ermine but of marabou feathers that she didn't dare tell him how cold she was.

The snow kept sifting over them like flour. "Now I know how angels feel on their way to heaven," Blanca Rosa said. She gazed admiringly at Jean-Baptiste, who reminded her of a prince in his black astrakhan coat buttoned up to the chin and his Russian-style hat. Then something strange happened: Blanca didn't feel cold anymore. Instead a fiery blaze began to burn her insides. She wanted to make love to Jean-Baptiste so badly she wished her breasts, her abdomen, her thighs were made of snow so she could melt in his arms.

They drove on until they reached Avignon and stopped there at a little café by the side of the road to have a cup of coffee and a croissant. Blanca could hardly get out of the car; she was stiff and her legs were numb. She felt terribly sleepy and kept stumbling on her silver heels. Jean-Baptiste had to help her to a chair. When Blanca asked if there was a ladies' room, a dirty-looking peasant hunched over a glass of wine pointed toward the back of the establishment, where there was an outhouse. Blanca gave up the idea of visiting it. Jean-Baptiste went, and when he came back to the car he rolled up its canvas cover. Blanca got in and fell into a deep sleep.

They arrived in Nice around four in the afternoon, the day after the ball. They took a suite in the Hôtel de Paris, the best in town. The hotel was right next to the Palais de Jeu and from their window that evening Blanca could see men in elegant tuxedos and women in long, glittering evening gowns stepping out of their cars and going up the casino's marble stairway.

When Blanca lay down on the bed she was shivering, whether from the chill of the trip or from the desire that raged inside her she didn't know. Jean-Baptiste undressed her slowly, blowing away the last snowflakes that clung to her marabou coat. Then he removed her Venus chiffon dress. When Blanca was totally naked she looked like an alabaster statue lit from within, her skin glowed so unnaturally. They made love passionately, then fell into a deep sleep. When Jean-Baptiste woke the next morning, the sun was streaming into the room and Blanca Rosa lay motionless by his side. She looked even more like an alabaster statue, but she wasn't lit from within any longer. She had died of hypothermia during the night.

Back in Paris Don Esteban had gone without news of his granddaughter for twenty-four hours and was almost beside himself. He had searched for her, room by room, at Versailles and had finally returned to the Crillon without her. When Blanca was still missing the next morning, he informed the police and a search was begun. The following evening Don Esteban received a telegram from Jean-Baptiste at the hotel, informing him of Blanca Rosa's death. Don Esteban immediately took a train to Nice.

On his arrival, he went straight to the police station, where Jean-Baptiste, the prefect of police, and a pathologist were waiting for him. "*Je suis désolé, Monsieur,*" the young man said as he tried to embrace Don Esteban, tears streaming down his face. But Don Esteban pushed him away. He had never gotten angry at anybody; he was a peaceful man. But he felt a noose of rage tighten around his throat when he saw the French count.

Blanca Rosa had died of overexposure during the night because she had driven almost all the way from Paris to Avignon in Jean-Baptiste's Alfa Romeo with the canvas top rolled down, the prefect of police explained to him. Don Esteban was incensed. He picked Jean-Baptiste up by the lapels of his coat and threw him against the wall. He threatened to call a lawyer and press charges against the young man. His granddaughter was a minor and Jean-Baptiste had carried her off from Versailles by force. But the prefect of police explained he couldn't do that, because Jean-Baptiste was the great-grandson of one of France's *grands maréchals*. Don Esteban clenched his fists and hung his head. At home he was an hacendado; the police wouldn't have dared ignore him. But in France he was an eccentric old man from an impoverished Caribbean island raving about an unfortunate accident that had happened to a young couple in love.

Don Esteban went to the morgue to identify the body and then to a nearby chapel to pray for Blanca Rosa's soul. He somehow managed to stay in control through the day. When he came back from the cemetery, he went to his granddaughter's hotel. He gave the concierge a twenty-dollar bill, asked for a key to her room, and gave orders to keep Jean-Baptiste and the reporters away. News of the unusual death had made the local papers, and a photograph of Blanca Rosa dancing with the French count at Versailles was published on the front pages.

Don Esteban locked himself in the room and began to pack his granddaughter's belongings methodically, making sure nothing was left behind for the reporters to pick over like crows. When he finished, he sat down on the double bed to rest for a minute. He could tell Blanca had lain there because a few strands of her hair still clung to the linen pillowcase. He slipped his hands beneath it and felt something curly with the tips of his fingers. Underneath were the false eyelashes Blanca Rosa had worn at the Versailles ball and had taken off before she died.

That insignificant detail made Don Esteban break down. The sensation of his granddaughter's golden eyelashes on his fingertips was too much for him.

He began to wail, pitifully calling out his granddaughter's name. "Blanca Rosa, my angel, what have I done to you? I should have sold not just my best farm but all my farms and my sugar mill as well, to buy you the warmest ermine coat in France. I wanted to save money, and God has punished me for my miserliness. He lent me your presence for a few years, but I didn't know how to take care of you, and he's called you back to His side."

He got up from the bed and knocked over two lamps, threw a chair out the window, swung at the crystal chandelier with his umbrella. In five minutes the place was a shambles. The hotel authorities rushed in and he was driven to the police station, where he was pronounced unbalanced.

Don Esteban was consigned to an institution at Aulnay-sous-Bois, an asylum run by Carmelite nuns. For a week he lay in bed as if he were dead. The nuns held his head up and fed him little spoonfuls of broth and recited the Rosary by his side. One morning he got up at daybreak and looked out the window of his cell. A wonderful peace emanated from the cloister, from the fishpond in the middle of the vegetable garden, from the gnarled olive trees planted around it. He listened to the nuns singing matins, their voices echoing like distant bells from the chapel. He recovered gradually and began to go to Mass every morning. He had never been devout, but his granddaughter's death had changed him.

When he felt strong enough, he returned to Guayamés. The Carmelite nuns had an old, dilapidated convent on top of a hill there, and Don Esteban began to visit them. The nuns did a lot of humanitarian work. They had a *hospitalillo*, a dispensary where they gave out food and dressed the sores of the needy. They usually had six or seven people in a special wing of the convent where they cared for the terminally ill.

Don Esteban donated money to have the convent's facilities restored. One Sunday he brought the nuns a case full of good things to eat: a canned Danish ham, a roast beef, a smoked salmon, which he knew they couldn't afford. He was sitting in the *portería* waiting for the nuns to open the door—no men were allowed into the convent except for its benefactor—when the Rivas de Santillanas' black Packard arrived at the convent's door and Tía Artemisa stepped out. She was bringing the nuns a basket of fresh fruits and vegetables from Emajaguas's garden.

Tía Artemisa was attracted to Don Esteban the minute she saw him. His back was straight and he wore his silver hair carefully combed to the side. He was polished and urbane in his perfectly cut blue linen suit. His slender face and hands gleamed like a spirit's in the half-light of the *portería*.

Tía Artemisa had heard about Don Esteban de la Rosa but she had never met him. She knew that he was a widower and that he lived alone in the family's old mansion on Cristóbal Colón Avenue, in the center of town, because his son and his only granddaughter had passed away. Don Esteban's father was a widower also. He had worked hard all his life and had retired to live in Europe on the income provided by the *central* Santa Rosa. He had left Esteban at the head of the mill, not wanting to be bothered with any of its problems. Don Esteban sent his father a generous amount every month so the old man could live with dignity.

The Santa Rosa was on the outskirts of Guayamés. It was one of the few sugar mills owned by the local hacendados that were still grinding cane and making money. Not a lot of it, but enough to let Don Esteban live reasonably well and pay for his father's expenses. The reason for the mill's success was that all the cane-producing farms belonging to Don Esteban were adjacent to one another. Once the cane was cut, it could be transported to the mill along the farm's interior roads rather than on the highway, which was heavily trafficked, full of twists and turns, and capable of sending trucks keeling over like overstuffed dinosaurs. The Santa Rosa had an excellent manager, a German who had lived on the island for more than twenty years and married a girl from Guayamés. Don Esteban never had to visit the mill at all.

Don Esteban was a very cultured man who knew a little of everything. He wasn't an architect, but he understood the laws of perspective, volume, and depth. He wasn't a painter, but he could extemporize on Renaissance painting. He wasn't a mechanic, but he could take his Buick's engine apart and put it back together again in no time at all. He was, in short, a dilettante who was totally inept at anything that had to do with making money but an expert at spending it. People in Guayamés were fond of him because he was very affectionate, but they knew he didn't like to work. They laughed at him behind his back and said he was like the Indian chief's son who loved to drink cane juice but wouldn't cut a stalk. Since his granddaughter's tragic death, Don Esteban had worked even less. He had become very pious and was always alone.

After meeting Don Esteban at the convent's *portería* three Sundays in a row, Artemisa decided to help the Carmelite nuns at the convent in Guayamés. They had asked her to assist with their nursing work. It would be a good experience, she said. Her mother believed her, but Miña knew she was lying. "You're in love with Don Esteban de la Rosa and you're figuring out how to catch him," she said. "You can't fool me, Artemisa. Your mother didn't name you after the goddess of the chase for nothing." "Goddess of the chase, goddess of the chase," Felicia, Miña's parrot, screeched, swinging from one leg to the other inside her wire cage.

The following Sunday when Tía Artemisa met Don Esteban at the convent, she invited him to come to dinner at Emajaguas, and Don

Esteban accepted. Artemisa knew Valeria would like him. He had money, he had an aesthetic sensibility, and he was a good man, the three prerequisites Abuela required of her daughter's suitors. But what was even more important, Don Esteban was an hacendado. Tío Venancio was a lawyer, Tío Antonio was a doctor, Aurelio was an engineer. Abuela Valeria's three sons-in-law all had respectable careers, but they were in a different category. Don Esteban owned a sugar mill and more than three thousand acres of land; he belonged to the almost extinct criollo sugar aristocracy. Valeria was sure that, wherever he was in heaven, Alvaro would be very pleased with Artemisa's future match.

Abuela Valeria invited Don Esteban for dinner on another occasion. That afternoon she assembled everybody at Emajaguas and told them they had to make Don Esteban *"declararse"*—ask Tía Artemisa for her hand. Gela, the cook, baked a guinea hen in passion-fruit sauce for him; Dido, who was home on a visit, recited Neruda's poetry from *Veinte poemas de amor y una canción desesperada*—"Twenty Love Poems and a Song of Despair"—at dinner; Lakhmé wore her flame-colored skirt with coins at the hem and did a belly dance to Rimsky-Korsakov's *Scheherezade*. Then everybody disappeared and left Don Esteban and Artemisa sitting by themselves on the living-room sofa. But Don Esteban didn't get the hint. After a few minutes, he kissed Artemisa's hand and politely said good-bye.

They went everywhere together: to Mass and Holy Communion in the morning, to the slums to do charity work and to the monastery to help out the nuns in the afternoon, to the movies in the evening. Don Esteban was a respectable older gentleman, so Abuela Valeria didn't think Tía Artemisa needed a chaperon; they always went out by themselves. But months went by and Don Esteban didn't make his move.

Don Esteban's mother had enjoyed diamonds, and when she passed away Don Esteban had inherited them. He traveled to New York and sold Harry Winston, the Fifth Avenue jeweler, all her diamonds but one, a perfect blue-white three-carat solitaire. Harry Winston paid half a million dollars in cash for the gems—a substantial sum at the time—and Don Esteban put the money in a safe-deposit box at the bank, together with the perfect diamond he didn't sell. When he started going out with Tía Artemisa he took the diamond to Guayamés's best jeweler and asked him to set it in a magnificent platinum mounting. He planned to give it to Artemisa as an engagement ring, but he kept postponing the date.

After Blanca Rosa flew back to God, it was as if a mantle of sadness had fallen over Don Esteban. Every time he saw something white—a feather, a white ribbon, a bit of lace—he thought of her, and because there were so many white things in this world, Blanca Rosa was always before his eyes. He talked to Tía Artemisa about his granddaughter: how much Blanca had cried when she was a year old and had stuck a piece of string up her nose, giving her a mysterious fever no one could cure, how she had slipped on her new shoes when she was two and had fallen headlong down the stairs and had to be taken to the hospital to have stitches in her forehead. Artemisa was very perceptive, and it didn't take her long to realize that something was terribly wrong. Don Esteban's heart was locked up tight against her because Blanca Rosa in her marabou coat was sitting on top of its lid. Her ghost needed to be put to rest.

One day Don Esteban told Artemisa he had decided to invest the cash from his mother's gems in the stock market. He didn't need the money, he said. He had a generous enough income from the Santa Rosa to send money to his father and live comfortably on what was left, but he wanted to do something that would keep him occupied. He thought playing the stock market was a good idea. He telephoned Pablo Urdaneta, a stockbroker from Guayamés who was a friend of his, and told him he wanted to see him. He had half a million dollars in cash in the bank, he said, and wished to invest it in something humanitarian.

Pablo Urdaneta knew that Don Esteban's son had been killed in the war, and he also knew that Don Esteban had become very religious since his granddaughter's death and was always doing charity work. When he got Don Esteban's telephone call he came running to the house carrying a large suitcase in his hand. Don Esteban invited Urdaneta to sit down in the living room. His friend put the suitcase on his knees, pushed the bronze springs on each side, and opened the lid slowly, as if he were about to show Don Esteban something very precious. Out came a captain's billed cap with a shiny leather visor, an infantryman's cap with a pair of tiny bronze rifles pinned in front, and a khaki shirt with epaulets and brass galloons.

Urdaneta handled the items delicately, almost as if they were sacred. Then he spread them out on one of Don Esteban's marble-topped tables. "Believe it or not, these items were made by Puerto Rican women to be worn by American soldiers fighting in Europe during the war. But now the war is over and we have no more government contracts; our seamstresses are dying of hunger. We need money to get started, so we can buy them sewing equipment and form a new company. This is a worthy cause, Don Esteban. Instead of investing in the stock market, put your money in the Puerto Rican needle industry. You'll be giving our seamstresses jobs and you'll be doing your patriotic duty."

Don Esteban stared at the uniforms and thought of his son who was buried in Normandy in an army uniform made by Puerto Rican hands. He got up from his chair, went to his study, and came back with a leather case full of money. "You may go ahead and invest this cash in the Puerto Rican needle industry in my name," he said solemnly.

Two months later, Urdaneta came to Don Esteban's house again. He told him that the needle industry had taken a dive and that clothes made on the island weren't sought after anymore. The Taiwan market had just opened, and the Puerto Rican industry just couldn't compete with the Chinese. In Taiwan, women didn't earn a minimum wage, had never heard of social security, medical insurance, or the right to go on strike. Taiwan was an investor's paradise, but it was hell for those poor women. Would Don Esteban consider investing in the Chinese needle industry? Maybe he could help the needle-workers there and at the same time recover a part of what he had lost. Urdaneta would need an additional five hundred thousand dollars if Don Esteban was interested.

Don Esteban thought about it for a few days. He didn't have the money, but he knew the bank would lend it to him if he put up the *central* Santa Rosa as collateral. He hated to think he had lost such a large amount of money—half a million dollars—in such a short time. But he took a loan for another half a million from the bank, called up Pablo Urdaneta, gave him the cash, and told him to invest it in Taiwan. When two weeks went by and Don Esteban didn't hear from Urdaneta, he telephoned his brokerage firm and was told the broker didn't work there anymore. He had taken the money and vanished from the island.

TEN

THE THICK SKIN OF MERCY

The next morning before Mass, Don Esteban told Artemisa everything. Tía Artemisa told Abuela Valeria, and Abuela informed the rest of the family. Don Esteban had lost a million dollars in bad business deals and there was no way to recover it. He would have to pay interest on the amount he had borrowed from the bank and his income wasn't going to be enough to cover the payments; the bank would soon take over the *central* Santa Rosa. The family cringed at the thought, especially Valeria.

Don Esteban didn't care what happened to *him*, he told Artemisa. He could live on bread and water and sleep in a cave like Saint Francis. But what would happen to his father? He was over eighty and was waiting for his monthly check; it was already late. The old man would be evicted from his apartment in Madrid, and all his friends would find out about it. The scandal would be so great it would probably kill him. Don Esteban would have to spend the rest of his life with his father's death on his conscience.

Tía Artemisa stared at Don Esteban in wonderment. She thought of her father, who didn't believe in credit and paid everyone cash. She simply couldn't understand how a million dollars could vanish into thin air. But Artemisa didn't lose her presence of mind. "Don't worry, Esteban," she said. "In the past, money was something one made by working hard, producing things with the sweat of one's brow. Today, however, one has to be very careful because money is not a thing but an idea. If one doesn't keep it under lock and key, it grows wings and the devil flies away with it. We'll pray to Jesusito and leave everything in his hands."

That night Artemisa couldn't sleep; she lay awake thinking how to help Don Esteban. At four in the morning, when she finally fell asleep, she had a dream. Jesusito appeared to her and told her the story of Saint Francis and Saint Clare. Francis and Clare belonged to the same family of rich merchants from Assisi, in the north of Italy. They loved each other, but they realized their mission in the world was to help the poor and that was much more important than their personal happiness. Each one had founded a religious order—the Franciscan friars and the Poor Clares—and lived by the most ascetic laws. Jesusito wanted Don Esteban to take a vow of poverty, too, and sell everything he owned. With the money, he'd be able to save his old father as well as his good name.

First thing the next morning Artemisa called Don Esteban and told him her dream. Don Esteban said he would do whatever was necessary; he was placing all his worldly goods in Artemisa's hands.

Next Artemisa called *El Listín Noticioso*, the local newspaper, and placed a classified ad. Don Esteban was holding an auction at his house on Cristóbal Colón Avenue, it said, and everything would be for sale—antiques, Persian rugs, Tiffany lamps, oil paintings, Limoges and Baccarat tableware. The money would be donated to an unidentified charitable cause. Artemisa didn't feel she was lying: with the crisis the *central* Santa Rosa was going through, Don Esteban's father was certainly a charity cause. Artemisa raised ten thousand dollars from the sale and went on to liquidate what was left in the house without feeling offended when her best friends called at three in the morning to ask her for a discount on some bauble they had liked.

Don Esteban immediately sent the money to Spain; it would tide his father over until he sold the land. He kept only his bed, a table, and a chair, which was a lot more than Saint Francis had after he took his vow of poverty, Artemisa said.

When everything in the house on Cristóbal Colón Avenue was sold, Don Esteban felt surprisingly lighthearted; he didn't have to look at things that reminded him of Blanca Rosa anymore. At last he felt free of her presence, and perhaps Blanca Rosa's ghost was also glad to be free of her grandfather's terrible sorrow, which had gnawed at her all this time.

Tía Artemisa came to visit him and Don Esteban walked through the empty rooms of the house with her. "Thank you for the wonderful idea of the auction," Don Esteban told Artemisa as they said goodbye. "I needed someone like you to blow away the cobwebs from my heart." And for the first time since he'd met her, Don Esteban kissed Artemisa, though on the cheek. Artemisa began to think that she was finally getting the upper hand in her struggle with Blanca Rosa's ghost and that she would be able to pry the girl from her poor grandfather's heart.

Don Esteban still had his sugarcane farms, and Artemisa asked Don Esteban for the key to his office and began to go there every day. She wanted to find out their location and how much they were worth. Every afternoon at four, after his secretary left, she tiptoed into the building, trying to make herself as unobtrusive as possible, and sat at Don Esteban's desk. Tall and straight in her yellow cotton dress, her back not touching the chair and her no-nonsense patent-leather flats planted firmly on the ground, Artemisa looked like a sunflower, her attention unflinchingly turned toward the lost gold of Don Esteban's farms. She began to look for land measurements, surveyors' plans, deeds of ownership, and other legal documents. Don Esteban was never at the office when Artemisa arrived; he left religiously at three o'clock for the Golden Sands Hotel, where he played a round of golf every afternoon.

Artemisa had inherited Grandfather Bartolomeo Boffil's courage. Once she located the farms, she exchanged her yellow cotton dress for a brown twill riding skirt and her patent-leather flats for a pair of black, scrupulously shined riding boots, got into a jeep with Contreras, Don Esteban's overseer, and a real estate broker from Guayamés, and the three of them drove out into the countryside. But when they got to the first farm Artemisa's heart sank: it was overrun by squatters. A shantytown of wooden shacks had sprung up, each house sitting on a piece of land, surrounded by barbed wire, where sugarcane had once grown. And what was worse, on the roof of each shack a flag with a red *jíbaro* wearing a *pava*—the sugarcane workers' hat—fluttered furiously in the wind, which meant the squatters all sympathized with the Partido Democrático Institucional, which had won the elections four years before.

In Puerto Rico there were two other political parties at the time: the Partido Socialista and the Partido Republicano Incondicional. Artemisa, like everyone else in our family, regarded the Partido Democrático Institucional as dangerous and despised its leader, Fernando Martín. Martín was the son of an hacendado, but to the Rivas de Santillanas he was a traitor and a hypocrite. Martín's speeches were always about social change. "The island's political status—statehood, commonwealth, or independence—isn't really what's important," he'd insist. "What matters is to put a dish of rice and beans on everybody's table." But of course it was all a lie. It was the old "*Quítate tú pa ponerme yo*"—"Get off the wheel so I can drive"—demagoguery all over again, and no one was going to convince the family otherwise.

Fernando Martín didn't really want to help the *jíbaros*; he wanted to get power into his own hands. He had taken his party's motto, "*Pan, tierra, y libertad*"—"Bread, land, and liberty"—from the Mexican Revolution, which meant he was practically a Communist. When Tía Artemisa saw the red *jíbaro* flags flying high from the roofs of the squatters' shacks, her conviction that Don Esteban should take a vow of poverty and sell everything he had went up in smoke. She was mad as hell.

In Artemisa's opinion, giving and taking were two very different things. Jesusito approved of giving but he disapproved of taking, and taking something that belonged to your neighbor was a mortal sin. If Don Esteban sold his lands and gave the money to his father or to charity, that was all right. But Artemisa wasn't going to stand by and let the lazy peasants—egged on by Fernando Martín—take away from Don Esteban lands that his ancestors had struggled to acquire. When Saint Francis and Saint Clare took their vows of poverty, they didn't cease to belong to the Italian upper class. They were poor, they had sacrificed what they owned in order to attain heaven, but they were still leaders in their society. They had established their own monasteries and had been entrusted by Jesusito to keep order in the world.

And even when people from the upper class sold their lands, as her own family had been forced to do, they still exercised that role. The poor couldn't just walk in and take their place.

No one knew when or how the squatters had arrived on Don Esteban's farms. At night the countryside was deserted, dark as a wolf's maw. There was no electricity or running water for miles. But by morning each squatter had a picket fence with a goat tied to it, several chickens and a rooster running around, and a lush vegetable garden in back of the shack.

When Tía Artemisa, the overseer, and the broker drew near the shacks they couldn't even get out of the jeep. The squatters immediately recognized them and began to throw stones and empty bottles. They had to drive back into town as fast as they could.

"How long has this been going on?" Tía Artemisa asked Contreras in a steady voice, trying not to sound upset.

"For the past two months," the overseer answered. "Before Miss Blanca Rosa's death, Don Esteban used to visit his farms regularly," he said. "But he never supervises them anymore. Three months ago the wire fences began to collapse because of the heavy rains. He didn't order them repaired, so it was easy for the squatters to move in."

Once they were near Guayamés, the real estate broker got out of Artemisa's car and climbed into his, which he had left parked on the outskirts, and drove back to his office. But the overseer sat shamefaced next to Artemisa in the jeep. Contreras was a stocky, hardworking man who had been with Don Esteban for over twenty years. He kept excusing himself. "I'm sorry, ma'am. I should have warned you of what was going on. But I wanted you to see it with your own eyes. I've tried to inform Don Esteban of the takeover many times." Contreras perspired copiously as he spoke and nervously wiped his forehead with the palm of his hand. Tía Artemisa listened patiently.

"You mustn't worry, ma'am," Contreras added, looking down at his shoes. "We're living in difficult times. Many people in Guayamés are going hungry, and since Fernando Martín's Democrats have begun to accuse the hacendados of paying the laborers too little, the peasants think it's all right to invade their lands. But of course what Fernando Martín is saying is all a lie."

"Don Esteban," Tía Artemisa said, clearing her throat, "has a heart of gold. It's not his fault that the price of sugar has fallen drastically in the world market in the last six months. When he has to pay his workers two dollars a week instead of three, it's because he has no alternative, not because he wants to." And Contreras sheepishly agreed with everything Tía Artemisa said.

Artemisa dropped the overseer off at the *central* Santa Rosa's clapboard offices and drove the jeep to Don Esteban's house on Cristóbal Colón Avenue. She was furious at him for being so irresponsible and letting the farm's wire fences fall into disrepair. She didn't care that people stared at her as she braked the jeep violently in front of the porticoed mansion and got out. She ran up the marble steps, still wearing her long riding skirt and her black riding boots.

"A mob of Fernando Martín's squatters has invaded your farms," she told Don Esteban angrily as soon as she walked in. "They've settled on them like locusts. And all because you let yourself get so depressed after Blanca Rosa's death." Don Esteban hung his head despondently and didn't answer. But when he saw Artemisa turn around to leave, he said, "We might as well let them stay, dear. The Bureau of Tax Returns called this morning to say they're about to expropriate the farms because I haven't paid my taxes in over a year. But you mustn't blame Blanca Rosa; it's not the poor angel's fault."

"Let them keep the farms?" Artemisa retorted, her face flushed with anger. "You must be out of your mind. You may *give* away the land if you want to, but you must never let them take it away from you. People in Guayamés won't respect you. They'll look at you like you're a chicken that doesn't mind being plucked."

The following day Artemisa called the police station in Guayamés and reported that hundreds of squatters had invaded Don Esteban's farms; would they please send a patrol over and remove them by force? The police officer who took the call laughed. The new laws put into effect by the Partido Democrático Institucional protected the squatters, even if their houses were built on privately owned land. Don Esteban would have to get a lawyer and a court order to force the squatters to leave peacefully.

Over the following week Artemisa visited the farms one by one in her jeep and counted the shacks from afar: there were two hundred and five. Then she called Don Esteban's lawyer and made an appointment. She went to see him and asked the best way to get rid of the squatters. The lawyer answered that an order of eviction would have to be prepared for each squatter and would have to be served by an officer of the law. Each eviction notice would cost Don Esteban a hundred dollars. But if he didn't act, the squatters had the right to lay official claim to the lands after five years of living on them.

Artemisa was on the verge of desperation. She kept repeating that since Fernando Martín's Democrats had come into power the world had been turned upside down. She wouldn't be surprised if rivers began to run uphill and pigeons began to shoot at guns. She put on a black lace mantilla and went to the cathedral, where the family had its own private chapel. Artemisa lit a candle and knelt before the altar. A few minutes later she heard Jesusito speak to her in the semidarkness: "You mustn't despair, my daughter. Things are not as bad as they seem. This last reversal you're telling me about may be just what Esteban needs because it will help him get free of Blanca Rosa's ghost."

Artemisa crossed herself and felt much better. She went to Don Esteban and told him what the lawyer had said. The evictions would cost him over twenty thousand dollars, and he didn't have that kind of money. But she had an idea and was going to try to make it work. They would visit the Bureau of Tax Returns together, but he must let her do all the talking.

The next day they drove there in Don Esteban's jet-black Buick, with a uniformed chauffeur at the wheel. The bureau was located in the old Spanish Casino, which had closed down a few years earlier when it was taken over by the Partido Democrático Institucional and turned into an office building. It had marble floors and twelve-foot ceilings, but the furniture—the marble consoles, gilded mirrors, and red velvet chairs—had all disappeared.

As soon as they were ushered in, Don Esteban asked which tax official had been assigned to them. The secretary himself, Manuel Felipe Sánchez de Montenegro, would see them, he was told. Don Esteban shivered when he heard the name. Manuel Felipe Sánchez de Montenegro was known among the hacendados as "the bulldog of Guayamés." Sugar, tobacco, coffee—it didn't matter what kind of plantation you owned; if you didn't pay your taxes to the penny, you soon had Manuel Felipe's bulldozers at the door. In a matter of hours the farm's crop would be razed to the ground and a sign reading "Government Property" would be nailed to the nearest tree.

Manuel Felipe's office was a stuffy cubicle with cardboard partitions that didn't even reach the ceiling. It was exactly like a dozen others down the hall. A metal fan whirred away noisily on the desk. Manuel Felipe was a light-skinned mulatto with a delicate frame. He sat on a beat-up swivel chair, working on a sheaf of documents piled before him. His hand resembled a bird's claw, steadily scratching numbers on the page and then punching them into an antiquated adding machine on his right.

Tía Artemisa sat in front of the secretary and smoothed her skirt around her slender legs; Don Esteban sat next to her, his Panama hat on his knee. Artemisa was wearing her yellow silk dress, her Mikimoto pearls, and L'Air du Temps, her favorite French perfume. Don Esteban wore an austere serge suit with a black ribbon on his sleeve. They were both thankful for the breeze that drifted in through the window that opened onto the Guayamés bay.

Don Esteban looked up wistfully at the caryatids holding up garlands of fruits and flowers in each corner of the ceiling, their naked breasts peeling and covered with dust. He had often danced under their gaze with his wife, Marina Lampedusa, and they made him feel crestfallen, reminding him of better times. Manuel Felipe didn't look up when Artemisa and Don Esteban came in; he continued to work on his documents. Artemisa coughed discreetly, but he still didn't look up.

Don Esteban knew Manuel Felipe by name but had never met him. The secretary was the son of Blanca de Montenegro, a girl Don Esteban had courted in his youth. Manuel Felipe was her only son. He had been brought up by his father, Manuel Sánchez, an illiterate gardener. Before what people in Guayamés called "her disgrace," Blanca de Montenegro lived in a house near the cathedral, on the main square, and she came from a very rich family. Her father, Don Hipólito de Montenego, was a Spanish merchant who owned a large tobacco warehouse on the waterfront. There he stored his bales as they were brought in from the countryside before being shipped to Europe.

Don Hipólito wanted only the best for his daughter. She had been raised by a governess, so she never went to school but learned everything she knew in her own home. When she turned fifteen she was invited to attend Guayamés's parties and met Esteban de la Rosa at one of them. They drove out to the beach for a picnic in Esteban's blue Chrysler convertible, then to Maravilla, a small town nestled high in the mountains behind Guayamés. After a few months, Esteban asked Don Hipólito for Blanca's hand and they were officially engaged.

Esteban liked Blanca very much, but he wasn't sure he was in love with her. They both read a lot and were always exchanging books. Esteban enjoyed looking at her, because he loved beauty in all its forms. Blanca's hair was pale gold; when they rode in his convertible and it was whipped by the wind, it reminded him of the *guajana*, the sugarcane flower. But Esteban's parents didn't think Blanca was a good enough match for their son and tried to discourage the relationship.

In Blanca's house Esteban felt like a stranger. The Montenegros had lamentably bad taste. They went about in a flashy silver Cadillac, wore bright-colored clothes from Martínez Padín, Guayamés's modern department store, and their servants were never in uniform. Don Hipólito was a millionaire and sold his tobacco all over the world, but the upper crust looked down on him. For this reason Esteban never liked to go into Blanca's house but always said good-bye to her at the door.

Esteban was weak-willed, and when his parents introduced him to Marina Lampedusa, he broke off his engagement to Blanca de Montenegro. Marina was a second cousin of his who lived in Sábana Verde, a town near Guayamés, and he felt comfortable with her. Marina was shy—almost mousy—and had an ordinary personality. Her family wasn't half as well off as Blanca's. Marina's father was a physics professor at Sábana Verde's public high school, but the family was an old, respectable one. After Esteban broke up with Blanca, he was surprised to discover how unhappy he felt, but never having been passionate about anything, he thought he had eaten something that didn't agree with him. He purged himself with castor oil and felt much better. He married Marina a few months later, and when a baby boy was born to them, he was named Valentín.

Blanca de Montenegro was terribly depressed when Esteban jilted her, but she didn't confide her feelings to anyone. As though her own disappointment weren't enough, she had to bear her father's constant criticism. He was furious at her for having lost "the best catch in Guayamés." He was sure Blanca would never get married, he said; she was as insipid as a glass of milk. She was always going around with a book in her hand and had never learned how to be coy or to flirt with boys. Blanca felt so bad she stopped reading and spent her days lying on her bed staring at the stuccoed ceiling.

Then, what Blanca's family called "her accident" occurred. There was an old almond tree in the Montenegros' garden, and every March its leaves turned blood-red and fell like large brittle handkerchiefs over Doña Ester de Montenegro's roses. Manuel, the gardener's son, was called to the house to help his father sweep them into a pile and set it on fire. Manuel was olive-skinned, green-eyed, and very athletic. He liked to swim in the bay and had crossed it several times just before dawn when the sea was the color of hammered pewter and rippled with small waves.

Blanca loved to watch the almond leaves burning; their smell was intoxicatingly sweet, like the smell of the nuts themselves. Blanca and Manuel had been friends for years, ever since they were children. Whenever he came to the house to help his father sweep leaves or weed the lawn she came out in her straw hat and sandals to help him. When the rose bushes had aphids that had to be eliminated, Manuel showed her how to mix arsenic with an organic compound. They both wore gloves and poured the white powder in a circular trench dug around each bush, later washing their hands thoroughly and changing their clothes.

That afternoon Manuel's father told him to rake and burn the leaves in the garden and went off to fix a leaky faucet in Doña Ester's bathroom. Manuel was sixteen. He had helped his father with the chore many times. He took off his shirt, poured gasoline on the leaves, and then lit them with a match. Perspiration made his skin gleam like burnished mahogany as he raked the leaves onto the lighted mound. Blanca de Montenegro was standing just behind him, dressed in a white cotton frock with a bit of lace at the hem. She looked at Manuel's muscular back and compared it with Esteban's puny torso. She wondered why she had been so in love with Esteban in the first place and why she had thought him the handsomest man on earth. "Why don't you have hair on your chest?" she asked Manuel, giggling. "Other men's chests are covered with it, and it makes them look like apes." "I don't know," Manuel answered. "I guess hair is supposed to protect white skin from the sun. I'm already dark-skinned; I don't need hair."

"Why don't you jump over the burning leaves, then?" Blanca went on teasing. "The sun is made of fire; this little one here shouldn't bother you." Then Blanca leaned forward and kissed him on the lips. Manuel was so surprised he turned around and leapt right into the flames, or rather, being an athlete, he jumped over them and landed on the other side. Blanca jumped after him, tripped, and fell on the pyre. Manuel pulled her out and smothered the flames with his hands. Blanca lay there quietly, smoke still curling from the hem of her dress. Then she looked into Manuel's green eyes. "Please take me away from this house," she said.

They eloped a few weeks later and went to live together in a bungalow near the Emajaguas River. They were both minors and knew they couldn't get married without their parents' permission. Manuel's parents helped them out as well as they could. Manuel's father, Felipe, was the best gardener in Guayamés and he had a lot of clients; he offered his son a steady job. After a few months, it was evident that Blanca was pregnant. Don Hipólito had cut Blanca off completely, but Doña Ester secretly sent her small amounts of money and helped the young couple survive.

When a baby boy was born to her, instead of feeling happy, Blanca felt even more despondent. The more she looked at the child, the stranger he seemed to her. He was neither white like the Montenegros nor dark like the Sanchezes; he was *café con leche*—coffee with milk. It was as if someone had mixed everything up inside him. She hated to hear him cry, but she couldn't pick him up from his crib to make him stop.

Blanca thought that maybe if the baby was baptized she could accept him. She took him to the priest in Guayamés but he said he couldn't baptize a child born out of wedlock. When she asked him to hear her confession, the priest refused because "to live in adultery is to live with one's heart full of worms." Blanca couldn't take it anymore. That afternoon when Manuel came back from work he found her lying on the bed, her mouth full of arsenic and a glass of water next to her bed. The baby was at Manuel's mother's house. Blanca had left him there that morning on her way back from church.

Don Esteban was grieved when he heard the news, and he sent a wreath of white roses with a purple ribbon to Blanca de Montenegro's wake. Don Hipólito offered to take his grandson, Manuel Felipe, into his house and bring him up as his own son. Some weeks after Blanca's suicide he drove to the Sanchezes' cottage in his navy-blue Packard to meet the baby. Manuel brought him out so Don Hipólito could see him, but he wouldn't let the baby's grandfather hold him. "I can bring my son up by myself," Manuel Sánchez said proudly. "I don't want a cent of your tobacco money."

With the small stipend his grandmother sent him on the sly, Manuel Felipe studied accounting and became a CPA. He married a local girl who had worked ten years as a maid to get her degree at the local secretarial school, and they had a daughter, whom they named Blanca. Manuel Felipe was crazy about her; he worked twelve hours a day six days a week, and on Saturdays did twelve hours of overtime so his daughter would have everything.

Manuel Felipe was a member of Guayamés's Partido Democrático Institucional. He came up slowly and surely through its ranks, until he became secretary of the Bureau of Tax Returns. He was an honest public servant; he truly believed that a nation's resources should belong to the people and not to a privileged few.

Manuel Felipe's behavior with Don Hipólito de Montenegro gave him a lot of credibility within the party. He set an example for how to treat the rich; he hadn't accepted a penny of Don Hipólito's money and had sent him packing. His daughter was brought up humbly, like most of the people in Guayamés, but with a solid education at the public high school. Several years later, when the government expropriated Don Hipólito's waterfront warehouse because the wharf needed to be enlarged, Don Hipólito visited Manuel Felipe at his cottage on the riverbank. The government had paid him a pittance for his property, Don Hipólito said. He had had to take out a loan to buy a second warehouse on the outskirts of town to store his tobacco, and he needed a government subsidy until he could pay the bank back. But Manuel Felipe shook his head. "It would look like nepotism," he said. "If we weren't so closely related, I might have been able to help you, but it's impossible." And Don Hipólito lost his warehouse and went bankrupt.

Don Esteban trembled when he remembered the story, which came flashing through his mind as he sat in Manuel Felipe's office. Tía Artemisa didn't know anything about Blanca de Montenegro or about her father, Don Hipólito. Don Esteban had never told her about them.

"Pleased to meet you," Tía Artemisa said, offering her snow-white hand over the top of Manuel Felipe's desk when the secretary stopped jotting down numbers for a moment to turn a page. Manuel Felipe had no alternative but to shake it. He sat back in his chair and smiled, folding his hands over his ample chest. He was dressed in a khaki shirt and pants. "My friend Don Esteban de la Rosa here is in a bind," Tía Artemisa said cordially. "As you know, the price of sugarcane has hit rock bottom, and Don Esteban hasn't been able to pay his taxes. He wants to sell some of his farms to meet the government's requirements, but they've been invaded by squatters and he can't get the people to move out. Maybe you could help Don Esteban get the squatters out, so he can pay his taxes." Tía Artemisa's voice was smooth. She sat on her chair holding her hourglass figure gracefully, as if posing for a portrait in *Vogue*.

Manuel Felipe looked squarely at Don Esteban. "And why doesn't Don Esteban de la Rosa say anything?" he asked. "I don't understand why Miss Rivas de Santillana is doing all the talking, since it's his farms we're discussing."

Don Esteban signaled to the black band on his arm. "My granddaughter died recently, sir," he apologized. "She was only sixteen. I'm afraid my mind hasn't been as clear as it should be since that awful day. That's why I've asked Miss Rivas de Santillana here to explain my situation. I agree with everything she said."

"I'm sorry to hear about your granddaughter. What was her name?"

"Blanca de la Rosa, sir. And she was the most beautiful girl in Guayamés."

"That couldn't be, sir," Manuel Felipe said, smiling, "because the most beautiful girl in Guayamés was and still is my daughter, Blanca Sánchez." And Manuel Felipe took a photograph from his desk and turned it around so Don Esteban could see it.

Don Esteban felt his heart ball into a fist. Blanca Sánchez looked just like Blanca de Montenegro, his old love. She had her grandmother's silver-blond hair and delicate features, and her smile was just as perfect. "You lost your Blanca, but I still have mine," Manuel Felipe said, shaking his head sadly. "Life has odd ways of getting even, doesn't it, Don Esteban?" Don Esteban realized Manuel Felipe knew all about him.

Tía Artemisa couldn't understand what they were talking about. "Is that your daughter?" she asked the secretary amiably. "She's very pretty. Has she made her debut yet? Because a cousin of mine was recently elected president of the Shooting Club and the cotillion balls there are extraordinary events. If you'd like me to, I could suggest your daughter as a candidate for this year's coming-out party." But neither the secretary nor Don Esteban was listening to her chatter.

"I know exactly why you've come, Don Esteban. I have the report right here. You mustn't worry about anything," Manuel Felipe said, picking up a sheaf of papers from his desk. "I promise that by tomorrow you'll get the squatters out and be able to sell your farms." And he stood up to shake Don Esteban's hand.

The next day Don Esteban awoke feeling ill and couldn't get out of bed. Tía Artemisa put on her riding boots, climbed back into her jeep, and drove out to Don Esteban's farms, but this time a government marshal went with her. She gave each squatter a little bottle of holy water, a color portrait of the Virgin of Charity, a scapular with Jesusito painted on it, and an order of arrest for any trespasser who didn't get off Don Esteban's land in twenty-four hours. The invaders left one by one, and a few weeks later Don Esteban could finally sell his land.

Tía Artemisa was exultant, but her happiness didn't last very long. Don Esteban had a heart attack and passed away six months later. In his will he left the *central* Santa Rosa, as well as all his land, to Blanca Sánchez, Manuel Felipe's sixteen-year-old daughter. The day after the funeral Artemisa received a small box in the mail, wrapped in brown paper and tied with a string, together with a handwritten note. The note was from Don Esteban, thanking her for everything she had done in Blanca Rosa's name and excusing himself for never having asked for her hand. Inside the box was the three-carat perfect solitaire, in memory of what might have been. Artemisa took the ring out of the box and solemnly put it on.

And that's why Tía Artemisa always dressed in widow's weeds and wore a diamond solitaire on her finger until the day she died.

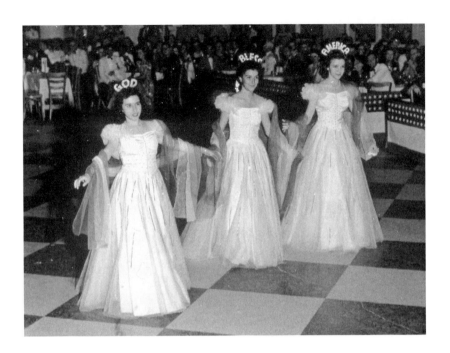

ELEVEN

THE VENUS OF THE FAMILY

In Tía Lakhmé's opinion, a beautiful dress was just as valid a work of art as a sculpture or a painting, because fashion had to do with imagination as well as with style. In fact, fashion was the truest of all the arts, precisely because it was so perishable. "A beautiful dress is like a butterfly," she'd say to Abuela Valeria when she wanted to buy a new gown. "It glitters in the sun for a few minutes, and then it's blown away by the wind. *La mode, c'est la mort.*" And if Abuela Valeria complained that the dress was too expensive and that Lakhmé already had three new ones in her closet, she would kiss and embrace her and tell her: "We have the money, Mother, why shouldn't we spend it? Are we going to take it with us to the grave?"

Tía Lakhmé was so beautiful she could have been a Hollywood star, and maybe that's why she was so unhappy. There's something about perfect beauty that puts people at its mercy; one doesn't want to disturb it or ask anything of it; it's a privilege just to be able to bask in its light.

Lakhmé was tall and willowy. She had red hair and curly eyelashes like Rita Hayworth's and the silky long legs of Marlene Dietrich. She wore only clothes by exclusive designers, such as Harvey Bering, Ceil Chapman, and Christian Dior, and she always made it a point to have her silk evening shoes dyed the same shade as her gown, whether it was ruby-red, sapphire-blue, or emerald-green.

Abuelo Alvaro died in 1926, when Lakhmé was only three, but Abuela Valeria didn't worry about her. Lakhmé was so beautiful Valeria was sure that one day she was going to marry a millionaire. When Tía Siglinda and Clarissa got married and left Emajaguas, Valeria gave their room to Lakhmé. She had it exquisitely decorated in white satin because she always saw Lakhmé as a future bride. It had white satin drapes, and the bed displayed a white satin bedspread under which Lakhmé shipped out every night to a world of dreams. Her dressing table had a three-paneled beveled mirror that surrounded her in its embrace; whenever she looked at herself in it she saw her perfect profile repeated in the distance ad infinitum.

Everybody at Emajaguas was a little bit in awe of Tía Lakhmé. She was always invited to the best parties and got to dance with the most sought-after partners, but she was terribly choosy and wasn't easily satisfied. Nobody dared find fault with her, although thanks to her perfect sense of taste, there were few opportunities to do so. Only Aurelio had the nerve to criticize her, and then strictly in jest. "You needn't be so proud of your good looks, Lakhmé," Aurelio would say. "Remember, you're the youngest one in the family, and as such, you're its tail end. And you know what hides under the tail."

When we were teenagers, my female cousins and I all wanted to follow Tía Lakhmé's example, but when we grew up and saw how many times Lakhmé got married, left the family home, and came back to Emajaguas like a plucked chicken after each divorce, we stopped wanting to be like her. Lakhmé was the perpetual bride, forever stranded on Emajaguas's shores.

Entering Tía Lakhmé's room was like entering a fashion boutique. We would try on her evening gowns and beg her to get rid of this one or that one because it looked *fanée* and was already a year old. I hated wearing my elder cousins' hand-me-downs, but I loved wearing Tía Lakhmé's. They made me feel like Cinderella dressed in her fairy godmother's clothes.

Like all but one of my aunts, Tía Lakhmé had attended the University of Puerto Rico. She had studied liberal arts for two years and always had books in her room, but I never saw her read any of them. Clarissa was forever poring over her books of agriculture, history, and sociology. Tía Dido's room was full of poetry books, and Tía Artemisa's reminded one of a sacristy, with prayer books lying all over the place. But in Tía Lakhmé's room, books served a very different purpose.

The minute my cousins and I walked through her door, Tía Lakhmé would make us all stand in a row and would balance a book on each of our heads. "You must learn how to walk keeping your chin up, my dears!" she would say. "If you look down, the world will look down on *you!*" And when she curled our eyelashes, trimmed our cuticles, and plucked our eyebrows with her steel tweezers, drawing them into perfect Cupid bows and making tears come to our eyes, she'd say to us: *"La que quiere azul celeste, que le cueste!"*—"She who wants cloud soufflé must learn to suffer!" But all her wisdom wasn't enough to teach Tía Lakhmé how to deal with the injustices of this world.

"I caught my first husband," Tía Lakhmé told us once, "when I was nineteen years old, and I was sure I had found my mate for life. It was 1942, and Tom Randolph was a first lieutenant in the marines, the handsomest man I had ever met. I fell in love with him at the pool at the officers' club in Guayamés. He was over six feet tall and looked just like Johnny Weissmuller.

"Our meeting was the result of an accident that was almost tragic. I didn't know how to swim, but it was terribly hot and the pool at the officers' club looked very enticing, so I decided to cool off at the shallow end. But the pool's bottom was slippery and it slanted abruptly; before I knew it I was sliding down with nothing to grab on to. Soon the water was over my head and my hands were the only thing above it. I tried to keep calm and walk back up, but I kept slipping toward the deep end. Then I panicked. I was sure I was going to drown. I looked around as if in a dream, my eyes wide open, staring at my own death. When I couldn't hold my breath any longer, I began to swallow tons of water. All of a sudden someone dived into the pool and came swimming toward me. He whisked me up in his arms and brought me to the surface in a second.

"He laid me on the ground and pumped the water out of my lungs. The minute he touched me, the positive current of the universe began to course through me. A week later, Tom came to Emajaguas to meet Mother. 'Lakhmé and I love each other,' he told her, 'and we want to get married before my ship sails. I'd like you to give us your blessing.'

"Valeria saw us holding hands and felt her heart grow heavy.

" 'There's nothing we can do with our lives except live them,' she said, shaking her head resignedly. 'If this man makes you happy, go ahead and marry him, Lakhmé. But please wait until he comes back from the war. Do you want to be a widow at twenty?'

" 'But he may never come back, Mother,' I begged. 'And then I'll never have known love.' So I kissed and hugged Mother and ran out of the house with my handsome marine to find a judge.

"Tom shipped out the following day, and for the next year he sailed the Pacific aboard a navy destroyer. He was at the battles of the Coral Sea and Midway, took part in the landing at Guadalcanal, and returned to the island when the war was over. He looked more like a god than ever as he walked through Emajaguas's door. He was still in uniform and his chest gleamed with campaign ribbons and medals, his officer's cap sitting jauntily on his head. When he saw me, he picked me up like a feather and kissed me on the mouth. It was the happiest day of my life.

"Mother gave us a wedding present of fifty thousand dollars, which was part of the money from the sale of La Constanza, the farm Father had singled out for me before he died. Tom and I bought a bungalow in the hills behind Guayamés with part of the money and we lived in seventh heaven for a few years.

"Tom was the perfect American husband. He was gentle and kind, he never touched alcohol or looked at other women, and he didn't mind helping with the housework. He dried the dishes and took out the garbage after dinner every night. But because of the severe wounds he had suffered in combat during his stint in the Pacific he couldn't hold a job. His nerves were shattered, and three years after we were married we had spent practically all our money on medical treatments. Then disaster struck. Tom had a massive heart attack and keeled over as he was working in the vegetable garden. I couldn't move him and there was no one in the house to help. I ran to the telephone to call Mother, and Urbano drove up the hill to our bungalow with the speed of lightning. But by the time we got to the hospital, my poor Tom was dead.

"Valeria invited me to travel to Spain with her, to take my mind off Tom. In Madrid I met Rodrigo de Zelaya, a swarthy-looking Spaniard who was ambassador to Morocco. Rodrigo was very handsome and he loved to swagger around Madrid in his riding habit—jodhpurs, boots, suede jacket, and all. The only thing odd about him was the nail on his right little finger, which was three inches long. Rodrigo used it to stir the perfumed Arabian coffee in his demitasse every morning.

"I met Rodrigo at a fox hunt at Villaviciosa, a *cortijo* on the outskirts of Madrid that belonged to a cousin of the king of Spain. I arrived dressed in a fashionable red hunting jacket, riding whip in hand, and English leather boots to my knees. 'Do you really know how to ride?' Rodrigo asked when he saw me so elegantly dressed. 'Of course I do,' I said confidently. 'My father taught me how.' And I easily mounted the black stallion he was holding for me, which was pawing the ground restlessly.

"I *did* know how to ride the delicate, small-framed *paso fino* horses of the *central* Plata. All you had to do was sit back in the western saddle and enjoy yourself. You could even drink a glass of champagne without spilling a drop as you rode through the cane fields, because they were as smooth as velvet and on level terrain. But I had never used an English saddle, much less in the Spanish countryside. I didn't have the faintest idea how to post, how to pivot my weight on my knees or lean forward to urge the horse into a canter. No sooner did I get into the saddle of the huge Spanish stallion than it sensed my insecurity and galloped across the plain like all hell. I hung on for dear life, but the beast was impossible to control. Rodrigo finally caught up with me. He made me get off my horse and had me climb onto his. I sat on the rump and held on to his waist, and the positive current of the universe began to course through me again. When Rodrigo asked me to marry him a few weeks later, I said yes.

"Rodrigo had lived in Morocco for ten years, and he had adopted many Arab customs. He had embraced the Muslim religion and asked me if I minded marrying him in a Muslim ceremony. We would get married in Rabat, he said, since mosques were forbidden in Spain. I thought it all marvelously exciting but Valeria was worried. 'Your fiancé reminds me of a one-clawed hawk. Once you go off with him to Rabat, you'll be in his clutches. Why don't you get to know him better in Madrid before you get married?' But I couldn't wait.

"Mother sailed back home full of foreboding. When she arrived in Guayamés, she sold another of my bonds and sent me a hundred thousand dollars through a bank transfer, four trunks full of clothes by ship, and all my jewelry by diplomatic valise. I deposited the money in a joint account in Rabat and gave Rodrigo a checkbook so we could both draw against it.

"At first I had a wonderful time. We lived in a beautiful palace made of blue mosaics, with Moorish gardens and fountains like murmuring mirrors—something out of the *Thousand and One Nights*. Rodrigo was a very good lover, and we made love almost every night. Arabs are experts in the art of sexual pleasure. He taught me dozens of secrets: he put mint leaves in my navel, jasmine leaves in my hair, ylang-ylang blossoms on my breasts, vanilla beans in my vagina, and then would smell and lick my body from head to toe. He had a young boy sit behind my bedroom's *masrabella*, the filigreed screen, and play the zither for us, while another boy caressed our naked bodies with a peacock feather as we lay in bed. Rodrigo's penis was large, like an ivory minaret capped by a pink dome, and I enjoyed myself enormously pretending I was its muezzin. I'd climb up on it and sing praises to Allah at least twice a day.

"But Rodrigo had one problem: he never talked to me. The Muslim religion discouraged conversation between husband and wife, and after a while I began to grow bored. I had been used to talking to my poor Tom all day and especially at night, after we made love. But with Rodrigo conversation consisted strictly of groans and sighs.

"I decided I would amuse myself alone, to take my mind off things. There was a wonderful bazaar in Rabat and I could visit it and buy beautiful silks and damasks that I could send to Paris to be made into gowns. But when I said I wanted to go shopping, Rodrigo told me I couldn't. A servant would go to the bazaar instead, and the merchants would bring the rolls of fabric to our house. He wanted me to wear a head scarf that covered half my face, as well as an awful ankle-length raincoat, every time I walked in the streets. I was incensed. I wasn't going to go around like a *tapada*, walking three steps behind my husband. I wasn't a Muslim and there was no way I was going to be made to behave as one.

"I determined not to pay attention to Rodrigo's orders. I began to see some of the European women I had met at the embassy parties, and in the afternoons we'd get together at the bar at the Hilton, which was near our house, to have a few cocktails and talk. But whenever I walked out the door in one of my designer dresses on my way to the hotel, people turned around and said shocking things to me.

" 'If you go on behaving this way, you'll destroy my reputation as an ambassador,' Rodrigo protested angrily. 'I've lived in Rabat for ten years and I respect Arab customs. The Koran sums it up very clearly: if women aren't covered, it's like giving a man salt to eat and then denying him water. And besides, women are much more attractive when they go around with their faces veiled.'

"I was getting angry, too, but I pretended nothing was amiss.

" 'And why is that?' I asked, smiling coyly.

" 'A woman's face is like her cunt—it belongs to her husband. She doesn't go around showing it to other men.'

"I burst out laughing"—and my cousins and I did, too, when we heard this part of Tía Lakhmé's story. "Of course I refused to put on a scarf or a veil, and Rodrigo and I had a violent argument.

"Another time Rodrigo invited several sheikhs to dinner at our house, and before the guests arrived he cautioned me: 'I know you're left-handed, Lakhmé, but when we sit down to eat on the dining room cushions remember to always use your right hand. Arabs use the left hand only for "unmentionable occupations." '

" 'And what are those?' I asked innocently.

" 'They use it to wipe themselves when they go to the toilet,' Rodrigo answered with a straight face. 'And to beat rebellious wives.'

"Again I burst out laughing"—and we did too, in Tía Lakhmé's silk-lined boudoir far away from Rabat and the fear she must have felt. "That evening I had a ball eating couscous with only my left hand from the huge hammered-bronze tray the waiters laid at my feet.

"Rodrigo was so incensed that when the guests left he took away my passport and my checkbook and forbade me to leave the house. From then on he screened all my letters and telephone calls and wouldn't give me any money at all. He had me followed everywhere by one of his servants and threatened to beat me up if I talked to anyone about my plight.

"The following Saturday was the maid's day off, so when the telephone rang, I answered it myself. It was Dido; she had arrived in Rabat with Antonio the week before, but every time she had called, the maid had said I was out. I asked them to come to the house for tea. We sat around talking on the red silk cushions of the living room, but Rodrigo was there also and I acted as if nothing were wrong. When Dido and Antonio were about to go I slipped a note into Dido's hand telling her what was happening: Rodrigo had kidnapped me; I was his prisoner and desperately needed their help. They should be at a certain address the next morning in a rented Land Rover to pick me up. We had to be very careful: under Muslim law, if Rodrigo caught me trying to leave the country without his permission he could have me thrown in jail.

"On Sunday morning I pulled on my gardening jumper and tennis shoes and discreetly put all my jewelry in my pockets. When Rodrigo left for the office I told the servant at the door I was going to prune my rose bushes at the back of the garden, and I climbed over the garden wall. Dido and Antonio picked me up at the appointed place not far from the house. Antonio was at the wheel and he didn't lose a minute. He drove the Land Rover south at full speed and soon we were deep in the Sahara desert. We didn't stop until we reached Mauritania.

"I arrived in Emajaguas a week later without a cent to my name but with all my jewels in my pocket. Valeria was so relieved to see me she didn't mind when I told her I hadn't been able to take my money out of the bank. 'Money's here today and gone tomorrow, dear, you mustn't worry,' Valeria said, comforting me. 'There's a remedy for everything in this world except death.' I was so relieved to be back home, I didn't shed a single tear for handsome Rodrigo de Zelaya.

"I married my third husband, Edward Milton, in 1957 in a huge wedding at the Guayamés cathedral. I had married Tom Randolph before a judge and my marriage to Rodrigo had been a Muslim ceremony, so neither of these counted in the eyes of the Catholic Church. Now I could have a true religious ceremony, with all the trimmings.

"I told Mother I wanted to have a veil ten yards long and a wedding dress with a train all the way from the street to the altar. I wanted this to be a true marriage. Valeria was glad I was finally going to be a proper bride. She went to the bank, took out the last fifty thousand dollars I had left in my account, and gave us the money as a wedding present.

"Edward Milton was a Presbyterian, but he agreed to be baptized and married in a Catholic church. He was of British descent and loved to brag that had his father stayed in London he would have had the right to sit in the House of Lords. I met him at a reception the British consul held at his house; all my old friends from Guayamés's best society had been invited. Having been married to an American who loved to live in the mountains and to a Spaniard who was half barbarian and had sequestered me in Rabat, I wanted very badly to return to the civilized world. Single women had a very limited social life in Guayamés. But once I married Edward I'd be invited to my friends' homes and be able to attend all their parties. Most important of all, I'd have an opportunity to wear beautiful clothes again.

"As soon as we got married, Edward bought a Rolls-Royce Silver Cloud and had a uniformed chauffeur drive us around town. He had a liveried butler—the first one in the history of Guayamés—open the door of our house, and I had a maid and a cook. Edward had his nails manicured and varnished by a beautician who visited our home every morning with a little wicker basket hanging from her arm, something truly unheard of in the *machista* culture of the island.

"Edward had studied at Oxford for a year and spoke English with a British accent. We often gave parties at home, but few of my friends came. Nobody liked Edward because he was so stiff and uppity. He had been born on a tobacco plantation near Raleigh, North Carolina, and was so wrapped up in himself he reminded everyone of a cigar. He never learned to speak a word of Spanish and the minute he walked in the door everyone had to start speaking English because it was bad manners to leave Edward out in the cold and he would immediately let you know that. If someone dared rattle on in the barbaric vernacular, Edward would start to criticize Puerto Rican men, the way they swore under their breath every time they had to wear a jacket and tie or the way they insisted that 'a man's dignity was in his balls.'

"Making love with Edward was something of a disappointment. He wasn't tender, like my darling Tom, and he wasn't exotic and erotically exciting like Rodrigo. His penis was like a cheap Flor de Oro cigar, the kind you can buy for five cents at any corner store on the island. And sometimes it got as prickly as an armadillo's. He couldn't stand it when I told him when and where to caress me so I could feel pleasure. He got very upset because he thought I was ordering him around.

"Edward invested our money in La Cacica, a small cigar plant in Caguana, which had a two-hundred-acre tobacco farm and a rundown shed where tobacco leaves were hung out to dry in the sun. He was completely confident because he had learned a lot about the tobacco industry in Raleigh. He discovered that Puerto Rican tobacco leaves were among the tastiest in the world. They were exported to Cuba and rolled there as gut leaves in the Montecristos and Partagás, although the Cuban tobacco manufacturers never acknowledged where the exquisite taste of their most expensive cigars came from.

"But what Edward enjoyed the most about his cigar business was the *tabaqueras*, the beautiful young women of Caguana who came to work every day in the factory. Processing the tobacco leaves was a difficult, delicate chore traditionally done by women. The *tabaqueras* first had to *despalar*, or break the stems off the leaves, then *deshilar*, or rip out the delicate veins, and finally spread the leaves out on their naked thighs to iron them out with their hands before they were hung to dry. Eventually their legs ended up as dark and perfumed as the tobacco leaves.

"Edward loved to smoke cigars, and that was probably the reason he was so attracted to the *tabaqueras*. He couldn't resist making love to them, because each time he buried his face in their perfumed thighs, he felt the same pleasure as when he was smoking a Puerto Rican cigar. Caguana is a secluded little valley outside San Juan and Edward didn't return until dusk, so unfortunately I didn't find out about this side of his business until much later.

"When I married Edward I expected him to be a haven for me, someone I could depend on for the rest of my life. I believed him when he swore he was a man of means, and when I visited the Milton family estate in Raleigh before we were married I was impressed. They lived in a turreted Victorian mansion on Main Street. But Edward had so many brothers and sisters that when his parents died the estate hardly paid him any money at all. After we were married, we had to depend solely on my income.

"In Puerto Rico, Edward's profits from La Cacica weren't enough to cover his expenses, let alone mine. After the Cuban Revolution in 1959 it became harder and harder to export Puerto Rican tobacco to Cuba, and finally the embargo stopped commerce completely between the two islands. Shipping rates went up drastically, as all products from the island had to be transported on U.S. freighters. I couldn't believe it when Edward told me he had to close down La Cacica. We were ruined and would have to live practically puffing on air.

"Edward sold the Rolls-Royce and got rid of the chauffeur and butler. I had to get rid of the maid and do the housework myself. My beautiful almond-shaped nails were the first thing to go, and my fingers turned into ugly stubs. I couldn't buy stylish clothes anymore. I couldn't even afford to go to the beauty salon; I had to fix my own hair. It was impossible to go on living like that.

"I packed my beautiful clothes in several trunks, put my checkbook and my jewels in my purse, and went back to live at Emajaguas with Mother. I left Edward the Gorham silver service, the Lenox porcelain set, and the Val Saint-Lambert glassware we had received as wedding gifts. And I would have left him much more in exchange for my freedom, because if I couldn't live for style, I couldn't live at all.

"Guayamés society is Catholic, apostolic, and Roman, and divorce isn't tolerated. I knew that if I divorced Edward I'd be cut off from the social scene completely and would never be invited to another important gathering again. I had no alternative but to try to have the marriage annulled.

"I wrote a letter to Rome asking the Vatican for information about annulments, but I never got an answer. So I went to see the parish priest in Guayamés. I told him about Edward's infidelities and how he preferred making love to the *tabaqueras* rather than to me. 'I want to have my marriage annulled and I don't know how to go about it,' I told Father Gregorio, sobbing quietly behind the confessional's red velvet curtain.

"Father Gregorio was a worldly Spaniard who loved good wine and was always amazed at other people's follies. He had come to Puerto Rico during the Spanish Civil War and was from a good family in Santander. But he had led a spartan life since arriving on the island.

I knew he would love to be invited to one of our family dinners. He pushed aside the curtain and peeked at me through the wooden grille.

" 'It's going to be difficult to give you a hand, my dear, but perhaps we can figure something out,' he whispered. I promised him that if he helped me get the annulment I'd see that he got invited to dinner at Emajaguas.

" 'There are three ways a marriage can be annulled,' Father Gregorio went on. 'If the groom is proven impotent at the time of the marriage, if the marriage contract was fraudulent—for example, if your betrothed was secretly underage or mentally unbalanced—or if one of the partners was unsure of the commitment before signing the marriage contract.' This last option, which Father Gregorio called 'the alternative of mental reserve,' was the most convenient for me, but it was also very expensive. Almost anybody could get an annulment that way, but not everyone could pay the Church forty thousand dollars in cash, the cost of the mental-reserve option.

"Father Gregorio advised me to claim impotence on Edward's part. Since we hadn't had any children it was a plausible allegation. The process of annulment was a complicated one. The pope in Rome would send a papal nuncio to conduct a detailed investigation on the island. All my relatives and friends would be interviewed. But if I could get Edward to play along, I'd have a good chance of success.

"I called Edward the next day and asked him if he was willing to make a deal. He said he wanted to go back to live in North Carolina, where one of his brothers had offered him a job, but he needed money to settle in Raleigh and he didn't have a cent. I offered to help him out. I told him all he had to do was tell the papal nuncio he was impotent, and I would give him twenty thousand dollars. Once the marriage was annulled, he could go back to Raleigh and his family with the money. Edward agreed and I sighed with relief.

"The next day I went to the bank with Valeria, who sold a bond for twenty thousand dollars and lent me the money. We sent the money to Edward. Father Gregorio wrote a letter to Rome with my petition and asked that an envoy from the Vatican be sent to the island to investigate the matter as soon as possible.

"The papal nuncio arrived four months later. He was thin and sallow, with long ears and sunken cheeks, and he wore a brown habit that made him look like he'd walked out of a painting by Caravaggio. He went around visiting everyone in the family—Valeria, Siglinda,

Dido, Clarissa—asking very private questions. The family was as solid as a brick wall. They covered my tracks so well the nuncio didn't even find out Edward was my third husband.

"Unfortunately, one day the nuncio traveled to Caguana and talked to the *tabaqueras* who still lived near the closed cigar factory. And once he had their testimony, there was no way to accuse Edward of being impotent. I had to get the annulment through the mental-reserve clause after all, and it cost me an additional forty thousand dollars, which Mother also had to lend me.

"After my divorce from Edward Milton I decided to remain single. I've been married three times, and I don't regret it. I've had my share of adventure in life. I know what a penis is like—the long, the thick, and the prickly short of it. And I can assure you none of it matters, my dears, because fashion is the secret of happiness. Since Edward, I've decided to live only for style, and I get a great deal of pleasure from it. But I can still teach *you* girls how to catch a husband, if you're interested."

PART III

CLARISSA'S TRIALS

We're all dead, children of the dead, the first man said.
No one dies, the second man answered.
—NAGUIB MAHFOUZ, *Málhamat al-Harafish*

TWELVE

ABUELO ALVARO'S LITTLE DIAMOND

The doctors were sure Clarissa wouldn't survive the first month of her life because of the rheumatic fever she developed when she was only a day old. Her heart murmur was so loud that the doctors could hear it without the aid of a stethoscope, simply by putting an ear to her little chest. She was placed in an incubator for a week, and when she didn't get better, the doctors told Abuelo Alvaro and Abuela Valeria to take their daughter home with them. There was nothing they could do but wait for the end.

When they got back to the house Abuela told Abuelo to find a nursemaid for Clarissa, because she was too distraught to care for the child. Abuela was only seventeen and she was terrified that the baby might die in her arms. That was when Abuelo Alvaro brought Miña Besosa to the house.

Miña was part Taíno Indian and part African, and she came from a very poor family. Her father, Triburcio Besosa, was a fisherman and her mother, Aralia, had died when she was very young. Miña had married Urbano, a black truckdriver who worked at the *central* Plata, when she was fifteen. When she came to Emajaguas she was already thirty-five and had had four children, who were among the healthiest in Camarones because of her abundant milk. One day Miña was washing Urbano's dirty clothes in the Camarones River when Abuelo Alvaro rode by on his horse. Urbano was holding on to her so that the current wouldn't sweep her away: Miña was about to give birth to her fifth child and so heavy that had she fallen, she would never have been able to make it back to shore.

When he saw Miña in the river, Abuelo Alvaro drew near, his horse playfully pawing the water. Miña's wet clothes clung to her body. She looked as if she were carrying a giant eggplant on her belly and two smaller ones on her chest.

"Congratulations on the happy event," Abuelo said to them, and pointed at Miña's swollen abdomen with a good-natured laugh.

"Good morning, *patrón*," Urbano answered. He had immediately recognized Don Alvaro Rivas de Santillana from the big house up at Emajaguas.

"My own wife has just given birth," Abuelo said. "How would you like to come to the house to nurse the baby? Since it's our firstborn, we'll pay you well." And he took a little bag of gold coins out of his pocket and jingled them above the horse's head.

Miña put her hand to her belly and looked fearfully at Urbano without daring to answer. "Of course she will, *patrón*," Urbano answered. "We'll be only too glad to oblige."

That night Miña cried herself to sleep. Just thinking that she would have to give the baby to her sister to take care of tore her heart. But Urbano was adamant. "Once you're working at the Rivas de Santillanas' house, we'll be secure. I'll come visit you every day, and we'll be able to buy our own house with that money."

Abuelo made some inquiries and found out Urbano was a responsible driver; moreover, he had never participated in any of the truckers' strikes at the *central*, and he had six years of schooling, which meant he could read and write. Also, Triburcio, Miña's father, had been to Emajaguas several times with the day's catch hung on a pole over his shoulders. Abuelo remembered him well. He had bought fish from him several times. Miña would be the perfect wet nurse for the baby at Emajaguas.

Back then, Puerto Rican ladies didn't breast-feed their children. They were supposed to be elegantly dressed at all times and to accompany their husbands to social events. All they did was rock the cradles and sing lullabies to their babies. Abuela Valeria was very proud of her breasts, which were alabaster white and just the right size, with nipples as delicate as rosebuds that Abuelo loved to caress at night. If she nursed the baby, her breasts would become swollen and dark, like those of mulatto women, and she certainly didn't want that. So a few days after Clarissa was born, Abuela asked the midwife to give her a special brew made from *retama* leaves that dried up the milk in her breasts, and two weeks later she was back to normal. She got all dressed up and went out to a party in San Damián with Abuelo Alvaro and soon forgot all about her baby.

When Miña arrived, Clarissa was lying in her crib, wrapped in her crocheted blanket and looking like a little wax doll. Miña was well endowed with fat; she was practically bursting out of her starched white uniform. "Poor little thing," Miña said as she picked the baby up. "She has a tiny warbler trapped in her chest, and she's so cold she can hardly breathe. But all she needs is a little warmth, and she'll come around." And she began to rub the baby down with camphor oil every two or three hours between feedings. She plastered Clarissa's chest and abdomen with pepper leaves; then she wrapped her up in long strips of gauze until the baby looked like a warm little *pastel de arroz*. Miña carried her around propped on her chest for three months, and Clarissa's *soplo* began to get better—her face turned a delicate pink. By that time she had gotten so used to Miña that no one else in the house could pick her up or she would cry her head off.

Abuela Valeria began to worry that Clarissa might never learn who her real mother was. Months went by and things remained the same. The baby would get red as a pepper the minute Abuela took her out of the crib and wouldn't stop howling until Abuela put her down. Finally, when the baby was a year old, Abuela told Miña to go back home. Clarissa howled all day in her crib but no one came to lift her. Abuela sat next to her for hours singing songs, but Clarissa didn't stop. It was terrible to think that the baby would grow up not loving her own mother.

Valeria realized she had made a mistake, letting Miña take over. She was going to do everything for her babies herself from then on, she said. She would change Clarissa's diapers, bathe her, feed her mashed potatoes from her little china plate and milk from a bottle. The time of snuggling into Miña's warm breast was over. But Clarissa wouldn't let Valeria get near her. She sat in her crib trembling with hunger and cold. But if she saw her mother approach with a spoon of porridge, she would flail her little hands in front of her and the food would go flying into Valeria's face. For two days Clarissa didn't eat anything or have a drop to drink. Everyone thought she was going to die.

"I can't stand hearing her cry like that," Abuelo Alvaro told Abuela Valeria on the second night as they lay in bed and he held her in his arms. "It's tearing my heart to pieces." Clarissa had been crying now for thirty-six hours without letting up. Her wail had become a whimper, like that of a kitten lost in the woods. Every once in a while Abuelo would heave a great sigh, his chest rising and falling like a mountain under the white linen sheets. "It's nothing," Abuela reassured him. "Today all the manuals say it's healthier to let babies cry than to pick them up. They get used to hardship and suffer less later on in life. Also, their lungs become stronger. Once I read in the papers that the mother of Adelina Patti, the coloratura soprano, never picked her up; she let her cry all the time when she was a child."

When the third day had gone by and Clarissa hardly had the strength to cry anymore, Abuela took her out of the crib and sat her on the floor. She put a bowl of milk, a plate of porridge, and a banana next to her and closed the door to the room. When Clarissa saw she was alone, she ate all the porridge with her little hands and licked the milk plate clean, but if anyone opened the door she began to howl again. When she was finished, she relieved herself on the floor like a small animal, and the maid had to come in and clean it up. This went on for a couple of weeks, with Abuela Valeria refusing to let anyone go into the baby's room, until Abuelo Alvaro couldn't take it any longer. He went in, picked Clarissa up, wrapped her in her little blanket, and sat her on his shoulder. But Clarissa went on crying. Then he took her out on the veranda to look at the sailboats going in and out of the Guayamés bay.

"Look how beautiful they are," he told her. "They look like swallows skimming the sky, free as the wind. One day you'll be like them and be able to do as you wish. If you give me a big smile and stop crying, I promise Mother will let Miña come back to work at the house." Clarissa, of course, couldn't understand a word he was saying, but his soothing tone calmed her down and she began to laugh.

Miña came back a week later, but instead of nursing and caring for Clarissa, she was put in charge of the housecleaning and the laundering. She was told never to get close to the little girl or she would lose her job, so when she walked by Clarissa's side, she always made a point of looking the other way, pretending there was nobody there.

After a while Clarissa began to ignore Miña as well and to act as if nothing had happened between them. She let everybody pick her up, feed her, and change her diapers, and her life returned to normal. Every once in a while, however, Clarissa would rub against Miña's legs when Miña came in to clean the bedroom or would lean against her as if by accident when Miña fed her. But Miña still ignored her.

When she was four years old Clarissa tried to get Miña's attention by other means. Miña loved parrots. "When they look at you with their golden pupils opening and closing their tiny kaleidoscopes," Miña said, "they are sharing an ancient wisdom with you. They always detect the thing behind the thing." But Miña wasn't able to afford a parrot.

From the terrace at Emajaguas one could often see parrots fly by in flocks, migrating from Santo Domingo to Puerto Rico on their way to the continent. Whenever she came out onto the terrace Miña would scan the trees for wings fluttering like pointed emeralds among the leaves. She would make cooing sounds but could never attract them. One day she bought a cage and sat for hours under the tamarind tree, a hopeful smile on her face. She made a wide circle of walnuts on the ground around her and kept a net tied to a long pole by her side, but the screeching parrots flew over her head and none came down.

When Clarissa saw Miña's disappointment, she ran to her room with her crayons. She came out an hour later, having drawn a beautiful green parrot in a cage just like Miña's, and gave it to her. When Abuelo Alvaro saw Clarissa's drawing, he went into town, bought a parrot, and gave it to Miña as a present. Miña hung the cage from a bronze hook in the kitchen and named the parrot Felicia, short for *felicidad,* and she loved her more than anything else in the world. Miña talked to her for hours, and Felicia always listened attentively, her head cocked to one side.

Abuelo Alvaro was sure Clarissa was cured. He filled her bathtub with toy boats and often took her to the seashore, all snuggled up in sweaters so she wouldn't feel the wind. He told her stories at night to put her to sleep, and when she grew up she always sat at his right hand at the dinner table. But what had happened with Miña had made a deep impression on Clarissa, and from then on she had a difficult time letting people touch her. It was as if a splinter of ice had remained buried deep in her heart. Love was the hardest thing in the world for Clarissa, because in spite of everything Miña had done to warm her, she always felt cold.

All that, of course, was many years later. But when Mother became a fat, happy baby thanks to Miña, everybody thought it was a miracle. That was why she was baptized Milagros soon after she was born. But when she grew older Abuelo Alvaro changed her name to Clarissa because she was so bright. By age two she could already speak clearly and when she was three she could read effortlessly. She was especially good with numbers, and by the time she was ten she was keeping a little notebook with a tally of every cent that was spent at the house, helping Abuela Valeria manage the family budget.

Abuelo Alvaro called her his little diamond because she always saw things in such a clear light. There was even talk of taking her to the United States to be evaluated at an institute for gifted children, but then Abuela got pregnant with Tía Dido. By the time Clarissa turned twelve, however, her development had slowed to normal, but she was always a little smarter than her sisters and brother.

Abuela Valeria named her daughters after the mythical characters in the works she loved. Every time a girl was born, Miña suggested a good, solid Spanish name to Abuela Valeria—for example, Juana, María, or Margarita—but Valeria had very definite ideas about what her daughters should be called. She named Siglinda after Wotan's daughter in *Die Walküre,* Dido after the queen of Carthage in the *Aeneid,* Artemisa after the Greek goddess of the chase, Lakhmé after the exotic Indian princess in Pierre Loti's poem *Le Mariage de Loti,* and Clarissa after Clarissa Harlowe, Richardson's sophisticated English heroine. Sons were important; one couldn't name them after fanciful characters out of literature or opera. Alejandro, therefore, was named in honor of Alexander the Great.

Clarissa was petite—barely five foot one—and she worried about not finding a beau. Abuelo Alvaro always reminded her that the best perfume came in small bottles. She was quick-tempered and proud. When she finally married Father she tacked his last name onto hers like the tail of a kite: Clarissa Rivas de Santillana de Vernet. This made her name so long she could hardly get it in at the bottom of her letters and checks, and it took her forever to sign them. She had been taught the Palmer method by the nuns of the Sacred Heart, and her penmanship, like everything else about her, was perfect. After the curlicued capital C of Clarissa came the elegantly flowing Rivas de Santillana, all the letters equally rounded at the bottom and pointed at the top, leaning slightly to the right as if swayed by the breeze that blew over her family's cane fields.

Even as a child, Mother was obsessed with perfection. She was very neat; her clothes were always freshly pressed, her shoes were never less than spotlessly clean, and she brushed and braided her own hair. She did her homework by herself and never got anything less than an A. She believed in the power of the mind and always finished what she began.

Clarissa was forever scolding and lecturing her sisters. Siglinda was too affectionate, kissing and hugging everyone; Clarissa called her "the sticky blob." Dido was a dreamer who floated around like a lost cloud. Artemisa was a *comesanto*, a sanctimonious holier-than-thou who never stopped praying and asking Miña to take her to Mass. Lakhmé was a birdbrain who lived for clothes and thought only about boys. There was no alternative but to make them do what *she* wanted, since she was the one who always knew best.

Abuela Valeria paid hardly any attention to Clarissa, so busy was she with her younger children. But Abuelo Alvaro idolized her, and he often took her along when he oversaw the farms, sitting her in front of him in the large western saddle that swayed to and fro across the cane fields like a rocking chair. When she was ten he bought her a pony and Clarissa became an excellent rider. She learned to love the land. "Never sell our farms," Abuelo said to her. "If things go wrong and you can't make ends meet, you may get rid of everything: the house, the silverware, even the *central* Plata—they are all replace-able. But once you sell the land, you can't start over, because you will have sold your heart." Clarissa promised that she would never sell it. And when Abuelo saw her gallop across the fields at his side, wearing jodhpurs, her hair cropped short over her earlobes, he cursed his luck that she hadn't been born a boy.

THIRTEEN

MIÑA'S SECRETS

Tía Siglinda was born one year after Clarissa, and Miña became her wetnurse too. Miña's milk was the best, Abuelo Alvaro said, and it was better if all the Rivas de Santillana children suckled from the same breast. This made them *hermanos de leche*, siblings in milk, as well as *hermanos de sangre*, siblings in blood. Alvaro hired Urbano as the family chauffeur, and Urbano moved in with Miña. They lived above the carriage house in an apartment Abuelo Alvaro had built for them. Miña was often pregnant, but she always had to send her own babies away to her sister in Camarones, who brought them up with the money Miña gave her. Miña's children lived together in a little wooden cottage by the Emajaguas River that Urbano bought for them, with a corrugated tin roof, a balcony facing the Guayamés road, and an outhouse in back, a luxury very few truck-drivers were able to afford at the time.

Miña was secretive and guarded. She seemed to be made of wood, so slow and sure were her movements, but she never made a blunder or left a chore undone. She never spoke unless spoken to, except to her parrot. She had high cheekbones and her gaze was like an eagle's; it seemed to assess you from a distance, as if measuring your strengths and weaknesses.

Miña got along very well with Clarissa and my aunts, but she couldn't stand Tío Alejandro. When he kicked his sisters or pulled their hair, Miña would stand in front of him, arms akimbo, and say: "You think that little prick of yours is your scepter because you're Emajaguas's prince. But you're no different from my other children. You've suckled my milk and gone to sleep in my arms, just as they have. There's a part of you that was born in the Camarones barrio and has slept on straw mats on the floor, four persons to a bed and four mats to a room, and has gone barefoot like I have, so you have no reason to get high and mighty and abuse other people." And Alejandro would bow his head and slink out of the room.

Miña was up before dawn because she was in charge of the cleaning and the laundering. Every Thursday she would set a huge cauldron over an open fire and sit patiently in front of the boiling soap and water, churning and swirling the family's underwear and bed linen with a long pole. I'm sure that was why Miña knew so many of our family secrets: because she was in charge of our dirty laundry. She always knew when Abuelo Alvaro and Abuela Valeria had made love, for example, and when a new child was on the way. And she also knew when they *didn't* make love and things were tense. Because she scrubbed the toilets, she knew when there was trouble at the mill: strikes gave Abuelo Alvaro diarrhea. She knew when my aunts became *señoritas* even before Abuela Valeria did, and she also knew when Tío Alejandro began to have wet dreams and to hate girls because none of them liked him. Miña also had to clean the bathtubs, so she knew when Alejandro stayed out late drinking at the bars in town, because the next day he always shunned baths.

But what really let Miña in on family secrets was the beautiful multicolored ball of soap she kept on a glass dish on top of her washbasin. She had fashioned it through the years, sticking together all the scraps of soap she had saved from the slivers she found discarded in the family's bathrooms. I saw it for the first time one afternoon when I went to visit her in her room. We had just arrived from La

Concordia and I scampered up the dark wooden staircase of the carriage house and hid in the bathroom, wanting to give Miña a scare.

I saw the soap resting on its dish, all shiny and larger than a softball. I picked it up, and it smelled of every single person in the house: of Abuela Valeria, Tía Siglinda, Tía Dido, Tía Artemisa, Tía Lakhmé, and Tío Alejandro. I turned it around slowly, inhaling everybody's secrets: Abuela's anger when she bickered with Clarissa, Siglinda's desire when she thought of Tío Venancio, Dido's excitement when she was writing a new poem, Artemisa's devotion when she was praying in church, Lakhmé's delight when she wore a new dress. And above all, Miña's smell, which held all the scraps of soap together in one marvelous perfumed globe. But I never dared ask Miña about the soap ball. I put it back gingerly in its dish and ran down the stairs and out of the carriage house.

FOURTEEN

ThE PRINCE OF EMAJAGUAS

When Tío Alejandro was born in 1904, Abuela Valeria let out a sigh of relief. She was afraid she was going to have to have a baby every year, because Abuelo Alvaro wouldn't be satisfied until he had a son who could be president of the *central* Plata. Tío Alejandro was the fourth child of my grandparents, and his arrival was duly celebrated at Emajaguas with a party. Champagne flowed, and all the hacendados of the region and their families were invited.

Tío Alejandro was a difficult child from the start. When he was born, Abuela Valeria asked Miña to nurse him, but Miña had just had a son of her own and wanted to go home. Abuelo Alvaro offered to pay her more because Alejandro was a boy, and finally Miña said yes. Miña was cautioned, however, not to overdo it. She was simply to feed the baby; his parents would provide him with affection. Miña didn't have any trouble with the arrangement. She never liked Tío

Alejandro much; he made her breasts sore because he could never get enough milk.

Alejandro had inherited Bartolomeo Boffil's height and solid physique, with a broad chest and strong legs. His name was an unfortunate choice, though, because in spite of being named for Alexander the Great, Tío Alejandro never grew to be taller than five foot three. His schoolmates laughed at him and nicknamed him Pepin the Short. What hurt Alejandro the most was that the girls in his class wouldn't look at him, and this made him bitter. Abuela Valeria told him not to worry, he was simply one of those late bloomers who would spring up all of a sudden in his teens. But Tío Alejandro never did. Valeria sent Miña to school every day with a special *ponche* for Tío Alejandro, a shake made with eggs, cinnamon, and cream, but even that didn't help.

Alejandro was Abuela Valeria's favorite child. When he was a baby Abuela called him her Apollo because he brightened her day. But in Clarissa's opinion Alejandro had very little in common with the god of harmony and light. When he grew up and went to school, Alejandro often got into fights and came home with cuts and bruises. He was tough, though, and never cried.

When Abuela Valeria realized that Tío Alejandro's height gave him an inferiority complex, she ordered special shoes made for him with leather platforms at the bottom and steel tips in the toes, which made him three inches taller and gave him a stiff, martial air when he walked. At school he loved to click his heels against the polished floors when he sauntered past his schoolmates, like a Fascist Italian prince. This made him feel better, and the steel tips were very effective when he got into fights because he could kick his opponents sharply in the shins.

If Tío Alejandro's height got him into trouble, he also had a lot of difficulty learning to read. Words were scrambled before his eyes as if he saw them reflected in a mirror. *Raw* became *war*, and *rat* became *tar*, and soon he was stuck in the alphabet's inky maze, unable to understand a thing. He felt awed by his sisters, but especially by Clarissa, because she was so good with words. He was afraid of her because she was smart and also very outspoken. It took Tío Alejandro two or three minutes to answer when he got into an argument. Clarissa's tongue was like a blade that could cut you to pieces in no time at all.

Abuela Valeria was convinced Alejandro didn't do well in school because he couldn't see the blackboard. She asked the teacher to seat him in the front row, but Alejandro still didn't learn to read. He had inherited Abuelo Alvaro's love of heraldry and would hide behind his textbooks to draw the family's coat of arms on a piece of paper —two swords crossed on a blue field covered with fleurs-de-lis. As the teacher droned on about multiplication tables, he'd fold it into an airplane and send it flying toward Mary Ann Cedros, the prettiest girl in the class and the daughter of the owner of the *central* Cambalache. But Mary Ann never paid him any attention.

Tío Alejandro loved to tease his sisters about the Rivas de Santillana name. When they got married, he'd say, they would all lose their last name and have to sign with their husband's, but when *he* got married he would give his name to his wife and children, and the Rivas de Santillana lineage would survive—thanks to him.

Abuelo Alvaro was often upset about his son's performance in school, but Tío Alejandro wasn't concerned in the least. After all, he was going to be president of the *central* Plata when he grew up, and to do that, one didn't have to be good with words *or* numbers; all one had to do was learn how to order people around. He didn't care at all about the farmlands he would inherit one day, which Abuelo Alvaro insisted were both a privilege and a responsibility. He never enjoyed riding across the fields to see the cane ripple like water in the wind, as Clarissa did. He thought the *central* Plata should make more money, and if he had to sell some land to raise working capital, he didn't see anything wrong with it.

What Tío Alejandro loved most was to go hunting up the Emajaguas River with the buckshot rifle Abuelo Alvaro had given him as a birthday present when he turned twelve. Every day after school he would lose himself in the river's marshes and return home with a piece of game, usually a mourning dove, which he would bring into the kitchen and give to Gela, the cook. Sometimes, however, he would deliver withered herons, limp silver owls, and even *guaraguaos*—our local eagles—their snow-white chests dripping with blood beneath their brown feathered hoods.

Abuela Valeria didn't like it when Alejandro brought dead birds into the house, but when he killed a blackbird one day and carried it to the kitchen and Abuela saw its crimson beak lying like wind-polished coral in the sink, she was furious. She made Abuelo Alvaro take away Alejandro's rifle and he was forbidden to hunt again. But Tío Alejandro went on hunting with a slingshot. He would roast his birds out in the field over an open fire and eat them all by himself.

Abuelo Alvaro was terribly strict with Tío Alejandro because he wanted the future president of the *central* Plata to learn to be disciplined early on. While his sisters' bedrooms had windows framed in frilly Swiss embroidery, Alejandro's room had no curtains, and there were no straw mats at the sides of his bed, so he had to step barefoot on the cold tiles when he got up to pee at night. He took an ice-cold shower every morning, and his four-poster bed had a hard, thin mattress made of horsehair, which pierced the striped cotton cover and pricked his skin.

Instead of a glass chandelier like the ones that lit his sisters' bedrooms, the lamp that hung over Tío Alejandro's bed was made of iron and decorated with a black medieval knight riding a horse. This was the last thing Alejandro saw before he fell asleep at night. His sisters had all the clothes and shoes they wanted; Guayamés's best seamstress was kept busy sewing gowns for them, and they often received charm bracelets, pearl necklaces, and rings from Abuelo Alvaro for their birthdays. Tío Alejandro had only two suits, one of coarse twill for every day and one of linen for Sundays, along with two pairs of custom-made platform shoes.

Abuela Valeria, on the other hand, spoiled Tío Alejandro behind Abuelo Alvaro's back. If Gela cooked a flan, Abuela always saved him the largest portion and served it to him secretly in the pantry; if there was fried chicken for dinner, Alejandro always got the drumsticks *and* the breast while the rest was rationed among the girls. Tío Alejandro was the only one of the Rivas de Santillana children ever to get a car for a present, a red Ford coupé with a rumble seat that Valeria had wrapped up in cellophane and parked under his window at Emajaguas one Christmas morning when he was eighteen.

Alejandro would try to win Clarissa over, asking her into his room to look at his stamp collection or letting her play *bolita y hoyo*—hole in one—with his swirled colored marbles. Clarissa never liked to play with dolls; she loved shooting pool in Abuelo Alvaro's game room and she could run faster than many of Alejandro's friends. She would have given anything in the world to join the baseball team at the Shooting Club, just down the road from Emajaguas. But when she got a hit and was running from second base to third, Alejandro would always put out his foot and trip her. She never made the baseball team.

At other times Tío Alejandro stole her notebooks and scribbled dirty words across her homework. Or he would enter her room without permission and steal her crayons and drawing books. Clarissa would run after him wielding a fork, screaming her head off and telling him to leave her alone. Tío Alejandro would twist her arm until he made her drop the fork. Clarissa would tremble with rage and squirm away, perspiration running down her face. They'd roll on the ground, clawing at each other like a pair of tiger cubs. Miña was the only one who could separate them and make them stop fighting.

Abuelo Alvaro always sided with Clarissa and scolded Tío Alejandro roundly. But Abuela Valeria insisted they were both to blame: "You need two to fight," she told Alvaro angrily. "One can't fight with oneself, so don't start accusing Alejandro of everything." And to Clarissa she'd say: "Your brother really loves you, Clarissa; he's simply trying to get your attention because he's bored and wants to play with you. If you were kinder and gentler, you wouldn't pay any mind to his pranks but would go along with him." Clarissa had to bow her head and do Valeria's bidding.

At the Sacred Heart in Guayamés, where Clarissa was going to school at the time, she was taught that God was always just. But the nuns were wrong, because God had made women weaker than men. "Someday, I swear, I'll kill you," she yelled at her brother once, "even if I have to go to hell!" Tío Alejandro laughed and, running to hide behind Abuela Valeria's skirts, accused Clarissa of trying to get back at him for every little thing.

FIFTEEN

TÍA SIGLINDA'S ELOPEMENT

Abuela Valeria wanted all her daughters to go to the university, something few young women were allowed to do at the time. This is something that always made me proud of being half a Rivas de Santillana. There weren't many families like Mother's in Puerto Rico at the time.

When my aunts were teenagers, Abuela gave them long talks about the importance of women getting an education. "You'll feel much better once you have a college degree," she told them. "You'll enjoy life more and acquire prestige in men's eyes. An education will make it easier for you to find a good husband and you'll be better mothers to your children." Her daughters all cheered when they heard this and kissed and embraced Valeria, because traveling to the capital meant they would attend all the social events there. They would make new friends and be able to take advantage of the cultural activities that Guayamés lacked—concerts, the ballet, the theater—and that they had enjoyed when they traveled to Europe with their mother.

Tía Siglinda was the only one of the Rivas de Santillana girls who didn't study at the University of Puerto Rico, because she always wanted to be a housewife. She dreamed of a white cottage with red roses blooming over her door, where she'd wait every afternoon for her husband to come home from work. Her hobby was sewing tablecloths, sheets, and shawls, and she sat for hours on the terrace of Emajaguas embroidering lilies, roses, and violets, as if a garden were constantly growing from her lap. She was convinced that her threads had magic powers and that once she gave someone a garment she had sewn, the person would never be able to forget her.

Tía Siglinda was Mother's closest sister; they had been born only one year apart and they were always together. They shared the same room, ate next to each other at the table in the pantry, and always took their baths together. Siglinda had inherited Abuelo Alvaro's happy disposition—she was always laughing and making jokes, while Clarissa brooded about every little thing. They were like two sides of the same coin, the optimist and the pessimist, the exuberant and the controlled, but they always gave each other support.

When Abuelo Alvaro and Abuela Valeria argued with each other and ashtrays and vases flew like missiles out the windows, the younger children would all run and hide under the bed, until Mother and Tía Siglinda stepped courageously between their parents. "Don't you love Mom, Dad?" Siglinda would ask Abuelo, laughing. "Don't you love Dad, Mom?" Clarissa would ask Abuela, sternly shaking a finger at her. And immediately their parents would stop insulting each other and begin to embrace, apologizing for the fright they had given their children and promising they would never fight again.

The first time Tía Siglinda heard Venancio Marini speak was in 1919, at her high school graduation. Siglinda was in the first row of the auditorium when Venancio, a Guayamés lawyer, began to deliver the commencement address. Venancio's family was of Italian peasant origins and had originally been very poor. His father, Javier Marini, had emigrated to the island thirty years before from Gaeta, a town in central Italy.

Tío Venancio was a brilliant lawyer, I heard Mother say many times. He had graduated from law school at the University of Puerto

Rico at nineteen. At twenty-two he was elected to the House of Representatives. By the time he was in his late twenties, he had made a reputation for himself working for American corporations that owned large sugar mills on the island.

The Partido Republicano Incondicional was in power at the time and Tío Venancio became one of its members. It proposed statehood as the solution for the island's economic ills and it sympathized with American interests. Thanks to his valuable connections, Venancio was elected mayor of Guayamés. That same year he was invited to give the commencement address at the public high school.

He was a wonderful orator. He was known in Guayamés as Pico de Oro, the Golden Beak, who never read from notes but "spoke from the heart," as the local newspapers put it. Siglinda looked up at him as he stood on the palm-decorated platform and was immediately smitten by his good looks. He had an imposing physique: he was six feet tall and his arms were as thick as a wrestler's from lifting weights every day. He was wearing a brand-new linen suit, two-tone shoes with the tips so polished he could see his face mirrored in them, and a diamond as big as a chickpea on his little finger. Tío Venancio modulated his voice so it felt like a cool wave of foam breaking over one's head. He was the kind of orator who compelled his audience to believe in everything he said, even if it didn't make much sense when his listeners went back home and sat in their own living rooms, beyond the magnetic power of his voice.

The night of Siglinda's graduation ceremony, Venancio noticed her unwavering gaze on him. She was a little overweight, but this only made her more appealing. He didn't like slender women; he was a man of substance and liked to embrace what he owned. Once the ceremony was over, he approached Siglinda during the party in the school's gymnasium and offered her a glass of punch. As she held it in her hand, he discreetly took a silver flask from his pocket and poured her a shot of rum. Prohibition was in full force, and if anyone had seen him, he would have been put in jail. But Siglinda was delighted, and she immediately drank up.

Abuelo Alvaro and Abuela Valeria didn't attend the graduation ceremonies, and Miña was busy talking to her friends in the school's kitchen, so Siglinda danced all night with Venancio. Before she said good-bye she invited him to visit her at Emajaguas. Venancio gladly accepted. Siglinda was enchanted. They had been dancing a rumba and it was very hot; when it was over she took out her fan and vigorously cooled herself.

"I love fans," she told Venancio. "I made this one myself, with sandalwood and a little bit of lace." Venancio looked at it closely. It was delicately embroidered, with a painted swan swimming peacefully on a lake.

"Do you know what Josephine de Beauharnais asked Napoleon Bonaparte when she met him at a ball in Paris?" Venancio asked Siglinda. Siglinda shook her head; she had a faint idea who Napoleon Bonaparte was but had never heard of Josephine de Beauharnais.

" 'What is the most effective weapon you've encountered in your military career, Monsieur?' Josephine asked. 'Your fan, madame,' Napoleon said." Siglinda giggled and Venancio kissed her hand. Then Siglinda said she had to go to the girls' room to take a pee, gave Venancio her fan for safekeeping, and disappeared from sight.

Venancio waited for Tía Siglinda for an hour but she never came back. He told his chauffeur to bring his De Soto around and drove home feeling very depressed. He couldn't sleep all night. He was torn between accepting her invitation to visit her at Emajaguas and his fear of repercussions. Siglinda was very young; he didn't want to do anything that would harm his reputation as a promising politician. He decided he wouldn't go. He put Siglinda's fan under his pillow and fell into a troubled sleep.

The next afternoon he had to drive by Emajaguas on his way to make a speech to the Girl Scouts Association in the next town. As he drove past the heavy wooden gate, he couldn't resist temptation and told the driver to stop because he wanted to return Miss Siglinda's fan.

It was raining as it can rain only in Guayamés; water was pouring down the roof of the house like a cataract. Venancio's chauffeur held a huge black umbrella over Venancio's head as he got out of the car. Venancio picked up the bouquet of red roses wrapped in green wax paper he had brought along for the head of the Girl Scouts Association, walked up the wide granite stairs to the house, and rang the bell. Miña answered and, when she saw the mayor, opened the door. "Is Miss Siglinda in?" he asked. "Please tell her Don Venancio Marini has come to call." And then he entered and folded his dripping umbrella in the hall.

With Taíno discretion, Miña tiptoed to Siglinda's room and knocked lightly on her door. "There's someone very important to see you in the living room," she whispered. Then she went back to the hall where Venancio was waiting, opened the frosted-glass doors to the living room, and politely ushered him in. She told him Siglinda would be right there.

Venancio sat down cautiously in a rocking chair. He was still holding the roses when Miña came in with a vase and put them in it. Venancio didn't dare get up from the rocking chair—he didn't want to break anything. He was a big man, and the living room was crowded with potted palms, delicately carved love seats, and half a dozen little marble-topped tables on which sat Abuela Valeria's biscuit porcelain baby dolls, all dressed in smocks and caps she had embroidered herself. Abuelo Alvaro walked into the living room by chance.

"Who let you in here?" Abuelo said coldly, without putting out his hand. Venancio got up from his chair. "Your maid, sir. I was just driving by and I thought I'd drop in to return your daughter's fan. She left it behind at the high school graduation party last night." Abuelo Alvaro stared at him. "Seventeen-year-old girls don't get visits from politicians, at least not *my* daughters," Abuelo Alvaro said. Venancio was an inch taller than Abuelo; both men were equally robust and they puffed out their chests like roosters, measuring themselves against each other. Siglinda entered the living room at that moment and drew near to introduce Venancio to her father, but Venancio cut her short.

"I'm Venancio Marini, sir, the mayor of Guayamés," Venancio said.

"I know that," Abuelo answered, "and I also know that it's raining outside." And he took the roses out of the vase and shoved them back into Venancio's arms, dripping water all over the mayor's suit. "I think you'd better leave," he said.

Venancio pretended he wasn't offended. He took the roses and placed them calmly over his right arm, pulled out his handkerchief from his pocket, and wiped the water from the front of his vest. Siglinda accompanied him to the door in tears. "Don't you worry, my little swan," Venancio told her, offering her a single rose. "One day you'll be my Siglinda and rid yourself of the moth-eaten Rivas de Santillana name." And head held high, he walked out into the downpour, leaving his umbrella behind.

Tía Siglinda was heartbroken; that night she woke Clarissa up with her sobs. Lifting the mosquito netting around her sister's bed, Siglinda slipped under the sheets with her. "What should I do?" she asked. "Venancio wants me to elope with him, but I don't want to upset Father."

"Do you love Venancio?" Mother asked. "Yes," Tía Siglinda answered, "and he loves me. But he scares me a little too. When I listen to him, I feel compelled to do what he wants. I can't control myself." Clarissa liked Venancio. He was a good mayor. He always had new projects: the dam at Río Corrientes, which had doubled Guayamés's electric power; the orphanage on Calle Méndez Vigo; the quay at the end of the main street, which permitted all the merchandise that arrived by ship to be unloaded and carted easily to the warehouses in the center of town. "Don't worry about it now," Clarissa told her. "Love has a funny way of solving life's problems." And she took Tía Siglinda in her arms and stroked her sister's hair until Siglinda fell asleep.

A week passed, during which Siglinda could think of nothing but Venancio. She dreamed about him every night and woke with the sheets wet with perspiration. Miña had secretly delivered several notes informing her that Venancio would be waiting for her every night outside Emajaguas's walls. The following week Tía Siglinda finally made up her mind. She got out of bed at three in the morning, went to the pantry for a loaf of bread, opened the back door of the house, and escaped down the backstairs. She ran out into the garden in her nightgown, threw the geese some bread as she hurried by their shed, so they wouldn't cackle at the commotion, climbed up a mango tree that grew next to the ten-foot-high fence, jumped down on the other side, and got into Venancio's blue De Soto, which was waiting for her at the curb. By the time it pulled away, Venancio had drawn the gray velvet curtain over the partition behind the front seat and Siglinda lay naked in his powerful arms.

When Abuelo Alvaro discovered the next morning that Siglinda was gone he was furious. He notified the police that his daughter, a minor, was missing. A patrol was sent out to find the couple, but Abuela Valeria bristled when she heard about it.

"Do you think that's wise, Alvaro?" she said, giving him one of her Boffil stares. "Venancio Marini is mayor of Guayamés. He's a very powerful man." Abuelo stared back at her with bloodshot eyes. "All politicians are corrupt. And this one's as vain as a peacock. How can you even consider letting him take Siglinda away from us? She's only seventeen," he said.

"She's going on eighteen," Valeria answered. "I was only sixteen when I married you. And Siglinda is stubborn. She won't care if she causes a scandal, which is just what I want to avoid. Once the newspapers get wind of what happened, our daughter's picture will be all over the front page and the mudslinging will be inevitable." Abuelo sat down dejectedly in front of Abuela. "All right, Valeria, I'll do as you wish," he said. "I'll notify the police to call off the search. But from now on, I forbid you to mention Siglinda's name in Emajaguas again."

Venancio bought Siglinda a beautiful house on Cristóbal Colón Avenue, the main boulevard of Guayamés, with a wrought-iron fence around it, a gingerbread *mirador* that looked toward the bay, and, in front, a trellis covered with roses. He wanted her to have servants, but Siglinda wouldn't hear of it. It was hot in Guayamés, she said, there was no breeze blowing in from the sea as it did at Emajaguas, and she enjoyed walking around the house naked to cool off. When Venancio came home from work they made love everywhere, on the heavy oak dining room table, on the yellow silk living room sofa, on the Persian rug with the Garden of Paradise woven into it, sometimes even on the bed, with the beautiful linen sheets Siglinda had embroidered herself. But every time Venancio asked Siglinda to marry him, she said no.

"What do you want me to be your wife for? To please Father and Mother? To keep the society ladies and the parish priest from gossiping about us? They'll gossip anyway. I'd rather remain your mistress."

When Abuela Valeria heard what was going on, she asked Clarissa to talk to Siglinda. Clarissa went to visit her sister, and they sat in the living room. They made an odd couple: Clarissa was snuggled up in the Mexican serape Miña had given her one Christmas, with the colors of the rainbow wrapped around her, while Siglinda sat naked on the yellow silk Victorian sofa Venancio had bought for her.

"You can't go on like this, Siglinda. You're getting love and lust mixed up," Clarissa told her. "Love comes from the soul and is pure. Lust comes from the body and can scorch you to hell."

"That's the difference between the two of us, sister," Tía Siglinda said, shaking her head. "I love Venancio more than anyone in this world, but it's impossible to separate body and soul. The body keeps the soul warm and the soul keeps the body cool, but if one of them dies, the other one will too. They're sewn together with the same magic thread."

"What thread?" Clarissa asked innocently.

"Pubic hair," Siglinda answered, laughing heartily. "The day you understand that, Clarissa, you won't feel so cold."

Tía Siglinda loved to shock people. When her well-to-do neighbors came to visit, wanting to verify the rumors that were flying around town, Tía Siglinda hurriedly ran to her room to get dressed, then sat demurely in the parlor. At first the conversation would develop normally, but out of the blue Siglinda would stare at her neighbors and say: "Each time Venancio fucks me, a red rose blooms over our porch." Coffee cups would start trembling, teaspoons would drop to the floor, but Siglinda paid no mind. "I know we should get married because I'm a Rivas de Santillana girl," she'd continue, fanning herself and following her flustered neighbor to the door. "But I like to go to bed with Venancio knowing I'm his procurer. I procure him whatever he wants—a tie or a tit, a cup or a cunt, or an earful of honey he can lick at will." And although few neighbors actually heard the last part of her speech, because by that time they were fleeing down Cristóbal Colón Avenue, Siglinda loved to whisper it to herself.

In 1920, a year after Abuelo Alvaro threw Venancio out of Emajaguas, Venancio sent him a magnificent present for Christmas—a case of Dom Pérignon champagne, Abuelo Alvaro's favorite—with a card wishing him a happy holiday and a good harvest for the *central* Plata in the new year. And as Venancio was by that time a close friend of the American governor on the island and the *central* Plata could certainly benefit from the government's financial incentives, Abuelo Alvaro and Abuela Valeria sent Siglinda and Venancio an invitation to join them for the Christmas feast at Emajaguas that year.

The dinner was a total success. Abuela Valeria and Venancio got along wonderfully, and Venancio couldn't stop talking about the marvelous inventions the Americans had brought to the island: the telegraph, the telephone, the electric generator, the electric stove. That was the reason he was for statehood, Venancio told Abuelo Alvaro: because he believed in the modern age. And since the Partido Republicano Incondicional was now protecting the sugar industry, it would be wise if Abuelo joined it and made a generous contribution.

Abuelo Alvaro thanked Venancio profusely and followed his advice. The next year, Tío Venancio was elected president of the Partido Republicano Incondicional. It was a position even more powerful than that of mayor. He met with the governor's cabinet in San Juan and named the party's candidates to the Senate and the House of Representatives. That Easter, Siglinda and Venancio had been married in the cathedral during High Mass. The entire town turned out for the wedding feast at Emajaguas.

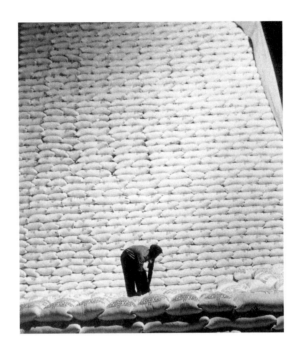

SIXTEEN

OKEECHOBEE

In September 1919 Clarissa traveled to San Juan and entered the University of Puerto Rico in Río Piedras. Before she left Emajaguas, she told Abuela gravely: "I want to go to the university to study, Mother, not to find a husband. When I grow up I want to be as free as the wind; I don't want a man hovering around me like a drone. And anyway, there's no nicer place to live than our own house." Abuela Valeria laughed, convinced that one day Clarissa would change her mind.

Clarissa installed herself at the Pensionado Católico. The food was bland but healthy; the beds were iron cots separated by sheets that hung from rods attached to the ceiling. The Pensionado was a large, four-storied building, with a long, balustered balcony, facing the campus. The grounds were planted with yellow trumpet vines, pink oleander, and red bougainvillea. A long avenue of royal palms led to an elegant Spanish Revival clock tower, whose pink ceramic pinnacles and green gargoyles ran with water every time it rained.

Dido and Artemisa followed in Clarissa's footsteps and arrived at the Pensionado two years later. Soon they were flitting around the social scene like a flock of swans, invited to all the parties and making new beaus at every opportunity. Clarissa didn't always go with her sisters. She spent a lot of time studying in the library, bundled up in Miña's Mexican serape.

The clock on the university's tower chimed its carillon every hour on the hour and gave Clarissa the feeling of being in a sacred place as she walked from one classroom to the next, her arms loaded with books. She had excellent professors, among them several American scientists and a famous mathematician. It made her heart beat faster, as she crossed the campus under the royal palm trees, to think that she was now part of an intellectual elite, that milling around her were the future doctors, judges, engineers, economists, and historians who would determine the fate of the island.

Clarissa majored in agronomy because she wanted to learn the most modern methods of sugar production. She thought her advice to her father might be helpful in managing the mill. They would be able to discuss the seeding, weeding, and harvesting of the *central* Plata's sugarcane in light of the latest technological developments. Clarissa also took classes in history and sociology and grew keenly aware of the importance of preserving one's natural resources, be it land or one's own mind and body.

At the Sacred Heart in Guayamés the nuns had taught Clarissa that God wanted women to be mothers above all and that Saint Paul had said they must obey their husbands. Valeria had agreed with the nuns, as long as her daughters were educated in the process. She got stinging mad every time she remembered how her own father had sentenced her to illiteracy. But although education was an advantage, even educated women from the upper classes usually couldn't find work. That's why Valeria always insisted marriage was the only career open to them.

Clarissa couldn't have agreed less. Education was necessary because it gave women the possibility of economic independence. You only had to drive down the road and meet a peasant woman, her belly swollen with child, a wailing baby in her arms, and a third one in rags trailing behind to understand that women were easily exploited by their husbands. Once they got old or had too many mouths to feed, the men simply took off for New York. But if a woman was educated enough to be able to survive on her own, she needn't let a man lay a hand on her unless he took responsibility for the consequences.

Women didn't even have the right to vote. Only men could vote on the island, which meant that women, from a legal point of view, were on the same level as prisoners, beggars, and the mentally retarded. Clarissa was indignant when she first learned this. The fight for women's suffrage was spreading in San Juan, so Clarissa became an activist in the movement. She joined several suffragette organizations, including the Liga Social Sufragista and the Liga de la Mujer del Siglo XX.

On her next visit to Emajaguas the first thing Clarissa did was to march into the kitchen and tell Miña: "Education is the first step in women's liberation! The right to vote belongs to those who have won it thanks to a university diploma. Educated women should be able to participate in the economic affairs of the country and have a say in its destiny." Miña stared at her in annoyance. "The vote should belong to all women, to those who can write and those who can't," she retorted, swirling her mop over Clarissa's patent-leather pumps and then wringing it out vehemently with her strong hands until the dirty water overflowed the bucket.

"To all women!" Felicia screeched, craning her neck inside her cage.

"Will you teach me how to read and write?" Miña asked.

"We'll start right now," Clarissa answered. And she took Miña to her room, sat her at the desk, gave her a pencil and a lined notebook, and began to guide her hand over the letters of the alphabet. When Clarissa's birthday came around a few weeks later, Miña gave her a present: a picture of herself, with "Miña Besosa" written at the bottom in her own hand. Clarissa had it framed and hung it on her bedroom wall.

One day Clarissa told Miña about Aurelio Vernet, a nice young man she had met at La Concordia, where she went to spend a weekend with a student friend from the university, Janina Figueroa, who was studying liberal arts. Janina was her roommate at the Pensionado Católico. Aurelio was at La Concordia for the holidays; he was studying to be an engineer at Northeastern University in Boston. Aurelio's father, Santiago Vernet, had a foundry and machine shop in La Concordia called Vernet Construction.

Aurelio was a nice young man, Clarissa told Miña. He wasn't cruel and selfish like Tío Alejandro. He had a slender build; he wasn't brawny and overbearing like most of the young men she knew. He loved to play the piano, and every once in a while Clarissa went to the university's theater, where there was an old Pleyel, to listen to him play. The only trouble was, she couldn't stand Aurelio's touching her.

"It's nothing serious, just an *amitié en rose*," Clarissa assured Miña. "You know I'm never going to get married, so stop looking at me like that. I'll never find another man like Father in the whole world." Nonetheless, Aurelio came to visit Clarissa at Emajaguas that Christmas, and although she wouldn't see him again until the summer because he had to go back to Boston, from then on the family considered him Clarissa's official suitor. In 1925 she graduated from the University of Puerto Rico at the head of her class with a degree in agronomy. Then she went back to live with her parents at Emajaguas.

During Christmas dinner that year, Abuelo Alvaro told the family the bad news about Okeechobee, which had begun to suck their fortune dry. Many years later Mother told me about that evening, which she believed was a turning point in their lives. The feast started out as usual; the food was prepared with love and the house decorated with the utmost care. Clarissa wore her favorite black velvet gown, cut low at the back. Tía Siglinda wore a red brocade evening dress; Tía Dido one of her Spanish *petenera* skirts; Tía Artemisa a blue silk robe that made her look like a priestess; Tía Lakhmé, who was only a child but already had exotic tastes, wore a necklace of tiny golden beads. The older sisters complimented one another as usual; it was like seeing themselves reflected in the mirror over and over. Finally, after exchanging gifts and bantering about who'd gotten last year's rewrapped *pasapalante*, saved from year to year because it was useless, everybody sat down at the table.

There was a lot of laughter and joking between my aunts and uncles as the wineglasses were filled again and again. At the time, only Tía Siglinda and Tío Venancio were married. My other aunts were still single. After a while, however, the tone of the family's conversation grew surprisingly plaintive. Abuelo Alvaro and Abuela Valeria became strangely silent as Tío Alejandro's voice rose in irritation above the rest.

He was twenty-one and was studying business administration at the University of Virginia. But he kept close tabs on what was happening at Emajaguas. He was complaining about an investment Abuelo Alvaro had made recently in Florida: a large sugar mill he had purchased on the shores of Lake Okeechobee, near the Everglades. A double disaster had struck: a severe frost as well as a hurricane had wiped out three thousand acres of sugarcane and destroyed the entire harvest. Thousands of dollars had gone down the drain.

"I told you Okeechobee was a bad investment from the start," Tío Alejandro said to Abuelo Alvaro bitterly. "But you chose to listen to Venancio." Lately Abuelo Alvaro had fallen more and more under Venancio's influence because Venancio had so much power with the government. He had come to depend on his son-in-law for the government loans he needed to keep the *central* Plata going.

"I bought the Okeechobee mill because I wanted to, and I'm not sorry I did," Abuelo said defensively. "Seventy percent of our island's valleys are in the hands of American sugar mill owners. It's time we turned the trend around and showed the Americans we, too, can be absentee owners."

"Your decision was obviously a mistake," Tío Alejandro retorted. "We've lost too much money already. We're small fry compared to American businessmen—we don't have the capital to wait it out until the weather gets better. Okeechobee will have to be sold."

Tío Venancio tried to calm Alejandro down. He was sure things would turn around the following year; a fabulous crop was expected and sugar was selling at an excellent price. He had suggested the purchase of Okeechobee not because of nationalist feelings but because he believed in statehood and was in favor of bringing Puerto Ricans economically nearer to the United States.

Abuelo Alvaro didn't answer. He had to admit that what Alejandro had said was true. Okeechobee *was* a terrible investment, and it was sold soon after that.

SEVENTEEN

ABUELO ALVARO SWIMS AWAY

"Your grandfather was only forty-five when he began to lose his mind," Mother told me once. "He was in the flower of his manhood. At first it wasn't very noticeable; he simply began to confuse the names of certain objects. He would be sitting at the table and ask Valeria to pass him the seltzer siphon instead of the wine carafe. Some days he would forget to shave one side of his face and go to the office with one cheek pink and smooth and the other one covered with a peppery scruff.

"He talked less and less, and one day after dinner he sat at the table with your grandmother staring off into space. I thought he was just depressed over some incident at the mill and didn't attach importance to it. But all of a sudden he took off his tie and began to unbutton his shirt. He took off his gold cuff links and then he removed his shirt. It was the middle of July and evenings were hot, so

Valeria thought perhaps he was just trying to cool off. But when Father got up from his chair and took off his pants and shorts, your grandmother and I began to scream.

"Fortunately we were the only ones there—Siglinda was already living in her own house in Guayamés, Lakhmé was sleeping, and my other sisters, as well as Alejandro, were away at the university—but we were terrified. Father paraded naked around the dining room and then walked toward the living room, where the windows were open and people could see him from the road. "I should never have been born! The Plata is near bankruptcy and I have to depend on my son-in-law's wiles to keep it going!" he cried. When Urbano ran into the living room and threw a bathrobe over him, Father punched him in the jaw. Mother and I locked ourselves in the bedroom and sent Urbano to get the family doctor. The doctor came with two male nurses, and between them and Urbano they held your grandfather down while the doctor injected him with a sedative that put him to sleep. But when he woke up, Father got out of bed, took off his clothes, and did the same thing all over again.

"The doctor came to the house once more and Father was again sedated. He was taken to the hospital in an ambulance for a thorough examination; the diagnosis was acute deterioration of the brain due to advanced arteriosclerosis. Valeria tried to keep him confined to his room, but when Father realized he couldn't get out he turned violent. He took his .44-caliber gun out of the closet, shot at the lock, and kicked the door open. The male nurses were called again, and they tied him to the bed. They bathed and shaved him, but it was like trying to subdue a wild bull. Alvaro strained at his bindings and hurled insults at Valeria, accusing her of keeping him a prisoner when there was nothing wrong with him. The whole thing broke my heart.

"I was the only person who could come into his room without his getting violent, so I brought him his meals on a tray every day. As soon as your grandfather saw me his eyes would light up and he'd smile, but he never spoke. Valeria hid his gun under her bed. Father was moved to a small room next to her bedroom that had iron bars on the windows. Mother was a strong woman; she refused to put him in an institution and tried to keep his condition a secret from her gossiping neighbors as well as she could. She had married Alvaro for better or for worse, she said, and would never be parted from him.

"The following months were a nightmare. One afternoon it was pouring and I went down to the basement to make sure all the windows of your grandfather's office were closed. I turned on the light and found stacks of unpaid bills on top of his desk, IOUs, receipts from dozens of people who owed him money. The Plata's economic situation was disastrous. When Okeechobee had gone bust it had depleted the family's resources. Now I understood why Father had become so distraught.

"One night the door to your grandfather's room was inadvertently left unlocked. He had been feeling better in the past few weeks; he seemed peaceful and was sleeping without any restraints. He got up at around three in the morning and went down the backstairs unseen. He walked down the road to the seashore, took off his clothes, and dropped them on the sand. Then he waded naked into the water and swam out to the bay.

"His body was never found.

"Your grandfather had made a will a few years earlier, when he was still in control of his mental faculties, and he had named Valeria executor of his estate. The will was read by Venancio to the family a few months after Alvaro was declared legally dead. Each of his children would eventually inherit a sugarcane farm of at least three hundred *cuerdas*, approximately three hundred acres. I would inherit Las Pomarrosas; Siglinda, La Templanza; Dido, La Altamira; Artemisa, El Carite; Lakhmé, La Constanza; and Alejandro, La Esmeralda, the most valuable farm of all because it was in the most fertile part of the valley. They were all choice properties and were free of liens. Each farm produced around twelve thousand tons of sugar a year— each *cuerda* produced forty tons—and the sugarcane was ground and processed at the Plata. Unfortunately, as long as Valeria lived, the farms would remain in her name and she could do with them as she wished. Alejandro would be the Plata's president as soon as he returned home from the University of Virginia. Meanwhile, an administrator would have to be found to manage the mill. Valeria appointed your uncle Venancio to do the job.

"The will also included a list of mementos belonging to your grandfather which my sisters, Alejandro, and I were to receive after he passed away. Valeria went around giving them to us the same day the will was read: Alejandro received Abuelo Alvaro's gold onion-shaped pocket watch and chain with the Rivas de Santillana name inscribed inside the lid; Dido, his Parker pen with a gold nib; Artemisa, the gold key that hung from his watch chain, which he used to wind the grandfather clock every morning; Siglinda, his wedding band, which he loved to twirl on the polished dining room table after dinner; and I got the mother-of-pearl switchblade he had always promised me. I went out onto the terrace and pressed the hidden spring to make the blade jump out. I stared at the mysterious inscription, R 4–24 L 6–32 R 3–22, wondering what the numbers meant. I could still remember the first time Father had shown me the knife in his closet, when I was just a child. I was about to put the knife in my pocket when Siglinda came bustling out and raised such a ruckus, insisting she had to have the knife, that I exchanged it for your grandfather's wedding band to calm her down."

EIGHTEEN

ALEJANDRO SELLS THE PLATA

"Valeria named Venancio temporary president of *central* Plata. The Partido Republicano Incondicional was still in power then, and Venancio was president of the party and mayor of Guayamés. He had very good relations with the navy. He knew the admiral in charge of the naval base at La Guajira and got him to pay a higher rent for the lands they were occupying near the coast of Rincón. Then he went to visit the owners of Caribbean Sugar, whose mill was adjacent to the Plata. Venancio promised he could get them a government subsidy for a new dam they needed in the upper reaches of the Emajaguas River that would make irrigation of their farms a lot more efficient during the dry months. The president of Caribbean Sugar returned Venancio's favor by visiting the president of the New York National City Bank in San Juan and pressuring him to loan the Plata an additional hundred thousand dollars—which was nothing to them, after all—at very low interest. Soon your grandfather's IOUs were all paid off and the Plata was free of liens.

"I offered to help Venancio out in the Plata's management. I visited the mill every morning, and in the afternoons I went down to the basement of Emajaguas, where your grandfather had had his office. I sat in Father's brown leather chair, opened his drawer, stared sadly at his pencils and pens, his glasses, his notepad. I couldn't reconcile myself to the fact that he was dead.

"I was dressed in mourning: black jodhpurs, black riding boots, and a white blouse with a bow at the neck. Every day I rode Father's horse, Bayoán, a beautiful black stallion, around the Plata's farms. I ordered the cane fields set on fire during the *zafra*, even though the burning reduced the sugar content in the stalks. I wanted to make it easier for the peons to cut the twelve-foot thicket of prickly leaves that tore at their flesh. Cutting cane by hand under a broiling noonday sun was an infernal job and I asked Venancio if there was something we could do to make it more humane. I suggested that we have a van deliver water and food to the cutters so they wouldn't have to depend on their children or wives walking all the way out to the cane fields to bring them their meals, usually rice, beans, and boiled codfish. Venancio agreed and the new system was put into effect.

"Alejandro came back to Emajaguas from school in June 1928. It had taken him a great deal of effort to graduate. He had flunked his senior year and had had to buckle down and study in order to pass the second time around. Valeria was relieved when Alejandro finally returned home. Venancio was still president of the mill and I was helping administer it. I was to stay in that position until Alejandro learned the ropes.

"Venancio was no longer mayor of Guayamés, but he had accumulated a small fortune. He had made a lot of money in a lawsuit he said he had won. He went around in a brand-new purple Packard with gray velvet cartouche seats and whitewall tires that was even more luxurious than your grandfather's old black Packard. Siglinda was always beautifully dressed. Venancio ordered fashionable crushed-velvet dresses and hats directly from Paris for her, and she wore rings with precious stones on all her fingers. Dressed in a silk shantung suit and wearing one of his colorful Italian ties with a tiny diamond horseshoe tiepin for luck, Venancio would drive Siglinda to the Shooting Club every day for lunch.

"No one at Emajaguas could understand how Venancio managed to live in such style. The Partido Republicano Incondicional was going through a crisis because of the economic slump, and it had lost the elections. Everybody connected with it was having a dreadful time. 'You lose one, you win another!' Venancio would say, flashing the diamond on his little finger as he caressed Siglinda's neck. 'The Partido Republicano has contributed greatly to the island's progress!'

"The following year, things didn't get any better. The Partido Socialista was in power, and it had eliminated all government subsidies and concessions to the sugar industry. Sugar production began to dwindle. As a parallel disaster, the American army and navy began to pull out, and many bases that were vital to the economy during the war were dismantled. La Guajira naval base was one of them, and the navy stopped paying rent for the Plata's lands. Soon the Plata had to take out a loan to meet the payroll.

"The day Alejandro came back to Emajaguas he went down to your grandfather's office in the basement. 'Time to move out!' he told me, standing in front of my desk, solid as a powder keg on his short, thick legs. The accountant, the two secretaries, the messenger boy—all stopped what they were doing and looked at him in surprise. Alejandro pushed my leather blotter, silver letter opener, pencils, and pens to one side with his riding whip to make space for a large stuffed *guaraguao*. 'Real management of the Plata is about to begin,' he said. 'I'd like to know whose idea it was to send free water vans and lunch baskets with hot food out to the workers in the fields. If the peons want welfare, let them work for the government. This is a private enterprise and its goal is to make money, not do charity work.'

" 'It was my idea, and Venancio agreed to it,' I answered defiantly. 'He's president of the mill.'

" 'He's not president now. From now on, I'm in charge of the Plata's operations. Mother's orders!'

"I immediately went to see Valeria. No hurricanes had whipped the island that year, but there had been too much rain, and the sugar content of the cane was low. The Plata's refinery had sold a third less sugar than the year before. The planting of the fields took place every three years and was due in two months. 'We're going through a crisis, Mother. This isn't the right time to change the Plata's management,' I told Valeria. 'You must let Venancio and me stay on.' But Valeria refused.

"I talked to each of my sisters and convinced them that it would be wiser if I went on administering the mill with Venancio's help for a while, until the sugar crisis blew over. But when my sisters told Valeria of their decision, Mother was furious. She went around the house pulling her hair and looking distraught.

" ' "Cría cuervos y te sacarán los ojos!"—"Hatch crows and they'll scratch out your eyes"—was one of your grandfather Bartolomeo's favorite sayings,' she cried, 'and he was right. Why did God give me such ungrateful daughters? Alejandro is my only son. He was brought up by your father to be a Spartan; we made him go through a lot of sacrifices in order to strengthen his character, so he could one day be at the helm of central Plata. You have to give him a chance!'

"At other times she'd say: 'You were brought up like princesses; you have clothes, jewels, even university educations. What more do you want? Why don't you find yourselves rich husbands? You have the Rivas de Santillana name, which is worth a fortune in social circles. There's no future more dignified than being wife to a powerful man and mother to his children.'

"Nothing could be done about it. My sisters all accepted Abuela Valeria's will in the end and left the management of the mill in Alejandro's hands. But Alejandro would have to prove his mettle, and only time would tell if he could do the job or not.

"Worried about the mill's future, I went on insisting. 'How are we going to finance the new crops, Mother?' I asked. 'In January we have to buy fertilizer and employ twice as many workers to plant the seeds in the fields, as well as pay the peons to cut the cane when the zafra begins. That's only six months away and Alejandro doesn't seem worried about it. Venancio can help us get the money. He's got contacts in the banking community and he's generously offered to lend us some personal funds, interest-free. He said we could repay him four years from now, when the Partido Republicano Incondicional wins the elections again.' But your grandmother refused.

" 'No thank you,' she answered dryly. 'Alvaro left half a million dollars in cash for this kind of an emergency. Alejandro is the only one who knows the combination to the safe, and we are simply waiting for all the provisions in Alvaro's will to be taken care of before opening it. But we'll open it tomorrow; the whole family has been notified.' My sisters were very surprised at this and for a while their hopes were rekindled, but I was skeptical.

" 'I hope the money's there, Mother,' I answered, 'because other-wise we'll soon have to take out another loan at the bank.'

"The next day the whole family went down to the basement to stand around as witnesses. I had seen Father open the Humboldt safe many times. It was a huge affair, a black iron box so large several people could stand up inside it. Alvaro had had it made to order in Germany, and it had taken twenty men to haul it down from the ship at the Guayamés bay and mount it on a sugarcane truck to bring it to the house. Every once in a while, Alejandro would go in with Abuelo, clicking his boots and smirking at me because I wasn't al-lowed to go in with them. I remembered seeing Father turning the wheel on the door slowly, its numbers tiny as hairs sliding silently around the rim.

"But when Alejandro opened the door, the vault was empty. A musty gust of air came out of its dark crevices. Alejandro blanched and had to sit down. He seemed just as surprised as everyone else.

"Valeria was the first one to react. 'Someone else must have known the combination,' she said, looking at me suspiciously. 'You were your father's favorite; maybe he told *you* the numbers also.' I was indignant. 'And what is the combination, Mother, may I ask?' Valeria handed me a piece of paper that read: R 4–24 L 6–32 R 3–22. I stared at Siglinda, then at Venancio, who was silently looking down at his shoes. But I still couldn't believe Venancio had taken the money. I was sure Alejandro was the culprit, so I kept quiet.

" 'I propose we all go to the bank together and ask if Alejandro has opened an account in his name recently,' I said loudly. But Va-leria wouldn't hear of it. 'Alejandro is your brother; he's incapable of behaving so despicably. You'd only shame him and he'd never forgive you.'

"Then Miña spoke up. She was standing behind me in the shadows, at the back of the office. 'About six months ago, a few days after Alejandro came back from school, I got up when it was still dark to boil the family's laundry over hot coals, and as I came out of the carriage house I saw a man opening the door to the basement,' she said in her deep voice, holding a wooden spoon up to command everybody's attention. 'I didn't get a good look, but I'm sure of one thing: the money's safely put away in a bank!' And no sooner had she said this than Felicia, perched on her shoulder, began to screech, spreading her yellow tail wide, as she always did when she was angry.

"Siglinda, Venancio, and Alejandro all left the room in a rage. The rest of my sisters were absolutely stunned.

" 'Alejandro is a hoodlum,' I whispered to Dido. 'He's severed the family's jugular!'

"A few months later Mr. Winston, one of the managers at Caribbean Sugar, the mill adjacent to the Plata, came to the house and asked to speak to Valeria. 'We'd like to make you an offer on Las Pomarrosas, the farm that's nearest to our mill. We're willing to pay a goodly amount.' The Partido Socialista was making the large American sugar mills bleed with higher taxes, and Caribbean Sugar was expanding its operations in a desperate effort to cut costs. They needed more land to produce more sugar. Valeria said she would consider their offer. Alejandro was in favor of it.

"When I heard about it, I hurried to Valeria's room. I couldn't believe that Mother could do such a thing, that she could so utterly submit to my brother's advice. 'You can't sell my farm, Mother. Father never intended you to sell *any* of the farms. I'll take you to court if you do,' I threatened. 'Go ahead and take me to court, Clarissa,' Valeria answered fiercely. '*Pleitos tengas y los ganes*,' she said, a gypsy curse which meant, in effect, 'May you wage lawsuits and win them all.'

"Alejandro tried to unruffle my feathers. He knocked on the door of the room I shared with Dido and asked to be let in. 'Don't take it so hard, Clarissa!' he said, sitting down on my bed. 'The sugar industry is doomed. Even the American sugar mills on the island will soon go down the drain, although they're so powerful they'll be able to survive a few years longer. We can't pay for the modern machinery they have, and they produce more sugar than we do. Do you know how many tons of sugar Caribbean Sugar produces? Fifty thousand tons a year. The Plata produces twelve thousand, and we have twice as much land. But it doesn't make any difference. It's better to cut our losses now, when the farms are still worth some money, than to sell later, when they'll be worth next to nothing. But if you don't want to sell your farm, Clarissa, we won't sell it,' he said. And he put his arm around my shoulders in a conciliatory gesture. I pushed him away. I didn't trust Alejandro anymore.

"Competition from Caribbean Sugar was fierce, and six months later the Plata was even more in the red. Valeria and Alejandro began to sell the farms one by one, all of them but mine. Without the land, the Plata had less and less cane to grind. Soon it was evident that the mill was going bankrupt. Caribbean Sugar made an offer of nine hundred thousand dollars, and after agonizing over the situation for a number of weeks, Alejandro decided we had to sell. Valeria agreed it was the wisest thing to do.

"Alejandro deposited all the money from the sale of the mill and the farms in Valeria's name, and she made a will leaving each of her daughters the exact amount their farms had sold for. Soon Valeria was reconciled with her daughters—except me. In my case it was different. I was the eldest and should have set an example. Instead, I had banded together with Venancio against my own brother, and that had been an abominable thing to do.

"Valeria forgave my sisters. She didn't spare any expense with them, and their lives went on as comfortably as before. They had clothes and money and traveled to Europe with Mother, but I didn't go with them. I stayed at Emajaguas with Miña and had almost no money. But when I asked Valeria to help me out, she told me: 'You still own Las Pomarrosas. You can pay your own expenses.'

"I took a job teaching history at the public high school. It was the only way to make some money and at least be partly independent from Valeria and Alejandro. But all this happened so long ago that I feel as if it happened to a different person."

NINETEEN

ALEJANDRO SAILS TO HEAVEN

A year after the Plata was sold, Tío Alejandro bought a fifty-three-foot Chris Craft Sports Fisherman and went fishing almost every day. It was a beautiful boat. It had a mahogany-paneled cabin, four bunk beds, an ample fishing deck at the back, and a wall-to-wall-carpeted lounge with a bar. He loved to go out in his boat because on the ocean there's no short or tall—only engine power matters.

Just as Tío Alejandro had foreseen, more and more local sugar mills were closing down because of the Partido Socialista's policies. The huge mills owned by American investors were in trouble also and began to cut production. It was a painless operation, however. Absentee owners lost a lot of money on the stock market, but their losses were strictly financial. To the local hacendados, on the other hand, bankruptcy was a social tragedy. Once they closed their mills they didn't belong to the local aristocracy anymore. They opened new businesses—car dealerships, department stores, insurance companies —but it just wasn't the same. Sugar money was at least two hundred years old, whereas the income from these new businesses put them on the same footing as the nouveaux riches.

The hacendados of Guayamés who had lost their mills tried to forget their disgrace with some kind of pastime, and fishing was one of their favorites. Tío Alejandro invited his friends to go boating and drinking with him, and they sometimes brought their party girls along. These women weren't exactly from the best families and usually wore high heels, *rumbera* turbans, and large hoop earrings. They were very gay and laughed at everything, especially when Tío Alejandro yanked off their shoes, which were making dents in his deck. But Abuela Valeria didn't care; she only wanted Tío Alejandro to be happy, with or without his picturesque party girls.

Alejandro loved fishing for blue marlin, and he had his yacht especially fitted out for it. He bought sturdy bamboo fishing rods that were so long you couldn't tell whether they were to cast over the sea or across the sky. He had a beautiful aluminum fishing chair made to order in Florida that looked like a throne, with its bright-red leather seat, upholstered arms, steel stirrups, and halter. Sometimes from the terrace at Emajaguas you could see marlin out on the water at sundown. They would spring out of the sea as high as twenty feet, flying over the ocean like giant one-winged angels. But although he dreamed about it every night, Tío Alejandro had never managed to catch one. He would sail off with his friends and often he would return home completely drunk. Urbano would have to undress him and put him to bed.

Once a year a marlin competition was organized by the members of the Guayamés Yacht Club. A golden cup was put on exhibit in a glass case, to be conferred on whoever caught the largest fish. Marlin could run up to a thousand pounds and measure anywhere from six to ten feet long. Alejandro promised Abuela Valeria he would win the competition that year and thereby regain some of his lost prestige. And if he didn't win the competition, he swore to his friends, laughing, a rum and Coke in his hand, he was still going to catch the biggest marlin of all. His sisters had been spreading false rumors about him in Guayamés, he said, blaming him for the Plata's bankruptcy and accusing him of having pocketed money from their lands. But when the marlin he was looking for finally swallowed his hook, he was going to prove them wrong. It would pull his yacht behind it like a winged chariot, and his reputation would be saved. That was what the red fishing chair was really for, Tío Alejandro joked to his friends as he stirred the ice in his glass. It wasn't for fishing at all—it was for the yacht's charioteer.

Abuela Valeria was upset when she heard Alejandro talk this way but she tried not to make an issue of it. Alejandro had her complete confidence—he was a good businessman and had invested the money from the Plata and the lands wisely. Thanks to him, the family had managed to weather the storm in spite of the disappearance of the money from the safe. But it worried her that on his fishing expeditions Tío Alejandro drank so much.

Whenever Tío Alejandro left on one of his trips at dawn, Clarissa would stand at the window shivering in her nightgown and watch him leave. Miña knew that intense look in her eyes and cautioned her: "Remember, Alejandro nursed at my breast just as you did. I don't like him any more than you do, but you're *hermanos de leche* as well as *hermanos de sangre*. If you wish him ill, you'll pay for it, because there's no greater sin on earth than fighting with one's own kin."

One day Tío Alejandro had been cruising off the north coast of the island, over the Puerto Rico Trench, a vast underwater abyss twenty-five thousand feet deep. A storm was brewing and the sea was churning into a lather when Alejandro's rod gave a tug. Alejandro pressed the release button on the fishing reel to set the line free and it went whirring over the water with the screech of an eagle. He ordered the captain to cut the motor, and the yacht lurched backward and forward for a few minutes, at the mercy of the waves.

Tío Alejandro shaded his eyes and looked toward the horizon. The sky was as clear as the sea. Not a single cloud was in sight, and the fishing line cut a path between sky and sea like a silver whip. All of a sudden, in the distance, a blue wing cleaved the water before plunging back into the ocean. Alejandro knew his moment had come. He put down his drink and stumbled to the fishing chair, his friends all gathering around him, cheering. He sat down, put his feet in the stirrups, slipped on the halter, and picked up the fishing rod. The reel was still unraveling at a dizzying speed. He was using a hundred-pound line and the brake would put a twenty-five-pound weight on the fleeing creature's mouth.

Alejandro knew he had to give the marlin breathing space, tire him out before he gave the line the first yank. The beast was large, he could feel it in the rod, but he couldn't guess how large. Alejandro grasped the rod more tightly and braced his feet against the stirrups. He struggled with the fish for over twenty minutes but the pull was still strong. All of a sudden the line went slack, and Alejandro was sure he had lost the marlin. Everyone held their breath as Alejandro unbuckled himself from the chair and went to look over the side, half expecting to see the monster slide silently from under the boat. But there was nothing there, so he sat down and began to reel in the line, buckling himself up just in case. Precisely at that moment the marlin bolted and the line got caught in the chair's pivot. The chair, with Alejandro still in it, was wrenched over the railing and went flying over the water. His friends couldn't believe what they saw: Alejandro still holding on to the rod, his captain's cap on his head and his legs stretched out before him as if he were on water skis, a huge wing flying in front of him. Then the chair began to sink with Alejandro still strapped to it, until at last the wing took a dive and Alejandro, chair, fish, and all disappeared into the depths of the sea.

Several of Alejandro's friends dove into the water but it was too late. He was never seen again.

Abuela Valeria was destroyed by Alejandro's death. Abuelo Alvaro's disappearance had been a heavy blow, but there had been no desperation in her grief. Alvaro had died of natural causes—he was terminally ill before he walked into the ocean, never to return. But Tío Alejandro's death was different. He was only twenty-nine, and Abuela Valeria was sure he was innocent of the vile rumors that were circulating about him. She couldn't reconcile herself to the undignified way in which he had died and the fact that everyone was gossiping about it. The drinking and the carousing that had supposedly gone on and the company Alejandro had been keeping—the spoiled playboys of Guayamés partying it up with their girlfriends— were very difficult to live down. From the point of view of Guayamés's upper crust, it was all proof of Alejandro's guilt, and his death was the price of his sins.

Abuela Valeria knew what was on everyone's mind, and yet she sat proudly at Alejandro's wake, not shedding a tear as the mourners milled and buzzed around her. I confess I admire her for the way she behaved. I'm sure she would have liked to caress Alejandro's face one last time, combed his hair with Eau Impérial, and sealed his eyes with a kiss. She would have liked to say good-bye to him when his coffin, with the Rivas de Santillana coat of arms engraved on the lid, went through Emajaguas's front door. But the empty space between her arms as she sat in the living room was all Abuela had to remember Tío Alejandro by.

Straight and proud, Abuela Valeria sat at the wake dressed in black silk from wrist to chin. She never once acknowledged the condolences her neighbors whispered in her ear as they entered and left the room; she never once answered the priest when he began to recite the Rosary, praying for Tío Alejandro's soul—each Hail Mary was born stone-dead on her lips. Her wound was so deep it hardly hurt at all.

TWENTY

CLARISSA AND AURELIO'S WEDDING

🙰 "I never considered getting married while Father was alive. But Aurelio wouldn't give up. He was patient; he could wait forever, he said. And when Alvaro passed away Aurelio knew he had a better chance.

"He courted me for years and came every summer from La Concordia to visit me on Sundays. In 1926 he graduated from Northeastern and returned to the island with a master's degree in electrical engineering. He had also obtained a diploma from the Boston Conservatory of Music. He immediately went into business with his father at Vernet Construction. 'Will you marry me?' he asked every time he came to Emajaguas, holding my cool hand in his. I told him how much I liked him but that I couldn't possibly marry him. Aurelio didn't pressure me to decide.

"A week after Father disappeared into the sea, Aurelio phoned me at Emajaguas. I was still devastated, but he wanted to know if it was all right to come visit, and I said yes. We sat out on the terrace, looking toward the bay, and Aurelio kissed me on the lips for the first time. 'I have a salary now,' he said. 'Will you marry me and come to live at La Concordia?' 'Yes,' I answered with a smile.

"And as proof of my trust in him I added: 'Father once told me never to sell Las Pomarrosas, "because once you sell the land, you can't start over, because you will have sold your heart." But since I'm starting over with you and I'm leaving Emajaguas, I want you to sell the farm. That way I'll be putting my heart in your hands.'

"The wedding was to be a small affair, as Valeria didn't want to spend any money on me. But Lakhmé, Dido, and Artemisa would all be there. And so would my dear Siglinda and Venancio. Aurelio's father, his three brothers and two sisters would also be present. Aurelio's mother, Adela Pasamontes, however, couldn't come to the wedding because she was seriously ill. I asked Mother if the ceremony could be held in the garden. I wanted to spend my last few happy moments with my sisters in the paradise I was leaving.

"The night before the wedding I went to bed early because I wanted to look rested the following day. But as soon as I lay down on the bed, sleep abandoned me completely. Valeria had hung my satin wedding gown on the closet door and laid my Brussels lace veil on a chair nearby. The dress was only faintly visible in the dark and glimmered like a ghost. The veil had settled next to my bed like a cold mist. I looked away and sighed.

"It was four o'clock in the morning and the stars were beginning to fade over the palm grove next to Emajaguas, but I was still awake. I felt like a warrior keeping vigil before battle, my armor laid out at my feet. Just thinking of Aurelio caressing me made me feel faint. Would love be the answer to all my problems, as Siglinda insisted? I kept hearing Father's voice when he used to take me to the beach to look at sailboats when I was a child: 'You can be like them when you grow up, Clarissa, as free and happy as the wind.'

"I finally got out of bed, wrapped my Mexican serape around my shoulders, and crept down the stairs and across the garden to the carriage house. I knocked timidly on Miña's door.

"Miña was putting on her uniform to come down to the house. Urbano had already left; I'd seen him feeding the animals in the cold morning mist at the back of the garden. Miña tied on her apron and began to comb my hair, which was slick and short like a boy's. Then we sat on the edge of Miña's bed, huddled next to each other.

" 'I can't go through with it, Miña,' I whispered. 'Aurelio is two years younger than I am, and I'm not sure I'm in love with him. I'm bowing out.' Miña burst out laughing.

" 'You can't fool me, Clarissa. That's just an excuse. You've been having second thoughts because you're thinking of your father. Forget Don Alvaro,' she said, patting my hand. 'He's dead and Aurelio is very much alive. Sure, you have doubts, but it's not your fault. It's that little piece of ice that got stuck in your heart when you were born.'

"And then she added, lowering her voice: 'Aurelio's a good man. He'll know how to melt it.' And she gave me a long hug. A few minutes later we went down the stairs together, and Miña brewed me a strong cup of coffee.

"The wedding took place on the morning of June 3, 1930. Everyone said I was a beautiful bride. I have a photo of Aurelio and me standing by one of the windows, encircled by the train of my gown as if we were standing in the middle of a silken pond. Aurelio is wearing his rented tuxedo and a top hat. We both look very serious, very much aware of the solemnity of the occasion.

"After a short reception and a champagne *brindis* in the garden, attended only by the closest family members, we changed clothes in separate rooms and ran laughing to the car under a shower of rice. We drove to La Concordia in Aurelio's convertible Pontiac coupé, which he had named El Pájaro Azul, The Blue Bird of Happiness. From then on, Aurelio was the center of my life."

TWENTY-ONE

THE HOUSE ON CALLE VIRTUD

"Your father, Aurelio, bought a small house for us in downtown La Concordia, near the train station. It was a middle-class neighborhood where the houses had corrugated tin roofs and stood in small lots so you could smell what your neighbor was cooking through the open windows. Aurelio bought the house with his hard-earned savings. It was made of wood and had a small balcony in front, then a living room, a dining room, and a kitchen, all in a row like carriages on a train; a long, narrow hallway in the middle led to the bedrooms at the back. The furniture was wicker, painted white, and there were lace curtains over all the windows. Aurelio had taken care of every detail.

"The only luxury we had at Calle Virtud was the Bechstein grand piano Aurelio bought with money from the sale of Las Pomarrosas. The farm brought three hundred thousand dollars, and the piano cost ten thousand. Aurelio put the rest of the money in the bank in my name, and ten years later, he invested the rest to help build the Star Cement plant. It was definitely a good business deal.

"The piano was so large it looked like a whale aboard a rowboat. To get it inside, Aurelio had to have our front door taken off its hinges. The piano took up most of the living room, so that there was nowhere left to sit down. It was an extraordinary object, totally out of place at Calle Virtud. But Aurelio loved it. Whenever he played it, music flooded the whole house."

"When I first arrived in La Concordia and stepped out of the Pontiac I felt faint. The heat of La Concordia was like a slap in the face. Aurelio had to help me up the steps. 'I'll get you something cool to drink; lie down for a while and you'll feel better. Our bedroom has a nice window that opens onto the back patio, which is shaded by a beautiful mango tree that rustles when there's a breeze, as if it were raining.'

"I did as Aurelio suggested and went into the bedroom. Aurelio followed with my two white leather suitcases. Then he went into the kitchen to make me a lemonade, but when he came back with the iced drink in his hand he found me sitting on the edge of the four-poster bed with my suitcases still closed. The gabled tin roof had trapped the heat under the attic and the room was an oven. 'I can't possibly stay here,' I said, about to burst out crying. 'The heat is stifling, but I'm freezing—I'll never be able to sleep. Please take me back to Emajaguas.' I was bathed in sweat and shaking all over.

"Miña had told Aurelio about my sickness just before the wedding; how, when I was born, I had come back from the hospital with a tiny splinter of ice lodged in my heart and Miña had had to carry me around the house strapped to her chest for a month until I finally grew warm. It was a strange story and it had worried Aurelio, but in his usual gallant manner he pretended nothing was amiss. He didn't say anything to me.

" 'Why don't you let me play something on the piano for you? It'll make you feel better before we drive back to Emajaguas,' he suggested. And he went into the living room, sat down on the piano bench, and opened the lid. 'Come and sit next to me, Clarissa,' he called. I stepped out of the bedroom shivering and sat next to my handsome young husband. He began to play Beethoven's *Appassionata* sonata. The music was so beautiful and Aurelio played so well that I gradually forgot I was cold. I calmed down and stopped shivering. When Aurelio finished playing he began to kiss me. He was a very good lover. He had delicate, almost feminine hands, which were as sensitive when he caressed my body as when he caressed the piano's ivory keys. Soon the little piece of ice that was stuck at the center of my heart began to melt. We went into the bedroom and made love on the four-poster bed. It was as if a tidal wave of music swept me away."

PART IV

THE VERNET FAMILY SAGA

When I was younger I could remember anything, whether it had happened or not; but my faculties are decaying now and soon I shall be so I cannot remember any but the things that never happened.

—*The Autobiography of Mark Twain*

TWENTY-TWO

SAILING DOWN THE CARIBBEAN

Santiago Vernet often talked to his children about his mother, and they enjoyed his stories. Elvira Zequeira was a rebel and a revolutionary who often hid *mambises*—black rebel soldiers—in her house at Santiago de Cuba. Elvira had a twin brother named Roque Zequeira, whose best friend was Henri Vernet. Roque met Henri in Paris. They both had studied engineering at the Ecole des Ponts et des Chaussées, and when they graduated in 1875, Roque suggested that Henri come to the island to try his fortune.

Henri was from the South of France and he came from peasant stock. He was born in Saint-Savinien, a drowsy little town on the bank of the Charente, where marshes abound and dozens of channels flow like arteries down the walls of a heart. Henri went to Paris to study engineering on a government scholarship because his father had been killed at the end of the Franco-Prussian War in 1870. It was an unfortunate accident; a truce had been reached and Charles Vernet's battalion was already marching home when a musket ball ricocheted off a tree and hit him in the back of the head.

Henri's mother made great sacrifices to send him to study in Paris; she waited for him in Saint-Savinien with her five children. She had high hopes for Henri. She was sure that, with his help, the family would finally pull itself out of poverty. But when Henri graduated, he couldn't resist the temptation to sail with Roque to America. He had nightmares of returning to the marshes of the Charente, where no one was ever in a hurry and barges floated lazily down the river laden with cabbages and artichokes. Henri had gotten used to life in Paris; the air sparked with activity and minds were razor-sharp. When Roque invited him to go to America, Henri agreed. Someday he would come back with a lot of money to help out his mother and little brothers.

They sailed to Santiago de Cuba together. Henri stayed in Roque's house. There Roque introduced him to his sister. "She's a little hummingbird," Roque said, picking Elvira up by the waist. "But watch out. When she wants you to do something you'd better do it or else find the lowest window to jump out of the house." Elvira looked at Henri's Sèvres-blue eyes and long, brown curls tied in a ponytail and fell in love with him. The fact that Henri was a soldier's son made it difficult for him to express his feelings, and it was Elvira who asked him to marry her. He said yes, and soon Santiago Vernet—Abuelo Chaguito—was on his way. He was born in 1879.

Roque and Elvira Zequeira were orphans; their parents had died within months of each other in a boating accident off Punta Santiago, the southernmost tip of Cuba—or so Chaguito used to say. The children inherited the large, rambling house on the outskirts of town. After he married Elvira, Henri moved in, and the three young people helped one another out in every way. Henri and Roque pooled their savings and, making use of their newly acquired engineering abilities, built the city's first commercial ice plant, Vernet Ice, which had its own electric generator—also the town's first. Santiago was the capital of Oriente, Cuba's richest province and the hub of much of its commercial activity. There were forty sugar haciendas in the outskirts; tobacco, cacao, and coffee flourished in the nearby Sierra Maestra. The city had magnificent homes and people gave extravagant parties all the time, so ice was a sought-after commodity.

Vernet Ice was a success from the start; delivery carts came by the dozen every hour to pick up blocks of ice that would be wrapped in hemp sacks and carried to private homes and businesses all over the city. Temperatures in Santiago could reach a hundred degrees in the shade. But once Vernet Ice was in business, people insisted, it was never as hot as before.

Henri had inherited the Vernets' bad luck. Once a short circuit cut off the plant's generator and Henri called out to Roque to go to the front of the building and pull the disconnect lever down. Then he went to the basement to try to fix the problem. Elvira had dropped Chaguito off at the plant while she went shopping, and he skipped down the stairs behind his father. It was dark and Henri had to light their way with a gas lamp.

Roque did as he was told. He pulled the lever down and then stood by the switch waiting for Henri to call again from the basement. Henri searched around by the light of the lamp and found a bare wire in one of the generator's cables; the frayed part needed to be cut and the cable connected again. "This is where the problem is," he told Chaguito, showing him the mat of wires inside the frayed cover. "We have to cut and repair the cable."

But upstairs one of the carts heavily laden with ice suddenly rolled out of the warehouse gate. There was a lot of traffic on the avenue, and the gatekeeper yelled, "Go ahead!" to the driver to let him know he could ride out. Roque mistook the driver's voice for Henri's and pushed the lever up. Henri landed three feet from his small son.

When he heard Henri cry out, Roque ran to the basement but in his haste forgot to pull the lever down. His friend was lying on the ground, his hands still stuck to the cable, and he was shaking violently. Roque was about to grab him by the arm to pull him away when Henri cried out, his eyes bulging, "Don't touch me! You'll only double the charge and kill us both! Turn the switch off!" Roque flew upstairs again, but by the time he returned, Henri was dead. Chaguito stood helplessly by, watching the smoke come out of his father's long brown curls.

When Elvira was told of the accident, she fell to the ground in a faint. Roque was overwhelmed as well. He felt responsible for Henri's death and kept seeing the terrified look in his brother-in-law's eyes as Henri struggled to free himself from the cable. Elvira tried to console him. "Some people are born under a good-luck star and others are born under an evil one," she said. "The Vernets belong to the second category. You mustn't blame yourself for what happened, Roque. Given his family history, Henri would probably have died young anyway."

Elvira was deeply concerned about her son. One night she came to Roque's room and knocked on his door. "We've both lost Henri, and nobody can bring him back. But we still have each other and shouldn't be bitter about it. I need you to help me look after Chaguito. He hasn't said a single word since Henri passed away. His teachers have threatened to expel him from school if he doesn't come out of his obstinate silence."

Roque agreed to try to help his nephew. In true Vernet fashion, the boy hadn't shed a single tear since his father's death, and Roque felt sorry for him. Chaguito was good with numbers, and to learn mathematics one didn't need to talk. If Chaguito didn't want to speak it was his business, but he could certainly count. Roque went up to the attic, opened an old trunk, and took out Henri's books of electrical engineering from the Ecole des Ponts et des Chaussées. He brought them down and opened them on the dining room table. Chaguito drew near and stared at them in fascination. They were all in French, and at first Roque thought this would make it impossible for Chaguito to understand them. But he was wrong. Soon Chaguito knew all there was to know about algebra, geometry, trigonometry, physics, and electrical and mechanical design, and along the way he had also learned to read French.

Years passed and in 1895, when Chaguito was a young man of sixteen, the War of Independence was raging in Cuba. José Martí was killed during a suicide charge at Dos Ríos, and the Zequeiras were incensed by his death. One time Roque took a potshot at a Spanish officer from a second-floor window of their house. Roque escaped but the house was ransacked, and the piano in the living room turned out to be full of bandages and cotton swabs. The Zequeiras' home was a nursing station for wounded revolutionaries. Elvira, Roque, and Chaguito all went to jail but were set free six months later, during a lull in the war.

When they returned to the house, Roque found an order to present himself for military service at the conscription office in Santiago de Cuba. He left the city and went into hiding in the *manigua*, the wild brush country near the town. Elvira hid her son in the attic. Chaguito was now seventeen and would soon be eligible for conscription. In spite of his small stature, he could only sit there; the ceiling was too low for him to stand. Late at night he crept downstairs to have a hot meal and be with his mother. All kinds of insects stung him—spiders, scorpions, and gnats—and his eyes were so swollen they looked like slits, but he had inherited Henri's military stoicism and endured his discomfort without complaint.

Elvira was very religious, and she made an altar in the attic where Chaguito could pray to the Virgen de la Caridad del Cobre, the patron saint of Cuba. He could light candles in the dark for the Virgin and watch the small red flames waver like hopeful flags around him. But Chaguito didn't pray. He slept with his back to the Virgin and swore that he'd make the family's bad luck change.

After a month Chaguito couldn't stand lying in the dark anymore. He was about to escape and join the *mambises* in the bush when his uncle Roque turned up at the house. Roque told Elvira that an electrical engineer was needed in Puerto Rico. The job was in La Concordia and involved mounting some new evaporators at the Siboney, a mill on the outskirts of town. His friends had passed on the information and were waiting for him outside the house. They were going to try to smuggle him off the island that very night.

"Take Chaguito with you, Roque, I beg you," Elvira said, pointing to the attic. "I don't care if I never see him again. I'd rather know he's far away and alive than nearby and six feet under." But when she told Chaguito, he didn't want to go; he didn't want to leave Cuba. So Roque and his friends knocked Chaguito out and smuggled him aboard the *Alicia Contreras*, a cargo steamer bound for Santo Domingo. Chaguito worked in the boiler room and fed coals into the furnace with such fury you would have thought he was feeding the anger that blazed in his heart.

In Santo Domingo the ship picked up a load of oranges, bananas, and green plantains, then sailed on to Puerto Rico. Chaguito and his uncle spent two weeks on a diet of bananas and oranges but arrived safe and sound at their destination.

TWENTY-THREE

CHAGUITO ARRIVES AT LA CONCORDIA

*"*Look at those *gachupines* marching up and down the square!" Chaguito exclaimed to his uncle Roque the day they arrived in La Concordia. He saw the Regimiento de Cazadores de la Patria —the Regiment of Hunters of the Fatherland—performing their military maneuvers in the Plaza de las Delicias. "They're an elegant-looking lot, but I bet they don't exactly hunt boar or fox!"

Chaguito was right. In La Concordia the Cazadores de la Patria tracked down citizens who wanted to overthrow the government and, once they had caught them, sliced off their ears, cut off their eyelids, or drove splinters under their nails until they confessed. And once they had confessed, they were shot.

La Concordia was unabashedly commercial. There were thriving businesses on every corner and only one or two churches in sight. Concordians were entrepreneurs; in his brief stroll through the city

Chaguito noted four factories: crackers, noodles, and Panama hats were all made in La Concordia, and tobacco was grown nearby. Next, he wanted to find out how many foundries there were in town. He stopped at a street corner, closed his eyes, and sniffed around like a dog. He was an engineer's son and he had iron in his blood; he could recognize the smell of liquid ore a mile away. Immediately he knew there were two in town, and he walked off in their direction. They were old-fashioned enterprises. One was owned by a Scotsman, Mr. McCann, who didn't want to spend any money modernizing his kilns, and the other by a Spaniard, Don Miguel Sáez Peña, who had made thousands of dollars building steam engines, conical wheels, crowns, and rollers for the sugarcane mills. But Chaguito saw that Don Miguel's foundry had an outdated steam boiler that was very run-down. Not surprisingly, it exploded a few months after he arrived in town.

Concordians were a practical, down-to-earth people who liked to call things as they saw them. The street the hospital was on was Calle Salud; the school stood on Calle Educación; the butcher's street was Calle Matadero. But the streets Chaguito liked best were Calle Armonía, Calle Hermandad, and Calle Fraternidad, representing the Masonic virtues.

Under Spanish law Freemasonry was strictly forbidden; membership in a Masonic lodge was punishable by death. But in La Concordia, Freemasons were all over the place, and Roque soon got in touch with them. He had served as grand master at the clandestine Masonic temple in Santiago de Cuba and he still had some influence in the fraternity. So the first thing he did after he arrived was to visit the Aurora Lodge, which was located in a ruined sugar warehouse on the outskirts of town, and ask that his nephew be accepted as a member. Chaguito was initiated soon after, and since all Masons were members of La Concordia's Firemen's Corps, he became a fireman as well.

The earliest photograph I've ever seen of Abuelo Chaguito was taken in 1900, four years after he arrived in Puerto Rico. He's sitting on a bench with twelve other firemen, and he's wearing the firemen's dress uniform: a red visored cap, a high-collared navy-blue jacket with gold trim at the neck, and a bronze saber at the waist. At five feet four, he was the shortest one of all—and his slight frame made his whiskers seem that much larger. At the bottom of the photograph someone had written in ink: "Fosforito Vernet—Little Matchstick Vernet—who loved starting fires as much as putting them out."

Precisely because they were so proud of their town, La Concordia's merchants had invested heavily in its fire brigade. The firemen had the latest equipment: horse-drawn engines, water pumps and hoses, tanks, axes, and ladders. La Concordia sat on a wide valley planted with sugarcane that was periodically set ablaze to facilitate harvesting. Hence the city often fell victim to fires sparked by flying embers of cane that landed on the roofs of the wood-frame houses of the poorer residents on the outskirts of town.

Two years after Abuelo Chaguito arrived in La Concordia, a tremendous fire broke out in the Plaza del Mercado Isabel Segunda. Since the wind was blowing from the south, the fire soon spread north toward the military powder magazine. The American army that had come with General Nelson A. Miles was stationed at La Concordia, and Colonel Hulings, the officer in charge, ordered everyone to evacuate. The fire seemed sure to reach the munitions depot and blow the town to pieces.

Chaguito was a lieutenant in the fire brigade and he disregarded the colonel's order. He drove his truck to where the fire was raging, and he and his men put it out. The next day the firemen were hailed as heroes by the citizens of La Concordia. But the army brought civil charges against them for disobeying military orders and the firemen were all put in jail. A large group of prominent men went to visit the American commandant and convinced him that what the firemen had done was heroic. La Concordia was as much a work of art as Paris, they said, only on a smaller scale, and saving it from destruction had been an act of humanity. The next day Colonel Hulings set Chaguito and the other firemen free.

The job of building the new evaporator at the Siboney had taken Roque and Chaguito two years, and when it was finished, Don Eustaquio Ridruejo, the mill's owner, commissioned them to install a new copper still for his rum distillery. But Roque wanted to return to Cuba. "The war is over now, sir. It's time to go home," he told Don Eustaquio.

"Your mother is waiting for us, lad," Roque told Chaguito. "She has no one in the world but us."

"You go on ahead, Tío," Chaguito said coolly. "I want to stay on at La Concordia for a few months. I'll install Don Eustaquio's copper still for him."

Tío Roque thought Chaguito was still angry at his mother because of the way she had had him put aboard the *Alicia Contreras*. So he carried his bags to the harbor himself and boarded the sloop that would take him back to Cuba.

But Tío Roque was wrong. Abuelo Chaguito wanted to remain on the island for other reasons. After the *Maine* had blown up in Havana's harbor, rumors had begun to fly around La Concordia that the United States was planning to invade Puerto Rico. Chaguito wasn't about to leave the island when things were just heating up. He had heard that President William McKinley's advisers at the Department of State had toyed with the idea of keeping Cuba after they invaded it—there were plenty of Cubans like Narciso López, who had wanted to annex the island to the United States in 1850—but it was too dangerous to attempt. Cuba was a rich and beautiful island, the largest of the Greater Antilles, but the mermaid might turn crocodile at any moment. It was much safer to take over Puerto Rico, the minnow to the south.

A month after the American invasion was over, Abuelo Chaguito wrote a letter to his mother in Santiago de Cuba. Bisabuela Elvira always kept it by her, and when she died not long after, Tío Roque mailed it back to Chaguito in Puerto Rico. It has been in the Vernet family for a hundred years. Aurelio kept it in his desk and showed an almost religious reverence for it.

Dear Mother: *November 25, 1898*
   I have received your letter and beg you not to worry, because I'm well and in good health. Things have calmed down a lot here, and people have taken up their usual routines of working, eating, and sleeping, even though now we have a very different flag in front of the alcaldía and the post office.
   I am working very hard for different haciendas near La Concordia, but this work is not new to me. You know how I struggled to learn to be a mechanic in several sugarcane centrales in Cuba when I was a mere boy of fourteen, and for a few months I even worked in a phosphate mine, where I carried ten-pound salt bags on my back to the cane fields

that needed fertilizing. Even so, I wouldn't have left my country if it hadn't been for the dirty trick you played on me.

I want you to know that on this island, which is poor and meager in size compared with our beautiful Cuba, I've learned a lesson I never understood while I was living at home: the need to respect other people's right to live as they wish. Even you, Mother, became influenced by General Valeriano Weyler's despotic methods when you had me put aboard the *Alicia Contreras* in the shameful way you did.

Since the Americans landed here, I have become an admirer of the United States. Religious tolerance and political compromise are the virtues that make democracy possible. Only by following the example of the United States will Cuba be able to rid itself of absolutism and Catholicism—the two millstones inherited from Spain that hang around its neck.

I suppose the Americans' arrival in Puerto Rico has been in all the Cuban newspapers, but I thought I'd give you a firsthand account of what happened. As a member of an elite Firemen's Corps in La Concordia, I had the opportunity to take a distinguished part in the invasion, and you can be proud of the way I behaved myself.

It was an odd situation. Americans are candid in matters of war. The place where they would land was supposed to be a secret, but everybody knew it in advance. The date, time, and place had been published in all the local newspapers, and housewives all over the island had cleaned out the grocery stores as if a hurricane were approaching. General Nelson A. Miles's fleet was expected to land in Fajardo, on the eastern coast, on the twenty-first of July. But when he got there, three regiments of Spanish troops were waiting for him, armed to the teeth. General Miles looks like an old walrus. I had the chance to meet him personally when he delivered a speech in La Concordia's Plaza de las Delicias right after he disembarked. He has white whiskers pouring down his cheeks and is large-jowled and hefty. But he's also a seasoned Indian fighter. A few years before he set sail for Puerto Rico, he defeated Crazy Horse, the Sioux chief who overwhelmed General Custer at Little Big Horn. So when he arrived at Fajardo and saw the warm reception awaiting him, he turned right around and sailed far out to sea again.

"If we could outfox the Sioux in Montana," Miles told one of his aides and later bragged to a reporter a few days after the invasion, "we can outfox the Spaniards in Puerto Rico and win the support of the peaceful natives along the way." Miles's four battleships—the Massachusetts, the Yale, the Dixie, and the Gloucester—as well as ten transport ships carrying 3,415 men, sailed north, as far away from the coast of Puerto Rico as possible, rounded Mona Passage in the night, all lights out, and landed at Guánica, a secluded bay on the Caribbean coast, at 5:20 on the morning of July 25. He wasn't expected at all there. Upon landing, he made a declaration to the people of Puerto Rico that was posted on fences all along the roads, on public buildings, and on school walls: "We have come not to wage war against the people of a country that has been oppressed for centuries but, on the contrary, to bring our protection to your citizens, as well as to your property."

Guayamés, Sabana Verde, Hicacos—all the western towns—surrendered peacefully to General Miles. Bands played in the streets, women threw flowers to the soldiers from balconies, the hated Spanish flag was burned in the town squares. The Spaniards, greatly outnumbered, began a hasty retreat across the mountains toward San Juan. Miles's fleet sailed victorious from Guánica to La Concordia, hugging the southern coast, and anchored in the bay. Then the ships, led by Commander Davis, aimed their cannons at the city.

Soon a United States army lieutenant bearing a white flag came galloping down the road from the harbor with an ultimatum from General Miles. If the Spanish troops didn't surrender, the city would be razed to the ground, Lieutenant Meriam said. But General San Martín, who was in charge of the garrison in La Concordia, said that military regulations prevented his accepting the ultimatum and that it was up to General Macías, the captain general of the island in San Juan, to accept it. The lieutenant then gave the town half an hour to answer before the cannons began to bombard the city.

We were all horrified! The message would have to be relayed to General Macías by telegram; nothing could be done in half an hour. You should have seen the chaos that ensued. Everybody ran here and there all over town, throwing their possessions into mule carts and trying to save whatever was portable. People began to leave the city by the hundreds, heading out toward the hills behind the town.

My firemen friends and I put on our helmets and joined a commission of foreign consuls and other respectable citizens, and we all rode together out to the harbor to try to negotiate a surrender. An hour had gone by already and the Dixie, the Annapolis, and the Wasp still hadn't fired their cannons at us. We talked to Lieutenant Meriam, a seasoned, stocky soldier who was still awaiting instructions, and asked him to relay our message to Commander Davis. We needed at least twenty-four hours to get an answer from General Macías in San Juan.

At ten o'clock that night the message finally came through, and General Macías ordered General San Martín to surrender. We put on our firemen's helmets again and drove our fire engine all the way to the Spanish encampment. As the city's private civil corps, firemen were allowed into the army encampments without problems. Instead of a water hose, however, we took out a flamethrower when we arrived. We stood there for several hours making sure the Regimiento de Cazadores de la Patria followed San Martín's orders and left the city. All through the night we had to make sure no riots broke out, and on several occasions we prevented the citizens from throwing stones and broken bottles at the retreating troops, so great was the hatred of Concordians for the Spaniards.

General Miles's army entered La Concordia peacefully at ten o'clock in the morning, dressed in heavy black-and-blue wool uniforms and sweating copiously under the blazing sun. They marched up to the alcaldía to the strains of the "Star-Spangled Banner," which soon turned into "There'll Be a Hot Time in the Old Town Tonight." The Hunters of the Fatherland had had a good military band, and when they retreated to the mountains, they left behind a magnificent set of musical instruments —tubas, drums, French horns, saxophones, cymbals. When the American soldiers saw them, they picked them up and began to play in the middle of the plaza. Everybody began to dance.

I love you, Mother, but I'm not returning to Cuba. I've become an American, a free man. Also, I'm a Freemason now. I'm no longer a Catholic. Down with Spain! Down with the Catholic religion! Down with despotism! Long live the United States of America! Soon I'll have enough money to send you a steamer ticket so you can join me here. The Vernets' good-luck star is finally on the rise.

Your loving son,
Santiago

TWENTY-FOUR

THE LOTTERY VENDOR'S DAUGHTER

La Concordia had a small electric plant, which supplied electricity to a few private businesses. The streets were illuminated with gas lamps; people cooked on charcoal stoves. When the Americans arrived, Stone and Webster of Boston was contracted by the U.S. government to wire the entire town. The firm's engineers built a large plant. Dozens of pine logs were shipped to the island from Montana, tarred from end to end like licorice sticks, and set up at every street corner. One morning Abuelo Chaguito saw the Americans setting up a log at the corner of Calle Fraternidad.

"You seem to have your hands full. Do you need help with the electrical part of the job?" Abuelo Chaguito asked one of the engineers from Boston.

"Do you know what the word *electricity* means, son?" the engineers asked, scoffing at him good-naturedly.

"Electricity is a force measured in volts, due to the presence and movement of electrons. It produces various physical phenomena, like attraction and repulsion, light and heating, or shock to the body. At least that's what the manuals say. But nobody *really* knows what electricity is," Chaguito said, leaning against a nearby fence.

"Who taught you that?" one of the Stone and Webster engineers asked in amazement.

"My father did," Chaguito answered. "And he also taught me the meaning of *electromagnet*, *electrotype*, and *electrode*. But he never told me what electrocution was, which was a pity because if he had, I might have been able to help him and he might still be alive."

"Your father was an electrician?" the man asked, wondering at Abuelo Chaguito's strange remark.

"He was an electrical engineer, sir, just like you. Electricity was his great love," Abuelo Chaguito answered. "Unfortunately, he's dead."

"Well, see if you can fix this piece of junk," the man said as he kicked a broken-down generator that was lying on the ground. Chaguito squatted and looked at it. "All you need is a new conductor coil; this one is all rusted. If you wait a minute, I'll run to the junkyard and get one."

"Bring it over tomorrow. And if you want to work for us, you're hired," the engineer from Boston said.

Chaguito went back the next day. He had an incredible ability with all things mechanical and could fix practically any type of motor. He was also very agile and, with spikes strapped to his heels, climbed the wooden lampposts to wire them for electrical power, a leather belt holding him to the post by the waist. The engineers from Boston were very pleased and invited him to come stay with them in the military camp outside La Concordia where all the government people lived.

And so Chaguito began to work for the Stone and Webster Electric Company and saved every penny he could. Someday he planned to open his own foundry.

One morning he was wiring a lamppost in front of an elementary school in Barrio Tibes when he saw a curious sign over its door: "The Good Luck School." An old man dressed in a faded black jacket and pants sat on the school's front stoop. He was obviously blind: his eyes were clouded as if someone had spilled boiled egg white in them. He kept tapping the ground with his cane to the rhythm of the multiplication tables the schoolboys were reciting inside. Chaguito could hear them perfectly through the school's open windows. The blind man held a sheet of lottery tickets in his lap, and when someone walked by he cried, "One thousand dollars for a quarter! Ten thousand for a dollar! This may be your last chance to buy a ticket to paradise!"

Chaguito thought it was an unlikely place for a lottery vendor to conduct his business, but he gave the old man a dollar and bought a ticket, number 202. Now the schoolboys were repeating the alphabet and he craned his neck to look in through the window. The schoolteacher was an imposing figure. She was six feet tall and her chest was as wide as an ocean liner. Dressed in a white blouse and a long madras skirt, she wore thick-heeled, no-nonsense shoes. Her hair was carefully combed into a starched bun.

Chaguito dug his spikes deeper into the lamppost and climbed a bit higher to observe what was going on. The teacher was strict with the boys; she held a long twig of hawthorn in her hand, and every time one of them lagged or made a mistake, she'd use her switch. Chaguito told himself she would make a wonderful mother. Boys were a good investment, especially when they worked for the family.

He spiked his way down the pole, walked to Agapito's Place, the cantina on the corner, and asked the bartender the name of the teacher. "It's Miss Adela," the bartender said. Chaguito went back to the Good Luck School at around four that afternoon. Miss Adela was just closing the door, and he waited for her at the bottom of the steps. The lottery vendor was still sitting there, sound asleep. The carriages that rolled down the street whipped up the dry mud on the pavement, and his black suit was covered with dust.

"Good afternoon, Miss Adela," Chaguito said, looking up at her. She was eight inches taller than he. "You certainly had your hands full today, teaching all those lads. And yet you look as fresh as if you'd just started. You remind me of a French rose!" Adela Mercedes Pasamontes had a very pink complexion, the only feminine thing about her, but it was the first time anyone had ever called her a rose. Men never said flattering things to her, and she didn't give a hoot. She was amazed when she heard what Chaguito said.

"I saw you this morning through the window," she said. "You looked like a monkey hanging from the lamppost. Aren't you afraid of those power lines?"

"Electricity *is* very dangerous, Miss Adela. The modern world begins and ends with it. But the law of probability is in my favor because it's already killed my father," Chaguito answered.

"I'm sorry to hear that. My mother died and Father is still alive, but he's blind," Adela said. And she stopped at the door to help the lottery vendor up from his chair.

"This is my father," she said, "Don Félix Pasamontes."

Chaguito felt less overwhelmed by Adela's size and self-assurance when she said that. At least they had one thing in common: they had each lost a parent.

"Have you been to France, young man?" Don Félix asked Chaguito. He liked to pop unexpected questions like that at strangers.

"*La France est un jardin, Monsieur. C'est le plus beau pays de l'Europe*," Chaguito answered in perfect French, without the shadow of an accent.

Adela looked at Chaguito with curiosity. He was twenty-one years old but his easy smile and slight frame made him look younger.

"Where did you learn to speak French?" Adela asked. "There are very few people in La Concordia who can speak it. It reminds me of Guadeloupe, where I was born."

"I've been around," Chaguito answered, helping her with her books.

Adela began to walk down Calle Fraternidad with her father and Chaguito. "My parents emigrated to Guadeloupe twenty-five years ago. They had a perfume and liquor store in Point-à-Pitre called the Rue de Rivoli," she said. "We had a good life there. Father sold liqueurs and Mother sold all kinds of perfumes—L'Heure Bleu, Shalimar, Joy. I didn't have to do anything. I just spent my days playing the piano. But nothing lasts forever," Adela concluded with a sigh. "Mother died last year, the same day I turned eighteen, and Father developed diabetes and went blind. We had to sell the store at a loss, close the house down, and even sell the piano. We came back to Puerto Rico, where Father has a brother, Francisco Pasamontes, who owns a prosperous tobacco factory, La Bella Cacica. Tío Francisco got him this job. He sells lottery tickets to the parents of the children I teach at school."

They were at the corner of Calle Fraternidad and Calle Salud. The street was busy with horse-drawn carriages and mule carts. Don Félix was carrying his cane, and he swung it in front of him in a semicircle to feel his way. He seemed always to know when some obstacle was in front of him. Chaguito watched in fascination; Don Félix was like a ghost dancer, padding softly down the market's crowded alleys without bumping into anyone.

Chaguito took Adela by the elbow when she began to cross the street. She was about to shake him off but didn't. He had an engaging way about him. He kept laughing and making jokes, and everyone they met on the sidewalk seemed to like him. It was as if he exuded some kind of substance that made people happy. So Adela crossed the street, letting him hold on to her arm.

She was headed for the Plaza del Mercado Isabel Segunda, which had been a gift to the city from Queen Isabella II of Spain. The street was crammed with vendors noisily peddling their wares; mules ambled along loaded with sacks of coffee and all kinds of produce from the mountains. The market itself was open, with a high, corrugated steel roof held up by ornate wrought-iron beams. Dozens of shops were crowded together on each side. It was like stepping inside a tropical rainbow, where the smells of cilantro, laurel, recao, mango, pineapple—all kinds of vegetables, flowers, and fruits—melded into an invisible perfumed arch above their heads.

Adela was excited. She enjoyed striking a bargain more than anything else in the world. In ten minutes she visited ten different stalls, laughing and talking as she carefully selected the merchandise. She took out her little brown purse, in which she had put Abuelo's dollar, and bought a chicken, rice, and potatoes, then gave it all to Chaguito to carry. Abuelo couldn't believe she had bought so much for so little money.

He took hold of her arm again. "Living with someone like you would be like having the Statue of Liberty holding up the roof of the house," Chaguito said gallantly. "You make one feel secure." Adela blushed with embarrassment and didn't answer. But what Abuelo really liked about Adela were her breasts, which were so large she would be able to nurse half a dozen boys with them.

When they reached Adela and Don Félix's house—a small wooden bungalow in El Polvorín, a barrio on the outskirts of town—Chaguito saw that it was badly in need of paint and that several louvered windows were askew. The narrow yard around it, however, was well tended and lush with rose bushes. Chaguito was about to leave when Adela asked, "Would you like to have dinner with us? I'm cooking coq au vin." Chaguito was delighted to stay. After that he came by the Good Luck School every day at five o'clock, walked Miss Adela and Don Félix home, and helped paint and repair the house in exchange for Adela's delicious cooking. He had fallen in love with Adela, but being a Vernet, he had a hard time telling her.

Some weeks later, when Chaguito was at work, he took a rest after lunch—he usually brought a ham sandwich and a thermos of coffee with him. He was sitting on the sidewalk with his back against a lamppost when a gust of wind blew an old newspaper down the street. He picked it up and saw the lottery list had been published. He'd completely forgotten about the ticket he'd bought from Don Félix, and as he flicked the pages he saw the winning number was 202. He couldn't believe his eyes. The paper was a week old and the prize had to be claimed that day.

Chaguito ran to his tent in the engineers' camp to look for the ticket but he couldn't find it. Then he remembered he had left it in the back pocket of his khaki pants the week before and had just given them to the washerwoman who came by the camp once a week. She took the dirty laundry to the Jagueyes River to wash. Chaguito ran across town.

He found the old woman kneeling on a huge boulder by the riverbank. She had just soaked his pants. "Did you find a lottery ticket in the back pocket of my pants?" he yelled from the shore.

"I'm sorry, Chaguito, I didn't look. But I'll look now." And before Chaguito could stop her, she put her wet, suds-covered hand into the pants' back pocket.

"No!" Chaguito cried desperately before she could take the ticket out. And he scrambled down to the water's edge and snatched the dripping pants from her. Then he ran down the road toward La Concordia. When he reached the school, he knocked on the door. "There's a ten-thousand-dollar ticket in that pocket, but it'll fall to pieces if I try to remove it," he blurted out to her. "I'd like to make a deal with you. If you rescue my ticket, I'll ask you to marry me."

Adela didn't answer. She quietly told her students to go home and closed the school for the day. Then she took Chaguito's pants to her house, made him sit in Don Félix's rocking chair in the living room, and built a fire outside. She hung the wet pants over it without trying to take out the ticket, and when they were dry she ironed them on a padded board. Chaguito waited patiently. When Adela finished, she carefully slid her hand into the pocket and extricated the dry ticket in one piece. "Here's your ticket to paradise, Chaguito. But you'll have to travel there alone because I'm never going to get married." And she pushed him unceremoniously out the door.

"But Don Félix sold me the ticket! It's only right that you should share in the benefits!" Chaguito cried, almost ordering her to open up. But Adela's door remained closed.

Chaguito ran to the lottery office and cashed in his prize: ten thousand dollars in a neat green pile. He counted the money meticulously and put it away under his mattress. The next day he went by the school again. He softened his tone considerably. "Please marry me, Miss Adela. We'll have half a dozen sons, so you'll be able to set up your own school. And I promise to take care of your father's eye operation."

When Adela heard Chaguito's pleading voice, she didn't have the heart to say no. She agreed to marry him.

The wedding took place on May 1, 1901, at La Inmaculada, a small chapel near El Polvorín. Chaguito kept as silent as a tomb about being a Freemason. He didn't want Adela to give him any trouble at the last minute. All during the wedding ceremony he knelt and mumbled softly to himself, pretending he was praying. When they stood at the foot of the altar Chaguito looked up at Our Lady of the Immaculate Conception, with her sweet face turned heavenward and a silver halo above her head, and thought that a church ceremony was a small price to pay if the Vernets' good-luck star began to rise.

TWENTY-FIVE

THE HOUSE ON CALLE ESPERANZA

Not long after Chaguito married Adela Pasamontes, he bought the house at 13 Calle Esperanza. Since thirteen was bad luck for everyone, he was sure it would bring *him* good luck. He had the house completely furnished with mahogany furniture from Casa Margarida: straight-backed chairs with square rush seats that made you feel as if you were sitting on a prickly cracker. The house was made of wood and painted light gray on the outside. But inside, the rooms were done in gay colors; Adela wanted to live in a place that reminded her of her life in Guadeloupe. The master bedroom was the color of peach brandy; the dining room was mint-green; the living room was Benedictine gold. Facing the street was a balcony, with a black-and-white domino marble floor, a silver-plated baluster, and three high, delicate columns ending in silver acanthus leaves. The gabled tin roof had two ventilators sitting on it like a pair of round steel helmets, and there was a deep patio at the back where Abuela Adela grew roses and Abuelo Chaguito kept his exotic parrots.

Abuelo also bought Adela an upright Cornish piano. He traveled to San Juan to buy it and had it shipped around the island to La Concordia. When Adela saw the movers taking the piano out of the crate she ran to the sidewalk, sat on the bench, and began to play. Out came the *zarabandas, danzas,* and *malagueñas* she adored but hadn't played since she left her beloved Guadeloupe. Soon everyone in the street was dancing.

The house was just around the corner from the marketplace, which Abuela loved to visit. But Chaguito had another reason for buying 13 Calle Esperanza: the new Adelphi Masonic Lodge stood just a block away. He knew Adela would be upset if she found out he was a Freemason, so he kept his visits to the lodge secret.

With the rest of the money from the lottery, on the outskirts of town Chaguito built the foundry he had always dreamed of: Vernet Construction. At first it was small, but gradually it expanded. In the structural-steel department, electric welders fused metal sheets for water and oil tanks, kilns, warehouse roofs, and sidings; in the machine-shop department, large and small lathes whirred and cut away all sorts of metals, and then the planers and shapers gave them form; the foundry department had a cupola furnace where Chaguito cast water pipes, tanks, construction rods, cast-iron balconies, and other products for local consumption. When he had saved enough money, he built a large oven, where he smelted the scrap iron he picked up at the city dump. He loved to pour the molten metal into molds, then watch the globs of fire cool off, sizzling in the water tank. What emerged were pulleys, wheels, and all sorts of valuable machine parts. The hollow casting molds were made of sand, and Chaguito designed them himself.

Chaguito was a gifted draftsman and he began to take orders and to design the machinery for the sugar mills and coffee haciendas near La Concordia: the iron crushing mills, evaporators, cogwheels, and piston rods used to process molasses into sugar, as well as the iron *tahonas* used to husk the blood-red coffee beans before they were spread out to dry in the sun. He was only modestly successful and couldn't sell many of them, though, because agriculture on the island was undergoing one of its periodic economic crises. The foundry business survived on the repairs that were needed at the sugar mills. But

Chaguito was never despondent. Ever the optimist, he saw the foundry as the springboard for his future success.

In 1902, a year after Abuelo and Abuela moved to the house on Calle Esperanza, Ulises was born. Aurelio was born the following year. Roque and Damián followed in quick succession. But when Adela gave birth to Amparo in 1912 and then to Celia in 1913, Chaguito was very upset. "I thought we were going to have a team of six boys, to get a successful business going," he told her.

Abuela put her foot down. "Women can do business too," she answered, bristling at Chaguito's attitude. "And in any case, not all business deals are made on earth. Some are made in heaven." As she said so, she kissed Celia, the new baby, on the forehead and made the sign of the cross over her.

Ulises and Aurelio slept in the cherry-liqueur bedroom, Damián and Roque in the mandarin-yellow one, Celia and Amparo in the anisette-pale blue. The boys' bedrooms were on the left side of the house and the girls' were on the right, next to the bathroom and the kitchen. All the bedrooms opened out onto a living room–dining room, which was divided by a freestanding wall against which the piano stood.

Despite Adela's colorful palette, the house had a martial air to it. The children's beds were all identical: wire-mesh iron-frame cots with thin horsehair mattresses next to plain night tables and chamber pots. Abuela and Abuelo's bedroom was on the left side of the house. They slept in a large canopied bed that was so high Chaguito had to climb a three-step ladder to reach it. Adela had a large pineapple carved on top of each bed column because in Puerto Rico pineapples are a symbol of hospitality.

Adela was a strict disciplinarian, which was the only way she could keep the household going on a meager budget. She asked my grandfather to cut a four-inch-wide leather strap from one of his belt pulleys, and she named it Santa Ursula. She went around the house with Santa Ursula tied around her waist and instilled the holy rule of obedience in her family.

Every morning as soon as the clock in the dining room chimed six, Adela, dressed in what Abuelo liked to call her Statue of Liberty robe, would sit before the Cornish piano and play something to wake up the brood: the Anvil Chorus or "Semper Fidelis." At other times, to keep Chaguito happy, she played a potpourri of "La Marseillaise" and the Cuban national anthem. The children all filed Indian-style into the bathroom, chamber pots in hand; they emptied the contents into the toilet, flushed it, brushed their teeth, washed their faces, and combed their hair. They had to be seated at the table in ten minutes flat or else they would be sent off to school without any breakfast. Everybody followed Adela's orders to the letter.

When breakfast was over, Chaguito would bring his horse-drawn carriage around and drop his children off at school on his way to the foundry. By seven-thirty everybody was gone. Adela would play the piano for an hour and then sit out on the balcony with a second cup of coffee and wait for the beggars of La Concordia to arrive. She was a good Samaritan and couldn't stand to see people suffer. In Guadeloupe she had learned what it was to go hungry. Every day beggars came up to the balcony and Matilde, the maid, would help her serve them bowls of chicken soup or put *cataplasmas*—an unguent made with olive oil and crushed mustard seeds—on their chests. Adela also held charity kermesses at her house to raise money for the poor who lived in La Concordia's slums.

Santiago wanted his four sons to be engineers so they could operate a large foundry. He tried to kindle in them an interest in science. Adela, on the other hand, wanted her children to learn to play musical instruments. She made Ulises play the flute, Roque the viola, and Damián the violin. Amparo, Celia, and Aurelio took piano lessons. She hired the best piano teacher in town, Monsieur Guillot, and would sit next to the children for hours as they practiced their scales.

For a while, the six Vernet children played as an ensemble at Adela's kermesses. La Concordia was a very musical place at the time. It had only fifty thousand citizens, but there were sixty small orchestras playing in its numerous social clubs. Opera and zarzuela companies came from Madrid, Barcelona, and Paris to perform at its famous Athena Theater, and Adela went to listen to all of them. She would get dressed in one of her black muslin Statue of Liberty robes, pin a black ostrich feather in her hair, and make Chaguito tell all his friends he was taking her to the theater to see *The Merry Widow* or *La Verbena de la Paloma*, although it was really she who was taking him. And because she had a very good ear, the next morning she would sit at the piano and play and sing for her children all the songs she had heard at the theater.

TWENTY-SIX

PRESIDENT ROOSEVELT VISITS THE ISLAND

For a long time Aurelio couldn't make up his mind whom he wanted to be like, his father or his mother. Both Chaguito's and Adela's families had known hard times. Chaguito's family had lost everything because of the Cuban War of Independence. Forced to hide in the attic, he had survived by sheer willpower. And so, when Vernet Construction finally opened its doors and he had to struggle to make it a going concern, his determination to succeed could sometimes be mistaken for indifference toward others. It wasn't that he was greedy or anything like that. He simply had no time for compassion for those who were as unlucky as he had been.

Abuela Adela, by contrast, had known beauty and privilege in Guadeloupe. Because of this, she never became hardened. Instead, she shared in her neighbors' suffering and believed in goodness. Aurelio looked up to Chaguito and understood his struggle to make

Vernet Construction a success, but he was secretly on Adela's side.

Aurelio toyed for a while with the idea of becoming a seminarian. He loved to go to Mass on Sundays, and one day he told his mother he wanted to become a bishop when he grew up. "How would I look dressed in purple silk, with an amethyst on my finger?" Aurelio joked. But Adela wasn't amused. "If you want to become a bishop, first you'll have to become a priest," she told him sternly. "But in order to be anything at all in this world, the first thing you have to do is love Christ and follow his example."

Abuela Adela believed that Jesus Christ was the only true God and that "He was above all things." Tía Celia used to tell the following story in illustration:

"When I was four years old," Tía Celia said, "Theodore Roosevelt visited the island. It was 1917, so he wasn't President anymore. He came to our house in the mountains for a picnic because he wanted to discuss public works for the island. Adela had put together a wonderful lunch in the garden and at the last minute she remembered our dog was named after Teddy Roosevelt. She didn't want to be embarrassed by any of us calling Teddy in front of Mr. Roosevelt, so she had the dog locked up. When the President came, he brought his family with him, including several of his grandchildren, and we played among the hydrangeas and the rose bushes. One of Mr. Roosevelt's grandchildren was very conceited; the fact that his grandfather had been President of the United States had gone to his head. He kept going on about how his grandfather had done this and his grandfather had done that, until finally I tweaked his ear and told him to shut up because his grandfather wasn't any better than my father. And to prove it, I let Teddy loose, and we all began to run after him, calling his name at the top of our voices, supposedly trying to catch him. Everybody found out our dog was named after the President. That night, after Mr. Roosevelt had gone back to town, Mother made me kneel facing a corner in my room for an hour as punishment for what I had done.

" 'His grandson said Mr. Roosevelt was better than Father,' I told Adela sullenly. 'I had to do what I did!'

" 'Christ is your only true father,' Mother told me. 'He's greater than your father *and* greater than the President. You had no reason to do what you did.' "

As a master Mason, though, Abuelo Chaguito convinced Aurelio that the Catholic religion was a thing of the past. Freemasonry was the modern way of helping humanity. At the same time, it could help the island become a part of the United States. To be a Freemason was to be of service to the people.

When Aurelio turned sixteen he was accepted at Northeastern University. As soon as Chaguito heard the news, he took him to the Adelphi Masonic Lodge and made him take the apprentice's oath. Many notable men in history had been Freemasons, and their names were inscribed in gold around the walls of the main hall: Benjamin Franklin, George Washington, Domingo Faustino Sarmiento, Mozart. Aurelio felt terribly proud as he stood under the Masonic triangle and compass in the white-columned gallery and swore to serve his fellow human beings. All the things Abuela Adela wanted him to do—go to Mass every day, gain indulgence by reciting the Rosary to the Virgen de Guadalupe, the patron saint of La Concordia, who stood on a little shelf in her bedroom, offer his discomforts in sacrifice for the souls of unrepentant sinners—seemed like a lot of nonsense to Aurelio after that. At Northeastern, students didn't pray in the hallways, as Adela wanted him to do. If you believed in science and the modern world, you couldn't believe in God—it was as simple as that. And Aurelio wanted to be modern, agnostic, and American, so he could serve his fellowman.

THE TWO FRIENDS

Soon after he arrived on the island, Abuelo Chaguito became friends with one of La Concordia's most prominent personalities, Alfredo Wiechers, better known as Bijas, because his red hair reminded everyone of the red *bija* with which Taíno Indians dyed their bodies. Bijas was a Freemason, like Chaguito, and they met at the Adelphi Masonic Lodge. They had a lot in common. "Architects and engineers are natural-born Freemasons because they are builders," Chaguito told Bijas. "That's why Freemasonry evolved in northern Europe from the medieval guild of stonemasons."

Bijas was the son of a German merchant who had been the Prussian consul in La Concordia around 1895, before the Americans landed at Guánica. Bijas graduated from the Special School of Architecture in Paris in 1896 and won the gold medal in his class. From there he went to study in Barcelona with Enrique Sagnier, the famous art nouveau architect. When the hacendados of La Concordia learned of Bijas's admirable skills, they wrote to him in Barcelona and asked him to return home because they needed someone like him to design beautiful homes for them.

Bijas was extraordinarily productive. In eight years he filled the town with his handsome buildings. He designed the Adelphi Masonic Lodge, the Athena Theater, the Rose Hotel, as well as dozens of private homes. Bijas made a lot of money and was soon a citizen of means. He became the darling of La Concordia and was wined and dined by the bourgeoisie. He and his father were among the prominent men who remonstrated with the American commandant when Chaguito and his fellow firemen were imprisoned for disobeying army orders.

In 1918, things were going relatively well at Chaguito's foundry. Abuelo decided to embark on a side venture. Buying an empty lot on Calle Fraternidad, he asked his friend Bijas to design a vaudeville theater, the Teatro Estrella, where one could see silent films as well. Up to then, films had been shown under a tent in the Plaza de las Delicias, where Aurelio used to play the piano for five cents and get to see the films for free. One Saturday afternoon Bijas came to the Vernet Construction offices on Calle Virtud. Aurelio was fifteen and happened to be there that day. Chaguito made Bijas sit at the sketching table where he himself worked every day for hours, carefully drawing the conical wheels, crowns, and rollers for the machinery that he advertised in mechanical catalogs and later cast at the foundry. But Bijas worked in a totally different way. He took a pencil and a large sheet of paper and, without using a ruler or a protractor, began to draw the Teatro Estrella's façade. His hand flew over the sheet, filling in all the details of a building that existed only in his imagination, but annotating with mathematical precision its exact measurements. That moment was a revelation for Aurelio. He saw the wonder of being able to imagine something completely original, of being able to bring it out from within, without any reference to the external world. Chaguito could never have done that.

"That's very nice," Chaguito said as the architect went on drawing. Chaguito was looking over Bijas's shoulder, and he was shivering with excitement. But he didn't want Bijas to know how much he admired him. Bijas was sketching in the theater's roof, which had to be much higher than the roof of a house to accommodate the movie screen.

"Remember, the walls are of brick, and a roof that high can be dangerous if there's an earthquake. Wouldn't it be wise to reinforce it with an iron beam?"

"That's the difference between you and me, Chaguito," Bijas said sadly, shaking his head. "You're an engineer, and engineers always have to be practical in order to head off catastrophe. Beams, steel columns, girders are all your specialty. But architects are dreamers, and we know that the real strength comes from within. You know how I hate beams. But I'll reinforce your theater with an iron girder, just to please you." And he drew a pediment on the building that looked like a garland of daisies.

During the First World War an atmosphere of xenophobia had developed in La Concordia. Everyone with a German name was seen as a possible traitor, and the Wiechers family was no exception. Bijas's father and mother had gone back to live in Hamburg, but he had stayed on. He had been born in La Concordia; it was his home, where he made his living. People gossiped and began to make him feel uncomfortable. They stared at him every time he went out, and the FBI had him followed. Bijas tried to win the agent over by lending him a pair of binoculars that could be used in La Concordia's port, where there was a constant lookout for the U-boats that circled the island. Wiechers forgot that the binoculars were a German brand, Zeiss, and his gift only made matters worse.

The war was almost over and Wiechers felt relieved to have weathered the crisis, when a formidable earthquake shook La Concordia, sending many buildings to the ground. Thanks to the iron girder, the Teatro Estrella remained standing. But Bijas's beautiful art nouveau house, which had a pink pergola on the roof where one could sit and see as far as the Plaza del Mercado Isabel Segunda, partially collapsed. His family ran out into the street in time, and fortunately nobody perished. People insisted he had it coming—it was his punishment for being a spy. Bijas suffered a nervous breakdown. He couldn't sleep at night, thinking the roof was going to collapse on his head. He was institutionalized, and when he came out he never drew plans for another building again. He made his living drawing pastels and watercolors, which he sold for practically nothing. Once he drew a special one of Chaguito, dressed up in his fireman's uniform. Underneath it he wrote, in a shaky hand: "In La Concordia, firemen will always be heroes."

Bijas finally couldn't take the gossip any longer. He sold his half-ruined home with all the furniture in it, and left with his family for Barcelona. Four years later Chaguito received a letter from him saying he was bankrupt and asking for a two-hundred-dollar loan. With the letter came a package wrapped in brown paper. In it were the Zeiss binoculars Bijas had lent the FBI agent, which the government had returned to him once the war was over. He wanted Abuelo Chaguito to have them as a keepsake. Chaguito sent him the two hundred dollars, and that was the last he ever heard of his friend.

TWENTY-EIGHT

AURELIO GRABS ULISES BY THE HEEL

I never knew Abuela Adela. She died in 1930, the year my parents were married at Emajaguas. But Father had a picture of her in our house in Las Bougainvilleas, an oval medallion of a dark-haired beauty dressed in black tulle with a fresh rose pinned to her breast. It was the only picture on his dresser, and he used to brush his hair and put on his coat and tie in front of her every morning. I also know how much Father loved her because once he showed me a linen handkerchief yellowed by age that he kept wrapped in tissue paper inside the small steel vault in his closet. "This handkerchief holds your Abuela Adela's last tears," he said to me. "Before she died, I dried her eyes with it."

Tía Amparo talked to me a lot about Abuela Adela when she came to visit us. "She was very perceptive," Amparo said. "Adela could tell more about people by how they looked than by what they said. If a man's shirt was buttoned wrong or if the shirttails were hanging out of his pants when he went by her house, Adela knew that he had made a bad investment. If a woman let her slip show or put on her makeup too heavily, Adela knew she was depressed and her husband was unfaithful. Chaguito couldn't understand how she did it; it was as if Adela could read people's minds. He even went so far as to accuse her of listening in on her neighbors when she sat outside the dark confessional at La Milagrosa, waiting her turn. But he was wrong. Your grandmother loved people; that was her secret."

One day something terrible happened. Ulises was six years old and he was playing in the empty lot next to the house, where he found a half-full can of gasoline. He wanted to build a bonfire to cook marshmallows, so he put some sticks together and soaked them with gasoline. Then he dropped a match on the pile. The blaze sprang up so high his clothes caught fire. He ran into the house screaming and Adela threw a basin of water over him. The doctor came and gingerly took off Ulises's clothes. His body was covered with second-degree burns. He had less than a twenty-five percent chance of surviving, the doctor said. Adela washed Ulises's blisters with distilled water, spread salve on them, rolled him in a blanket, and put him to bed. Nothing more could be done but to pray.

Aurelio was five. He never forgot the foul smell of charred flesh and the uproar Ulises's accident caused. The family forgot all about him and he hid in a closet. He was terrified. The word *death* went swishing around the house like a sharpened sickle. It was the first time Aurelio had heard it, and he was surprised to learn that someone could "pass away," simply cease to exist. When he tiptoed out of the closet, he was forbidden to enter his brother's room, but unseen he peered at him through a chink in the wall. Aurelio saw Adela and Chaguito kneeling next to Ulises's bed, praying and holding hands. Ulises was their first child, Adela sobbed. All their dreams were pinned on him. Aurelio was dismayed; he realized he was in second place—*el segundón*—and he was afraid his parents wouldn't love him.

Ulises pulled through, thanks to Adela's unfailing energy—she spent three days and nights dressing Ulises's wounds and praying. And from that moment on, Aurelio knew that his mother's love was the foundation on which the house on Calle Esperanza stood.

Abuelo Chaguito was wonderful, but he was not altogether dependable. Tía Celia told me the story of how Abuelo sent Ulises to Boston University in 1920, but although Father was to start at Northeastern the same year, Chaguito said there was no money to pay for his steamer ticket. Abuela Adela was furious at her husband, but she still felt a lot of respect for him. She controlled her temper and said sweetly, "I have some money laid by under the mattress, dear. Why don't we buy Aurelio's ticket with that?" It was her savings for the last five years, but she didn't hesitate to part with it.

After Adela's quarrel with Abuelo Chaguito over Aurelio's future, she was so hurt she moved out of their bedroom. From then on she slept next to Tía Amparo and Tía Celia and Abuelo slept by himself in the huge canopied double bed next to Aurelio and Ulises's room. Something had broken inside her, perhaps her confidence in Chaguito. She never explained her decision to anyone.

Abuelo didn't move out of the house, but he never came straight home from work after that. He had many friends in town and visited them until late at night. The house at Calle Esperanza was split in two: the men slept on the left and the women on the right.

Tío Ulises looked the most like Abuela Adela: he was pudgy and had Pasamontes eyes, which were small and close-set. This made him look slow-witted, as if he were zapping flies, decidedly an advantage because Tío Ulises was sharp as could be. He had inherited Abuela Adela's ability to make a good deal, and with his short, fat fingers could count dollar bills faster than anyone.

Aurelio took after the Vernet side of the family; he had inherited Henri Vernet's silky brown curls, wide-set eyes, and long, slender fingers, which were perfect for playing the piano. He also shared Bisabuelo Henri's love for science, combined with Adela's passion for music. Aurelio was as incapable of telling a lie as Ulises was of speaking the truth. But Aurelio never told on his brother when he did something wrong.

One day, Abuela Adela sent them to buy a loaf of bread at the *panadería*, and on the way back to the house Ulises made a small hole in it and ate half the insides. When they brought the bread to the table and Abuela sliced the first piece, the whole loaf crumbled and fell apart. Adela picked up Santa Ursula, and Aurelio took his punishment like a man. But when Abuela Adela went looking for Ulises, she couldn't find him anywhere.

"Where's that devil of a brother of yours?" Adela asked Aurelio, shaking Santa Ursula in his face. "I'm sure you know where he's hiding. You two are as close as chiggers!" Aurelio wouldn't tell.

Ulises had climbed on top of Adela's wardrobe, and he stayed there for three days. He came down only to pee and drink milk at night. On the third day Abuela was so worried she called the police.

"It's as if the earth had swallowed him up. He's disappeared!" she told the officers in tears when they came to the house. "I thought it was all a game and that his brothers were hiding him, but he must have run away! Poor child, it's all my fault. I shouldn't have been so strict with him!" When Tío Ulises heard this, he crept silently down the back of the wardrobe and slipped out the kitchen door. A few minutes later the police found him lying in the middle of the street unconscious; he had fainted from hunger. Abuela Adela was so happy they found him that Aurelio was the only one who was punished.

Ulises was always trying to win his mother over. He became a friend of most of the vendors in the marketplace and bought Adela all kinds of special fruits and vegetables with the money he made on the sly selling combs and chewing gum at school. He could sell anyone just about anything—especially if it was something the person didn't need. "Selling is the oldest of all the arts," he'd tell Father. "Every time you sell something, you're selling yourself. That's why you can't be a successful businessman if you don't think you're the greatest fucker on Earth." Father winced at Tío Ulises's foul language and told him to shut up, but Ulises only laughed.

There was nothing in this world that Tío Ulises liked to do more than sell. Sometimes he would take things from the house and sell them in the marketplace. He would take one of Adela's scuffed silverplated serving pieces, for example, polish it so that it looked like sterling, and get a ridiculously high price for it. Then he would run back home and tell Adela, "Here's the money from your chafing dish, Mother. It looked a little beat up, and I sold it so you could buy a new one." Adela would scold him angrily and make him kneel in front of an image of the Virgen de Guadalupe, but she always forgave him in the end.

When Ulises grew up he enjoyed selling as much as he did making love. "Both activities are an affirmation of life," he'd say, "from both you derive the thrill of conquest. When you fuck, you vanquish by will; when you sell, you conquer by wile." Abuelo Chaguito agreed with Tío Ulises in this respect; they both saw doing business as a kind of game in which the better team always won. Later, when Aurelio and his brothers were all back from their studies in the States, Vernet Construction became a team with four players, and Abuelo Chaguito was its captain. Their game was hardball: the winning team got everything and the losing team got nothing. It was sad, but those were the rules.

Aurelio, my father, was so softhearted he couldn't see a dead dog lying in the road without getting out of his car to bury it, and if the dog was hurt he'd take it home and nurse it back to health. Once he was driving home late at night from one of his jobs installing machinery at a sugar mill when he saw two drunks slashing each other with their machetes. Father got out of the car and stood between the struggling men. They didn't want to kill a stranger, so they had to stop fighting.

He was sentimental and romantic and tried to win Adela's heart by learning to play the most difficult piano pieces. In 1916, when he was thirteen years old, he played Mendelssohn's *Rondo Capriccioso* in a high school competition. Several students were participating, and his cousin Mariana Pasamontes was one of them. Mariana was eighteen, and she was a much more advanced student than Aurelio. Aurelio gave a commanding performance the day of the competition and won first prize. But when the principal came on stage to present him with a medal, he said he didn't want it. He asked that the medal be given to Adela instead.

Aurelio was something of a child prodigy, but his precociousness was due to his desperate effort to catch up with Tío Ulises. He skipped eighth grade and graduated from high school at sixteen, at the same time as Tío Ulises. They both went off to study in Boston and finished in record time, each with a college diploma under his arm—but Father also had a master's degree. Tío Ulises was full of fun; he liked to drink and dance and go to parties. He had half a dozen girlfriends and knew all the artists in La Concordia, but Father never had any fun.

While the brothers were in Boston they lived together at 22 Kingsbury Street, in a boardinghouse near Fenway Park. After school Aurelio worked as a waiter at a coffee shop on Huntington Avenue, near the Boston Conservatory of Music. Ulises got a job at a hardware store on Commonwealth Avenue. Being a born salesman, he immediately began to make more money than Aurelio. Every week Father received a letter from his mother telling him not to abandon the piano but to study at the conservatory no matter what the cost; his weekly letter from his father told him to quit the piano and do his best to get through Northeastern in three years.

Aurelio would go directly from his classes to the piano and practice two hours every day. Then he would work at the coffee shop and study for his engineering courses until two in the morning. During his senior year he signed up for a course in circuits and devices and then forgot all about it. He didn't go to a single class. When he was notified that the exam was the next day and that if he didn't pass it he would fail the course—which meant he wouldn't graduate—he pulled an all-nighter, took the exam the next morning, and just squeaked by. He didn't know what the word *tired* meant. He was like a little lead soldier, always marching across the battlefield.

Scrimping and saving, Abuela Adela and Abuelo Chaguito managed to send Roque and Damián to study at Northeastern too. Roque studied civil engineering and Damián chemical engineering, but as students they weren't as good as Ulises and Aurelio. Roque was a slow learner and he had to cram for hours in order to pass a course; Damián was very intelligent but he was sensitive and sometimes got so nervous when he had to take an exam that he panicked and flunked. Adela had to keep writing them letters giving them moral support. She also threatened not to let them come home for summer vacation unless they passed their courses.

TWENTY-NINE

†HE ØBEDIEN† GIAN†

In 1926, Tío Ulises married Caroline Allan, a platinum-blond Boston heiress whom he'd met while studying at the university. Abuelo Chaguito was too busy to go to the States and Abuela Adela wasn't feeling up to traveling alone, so Aurelio was the only family member who attended the wedding. He was Tío Ulises's best man and had to pawn his wristwatch—Adela's graduation present to him that summer—to rent tails for the ceremony.

Caroline came to live with the family at the house on Calle Esperanza, and she was like a daughter to Abuela Adela. For two years she kept Adela company and was a great help; Adela's health was already fragile and she couldn't move about easily. Caroline was Tía Celia's best friend, and Caroline taught her perfect English. Adela felt sorry for Caroline for having married Ulises, the rascal of the family. She wished she had married my father instead, but Aurelio was already in love with Clarissa. Mother was a little stern for Adela's tastes, and she was always going on about the Rivas de Santillana as if they were God's gift to humanity.

In 1925, the year before she married Tío Ulises, Caroline had graduated Phi Beta Kappa from Radcliffe. Her family had a "cottage" called Valcour in Newport, near The Breakers, the Vanderbilt mansion. Valcour had sixteen bedrooms, six bathrooms, a swimming pool, and a tennis court. The bathtubs ran both salt water and fresh water, hot or cold. The family also owned a yacht, the *Cormorant*, which sailed to the Bahamas every summer.

"Why would an heiress marry an odd little mustachioed Latin lover and come to live on an exotic Caribbean island where half the population goes barefoot, doesn't have enough to eat, and lives in palm-thatched huts with no sanitary facilities?" I asked Tía Celia once. "To run away from her family, of course!" Celia exclaimed.

Caroline was madly in love with Tío Ulises. This was something I found extraordinary because Ulises was far from good-looking. He was short, and his close-set eyes, fleshy cheeks, and thick mustache made him look like a satisfied beaver. But I suppose it is true that a man as passionately in love with life as my uncle Ulises could make a woman feel rapturously happy.

As long as she had her beloved Ulises at her side, Caroline didn't mind sharing the only bathroom in the house with eight other family members, having the dogs' ticks crawling up the legs of her bed, or passing the serving dishes around the table at dinnertime. She was a moonlit beauty who appeared cold and aloof on the surface. But her heart was a regular little volcano in a constant state of eruption. Like Abuela Adela, she was a woman with a mission, but hers was women's suffrage. When she learned that women in Puerto Rico could not vote, she was horrified. In the States, women had secured the franchise in 1920, thanks to the Nineteenth Amendment.

For two years Caroline worked with the suffragettes in La Concordia, organizing meetings in support of women's right to equal pay and employment opportunities as well as to the vote. When Tía Celia began to talk of going to Nepal to be a missionary, Caroline gave her her full support. "The Vernets talk a lot about justice," she said to Tío Ulises once, "but Amparo has studied only as far as high school. And Celia wants to be a missionary, but Chaguito won't let her. What kind of justice is that? Where is the equality the Vernets are always touting?"

As soon as my uncles returned to La Concordia, they went to work at Vernet Construction with their father. Adela wasn't sorry to see Ulises become a businessman—he had commerce in his blood. But Aurelio was different. It made her cry to see how he never had time to sit down at the piano to play even a short little *danza* like "No me toques" by Morel Campos, which made her wish Chaguito were tickling her and they were sweethearts again.

The twenties were a very difficult time on the island. Sugar prices plummeted after the First World War and Puerto Rican coffee couldn't compete with Colombian, which sold for half the price on the mainland. In 1929 the Wall Street crash sent the economy reeling. But the island had already suffered another, even more severe blow: in 1928 San Felipe had struck.

San Felipe was a flying sawmill that mowed down everything in its path. It arrived from the south and left through the north with winds so strong that anemometers were bent out of shape. None of Adela's prayers worked, not even the novenas to San Antonio and Santa Agata, two saints who scare off rain because they like cats. Nobody was prepared for the catastrophe: communications were completely inadequate, and people had no way of knowing a hurricane was coming. My grandparents had to rely on the avocado tree in their garden, which plopped unripe fruit to the ground when there wasn't a trace of wind. Suddenly the sky began to grow black and before long everything on the island was being shooed like a stray dog across the Caribbean. Even furniture had to be tied down if you didn't want to find your living room rocker, your kitchen stove, and even the roof of your house hanging from a mangrove in Florida.

On Calle Esperanza they were just as unprepared as everywhere else. Luckily the storm came in September and Tío Roque and Tío Damián were home for summer vacation. Ulises and Aurelio helped Abuelo Chaguito board up the windows and doors at the last minute. But when the hurricane began to blow full blast and the corrugated tin roof began to wobble like a kettledrum, Adela panicked and started to scream. Chaguito ordered his four sons to climb up to the attic and nail the beams of the ceiling to the walls of the house. The hurricane passed and Chaguito was euphoric. "Thanks to me, catastrophe was avoided!" he bragged with his usual modesty. Adela always wondered how close she had been to seeing her four sons fly off, hanging on to the roof's wooden rafters.

For months after San Felipe, the poor of La Concordia survived on flour, margarine, dry crackers, and powdered milk doled out by the U.S. Army. Over 10,500 residents were homeless. There was no gas, electricity, or running water. The sugar, coffee, and tobacco planters, who lost all their crops, usually had their machinery repaired at Vernet Construction, and when San Felipe flattened the island they delayed their payments even more than usual. Tío Ulises and Father had a terrible time bringing home enough money to meet the payroll. Aurelio spent most of the week on the road, driving from one hacienda to the next down winding back roads. He often had to sleep in the family's old Model T. Once he woke up with a cow sticking its head through the window to lick his cheek.

The large American sugar mills—Eastern Sugar, Guánica Central, and Aguirre—owned forty-six percent of the sugarcane-producing land on the island, but they refused to buy machinery from the Vernets. Abuelo Chaguito would rail against them in disbelief: "We're American citizens, just like they are! We could repair and even build all the equipment for their mills at Vernet Construction!" But when he approached them, they always said the same thing. "Of course you could repair the mill's evaporator. But how long would it last? We'd rather ship it to the States and have it repaired there to make sure it won't break down again." Chaguito refused to believe Americans could be so unfair. But since he couldn't speak English and had to talk to the sugar-mill managers through an interpreter, there was no way he could convince them to the contrary.

Once Ulises and Aurelio came back from the States, however, things began to change. They were fluent in English—with a Boston accent, to boot—and made a good impression on the American managers, who began to give Vernet Construction the contracts for repairs of the mills' machinery and even to buy equipment. But then San Felipe struck, and the Americans couldn't afford to buy any new machinery.

To make matters worse, the only way Abuelo Chaguito could calm his anxiety was by spending money. Adela would yell at him that there was a boiling cauldron in hell just for him, full of all the gold he had wasted in his life. But it was as if it were raining in Hades.

First it was parrots. Every week Abuelo Chaguito brought home a new one, and soon he had a collection. They were beautiful and shone like jewels inside their cages at the back of the garden. But they were also nasty and tried to bite Adela every time she fed them.

"How can anything so beautiful be so vicious and make such an infernal noise?" she asked Chaguito, putting her hands to her ears to fend off the screeches and hoots. "If you bring one more of those devils dressed up in colored feathers to the house, I swear I'll wring its neck and drop it into the soup pot."

But Chaguito went on with his extravagant hobby. He bought an emerald-green yellow-nape parrot from Venezuela for fifty dollars, then a red, green, and gold macaw from the Amazon for a hundred, and a deep-blue cockatoo from Paraguay for two hundred and fifty. Chaguito loved to tame them. He would let one out of its cage, perch it on his gloved hand, and take a large walnut from his pocket. The parrot would inspect it suspiciously, turning it this way and that on the tip of its beak, then crack open the shell and remove the sweet, crumbly meat with its tar-black tongue. Chaguito scratched its head as it ate, softly calling out, "*Piojito, piojito*," until the parrot became drowsy and stopped wanting to bite him.

"Taming parrots is simply a struggle of wills," Chaguito would tell Adela. "I love to see how they lose some of their fierceness every time I feed them a nut."

But Abuela Adela had really begun to worry long before, when Chaguito started collecting automobiles. In 1907 Don Rafael Escribá, the owner of the Ridruejo sugar mill in Caguana, had offered to pay for a major repair to his evaporator with his two-year-old black Reo instead of cash. Chaguito was particularly attracted by the Reo's canvas top and the wooden spokes on its wheels. So he brought home the Reo. Then in 1908 Don Marcelino Marfisi had wondered if he could pay for a new *tahona* with his blue sports Parry, which had patent-leather mud guards and bright steel spokes. It was practically new but Don Marcelino had almost perished when the car went off the road. Chaguito loved it. He could repair the damage at the foundry for nothing at all, and he accepted it as payment for the *tahona*. In 1909 he had repaired the cogwheel at the Antonsanti sugar mill, and instead of the thousand dollars they owed him, they asked if they could settle the account with a brand-new fire-engine-red Stutz Bear Cat. Mr. Antonsanti wanted to get rid of it because the price of sugar had dropped even more and he couldn't meet his payments. Again Chaguito accepted the deal.

Until then, Abuela Adela had behaved like an obedient giant. She was always asking Abuelo Chaguito how much she should spend on the house. When Chaguito gave her fifteen dollars and told her to buy enough food to last the family a whole month, she never complained. Abuelo Chaguito was older than Adela, and he had the wisdom of experience. The minute Chaguito walked into the house at the end of the day, Adela would stop whatever she was doing—whether teaching Tío Ulises to read or giving Aurelio a bath—and run to make him feel at home. She'd take his jacket and hang it up, put his straw hat on the stand, and demurely ask if he needed anything.

Chaguito would tell her to bring him his slippers and a glass of iced lemonade and would walk out onto the terrace complaining about the heat. By the time he reached the shade of the mahogany tree at the back of the garden, where he loved to sit reading the newspaper, Ulises and Aurelio would be flying down the street like a pair of barefoot devils, because they knew she wouldn't be paying attention to them for the rest of the afternoon.

But the night Abuelo Chaguito drove the Stutz Bear Cat to the house, honking its silver horn all the way down Calle Esperanza from a party at La Concordia's casino, Adela reached the end of her tether. It was two in the morning and she was sitting next to Damián, who was lying in bed with an asthma attack, when Abuelo Chaguito stepped gaily into the room all dressed up in his fireman's dress uniform. Tío Damián's chest was covered with a cheesecloth smeared with *benjuí*, a black unguent that was applied hot to make breathing easier, and Santa Ursula was beside Adela on a chair. Abuelo Chaguito was thinking how lucky he was to have such a wonderful wife who could bring up his children, cook, and clean on practically no money at all. He was feeling very affectionate. "And how is my Statue of Liberty tonight?" he said, drawing near to give her a kiss on the cheek. But Adela turned her face away.

"How much did that piece of junk cost?" she asked, looking angrily out the window at the Stutz parked across the street.

"One thousand dollars. But you wouldn't understand, dear," Chaguito added diffidently. "A Stutz is a collector's dream. It's worth every penny."

Adela got up slowly from the bed and towered over Abuelo Chaguito. "Do you mind showing me the palms of your hands?" she asked in a controlled voice. There was an uncomfortable pause, but Chaguito decided to humor her. He spread his hands in front of him, palms upward, and gave a nervous little laugh. Adela examined them carefully. "That's funny. I don't see a hole in either one. And I'm sure there must be one because I've never met a wastrel like you in all my life. Tomorrow you're going to take that nickel lobster back to Mr. Antonsanti and ask for the money he owes us, or else you'll have a taste of Santa Ursula like everyone else in this house."

Abuelo Chaguito gave in and returned the Stutz to Mr. Antonsanti the next day, asking to be paid in cash. From then on, none of my grandfather's smiles and tricks did him any good. Adela took the helm and managed the family budget. And if something ever went wrong, she had only to grab hold of Santa Ursula, the walls of the house would begin to tremble, and Abuelo Chaguito, as well as everyone else, would run for cover.

THIRTY

TÍA CELIA'S BLUE DOLL

Whenever Abuela Adela fell ill, Aurelio would take her place at the head of the table. He was worse than a drill sergeant. Abuelo Chaguito was so busy he often didn't get home until after dinner. Tía Celia told me a story about Father once that gave me an idea of what he was like at the time.

Meals at the house on Calle Esperanza were very different from the lavish dinners at Emajaguas. The Vernets always ate plain fare: steak and onions, French-fried potatoes, corn on the cob, fried eggs over white rice, and *guineitos niños*—baked baby plantains. Everything, though, was served in generous portions. Seafood and salads were luxuries that didn't give you the calories necessary for hard work. (Aurelio had never tasted an oyster or a shrimp, much less a lobster, until he met Clarissa.)

The Vernets' table was bare—a tablecloth was used only on special occasions. The tableware was stainless steel, and the dishes and glasses were from the local hardware store. The dining room opened onto the balcony at the back of the house, and Abuelo Chaguito's German shepherds, Siegfried and Gudrun, were always lying in wait under the table to snap up whatever morsel might fall to the floor. Years later Abuelo Chaguito had sculptures of them cast in cement and set them up on either side of the steps that led down to the garden.

The Vernets had neither the time nor the patience to indulge their taste buds. Nonetheless, etiquette at the table was important. There was only one servant, and Aurelio had given strict orders that no one should begin to eat until everyone had served himself. Once, at lunch, Tía Celia couldn't resist popping one of the *bacalaítos fritos*, the crunchy golden cod fritters that were her favorite dish, into her mouth before the others had food on their plates. At first Aurelio didn't notice, but when Celia munched on the fritter, it was so crisp it made a loud noise. Aurelio looked up. "Who's eating?" he asked archly, looking around the table. Celia giggled behind her napkin, but Aurelio was indignant. He ordered Celia to her room; that day she would have no lunch. But Ulises later sneaked into Celia's room with his pants full of *bacalaítos fritos*. "You mustn't pay attention to Aurelio," he said as he took them out of his greasy pocket. "He loves to boss people around and never has any fun. But you and I know that having fun is what heaven is all about."

Tía Celia was the runt of the family. When she was a child, Tío Ulises nicknamed her Volleyball because she was always bouncing around the house on her short, thick legs. But she had beautiful pale-blue eyes—the color of the sky at dawn—and a fair complexion.

Celia was Abuela Adela's favorite daughter and Adela gave her a lot of attention. She taught her to read and write and they recited the Rosary together every day before the Virgin of Guadalupe's image.

Once Adela said to Tía Celia: "To reach heaven one must make sacrifices. Praying and fasting and helping the poor are not enough. Every sacrifice we make brings us closer to heaven." Celia didn't know what *sacrifice* meant, but she smiled and agreed wholeheartedly with her mother.

A few days later, when Abuela Adela was sitting on the balcony with Celia, a beggar woman whom Adela knew well went by, leading an emaciated little girl by the hand. They stopped to talk. It was Three Kings' Day, or Epiphany, and the marketplace across the street was crowded with vendors' stalls exhibiting their toys. Rocking horses, tin horns, gaily ribboned drums all gleamed in the sun. The beggar's child looked at everything wide-eyed from where she stood, but her mother couldn't buy her anything. Celia was sitting next to Abuela. On her lap was a beautiful doll dressed in blue gingham with white ribbons at the neck that the Three Kings had brought her.

All of a sudden Abuela said, "Celia, didn't the Three Kings bring Aralia's little girl a present last night too?" Celia immediately understood what her mother meant. "Of course they did! They brought her a doll!" she said. And she ran to her room to get a doll whose pink gingham dress was a little faded—last year's gift from the Magi—but still very nice. She came back to the balcony and generously handed the doll to the little girl. "Not that one! The new one. Don't you remember, Celia?" And Tía Celia, with tears in her eyes, went back to her room to get her new doll, and handed it to the little girl. Now she knew the meaning of sacrifice.

Tía Celia was always climbing trees and riding her bicycle, and later she became a star baseball player at La Concordia's country club. She once showed me a picture of her First Communion, and I found it amusing and at the same time revealing. Celia is kneeling on a carved dark-mahogany prie-dieu. Her head is covered with a veil crowned with large white roses. In one hand she holds a small missal, and in the other a large Communion candle. But instead of holding the candle devoutly in front of her, Celia has slung it over her shoulder like a baseball bat. Many years later, when Celia became a nun, she had that same wholesome approach to religion—a "coming up to bat" style—that enabled her to do a lot of good in the world.

THIRTY-ONE

ADELA PASSES THE BATON

Adela's right leg began to swell and acquired a gray hue that made it look like an elephant's foot. Nobody knew what was wrong with her, and she refused to see a doctor. "It's nothing, just a bad mosquito bite," she'd say to her children. She bathed her leg at night in *sal de heno*—Epsom salts—diluted in warm water, and sewed several more long muslin Statue of Liberty robes, which she wore when she went out so no one would notice her swollen limb.

La Concordia was overrun by poor peasants who had come from the hills looking for shelter from San Felipe; the epidemics of cholera and typhus that followed brought even more refugees. Slums sprouted like tumors all around the beautiful nineteenth-century city; its gleaming white buildings were surrounded by shacks that had no sanitary facilities, no electricity, and no running water. Adela felt terribly guilty to be living in a nice house and even having a servant to help with the housework. Her family tried to tell her there was nothing one could do about it, but she didn't agree.

One time, having come home from an initiation ceremony, Abuelo Chaguito forgot to put away his trowel and Freemason's apron, which he usually kept under lock and key in his desk. Adela found them and at first she was terrified. The parish priest had told her that Freemasons celebrated demonic rites in their temples, and she was sure Chaguito would go to hell. But when she learned that Abuelo had made Aurelio, and later the rest of her boys, join the fraternity and that they had taken the oath of brotherly love because they were sure it would help them in the building trade, Abuela was almost hysterical. She couldn't even go to the Adelphi Lodge to denounce Chaguito's heresy, because women weren't allowed in Masonic lodges.

Adela redoubled her efforts at charity work and began to visit the slums of La Concordia on foot, to pay for Chaguito's sin and prevent her sons from going to hell.

The streets of the slums were unpaved, and Abuela Adela took off her shoes and walked barefoot to do penance for her husband and her sons. Her Statue of Liberty robe got spattered with mud and she arrived home exhausted every afternoon. One day she felt so sick she couldn't get out of bed, and a doctor was brought to the house. He examined Abuela and told Chaguito that a parasite had wormed itself into the tissue of her right leg; the illness it was causing was deadly. Eventually the parasites would invade her whole body, but fortunately their progress was slow. Adela might live for another two or three years. Chaguito, ever the optimist, felt sure the Americans were bound to discover a cure in that span of time.

After a while Abuela Adela felt better and got out of bed. She could walk around the house with a cane, but she couldn't go out. She had to stop her charity work in the slums. She knew she had to settle the matter of who was to be the head of the family when she passed away. Staying at home, she began to see things a little more clearly, especially when the subject of Tía Amparo's and Tía Celia's education came up.

Abuelo Chaguito didn't think women needed to go to college at all. He thought they should get married, have children, and take care of them. "A man without a profession isn't worth a cent. But a woman can marry a professional and help him be a success in life," he told Tía Amparo one time.

Abuela Adela couldn't have agreed less. She believed the education of women to be of vital importance, and she was much more modern than Abuela Valeria in that respect. Valeria believed women should go to college to be more attractive to men and make a good marriage. But Abuela Adela wanted her daughters to be educated so they could be free and live fuller lives—with or without men.

She didn't want Amparo and Celia to stay home as *she* had; she wanted them to have a completely different life. Adela had loved being a schoolteacher, but because Chaguito had promised to have her father operated on, she had consented to marry him. The operation had been a success, and Chaguito had proved to be very kind. Once they were married, Don Félix Pasamontes never had to sell another lottery ticket in his life; Chaguito took care of his every need. But he died only a few years later, so Adela ended up sacrificing her career as a teacher to raise Chaguito's brood.

From the start, Abuela Adela tried to instill in her daughters a spirit of independence, something Abuela Valeria never did. She planned to send them both to college abroad, just like her boys. Then in 1928 the two catastrophes occurred: San Felipe hit the island like a freight train and brought Vernet Construction to the brink of ruin, and Adela discovered that Chaguito and her sons were Freemasons.

Adela's priorities changed, and she began to see the matter of her daughters' education in a different light. Even if college for the girls was now out of the question—the income from Vernet Construction was barely collateral for the bank loan Chaguito had had to take when Roque and Damián entered Northeastern—they could still have their own careers. Amparo and Celia would become missionaries of the Catholic Church and go abroad to preach the Gospel to the heathen. So Abuela nailed a map of Kenya to Tía Amparo's wall and a map of Nepal to Tía Celia's wall.

"Wouldn't you like to travel to Africa and Nepal when you graduate from high school?" Adela asked them quietly. She didn't want Abuelo Chaguito to hear. "If you become missionaries you can go there for free, and you need only a high school diploma to enter a missionary order. That way you'll be achieving three important goals. You'll travel and see the world, gain souls for the Catholic Church, and also be helping to save your father and your brothers from going to hell."

Tía Amparo was so horrified when her mother told her she'd be going to Africa to do missionary work that she decided not to graduate from high school. Amparo was a senior and had almost finished her second semester; graduation was just around the corner. But she stopped studying and nearly flunked her final exams. Abuela Adela was upset. She couldn't figure out what was wrong with Amparo and asked Tío Ulises to talk to her. Ulises was very close to Amparo. They both loved to party and covered up for each other when they came home late at night, climbing over the wall at the back of the garden and sneaking in through the terrace when everybody was asleep.

Tía Amparo was attractive in a blowsy sort of way. She was tall and soft-featured, with a delicate complexion and dark hair. She was very kind, but she had a weak core. As a baby she loved to be carried and didn't learn to walk on her fat, rosy legs until she was two. She was also large-bosomed like her mother, which was why boys were always swarming around her. Tío Ulises and Father were constantly on the lookout and shooed her suitors away. Tía Celia didn't need looking after: she was short and muscular and could take very good care of herself.

When Amparo told Ulises of Adela's campaign to turn her into a missionary, he took the money he had saved from his job at the hardware store in Boston and bought Amparo a pair of silver dancing slippers with rhinestone heels. He put them on her desk. "They'll be yours on graduation day," he said. "And don't worry your pretty head about traveling to Africa to baptize the little heathen children in Mombasa anymore. You're too good-looking for that. I'm sure this summer you'll meet the man of your dreams."

Tío Ulises was right. That summer Tía Amparo met Arnaldo Rosales, the son of one of the richest sugarcane hacienda owners on the island. They got married at the end of the summer and Tía Amparo went to live in Maracai, a town on the eastern coast. At first Abuela Adela didn't like the idea of the marriage because she was losing one of her combatants in her battle to win back the family's lost souls. But Arnaldo Rosales was a good man and she wanted Amparo to be happy.

After Amparo left to live in Maracai with Tío Arnaldo, the house on Calle Esperanza was even more divided. The men in the left wing—where Abuelo Chaguito and his sons slept—read books on physics, chemistry, manufacturing, and banking and dreamed of the day they would establish a business that would make them rich. Ulises's favorite mottoes became "E Pluribus Unum" and "Novus Ordo Seculorum"—stamped on dollar bills beneath the pyramid with the eye of God floating above. The women on the right side of the house—where Tía Celia and Abuela slept—recited the Rosary every night, read the *Lives of the Saints*, and talked about when Celia would go to Nepal to do missionary work. Aurelio hovered in between. Even though he slept on his father's side and wanted Vernet Construction to be a success, he was also determined to fight for justice. The purpose of life was not just to accumulate money and make the Vernets' star begin to rise but to help humanity live in a better world.

When Celia was a junior in high school she was a very good student and got straight As. She noticed that her parents never embraced or kissed anymore and that they slept in different rooms. If going to Nepal would bring them together again, she told herself, she was willing to do it. Celia fell asleep every night dreaming about Nepal. She found out everything she could about it and couldn't wait to graduate from high school.

Once, Father saw Celia poring over a map of Asia spread out on her bed. "Why are you suddenly so interested in Nepal?" he asked her.

"I'm going to travel there as a missionary as soon as I graduate from high school next year," Celia answered. "And once I'm there, nothing will prevent me from becoming a saint and I'll be able to save your soul." When Celia felt passionate about something, her blue eyes grew paler and shone with an intense light.

Aurelio looked at Celia in amazement. "That's preposterous. Who's been talking nonsense like that to you?" he asked. But Celia clammed up. Aurelio never talked to her except to scold her. Why should she start confiding in him now?

"No one. I just made it up."

But Aurelio didn't believe her, and he went to Adela's room to find out what was going on.

"Celia wants to go to college and your father has no money to send her," Abuela said. "The next best thing we can do is let her travel. The Sisters of Loretto will pay for her steamer ticket to Calcutta. From there they'll take her by train to Nepal. The sisters have a mission in Kathmandu. She'll be all right there, she'll learn Nepali, work hard, and see the world."

Father was shocked. The next day he went to Abuelo's office to tell him what he'd heard. "Celia says she's going to Nepal as a missionary if you don't send her to study at a university in the States. And Mother is her ally. If I know Mother, Celia will end up in Kathmandu in a year's time." Abuelo Chaguito was even more incensed. "No daughter of mine is going to become a nun unless it's over my dead body! Can you imagine what my brother Freemasons would say if they heard about this? We're supposed to eradicate the Catholic Church, not add to its members! Anyway, it's impossible to send Celia away to study, because I'm already in debt up to my neck."

Aurelio decided to take out a personal loan at the bank and send Celia to college on his own. It was a difficult decision; he was courting Clarissa at the time, but he didn't give it a second thought. When Abuela Adela heard the news, she was entranced. "I knew you could do it. I knew you'd come through for us!" she told Aurelio. "Celia will be grateful to you for the rest of her life."

Aurelio lied to Celia. "I found the money," he said. "We made a very good deal in San Juan selling cogwheels to a new sugar mill. Next year you'll be going to a first-rate college in the States."

But Celia said she didn't want to go to college anymore. "I'd rather be a missionary and go to Nepal," she informed Aurelio, pale-blue eyes burning. "That way I'll keep all of you from going to hell." Every night Celia prayed for hours, her arms extended like those on a cross. She stopped eating her favorite dishes—even *bacalaítos fritos*—and lost ten pounds. She put pebbles in her shoes and in her bed and offered up the pain for the salvation of unrepentant souls. During the day she went to school and acted as if nothing were wrong.

One evening Aurelio knocked on Tía Celia's door. "I think we should talk with Mother about your trip to Asia," he said. And he went with his sister to his mother's room. "Celia insists on going to Nepal, and I think it's a good idea, Mother. But she'll be able to do a lot more good if she has a college degree first. Don't you agree?"

Abuela Adela said yes, and as Tía Celia was always respectful of her mother's desires, she agreed to do as Aurelio suggested. But things turned out differently.

On September 7, 1930, Abuela Adela woke up feeling very ill. She realized she was going to die. The family was in chaos, but in true Vernet tradition, none of them expressed what they were feeling. Tía

Amparo was notified and came immediately from Maracai to stay at the house. Tío Damián and Tío Roque were there also, having just graduated from Northeastern.

Only Father was away; he had had to travel to Tallahassee, Florida, to see about a possible contract for a sugar mill, and it took him several days to return to the island. Everybody stood around Abuela Adela's bed holding back the tears. They knew the moment had come for her to pass the baton to one of her sons, and they wondered who it would be.

Tío Ulises put himself in charge of the situation. He made the arrangements at the funeral home and picked out a coffin. Then he called the hospital and had several orderlies come to the house to help carry Abuela Adela to the large mahogany bed she had shared with Abuelo Chaguito. Framed by the bed's columns, with their giant pineapples on top, she looked like a dying Amazon on an altar.

Two long days passed. Adela was suffering: the parasites had gotten into her bloodstream and every movement was horrendously painful, but she didn't complain. She hadn't said a single word in twenty-four hours or shed a tear. She looked at her family and smiled courageously but wouldn't let anyone touch her, not even Ulises, who tried to soothe her by mopping her forehead with a handkerchief soaked in eau de cologne. Even the graze of a hand on her skin caused her an unbearable flash of pain. The image of the Virgen de Guadalupe was placed in front of Adela's bed, surrounded by a dozen burning candles. Abuelo Chaguito, Ulises, Roque, and Damián all stood silent on one side of the bed, their hands clasped behind their backs and their eyes sand-dry; Amparo and Celia knelt on the other, reciting the Rosary and asking God to be merciful by taking their mother away so she wouldn't suffer anymore. Ulises was profoundly distressed. He couldn't understand why Adela wouldn't talk.

On the third day, the parish priest of La Inmaculada, where Abuela Adela had done so much charity work, came to give her Holy Communion and anoint her forehead. But even then, Abuela wouldn't speak. Hours passed. Every once in a while she groaned, opened her eyes, and asked for Aurelio, who still had not appeared.

At four o'clock in the afternoon, Aurelio finally arrived. He drew near the bed and leaned over his mother to give her a kiss. Adela opened her eyes and two large tears rolled down her cheeks—the first she had shed since she had been taken ill. "Aurelio, I'm glad you're finally here! God bless you, my son!" she whispered. And heaving a great sigh, she passed away.

And with that special blessing, imparted only to Aurelio before she expired, Adela let her family know whom she wanted to be in command.

THIRTY-TWO

THE MASONIC DOVE

Within a year Vernet Construction was making enough money for Aurelio to be able to pay for Tía Celia's education without having to take out the loan. Tía Celia had no trouble getting accepted at Marymount College of the Sacred Heart in Washington, D.C.: she had graduated from La Concordia's Sacred Heart Academy at the head of her class. When September came around, Celia had everything ready, and Amparo helped her buy new clothes.

But after Adela's death, Abuelo Chaguito didn't want Celia to leave. He was deeply grieved by Abuela's passing. All his life he had drawn his strength from Adela, and he no longer had the Statue of Liberty to hold up the roof of his house.

Being short had never bothered Abuelo, but now he felt small and vulnerable. He was so sad he shaved off his mustache and went around with his clothes frayed and his tie rumpled and stained. His face betrayed a vulnerability that had never been there before. Without his mustache, it was as if he were exposing his sadness to the world.

"Please don't go yet. You're my youngest, my turtledove. Who's going to take care of me after you're gone?" he said to Celia, his eyes glistening. And when Celia didn't answer, he added: "Amparo deserted me, Adela passed away, and now it's your turn. Perhaps God is punishing me for having left my mother behind in Santiago de Cuba to come to this island years ago. But if I hadn't come, I wouldn't have met your mother and none of you would have been born."

Tía Celia could see that Abuelo Chaguito needed her. The house had begun to look like a college dormitory in disarray. There were clothes scattered all over and the furniture was covered with dust. Matilde, the maid, had so much work that she might leave at any minute. And if she did, what would happen to Celia's father and brothers?

So Celia did what her mother had taught her. She rose to the occasion and decided to make a sacrifice. "All right, Father, I'll stay and take care of you. But promise me that three years from now, when I'm twenty-one, you'll take me to study in the States."

Abuelo Chaguito gave a sigh of relief and promised her. Celia was eighteen, she was in the prime of life. Who knew what might happen in three years? With her curly auburn hair and her clear blue eyes, she could meet a nice boy from La Concordia and fall in love. Meanwhile, he wouldn't be alone.

For three years Tía Celia helped Matilde with the housework. She played the piano for her father every evening and kept him company. Aurelio offered her a job as a social worker at Vernet Construction, and she spent part of each day visiting the families of the firm's employees. She was patient; she had promised her mother she would go to Nepal one day, and she swore to herself she would.

A few months before Tía Celia turned twenty-one, she wrote to a convent belonging to the Maryknoll order in Chicago and was accepted. The morning she received the letter, she reminded her father of his promise as he was having breakfast. But Chaguito said he didn't remember having said any such a thing. Celia was furious. She began to throw pots and pans into the sink and accidentally scalded Siegfried's and Gudrun's backs.

Aurelio had to step in when he heard the racket. He tried to be as diplomatic as possible. "You promised Celia you'd take her to the States to study to be a nun, Father. Today is her twenty-first birthday—the time has come," he said.

"I said I'd take her to the States to study, not to be a nun," Abuelo answered, without looking up from his desk. "She's twenty-one. If she wants to go, she can go."

"You're taking her to the States to *study to be a nun,* Father. The same way you took the three of us to learn to be engineers and Ulises to be a businessman. You have to do the same for Celia. You can't let her go alone." And Abuelo had no alternative but to keep his promise.

The following week, Abuelo boarded the steamer *Borinquen* with Celia. Before they left, Aurelio gave Tía Celia Adela's jewels, the ones Abuelo Chaguito had bought her on the birth of each of her sons though he couldn't afford them. Adela had kept them because she didn't want to hurt his feelings: a pearl necklace, a pair of small diamond earrings, a sapphire ring and brooch. "Make good use of them, little sister," Aurelio said, giving Celia a kiss on the cheek. "Wear them and make yourself beautiful, or give them to the poor. Whatever you do, put them someplace Mother will see them from heaven."

Abuelo and Celia landed in New York and from there took the train to Chicago. When they arrived at the convent, a large, forebiding Victorian mansion of gray limestone with seven turrets, Tía Celia said: "Don't come in with me, Father. It's late and you should go back to the hotel." She knew that the moment she entered its doors, she would be a novice and eventually would take vows, and she didn't want her father to know the truth. Aurelio had said that she was going to a college in Chicago to *study* to be a nun.

But Abuelo Chaguito insisted. He was too much of a gentleman to leave his daughter standing on the sidewalk with all her luggage around her. He rang the bell and three nuns opened the door. "We've been expecting you, my dears," they chanted in unison, ushering Abuelo Chaguito and Tía Celia in cordially. The nuns took Abuelo's hat and cane, as well as Tía Celia's suitcases, and made him sit in the waiting room. Celia disappeared into the cloister. An hour later, it was Abuelo Chaguito's turn to learn what the meaning of the word *sacrifice* was: a door opened and Tía Celia emerged before him, shorn of her long auburn locks and wearing the Maryknolls' severe habit of heavy black wool, her face beaming with joy.

Abuelo Chaguito took the train to New York the next day and left for the island by steamer the following week. Tía Celia stayed in the convent for years, taking vows of poverty, chastity, and obedience. She donated Adela's jewels to the convent, and they were used to adorn the monstrance in which the Holy Host was exposed. Every time Celia knelt in front of the monstrance to pray, she felt Abuela Adela watching her from heaven. This helped her persist in her vocation and overcome the many trials she had to face during her difficult novitiate.

Tía Celia took her perpetual vows in 1940, and for ten years she did missionary work in the Bronx and then in the Appalachian Mountains of Alabama. She taught blacks, Italians, and Puerto Ricans and never again thought of going to Nepal. Eventually she was put at the head of one of the Maryknoll congregations and asked Abuelo Chaguito to create a design the sisters could use on a processional pennant. Abuelo Chaguito was more than glad to oblige: he drew a triangle that looked suspiciously like a Masonic pyramid, and inside it, in place of the all-seeing eye, he designed a dove, its wings open in flight. "The triangle is the Holy Trinity and the dove is the Holy Spirit, of course," Abuelo explained to Tía Celia in a letter. But Celia knew that when her father had placed the dove inside the Masonic pyramid he was thinking of her.

THIRTY-THREE

THE CRIOLLO VALKYRIE

Abuelo Chaguito met Brunhilda Casares, my stepgrandmother, after he left Tía Celia at the convent in Chicago. Brunhilda was a pastry maker from Caguas, and I've never been able to eat a piece of wedding cake without thinking of her, because her hair was the exact color of the golden batter she poured into her cake molds. She always kept a tin can full of freshly baked ladyfingers at her house, and whenever Abuelo Chaguito's grandchildren came to visit, she'd offer us some. The ladyfingers were just like her, much too sweet and full of air.

After leaving Celia at the convent, Abuelo Chaguito boarded the *Borinquen* in New York and set sail for Puerto Rico. He was very depressed. He dreaded sleeping by himself in his cabin and going back to the house on Calle Esperanza alone. He was strolling sadly on deck, cane in hand, watching the Statue of Liberty slide by on the port side and thinking of Adela, when he saw a large woman leaning on the railing, her blond hair braided around her head in a golden crown. When she turned around and faced him she was laughing merrily— apparently at nothing, since she was completely alone.

Chaguito approached her and introduced himself in English, thinking she was an American. She answered in Spanish:

"I'm Brunhilda Casares. Very nice to meet you."

"Have you been traveling long?"

"I spent a month in New York. My husband recently passed away, and I was staying with relatives." And she laughed her silvery laugh, winking at him puckishly though neither of them had said anything funny.

Chaguito made a bow and kissed her hand. "I like women like you, with an ample provision of everything: caramel tresses, guava flan hips and derrière, and large coconut-custard tits full of laughter."

Chaguito surprised himself. He wasn't usually so forward, but he was sick of musty black habits, clouds of incense, and mumbled talk of salvation, immolation, and sacrifice. And he was enchanted by Brunhilda's laughter. Adela had never laughed like that; she was usually as stern as a sphinx. Brunhilda looked at him as if what he had said was the most natural thing in the world and giggled softly, fixing a loose hairpin that sparkled in the afternoon sun. Her good humor seemed to spread out glimmering over the sea in beckoning waves. Three dolphins sprang immediately to the surface and began to swim next to the ship, curving their sleek backs playfully in and out of the water. Brunhilda pretended to be afraid of them and drew closer to Chaguito so he could smell the Bal à Versailles essence she had dabbed under the gauze flounces of her dress.

Chaguito didn't have to spend the night alone in his stateroom after all. He slept enmeshed in the sweet net of Brunhilda's hair. After making love several times, he said to her: "I'm so happy I met you, I swear I could die in your arms."

When they arrived in La Concordia they were already married. Chaguito walked through the door of 13 Calle Esperanza with Brunhilda proudly clinging to his arm. "No one will have to worry about me from now on!" he told his children heartily as he greeted them. "Brunhilda is young and strong. With her to take care of me, I'll never be a nuisance to anyone, and a few years from now you'll save yourselves a pretty penny because you won't have to put me in a nursing home." At first the family was concerned, because Brunhilda was only twenty-eight years old, half of Abuelo's age. They were afraid she might be a scheming, greedy woman. But when they saw how she laughed at every little thing and refused to take anything seriously, they stopped worrying. They were convinced she was a complete dunce.

The first thing Brunhilda did was to bake Chaguito her special *ponqué*. "I'm an artist in my own right," she said as she brought the cake into the dining room. "It's not my fault that gourmet food is the most perishable of all the arts. It's very difficult to cook one's way to immortality because the tongue has such a short memory and gives only ephemeral pleasure." She had been a locally famous pastry maker before she met her first husband, a Dr. Mediavilla, and had had her own catering shop in Caguas. Dr. Mediavilla managed a nursing home for the terminally ill in San Juan, El Angel de la Guardia, and he had many patients. When they were married, Brunhilda closed her pastry shop and moved to San Juan.

Brunhilda knew how to make all kinds of delicious desserts—meringues, pies, puddings—all of which she sold to her exclusive clientele in Caguas. But her specialty had always been the *ponqué*. She had her own secret recipe: a dozen egg yolks beaten to a lemony yellow, a pound of pure butter, three cups of sifted flour, a cup of sugar, half a teaspoon of baking powder, and a pinch of salt—everything folded together as intimately as lovers. The mixture was poured into a round aluminum mold with a hole at the center, put in the oven *a fuego lento, al baño de María*—at low temperature, in a pan of water—for forty-five minutes, until an aromatic golden ring emerged. It was said that Brunhilda's butter-and-egg cake had magical qualities and that once it was tasted by the groom he would never be unfaithful to his bride. But Brunhilda gave all that up when she married Dr. Mediavilla, and she hadn't baked a cake for years.

Brunhilda enjoyed the finer things in life, and my grandfather soon recovered his joie de vivre. The day after her arrival she began to poke about the house to see what was inside the cabinets and cupboards. From the sideboard in the dining room, she took out the fine linen tablecloth, hand-decorated china, and Fostoria glassware that Adela used only on special occasions. She ordered the maid to set the table with them and throw out the everyday tableware and glassware. When Chaguito expressed his surprise at lunchtime, she told him: "I don't see the point in living like a pauper when we have such nice things. What are you saving them for? So your children can enjoy them after we die? Let's take pleasure in them ourselves!" Chaguito found this preposterous and laughed his head off. Brunhilda's exuberant potlatch was a refreshing change from the thriftiness of Adela, who had saved every penny as if it were gold.

Chaguito was still in his fifties, but he had had a difficult life. He had worked fourteen hours a day practically since he was a child, struggling against hell and high water to keep his family afloat. But the effort had taken its toll and he looked much older than his age. He was almost completely bald, and his mustache was snowy white. Chaguito loved to wear old clothes, the kind that feel they wear themselves on you. But his wife enjoyed buying him elegant Belgian linen suits, French ties, Spanish cordovan shoes. She soaked his handkerchief in Jean-Marie Farine eau de cologne and took him out for a ride every afternoon in the shiny blue De Soto sedan she had also purchased. Chaguito didn't mind any of it. He remembered with nostalgia the days when he had admired beautiful cars. Now he was tired and could find little enthusiasm for them, but he wanted Brunhilda to enjoy herself.

Brunhilda loved to show Chaguito off whenever they went out on visits. "And how does my Puss in Boots feel today? Doesn't he look like a sugar granddaddy?" she'd say to her friends, laughing, as she patted Chaguito's cheek and combed his perfumed mustache with a tortoiseshell comb she had ordered from Paris. Abuelo would blush with embarrassment, but he didn't dare complain lest he hurt Brunhilda's feelings.

Brunhilda was very wise in the ancient ways of love and soon had Chaguito lighting up like a match every night. The first time they made love Chaguito climbed on top of her and felt like Captain Ahab astride his mythic whale, cruising the seas of immortality far from the sight of shore. Brunhilda banished Abuelo's German shepherds from under Chaguito's bed, where they had reigned supreme. In the early morning she loved to walk around the house in her semitransparent nightgown, looking exactly like Rubens's Venus in *The Judgment of Paris*.

A few months after her marriage Brunhilda began pleading with Abuelo Chaguito to buy new living room furniture because the old mahogany and wicker chairs and settees that made one sit up at attention were reminders of Abuela Adela. Chaguito rushed to humor her and bought comfortable new Henredon sofas and chairs upholstered in silk shantung. He also got rid of Abuela Adela's four-poster bed with its pineapple finials, which he sold at a very good price since it was an antique. Brunhilda replaced it with a queen-size Beautyrest mattress with a cushioned headboard upholstered in blue satin. She had a modern bathroom installed in the house that was the talk of the town. All the fixtures were of gleaming black porcelain: the toilet looked like a throne from the pharaohs' necropolis at Luxor, the tub like a Roman coffin, and the sink like a basin for ravens. The walls were done in black tile, which Brunhilda decorated with transfers of naked women from exotic countries the world over so Chaguito would realize the great advantage she held over all of them.

Where Brunhilda made the most striking improvements to the house, however, was in the kitchen. She ordered a stainless-steel range and an oven, each of which cost five thousand dollars and was large enough to make King Farouk's chef die of envy. She purchased a Mix Master electric beater for a thousand dollars and had it hung from the ceiling so that it looked like a windmill. The refrigerator was as large as the one installed at the Condado Vanderbilt, the largest hotel in San Juan at the time, and cost three thousand dollars.

When Aurelio learned that Abuelo Chaguito had spent over twenty thousand dollars on the house, charging all the expenses to Vernet Construction's account, he told his father: "Have you forgotten how hungry you were when you arrived in La Concordia from Santiago de Cuba, after eating only bananas and oranges for weeks? That day you swore you'd make the family's bad luck change! If you go on like this, you'll make us go bankrupt."

Chaguito was filled with confusion and dread. His past came rushing back at him and he gave a great sigh. "What do you suggest I do?" he asked, fidgeting uncomfortably in his chair. "You must put your shares of Vernet Construction in our names, Father," Aurelio said. "Then you must close your bank account, and we'll give you a weekly allowance to live on. I'll be your accountant from now on. That way we'll be able to keep track of every penny Brunhilda spends."

When Brunhilda found out about this, she stopped laughing. "So that's the way things are going to be!" she fumed at Abuelo Chaguito. "I guess I'll just have to go back to work." And she opened up a pastry shop in the house at 13 Calle Esperanza.

Soon Brunhilda became famous in La Concordia for her wedding cakes. Every young lady of social standing wanted a Brunhilda original at her wedding. There were golden ziggurats all over the house: on the heavy oak table in the dining room, on the marble-topped sideboard, on the delicate oval end tables in the living room, even on the piano bench—six- and seven-tiered constructions that Brunhilda said were her palaces of love. The cakes were covered with satiny icing and decorated with bouquets of roses sprinkled with silver globules, glass lakes with swans skimming the surface, stairways beneath arches braided with ribbons, extravagant gazebos where white doves kissed and nuzzled, just as Chaguito wanted to do every night—except Brunhilda now kept him at bay. And on the base of each cake Brunhilda wrote with a frosting nib trailing creamy sugar mixed with egg white: "Love is a wicked poison and also a divine balm. Its antidote is unknown, but only thanks to love does man survive."

To please her clientele in La Concordia, Brunhilda added a special detail to each cake, a reproduction of one of the beautiful buildings the citizens were so proud of, baked separately and then covered with icing: the Athena Theater, the casino, the Adelphi Masonic Lodge, the cathedral, the firehouse. Before the bride and groom sliced the first piece of wedding cake with a silver knife, they had to take the building off the top and eat it piece by piece until not even a crumb was left. This architectural cannibalism of his beloved city almost made Chaguito cry. He thought Brunhilda was purposely ridiculing his respect for a city that had been built as a monument to individual entrepreneurship, and he wondered what his long-gone friend Bijas, the architect, would have said if he had seen such a sacrilege: La Concordia's beautiful buildings crumbling under the dainty teeth of young brides and grooms. But by now Brunhilda had her own money—she was paid hundreds of dollars for each cake—and Abuelo Chaguito couldn't remedy the situation.

THIRTY-FOUR

THE KINGDOM OF CEMENT

Almost no one on the island remembers the thirties anymore, *los años de las vacas flacas*—the years of lean cows. But Father never forgot them. He was always looking to save something for hard times. *"El que guarda siempre encuentra"*—"He who saves always finds"—was one of his favorite sayings, which was very different from Tía Artemisa's *"El que da lo que tiene a pedir se atiene"*—"If you give away what you own, one day you'll have to beg."

In 1932 San Ciprián left the island's coffee industry in ruins. The forests of mahogany, oak, and *yagrumo* trees that served as a canopy for the delicate red coffee beans were decimated, and the mountains looked as if they had been blasted by a bomb. Coffee never recuperated, but although the sugarcane fields around La Concordia were flattened, that industry soon began to revive. La Concordia's merchants and hacendados were a tough breed, and they immediately set to work to rescue their crops.

First they set fire to them. Then they planted new seeds. A year later, the rustling cane stalks were almost ready for cutting again. Orders for the crushing mills and the evaporators used to process molasses into sugar began to pour into Vernet Construction. Father was relieved, but Fernando Martín, the leader of the Partido Democrático Institucional, was furious. He had believed that San Ciprián, coming four short years after San Felipe, was sugarcane's coup de grâce, that the *yerba del diablo*, or devil's weed, had been stamped out for good. The island would finally rid itself of the absentee sugar consortiums, as well as of the exploiting criollo hacendados. But the weed was springing up again all over the island.

Fernando Martín was still a fledgling politician then, but he had a lot of influence in Washington. He supported the Costigan-Jones bill, which set a quota on sugar-producing mills—domestic and foreign— and was particularly onerous for the Puerto Rican sugar industry. In February 1934, the U.S. Congress made the bill law. Father himself told me the story.

The Partido Republicano Incondicional—Tío Venancio's and the sugar barons' party—was in power. But although the crisis in the sugar industry had eased and the cane fields were producing again, sugar prices kept falling drastically in the States. Shiploads were imported from Cuba, which was thirteen times larger than Puerto Rico and produced much more sugar. To make matters worse, Hawaii, though thousands of miles away, was not so far that it couldn't compete with us, and soon it added to the avalanche. Sugar beets, moreover, were now produced by the ton in Louisiana. The United States was awash in sugar.

Many years later, when the Vernets had established themselves, Abuelo Chaguito used to say with relish that the Costigan-Jones law had been to the Puerto Rican sugarcane aristocracy what the guillotine had been to the French. In 1933 sugar production on the island had reached 1,101,023 tons, but the quota for 1934, imposed by the Costigan-Jones law, was 826,000 tons. This was a hard blow for La Concordia, where sugar was everything.

The American consortiums that had taken over the sugar-producing industry in Cuba, as well as those in Louisiana, were a lot more powerful than the mainland owners of Aguirre, Eastern Sugar, and Guánica Central, so their sugar quotas were much higher. In Cuba, Fulgencio Batista had just come to power, and he promised to let the United States build naval bases on the island if Cuba's sugar quota was respected.

Vernet Construction immediately began to feel the pinch. Aurelio, Ulises, Roque, Damián, and Abuelo Chaguito went spinning around the island trying to get the sugar barons to pay their debts. Not one of them did. *Centrales* Machete, Bocachica, Cortada, Constancia, and Carambola—the five criollo mills that surrounded La Concordia— began to list like ships about to go down. The large American sugar mills had a hard time keeping afloat as well. There was nothing the brothers could do but stare in horror at the multiple catastrophe, aware that Vernet Construction, tethered as it was to the sugar mills, might soon end up at the bottom of the ocean.

Organized labor was the next blight, and strikes ravaged the sugar mills. In November 1934 it was rumored that the Partido Socialista was going to carry the elections. But people were shot by mysterious agents for trying to prevent the sugar barons from locking them up in cattle pens on election day, and things stayed as they were. The Partido Republicano Incondicional won.

The turmoil continued and the workers of Vernet Construction also went out. Abuelo Chaguito had to reduce the workweek to three days and lay off ten of his workers at the foundry. Salaries were cut twenty percent. Abuelo felt terribly guilty, knowing his employees were already on the verge of starvation, but it was the only way he would be able to refinance his debt to U.S. Steel in Michigan.

Then something extraordinary happened. In 1936 Eleanor Roosevelt visited Puerto Rico. The President had sent her to investigate accusations that the Costigan-Jones law had benefited only the mill owners, who received cash compensation for a reduction of their quotas, while cane laborers by the hundreds were left without work. Governor Blanton Winship received Mrs. Roosevelt at the gubernatorial palace with a dozen roses wrapped in cellophane, but Mrs. Roosevelt wasn't interested in the elegant reception the governor had organized for her. She asked him to cancel it, climbed into a Model T Ford, and went to visit the slums. She had a horsey face and was much too tall to be beautiful by Puerto Rican standards. But she talked to the women in the needle workshops and told them not to forget to exercise their right to vote, which they had just recently acquired. She talked with children about the importance of washing their hands before meals, brushing their teeth at night, and saying their prayers; she spoke in old people's homes about the Social Security Act, which included the provision for retirement insurance her husband had succeeded in getting passed in 1935. Everybody loved her.

When she visited the schools she was amazed to see young girls embroidering lace handkerchiefs during their lunch hour in order to add a few pennies to the family income. She also visited the shacks of the sugarcane laborers and the factory workers. Typically these consisted of two rooms with no windows. The back room was dark; the front room's only light came in through the doorway. There were no screens, no plumbing, no toilets, and women cooked outside on little coal stoves. It was like the Stone Age, and she was horrified.

Mrs. Roosevelt evidently had the President's ear, because four months later he visited the island. He landed in La Concordia's bay, where General Miles had landed forty years earlier. His caravan went up Calle del Real de la Marina, to the wild cheers of the crowd. The street was lined with American flags, and a triumphal arch had been set up at the entrance to La Concordia, with a lion—the city's emblem—standing on each side. President Roosevelt saw that everything his wife had said was true, and as a result he assigned seventy million dollars to the island through the Puerto Rico Emergency Reconstruction Administration, better known as the PRERA. When he arrived at Plaza de las Delicias, the President gave a speech and pointed out the purpose of his program: relief for unemployment through public works. Housing projects would be built to relocate people living in the slums, aqueducts and sewer systems would be installed, streets would be paved and sidewalks laid.

"I went to hear the President's speech," Father told me once. "I had to stand on top of one of the lions surrounding the fountain in the plaza in order to see him, but I didn't miss a word. When I got home I immediately summoned my brothers to Father's office. 'President Roosevelt is offering Puerto Rico an extraordinary opportunity,' I said to them, and I described the public projects planned. 'By next year, the demand for cement on the island will be three times what it is today. Why don't we build a cement plant with the funds the federal government is willing to lend the island? We can raise part of the money for the plant by putting Vernet Construction itself up as collateral. I'm sure that if Ulises and I travel to Washington, we can get the rest of the funds.'

"But Ulises didn't think it was a good idea, because it hadn't occurred to him first. 'Sugarcane will always be the backbone of our island,' he said. 'The mills will come out of their slump soon and they'll be able to pay what they owe us. But if we try to build the equipment for the cement plant at the foundry and stop taking the hacendados' orders, they'll go someplace else and cancel our contracts. If the cement plant is a failure, Vernet Construction will never be able to recover. I think we should build a plant to manufacture chemical fertilizer instead.'

" 'Fertilizer?' I asked Ulises, laughing so hard I almost fell out of my chair. 'You must be out of your mind! Agriculture is dead. Cement is the future, sugarcane is the past.' "

But my father was afraid of getting Vernet Construction even more deeply into debt. He knew the cement plant would cost at least two million dollars and that the federal government wouldn't lend such a large amount to a Puerto Rican enterprise. "Let's wait a while and take advantage of the building that will soon be done in La Concordia by the PRERA," he said to his brothers wisely. "The aqueduct and sewer system, the bridges—we can do all that easily at the foundry. That way we'll save money and have more capital to invest in the cement plant when the time comes."

Father turned out to be right. The PRERA announced a half-million-dollar loan to Governor Winship to build a cement plant in San Juan; a Baltimore firm would supply the machinery. Later the PRERA lent Winship an additional million dollars, and in three years the cement plant began to operate. But thanks to the New Deal's reconstruction plans, the demand for cement on the island was more than the government's plant was able to supply.

For the next five years Vernet Construction made miles of iron pipe for the sewage system of La Concordia and helped install it. It also built the city's aqueduct, which brought water from the mountains. Thirty-five kilometers of street were paved and dozens of iron bridges spanning the island's rivers were forged at the foundry. All of it was paid for in cash by the PRERA. By 1940 my grandfather and his four sons were almost ready to embark on their great adventure: building the Star Cement plant.

Abuelo Chaguito was euphoric. He danced around the living room singing "La Marseillaise," with Siegfried and Gudrun barking after him. He was still a fireman at heart and cement was, in his eyes, the answer not only to his family's troubles but to La Concordia's. The Vernet family enterprise would at last be free of the scoundrel hacendados who had tortured him for so long. They had refused to pay for the equipment the Vernets had built and installed on commission and had left him so saddled with debt that it was a miracle Vernet Construction was still afloat.

Cement would now be produced at La Concordia, the most beautiful city on the island and the pride of the Masonic world. Star Cement would be made with Puerto Rican lime and Puerto Rican sand; the city would become practically indestructible. Bijas, Abuelo Chaguito's architect friend, would have been proud of him! Chaguito wrote Star Cement's first advertising ditty himself, and it went like this: "Build your house with Star Cement / And sleep secure at night, / Safe from fires, hurricanes, and termites, / That's right!" It was sung over and over on La Concordia's radio stations for years.

• THIRTY-FIVE •

THE VERNETS' STAR BEGINS TO RISE

Tío Roque and Tío Damián were as important in the building of the cement plant as their elder brothers. But unlike Aurelio and Tío Ulises, they were shy and didn't tout their achievements all over town. The competition between Aurelio and Ulises, by contrast, never ceased. Aurelio needed to prove he was worthy of Adela's trust every day of his life. Ulises was so absorbed in everything he did, he didn't even notice that his brother was snapping at his heels.

Tío Roque was the most ungainly of the Vernet brothers. Short, with long ears and a thick nose, he looked like a bloodhound. He never did as well as his elder brothers in college, except during his junior year. That was when he took a course called Archaeology in Lowland South America and the Caribbean as a distraction from civil engineering. It was like discovering a lost paradise. He dropped all his courses in construction management, structural analysis, behavior of reinforced-concrete structures—subjects in which he was just scraping by—and signed up for a program in the prehistory of the Amazon region.

Roque was overwhelmed with admiration for the Taíno Indians, who were living on the island when Columbus discovered Puerto Rico in 1493. The Taínos lived in harmony with nature, following the rhythm of the sun, the moon, and the tides in their daily lives. They bathed two and three times a day in the island's pristine rivers, smoked tobacco and *campana* leaves to cleanse themselves and communicate with the gods, and made love as often as they could in their hammocks of rainbow-colored twine braided with hummingbird feathers. Tío Roque thoroughly agreed with the Taíno Indians' way of life.

After he began to study the Taíno culture, Roque decided he didn't want to go back to the island. He wanted to live in Venezuela and look for the remains of the Ignery, the ancestors of the Taínos, in the Amazon basin. When Aurelio heard about his brother's plan, he was incensed. It was not for this that Chaguito and Adela had sacrificed to send Roque to Northeastern. He took the first steamer to New York, arriving at Northeastern two weeks later.

The new cement plant, although still years off, was already on Aurelio's mind, and he knew that without Roque's help it would be impossible to begin building it. As a civil engineer, Roque would be essential in the assembling of the steel structures which would house the kiln and the heavy mill. But Aurelio didn't scold him or tell him he was behaving selfishly, changing his plans at the last minute and letting his parents and his brothers down.

"Did you know the limestone quarry behind the site where we're hoping to build has a Taíno Indian burial ground that's two thousand years old? Hundreds of pottery shards, bones, and seashells were found in it recently—*El Diario la Prensa* just reported it. The Smithsonian Institution has expressed an interest, and we plan to mine the limestone around it and save as many of the Taíno artifacts as possible. If you come to work with us, you can oversee the job yourself." Aurelio had made the story up on the spur of the moment.

"Really?" Tío Roque asked, his eyes lighting up. "I'd love to do that. I'll help you build the cement plant if you promise to let me supervise the excavation of the burial ground."

Tío Roque studied hard and managed to graduate a year later. He went back to the island and helped his brothers build the cement plant, erecting the iron beams and reinforced-concrete pedestals that would hold up the long revolving gut of the mill. As soon as the plant was ready to produce cement, the electric shovels started to eat away at the nearby limestone quarry, which later was known in town as Vernet's Cheese.

Tío Roque discovered that what Aurelio had said was true—the limestone hill turned out to contain several Taíno tombs. A square hole in the ground was discovered at the top, where apparently a chieftain had been buried. A *dujo*, or low chair, carved in stone with a lizard's face protruding in front, was found at the site, as well as an elaborately carved *macaná*, a fighting club. Tío Roque was ecstatic. He carefully removed the relics and gave orders that, as soon as another tomb was found, all work at the quarry should stop and he should be notified. It wasn't long before another tomb was located. Roque ran to the hill and crept into the square opening, at the bottom of which he found more priceless relics. He spent hours kneeling on the ground under a merciless sun, a small spatula and a brush in his hands, slowly unearthing the ancient objects and sniffing around to see if he could find more. Naturally, when the operators of the bulldozers, Caterpillars, and electric shovels—whose incomes depended on how fast Vernet's Cheese disappeared under the jaws of their machines—realized what was happening, they were upset. From then on, the minute a Taíno *yacimiento* turned up, they would dig away at that side of the quarry as fast as they could, until it was buried under tons of debris. That was why, after the first couple of extraordinary archaeological finds, Tío Roque never discovered any more Taíno remains in Star Cement's limestone quarry. He had to go scouting for Taíno relics elsewhere.

Tío Damián was Father's favorite brother, as well as his protégé. He was short and had a frail constitution. When he was born the doctors diagnosed a delicate heart—it didn't pump blood as effectively as it should. Asthma attacks worsened his condition, because every time he had to inhale cortisone, his heart felt the blow.

He had thinning blond hair and blue eyes like Tía Celia, and his skin was very white. He had a delicate beauty, and when he was a child, Ulises, Celia, and Adela affectionately called him White Jasmine. But Amparo and Roque liked to tease him and dubbed him the White Mouse. He always wanted to be good, and when he went to confession on Saturdays and the priest asked him if he had misbehaved that week, he'd whisper guiltily that Ulises had slapped him, Amparo had tripped him, and Roque had yanked his hair.

When Damián arrived in Boston to study at Northeastern, Aurelio helped him with everything. He steered him through registration and showed him how to pick out his courses, settled him in his dorm, and gave him half his sweaters and woolen socks because he was terrified Damián might die of pneumonia. But what really saved Tío Damián from perishing in the merciless Boston winters was the yellowish-brown muskrat coat Aurelio bought him. Father had only one overcoat: an ugly green army greatcoat he stuffed with newspapers every time he had to cross the bridge over the Charles River by foot because he couldn't spare the ten cents for the trolley. So he walked over to the Salvation Army on Commonwealth Avenue and asked if anyone had donated any fur coats recently. He was told that the one person who had had been shot twice in a barroom brawl; the coat might bring bad luck. Since Tío Damián didn't drink, Aurelio purchased the coat for a dollar and took it to his brother. When Damián put it on, it fell to his heels, and with his balding pate and long nose it made him look like a ferret. "No one will say you look like a white mouse anymore!" Aurelio told him.

Tío Damián had long, slender fingers and what he liked to do most in the world was play the violin. When he was a boy, he sometimes played while Aurelio accompanied him on the piano, but Aurelio always drowned him out. Damián's violin notes were blown away like gossamer threads in the hurricane of Father's music.

As grown men, Aurelio lived for politics and statehood, Ulises to make money and conquer women, and Roque to sniff out the trail of the Taínos. But Tío Damián lived for beauty. A poem, a sonata, or a sculpture was good only if it was beautiful, but evil if it was ugly. And the same was true of people. There were those who were able to feel beauty and those who couldn't—the hardened, the indifferent, and the selfish.

When Tío Damián went to Northeastern, he put aside his beloved violin and dove into his studies. He emerged four years later a full-fledged chemical engineer, but without having played a single note on his instrument. He didn't have the energy to pursue two careers at the same time. Aurelio couldn't understand it. When Damián returned to the house on Calle Esperanza, Aurelio scolded him roundly for not having graduated with a degree in music as well as in engineering, as he had.

Damián went to his room and locked the door. Soon a sad, beautiful melody began to filter from under his door like a long sigh of regret.

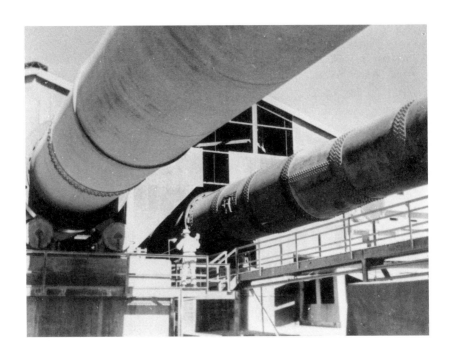

LA TECLAPEPA

There was quite a gulf between Abuelo's dream of a cement plant and reality. The first thing the brothers did was pool their capital. The family had around half a million dollars saved; Vernet Construction was mortgaged for another half a million; Tío Arnaldo Rosales, Tía Amparo's husband, put up two hundred thousand; and Aurelio invested Clarissa's two hundred and ninety thousand, which was sugar money and originally came from one of the *colmillús*, or "long-fanged ones," the sugar barons Abuelo Chaguito hated so much. But since the Plata had gone bankrupt, Chaguito didn't mind. The family still needed another two million, and they knew they would have to go to the PRERA. Every time Abuelo Chaguito thought about it, he cringed.

With the outbreak of the Second World War, the U.S. Army and

Navy desperately needed cement produced in Puerto Rico. Moreover, with Germany carrying out massive air attacks on London, the British asked Washington for a bay large enough to harbor the Royal Fleet in case the Nazis invaded England. Puerto Rico was pinpointed as a likely haven. A search was begun, and finally the U.S. Navy decided to build a dry dock on the eastern coast, near the town of Fajardo. It would be one of the largest dry docks in the world. Thousands of tons of cement would be required, and the navy needed them in a hurry.

The first loan from the federal government for the Vernets' cement plant—half a million dollars—came three months later, with the endorsement of both the U.S. Navy and the U.S. Army. Aurelio and Tío Ulises traveled to Pennsylvania and bought a used cement kiln, a mill to grind the clinker, and an electric generator. But German U-boats patroling the Caribbean sank the ship carrying the equipment before it reached the island. The operation was repeated three times, and three times the kiln and the mill ended up at the bottom of the Atlantic Ocean. The fourth time the brothers were successful. The mill and the kiln arrived safely, but the electric generator and the mill's driving gear, which were transported in another ship, did not. The submarines sank that too.

Chaguito's sons were about to give up, but he was adamant. "There's nothing impossible for a Vernet!" he reminded them. "We can build the equipment ourselves."

Machinery as large as the cement mill's driving gear had never been built at the foundry. Four feet in diameter and one foot thick, it would weigh several tons. The foundry's oven, where the Vernets cast the crushing mills for the sugarcane *centrales*, wasn't big enough and would never stand the weight. But Abuelo Chaguito's capacity for improvisation was endless. He ordered his sons to solder two-inch iron sheets together into a four-foot-wide cylinder and then cut out the pinion's teeth by hand, one by one. When the handmade driving gear was finished, it was a jewel.

Father would be in charge of the plant's electrical equipment, Roque of the mechanical side, and Damián of the chemical end. Ulises would scout the banks for a loan to begin production. Soon, thanks to the persuasive commercial abilities he had inherited from Adela, the Federal Financial Reconstruction office lent Ulises a million dollars at very low interest, accepting as collateral the plant itself. Chaguito was elated. From then on, Tío Ulises was known in La Concordia as El Mago de las Finanzas, the Financial Wizard.

The family purchased a sugarcane plantation on the outskirts of La Concordia, at the foot of a small, rocky hill where the Vernets could extract lime. The cane was stamped out and the plant's first kiln— the one that had escaped the German U-boats—was put in place. A small kiln, it measured only 189 feet in length and 10 feet in diameter, and it arrived in two segments, which the brothers riveted together at the foundry. They also bought a secondhand mill in Pennsylvania that had originally been used to grind flour. It was much larger than they needed, but it was being sold on the cheap at a flour-processing plant in Philadelphia.

The mill's motor was a 1,000-horsepower Allis Chalmers. It operated with an unusual system of switches, which Aurelio found fascinating. The stator—the stationary part of the motor—and not the rotor, was what made it begin to roll. Father fell in love with it the minute he saw it. He named it La Teclapepa and often took me to see it when I was a child. We would walk up the four concrete steps, a little iron door like the visor of a helmet would open, and Father would hold me up in his arms, placing a mask with round purple glasses before my eyes. Inside the revolving inferno, liquid cement rolled around in waves.

The kiln reminded me of the hell the nuns and priests were always talking about in school to make us behave. If the devil existed, his gut would be like La Teclapepa's. When he swallowed up the souls that died in mortal sin, they'd fall into a cement mill and spend an eternity going round and round in a white-hot mess, sliding down the brick-lined cylinder, unable to get out.

Whenever Mother got angry at me, she'd tell me I was going to end up in La Teclapepa. This scared me at first, but I stopped being afraid when I saw how well Father took care of La Teclapepa: any time there was a breakdown, even if it was at three in the morning, he'd run to the plant to fix it himself because he could work faster and more efficiently than any of the engineers and a few hours of stoppage meant thousands of dollars down the drain. I was sure La Teclapepa was a benevolent monster. Instead of sin and punishment, I associated it with the family's economic well-being, because it turned clinker stones into gold.

When the plant opened, La Teclapepa produced 4,000 sacks of cement a day. By 1944 three more kilns had been installed, and the Vernets' cement plant was producing 1,626,059 sacks of Portland cement a month, most of it destined for the U.S. army and navy bases on the island. By 1945, when I was seven years old, the four Vernet brothers were millionaires.

None of the Vernet men was drafted during the Second World War; their plant was deemed essential to the national defense. Army, air force, and navy bases went up all over the island, and they were all built with Star Cement.

More important, the Vernets had made their fortune cleanly, without taking anything away from anyone. Theirs was a very different situation from that of Abuelo Alvaro, for example, who had made his money by fighting tooth and nail to keep his precious acres of land from his neighbors, the powerful American sugar mills.

Once the military bases were built, a second project came along that helped consolidate the Vernet brothers' fortune: the Federal Housing Administration announced that it would issue thirty-year home loans but that the houses had to be built of cement. That way they could be used as collateral for the loans. Cement homes began to mushroom all over the island. In San Juan, two major new thoroughfares surrounded by middle-class projects were built on what was then the outskirts: one was wide and palm-lined and named Avenida Franklin Delano Roosevelt; the other was a narrow, busy street that ran parallel to it, the Eleanor Roosevelt. One could imagine the four Vernet brothers standing at the ends of these avenues, smiling from ear to ear, selling paper sacks full of cement.

Aurelio never forgot Adela's blessing on her deathbed. As soon as the Star Cement plant was running, he implemented the same Masonic principles he had enforced at Vernet Construction: he saw the plant's three hundred employees as his personal responsibility and established a health-care plan for them. He also set up a retirement fund. He made Star Cement the first Puerto Rican enterprise to pay its workers the federal minimum wage, a dollar an hour at the time. The workers at Star Cement were considered part of the Vernet family. Every year at Christmas its members would assemble at the foundry grounds—the site of the Vernets' original business—and the Vernet children, dressed in their best clothes, would share with the workers' children the toys Santa Claus had brought them.

THIRTY-SEVEN

STATEHOOD AND SAINTHOOD

"My struggle against the pressures of being a Vernet began in 1944," my mother told me. "That's when Star Cement gave your father the opportunity to fight for statehood. Aurelio had enough money to enter politics then, and he ran for mayor of La Concordia on an independent ticket. He was soundly defeated, but it didn't daunt him in the least. He was willing to bide his time.

"Aurelio had inherited your grandfather Chaguito's ardent belief in statehood. It was Chaguito's friendship with the Stone and Webster engineers that had given him the idea of sending his four sons to college in Boston. The American government had lent him about half of the money needed to build the cement plant, and then they had bought the cement from him to build the new military installations on the island, as well as the New Deal housing projects.

"But Aurelio's faith in statehood had an older, deeper root. When he was seven years old, he told me, he was standing next to Adela on the balcony of 13 Calle Esperanza when he saw Chaguito riding toward the house. Sitting next to him in the horse-drawn carriage was Don Francisco Pasamontes, Adela's uncle, who had given her family a helping hand when they emigrated from Guadeloupe. Tío Francisco's face was covered with blood, and he was pressing a hand-kerchief to his forehead. Adela ran to the sidewalk and helped Chaguito carry Tío Francisco into the house. Fortunately, a doctor was able to stop the hemorrhage, but for several hours Tío Francisco's life hung in the balance.

" 'What happened to Tío Francisco, Mother?' Aurelio asked in a terrified whisper.

" 'He was stoned at a statehood rally by an independence sympa-thizer,' Adela answered. She brought out her best sheets for Tío Fran-cisco, who stayed at 13 Calle Esperanza for several days. Adela recited the Rosary by his bedside, comparing Francisco to Saint Stephen, Christianity's first martyr, who had died by stoning. Aurelio knelt beside her and said the Rosary also, and since that time statehood and sainthood had remained strangely yoked in his mind.

"Cement, the foundation on which our family's well-being rests, made your father's battle for statehood possible, but it was at odds with Emajaguas's credo. Faith in inspiration, the importance of aes-thetic experience, and love of nature—these were beliefs I had ac-quired as a child. When Aurelio began to get drawn into politics I immediately saw that statehood would mean dozens of shopping cen-ters, more cement roads, and urbanization all over the island. 'De-velopers have no respect for the land, for growing things!' I'd say to him when still another forest was razed to make way for a new project on the outskirts of La Concordia. 'Everything is interconnected. If we destroy our environment we'll never be free!' But Aurelio never lis-tened to me.

"Politics is a sordid arena and I don't believe in it. I've always made fun of the local patriots who have statues erected to them in the middle of the town square, their heads convenient landing spots cov-ered with bird droppings. When I was young I believed political ac-tion could change the world and I joined the Liga Social Sufragista and the Liga de la Mujer del Siglo XX. I was exultant when we won the right to vote. But after so much struggle, women didn't know what to do with the ballot. Most of them voted as their husbands told them to. After the First World War many women on the island became professionals and struggled to lead independent lives—I was one of them. But the independent spirit I had inherited from my grandfather Bartolomeo Boffil didn't do me any good when I came face-to-face with my brother, Alejandro. *'Que te parta un rayo y que te pise un tren'*—'May lightning strike you and a train roll over you'— I kept wishing my brother. And when the moment came, he kicked me out of the Plata with Mother's consent.

"Then I met Aurelio and fell in love. My husband is the kindest person in the world. He believes that statehood is the most effective way to help the poor, wipe out sickness and hunger, eliminate the slums, give everybody electricity, running water, and a deed of ownership to his own house. He's probably right, but my soul remains tied to the land. I'm Puerto Rican before anything else. For this reason, every time elections come around, I leave a blank space where I should make a cross. But I keep quiet about it because I see how important statehood is for Aurelio, and I'm afraid to lose him.

"From the beginning I saw politics as a fearsome rival competing for Aurelio's love. My father, Alvaro Rivas de Santillana, lived only for his family: Valeria was his queen, his daughters were his princesses, and Emajaguas was his kingdom. He would never have lent himself to the hullabaloo of politics. My father led a dignified, productive life and reared his family in peace, as far away as he could from the turmoil of the crowd.

"I knew Aurelio had the best intentions at heart, but I couldn't help feeling resentful. I had given up so much for him. My studies in agronomy and history were diversions, and their effect on me cosmetic, as Valeria had predicted. I was no longer Clarissa Rivas de Santillana, who had once planted Guayamés's sugarcane valleys and taken responsibility for the family business. I became Aurelio's comforter, his adviser, the university-educated mother of his children. I lived by reflection, like the moon—basking in the light of my husband's successes. It was very hard for me.

"After Father passed away, I loved Aurelio more than anyone else in the world. Aurelio loved me, but I always feared politics would take him away from me."

THIRTY-EIGHT

FERNANDO MARTÍN'S MUSTACHE

The year my father ran for mayor of La Concordia, Mother and I attended our first political rally, and we had to do it on the sly. Women seldom went to political rallies. Meetings—*mítines*, as they were called—were often held in dangerous barrios where the men ended up getting drunk and whipping out their machetes the moment there was a disagreement. Clarissa was under strict orders from Aurelio not to attend any *mítines* alone.

But one night, when Father was away campaigning in a distant barrio, Mother took me along to a *mítin* the Partido Democrático was holding in Barrio San Martín de Porres, near Río Flechas. I was only six, but like Mother I wanted to know what the opposition was saying about Father.

Mother wore a frumpy old dress and a wide-brimmed hat, and she made me wear a pair of beat-up overalls and tennis shoes. We elbowed our way into the noisy mass of people milling around a wooden platform on the dry river's edge. Mother picked me up in her arms so I could see what was going on, and what I saw will remain branded in my mind forever. On the platform, the Democrats had built a wooden gibbet, from which hung a straw doll wearing an old guayabera with an American flag wrapped around its neck like a bib. Every time one of the men on the platform pulled the cord, the straw doll's head jerked, the crowd cheered, and the doll danced in the air like a drunkard who had been hanged. During one of its turns it faced our way, and we recognized the delicate mustache, the straight nose, the warm brown eyes. It was Father's image. I started to cry and kicked Mother in the stomach until she put me down. We both ran home, not daring to look up. Now I knew why Mother got so upset every time Father left for a political rally.

For a while after losing the race for mayor, Father stayed out of politics, which was a relief for Mother and me. But in 1945, Tío Venancio approached him and suggested that he join the Partido Republicano Incondicional. Tío Venancio was a very able politician. He had been president of the party for twenty years and had fought for statehood for just as long. When Venancio generously offered to teach Aurelio the ropes, Father took him up on the offer. He joined the party.

Partido Republicano billboards appeared on every major avenue of San Juan, La Concordia, and Guayamés announcing the political partnership of the brothers-in-law. A stern Tío Venancio, the president of the party and its candidate for governor, loomed against the sky in an elegant dark business suit with a tiny diamond horseshoe pinned to his tie, looking down at the cars stuck in traffic. A smiling Aurelio, the party's vice president and candidate for resident commissioner, stood next to him in a short-sleeved guayabera, a sacrificial expression on his face. It was hoped that Tío Venancio's image would speak to the well-to-do voters, while Father's would appeal to the poorer people from the barrios.

Political leaders began to visit our house loaded down with chickens, goats, roosters with slick red feathers curling jauntily in their tails; baskets overflowing with navel oranges, ripe plantains, and *pan de azúcar* pineapples; with portable ice boxes filled with red snapper, blue shad, and silver grouper. When Mother saw them at the gate she smiled her delicate Cupid's-bow smile at them, carefully hiding her feelings. Those generous gifts and eager handshakes meant only one thing: if the Partido Republicano Incondicional ever won the election, Aurelio would become a public figure and she would have to share him with these strangers.

What was worse, she would no longer belong to herself. She would lose her anonymity—which of course meant being approved or disapproved of by everyone in La Concordia. Already her face often appeared next to Aurelio's in the party's leaflets. Her spirit would remain trapped inside the wooden ballot box. But Mother went on giving Aurelio her unconditional support.

From 1942 to 1946 Fernando Martín consolidated his power. He was very Latino-looking, though with a twist. He had swarthy skin, charcoal-black hair, and a carefully clipped mustache. But he was tall and brawny and gave an impression of solidity that was new to the image. He had grown up in Greenwich Village and had worked as a reporter in the States for years, so he spoke English without an accent. All this was unfamiliar to American congressmen. Until Martín's election, Congress and the President were used to dealing with members of the Partido Republicano Incondicional, most of whom were fair-skinned and very European-looking and spoke perfect English. Many members of the Partido Democrático, by contrast, knew hardly any English at all and were proud to speak through interpreters.

Martín was an astute politician. He realized that it was important to mix with the people, that the years of preaching politics across the family moat, as the wealthy hacendados had done, were over. Instead of relying on the radio and newspapers, Fernando Martín got on a mule and rode out to spread his word to the common people. The parallel with the Gospels was well thought out: Christ rode on a mule into Jerusalem; Martín rode on a mule into the mountains at the heart of the island. He sat down with the *jíbaros* in their huts and drank their bitter sugarless coffee. He slept in their ragged hammocks and drank their illegal *pitorro* rum. The Partido Democrático Institucional was the workers' party and they should "lend" him their vote. "Your vote is the same as your machete; it's your manhood," he told them. "No pair of shoes, no three-dollar tip, no bottle of rum can ever buy it. Whoever sells his vote to the hacendados instead of wielding it to defend himself is selling his soul." And in 1946 Fernando Martín's broomlike mustache swept the island. He won the election by an overwhelming majority.

Father was crushed, but Tío Venancio told him, "It doesn't matter. We'll win the next one. But we must go on fighting to help the sugar industry. If we're poor, the United States won't want us as a state. We must make the sugar mills prosper, because that way the whole island will thrive."

Aurelio's heart was in the Star Cement plant and he didn't think the sugar industry was very important anymore. Industrialization, Fernando Martín's goal, was more up his alley. But he didn't contradict Tío Venancio. Secretly he admired Martín for defending the peasants' right to vote. In the past, when election time came around, many peasants sold their votes. And Martín was right to blast the Incondicionales for their corrupt practices—for locking up the peasants in cattle pens on election day, for example, and handing each of them a bottle of rum. When nothing else mattered but the fire in their veins, the peasants were made to file by the ballot box, which was placed at the end of the same mud path the cattle used when they were led out into the open field. There the peasants were made to vote with an X under the Incondicional symbol. But Father was convinced that Tío Venancio had mended his ways and that the party's corruption was a thing of the past.

Father knew all about Fernando Martín's campaign; he read *El Bohío*—the Partido Democrático Institucional newspaper, which Martín himself wrote—and even went incognito to a few of Martín's rallies. When Martín won the election in 1946, Aurelio was almost glad, in spite of the fact that Martín didn't believe in the concept of a commonwealth. "Economic progress is not the most important thing in this world, you know," Father reproached Tío Venancio once. "Individuals are much more important. And if they're hungry and sick, we have to help them first." But Venancio got very angry every time he heard Fernando Martín spewing fire and brimstone against the sugar industry.

Tío Venancio and Father saw each other frequently at Emajaguas and they remained close political allies. Mother and Tía Siglinda, moreover, were very close. Venancio was pleasant; he was always cracking jokes and making people laugh. It was hard for Father not to like him, even if he didn't always agree with his shady political maneuvers. We all knew that Venancio had done a lot of good things as mayor of Guayamés.

Venancio kept the Partido Republicano Incondicional's machinery in good shape, constantly oiling and tightening its nuts and bolts. "Knowing how to win your followers' loyalty is the most important aspect of a politician's career," Venancio often advised Aurelio, and Venancio certainly knew how to do that; he kept tight control over his party's budget. Every four years the government gave each party a certain amount of money for the political campaign, and Venancio doled out every cent of this kitty to his followers, not always justly.

Most Incondicional voters were faithful to Venancio because of the beautiful way he spoke Spanish. He would climb the platform and open his arms wide, his three-carat diamond ring glinting on his little finger, and begin to extol the need for loyalty to "the cause of statehood." "*Amigos y compatriotas,*" he would say, "*hay que saber sacrificarse por la causa*"—and immediately the crowd would fall silent.

But Tío Venancio never bothered to explain the exact meaning of "the cause of statehood." Unlike my father, he had never read Thomas Jefferson, much less Abraham Lincoln. In fact, Venancio hardly spoke English at all. That was what was hilarious about it. He wanted Aurelio to join the party because Aurelio was fluent in English. He alone could travel to Washington and talk to the senators and representatives the way Fernando Martín did about Puerto Rico's serious problems.

THIRTY-NINE

THE WEDDING PIANO

I may as well admit it: I was in love with Father from the instant I was born. When they brought me out of the delivery room and put me in his arms, I must have looked at him with adoring eyes, because he said: "Elvira looks just like a *Virgencita*! How wonderful that now I'll always have someone to love!" From that moment on, I unwittingly became Clarissa's rival.

I was always my father's daughter, and I always wanted to be like him. When I was on vacation from school at the Sacred Heart I'd go with him to the office at Vernet Construction, sit next to his desk on a swivel chair, lick his stamps, serve him cold water from the cooler in Dixie cups, and put his paper clips in order, arranging them by size. I didn't care what I did, as long as I was near him. I preferred it a hundred times to staying home with Mother or playing with girls my own age.

Clarissa always made it clear that I was born solely as a result of Father's whim. After my brother Alvaro's birth, Father had to plead with her to have another child. Clarissa was perfectly happy with my brother; she didn't want another pregnancy. She had a delicate frame, and being pregnant with Alvaro was torture for her, physically as well as psychologically. "A balloon with legs! Who wants to feel like that?" she complained to Father. "A pregnant woman can't sleep or walk. She can only roll around!" Finally she relented, perhaps because Father continued to mourn for Abuela Adela and she felt sorry for him. One year after Alvaro, I came along.

Mother was always pointing out to strangers how much I resembled the Vernets. I had inherited their clumsy way of moving and was always overturning the milk at the table, spilling gravy on my dress, or stumbling on the pavement when I walked down the street. And every time I had one of these little accidents, Mother shook her head disapprovingly and said, "Just like your father!" Alvaro, on the other hand, was perfect in her eyes. He looked a lot like Mother: he had her chiseled nose, marble forehead, and smooth ivory skin. When I came along looking just like Father, with my bowler forehead and ruddy skin, the die was cast. There was no getting away from him.

Father saw me as an extension of himself. I could do no wrong because I was what *he* would have been if he had been born a girl. Through me he could embrace more of life, experience it vicariously.

Father loved his Bechstein, and he'd play it for hours at a time. Listening to Father, I was sure that music was all about seduction. He made me fall in love with him the same way he wooed Clarissa. As I stood next to him, my eyes barely above the keyboard, I could see his hands flying like eagles above the clouds. Right then and there, an invisible thread spun out of those musical notes and wound itself around my heart.

The black keys held all the sadness in the world. They were high and narrow and delicate as coffins and made me feel balanced on the edge of the world before I fell asleep at night. The white keys, by contrast, were all happiness, flat and sunny like the flagstones in the middle of our garden, which flew under my feet when I ran to meet Father as he came in the gate for lunch.

The Bechstein grand had traveled to New York from Germany on the *Hindenburg*. The idea that our piano had floated all the way from Germany to America on a hydrogen-filled balloon and then traveled by ship to the island fascinated me as a child. I imagined being curled up in its belly as it drifted across the Atlantic, and I loved to pretend to crawl under its black folds as Father's music engulfed me.

Father studied music because of Abuela Adela. He never became a professional musician, but he played the piano for her every day of his life. It was his secret way of keeping alive the illusion, like a tiny flame about to go out, that one day he would become a pianist and make her happy.

For Abuela Adela, music was like religion. "Listening to music," she told Father, "is like dropping a plumb line down the well of your soul. It's the only way to keep in touch with God." Her dream of salvation began at a very pedestrian level: in her insistence that Father practice his scales every day on the Cornish upright piano at the house on Calle Esperanza.

When my parents got married there were very few phonographs in La Concordia, and they were of the kind you had to crank up before they scratched out music on a Bakelite disk. Our house was always full of music. Mother knew how to play the piano, too. But she played only for pleasure. She never tried to become a serious musician like Father.

Once, when I was six years old, Father stood me on the piano bench and opened the lid, which spread its huge black wing over our heads. Propping it up on a varnished pole that ended in a bronze nib, he showed me the piano's insides. A horizontal harp lay inside the box, and it had dozens of strings ending in little green felt-covered hammers that looked like tiny birds. Each bird was connected to a different musical key. One pressed a middle C and the corresponding hammer pecked at a string that sang C for a long, long time, almost for as long as a finger wanted.

I studied the piano for eight years but I could never play as well as Father. Clarissa sat next to me every day to supervise my lessons, making sure I learned my Czerny arpeggios by heart. But if I made the same mistake twice, she would pinch my arm or pull out a tuft of my hair, so that by the end of the lesson my arms were black and blue and my braids were in tatters.

FORTY

FÓSFÓRITÓ VERNET

Abuelo Chaguito lived in a house across the street from ours in Las Bougainvilleas and I visited him there until he was seventy-five years old. By that time he was deaf and walked with a cane, but he still had a merry glint in his eye and enjoyed sharing a good laugh.

There must have been a lot of the Abuelo Chaguito I knew and loved as a child in the spunky seventeen-year-old Santiago Vernet who arrived in La Concordia in 1896. The same subtle laughter, the same mischievous wink in the eye. Was his Cuban accent more pronounced when he arrived on the island? Fifty years later he still had it and would use words I'd never heard before, like *congrí*, instead of *arroz con habichuelas*, for black beans and rice, and *fruta bomba* instead of *lechosa*, our name for papaya. And I remember his telling me that I should never, ever say *"Qué vaina!"* because in Cuba it meant something terribly indecent, especially if said by a woman. I knew it referred to the flame tree's seed pod, but many years later I found out it also referred to a woman's vagina.

Chaguito loved animals. When he traveled to South America to assemble the crushing mills that were cast at Vernet Construction he brought back monkeys, sloths, and once even a baby jaguar. He raised sheep on the cheddar-colored hill where Vernet Construction dug its lime for the cement plant, and on my eighth birthday I asked him for a lamb. He immediately had one bathed, combed, and perfumed and brought it to my birthday party with a red ribbon tied around its neck. But when Serafina grew up and became a ewe, butting everybody who got in her way, Mother decided to make a stew out of her. Abuelo immediately came to our house to rescue her, and she went back to the lime quarry. "You must never eat a friend," he said. "Serafina made you happy; we must pardon her."

Chaguito fed Siegfried and Gudrun pieces of bread dipped in his own *café con leche* every morning, and the dogs spattered everyone at the table when they leapt up to catch them. Often he had ticks crawling up his pant legs. Unlike him, Abuelo Alvaro had always worn clothes that were freshly starched and pressed, and he was a little distant from everyone.

Abuelo Chaguito played a special role in my childhood. When Tía Celia left to study in the States and became a missionary, Chaguito was terribly distressed because Celia was the happy-go-lucky one in the family and always made him laugh. They shared an impish sense of humor that none of the other Vernets had. So when all my cousins went to boarding school in the States, Abuelo asked my parents not to send me.

We spent a lot of time together. Chaguito loved dominoes and taught me how to play. He often took me with him to his house in the mountains, which had a strawberry patch in the back, and we ate freshly picked strawberries together. He carried a picture of me standing in a field of blue agapanthus in his wallet; he didn't carry photographs of any of his other grandchildren. He told me that when I was born he insisted I be named Elvira. That had been his mother's name, and he felt bad because she had died in Cuba without his ever having seen her again. But after I grew up, I hardly ever went to visit Chaguito. It must have broken his heart, but he never complained. He was my first abandoned lover.

There was a reason, as there always is. In 1951, when I was in the eighth grade at the Sacred Heart, my life had become full of the normal activities of girls my age: going to parties and picnics, visiting girlfriends, talking about boyfriends, but also attending ballet classes. One day Chaguito went to see me dance at the Athena Theater and realized I was serious about ballet. He knew me better than my parents and he was terribly upset. "She's stubborn; she wants to be a dancer and she'll find a way to do it. You have to do something to stop her." My parents immediately took me out of ballet school.

I never forgave Abuelo. I brooded and cried for a month and began pestering my parents to send me to study in Boston. Perhaps my insistence had something to do with the fact that I knew how much it would hurt Abuelo Chaguito; I wanted to get back at him for having made me give up ballet. After all, I was only thirteen and I wasn't fluent in English, although I had learned to read it well enough at the Sacred Heart. In retrospect, it should have scared me to death to think of going away, of leaving my family and my friends, and yet I have no recollection of fear.

My family finally agreed to let me go away to study. When the question of what type of school I should attend came up, Chaguito suggested that I attend a Protestant one because in his opinion there were no first-rate Catholic schools for girls. When I observed, echoing the nuns' comments, that I might be putting my Catholic faith in jeopardy, Abuelo said that there wasn't one faith, there were many, and that understanding this was part of being a Vernet.

My parents sent me to study at Danbury Hall, a Protestant boarding school in Newton, Massachusetts. I loved Danbury. For four years I didn't have to go to confession; I confessed my sins to myself instead of to a priest. I didn't have to get up early to go to Mass on Sundays; instead I went to vespers on Friday evenings, where we sang hymns and didn't have to kneel. When the Protestants prayed "Our Father, Who art in Heaven," they added a little tail to the prayer, "for Thine is the kingdom and the power and the glory for ever and ever. Amen," which Catholics never said. But I didn't feel the least bit guilty about it. I had become a Vernet.

PART V

THE VERNETS' QUADRIGA

We go back and back; forever we go back all of us to the very beginning; in our blood and bone and brain we carry the memories of thousands of beings.

—V. S. NAIPAUL, *A Way in the World*

FORTY-ONE

CLARISSA'S HOUSE

By 1948 the Vernet brothers had made so much money that Aurelio, Ulises, Roque, and Damián all moved to Las Bougainvilleas, the most elegant district in town. The houses were all constructed of Star Cement in what was known as the Hollywood style: sloping red-tiled roofs, stuccoed white walls, cool inner patios with fountains and arched galleries to minimize the heat, wide front lawns with orchids, frangipani, ylang-ylang, and many other exotic blossoms and trees. The Vernet homes were set in what used to be a cane field and were lined up next to one another on Avenida Cañafístula like four ornate chariots competing for elegance and speed.

Father was the first of the brothers to build a house at Las Bougainvilleas. We had never lived in a cement house before, and it was almost like living in the States. It meant we didn't have to worry about "fires, hurricanes, and termites" anymore. We could escape all the plagues of the tropics.

When the house at 1 Cañafístula was being built we were still living on Calle Virtud. Father would take me to the two-acre lot on the outskirts of town early in the morning, before I went to school. The workmen were already there, waiting for us to arrive. The minute we got out of the car, they began to pour the cement powder into a circular trench. Then they added three parts sand and one part gravel and poured some water from a hose into the center of the little gray volcano. Next they carefully mixed the Star Cement with the rest of the materials, lifting it from the edges and throwing it into the center with their shovels. The mixture was similar to the cake batter Mother made in the kitchen, except the cement was gray. The workers would stand in a line and pass bucketful after bucketful of cement over to a wooden mold with iron rods sticking out of it and then pour in the contents. In a week, the mold would be removed and a new room, a new terrace, a new hallway would be standing there—something that hadn't existed before.

The house had two wings that were perpendicular to each other: the living room and dining room were on one side and the bedrooms on the other. A long arched veranda that ran along both wings opened onto the garden. A sloping roof at least twenty feet high was painted a deep turquoise, as if Aurelio wanted to bring La Concordia's perfectly blue skies into the house. It was an optimist's color, just as the solid concrete foundation was an expression of Father's faith in the American way of life.

The house was surrounded by a vast expanse of lawn that needed to be watered constantly, since it seldom rained in La Concordia. The garden was lush with royal palm, oak, and mahogany trees, as well as with myrtle, frangipani, jasmine, and *dama de noche* blossoms that left perfumed wakes around the rustling trees and bushes whenever a breeze came up.

The garden was Clarissa's hobby, and her bedroom window opened directly onto it. As soon as she got out of bed she leaned out the window in her nightgown and from there would direct Confesor, the elderly gardener who had worked for our family for many years, to prune a hedge of myrtles over here or water the frangipani over there.

It was the happiest part of her day, and she would spend hours trying to create, at Avenida Cañafístula, an exact copy of the garden at Emajaguas.

If you walked by our house in the evening you could often hear the music of Liszt, Schubert, Chopin, and Beethoven spilling over the garden wall. Concerts were frequently held on Saturday evenings, and friends who played the violin, the viola, and the flute came to accompany Father and Mother's piano. During these concerts I was expected to sit in the living room for hours as though I were in church—never getting up or interrupting under any circumstances. Classical music was like God. Its beauty was absolute, merciless, unyielding. There was no way to establish a dialogue with it; it left you absolutely mute with its perfection. And to make matters worse, it had all been composed by men.

My parents couldn't stand it when I played popular music on my Victrola: the boleros of Rafael Muñoz, sung by Bobby Capó, or the *guarachas* and mambos played by Mingo and His Whoopee Kids, El Trío Vegabajeño, and La Sonora Matancera. Mother practiced the piano in the morning and Father practiced in the afternoon, after work. She played minor works by Chopin that made you feel weak and want to lie down, while Father's music was always exuberant and energizing—Beethoven's *Emperor* Concerto, Liszt's Sonata no. 123, Chopin's Concerto no. 2—and when he played, the sun shone like a golden orb outside our windows. Mother loved Chopin's preludes, especially the ones he had composed at Valdemosa, where he stayed with George Sand when he was ill with consumption. The minute Clarissa began to play them I would have trouble breathing, my hands and feet would grow cold, and I would be sure I was about to spit blood. I would run to my room and grab a volume of *Tarzan* by Edgar Rice Burroughs, and only then would my spirits revive.

Music was Father's great escape; reading was mine. As a child I loved to read, and I soon discovered Father's library on the second floor, above the bedrooms. I would sneak in, filch a novel, and tiptoe with it to the small, narrow balcony of the guest room that jutted out over the garden. No one ever went up there. The windows were always closed to keep out the dust, and it was kept dark so the curtains and bedspreads wouldn't fade. The balcony had cast-iron balusters through which one could look down at the lawn spread out beneath one's feet like a steaming green lagoon. A huge vine of purple bougainvillea clung to the balcony's red-tiled gable and kept out the rain.

I squeezed myself against the railing to shut the double doors behind me, sat down on the floor, opened my book, and began to read. Inside that prickly grotto, suspended in midair like a bird in its nest, I became acquainted with Emma Bovary, Eugénie Grandet, Catherine and Heathcliff, Jane Eyre, Becky Sharp, Tom Sawyer, Cyrano de Bergerac, Don Quixote, and many other heroes and heroines who have accompanied me through life. I could hear Mother and the maids, twenty feet below, calling me to come do my homework, practice my piano lessons, or take a bath. But they never found me. When I got tired of reading, I'd stand on the balcony and look out toward La Concordia, wondering what went on in all those houses and how many plots of novels were being acted out in them.

Once, in an unexpurgated copy of *A Thousand and One Nights* I came upon a passage that said: "When Jazmina, the sultan's daughter, became betrothed to Aladdin, she was taken to the baths by the women of the harem, and they shaved her pubis until they left it as smooth and pink as the palm of her hand." I racked my brain, but I couldn't understand why anybody would do that. I went downstairs and ran into Abuela Valeria, who was staying with us for a few days. I read her the passage and she was shocked. She snatched the book away from me and gave it to Father, who promptly locked it in a cabinet.

Fortunata y Jacinta, by Don Benito Pérez Galdós, was one of my favorite novels, and I read almost all of it in my secret hiding place. It was the story of two girls: Fortunata, the rebel chicken vendor who defies society's conventions and gives her lover, a high-society *señorito*, raw eggs to eat before making love to him in a haystack, and Jacinta, the well-brought-up society girl the *señorito* marries, who never complains, accepts a woman's place in the world, and dies young but at peace with herself. Right away I identified with Fortunata. When Mother asked me what costume I wanted to wear to the carnival at La Concordia's casino that year, I showed her the novel I was reading and said I wanted to go dressed as Galdós's chicken vendor, who fed her lover raw eggs. Mother slapped me, took the novel away, and didn't permit me to go to the carnival that year. After those two episodes, I didn't tell anybody in the house what I was reading.

Looking through some old books one day, I found my brother's and my baby albums. Alvaro's was beautiful: bound in blue silk, with a baby sitting on the cover with a tiny crown on its head. In it Mother had kept a day-by-day account of Alvaro's progress: when he first sat up in his crib, when he began to teethe, when he took his first steps, when he gurgled his first words. Stored neatly in a box next to this album was a curl of Alvaro's dark hair tied with a blue ribbon; his first shoes, dipped in bronze; his baptismal certificate; his early report cards; his vaccination certificates; the ribbons he won in school; and the cloth book Mother taught him to read from. I had never seen a book like it; it was a book one could sleep with, like a pillow, and I immediately fell in love with it. But when I asked Mother if I could play with it, she said, "No, that was Alvaro's first book," and gently put it back in the box.

My album had a pink silk cover with a hand-painted stork carrying a baby swinging from its beak. As I opened it my heart trembled in anticipation. But after the first few entries—the hospital I was born in, the time of day, the name of Mother's obstetrician—the pages were blank. There was nothing on them; some even smelled brand-new. I felt as if I had fallen out of the stork's beak and was tumbling into space.

Right then and there I decided to fill in the empty pages. For the next few weeks I pestered Mother with questions like: "When did I first begin to walk?" "What were my first words?" "When did I learn to read?" I snipped off a lock of my hair, tied a ribbon around it, and pasted it to the album's pages. I found an old pair of baby shoes—I couldn't be sure if they were my first, but they would have to do—and asked Mother to have them dipped in bronze like my brother's. She gave them to Father's secretary in my presence and ordered him to mail them to Macy's baby department "to be dipped in something or other to preserve them." She was humoring me and I knew it, but I didn't care. I went on looking for the missing documents: I asked Tía Celia to get me a copy of my baptismal certificate; I asked for copies of my report cards at school; I searched the house for all the photographs Father had taken of me when I was a baby and pasted them in my album. When I finished, it was as complete as Alvaro's. It was like giving birth to myself.

Mother often sang me to sleep when I was a child. We'd sit in a rocker and she'd always sing the same song: *"Una góndola fue mi cuna, el Adriático me arrulló, y una sútil y azul laguna, mi tranquila niñez pasó"*—"The Adriatic was my crib, a gondola rocked me to sleep, and my peaceful, happy childhood was spent on its blue lagoon." When I'd ask Mother where Venice was, she'd say that it was a city far, far away where honeymooners went but that I shouldn't go there or get married for a long time because then I would lose my way back to Las Bougainvilleas, just as she had lost hers to Emajaguas. That's what had happened to her, she'd say, kissing me softly in the dark.

Mother was beautiful. I remember how much I wanted to be like her even though I looked like Father, as she constantly reminded me. The stories of how smart Mother had been in school—how she had won the First Medallion at the Sacred Heart in Guayamés and then had been valedictorian of her class at the University of Puerto Rico in Río Piedras—were like myths in our family. Alvaro was just as smart; he never got anything less than an A and was always at the head of his class. But I got As, Bs, and Cs; sometimes I was at the head of the class and sometimes at its tail. There was nothing I could do. I would never have the chiseled Rivas de Santillana nose or Clarissa's brilliant mind.

I was afraid of losing Mother. Whenever we drove to Emajaguas I was terrified that she'd stay there and that Cristóbal and I would have to return to La Concordia alone in the family car and explain to Father why Mother wasn't with us. Other times I fell into a panic, certain that I would be left behind, a feeling that never left me after my roller-coaster adventure.

I was seven years old when we traveled to New York for the first time. It was the fall of 1945 and the war had just ended; a spirit of optimism reigned in the city. We stayed at the Essex House in a beautiful room overlooking Central Park. Around the corner was the Automat, a cafeteria we loved to go to, where you could put a dime in a post office–type box and take out a dish of lemon meringue pie, a ham-and-cheese sandwich, or a shiny red apple.

We visited the Metropolitan Opera House, Carnegie Hall, the

Statue of Liberty, and the Empire State Building, which swayed slightly in the wind and filled my heart with wonder when Father told us how the observation tower was originally intended to be a mooring station for zeppelins. But what I loved most was the roller coaster at Coney Island, where Father took me twice. The first time was wonderful. The second time was a nightmare.

We sat in a red car made of wooden slats, lowered the iron bar that imprisoned us but kept us safe, and didn't come back to earth for almost an hour. Whenever the ride came to an end, Father would pay the ticket taker and we would go around one more time, yelling and hugging each other tightly against the rushing wind. The car would climb slowly to the top of the tracks, stand there poised for a few seconds, and, as we contemplated the beautiful tapestry of the Palisades Park and the Atlantic Ocean, plunge us headlong into an abyss. The speed of what felt like a free fall made us drunk with pleasure.

The following Saturday I asked Father to take me to Coney Island again, but this time Mother said she wanted to come too. We left Alvaro with my cousins and took the subway from the city. I was quiet the whole time, sulking over the fact that Mother undoubtedly wouldn't let Father ride in the roller coaster with me more than once—she was sure to prefer the carousel. A few stations before we arrived at the Coney Island stop, I let go of Father's hand and went to stand by myself near the door. My parents, deep in conversation, didn't notice my absence. When the subway came to a stop a crowd of people surged in and I was forced out of the train. It was impossible to get back on because of the packed bodies. The doors slammed shut and the train took off with a deafening roar. As I watched in horror, Father and Mother realized that I was missing and rushed to the window. They waved at me frantically, giving me instructions I couldn't hear or understand. I sat down on the station floor and began to cry.

My parents got off at the next stop and immediately telephoned the police. Ten minutes later two officers came by and began asking questions. Soon one of them had me sitting on his shoulders as he carried me to the nearest precinct house, where my parents were waiting for me. But for a long time I had nightmares of Father and Mother thundering away on the subway, smiling and waving their hands as they left me behind.

FORTY-TWO

MIRROR, MIRROR, ON THE WALL

At a cement plant, the product is constantly monitored: a small cylinder of cement is placed in a hydraulic testing machine thirty-six hours after it has been cast, and three thousand pounds of pressure are applied to it. If the cylinder crumbles, it means something is wrong with the mixture: it may have too much lime or too little silica, or maybe the temperature of the oven wasn't quite right when the mixture of sand and lime was made into clinker, the shiny black stones that sound exactly like their name before they are ground into cement powder.

Not everybody in my family was able to stand up to the pressures of being a Vernet. Tío Roque and Tío Damián were in a way victims of Star Cement. And so, too, was Mother.

Mother's world had changed drastically since she had left Emajaguas: agriculture had disappeared, the lush sugarcane fields around

Guayamés that she loved to ride across on horseback lay fallow and weed-ridden, and now her nerves were out of kilter. Star Cement had never really interested her, and yet the cement plant had shaped her life. She lived constantly under its threatening shadow. I swore to myself that I wouldn't crumble because of the pressures of being a Vernet, that what had happened to her wouldn't happen to me.

Once I told her smugly, "When I grow up I'm going to have my own career. I'll be a doctor, a businesswoman, a reporter, maybe even an agronomist. Anything but a housewife!"

"Is that right?" she asked. "We'll see about that, Miss Liberty!"

There was never a chance of Mother's working. Father wouldn't permit it. He suspected unknown dangers around every corner. She might be kidnapped and held for ransom. Or worse, she might be ridiculed, laughed at. "You mean you want to work?" he asked in disbelief when she raised the question. "What in the world for? Why should you get up at seven every day and trudge to the nearest high school to teach a bunch of undisciplined children history or agronomy?" If she answered, "Because I want to feel proud of what I can do," he would reply: "But you're already a Vernet. Isn't that enough?" As if, for her, self-pride must reside in being, and not doing. And he would look at Mother with disapproval for wanting to be more than she already was.

Father was conscious of the dangers of being a Vernet and tried to protect Mother as much as he could, but that only made matters worse. He surrounded her with servants and discouraged her whenever she wanted to go into town; she should stay at the house and take care of her beautiful garden, he said. He made Cristóbal, who was tall and brawny, drive her everywhere in the family's new blue-and-white Cadillac. Clarissa did as Aurelio wished; when she wasn't visiting Emajaguas, she lived in isolation, taking care of her garden and eventually losing contact with the world outside its walls.

Mother and I spent very little time together in Las Bougainvilleas. I don't remember ever seeing her in a bathing suit or taking a stroll barefoot on the beach with me. It was Father who taught me how to read and write, how to ride a bicycle, and how to swim. Mother belonged to a sewing club, Las Tijerillas, and the members met at our house every week. They were good friends of Mother's and exchanged recipes and gossip with her. Most of them didn't have a college education and didn't belong to La Concordia's sugarcane aristocracy.

They were middle-class women, the wives of Star Cement plant managers, of the sales executives, of the low-level engineers, and they all did their own housework. Mother couldn't stand La Concordia's well-to-do ladies, who did their shopping in Miami and spoke a Spanglish peppered with *honeys* and *darlings*. These were women hopelessly spoiled by their husbands, just as Father spoiled me.

When Father went on a trip he always brought back two beautiful presents, one for me and one for Mother. Once he went on a business trip to Mexico and bought her a magnificent silver and turquoise bracelet. I got one exactly like it, only daintier. When he traveled to the island of Margarita, off the coast of Venezuela, he bought her a magnificent freshwater-pearl crucifix and brought me one just as beautiful, only smaller. I never wore the jewelry, but I kept it as a token of Father's love.

Mother loved Father, but the protected domestic life she led in Las Bougainvilleas slowly ate away at her self-respect. Father, in turn, adored her, but there was a blind spot in his love. I remember one Saturday morning when I spilled ink on an antique French Provincial chair in Mother's bedroom. Going to fill my Parker pen at her marble-topped vanity, which doubled as a desk, I stumbled and carelessly dropped the ink bottle. I tried to take out the stain with milk, but it spread all over the silk upholstery. When Mother came home from shopping she was furious. She slapped me and called me a scatterbrain. She ordered me to my room for the rest of the day. Father laughed and told her that a chair was just a chair and that I was only trying to do my homework; she shouldn't lose her perspective. Mother burst into tears and shut herself up in *her* room. I apologized through the locked door, but secretly I rejoiced. I stood there next to Father and took his long, slender hand in mine. Mother couldn't stop crying. Father winked at me, gave me a kiss on the cheek, and quietly locked me in my room. I felt betrayed.

Another time, the three of us went to visit Abuela Valeria at Emajaguas and stayed overnight. Alvaro had a baseball game and didn't come. When I woke up I discovered I had my period. I hated having it. It kept me from swimming, going out to play baseball, behaving like a tomboy. I locked myself in the bathroom, rinsed my pajama pants, and hung them to dry over the curtain rod. I wanted to pretend nothing had happened. Rather than ask Mother for a sanitary napkin, I stuffed my panties with toilet paper.

After lunch we got into the car; Father was driving. We had been traveling over an hour and were halfway to Las Bougainvilleas when Mother asked if I had packed my new pajamas in my overnight bag. "I forgot them at Emajaguas," I said. "I got the curse last night." Mother dug her nails into my arm. "We'll have to drive back to get them then. Aurelio, turn the car around." Father tried to calm her. "We can get them the next time we visit your mother, dear. We don't have to go back right now." But Mother was beside herself. "You little idiot!" she said. "Why do you have to be so careless? Your head's always in the clouds."

Father ignored us. He looked out the window and turned the car around at the next curve; soon we were speeding back to Emajaguas. I was in tears, not because of Mother's scolding but because I was convinced Father loved Clarissa more than he loved me.

FORTY-THREE

FATHER RUNS FOR GOVERNOR

In 1956 Tío Venancio approached Father and said, "I've run for governor too many times and people are tired of my image. I think we'd stand a much better chance if you ran this time. But I'll still be president of the party. I'll go on taking care of the strategy and organization. Together we'll keep the Partido Republicano Incondicional afloat."

Venancio's wheelings and dealings with the sugar barons were hurting him at the polls. Still, the Partido Republicano Incondicional stood for statehood, Father's sacred cause, and every four years at election time "*el ideal*" carried a large portion of the island's votes.

Father accepted Tío Venancio's offer and ran for governor. There were many towns to visit, many speeches to make. The Partido Democrático Institucional had a formidable political machine and was very difficult to defeat. Mother was terrified that something might happen to Father at one of the *mítines*. His absences were a torture to her, as she could hardly sleep at night.

Father became a politician, a public figure, and sometimes a bit of a ham actor. The moment he climbed the steps of the stumping platform he cast himself in the role of *"padre de la patria."* During his campaign one of the most popular of the party's songs, sung by groups of children clapping their hands delightedly, was *"Vernet, Papá, queremos estadidad!"* Aurelio loved it all: he patted, hugged, and kissed people so effusively that he became infected with mange more than once; his hair began to fall out and he got blisters all over his skin, just like the stray dogs that wandered the streets of La Concordia. Every time I heard that song I got stinging mad. My father was my father, and that stupid slogan relegated me to the status of a distant cousin.

As the campaign progressed and Father's absences grew more frequent, Mother grew jealous of other women. She was constantly on the lookout, imagining that Father had a lover in every town. She was suspicious of his secretaries, and she made him fire all the female ones and hire only males. When she walked down the street with Father, if a woman passed by swinging her hips and batting her eyelashes because she recognized the handsome candidate for governor, Mother would narrow her eyes, whisper, "Bitch!" and hang on even more tightly to his arm. Once, a particularly good-looking party functionary walked by during a party convention, and Mother strode up quickly behind her, smacked her on the behind, and yanked a tuft of hair from her head. Then she ran down the aisle and out into the street, where she waited around the corner until Father got the car to take her home. Fortunately, Aurelio was so popular with the female constituency that these episodes never had serious consequences.

Mother's temper tantrums began to get worse. She grew furious at the new gardener, who was a drunkard and never watered the plants; at the maid, who was a *puta* if she visited her boyfriend on her day off. Eladio, the Chinese cook, once got so upset at her when she called him a *carbonero*—a coalman—for overcooking the London broil that he threatened her with a knife, and Mother had to run and lock herself in her bedroom. She was jealous of the maids and cooks and treated them so poorly that they never stayed long. It seemed as if a different one walked through the door every month.

She would have Cristóbal drive her to the slums in the Cadillac to look for the daughters of poor but decent families whom the Siervas de María had recommended to her as maids, but after a while she couldn't find anyone. The shantytown huts were made of flattened tin, bits of wood, and cardboard, and the streets were labyrinthine. The Cadillac would turn left and right a dozen times before it arrived at the right address; often people would "accidentally" throw garbage out their windows as the car went by. This would give the girls time to hide under the bed or scurry out the back door of the house as soon as they heard the Cadillac coming, and their parents would claim to be childless.

One time Mother went to confession at La Inmaculada, the chapel where Abuela Adela had done her charity work. It was near a slum where many of the girls who worked as maids in Las Bougainvilleas lived, so the parish priest knew many of them personally. When Mother knelt in the confessional and began to excuse herself for her short temper, the parish priest grew curious and asked her name. When she identified herself, the priest said: "I've heard a lot about you from my parishioners, my dear—and I'm very interested in what you have to say. A bad temper may be only a venial sin, but when you deprive someone of his dignity, it can also be a path of red-hot bricks that leads to hell!" Mother's face flushed and she wished the earth would swallow her up. She was so embarrassed she did her best to control her temper for a while.

Most of all, I think, Clarissa was jealous of me. I was half a Rivas de Santillana; it didn't matter how much she insisted I resembled the Vernets. When Father's political campaign intensified and Clarissa was too tired to accompany him, he asked me to stand beside him on the platform when he spoke. I was eighteen and this made me feel important. Father needed me, I told myself, and my presence in this world made Mother's just a little bit less necessary.

Father had to travel to New York in search of funds for his campaign. He took Tío Ulises along, which galled Mother, who regarded her brother-in-law as a relentless skirt chaser. But Father set her mind to rest by assuring her that Ulises was essential because of his excellent connections with the mayor of New York, who arranged for them to rent Madison Square Garden for a nominal sum. The Partido Republicano would hold a Puerto Rican rally there to raise money for the statehood campaign.

It was past midnight when Father returned a week later. As soon as I heard his car turn into the driveway, I got out of bed and flew across the yellow and gray tiles of the terrace to the door. Dressed in his navy-blue wool suit and gray silk tie, with his cinnamon-colored hair, light brown eyes, and delicate mustache, he was the handsomest man on earth. I wrapped my arms around him and kissed him on both cheeks.

Mother, strangely enough, stayed in her room. When Father went to the master bedroom calling her name, I followed, ignoring the fact that they probably wanted to be alone.

Mother sat propped up in bed in one of her silk georgette night-gowns. Her table lamp, a Sèvres shepherd dressed in a blue jacket, threw a delicate oval of light over her embroidered coverlet.

"Did you have a nice trip?" she asked Father coolly, without glancing up from the novel she was reading.

Father said yes and sat on the edge of the bed. He leaned over to give Mother a kiss. "Siglinda called this afternoon," Clarissa went on. "She said she saw a picture in the *Daily News* of Ulises and you at Madison Square Garden. She said you weren't alone; there was a platinum blonde hanging on to each of you."

Aurelio burst out laughing. "You can't be serious!" he said. "We've been married for more than twenty years and you're behaving like a jealous bride!" he said. He turned and winked at me. "They were campaign aides. Didn't you notice the statehood flags draped across their chests?"

I laughed, too, and looked down sheepishly at the floor. I didn't dare look at Mother. "I have the proof right here that I was thinking of you the whole time!" Father added, pulling a small black suede box from his pocket and putting it on Mother's lap. "Open it," he said, smiling broadly. Mother looked at him, eyebrows knit. She took the ring out of the box: it was a three-carat star sapphire. But instead of putting it on her finger, she threw it angrily toward a corner of the room.

I stood there petrified. Father got up laughing from the bed and went looking for the ring under the wardrobe. When he found it, he came over to where I was. "You take it, darling," he said, slipping the ring back in the box. "Your mother's right not to want it; she deserves something much better. I should have bought her a diamond."

"Don't you dare, Elvira! Your father has a guilty conscience and he's simply trying to make amends!" Mother shrieked from the bed.

But I took the box, opened it, and carefully slid the jewel onto my finger.

"Thank you, Daddy," I said, kissing him again.

FORTY-FOUR

†HE QUEEN OF MUSIC

There were few cultural activities in La Concordia; the Athena Theater seldom presented operas or ballets, and there was no public library. Probably because she was bored, Mother one day accepted an invitation to a bridge party at the house of Rosa Luisa Sheridan, the wife of a distillery owner. Not everyone in La Concordia got invited to Rosa Luisa's parties, but Mother belonged to the sugarcane aristocracy of Guayamés and Rosa Luisa considered her one of her own.

The sugar barons of Las Bougainvilleas still managed to live relatively well, thanks to rum's golden ambrosia. Most of them had their own distilleries—Ron Llave, Ron Palo Viejo, Ron Bocachica, Ron Caneca, Ron Carioca, Ron Agüeybaná—which stood on the outskirts of La Concordia. But with the sugar industry on the wane, the reign of King Rum was coming to an end also, and the sugar barons knew it. Every once in a while, a distillery would be uprooted piece by piece like a half-rusted dinosaur and shipped to Santo Domingo or Venezuela, where it would be reassembled and the sugar barons would begin to make money thanks to the meager salaries paid to the peons.

The only thing the sugar barons could do was resign themselves to seeing their fortunes dwindle and live it up as best they could with the last swigs of rum at the bottom of the barrel. Probably for that reason the expression for getting plastered at the time was *darse el palo*, literally "clubbing oneself to death."

Every sugar baron's house in Las Bougainvilleas had a bar made of glass blocks, with colored lights, a brass rail, nickel-bright stools, a polished mahogany counter, and shelves loaded with liquor at the back. The barroom usually had no windows, which added to the shadowy cabaret atmosphere, already clouded with cigarette smoke. A phonograph with huge Philco speakers ensconced in a "built-in" wall unit exuded mood music, and an air conditioner was usually kept going full blast, so the sugar barons could pretend they were in New York. Pickaninnies with corkscrew penises, Coca-Cola openers shaped like steel breasts, pin-up calendars with naked models of all shapes and sizes were part of the usual decor. The exception to the rule was our house at 1 Avenida Cañafístula, where Father and Mother would have had their heads chopped off before allowing a bar. Whenever they gave a party, they stopped serving drinks at midnight, a hint for everybody to go home.

These bars often had a door leading to the back of the house, where gentlemen met their paramours and could make a discreet exit without their wives noticing anything amiss. Rum and sex were, in fact, the two main entertainments in Las Bougainvilleas. The men pursued them openly. The women, on the other hand, drank like fish but had to be careful about the sex. Female infidelity was not permitted—shooting your wife if you caught her *in flagrante* was a sport husbands practiced successfully—and ladies were forced to socialize only with other ladies. Mother, isolated at 1 Cañafístula, was unaware of this situation when she went to Rosa Luisa Sheridan's bridge party.

She got there late, delayed by a dental appointment, and found the front door ajar. She stepped in, pushing it fully open with her umbrella and calling out for Rosa Luisa. Soft music wafted out from the bar. Instead of the elegant little card tables she was expecting, with ladies shuffling the deck and betting in low voices, she saw a group of women dancing and others lying on cushions strewn on the floor. They were kissing and rubbing slowly against one another, and they were so drunk they didn't even notice Clarissa standing there. She turned and ran out of the house, her face flaming.

Aside from backroom bars, coronation balls were another form of escape for the sugar barons. They were held every year at the Sports Club, located in an art nouveau building designed by Bijas at the beginning of the century. It had once been a beautiful building, and one could still pick out the elegant prairie-style design of its over-hangs and courtyards. But now the structure was eaten through by termites, and the ballroom's plank floor was full of holes. There were coronation balls for everything: for the Carnival of Pirates, for the Carnival of Animals, for the Carnival of Planets, for the Carnival of Birds, for the Carnival of Dolls. Clarissa and Aurelio had each taken part in a carnival when they were teenagers: Clarissa had been Queen of the Dolls and Aurelio King of the Planets. When I heard about this, I told Father I wanted to be Queen of the Carnival at the Sports Club also. Father probably would have said no if it hadn't been 1956 and he hadn't been running for governor.

My parents offered to pay all the expenses of the carnival that year and I was named Queen of Music. I was exultant. The ball was to be given in June, and Mother ordered a beautiful dress for me from Saks Fifth Avenue (this was a formal affair and Monserrate Cobián was simply not up to the occasion). The ball was a perfect opportunity for political fund-raising, as was the cocktail party preceding the ball which would be thrown in San Juan.

My dress and train were of billowing white organza embroidered with musical notes, and the skirt was held in place by a huge hoop petticoat. A crown with a giant rhinestone C clef sat on my head. Father himself, dressed in tails, played the first movement of Chopin's second piano concerto on the Bechstein, specially brought over to the club for the night.

Followed by my pages and maids of honor, I strutted up the stairs to my throne—a huge lyre, done in pearl-colored silk—and regally seated myself. From up there I saw Mother hiding behind a column, dressed in black and clutching the little white lace handkerchief with which she had been dabbing powder on my face a few minutes earlier to dry my perspiration and take away the shine as she prayed that nothing would go wrong.

As carnival queen I accompanied Father to many banquets, balls, and rallies that summer, driving through the towns of the island. Mother usually stayed home.

FORTY-FIVE

VENECIA'S PASSAGE TO HEAVEN

Our house was next to Tío Ulises's, and separated from it by a low stuccoed wall with an arched doorway. The door was later walled up, but its outline remained there for years, and it excited my curiosity as a child. Why had it been cemented over? I didn't unravel the mystery until many years later.

Tío Ulises's house at 2 Avenida Cañafístula had a showy wrought-iron fence decorated with white scrolls and spirals that gave it a festive look. Ours had a seven-foot-high wall around it that created a cloistered atmosphere that Clarissa cherished because it reminded her of Emajaguas. Next to Tío Ulises's house came Tío Roque's, and next to Roque's was Tío Damián's, both as beautiful as their elder brothers'. On the other side of the street was a handsome plot of land the Vernets bought for Abuelo Chaguito, hoping to convince him to build there someday. Several years after Abuela Adela's passing,

Abuelo Chaguito was still living with Brunhilda in the old wooden house on Calle Esperanza in the center of town. He didn't want to leave; there were too many memories there of his life with Adela.

Tío Ulises was an advocate of laissez-faire, and I remember his two favorite sayings: "Money has no ideology; it grows both to the right and to the left" and "He who tries to control energy will only destroy himself." Perhaps because he believed that nothing lasts forever and that the world is in a state of constant change, he would give money to the Catholic, Evangelical, and Lutheran churches, all at the same time. In politics he was just as flexible, contributing to Fernando Martín's Partido Democrático Institucional, to Tío Venancio's Partido Republicano Incondicional, and to the Partido Independentista. At election time you would see all three flags flying from the roof of his house: the Partido Democrático's red *pava*, the Partido Republicano's tricolor, and the Independentistas' white cross on a green field. He probably voted for all three parties, because he had friends among the voting officials and they let him into the polls long after they were closed.

But Abuela Adela's death continued to affect Tío Ulises. Her blessing of Aurelio on her deathbed had been a terrible blow to him. Ulises was the eldest son, the one who resembled Adela the most. He had inherited the Pasamontes' financial abilities, and yet Adela had preferred Aurelio over him and had made his brother the head of the family. Ulises couldn't understand it. If Aurelio was smarter, Ulises at least would be more of a man. And yet, if his mother didn't love him, no woman would ever love him. And so Tío Ulises began to feel that Caroline Allan's love wasn't enough; he needed to prove that other women loved him also. That was when he began to run after every available female who crossed his path, "even if she looked like a broom," as wags in La Concordia said.

Tío Ulises had a different girlfriend on every street corner. Whenever he spent the night out, Caroline would angrily demand where he'd been, but he wouldn't tell her. She could ask anything she wanted except his whereabouts, because they fell under the heading of laissez-faire. "Sexual energy is like money—it cannot be controlled," he told her. "He who tries to control it will be destroyed." Caroline eventually fell ill and her family came to get her in the *Cormorant*, their yacht. They forced her to return to Boston, and she divorced Tío Ulises in 1931.

For the next several years Tío Ulises remained a bachelor, and when the Star Cement plant began to make millions of dollars, he closed up his house and decided to go to Europe. He traveled for three months all over the continent and liked only two things: the Lido in Paris—where he saw more bouncing breasts and bejeweled pussies than he had seen in his entire life—and Venice. In Venice he had a magnificent time. He rented a motorboat and spent a week roaring around the canals at thirty miles an hour, swamping every gondola he ran across and wondering why tourists found them so romantic when they were so maddeningly slow. He fell in love with the Byzantine basilica's four golden domes and with the doge's campanile on Piazza San Marco. "Venice," he told Aurelio and his brothers when he got back to La Concordia, "is the passageway to heaven." He also admired Venetian merchants enormously, and above all, the doge Enrico Dandolo, because he had dared defy Pope Innocent III's papal bull and had turned the Fourth Crusade to Jerusalem into a commercial venture.

A few weeks after Ulises's return, Abuelo Chaguito sent him on a business trip to San Juan. He drove across the island in his sporty blue Morris. He was passing through Maunabo, a little town on the east coast, when he saw a young girl standing by the side of the road selling mangoes under a palm tree. The mangoes were ripe, and they shone like golden globes at the bottom of a tin pan at her bare feet. The girl was very tall, and as she stood there, she swayed in the wind this way and that, just like the palm trees behind her. Her clothes were too tight for her, and her breasts rose like perfect spheres from beneath her white cotton blouse. "Has anyone told you look like a Byzantine cathedral?" Ulises asked her, getting out of the car. "Your breasts remind me of the domes of Saint Mark's basilica, your neck of Giotto's campanile, and your arms are made of the same bronze Ghiberti used to cast the doors of paradise." The girl thought he was crazy and burst out laughing. "I have no idea who those gentlemen are, but if you buy half a dozen of my mangoes, I'll close shop and go back home. I've been standing here in the sun all afternoon with no luck."

Tío Ulises bought all her mangoes and invited her to get into the car. The girl did so, and Tío Ulises began to hum a song the Trío los Panchos used to play a lot: "*A la orilla de un palmar, estaba una joven bella, su boquita de coral, y sus ojitos de estrella, al pasar le pregunté, que*

quién estaba con ella, y me contestó llorando, sola vivo en el palmar"—
"At the edge of a palm grove I met a beautiful girl, her lips like coral,
her eyes like stars. I asked who was with her and she answered, crying,
'I live alone among the palms.' "

After a while, Ulises asked her where she lived, and the girl pointed
out a run-down establishment near Maunabo's town square. "My father, Francisco Martínez, owns a *colmado* in town, La Cócora de Pepe.
My mother and my three little brothers live in two rooms at the
back," she said. Tío Ulises drove up to the town square, walked into
La Cócora de Pepe, and introduced himself. Then he asked the man
what his daughter's name was and learned it was Filomena Martínez.

"I want to buy everything you have in your shop," Ulises told him.
The girl's father stared at him. Tío Ulises's face seemed familiar, and
before telling him to get out, Don Pepe asked him what his last name
was. When Tío Ulises said it was Vernet, Don Pepe said he'd sell
him the whole store: rum, potatoes, rice, beans, plantains, yams,
yucas. Ulises could even take his daughter if he wanted, all for ten
thousand dollars. A few minutes later Filomena Martínez was sitting
in Tío Ulises's convertible roadster. Ulises took her to his home in
La Concordia.

Filomena loved the house. The first thing she did when she got
out of the car was to take off her shoes and walk barefoot through
the gate. Tío Ulises liked everything about Filomena except her
name. So the next day he took her to La Concordia's cathedral, sprinkled holy water on her from the baptismal font, and baptized her
Venecia Vernet. He married her before a judge, bought her a trunk
full of beautiful clothes, a necklace with two hundred diamonds, and
a marquise diamond ring worth half a million dollars. They traveled
together to Venice, where he showed her Saint Mark's basilica, the
campanile, and the Grand Canal and asked if she saw how similar
she was to her namesake. Venecia laughed, but since she had always
been poor and Ulises was a kind man, she didn't mind his eccentric-
ities. When Ulises went to bed with her and began to call out Adela's
name in anguished tones when they made love, Venecia felt sorry for
him and treated him very gently. Eventually Tío Ulises fell in love.

Tía Venecia was a free spirit and in that respect she was very much
like Tío Ulises. She had grown up almost as a child of nature in a
palm-thatched hut by the sea. Her father was a *mallorquín*, a merchant
from Mallorca, who had come to Puerto Rico long ago and had fallen

in love with a local girl from Maunabo. Venecia had only an eighth-grade education, but she was naturally intelligent, and as soon as she was settled, she began to read everything she could lay her hands on. She taught herself to speak English and she became a charming hostess to all the bankers and businessmen of La Concordia who came to dinner when she and Ulises moved to the spectacular new house at 2 Avenida Cañafístula.

Tía Venecia was beautiful and she knew it. Her body was lithe and voluptuous, and with her golden skin and dark eyes she caused a sensation wherever she went. Before she met Tío Ulises she loved to swim naked at the beach in Maunabo at night, where—because the continental shelf is very shallow there—waves travel long distances and pull silver manes of foam behind them. She loved to stretch her body over the water like the bow of a violin and feel the sea flow over her breasts and between her legs. She had had many lovers and she would lie with them on the beach under the stars.

After she had lived with Tío Ulises for a while Tía Venecia realized Ulises would never be completely faithful to her. Every time the family made a new business deal—if they needed money for a new cement mill or if they were planning to build a new kiln and Ulises had to go on a business trip—he would get terribly anxious and miss Adela. Then he'd find himself a prostitute and bury his head in her groin until he wallowed in her acrid smell, and only then would he be able to forget his mother and make the deal. Venecia was very understanding and didn't object to Ulises's behavior. But she made him move to the back of the house, where he built himself a bachelor apartment, while she kept the front of the house to herself. The red-light district of La Concordia was nearby, and this was very convenient because once in a while Tío Ulises could bring a woman into the house without anyone's noticing.

Venecia didn't want to become resentful; jealousy was a petty emotion she considered beneath her. Furthermore, she loved Ulises, so she decided to go on living with him on condition that he spend at least four nights a week with her and the other three in his bachelor apartment with whomever he wished. That way she would be able to keep her dignity and also hold on to her husband. Tío Ulises was erotically very inventive, and he built a secret passageway that connected both sides of the house. There he could run naked after his wife at night, and they could search for each other, laughing and playing hide-and-seek. Every time Tío Ulises found Tía Venecia in the dark, he felt so happy he was sure he was in heaven. And after they made love, they went back to their respective suites.

Most of the family remained ignorant of their goings-on and believed Tío Ulises had finally settled down to a normal family life. But we lived next door to Tío Ulises, and Clarissa once saw a strange woman running naked in the garden at the back of the house. From then on she forbade me to visit my cousins Catalina and Rodrigo unannounced. It was at that time that she had the door in the wall between the two properties cemented over, without telling anyone the reason.

The episodes of Tío Ulises's promiscuity were few and far between, so Tía Venecia remained relatively happy. They decorated their house with lavish frescoes executed by Puerto Rican artists that portrayed folkloric scenes such as cockfights, the sugarcane *zafra*, and the coffee harvest. Everything in their house was on a grand scale—the thirty-foot-high ceilings, the salons the size of ballrooms, the gilded furniture. The gardens were filled with parrots, peacocks, and even a declawed baby leopard. And when the two of them sat down to lunch in front of their beautiful garden, served by liveried waiters, Ulises would joke with Venecia, a tinge of condescension in his voice: "I wonder what the middle class is doing right now."

FORTY-SIX

FRITZI'S WAKE

My cousin Rodrigo was Tía Venecia's favorite. He looked like her and had the same delicate frame. When Rodrigo grew up he would be able to do all the things Venecia had never been able to do and would do them with her face. It was as if at birth a mischievous spirit had switched the sex of her child.

For Rodrigo's seventh birthday, Venecia had three miniature houses built on the terrace of her mansion in Las Bougainvilleas, one made of straw, another of cardboard painted to look like wood, and a third of cement blocks carefully arranged one on top of the other. Alvaro, Catalina, and I were to act out the story of the three little pigs, and Rodrigo would play the part of the wolf. Venecia read the story from behind a screen of green bushes, which was supposed to be a forest. Alvaro, Catalina, and I approached the three houses, laughing and giggling with delight. Rodrigo huffed and puffed, and first the straw, then the cardboard house fell down (thanks to a push from Tío Ulises, who was hiding behind them). But when it was time for the cement house, the wolf huffed and puffed and the house stood firm. We all cheered.

My cousin Catalina often came to our house to play, and I went to play at hers. Catalina had a miniature dachshund named Fritzi, and she was crazy about her. Fritzi had long, shiny ears and a torso as sleek as a black torpedo skimming the ground. When Fritzi died, Catalina was terribly upset, but she pretended she wasn't. She called me over to her house and said, "Fritzi just passed away and I'd like to do an experiment with her. Let's bury her in the garden and dig her up in a month." We put Fritzi in a large shoe box—one belonging to Tío Ulises, who had large feet—and trooped solemnly down the stairs with it. We dug a hole under a hibiscus bush, put the box in, covered it with flowers, and filled the hole with dirt. A month later Catalina reminded me of our experiment, and we dug up the box. But when we opened it, there was a mass of creeping worms inside that stank to high heaven. We dropped it on the ground and ran as fast as we could into the house, and when we stopped to catch our breath, we were both crying. "It's not Fritzi," I told Catalina, trying to calm her down. "Fritzi's in dog heaven. That's just a rotten sausage the cook threw away."

Catalina was short and heavyset, with a thick neck. Tía Venecia was forever making fun of Catalina's looks; Catalina's body, not surprisingly, became a source of anxiety for her. Venecia had caught Tío Ulises thanks to her extraordinary beauty, and she was afraid that, when the time came to get married, Catalina wouldn't be able to do as well for herself.

I liked Tía Venecia a lot—she was always laughing and she dressed in bright clothes, while Mother dressed only in black and was always complaining about something. Venecia liked doing things with us. She took us on picnics in the mountains and organized Halloween outings and Easter egg hunts. She was affectionate and intelligent and very kind to me. But she had no empathy with her own daughter.

I hated when Tía Venecia was cruel to Catalina. I wondered why mothers were always looking into their daughters' faces and never liked what they saw. Were they so unhappy with their own lives?

"Stop dragging your feet, Catalina, you look like a platypus dragging your tail!" Venecia would tell her. Or "Don't stoop when you walk. You look like a doggy bag!" Unfortunately, Tía Venecia was always setting me up as an example: "Why don't you try to walk like Elvirita? Try to hold your neck up so people will see you *have* a neck!" Every time I heard this I cringed because Catalina would look at me with hatred. I knew exactly how Catalina felt when Tía Venecia scolded her, because Clarissa did the same thing to me. "Go put some clean clothes on! You look like a beggar girl," she'd tell me when I came in from playing basketball at the club. I loved sports and Clarissa couldn't endure them. They were *marimacha* games that fostered familiarity between boys and girls.

Catalina and I were very close, and when Tía Venecia and Tío Ulises went to live in Florida, I missed her very much. Like everyone else who surrounded Tío Ulises, my cousins disappeared one day, and I never heard from them again.

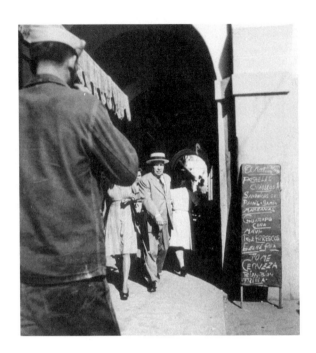

FORTY-SEVEN

†HE FINANCIAL WIZARD

In an initial effort to industrialize the island, Fernando Martín's government invested heavily in four new plants for the production of glass bottles, cardboard and paper, clay bricks, and cement. But two factors worked against the project. In the first place, the mainland investors who were being wooed to open additional manufacturing businesses in Puerto Rico were afraid of the socialist image Martín's party presented—the *pan, tierra y libertad* that had so infuriated Tía Artemisa when she saw the red *jíbaro* flags fluttering in the wind over Don Esteban's lands. It was rumored that, once the Americans had invested their capital, Fernando Martín would nationalize all the new plants. In the second place, the government was a poor administrator. In 1955, three years after the four plants opened, thousands of dollars were going down the drain, and Fernando Martín had no alternative but to put them up for sale. But nobody wanted to buy them.

Because of his many friends in the Partido Democrático Institucional, Ulises was the first to find out about the sale, and he told Aurelio about it. Abuelo Chaguito immediately ordered Tío Ulises to raise the money, and Ulises began to scurry here and there, nosing up and down the government's corridors and burrowing all over the place like a groundhog. First he went to the Banco de Fomento and asked the government itself to lend the Vernets the first two million dollars, since it was in such a hurry to sell. Then he withdrew funds from several other accounts until the family finally got the money together and bought the plants. Six months later, thanks to the management skills of Aurelio and his brothers, all four plants were making money.

The plants were owned by Vernet Construction, which became the family's holding company, and Aurelio was made president. Adela had wanted him to be the head of the family, and Chaguito had respected her wish. Each brother was issued an equal number of shares (the women didn't count because they "didn't work"). But Tía Venecia began to feel that the family's good fortune was entirely the result of Tío Ulises's financial savvy and that he should have more shares and head the company. She was always bragging about his achievements and making the rest of the family feel as if we owed him everything. As far as she was concerned, Aurelio was a nincompoop who did nothing but ride the coattails of others.

The first time I heard Tía Venecia talk like that about Father, I stopped liking her. She was ambitious, much more so than my uncle, who always remained Adela's son at heart. Venecia loved Tío Ulises so much she would have given him the world to play with if she could have. But for Ulises, making money never had anything to do with controlling other people's lives; it was a sport he played, and he wanted to play it better than anybody else.

Ideas for new business deals spurted out of Tío Ulises like a geyser; Aurelio couldn't understand how Ulises could think up so many schemes at once. No sooner had the family bought the four government plants than Ulises suggested to Aurelio that they buy a cement plant in Santo Domingo, which he named Cementos Titán, in honor of himself. Then he acquired a glass-bottle factory in Colombia that he had heard was going for a very good price and that he named Cristales Odiseo, again in honor of himself. A few months later, Aurelio and his brothers had these plants making money as well.

At dinner Ulises would say to Venecia: "Life is like a bonfire—it's worth living only if you're dancing on the tip of the flame. Poverty is just lack of energy. I could never stand being poor again." And when Venecia didn't answer but looked at him with adoring eyes, he'd add: "Don't worry about it, my little duck, just serve me another glass of champagne. I wonder what the middle class is doing right now."

Meanwhile, his brothers and his father tried to administer the new plants as best they could, but it was like trying to manage the Greek empire after Alexander the Great had galloped across it astride Bucephalus. The family was spreading itself too thin. Aurelio began to look for ways to control Ulises.

Tío Ulises, however, had begun to believe Tía Venecia when she assured him that he was a genius. He bought a twin-engine Cessna and flew around the island like Hermes, the mythical merchant, selling cement, glass, paper, cardboard. He didn't care what he sold as long as he put money on the line and moved the merchandise. Entropy meant ruin, and ruin eventually spelled death. He also began to have more love affairs. Well aware of his reputation for giving his girlfriends extravagant gifts, women batted their eyelashes at him, flirted shamelessly, and did everything they could to yank him away from his wife.

Tía Venecia had other problems that made her unhappy in Las Bougainvilleas. Because Tío Ulises had divorced his first wife, he couldn't marry Venecia in church. As a result, Catalina hadn't been admitted to the Sacred Heart Academy, where all the girls from good families went. Venecia hired an English governess to teach Catalina at home, but consequently Catalina had few friends and was growing up a lonely child. Furthermore, Venecia didn't get along with Clarissa. Tía Venecia thought Clarissa looked down on her. She resented the fact that Clarissa had invested almost three hundred thousand dollars in the cement plant, when she herself couldn't provide a cent. She would have invested much more than Clarissa if she could have, in order to have Ulises run the family business. She insisted it was thanks to Clarissa's money that Aurelio was president of Vernet Construction.

Venecia grew more and more frustrated and eventually decided that she wanted to leave Puerto Rico. She began to pressure Tío Ulises to strike out for himself in Florida. "This island is too small for us; there's no breathing space. Think of all the business deals you could make if we lived in the States. We'd be in the big leagues there, like the Rockefellers."

But Tío Ulises didn't want to live so far away from his family. As president of the glass-bottle plant in Colombia, he took out several bank loans, putting the company up as collateral without telling his brothers. With the money he secretly bought extra stock in Star Cement. His equity in the company increased by twenty percent and he began to put pressure on the family to make him president of Vernet Construction. But no one wished to. Aurelio humored him. "Your work is very valuable, Ulises, but you know I'm the leader of the pack. This is all Venecia's fault. Remember Father's saying: 'All for one and one for all.' *En la unión está la fuerza.*"

Ulises's efforts to gain more power within the family didn't appease Tía Venecia. She began to search for a way to make Ulises's life impossible: she decided to renovate their house. Ulises was perfectly happy with it the way it was and indeed would have preferred a much smaller one, as anything that took time away from new business deals was torture for him. But Tía Venecia wanted everyone in La Concordia to know that of the four Vernet mansions standing in a row, theirs was the largest and the most luxurious. Ulises was the financial wizard, the leader of the Vernets' *quadriga*, and even if the family wouldn't admit it, the Vernets owed him everything they owned.

Every day dozens of workers would come to Venecia's part of the house and we would hear their picks and shovels, their hammers and drills working well into the night. But the workers never finished what they began. No sooner was a living room completed than Venecia would order it demolished so a larger one could be built in its place. As soon as a bathroom was redone, she'd make the workers rip out the pink marble and carry away the pink toilet because she had changed her mind: now she wanted everything done in green. Sometimes, on exceptionally dark evenings, we would see lanterns floating in the garden and hear loud, rough bursts of masculine laughter that certainly didn't come from Tío Ulises. Clarissa had no idea what was going on and she wouldn't look out her bedroom window to find out, but she hoped Venecia was getting even with her scoundrel husband by fucking all the construction workers in the ruins of her house.

Ulises heard of a cement plant for sale in Fort Lauderdale, Florida, and urged the family to buy it. If they weren't interested, he'd buy it alone, he said. He was tired of having to tout his achievements louder than Aurelio all over the island. Since Aurelio had entered politics he had an unfair advantage because he got more publicity. But that didn't mean Aurelio was the leader of the Vernet pack. Ulises was the eldest, and the Vernet empire was *his* doing.

Aurelio didn't say anything. He called the family together, and it was agreed that Tío Ulises should buy the Florida plant if he wanted to. Since he insisted on managing it alone, he would have to go into it by himself and leave the family out.

Ulises then asked his brothers to buy his shares in Vernet Construction, and they agreed to pay him fifty million dollars. Each brother took out a loan for sixteen million dollars to buy his shares. With the money, Ulises moved to Sarasota with Tía Venecia and his two children. He bought a mansion on Bayview Avenue that was three times the size of the house at 2 Avenida Cañafístula, but Tía Venecia didn't get to enjoy it for long. A year later, she began to have dizzy spells and the doctors discovered an abnormal widening of the aorta that would gradually result in an aneurysm. She could live another five to ten years without doing anything, they said, but eventually she would have to be operated on. Tía Venecia decided she wanted the operation right away. She was a free spirit; she couldn't live under a death sentence. She chose to die on the operating table rather than live by halves.

After her death, Tío Ulises was like a kite without a string; he got lost in the limitless sky of his erotic fantasies. He married three more times and was divorced an equal number. He married a lion tamer from the Ringling Brothers circus in Sarasota, a topless dancer, and a nurse, in that order. By the time of his last marriage, his cement plant in Fort Lauderdale had gone bankrupt. The oil crisis of the 1970s had caused a debacle in the construction industry, and Ulises ended up owing the National City Bank of Florida a hundred million dollars, twice his original capital. When Aurelio and his brothers heard the news, they were distraught, but they couldn't keep a hint of pride from creeping into their voices when they told their friends:

"Ulises owes the National City Bank so much money it's afraid of proceeding legally against him because it might go broke!"

Tío Ulises's economic disaster caused the family a great deal of anguish. The National City Bank officials didn't believe Aurelio when he told them that Ulises had sold his share of the family business and that he had nothing to do with Vernet Construction anymore. A squadron of bank lawyers and officials from the States flew to the island and descended on Vernet Construction like vultures—with permission from the State Department—to scrutinize all of Vernet Construction's economic statements and corporate documents. The investigation went on for months, during which time all the family's accounts were temporarily frozen. But my brother, Alvaro, proved at that moment to be a worthy leader of the Vernets' quadriga. He surrounded himself with a battery of lawyers and, after several months, managed to prove that the deal with Tío Ulises had been a clean surgical cut and that there were no ties that made the family liable for his debts.

This was around the time that Robert Vesco fled Florida and sought refuge in Cuba for owing U.S. banks a similar amount of money. But Tío Ulises, being the beaver that he was, simply went underground. He disappeared from sight and went to live with his daughter, Catalina, in an isolated cottage on Sanibel Island, where he hibernated for years under a different name. Catalina, much to everyone's surprise, had done very well for herself, even though she had remained single. She had studied business administration at the University of Florida and owned her own communications firm. She took care of her father and looked more like him every day. She never returned to La Concordia.

Years later Tío Ulises called Aurelio from Sanibel Island and asked him for a loan; he wanted to return to Las Bougainvilleas. Aurelio tried to discourage him. He'd be terribly bored, he said, there was nothing to do in town. Most of his friends were dead and nobody remembered him anymore. "It's not just a whim, Aurelio," Tío Ulises said. "I want to come home to die." Aurelio laughed and told him not to joke like that, but when Ulises insisted, Aurelio sent him the money.

The house on Avenida Cañafístula was still his, and although it was more a ruin than a house, Ulises moved in. A few days later he came to visit me in San Juan as if nothing had happened. I hadn't seen him in sixteen years and everybody else related to him had disappeared from the island: Caroline Allan, Tía Venecia, my cousins Catalina and Rodrigo. But Tío Ulises had turned up again, like the proverbial bad penny. I was forty-six years old, but when he saw me he smiled his happy beaver's smile, kissed me on the cheek, and called me nena, just like old times. He'd be living in his bachelor apartment in Las Bougainvilleas from now on, he said, and would be glad to be of help if I needed anything.

Tío Ulises didn't socialize very much. He stayed at home, looking after his parrots and peacocks, and almost every day he went to visit Abuela Adela's grave, which stood on a hill near the Star Cement plant, on the outskirts of town. There he swept the cement dust that collected on the marble slab, put fresh flowers in vases, and said a prayer or two before returning to his rambling ruin.

One time Tía Celia, who was living in the convent near the Vernets' old foundry, came to visit Tío Ulises at the house. She opened the ornate iron gate and knocked several times on the dilapidated front door, but getting no answer, she walked around to the back. She rang the bell to Tío Ulises's apartment, and almost dropped dead when a beautiful naked young redhead opened the door. Tía Celia was used to dealing with delinquents of all sorts in the slums of La Concordia, where she did missionary work, so she calmly asked to see Tío Ulises. The girl smiled broadly and invited her to come in as naturally as if she'd been dressed to the nines. Then she disappeared into one of the bedrooms.

"And who is your little redheaded friend?" Celia asked Tío Ulises without a hint of a smile when he walked into the apartment's sitting room.

Tío Ulises laughed and said: "It's not what you think, Celia, don't worry. Nanette is my daughter. She was born to my fifth wife, Marion, the nurse from Sarasota, eighteen years ago. She's a nurse also, and she's taking care of me."

"And why, pray tell, must she go around naked?" Tía Celia asked dourly, staring at him with her pale blue eyes.

"It's just a fancy of mine, Celia. You know how much I loved Venecia and how I always said she was 'my passage to heaven.' When I see Nanette without her clothes on, she reminds me of her."

A few days after Tía Celia's visit, Nanette called her at the convent at 5 a.m. to tell her that Tío Ulises had just passed away. Celia phoned Father, who was in La Concordia at the time, and they converged on the house. Nanette had disappeared. But they found Tío Ulises in bed completely naked, his penis half melted on his thigh, and a beatific expression of happiness on his face.

FORTY-EIGHT

JOINING THE HOLY ROMAN EMPIRE

Tío Roque was Tía Celia's favorite brother, and she was the one who told me about him. "My earliest memory of Roque," Celia said, "is of watching him climb a mango tree, limber as a Taíno Indian, to throw the ripe golden fruit at me."

Tío Roque married Clotilde Rosales, his childhood sweetheart, after he graduated from Northeastern. They lived in the most conservative of the four Vernet houses, the one next to Ulises and Venecia's. It was an old house that had originally stood in the middle of the cane field when Las Bougainvilleas was built. Roque had it renovated and built a new wing for the kitchen and bathroom. The house had red polished-cement tiles of the kind manufactured on the island at the time, and an old-fashioned balcony shaded by green-and-white-striped awnings where Clotilde liked to sit rocking herself and gossiping with her sisters. But its most striking feature was the modern, air-conditioned laboratory Tío Roque built at the rear of the house, with fluorescent lights and all kinds of chemical beakers on white enamel trays, which he used to help preserve his collection of Taíno artifacts and fossils.

Tía Clotilde's last name was Rosales, but she was not related to Tía Amparo's husband, Arnaldo. She belonged to the poor Rosaleses, not to the rich ones, as she immediately pointed out to you with pride when she was introduced. Her father didn't boil molasses into sugar, paying his workers two cents a day, as Arnaldo's did.

Tía Clotilde had dull black hair and a sallow complexion. She never spent any time grooming herself, which was odd because Tío Roque—though he wasn't exactly the Clark Gable of the family—loved to dress in fine clothes, splash himself with quantities of eau de cologne after taking each of his several baths a day, and preen and admire himself before the mirror for hours. Girls were always falling all over Aurelio, who was the *nene lindo* of the family, but they also liked to be near Roque, whom they considered the sexiest of the Vernets. When Tía Clotilde began to ask Tío Roque to dance with her at parties and smiled at him coyly when they met in the street, Tío Roque preferred her above the rest. Clotilde was mysterious and he wanted to teach her the Taínos' secret: men and women were born to enjoy the pleasures of life, not to work themselves to death.

Tía Clotilde's father, Don Emiliano Rosales, owned Portacoeli, the only funeral home in La Concordia with a crematorium. He was an atheist and everybody in town knew it. He was also a rabid anarchist and labor leader, who saw God as the "antihuman principle."

Don Emiliano Rosales thought a crematorium was needed in La Concordia, not only because it provided a cheap way for the workers to dispose of their loved ones but because in cremation we are all made equal through purifying fire. Carved over the doorway of Don Emiliano Rosales's crematorium was "Dust to dust and ashes to ashes"—the only versicle from the Bible he believed in. And when the ashes had all been mixed together—which is what Don Emiliano Rosales did when he handed family members the remains of those they thought were their loved ones—social and economic differences were obliterated and class distinctions were transformed into anonymity. But the Catholic Church banned cremation and saw it as a mortal sin, which was why Tía Clotilde and her family were rarely invited anywhere.

Tía Clotilde, too, was an atheist, and the first thing she told Roque when she started seeing him was that she didn't believe in God. Roque wasn't a religious person, but he had loved Adela and after she passed away he revered her memory. He believed in a "superior spirit" and prayed to it once in a while because someday he hoped to see Adela again.

This upset Clotilde. In her opinion, God was a projection of the threatening father figure on which the whole unjust capitalist system was founded. Roque told her not to worry, that he was a Freemason himself and didn't go to church. But Clotilde got mad at him anyway.

"An atheist is something very different from a Freemason," she said. "Atheists deny the existence of a 'superior spirit' and believe resolutely in themselves."

Because of these convictions Tía Clotilde made very few friends after she married Tío Roque and moved to Las Bougainvilleas. Her childhood friends from La Victoria, the workers' district where she was born, didn't like to visit her now that she was a millionaire's wife. She rarely ventured outside the confines of her own home and became so sad it was as if her mouth were always full of ashes; she couldn't talk without spewing and blowing them all over you. She always wore dark glasses, whether indoors or out, so no one knew the color of her eyes. "Atheists," the parish priest used to say from the pulpit at the cathedral, "seek to poison God's world out of despair of loving, and being loved by, Him." And that was precisely why Tío Roque loved Clotilde. He was sure he could teach her to be happy; she would learn to live in the light instead of in the dark.

In 1948, Tía Celia made her first trip back to the island in years and the first person she visited was Roque. They spoke in his laboratory, surrounded by the dusty Taíno bones and pottery shards Roque was patiently trying to piece together. Celia told him all about the missionary work she was doing in the Appalachians, roaming through Alabama in a beat-up pickup truck with a platoon of nuns or taking a Catholic census among the coal miners and baptizing them whenever she could, with the aid of a parish priest.

Celia had received a telegram from Monsignor MacFarland, an Irish bishop who had recently arrived on the island, ordering her to come home. She asked Tío Roque if he knew what it was all about. Perhaps it was the new Catholic university the bishop wanted to build in town, Roque replied, but he was sure Tía Celia would soon find out for herself. Tío Roque was right; the next day MacFarland summoned Celia to the bishopric.

"The Puerto Rican bourgeoisie is very tightfisted, and it's difficult to get them to give money for the public good," he said. "But your mother, Adela Pasamontes, was different. She suffered deeply when she saw others go hungry. She was generous with the poor and used to visit the slums to feed them."

Celia looked at the bishop, her eyes flashing. She had lost a lot of weight lately—there was seldom enough to eat in Appalachia—but she was still a live wire. She wore her summer habit, which was made of heavy white wool, and a little round straw hat. She didn't look hot at all. The bishop, on the other hand, who loved good food, looked like a sweating eggplant in his purple silk robe.

"Mother was right, feeding the poor *is* very important, Your Excellency," Celia answered circumspectly. "Do you know how I guessed when to knock on someone's door in the Appalachians? If it smelled like sauerkraut or chop suey I didn't knock because I knew they were either Jewish or Chinese and wouldn't invite me in. But if it smelled like spaghetti or rice and beans, I'd knock on the door right away, because I might be able to baptize a sick baby and also snitch a free lunch." The bishop smiled condescendingly. Being Irish, he hated spaghetti but he made a mental note that, as bishop of La Concordia, it was his duty to find out what rice and beans tasted like. He'd have his cook make some for him that very day.

He began to question Tía Celia and learned that while Abuela Adela and her daughters had all been pious her sons, as well as her husband, were Freemasons. This had caused Adela to suffer deeply before she passed away, but it also meant that, hidden away in a corner of the Vernets' minds, they had guilty consciences.

"Are your brothers as selfless as you, my daughter?" the bishop asked Tía Celia affectionately.

"My brothers are all very generous," Tía Celia answered. "They love to give away money: Aurelio to politics, and Ulises and Roque to their girlfriends. If we can convert them from Freemasonry to Catholicism, I promise you, it'll be worth it."

A few days later MacFarland, accompanied by a smiling Tía Celia, visited Abuelo Chaguito and Aurelio and suggested that, if they donated to the Church the sugarcane farm they had acquired on the outskirts of La Concordia for a possible expansion of the cement plant, the institution that would rise there would be called La Universidad de las Mercedes, in honor of Abuela Adela, whose full name had been Adela Mercedes Pasamontes. This generous donation, the bishop promised, would open the doors of the Holy Roman Empire to the Vernet family. The Order of Saint Gregory would be conferred on Abuelo Chaguito at Saint Patrick's Cathedral in New York by Cardinal Spellman himself in a solemn ceremony—but only if Chaguito renounced his Masonic beliefs.

Aurelio brought the male members of the family together in the dining room at 1 Avenida Cañafístula to discuss the issue. Abuelo Chaguito said he would consider the donation: Freemasonry was on the decline worldwide, and taking a leading role in the Catholic Church could bring the family important prestige. But several terms would have to be added to the negotiations. Catalina, his granddaughter, would have to be admitted to Sacred Heart Academy; Tío Ulises's marriage to Caroline Allan would at last be annulled without Ulises's having to pay a cent for the annulment; and most important of all, Tía Celia would have to be allowed to return permanently to the island to do her missionary work in La Concordia—something Abuelo Chaguito had sought for years because he missed Celia so much. Bishop MacFarland agreed to all of Abuelo Chaguito's terms.

Soon afterward, Abuelo bought an old house near Vernet Construction and presented it to the Maryknolls as a gift. Tía Celia and her missionaries moved in and they began to work in La Concordia's slums—Las Cajas, Pantanales, Despeñaperros, Riachuelo Seco.

The first stone of La Universidad de las Mercedes was laid on September 10, 1950, the twentieth anniversary of Abuela Adela's death. Bishop MacFarland officiated at a High Mass in La Concordia's cathedral to commemorate the event, and Abuelo Chaguito, his four sons, and their wives—except Tía Clotilde—all received Holy Communion. It was Tía Celia's day of triumph. She had won the battle for her brothers' and her father's souls.

A year later the university opened its doors. The consecration was attended by the island's highest clerical officials. A raised platform decorated with bouquets of white lilies was set up in the middle of the campus, where sugarcane had grown less than a year before; yellow-and-white banners—the colors of the Catholic Church—flapped in the wind. A portrait of Pope Pius XII hung over a red velvet curtain that served as a backdrop. Bishop MacFarland and the Vernet family sat on high-backed Spanish-style chairs above a sea of heads. Bishop MacFarland wanted to hold the family up as an example to La Concordia's bourgeoisie, to see if he could generate more donations for the university.

Abuelo Chaguito wore the medal of Saint Gregory pinned to his chest. The bishop's round face beamed above the golden crucifix with a large amethyst at its center. Tía Celia and Tía Amparo, both dressed in white, sat next to Chaguito and the bishop. The four Vernet brothers and their wives sat behind them, the men in elegant business suits. Everybody was smiling except Clarissa, who looked with melancholy eyes at what remained of the sugarcane in a field nearby; soon it would be gone too. Unfortunately, Tía Clotilde had to sit under the portrait of Pope Pius XII, which made her particularly uncomfortable. As usual, she wore dark glasses and a large hat and didn't try to hide the mocking smile that played on her face. She was amazed at the change that had come over the Vernets—from Freemasons to exemplary Catholics in one year.

FORTY-NINE

†HE FIRE ENGINE

Tío Roque and Tía Clotilde had two sons, Enrique and Eduardo Vernet. When Eduardo, the younger, was born in 1938, Tía Clotilde said to Roque: "We're a family now. Why don't you strike out on your own? Aurelio and Ulises are in control of Vernet Construction, and Damián always does what they tell him to. You can't make decisions without consulting them first. Right now you work well together because you're brothers. But what's going to happen when Enrique, Eduardo, Rodrigo, and Alvaro grow up? Cousins don't always get along. It's better to divide things now, while your father is still alive, so that each can take his money and do what he wants with it."

But Roque kept putting it off. And when Ulises broke away from the family and the brothers had to raise fifty million dollars to buy him out, it became impossible. "I'd be afraid to go out on my own,

Clotilde," Roque said. "My stocks are so valuable, Aurelio and Damián couldn't buy them if they wanted to. We'd have to sell the cement plant, which would definitely be a mistake. Anyway, the truth is that I don't want to go into business for myself. I prefer to work a few hours a day at the plant and go on my archaeological digs in my spare time. If I sell my shares and go out on my own, I'll have to work twice as hard as I am now."

"We're living a lie," Tía Clotilde retorted. "We have everything we want—money, a beautiful house, a nice car—everything except self-respect. I want to feel proud that you're my husband." But Tío Roque wouldn't relent. Instead, he shut himself up in his studio at the back of the house to study his *dujos*, his *macanás*, and his carved stone *cemíes*. Tía Clotilde shouted at him from the other side of the door: "All right, we'll do as you say, Roque, and keep on sucking from Star Cement's golden tit. But from now on, my children will call themselves Vernet Rosales, instead of just plain Vernet. And don't expect me to go have lunch at the house on Calle Esperanza on Sundays anymore, because I'd rather stay home."

Enrique and Eduardo weren't baptized when they were born, but Tía Clotilde didn't let anyone know. When the time came for them to go to school, she sent them to the same Catholic school Alvaro and I went to, the exclusive Academia de los Padres Paules. Clotilde's brothers had gone to public school, like all the other children from La Victoria. But since she was now married to a Vernet, her sons were accepted at Los Paules.

Although Los Paules was a boys' school, the fathers accepted girls until the fifth grade. Clarissa, ever faithful to the Rivas de Santillana tradition of thriftiness, decided to send me there for elementary school (instead of to the Sacred Heart, where the girls of good families went), in order to save gas. In 1944, when I entered first grade, gasoline was being rationed. Cristóbal would have to make only one trip each way.

There were two or three girls in my class and ten to twelve boys. We all wore khaki uniforms, Buster Brown shoes, and ties the same color as our uniform. The girls mingled freely with the boys, and there was absolutely no special treatment given to them. I loved Los Paules. Studying there, I was convinced that there was absolutely no difference in intelligence or spunk between boys and girls and that we could succeed equally in life.

Tía Clotilde didn't have a chauffeur and Tío Roque never learned to drive a car, so their children went to school by taxi. But when Tía Clotilde heard that Cristóbal drove us to Los Paules in a Cadillac, which Father bought after the Pontiac, she was very upset. She didn't want her sons to grow up with an inferiority complex, so she called the fire department, where Abuelo Chaguito still had many friends, and asked if they couldn't pick her children up in the afternoons.

The students would all be playing in the school yard, running after one another and screaming and yelling like devils on the loose, when La Concordia's fire engine would charge through the gate, bells clanging and siren screaming. Everybody would freeze as my cousins walked single file to the front of the engine and climbed in next to the driver. Then the firemen began clanging the bell again and drove to 3 Avenida Cañafístula at full speed.

Once I entered Los Paules, it didn't take me long to realize that my cousins were no match for my brother and that someday Alvaro would be president of Vernet Construction and of Star Cement.

I was Father's spendthrift daughter, and Alvaro was the practical, reasonable child. I always pressed the new tube of toothpaste in the middle, so that after a while I had to struggle to get anything out, while my brother always curled his tube from the bottom, evenly and systematically, until all that was left was a flat, empty noodle he could throw away with a clear conscience.

The differences between my brother and me didn't worry me when I was young; in fact, I wasn't even aware they existed I was so busy dogging Father's footsteps. I could do everything my brother did: I could swim like a fish, bat a baseball, and even hit a home run once in a while. But things changed the day my brother got into a terrible fight with our cousin Eduardo Vernet.

Eduardo loved fistfights, and he looked it. He reminded me of a cross between a powder keg and a pork barrel. At Los Paules he was always picking on children who were smaller and weaker. His grandfather Rosales had been a worker at one of La Concordia's foundries—competitors of Vernet Construction—and he still lived in La Victoria, where Eduardo often visited him. There bigger children were always trying to bully him, so he'd taken his fair share of punches too; he didn't seem to mind. Moreover, his grandfather's crematorium made him the butt of jokes: "Broil a friend and gift wrap him for Christmas," someone would yell at him at recess, and Eduardo's right fist would spring out like a sledgehammer and punch the smartass in the mouth.

Once, when he was playing in the school yard, Eduardo punched ten-year-old Luis Martínez between the shoulder blades for no apparent reason, just as at La Victoria he himself had been attacked. Alvaro saw him and sauntered over. Eduardo was glowering at the younger student, who lay flat on his chest across the basketball court's center line.

"Do you think being a Vernet gives you the right to bully people?" my brother asked in an icy but polite voice.

"No. But being a Vernet Rosales does," Eduardo answered. "I'm not a Rivas de Santillana pansy who's a mama's boy."

The insult was heard all around the court, and instantly there was a crowd of students jostling Eduardo and my brother. I pushed my way through the ring of boys, conscious of the sweaty smell of puberty. Alvaro was slender, not brawny like Eduardo, who had three hundred and sixty muscles in his body, the thickest one in his head. My brother looked down on fistfights as well as on basketball and baseball, games only plebeian students played; he loved tennis because it was an aristocratic sport.

Alvaro and I lived sheltered lives in Las Bougainvilleas, and it never occurred to my brother that something was expected of him after Eduardo's insult. Alvaro was helping Luis up off the ground amid jeers and I was standing by his side, holding the thermos that I brought to school every day filled with tomato juice, when Eduardo's sledgehammer swung out of the blue. Alvaro saw it coming out of the corner of his eye and ducked just in time so that it swished over his head. He turned and began to walk away, but Eduardo sent an unerring right straight from the shoulder, and his fist landed squarely in Alvaro's face. I began to jump up and down in frustration and threw my tomato juice in Eduardo's face.

By the time we got home, Alvaro's bloody nose had grown to twice its size; it no longer had that elegant, chiseled Rivas de Santillana look. But Alvaro clammed up and wouldn't tell our parents what had happened. I was the one who confessed, between hiccups and tears. Eduardo had punched Alvaro, as well as a younger student, and all three had been put on probation.

"Did you hit Eduardo back?" Father asked. Alvaro flushed and said no, he hadn't had the chance. Father nodded his head approvingly.

The important thing was to keep the peace in the Vernet family, Father said.

But Mother thought the whole thing was preposterous. "Keep whose peace, the Vernets' or the Rosaleses'?" she asked Father, her eyes glinting. That very afternoon she went into town and bought two pairs of twelve-ounce red boxing gloves that looked like huge ripe tomatoes. She made Father and Alvaro prance around the garden in Las Bougainvilleas all week, taking jabs at each other. For three weeks they kept it up until Alvaro was ready for his revenge. Then at recess he punched Eduardo in the jaw and knocked him out cold. That was the day I learned I was really very different from my father and my brother. Brute force—something that men took for granted but that was completely beyond women—was what set us apart.

FIFTY

ROQUE'S RUSSIAN ROULETTE

My cousin Enrique was tall and gangly and looked like a grass-hopper. He was very shy. He stuttered severely and sometimes you had to wait three or four seconds before he could pronounce a sentence. The other children would laugh and chant: "*Soy ggggago porque no caggo!*"—"I stutter because I can't shit!" They were cruel, and they were also envious of him for being a Vernet. Enrique couldn't have cared less. He just wanted to be left alone.

Enrique got bad marks and was held back twice—in second *and* third grades—but not because he wasn't intelligent. His teachers were impatient with him, and when he couldn't answer questions as quickly as the other pupils, they thought he was unprepared and yelled at him mercilessly. Enrique would freeze in terror and forget his lesson at once.

Enrique's speech impediment made him self-conscious and he had few friends. Tía Clotilde, moreover, never came to school, because she didn't want to mix with the Catholic parents of the other children, so Enrique was rarely invited to his friends' homes. One day Enrique told his mother he didn't want to go back to school at all. Tía Clotilde unwisely gave in, and since they could afford it, had a private tutor come to the house. But Enrique grew sadder and sadder and finally locked himself up in his room and wouldn't emerge for days. Tía Clotilde would take food to him on a tray and beg him for hours to open the door so he could eat something. Finally, one night when the house was asleep, Enrique stole Tío Roque's gun from his desk in the study and shot himself in the head. He was only fourteen years old.

The tragedy affected all of us, but especially Abuelo Chaguito, who mourned for the child and feared it was a bad omen. There had been no violent deaths in the family since his father, Henri Vernet, had been electrocuted in Cuba, and he was afraid it might mean the family's star was on the wane. Adolescent suicides were practically nonexistent in La Concordia at the time, and he blamed Tía Clotilde for Enrique's troubles. "Who wants to have an atheist for a mother? I'm not surprised no one wanted to play with the child at school. Clotilde should convert to Catholicism and have Eduardo baptized. That way, all her troubles would be over." Tía Celia went to the house and tried to comfort Tío Roque, who was destroyed. He had been a Freemason most of his life and didn't even remember how to pray.

"He died a heathen, Celia," Roque said, crying. "His soul will float around forever in limbo, unable to fly up to heaven. My poor son!"

"Don't cry, Roque," Tía Celia replied. "Enrique had no sins. His soul went straight to heaven, whether he was baptized or not. We'll bury him next to Mother in the family mausoleum, and she'll take care of him."

But Tía Clotilde wouldn't give in. She refused to let Enrique be buried in the Catholic cemetery and had him cremated at Portacoeli. Then she took his ashes in a little bag and threw them toward heaven herself from the top of La Atalaya, a windy hill behind La Concordia.

Tío Roque went on digging for Taíno Indian bones, but they made him feel even sadder. He saw the careful way Taínos buried their loved ones, accompanied by their dogs, pottery, vessels, and all sorts of good-luck amulets for the journey to the other world, and he thought of his son, who would never be able to find his way back to Las Bougainvilleas on the day of the Apocalypse. He also felt unhappy because he had less and less work. Aurelio and Ulises had surrounded themselves with ambitious young engineers clawing their way up the executive ladder, and they had relegated him to the background. But his brothers were very generous and he went on receiving the same salary. Nonetheless, he felt smothered, useless.

In his despair, Tío Roque became infatuated with a seamstress from Riachuelo Seco, one of La Concordia's poorer neighborhoods. Roque met Titiba Menéndez at the house when she came to alter his shirts. Roque's arms were short and he always had to have his sleeves taken up at the cuff. Tía Clotilde wasn't at home at the time and they ended up in bed, making love like rabbits—as quickly and as many times as possible—terrified that Tía Clotilde might walk in the door any minute. Titiba had Taíno blood, and the minute Roque saw her he was entranced. She looked like the first Taíno Indian woman Cristóbal Colón had described in his diary, the *"Libro de la Primera Navegación y Descubrimiento de las Indias"*: "She had large black eyes, copper-colored skin, and hair as silky as a horse's mane, cut straight above her eyebrows in thick bangs."

After that first meeting, it was as if Tío Roque had ingested a drug. He couldn't live without the pleasure Titiba gave him. He bought her a house in Las Margaritas, the same middle-class suburb where Alvaro and I were born. And, unknown to Tía Clotilde, they had three children. Tío Roque moved his collection of Taíno artifacts and pottery shards to Titiba's house and spent two or three afternoons a week there. He wanted to enjoy life, and Titiba was always in a good mood. He was tired of living next to a volcano that was constantly erupting and blowing ashes in his face. Roque knew that he was playing Russian roulette by keeping this arrangement and that Tía Clotilde would have his skin on the day she found out. But he was too happy with Titiba to care.

FIFTY-ONE

THE ROLLING COFFIN

It wasn't until Roque was sixty-three years old that Tía Clotilde discovered his secret family. The Vernets were going through the perilous financial crisis that Tío Ulises's bankruptcy had unleashed upon them. There were IRS inspectors and auditors from the National City Bank crawling all over, analyzing the corporate bank accounts. Unexpectedly, Roque found himself in tight economic straits. He spent no money on himself and dressed in shabby clothes. But he had two households, each with servants and all the usual expenses; moreover, he had Titiba's three sons to put through college. His salary of a hundred thousand dollars a year from the cement plant was temporarily attached by the IRS. Still, he wasn't worried, because he had a million dollars in cash stashed away in a box in his closet at 3 Avenida Cañafístula—or so he thought. When the time came to draw on it, he discovered it was gone. Eduardo had stolen it and disappeared. Reportedly, he was living in Spain.

Tío Roque was overcome with fear. Unable to face either Tía Clotilde or Titiba, he decided to go away. He stuffed a beat-up alligator suitcase with dirty underwear and went to visit Tía Celia at the convent.

It was Sunday and Tía Celia was at home. For a while Roque sat in the garden without saying a word while she fed her parrots. Tía Celia wondered where he was going, but she didn't dare ask because he looked so sad. He had forgotten to shave that morning, and his long bloodhound's ears had turned ash-gray; his heavy eyebrows hooded his eyes in shadow. When Roque finally got up to leave, Tía Celia said: "Why don't you come and have lunch with us a little later? We're having pig's knuckles and garbanzos, one of your favorite dishes. I'll put an extra plate on the table for you." Tío Roque agreed and left, heading with his battered suitcase toward the old Vernet Construction offices, which stood next to the foundry.

The building had been constructed in the 1950s, and although it was a rough affair it had a certain charm. It was a plain square structure made from large red clay bricks manufactured at the Vernet plant. Four stories high, it had two flagpoles sticking out over the entrance door. From one of them waved the American flag, from the other the family flag: four golden stars (which stood for the Vernet brothers) linked to one another and contained within a larger star (Abuelo Chaguito's) on a navy-blue field. There were no stars for Tía Amparo or Tía Celia.

The building was practically empty. The Star Cement plant was still in La Concordia but Vernet Construction's management had moved to San Juan. The foundry, welding shop, and machine shop were still in operation but business was very slow. With the demise of the sugar industry the town had suffered a severe economic depression and the population had decreased from around two hundred thousand inhabitants in the 1960s to approximately a hundred and fifty thousand, the result of emigration to the mainland.

Roque walked past Aurelio's and Ulises's offices, which were at the front of the building. Their names were still engraved on the frosted glass, laying claim to the most important rungs on the company's ladder—first vice president and second vice president. Roque's footsteps echoed down the hall, and he peered into Tío Damián's office, which had an ocean view and plenty of sunlight. Damián was away on one of his frequent trips to Europe in search of works of art. He and Roque had grown very close after being left behind in La Concordia by their elder brothers. Tío Damián's portrait hung from the wall as usual. He was dressed in an elegant light-blue suit the same color as his eyes, and his thin lips were drawn into a delicate ironic smile. Roque walked on to his own office, at the back of the building. It was the darkest one of all and looked out on the foundry's back yard, where the scrap iron and discarded machinery were dumped. He locked the door behind him and sat down at his desk. From beneath the bundle of dirty underwear in his suitcase, he took out a gun, aimed it at the left side of his chest, and fired.

A few minutes later the caretaker—who had heard the shot ring out in the almost-empty building—ran up the stairs. He opened the door to the office with a master key and found Tío Roque lying slumped on his desk in a pool of blood.

That afternoon, while Tía Clotilde made arrangements for Roque's funeral with Tía Celia's help, Titiba Menéndez went to the house at 3 Cañafístula. She was ushered into the living room by the maid, who was trembling with fear because in La Concordia everybody except Tía Clotilde knew who Titiba Menéndez was, and she wasn't one to beat about the bush. The minute Tía Clotilde walked in, Titiba asked her if they could share Roque Vernet in death as they had in life. Tía Clotilde wanted to know what on earth she was talking about and Titiba confessed everything: Roque had been her lover for years and they had three boys, all of whom wanted to attend the wake. And so did she, because she had loved Roque with all her heart. Titiba suggested that, since Tía Clotilde's family owned Portacoeli, both families could hold the funeral service together.

Tía Clotilde was shocked, but she agreed to the odd petition. She was touched by the fact that Roque, a man of simple tastes, had chosen Titiba, a woman of humble origins like herself, as his paramour, instead of one of the rich bitches who were always after the Vernet brothers. She invited the whole Vernet family to the wake, but only Tía Celia and Aurelio went. Celia was terribly upset by Tía Clotilde's decision to cremate Roque's body and by the fact that there would be no religious ceremony. But Clotilde's atheism was very important to her. It was her way of proclaiming her right to be different from the Vernets. In spite of the Vernets' role in La Concordia's society and of the dignity and prestige that the Catholic Church had conferred on them, she stuck to her guns and refused to allow a Catholic ceremony for Roque.

Tía Clotilde ordered two adjacent chapels at Portacoeli to be filled with flowers—one for the Vernet and Rosales families and one for the Menéndez family. Tío Roque's silver-gray casket was mounted on a little car with wheels, and he spent the whole afternoon commuting between the two families before entering the oven's sad tunnel hidden by velvet curtains. He would spend two hours with the Vernet and Rosales families at their chapel and would then punctually be wheeled to the Menéndezes in the adjoining chapel. And all the time, Tía Celia walked behind her favorite brother's coffin, crying her eyes out and reciting the Rosary out loud, remembering how Tío Roque had loved to throw ripe mangoes at her from the tree as if he were a Taíno Indian.

FIFTY-TWO

THE WHITE JASMINE

Tío Damián's house, 4 Avenida Cañafístula, next to Tío Roque's, was the last one in the row. It was exactly like our house, only smaller, because Tío Damián and Tía Agripina had no children. Inside, it was full of the beautiful sculptures and paintings Tío Damián had brought back from his frequent trips to Europe. But the thing I remember the most about it was the collection of medieval armor, the swords and spears that lined the walls of the study, and the huge white polar bear rug in the hallway, legs spread apart and red tongue lolling out between white fangs.

Clarissa and Aurelio were always teasing Tío Damián and telling him to get rid of the moth-eaten shag—something totally out of place in a town like La Concordia, where the heat could be unbearable—but he never did. I loved the polar bear; the first thing I did when we visited Damián was throw myself on the rug and roll around on it. I felt I knew why it was so important to my uncle. He had to impress upon the family the fact that, even though he was the most reserved of the Vernets, his spirit was as strong as a bear's.

Tío Damián hardly ever spoke when the family came to visit him: he let Aurelio and Ulises do all the talking. But he wasn't shy with children. He was a bit of a ventriloquist and loved to do magic tricks. Whenever we went to his house, he immediately picked me up and squeezed pennies out of my ears or pulled quarters from his shirt-sleeves and gave me the money to buy candy. When he finished his act, his index finger would buzz all around me like a mosquito and end up tickling my underarm.

Tío Damián married Tía Agripina, but instead of helping him become a more self-assured young man, Agripina only added to his insecurity. She was from a good family in San Juan, the Leclercs, and everybody was surprised when she decided to marry Damián Vernet, who had no social standing whatsoever. The Leclercs had lost most of their money during the First World War. Agripina's father, Roberto Leclerc, was a daredevil pilot and a friend of Abuelo Chaguito's, but he was killed at the battle of Verdun. Still, they had a very prestigious name.

Agripina's mother had brought her up as a society belle. She graduated from a finishing school in Newport, Rhode Island, where she learned to embroider Madeira tablecloths and decorate porcelain plates with apricots and roses, but she could do virtually nothing that was useful. During Hurricane San Felipe, for example, Agripina had been no help at all. Her mother was going crazy, trying to fill tubs with water and prepare enough food to tide them over for several days. But when the 150-mile-per-hour winds started to blow and the tin roof began to rattle, Agripina dove into a kitchen cupboard and stayed there throughout the hair-raising ordeal.

A year after they were married, Agripina said to Tío Damián: "I wonder why I haven't gotten pregnant yet. Are you sure you're not consumptive? You know, one of the reasons I married you was because I wanted to have children. I'm sick of society life." Tío Damián laughed and told her she was being silly; it was much too early to start worrying. "This way we can enjoy ourselves a little longer before getting tied down: go to the movies, play tennis, visit our friends as much as we want." But Agripina began to cry and said, "I have no one else in the world but you. If anything happened to you, I'd be completely alone."

She hadn't always been like that. Before she met Tío Damián she had lived a flapper's life. "Flappers live heroic lives," she'd say to her friends. "When they defy convention they lend a special brightness to things." In Agripina's opinion there was little difference between a daredevil pilot and a flapper—both were equally intense. The main thing was to escape boredom, to defy the bourgeois mentality by living on the edge. And so Agripina smoked, drank, and frequented all the speakeasies in San Juan.

One night she dropped by the Pif-Paf-Pouff, a nightclub hidden away in a cellar. Even young ladies were obliged to enter it by sliding down a chute, at the bottom of which a group of young men in tuxedoes helped them up from silk cushions, inevitably complimenting them on their lace panties. She got so drunk that the next morning, when an M.P. found her, she was sprawled on the sidewalk. She had passed out after vomiting all over her sequined black tulle evening dress. The M.P. helped her into his car and drove her to the police station near Fort Brooke. After a phone call from her mother, Marina Leclerc—who had powerful friends—Agripina was released. The incident created a scandal. The photograph of her lying drunk on the sidewalk was in all the local newspapers and left her seriously shaken. For several months afterwards she woke up in the middle of the night dreaming she was hurtling through space strapped in a blazing biplane—which was exactly how her father had died.

Agripina's mother was so disgusted she told her daughter to leave the house, and Agripina took refuge with one of Tía Amparo's friends. Tío Damián met her there on a visit to San Juan; she was already on the wagon and had changed her ways. Tío Damián was so shy he never dared ask any girls out. When Agripina discovered what a sweet man he was and began to call him at La Concordia every day, he was overwhelmed with gratitude that such a good-looking girl should notice him and asked her, over the telephone, to marry him.

La Concordia was just what Agripina needed. She wanted peace and tranquillity, and the first few months there were a balm for her. Agripina did volunteer work at the Hospital de las Siervas de María, a beautiful pink building from Spanish colonial times, where the nuns glided silently down arched corridors with huge starched coifs fluttering on their head. But Agripina still woke up in the middle of the night feeling an unendurable emptiness. "I feel like a plaster cast instead of a woman: beautiful on the outside and hollow on the inside," she complained to Tío Damián every night before she fell asleep. "I want a baby more than anything else in the world."

For five years Agripina tried to get pregnant, and then Damián went to see a urologist. The urologist examined his testicles and discovered that they were diminished in size. He asked him about his childhood illnesses and it turned out that Damián had suffered a severe case of mumps when he was fourteen. The infection had left him permanently sterile.

When Damián told Agripina the news, she was shattered. He took her in his arms and tried to comfort her. "We can adopt a baby and bring him up as our own. There are dozens of abandoned children in the orphanage." But Agripina wouldn't consider it. She was terrified of adopting a child who might have inherited who knows what horrible defects. She decided to help out at the orphanage anyway.

The work was good for her. It made her feel less guilty for her past sins. But whenever she and Damián made love and she was about to let herself be engulfed in an avalanche of pleasure, she saw a tiny baby floating on the crest of a wave, stretching out its arms to her, and all the pleasure she was feeling would ebb away like a retreating tide.

In spite of his personal problems, Tío Damián proved instrumental in the success of Star Cement. As a chemical engineer, he became one of the plant's principal administrators and helped his brothers and his father turn around the businesses they acquired from the government. He had as much money as he wanted, and he loved Tía Agripina deeply, but he wasn't happy. He was in a constant state of anxiety, threatened by invisible dangers. That was when he began to collect medieval armor, swords, and pikes and hang them on the walls of his study. Then he bought the white polar bear skin and spread it out in the entrance hallway of his house in Las Bougainvilleas. Tío Damián felt he had to defend himself from something, but he didn't quite know what it was.

He suspected that his opinions were never taken into account at Vernet Construction. Although Aurelio and Tío Ulises were always very polite and affectionate with him, they made the really important business decisions behind his back. Each of them had a battery of executive advisers, but Damián had no one. He didn't tout his achievements around town or have a reputation as an investor or a politician. No one was interested in what *he* had to say.

In 1968, after Aurelio moved the management of Vernet Construction to San Juan, Ulises sold his shares and moved to Florida. Damián and Roque were left in charge of the huge, half-empty Vernet Construction building in La Concordia, where doors creaked open by themselves and Abuelo Chaguito shuffled in every afternoon, leaning on his cane. He'd post himself at the door to the building and turn back everyone who tried to leave the office at half past four, twenty minutes before the bell rang.

To take his mind off things, Tío Damián began to travel to Europe with Agripina more often. They would board the *Queen Mary* in New York and spend three weeks at the Savoy in London. Then they would sail to Le Havre and spend a week at the Plaza Athenée in Paris. Then on to Florence, Venice, Rome, Athens. They came back from each trip loaded with art treasures: paintings, sculptures, antique silver. The house in Las Bougainvilleas began to resemble a museum. But Tío Damián was still melancholy and talked less and less. Agripina's perpetual complaints about his sterility didn't help.

When Tío Roque committed suicide in 1970, Abuelo Chaguito stopped coming to the Vernet Construction offices altogether; Damián had to go there alone every day. The old foundry next to the offices, though still operating, was losing money. Tío Damián was supervisor, and he made his rounds every morning. He checked to see that the welders were wearing their protective masks. He visited the machine shop and verified the new orders for crushing mills and cogwheels, which were fewer and fewer as the island's sugar mills closed down. He visited the warehouse, where the steel and iron beams were stored. Then he went up to his office and sat at his desk looking out the window at the ships unloading their cargo on the nearby dock.

After a while, the contours of reality began to disintegrate, and he got lost in a fog of speculation. One evening at nine Agripina telephoned the office to see if he was still there. No one answered the phone. Agripina drove over in her Lincoln Continental and had the janitor open the building. They found Damián sitting at his desk in the dark, as if in a trance, staring out the window.

This was in 1972, when Aurelio was still spending a lot of time in

San Juan. Agripina telephoned him and he flew to La Concordia the following day. They decided Damián should be hospitalized and arranged to have him admitted to New York's Flower and Fifth Avenue Hospital, which had one of the best mental clinics in the States, where Dr. Lothar B. Kalinowsky was world-renowned for his electroconvulsive therapy. Tío Damián was administered several electroshock treatments during the following months, and his recovery was spectacular. A few weeks after his third treatment he was as good as new. He had come out of his catatonic stupor and talked normally with Tía Agripina and everyone else. He immediately began planning a trip to Mexico City with her, because they had never been there.

One night, while Damián and Agripina were traveling in Mexico, Aurelio woke up bathed in perspiration. It was three o'clock and he had had a harrowing nightmare. He had dreamt that Damián was buried alive inside one of the pyramids of Tenochtitlán and was calling out desperately, begging Aurelio to rescue him. At the foot of the pyramid there was a plumed serpent carved in stone with its jaws open wide. It looked like a water spout but was actually an *almoducto*, a pipe through which the souls of the sacrificed traveled from the center of the pyramid to the outside.

"If you stand in front of the pyramid for a few minutes, you'll see Damián's soul come out of the stone pipe and be able to take it home with you," Aurelio heard somebody say in his dream. "But his body belongs to us. He'll be buried in Mexico, because when he was alive you never listened to him."

Father got out of bed. His heart was racing. He crossed the terrace, walked over to the piano in the living room, and started playing. Nothing helped. Suddenly the telephone rang. It was Agripina, calling from Mexico City. Damián had just died. They were having dinner at a restaurant in La Zona Rosa when he felt an acute stab of pain in his chest. By the time the ambulance got him to the hospital, he was dead.

Father flew to Mexico City and drove immediately to the hotel where Tía Agripina was staying. Damián's body was still in the morgue. On the way there, Aurelio asked her if the doctors had discovered the cause of Damián's death.

"They wanted to do an autopsy and I wouldn't let them. But he probably died of a heart attack," she answered, trying to hold back the tears. "We're at almost eight thousand feet here, and Damián's heart was weakened by the electroshocks. It never occurred to us when we planned the trip to Mexico City, but he probably couldn't stand the altitude."

Aurelio thought her theory was plausible. He took her in his arms and tried to console her. Then Agripina added: "When he was dying in the ambulance, around one o'clock in the morning, Damián kept calling out your name. He wanted you to come and get him. He was convinced that only you could save him."

Aurelio felt his hair stand on end but he didn't tell Agripina that he had heard Tío Damián calling out to him in his dream at that very hour. Since Mexico was two hours ahead of Puerto Rico, it was then three o'clock in San Juan. In the meantime, the Mexican authorities were alleging that, since the cause of death was unknown, Tío Damián's body couldn't leave the country until a thorough criminal investigation was conducted. A mandatory autopsy had to be performed and it could take several months because Tío Damián had to wait his turn. Aurelio was furious. He wasn't going to let the Aztecs cut his brother up or leave parts of him behind. He was going to get him out of the country in one piece if he had to bribe half the Mexican government to do it. It cost him ten thousand dollars, but three days later they were on their way to the island with the body.

When Tío Damián's coffin finally arrived in La Concordia, Agripina had it taken to their house at 4 Avenida Cañafístula. Father, Mother, and I said good-bye to him there, together with all his friends. When the wake was over, Father and his brothers carried the coffin across the street to Abuelo Chaguito's house, before placing it in the hearse.

Abuelo Chaguito had moved to Las Bougainvilleas some years back to be near his sons and grandchildren. Now in his nineties, he stood on the stoop of his house at the corner of Cañafístula and Flamboyán and took off his straw hat as the coffin approached. Then he slowly came down the steps and put a trembling hand on the lid. Aurelio, who was helping carry the coffin, drew near and stood next to his father.

"What did he die of? Did they finally find out?" Abuelo Chaguito whispered uneasily so the reporters wouldn't hear.

"He died of silence, Father," Aurelio answered, tears welling up in his eyes. "It was all our fault. We forgot Damián had a delicate heart and we didn't listen to him."

FIFTY-THREE

FOSFORITO VERNET'S LAST SPARK

Abuelo had designed a house for himself in Las Bougainvilleas that was very different from those of his sons. Modern and practical, it had a cantilevered cement roof that no hurricane could blow away and lozenge-shaped louvered windows that reached all the way to the ceiling and let in a lot of light. The house was completely white, and the floors were a cream-colored terrazzo that always made me think of tapioca pudding. When he moved from Calle Esperanza, the only thing Abuelo brought with him was Adela's rosebushes, which flowered profusely all year round. He planted them in a small garden at the back of the new house and took care of them himself.

Brunhilda always said she had worked as a nurse for her first husband at the nursing home, but later we found out it was a lie. What she had really done was prepare the dead for burial. She loved to do this. It was a kind of victory to feel young and alive when you had death lurking about. As soon as a patient passed away, Brunhilda took over. She went to his room and locked the door. Then she pressed down his eyelids with coins, tied a handkerchief under his chin, bathed him, and dressed him in his best clothes. If the patient was female, she carefully brushed the woman's hair, put nylons on her legs, and slipped heels on her feet. Once she told me how she had had to struggle to pull a girdle on a lady who was overweight and whose relatives would have been disheartened had she not looked her best. Brunhilda's description gave me goose bumps.

Brunhilda would console the relatives and tell them not to worry, that soon their loved one wouldn't look sick or old at all. They would be in tears and hardly anyone would dare look at the body. They would stare at the floor as they recited the Rosary and waited for the undertaker to carry their loved one away. They would sneak a look now and then, however, and discover that Brunhilda was right. As soon as the body cooled and the flesh began to get hard, the sunken cheeks filled out, the rings under the eyes disappeared, and all the wrinkles of age slowly vanished from the deceased's face so that Grandfather or Grandmother ended up looking like a pale young man or young woman who had simply fainted away.

A year after Damián passed away, Chaguito was working in the garden and felt a heavy pressure in his chest. An intense pain seared his left shoulder and arm; even his teeth and jaw felt as if they were on fire. He keeled over into the rose bush he had been pruning and passed out. When he came to, he was in the intensive-care unit of the Hospital de las Siervas de María, where he would remain for two weeks. When Abuelo returned home, Aurelio said to Brunhilda: "Please take good care of Father. You know how much he loves you, and I assure you we'll make it worth your while." Brunhilda smiled and answered warmly: "Don't worry, Aurelio. I'll do my best."

Abuelo Chaguito had to stay in bed and rest as much as possible. The attack had done considerable damage, and if he didn't take care of himself, he could die of massive heart failure. "At least Brunhilda has had some experience as a nurse. She can keep your nitroglycerin handy, take your blood pressure, and bring you the bedpan at night so you don't have to get up," Aurelio told Abuelo reassuringly. "And I can fly here from San Juan in an hour if you get sick."

Abuelo was almost completely deaf. I think he went deaf on purpose so as not to have to listen to Brunhilda's constant cackle—which is what her silvery laughter had turned into. He looked skeptically at Father, but he didn't say anything. Brunhilda had very little patience with him. She slept in a bed next to his but when he needed to pee at night he never dared to wake her up. She'd bring him the bedpan, and then, as he tried to urinate, she would pinch his arms and whack his ribs, telling him to hurry up because she was exhausted and needed to go back to bed. Abuelo Chaguito was a gentleman, and above all, he was a fireman of La Concordia. He would never complain to Aurelio about Brunhilda.

One night Abuelo Chaguito awoke with an acute fibrillation. His heart was racing like a hare's, but he didn't wake Brunhilda up. If he was dying, he preferred to die in peace. He looked around in the dark and saw that she had lit a votive candle in front of the plaster image of the Sacred Heart on top of his dresser. The image made him shudder because Christ's heart, which was exposed in the center of His chest, was bleeding as if it were a pomegranate and someone were squeezing it. He looked away, trying to calm himself, and he tried to think of pleasant things. He began to imagine La Concordia's streets, and in his mind he went walking up and down its elegant sidewalks, admiring the beautiful buildings. He remembered the day he arrived from Santiago de Cuba and first noticed that the streets were named after the Masonic virtues: Calle Fraternidad, Calle Hermandad, Calle Armonía. How happy it had made him feel! He sensed he had come home.

He meditated on the many happy coincidences in his life. In his heart, he was already a Freemason—like his father and his father's father before him—when he arrived in La Concordia. Then his sons had become Freemasons and had built the Star Cement plant, cement being the mason's material par excellence. Thanks to Star Cement, the city was in a constant state of development, a living organism, changing and transforming itself. Its buildings kept growing ever higher and lovelier, like flowers blooming in a tall vase. Chaguito was terribly proud of La Concordia. It was his city. He had saved it from destruction as a fireman and then had helped rebuild it many times.

He didn't want to die, because he didn't want to leave it. In the more than seventy-five years he had lived in Puerto Rico he had been away only once—when he traveled to New York and Chicago to take Celia to the convent. His children and his grandchildren, on the other hand, had traveled all over the world and then they had all left town. Aurelio still lived in Las Bougainvilleas, but since Vernet Construction had moved to San Juan, he practically lived there also. Ulises had shot off like a cannonball to Florida. Amparo had gone to live in Maracai with her husband. Then Roque had committed suicide and Damián had died of a heart attack. His grandchildren, too, had dispersed. Both Alvaro and I had gotten married and were living in San Juan. Rodrigo and Catalina had settled in Florida. Enrique had committed suicide, and Eduardo had disappeared with his father's money.

Abuelo couldn't understand why his children and grandchildren had all moved away. When he left Santiago de Cuba, Chaguito was dirt-poor and had barely escaped a bloody war. His children and grandchildren had everything—the best education money could buy, a comfortable situation, good health. And they lived in a democracy, protected by the flag of the United States. But they were like turbines without an axle, running wild all over the world. Why couldn't they be happy in La Concordia? What were they running away from? He didn't know.

Only Celia had stayed, and she visited Abuelo often. He had grown very close to her in the last few years. She was an extraordinary woman, and thanks to her, Abuelo had come to realize that La Concordia was beautiful not only for its buildings but also for its people. They were indestructible. They had suffered one crisis after another: devastating hurricanes, massive migration to the mainland, the collapse of the sugar market, the failures of the local oil refineries and tuna canneries. With the sugarcane industry all but wiped out, the foundry, steel welding, and machine shops had finally closed down. The Star Cement plant was still operating, but the rising cost of electricity meant it was just scraping by.

When the foundry had gone bankrupt the port area had turned into a dreadful slum. The houses of the workers became shacks and hundreds of new ones sprouted up in the marshes nearby, where land didn't belong to anyone because it was deemed uninhabitable. These homes were set on stilts and made of wood, with tin roofs covered with stones. Abuelo asked Tía Celia what the stones were for and she explained that the youngsters threw them whenever they saw a stranger, so angry were they at the world.

Celia visited the slum every day, jumping from board to board over the stinking quagmire and avoiding the rocks that flew her way. She

opened a medical dispensary next to Vernet Construction. Later, Celia added a Center of Orientation and Services to the dispensary, and
then a School for Arts and Crafts. She didn't want to mention religion, because she knew that, in the heated atmosphere of the slum, to
talk about sin and repentance would have been to sink the ship before
it set sail. By 1970 her School for Arts and Crafts had become a
university with hundreds of students and achieved academic accred-
itation at the national level by the Middle States Association Board.
Abuelo Chaguito was so impressed he gave Celia's missionary center
every penny he could hide from Brunhilda.

As he lay sleepless in his bed thinking of La Concordia's troubles,
Abuelo Chaguito remembered Tía Celia and slowly a peaceful smile
spread across his lips. His heart quieted down, and he fell asleep.

Abuelo Chaguito didn't open his eyes until late the next morning—to the rumble of a cement mixer outside his bedroom window.
He didn't have to see it to know what it was: the sound of gravel
mixed with sand, cement powder, and water going round and round
inside the giant cylinder was the most beautiful sound in the world.
Brunhilda had long since gotten up, so he rang the bell next to his
bed and Amalia, the maid, knocked on the door. He asked her what
was going on.

"It's the workers from the cement plant, sir. They've finally come
to do the job in the garden."

"What job?" Abuelo Chaguito asked, his voice trembling. And he
had Amalia help him out of bed and hand him his cane.

"Doña Brunhilda is redoing the garden, sir. She's modernizing it."

Abuelo Chaguito put on his slippers and his bathrobe and shuffled
out of the bedroom and into the family room as quickly as he could.
He opened the louvered windows and looked out. The workers were
pouring cement, his cement, where Adela's rosebushes had stood.
Chaguito paled and grabbed a chair for support. At that moment,
Brunhilda walked in, a satisfied smile on her face.

"It'll look fine when it's finished, dear. We have so little household
help these days; there's no one to sweep the leaves, and the garden
got into a terrible state while you were ill. But I'm having a decorator
pave the cement with Talavera ceramic tile; it'll be very colorful and
we won't have to sweep leaves anymore."

Abuelo Chaguito went back to bed again, feeling terrible. The pain
in his chest returned, as well as the fibrillation. Aurelio was sum-

moned from San Juan and Alvaro and I flew with him to La Concordia. When we walked into the room an hour and a half later, the doctor was there, and he told us that Abuelo Chaguito was dying. Brunhilda was holding him in her arms and Chaguito was gasping like a fish out of water. He didn't speak, but Father realized he didn't want Brunhilda near him. His arms and chest were covered with bruises, and he looked at us with pleading eyes.

When Brunhilda saw Aurelio, she got up from the bed and left the room. We all stood around Abuelo and held his hands. The doctor began to massage Chaguito's chest vigorously, and a nurse gave him a shot of nitroglycerin. "Go on, Doctor, keep trying, keep trying! Don't give up!" Abuelo kept saying. "Life is a precious gift—it must be saved at all costs!"

But it was no use. The heart attack was massive and Chaguito eventually fell silent. Aurelio closed his father's eyes gently, but he refused to cry. Abuelo Chaguito had passed on like a true fireman, his courage undaunted.

PART VI

THE I WITHIN THE EYE

Telling a story goes hand in hand with the knowledge of life: the knowledge of oneself, in oneself, by oneself.

—SCHEHERAZADE, *A Thousand and One Nights*

FIFTY-FOUR

XOCHIL'S CONVERSE SNEAKERS

Mother's difficulties with the servants at our house grew worse as Father's political campaigns intensified. A new servant would begin working at 1 Avenida Cañafístula, impressed by the fact that she was employed by the handsome Aurelio Vernet, whose photograph was plastered on all the fences and walls of La Concordia. She was usually a slender, humbly dressed young woman from the slums with a glow on her cheeks, fresh red lips, and the cleft between her breasts clearly visible above her uniform's starched white apron. But a week didn't go by before Mother was getting into an argument with the new maid because she had come into the master bedroom without knocking or had brushed too close to Father when she was serving the table and had stared at him doe-eyed.

When more than a dozen local girls had come and gone, Mother convinced Father that they should hire someone from Guatemala.

American companies—the tuna canneries and transistor-radio factories that had sprung up around La Concordia in the fifties and that employed only women—had completely spoiled the working population. They all had to be paid the minimum wage as well as social security, they answered back tartly if you corrected them, and they wanted to go out on the town every Friday and Saturday night. But Guatemala was undeveloped enough that a young working girl was sure to be unspoiled. She would be submissive and obedient and work for a lot less.

Father contacted an agency in New York that brought temporary immigrant workers into the country with the aid of a subagency based in Guatemala City. He said he was willing to pay for her ticket and whatever expenses the trip might entail. My parents had never traveled to Central or South America and knew very little about those areas; it never occurred to them that Xochil Martínez, the girl the employee agency finally contracted for us, might be an Indian. At the time, very few well-to-do people in La Concordia had visited Central America, which they supposed was a lot like the island. We had enough backwardness at home, Mother said: telephones often didn't work, water came out muddy from the tap whenever it rained heavily, and roads were often unpaved. When Father had time, we always traveled to Europe and the United States, treating ourselves to vacations in civilized countries.

Mother was eager to show the new maid off to her friends, the ladies of her sewing club, Las Tijerillas. But when Xochil stepped out of the family car, Mother almost fainted. Xochil looked like an Olmec idol. She was solidly built, with slanting eyes and a flattened nose, her round head resting on her shoulders as if she didn't have a neck. She spoke hardly any Spanish. She wore a beautiful Mayan *huipil*, a square-cut robe embroidered with birds and stars that reached below her knees—and she carried all her belongings in a satchel. What impressed Mother the most were Xochil's feet, which were bare and as big as a baby elephant's. She had walked barefoot from the edge of the forest of Petén to Guatemala City. Once there, she had approached the first Catholic church she saw, showing the priest the letter from the employment agency in New York and the special permit the immigration authorities had sent her in the Petén and asking him if he could please take her to the airport. The priest complied, and soon Xochil Martínez was on her way to the island.

When Xochil arrived at our house in Las Bougainvilleas, she smiled sweetly and walked softly to the kitchen, where she sat down to have some lunch. She hadn't eaten anything on the plane, she said, because she was afraid of getting sick. Mother served her a plate of rice and beans and a fried pork chop, which Xochil thoroughly enjoyed.

Xochil was obedient and submissive and always tried her best to please Mother. But she had never seen a telephone and was too terrified to answer when it rang. At night, she never listened to the radio or watched television: she sat by herself in the garden, singing softly in Mayan and weaving beautiful grasshoppers, butterflies, and hummingbirds with the palm leaf stalks she picked from the garden. She didn't like to sleep indoors in the stifling heat of the servant's room but took her *metate* outside, where on clear nights she slept under the fan-leafed breadfruit tree, a beatific expression on her face.

Mother decided to make the best of the situation. She disliked fat people, because they offended her Emajaguas aesthetic sensibility, so she put Xochil on a diet. She locked the cupboard in the pantry and ordered the cook to serve the new girl only a small portion of rice and beans, a small salad, and a *tostón* at lunchtime every day. A glass of milk at dinnertime and another one at breakfast would complete the menu.

Xochil didn't complain but quietly obeyed Mother. She had been on a diet for a week and had already lost ten pounds when one afternoon a political *cacique* from one of the nearby towns brought Father a magnificent stalk of *guineos manzanos* as sweet as honey. There must have been more than fifty short, thick bananas on it, and they were so ripe they were already beginning to burst through their delicate yellow skins. Their white flesh was partly visible and their luscious aroma filled the whole house. The *cacique* gave Xochil the bananas to put away in the kitchen cupboard while he sat down to talk to Father on the veranda. Mother was taking a nap, and the cook had already left for the day, so Xochil was left alone with her terrible temptation. When Mother woke from her nap and came into the kitchen to help Xochil with dinner, she found her unconscious on the floor, having consumed fifty *guineos manzanos* on an empty stomach.

Xochil eventually lost fifty pounds, and Mother was able to dress her up in a size fourteen starched white uniform with lace edging on the collar and sleeves, but she still couldn't show her off to Las

Tijerillas. Xochil's feet were so large that no shoes fit her. Mother took her to all the stores in La Concordia, but women's shoes simply didn't come in her size. Xochil couldn't serve the table barefoot— that would have been unthinkable. Mother was practically in tears about the whole situation.

One day I hit on a solution. I took Xochil to La Concordia's sports shop and told the salesman to bring us a pair of Converse sneakers size fifteen and a half EEE, the kind basketball players wear. Xochil put them on and they fit like a glove. After that she was able to serve the table at teatime and pass the silver tray with the dainty asparagus rolls and the creamy chicken puffs to Mother's elegant lady friends.

Xochil lasted two years with us, longer than any young woman from La Concordia's slums, without a word of protest ever issuing from her lips. But one day when she had saved enough, she quietly disappeared.

THE CARDINAL'S DINNER SERVICE

Mother worried that Father was going to drive us into bank-ruptcy. In 1944 he had spent a fortune on his ill-fated cam-paign for mayor of La Concordia, and in 1948 Bishop MacFarland had sweet-talked the Vernet brothers into donating the land for the Universidad de las Mercedes, plus three hundred thousand dollars more for a science building. Mother didn't believe in throwing money away on politics, but she was glad to help out the Church; the uni-versity was certainly a worthy cause. Philanthropy, however, should be practiced in an orderly fashion.

As a Rivas de Santillana, Mother felt it was her duty to be thrifty. But the Vernets had made more money than she was capable of com-prehending. Instinct told her that she was in a dangerous situation. Once you were a millionaire it was very easy to lose control. You were awash in your money like a sailor on a raft: wherever you looked there was a wave of cash drifting away from you, and there was no way to control the direction of the swells. So Mother stuck to her frugal ways; she never spent a penny more than was necessary and lived as she had before.

Whenever she went shopping, Mother always bargained. There was nothing unusual in this at the Plaza del Mercado, where housewives haggled with the fruit and vegetable vendors for hours, trying to save a few pennies. But Mother did the same thing when she went shopping in the elegant department stores and boutiques of La Concordia, where no one ever discussed money. She bought her clothes on sale whenever possible, and when she visited an expensive shoe store, she always asked if they had any samples left. Samples were the shoes the mannequins in the windows wore, which were usually so small they didn't fit anybody and thus were disposed of for a pittance. Mother wore a size five and she always took advantage of it. Her beautiful Papagallo and Bally shoes never cost her more than four dollars.

A few days before the laying of the cornerstone of La Universidad de Las Mercedes, Father asked Mother to prepare a formal buffet dinner at home; he wanted to celebrate the event in style. Cardinal Spellman was coming from New York to bless the foundations of the new buildings, and Bishop MacFarland and a dozen other Church dignitaries would also be present. At least thirty dinner guests were expected. Mother had the best catering service in town prepare the food: Cornish game hens stuffed with wild rice, shrimp jambalaya, and a special "prime blue-ribbon" roast beef flown in on ice from New York. She ordered her silver trays polished and her Venetian glassware rinsed. But when Mother took out her Lenox dinner service, she realized she had only twenty-four place settings, and she rushed to El Imperio, the best department store in La Concordia, to see if they had a set to match hers. They did. One had just arrived and they were exhibiting it in the store's main show window. Turquoise-blue, the plates had a delicate twenty-four-carat gold scroll around the rim. It was very expensive, but Mother loved it. She took it home on approval, to see how it looked next to the Lenox set she already owned.

Aurelio was excited about the new university, and the day before the dinner he went to La Concordia to shop for wine and champagne. He met half a dozen friends hurrying down the street and invited them all to come to the party the following evening. When Mother found out, she was furious. "What will Cardinal Spellman think of the Vernets when he walks up to the buffet table, plate in hand, and the roast beef is carved to the bone? We'll never live it down!" She made Aurelio telephone his three brothers that night and tell them and their wives not to serve themselves any roast beef.

Ulises, Venecia, Damián, Agripina, Celia, and Roque laughed the whole thing off. They knew how impulsive Father was and how he loved inviting guests to his house at the last minute. The following evening they served themselves only salad and bread and stood to the side drinking wine and champagne and talking among themselves while everybody lined up in front of the buffet. But Tía Clotilde took her beautiful turquoise Lenox plate with its golden scroll, walked up to the table, and served herself a juicy slice of roast beef. When he saw what Tía Clotilde was doing, Aurelio hurried over to her and whispered that Cardinal Spellman still hadn't served himself and that she should put the meat back on the platter. Tía Clotilde was furious. She set her plate down with a bang, took Roque by the arm, and steered him out of the house just as Cardinal Spellman was pronouncing the benediction. Still, dinner was a success and when Cardinal Spellman left, he extended to Mother his beautiful amethyst ring to kiss and blessed Aurelio, Alvaro, and me, gently placing his hands on our heads.

By three o'clock in the morning Mother still hadn't been able to fall sleep. She tossed and turned, thinking of the extravagant Lenox dinner set that she didn't really need. The set had cost three hundred dollars, which now had to be added to the three million the Vernets had donated in land and to the three hundred thousand they had donated for the science building. Clarissa felt that the family had gone overboard and that it was her duty to economize. So the next day she carefully packed the Lenox dinner set in its crate again and had it taken back to El Imperio, where she asked for a credit because the design of the plates hadn't blended in with her own, after all.

A few days later Tía Clotilde was in town to do some errands and she went by El Imperio. She was amazed to see Mother's turquoise-and-gold dinner service exhibited in the window as an exclusive new arrival. She went in and asked for the manager. "Did you sell an identical dinner service to Clarissa Vernet a few days ago?" she asked, pointing to the window, her face wooden. "No," the manager answered. "This dinner service is very expensive. Our store ordered only one. But we did let Mrs. Vernet take the plates home overnight on approval, because she wanted to see if they matched her own." Clotilde arched her eyebrows and looked at the woman with venomous eyes. "The whole Roman Curia ate off those plates three nights ago," she said vindictively. "Clarissa Vernet gave a dinner for Cardinal Spellman and thirty-odd priests at her home, and he ate roast beef, wild rice, and shrimp jambalaya on them. I know, because I was there. Are you still going to sell the dinner service as if it were new?"

The manager was astonished and immediately telephoned Mother. She rushed to the store, paid for the dishes in cash, and took them home with her. The story soon spread to the rest of La Concordia's more fashionable commercial establishments and Mother never again dared take anything home on approval or even ask for a discount. But whenever we traveled to New York and went shopping for clothes at Bergdorf's or Saks Fifth Avenue, she couldn't resist temptation and always asked the salesladies in the designer salon for a discount, to my embarrassment.

FIFTY-SIX

THE FAMILY'S SACKS OF GOLD

In May 1956 I graduated from Danbury Hall, and in the fall I entered Saint Helen's College. During my four college years—from 1956 to 1960—I studied hard and lived an austere life. Saint Helen's was very different from what it is today. Then it was an all-girls' college run by nuns. Students slept in army-style iron cots, there were no rugs on the bedroom floors, and you had to step on cold cement when you got out of bed in the morning to go to the one bathroom at the end of the hall. When I took my granddaughter there on a recent visit, I marveled at the aqua wall-to-wall carpets, nice soft mattresses, and beautiful tiled bathrooms shared by adjoining suites. But the spartan conditions of Saint Helen's were good for me, if only because at home my parents spoiled me so much.

Since Saint Helen's was a Catholic school, I would get salutary doses of religion. Father regretted having yielded to Abuelo Chaguito's Masonic promptings and sent me to Danbury. Thanks to Bishop MacFarland, he had become conservative and now went to Mass and Holy Communion regularly, following in Abuela Adela's footsteps. Saint Helen's was a forty-five-minute train ride from New York City, that den of sin and iniquity, and my parents were terrified that I would venture there without a chaperon or, worse, accompanied by crazy Irish girls looking for a bar and a good time. But unlike nondenominational colleges and sophisticated universities like Stanford or Berkeley, Saint Helen's allowed its students' parents to choose to have their girls confined to campus. Every weekend, when Saint Helen's rolling acres were as deserted as the Russian tundra, I had to stay in my dorm. I could get together only with the Turkish, Arab, and Japanese girls whose parents were as conservative as mine, or sign up to go to the movies in town with one of the school's chaperons.

Fortunately, my isolation was countered by my deep interest in my studies. I was fascinated by Abd ar-Rahman III, the great Umayyad emir of tenth-century Spain; the French poets Pierre Ronsard and Paul Verlaine; the anthropologists Ruth Benedict and Margaret Mead. So passionate was I that in winter I would sometimes strap tennis rackets to my shoes to trek to the library through the drifts of snow. But when I returned to La Concordia for summer vacations, I didn't open a single book. I got up at ten and slept in a French Provincial bed with gold trim. My room had a V'soske carpet and a Venetian chandelier. Summer threw me into a whirlwind of social activities and I was invited to parties almost every night. I had dozens of ball gowns and went on daylong picnics with friends to Isla de Pargos on the *Chaguito*, the sixty-foot Norseman yacht that the Vernets all shared. Anyone would have thought I was the happiest girl in the world. I was bored to death.

As soon as I arrived home for summer vacation, I was recruited for Father's political campaign, which was now active even between elections. It was more interesting than going to the parties of the girls and boys my age. I enjoyed the banquets and balls, the small-town stumping, the caravans and parades. I loved to appear by his side, beautifully coiffed and dressed in an Oscar de la Renta outfit. Mother went to many of these events also, but she stayed in the background, dressed in black and holding on to her precious anonymity. The futility of these outings wasn't lost on me: ladies weren't allowed to speak at rallies or to meet the people from the towns to discuss with

them the issues at hand. We simply stood next to the political candidate, smiling, adding beauty and respectability to his image. I was
so desperate for a career, however, that I hoped that some of Father's
charisma would rub off on me.

My quarrels with Clarissa during those four years escalated from
mere skirmishes to full-blown battles. I had a voluptuous physique. I
was six inches taller than Clarissa and wore size ten shoes. My hips
were wide, and I had a hard time keeping my generous breasts inside
my bathing suit because I didn't just lie about like the rest of my
friends, sunning myself at the pool; I liked to dive and swim. I loved
sports and played a lot of basketball and lacrosse at Saint Helen's and
had developed strong thighs and calves. Having been away from home
for years, I had become a stranger to Mother. She wasn't sure who
this giant of a daughter was anymore.

When she saw me dancing with a boyfriend, the romantic memory
of the love she had experienced in the garden at Emajaguas when
Father had courted her vanished like a mist. My kind of love wasn't
a spiritual affair like Rima's in *Green Mansions*, an emotion as delicate
as the flutter of a bird's wings. She saw it as an avid grasping of the
flesh, a prosaic grappling of the sexual organs—an image undoubtedly
nursed by the steamy, provocative films of the period: *East of Eden*,
A Streetcar Named Desire, and *Cat on a Hot Tin Roof*.

In my mind the difference between sex and love was clear. I hadn't
read Margaret Mead in vain. In spite of the nuns' fascist rules at Saint
Helen's there were always opportunities to see boys alone—for example, when I stayed overnight at a friend's house. I thought about
sex all the time—it was like a flame burning inside me, something
I'd never felt before. It lit up everything around me, got rid of the
cobwebs, and energized me. But it was far too dangerous to indulge
in.

The minute I arrived back in Las Bougainvilleas for the summer,
Clarissa would let me know who was in control. I couldn't step out
of the door without asking her permission, and I had to go to all the
parties with a companion—usually Clarissa herself or one of my girlfriends' mothers. Clarissa would sit close to the dance floor scrutinizing my every move, and if she saw me dancing a bolero too close to
my partner—riveted limb to limb, the way I liked—she would get up
from her chair, draw near to where we were swaying dreamily to
Rafael Muñoz's "Perfume de Gardenias" or Lucho Gatica's "Piel Ca-

nela," and separate us with a sharp push. Then, in the privacy of the ladies' room, she would lecture me on how a well-brought-up young lady didn't let a man rub his penis against her thigh. Finally she would take a little lace handkerchief out of her purse and spread it across my low-cut dress. I hated her then and wished with all my heart that she would die.

Soon, of course, the rumor flew around town that Mother was some kind of sexual Gestapo, and young men were afraid to ask me to dance. This was made worse by the fact that I was the daughter of an important public figure. All of a sudden I became a wallflower, off-bounds to boys my age. I could dance only with my "official" partners, the political aides who accompanied us to all the parties. Weeks passed and the telephone at home never rang.

Father wanted to keep me shut up like a jewel in a silk-lined boudoir, just as he had kept Mother. My problem was that I wanted someone as bright, good-looking, and kind as he, but with a different name.

In July 1958, I was selected carnival queen again, this time of San Juan Casino. The theme of the ball would be "The Printed Word" and everything related to it: all the letters of the alphabet, of course, books, magazines, newspapers, tabloids, gazettes; as well as printing presses, rotary presses, handpresses, flatbed presses, roller presses, electrotype presses, rotogravure presses. The ingenuity of San Juan's social set was taxed to the extreme as well-to-do parents rushed to come up with appropriate costumes for their children. The carnival was important for Father's new gubernatorial campaign: reporters from all the newspapers on the island would be present at the ball. There would be maximum exposure for the father of the queen, which would come in handy for fund-raising.

This time I would be attired in a black sheath and train, making my entrance in the casino's ballroom as Lady Ink, my costume embroidered with hundreds of shimmering onyx beads, symbolizing ink drops; and on my head I'd carry a cut-crystal urn, supposedly my inkwell. For weeks I had to go through the whole rigmarole of rehearsing the coronation, practicing the waltz, going for fittings. I took everything very seriously and didn't find any of this ridiculous, since I was helping Father. But I was getting tired of being trotted out like a mannequin each summer and swore this would be the last time.

Since I was older now, I would no longer be escorted by Father.

Instead I was assigned a king, Víctor Matienzo, a tall, gangly bachelor with a nose as large as De Gaulle's but a brain considerably smaller. We went to several preball cocktail parties together and he bored me so badly I had a hard time suppressing my yawns. Years later I learned he didn't like women at all.

My parents and I had just come into the casino's ballroom the night of the coronation when the orchestra began to play "*Lágrimas Negras*"—"Ink Tears"—the song Víctor and I were supposed to waltz to. Unfortunately, my headdress weighed at least ten pounds and was beginning to give me a headache, so I went to get some aspirin. When I walked back to where my parents were standing I overheard Mother say something that stopped me in my tracks: "We have to be careful now that you're a candidate for governor again. As long as Elvira is with Víctor she's all right, but unfortunately he won't be her partner through the evening. The young men buzzing around her could be scoundrels. They're probably more interested in our money and position than they are in her."

I flushed with anger but controlled myself.

After Víctor and I danced the waltz, which marked the beginning of the ball, I excused myself and said I had to go to the ladies' room to freshen up. Clarissa followed me. She was about to pinch me and take out her little lace handkerchief to tuck into my plunging neckline when I asked her angrily if she was covering up my breasts or the family's sacks of gold.

Clarissa was furious. She lifted her hand to slap me, but I stopped her in midair. It was easy; I towered above her, and for a second I saw my own hatred shining back at me in her eyes. Then something terrible happened: Mother cringed and began to cry.

I walked out of the ladies' room trembling. That was the last time Mother tried to hit me, and I was never afraid of her again.

I refused to attend any more parties or political gatherings that summer and decided to get a job. I worked as a volunteer at the Municipal Children's Hospital in the mornings and as a proofreader at *El Listín Noticioso*, a small local newspaper, in the afternoons. Then I did some scouting around town and published several articles, one of them about the old cemetery of La Concordia, which was shamefully neglected because of the town's fiscal crisis; I had seen dogs chewing human bones there. But since Father had recently acquired the newspaper—after the success of my coronation ball he realized the importance of the press in a political campaign—the editor believed he was doing me a favor and didn't give me any encouragement or pay me for my work. I left the job, and the summer dragged on like a sack of stones until, thankfully, September came around again and I left for Saint Helen's. There I could live and study all I wanted, and no one knew who Father was.

FIFTY-SEVEN

REBELLION AT THE BEAU RIVAGE

In the spring of my junior year I wrote a letter to Father asking him to let me attend the University of Geneva during the summer. Alvaro, who was at Princeton, had done the same thing the summer before, and he had spent three months studying French at the Sorbonne, living by himself in Paris. Saint Helen's offered an exchange program in Geneva and I could take French courses for credit.

I wanted to go on studying and get a doctorate in English literature when I graduated from Saint Helen's. Graduate students could live in boardinghouses; they didn't have to stay in dorms, and there were no rules for parents to enforce. In the States, women were considered adults at twenty-one and could do more or less what they wanted— find a job and live by themselves, for example. Only in places like Iran, Saudi Arabia, and Puerto Rico were they treated like little girls until they were so old no one cared anymore.

Several girls I knew at Saint Helen's were going to study in Geneva that summer also and would live in a boardinghouse near the university campus; we could keep one another company. Father agreed but suggested I accompany Mother and him on the first leg of a European trip they themselves had planned. First we would go to England and France, then to Switzerland, where he promised to drop me off in Geneva at the university at the beginning of July. I could stay there by myself for two months and at the end of August fly directly to New York after finishing my courses.

Everything went as planned, and we arrived in Geneva from Paris after having spent the night on the train. We stayed at the Beau Rivage, a beautiful hotel on the shores of Lake Geneva with red geraniums on the windowsills and an elegant restaurant overlooking the water. A wide marble staircase led from the terrace to the suites on the first floor where we were staying. The lake's famous geyser was clearly visible from my window. It fluttered in the wind like a huge ostrich feather, gracefully swaying this way and that over the silvery water. We were having lunch on the terrace two days later, under a Martini & Rossi umbrella, when I said to Father: "I've contacted my friends from Saint Helen's and I have all the information for the French courses I need—they look fascinating. I can move to the student pension tomorrow; my bags are all packed."

Father looked around, as if he hadn't heard what I said.

"Look who's sitting at the table next to ours," he whispered to Clarissa, smiling conspiratorially. "It's Grace Kelly, and that's Prince Rainier sitting next to her."

"You're right!" Clarissa answered, a little too naïvely. "And I think I recognize the Shah of Iran a few tables down, with Farah Diba. *How exclusive!*"

I looked at Father over the *coupe gelée à trois saveurs* and slowly set my spoon down on the table. I didn't even bother to look at Mother; I already knew what she thought. "You promised, Father. You gave me your word in the letter you wrote me at school," I whispered, my voice full of apprehension.

Father sighed deeply and finally looked at me.

"This is a beautiful hotel, isn't it? I'm sure you don't have a view of the lake from your window at the pension. Your mother and I have decided to stay in Geneva for three weeks so you can be with us. You can still audit the French courses at the university. You don't really need those credits, and in three weeks you can learn all you need."

"I'm twenty years old, Father. I can take care of myself. I want to take those courses for credit and stay at the pension with my friends."

Clarissa aimed one of her flamethrower looks in my direction. "Your father never changes. He's always making promises he can't keep. You're not staying by yourself at the pension and that's final. I never did such a thing, and you won't either. It's the duty of a well-brought-up young lady to sacrifice herself and obey her parents. You can't throw your reputation to the wind."

A cold breeze rose from the lake as I sat there stone-faced. I was pondering the many meanings of the word *sacrifice*. For Tía Celia it had meant celibacy *and* freedom; she had taken a vow of chastity but she had also lived a life full of adventure and had traveled all over the world, going where she was most needed. Mother had remained a hostage at Emajaguas until Father came along. Then she had willingly entered another prison, the house on Avenida Cañafístula. I was supposed to follow in her footsteps—except that my jailer might not be as kind as Father.

I got up from the table and slowly walked up the wide marble staircase that led to my room on the first floor. As I went up I opened my handbag and searched for my wallet, saw it was empty, and threw it over the banister. Then I took out the key to my room. I confirmed that I had no passport or plane ticket in my purse; Father had taken them both, to keep them safe for me. So I threw my purse over the railing also, and it fell down the stairwell with a clatter and landed on the restaurant floor. When I got to the landing I walked down the hall to my room and took out my suitcase. I opened it wide and emptied its entire contents over the banister. My Saks Fifth Avenue shoes, my lace Blackton panties and bras, my Ceil Chapman dresses all landed on the heads of Grace Kelly, Prince Rainier, the Shah, Farah Diba, Mother and Father, and the rest of the exclusive guests of the Beau Rivage. When the suitcase was empty I threw it over the banister as well, but luckily for me it fell on one of the waiters and not on the head of Prince Rainier.

Then I slowly walked down the stairs and back to our table, where Father and Mother stood staring at me. As the alarmed guests whispered among themselves, I sat down and finished my ice cream. That night I swore I was not going to be like Clarissa; I would never sacrifice myself.

FIFTY-EIGHT

CLARISSA'S PASSING

Recuerde el alma dormida,
avive el seso y despierte
contemplando
cómo se pasa la vida
cómo se viene la muerte
tan callando.

—JORGE MANRIQUE,
"Coplas a la muerte de su padre"

That November Aurelio ran for governor against Fernando Martín a second time and was defeated once more. Martín's popularity was overwhelming: he had dominated island politics for twenty-four years. Mother gave a sigh of relief. She didn't mind Father's obsession with politics as long as his chances of winning were nonexistent. I suspect Father himself was relieved. Running against Martín had become something of a futile effort, like trying to bring down an elephant with an air rifle. Nobody expected Father to win, but in the meantime they admired him for his heroic attempt.

Over Christmas vacation I met Ricardo Cáceres, a young man from a good family in San Juan. Ricardo was studying business administration at Cornell University, and he would soon be graduating. He planned to work with his father in the family's insurance company. Father and Mother couldn't find anything wrong with him.

Ricardo was serious and determined. He wasn't a playboy or a candidate for some fledgling political post, like so many of the young men I had met during the past few summers in La Concordia and San Juan. Ricardo and I went out a few times during our short stay on the island, and after we returned to our respective colleges in the States, he came to Saint Helen's to visit me several times. At the end of the semester he proposed to me. It was spring, just before graduation, and we were taking a stroll around the campus. The flower beds were full of tulips, but they hadn't bloomed yet. A few days later all of them would open, and the campus would look as if hundreds of elves were clapping.

Ricardo had just given me his Cornell ring, and I put it on my finger.

"Will you marry me after we graduate?" he asked.

"Will we live in San Juan?"

"Of course. That's where Father's business is."

"I'll think about it," I said, without looking at him.

Holding hands, we walked silently to a far corner of the campus, where a complicated hedge of boxwood was pruned to perfection. I took a deep breath. I wondered why I loved the smell of boxwood; I suppose it made me feel at home—trapped in a beautiful labyrinth. We kissed passionately behind some bushes. My life had no direction, but with Ricardo maybe I'd melt right off the surface of the earth.

Ricardo was very traditional: he wanted a wife with whom he could enjoy sex, a woman who would bear his children and take care of his house. He definitely was not the intellectual type. I agreed about the sex, but I wasn't sure about the rest. I kept my thoughts to myself, however, and pretended to be exactly what Ricardo had in mind.

During that last Christmas vacation in Las Bougainvilleas I had told my parents: "When I graduate from Saint Helen's College in

June, I want to go on studying and get a doctorate in English literature. I've applied to Harvard and I think I have a good chance of being accepted." It was late Sunday morning and we were sitting out on the terrace. We had just come back from Mass and were waiting for Tío Damián and Tía Agripina, who were joining us for lunch. The scarlet bougainvilleas were in full bloom and the wall around the garden was covered with an exuberant mantle. Father was feeding his nightingale some grapes and was standing next to the large aluminum cage with his back to me. He said nothing.

I thought it was about time a Vernet–Rivas de Santillana girl had her own career. Abuela Valeria had grown up illiterate because of Bartolomeo Boffil's selfishness, and for that reason she had insisted on her daughters' having a university education—an extraordinary thing at the time. But it seemed that their education was an end in itself; marriage was the only possible career for women. Even Clarissa, who had been such an enthusiast in her defense of women's education when she was at the University of Puerto Rico, had given up in the end. And in Father's family it was even worse. Tía Amparo had gone only as far as high school and Tía Celia had become a nun to pursue a career as social worker disguised as missionary.

More than twenty years had passed since Tía Celia's rebellion, but things hadn't changed at all. The idea of a single girl from a good family finding a job and living by herself in a place like New York or Boston and earning her own salary (without becoming a nun) was out of the question. My doctorate was the only way to postpone my return to La Concordia and escape my family's influence.

"What on earth do you want to go on studying for?" Mother answered with a little laugh as she took a sip of her vermouth. "You don't have to work, you don't need the money! Don't tell me you prefer New York's grim weather to our sunny Decembers! Maybe if you wanted to study something practical like accounting, nursing, or even agronomy . . . But literature is different: you can read all the books you want in your father's library. You've been away from home for eight years now, dear. It's time you spent some time with us."

She said it with affection; I realized Mother had missed me, and for a moment I was almost convinced that she wanted me by her side. But our disagreements had been going on for too long, and I was unable to feel sorry for her. I remembered a story I had read long ago called "The River's Orphan." In it a little girl's mother drowns herself in a river. Every day the girl goes to the riverbank and stares into the water, hoping her mother will come back. The little girl sees only herself, but as time goes by she resembles her mother more and more. Finally she is sure her mother has returned because the image in the water looks just like her, and she reaches out her hand to help her mother back to shore. But the little girl loses her footing and falls into the river and drowns. I was terrified the same thing might happen to me. Mother needed help, but so did I.

When I saw there was no alternative but to come back home and live with my family, I accepted Ricardo Cáceres's proposal of marriage. At least I would be warden of my prison and live in my own house. The wedding took place in August at the cathedral in La Concordia. We had a reception at the house on Avenida Cañafístula, but I didn't feel like celebrating. I didn't love Ricardo. He had no imagination or artistic sensibility. But he was my door to freedom from Mother's hell.

A few weeks after we were married, Mother sent me four myrtle bushes she had planted herself in empty yellow-and-brown Café Yaucono cans. "Myrtle summons the spirits; when it blooms, ghosts like to gather around it, especially when the rain lets up at night. I brought some of these myrtle bushes with me from Emajaguas when I married your father, and I thought you'd like to plant them at your new home," she had scribbled on the back of a used envelope. "Plant them near your open window or on your balcony. That way you'll be able to smell them at night, and they'll give your house a cozy, lived-in feeling." I did as Mother suggested.

Clarissa liked Ricardo. They were both born under the sign of Capricorn, and they got along famously from the start. Ricardo had a strong character and Mother respected that; she felt I needed someone who would keep me in check. The only thing she didn't like about Ricardo was his teeth, which were crooked and much too large for the narrow arch of his mouth. Rather than hurt Ricardo's feelings by telling him he should do something about them, she wrote him an anonymous note in her beautiful Palmer script, suggesting that he see an orthodontist. Ricardo didn't say anything to me about the note, but he saw a dentist a few weeks later. A month after he got the note, we went to La Concordia to spend the weekend. When we arrived, Ricardo kissed Mother on the cheek and then smiled widely, a shiny stainless-steel smile. Mother burst out laughing. She knew *he* knew who had written the note.

Mother enjoyed making fun of the American First Ladies with Ricardo. Behind Father's back they compiled an album with photographs from the newspapers. Mother liked Mamie Eisenhower because she was thrifty and never hogged the limelight the way Jackie Kennedy did. She liked Mamie's little straw hats with their white point d'esprit veils floating above her head, and whenever Mother traveled to the States she wore hats just like them. Lady Bird Johnson she disliked the most; she insisted she had no table manners. Whenever Lady Bird was photographed eating, she'd be caught with her mouth wide open, sometimes even sticking a fork into her mouth with a piece of steak at the end, which Mother found disgusting. Once she cut out a photograph of Lady Bird and taped it to the wall next to her bed, it made her laugh so much.

A year after Ricardo and I were married, I went on a cooking strike. "I'm tired of cooking Spanish food. It's too complicated and it takes too much time. From now on," I said to Ricardo one evening, "we're going to eat more Italian and American food: things like spaghetti or broiled steak and mashed potatoes." I would be in graduate school soon at the University of Puerto Rico, and that's all I'd have time for. I'd already signed up for three courses. Ricardo didn't answer but simply went on eating his *bacalao al pil pil*—codfish fried in parsley, one of the delicious recipes his mother had given me—and dipping his bread in the garlicky oil.

The following evening I boiled some spaghetti and made a plain marinara sauce for it, practicing for my upcoming university days. Suddenly, Ricardo took his plate of spaghetti and threw it against the kitchen wall. "I don't like my spaghetti al dente," he yelled as I sat openmouthed, watching the vermicelli in red sauce trickle down the yellow wallpaper like a Jackson Pollock painting. "And I don't want my wife chumming around with male students half her age. You should have asked me before you signed up for those courses."

I still didn't know my way around Ricardo, or if there *was* a way around him. I lowered my head and didn't answer.

I soon realized that Ricardo was a violent, intractable man. If I contradicted him, he yelled and threatened to hit me. But I really grew afraid of him when he began to collect hunting rifles and spend all his free time oiling and cleaning them on the front porch of our house. He had picked up hunting as a hobby and often traveled to Santo Domingo with his friends on birding expeditions.

We remained married for nine years. I did a lot of serious thinking during that time. I realized the folly of deluding myself into believing I could acquire a career by osmosis. We weren't living in England, where the nobility inherited their power by divine right. In Puerto Rico the most I could aspire to be as Father's daughter was carnival queen. Worst of all, I began to feel I had been used. I was thirty-one years old, my self-respect was in shreds, and I had nothing to be proud of. And I was married to a man I hated and feared.

I wanted to get a divorce but I had no money of my own and was too proud to ask my parents. I also feared having to live under the same roof as Mother. First I had belonged to Father and now I was Ricardo's. That's why women understood the politics of colonialism so well: if you treat them well, feed them, clothe them, and buy them a nice house, they won't rebel. Except that hatred keeps smoldering inside them.

I chose Ricardo's physical threats over Mother's psychological battering and decided not to get a divorce. I stayed home, took care of my children, and gave them as much affection as I could. I also read voraciously. I never gave up hope of going back to the university to get a doctorate in literature. But I lived in constant fear that my sons would grow up to be as belligerent as their father. There was simply no way out of the situation. I struggled to keep all the balls in the air while trying to appease Ricardo. In the eyes of San Juan society, I was the perfect wife.

In the meantime, in 1966, something unexpected had happened. Fernando Martín, feeling very sure of himself, announced that a plebiscite would be held so that Puerto Rico could approve commonwealth as its definitive status. Tío Venancio decided the Partido Republicano Incondicional wouldn't participate. The party's constituency had been decreasing steadily, and he was afraid it might be completely wiped out. Father was incensed. Venancio was more concerned about the party and his own position as president than about statehood—*el ideal*. For the first time in his life he fought openly with Tío Venancio. Statehood *had* to be an option at the polls.

He broke with Tío Venancio's Partido Republicano Incondicional and founded his own political party, the Partido Estadista Reformista, which pledged to defend statehood in the plebiscite. In a single year he put together a successful campaign, paying for much of it out of his own pocket.

The plebiscite was a momentous event. The outcome showed the island to be equally divided between those for statehood and those in favor of commonwealth status. All those years the island had been voting for Fernando Martín and against Tío Venancio, not against statehood, as his opponents insisted. Aurelio ran for governor again the following year, but this time it was different. Fernando Martín had retired. The polls indicated that the Partido Estadista Reformista had a good chance of winning. Free of Tío Venancio and of the *colmillús* shadow, Father was running on his own.

Aurelio was having the time of his life. More and more, he enjoyed mixing with the crowds, listening to their grievances and taking note of their needs and wants. He chose the *almácigo* tree as a symbol of his party, a happy choice. In pre-Columbian times the *almácigo* represented the home: the Taíno Indians used its bark to cure all kinds of ills and sometimes thatched their huts with it. He was convinced that life couldn't hold defeat or failure.

As soon as speculation about a possible victory for Father began to spread, Mother became ill. She complained of a sharp pain in her chest that made breathing difficult. A thorough medical examination revealed that her childhood *soplo*, the little murmur in the aorta, had gotten worse. At the same time she had developed calcification of the arteries, and this made her situation very dangerous. Her brain was slowly being deprived of oxygen, and she could have a hemorrhage at any moment. The heart specialist ordered her to remain in bed, inside an oxygen tent.

In the last month of the campaign Mother and Father grew closer than they had ever been. I noticed it every time I went to visit them in Las Bougainvilleas. Father made a point of spending the night at home no matter how far he had to travel during the day to give one of his speeches. They talked for hours—the master bedroom was next to mine, and I could hear their murmuring voices well into the night. In the morning, before he left for his campaign appearances, Father would sit next to Mother's bed and she would tie a little string around his wrist. He couldn't leave until he had described in detail his schedule for the day: the towns he would visit and the number of speeches he would make. She knew she was very ill. It was the only thing she could do in solidarity.

On November 1, 1968, four days before the election was to take place, I was in La Concordia visiting Mother. I tiptoed into her room to see if she was awake. Two oxygen tanks, like steel missiles with pressure valves on them, stood next to her bed. I peeked into the plastic tent spread over it. She lay quietly on her lace pillows, her chest hardly moving, so the oxygen could go straight to her lungs. She had her eyes closed, and there wasn't a single wrinkle on her face. She was sixty-seven, but she didn't look a day over fifty.

Clarissa opened her eyes and smiled at me. I slipped my hand under the tent and held her icy hand in mine. "Are you cold, Mother?" I asked as I tucked Miña's old rainbow-colored serape around her legs.

"No more than usual. I didn't hear you come in, Elvira. When did you arrive from San Juan?"

"Just a few minutes ago. The plane hit a thunderstorm as we flew over the mountains."

"And how is Ricardo?"

I was silent for a few moments, then looked straight at her. "The same as usual, Mother. You know how it is between us."

Clarissa let out a deep sigh. "Ricardo loves you in spite of his bad temper, and the children need their father. You're letting happiness slip through your fingers like sand."

I didn't want to argue with her—we had been over this many times already. But I never dared make a decision; I just hung on. Mother knew what I was thinking.

"No Rivas de Santillana has ever gotten a divorce except for Tía Lakhmé, and everyone knows she's crazy," Mother said. "If you do, your grandparents' ghosts will follow you around and push you down the stairs or in front of a car. Your aunts and uncles will be furious. The whole family will be up in arms. You must be out of your mind, Elvira."

Mother looked at me as if she were at the bottom of a pool, she seemed so far away. Her hair had turned completely white and was cropped closely around her head like a halo.

"Remember those myrtle bushes you sent me years ago, Mother? They're in bloom and my house is full of ghosts. I guess there's something to nature after all, like you always said."

"Really? And do they talk to you?" Clarissa asked me, half in jest.

"They talk to me every day," I answered seriously. "Abuelo Alvaro and Abuela Valeria, Abuelo Chaguito and Abuela Adela pull up their chairs and sit next to me. They tell me to leave Ricardo and go look for a job."

Mother laughed, and looked at me reproachfully.

"Ricardo has been a good husband," she said. "He's a good provider and has never been unfaithful to you. And that's the only reason to get a divorce."

I paced around the room, wanting to say something and not finding the words.

"Tell me something, Elvira," Mother murmured. "All your life you've insisted you were a Vernet. But you have some of Tía Lakhmé in you, because you love beautiful clothes; you've got some of Dido, because you love literature; some of Siglinda, because before you married Ricardo you were crazy about boys. You've got some Rivas de Santillana in you, after all, even if you refuse to acknowledge it."

I was surprised at what she was saying. But she went on: "Having money, a career, is not that important. Nature, the positive current of the universe where everything is interconnected, is what really matters. Our duty is to partake of that unity, not of its differences. To try to understand ourselves and, by the way, to find God. That's why getting a divorce from Ricardo in order to live like an independent woman won't do you any good. You have to be independent in your own soul."

I couldn't bear it anymore. "That's not true!" I whispered desperately. "Don't tell me *you* weren't sorry to sacrifice your career. And you *never* wanted Father to get into politics." She didn't answer.

"Why didn't you try to dissuade him?" I asked. "Wasn't politics a way of being unfaithful to you? Didn't you see how it was harming me? Why have you always kept quiet about everything that really mattered to you . . . to us?"

"Because I love your father. It's important for men to do what they have to do."

"That's bullshit, Mother!"

She fixed an icy gaze on me from behind the transparent tent. "I won't stand your being disrespectful to me," she said in a trembling voice.

"Well, I'm not going to follow your example, Mother. I'm leaving

Ricardo, even if I have to starve. And the children are staying with him. Let *him* take care of them for a change!"

I began to sob as if my soul were being wrenched from my body. "You never loved me, Mother. That's why you were always telling me how much I looked like Father."

All of a sudden I felt Mother's hands as cool as snow on my shoulders. She had pushed aside her plastic cocoon and was pulling me close to her. Then she began to rock me as if I were a child.

"Shhhh! Don't cry, Elvira! Everything will be all right. I said you looked like your father because you liked to hear it so much. But you've always been my spitting image. And I love you very much."

Then she closed her eyes and lay back on her pillows. She was too weak to talk to me anymore, so I tiptoed out of the room.

I flew back to San Juan that same afternoon steeped in sadness, fearing that I had found my mother just when I was about to lose her.

The election had a momentum of its own. Four days after my conversation with Mother, Father was elected governor of the island. No one was more surprised than he was. He was in Las Bougainvilleas, sitting next to Clarissa's oxygen tent, when he heard the news from party headquarters in San Juan. His victory was decisive; there was no question about it. This was the third time he had run for governor, and he had been sure he was going to lose.

Over the next few days the whole family rejoiced and congratulated him, Clarissa most warmly of all. They would now live in La Fortaleza, the governor's palace in Old San Juan. A month later Mother made the trip from Las Bougainvilleas to the capital in an ambulance. She was very brave about it. She knew she was never coming back, but she didn't cry. She said good-bye to everyone with a perfect smile: to Martina, the cook; Confesor, the gardener; Cristóbal, the chauffeur; all her neighbors and friends. She was leaving behind the house she had lived in for thirty-eight years; her gilded Louis XVI furniture, decorated with delicate bouquets of roses; her silver and china; her family photographs from Emajaguas. Most painful of all, she was leaving behind her beautiful garden.

Clarissa's hospital bed, with its oxygen tent, was set up in the governor's private apartments on the third floor of La Fortaleza. The massive Spanish-colonial furniture that the governors traditionally used was carved dark mahogany, and it was more than two hundred years old. The double bed was especially forbidding, it was a large boxlike affair with a flounced red canopy where Fernando Martín— Father's longtime antagonist—had slept so many years. Mother thanked God she didn't have to sleep in Fernando Martín's bed; it would have given her nightmares. She would have been kept awake by the song she had sung so often at rallies: *"Abajo la pava, abajo el pavín, abajo el bigote de Fernando Martín!"*—"Down with the big *pava*, down with the little *pava*, and down with Fernando Martín's mustache!" Aurelio, however, didn't mind sleeping in the governor's bed at all. In fact, he slept like a rock. His sleeping there meant that the American way of life, with better living conditions for the poor and democracy for all, was finally on its way to Puerto Rico.

La Fortaleza had originally been a military fort, and the governor's apartments were located in the old part of the building, dating from the sixteenth century. The rooms had walls three feet thick, ceilings supported by dark *ausubo* beams, and very small windows. The windows had angled sides from which soldiers had shot their muskets to defend the palace from pirate and Indian attacks.

The governor's private apartments consisted of a bedroom and a small living room, where Father's Bechstein was immediately installed. It was the only piece of furniture that was moved from our house in Las Bougainvilleas. Father still practiced the piano for an hour every day. None of Mother's gaily decorated furniture was brought along: it wouldn't have fitted in with the severe colonial decor.

Mother pined away for two years in these dark, solemn rooms, looking out the small windows at the traffic jams in the narrow streets of Old San Juan. The governor's palace was surrounded by beautiful gardens, planted by the count of Mirasol in the eighteenth century, but Mother never got to see them up close. She was too weak to go downstairs to the ground floor, but she never complained. She simply refused to talk about her illness.

Aurelio's office was on the first floor of La Fortaleza, and one day, while working on a speech, he got a telephone call from the doctor to come up to the private apartments immediately. Mother had taken a turn for the worse. He ran up the staircase three steps at a time; he couldn't wait for the elevator. When he arrived at the third floor he was told Mother had had a cerebral hemorrhage. She never knew she was dying—she passed away without regaining consciousness. Father couldn't believe what had happened. He stood by the bed holding her hand, reassuring her she had nothing to be afraid of because he was there by her side, but she was already dead. The doctors came up to him and took him gently away. Aurelio stumbled into the next room, overwhelmed.

I arrived at La Fortaleza a few minutes later. Nobody had called me at home to tell me Mother was dying. I was sitting out on the terrace writing letters and paying my monthly bills when I felt a sudden urge to visit her. She hadn't been feeling well lately, but her ups and downs were frequent and the family had become accustomed to them.

When I entered the private apartments, I saw several of Father's bodyguards whispering and milling about the hall. Then the door to the bedroom was flung open and Father walked hurriedly by without seeing me, his hand over his eyes. I called out to him, but he disappeared rapidly down the hallway. I thought it was odd, because at the end of that hall there was only a dark sitting room where no one ever went. I stopped at the door and saw Mother's head from behind. She was lying uncovered on the bed, the plastic oxygen tent pushed to one side. The doctors and nurses were still there, picking up needles and cotton swabs from the floor and from the night tables. I walked into the room and slowly turned. I saw that Mother was dead.

I stood there, stunned. My skin felt dry and I couldn't understand why—I felt as if I were drowning. Mother had fallen into a dark pool, and I was falling in after her.

It was strange to see her without the plastic cover separating us, as if she had suddenly been stripped of the armor that had protected her from the world. A nurse, Mrs. Gómez, led me to a chair, and I sat down, trembling. She brought me a glass of water.

"Your father asked me to bathe and prepare her before she's put in the coffin," Mrs. Gómez said. "He wants the wake to take place in La Fortaleza; he doesn't want her to be taken to a funeral parlor. Why don't you go into the next room and wait with your father until the rest of the family gets here?"

I refused. Mother needed me desperately.

I thought of Brunhilda and thanked God she was at La Concordia; otherwise she would have been here, insisting on doing the job herself! We locked the door and I stood next to the bed, facing Mother. I watched Mrs. Gómez bring a bowl of water, a sponge, and a bottle of Jean-Marie Farine, Father's favorite cologne, which Mother had also taken to wearing. She took off Mother's nightgown and began to bathe her. Mrs. Gómez had soft, gentle hands and moved Mother's limbs as if she were still alive and could feel what was being done to her. A sickly-sweet smell filled the room, filtered into my nostrils, and stayed there. For months afterward I had to put myrtle boughs in vases all around my house so one smell would mask the other.

When Mrs. Gómez was finished, I kissed Mother lightly on the forehead. She looked frail and vulnerable; I was surprised at how much weight she had lost. There was so little left of her.

So this was Mother's death! I had imagined it otherwise. Her skin was white as unspun silk. The stillness—not even an eyelash stirring. The chest a calm receptacle for a quiet heart. It was over; there was nothing else to be done: she was finally reconciled with herself.

I thanked God she had had a peaceful death. No wounds marked her body, no grimace of pain distorted her beautiful, cameolike profile. She had a death worthy of the Emajaguas philosophy of life. "If one accepts one's destiny, the pain is sublimated and there is no sacrifice," she had said to me over and over again. She had been right, preaching obedience and acceptance to me for so long.

And then something astonishing happened. Mother was allowed one last act, perhaps even more overwhelming because it happened after her death. When the nurse turned Mother's naked body to bathe her back, a mouthful of fresh blood spilled out and stained the white sheet a bright red. I stared at it, horrified.

For days after Clarissa passed away, Aurelio refused to speak to me. He sank into a deep state of melancholia unlike any I had seen before. Sadness turned his mouth into a bloodless wound. He wore only dark suits and black ties to the office. He seemed resentful of the world, but especially of me. One evening I went to visit him at La Fortaleza and walked up to the private apartments. He was playing Beethoven's *Moonlight* Sonata on the piano. I sat next to him and tried to put my arms around him, but he pushed me gently away.

"I'm sorry, Father. I know you're in pain. But you must look ahead, you can't look back. You're free now, you'll go on being a wonderful governor. And you'll never be alone, because I'll always be with you!" Father turned and looked at me in astonishment.

"You could never take her place," he said in a grieving voice. "I loved her more than my life. She was my inspiration in everything."

I got up from the piano bench, tears streaming down my face, and went home.

Mother's death cast a pall over Father that was so overwhelming he was unable to shake it off by the time of the election campaign two years later. He had lost his formidable élan vital, that endless fountain of energy that had made everything seem possible.

A few months after his defeat in 1972, Father had a baby Bechstein delivered to my house as a birthday present. He was almost inconsolably lonely, he said, and wanted to come by to practice once in a while after he left office. When I saw the movers carrying the piano out of the truck and bringing it through my front door, I didn't say anything. I was grateful for Father's magnificent present and wanted to help him. I knew how important music was to him, and that there was nothing sadder than playing for an empty house. But my heart was tight with fear.

Ricardo and I had been separated for three years, and while it took some time, I had begun to date different men. They telephoned often and sometimes came to visit in the evening. But now my house was flooded by Beethoven's *Appassionata*, Debussy's *Clair de Lune*, Chopin's mazurkas and études, the same music Father had played for Mother. Word got around that the ex-governor came to visit me every afternoon, and my telephone soon stopped ringing. If someone approached the house, the minute they heard Father's energetic pounding on the keyboard, they stealthily got back in their cars and drove away.

I grew so angry at Father I couldn't breathe. I called the piano showroom and asked for the owner. When he came to the phone, I was in a fury. "Come and take this piano away right now!" I said. "If you don't, I'll have it carried out into the garden, open the lid, and leave it there until the rain makes the strings burst and washes the ghosts away!" The owner must have thought I was crazy. The piano movers arrived within an hour, carried the Bechstein out of the house, and took off with it as fast as they could.

When Father came by the house the next day, he was amazed that the piano wasn't there. He looked at me in dismay. "Where's the piano?"

"I sent it back to the store, Father," I answered, holding back the tears. "The little green felt-covered hammers that look like tiny birds were pecking away at my heart and I couldn't stand the pain." Father didn't say a word. I gave him a kiss on the cheek, and he turned quietly away and went back to his house. What was there to say after so many years of not saying what we really felt?

I had no way of knowing that Mother's death would affect me so deeply. I began to have a recurring nightmare: I would be sitting in a chair watching Mrs. Gómez give Mother her last bath. All of a sudden Mrs. Gómez would turn Mother's body over and fresh blood would again pour from her mouth. I would wake in terror, trying to understand what the dream meant, but I didn't have an inkling.

Eventually the nightmares stopped and things went back to normal. With the money I inherited from Clarissa, my life changed radically. I got up the courage to ask Ricardo for a divorce, which he didn't contest. Time cools even the most intractable tempers and Ricardo wanted his independence as much as I wanted mine.

With Mother's money, I bought a house of my own and moved into it with my children. A few years later, when they were old enough to look after themselves and to leave under the care of a nanny, I went back to the university and finished my doctorate. Soon I was teaching to my heart's content. Mother's passing had made possible for me what she had wanted for herself when she was young: a career that would lead to self-respect and economic independence. Ironically, that freedom came at her expense.

I dreamed about Mother one last time. We were crossing Río Loco and the family's temperamental Pontiac had stalled on us again. The river was rushing past, but instead of dogs, pigs, and goats being pulled along by the murky rapids I saw Abuela Valeria, Abuela Adela, Tía Lakhmé, Tía Dido, Tía Artemisa, Tía Amparo, all swimming desperately against the current. Clarissa and I sat safely inside the Pontiac, dressed in our Sunday best. She took a dollar out of her purse, rolled down the window just enough so she could wave the bill at the men on the riverbank, who soon came and pulled us out. And as we drove away I could hear through the open window the voices of those I could no longer see, but whose stories I could not have dreamed.

52

$60^{\underline{o}}$

M/F

I'LL CRY WHEN I KILL YOU

Also by Peter Israel

The Stiff Upper Lip
The French Kiss
Hush Money
The Hen's House

I'LL CRY WHEN I KILL YOU

A MYSTERY

PETER ISRAEL

THE MYSTERIOUS PRESS

New York • London

The Mysterious Press, 129 West 56th Street, New York, N.Y. 10019

Printed in the United States of America

First Printing: February 1988

10 9 8 7 6 5 4 3 2 1

Library of Congress Cataloging-in-Publication Data

Israel, Peter, fl. 1967–
    I'll cry when I kill you.

I. Title.
PS3559.S74I4 1988   813'.54   87–7836
ISBN 0–89296–268–2

For my darling girl . . .
Happy Birthday

I'LL CRY WHEN I KILL YOU

PART ONE

PART ONE

CHAPTER
1

People jog in the suburbs, too, it turns out. The men get out first with the birds, before the sun. Some wear reflector armbands. The women come later, heel-and-toeing under the tall shade trees in their sweat suits, looking like they hate it like women joggers everywhere. Jogging's like life, somebody told me: the boys have all the fun.

I was into my second half hour of it that morning when the car stopped me. I'd come downhill out of the estate area, which was like some dark, forested graveyard, and into tree-lined streets where the early sun dappled onto sidewalks and there were signs of morning life like from some time warp. I saw teenage kids delivering newspapers off bicycles and dogs sniffing at green plastic garbage cans. Once I passed a milk truck and heard the clinking of bottles inside. There were birds chirping in the trees, sprinklers working the lawns and every so often the cough of a motor. But there was more human traffic than car, and it was the kind of community where the walkers and joggers wave at each other regardless of race, creed, sex or color.

3

For good reason, if you stop to think about it.

Pure Wasp America, in other words, and it felt a long way from the Central Park Reservoir, even though a crow could have made the trip in thirty minutes give or take.

The car broke my concentration. It was a Mercedes, gunmetal gray, and the driver wore a suit to match. It slowed down as it passed and parked some twenty yards up the street, diagonal to the near curb. The driver reached across the front seat and opened the door on my side.

He knew who I was. No matter that I'd never seen him before.

"He wants you," he said, when I pulled up abreast.

"Who's He?" I asked.

No answer.

The driver was big, blond, young, and he wore a blue button-down shirt and navy knit tie under the gray suit. I suppose from his point of view there was only one He. With a capital *H*.

"What's He want me for?" I asked, swinging into the front seat next to him. I was a little annoyed. It was 7:17 A.M., this was my first morning on the job, and I didn't work for Him anyway. I was only on loan, so to speak, a gift from my boss, who also happened to be His attorney. Although, knowing the Counselor, the client would be billed amply for my services.

The driver didn't answer that question either. His mission, apparently, was just to pick up the package and deliver it. The Mercedes did a well-oiled K-turn maneuver. Five minutes later we were winding our way up through the broad lawns and deep woods of the estate area, glimpsing some great gray fieldstone mansions, and up to the spiked iron gates of Bashard's domain—the crenellated, betowered Victorian pile near the top of the hill from which, as I'd seen from my tower window the night before, you could make out the distant lights of the Big Apple.

When I'd gotten there the night before, I'd had to wait outside the gates until identified. This morning, the driver of the Mercedes executed a series of signals with the brights and dims, and the tall gates slid back on tracks automatically, and in we went.

Twenty minutes later, I was toweling down after a shower and shave when my bathroom phone rang.

"Mr. Bashard's waiting for you in the second-floor study," a male voice told me. Then the phone went dead in my ear.

Raul Bashard, Raul R. Bashard, Raul Rogan Bashard. You'd have to have been blind, deaf and/or asleep not to have recognized the name, even if you were part of the third of the country that's supposed to be illiterate. I guess a lot of people must have thought he was dead, along with that older generation of science-fiction buffs who went back four or five decades to when Raul Bashard was contributing to magazines like *Amazing Stories* for a penny and a half a word. By the time I discovered his writing, which wasn't yesterday either, he was already known as the Dean of Science Fiction, and you'd see pictures of him and his wife in the papers, crossing the Arctic Circle on an ice floe, found (after having been lost) in the Andes, or shaking hands with the astronauts just returned to Earth. The wife died; Bashard lived on, wrote on. The last publishing contract I ran through the word processor at the office called for a two-million-dollar guarantee to the Author.

The Counselor and Raul Bashard went way back, back before me, certainly, and the Counselor's Wife, and the five-story town house in the East Seventies, back at least to The Firm, which the Counselor abandoned years ago (to, as he liked to put it, "go private" with his clients). Bashard's wealth and the Counselor's had grown together, only Bashard's grew faster. He used our office for most of his affairs, including the real estate (of which the Victorian pile was but one holding), the sheltered investments, the foreign accounts, the trusts, the charitable endowments. Strange, then, that not only had I never laid eyes on the man before that morning but had never so much as talked to him on the phone. When Raul Bashard wanted his attorney he invariably had an intermediary place the call, and he wouldn't get on the line himself till he knew the Counselor was waiting.

Wealthy beyond what most of us dream about, adventurer, guru, recluse, a paranoid as I found out, Bashard was also something of a medical freak. Brain tumors, heart attacks, cancers, all the modern-day scourges—Bashard had confronted them all, and if he'd lost a battle here and there, he was still ahead in the war. At least for the time being. What he looked like now, though, few people knew. Once he'd been a striking figure of a man, that you could tell from the picture on his book jackets, but they hadn't changed the photo in years.

In other words, he'd been reported dying so many times you sort of assumed he was dead. Until, that is, the manuscript of the new novel arrived, not a comma to be changed without permission of the Author, "created and written by Raul R. Bashard," as it always said on the title page—and the million-dollar contracts started spewing out of our word processor.

I went down by the central staircase, one of the most imposing features of the mansion. Its wide stone steps circled back on themselves, leaded windows at the half-landings gave out on the rear sward of the estate, and the center airwell was wide enough for a little wrought-iron elevator to run up and down inside.

By the standards of the place, Bashard's second-floor study turned out to be a small room, almost cozy. It had a mahogany and marble fireplace and floor-to-ceiling bookshelves wherever the doors and windows would allow, with a polished mahogany stepladder on wheels for the higher shelves. I didn't realize it at first, but every volume on the shelves was a Bashard, arranged by country, and most were in mint condition. Brass plaques fixed to the shelf fronts identified the countries. There were leather-bound editions, hardcover editions, book-club editions, illustrated editions, paperbacks, translations, anthologies, copies of old magazines in plastic slipcases.

Tall leaded casement windows, framed by drapery, gave out over the front of the house. The trees on this side were too tall to give you much of a view, but you could see the graveled driveway circling up to the stone portico of the main entrance and beyond it part of one of the fieldstone outbuildings.

In front of the windows, a computer layout—an oddity in that Victorian setting—sat on a long, glass-covered, mahogany table. CRT screen, television screen, modem, keyboard, printer, all forming a kind of control center. And Raul Bashard, his back to me, bent forward, palms on the glass top, scrutinizing the television screen.

Second oddity: If you didn't already know, you'd never have guessed he was seventy-nine. And sick. Possibly he'd shrunk a little, I thought, and his hair, slicked to his scalp as it always had been in the photos, might have thinned, and there were other signs, as I'd soon notice, that he couldn't always hide. But his bearing was as strong and erect as an officer's on a parade ground; his facial skin, apart from the trim white mustache, was pink, glistening, clean-shaven and devoid of wrinkles; his clear dark eyes pierced, appraised, accused like a cat's.

Not a man, in sum, who looked afraid for his own life.

But he was. Or so he said.

His clothes, with one exception, bore out the military impression. He wore a tailed tweed jacket over a pale green turtleneck that seemed molded to his body. Olive-drab flannel trousers were creased to a knife's edge. The one anomaly—the more remarkable for his otherwise impeccable look—was a pair of yellowed and dirty white sneakers.

A quick word about the sneakers. I noticed there was no carpet in the study, only a gleaming floor of inlaid parquet squares. In fact there was no carpeting anywhere in the house other than a few Oriental rugs in the formal rooms, and these were small. The Master, you got the feeling, didn't like people getting close to him unannounced. Whereas he went around in sneakers.

"What use are you to me, Revere, if you're not here when I need you?"

He spoke sharply, without turning from the television screen.

"I didn't know you needed me," I think I answered.

"If I didn't need you," he snapped back, "you wouldn't be here. Jogging will ruin your body anyway. If you can jog, you can run. If you can't, walk. I used to walk eight miles a day, thirty inches to the pace. I did it up to two years ago. I don't anymore. Jogging belongs to the contemporary idiocracy. Look at this one!"

His voice grew agitated, angry. He waved me forward toward the television screen. It showed, in color, a middle-aged woman in gray sweat suit and running shoes, a white towel wrapped around her neck, laboring uphill on a paved road under an umbrella of oak trees. She gasped and flailed her forearms as the camera followed her. I thought the road, the trees, looked familiar.

"Ruthven, Eleanor," Bashard called out next to me, his fingers pushing buttons on the computer keyboard. "Function: housewife; age: forty-one; sign: Taurus; spouse: Ruthven, Ed; function: senior vice-president Chase but he'll go no further; age: forty-two; sign: Virgo; inhabit: Four Puck Road, 3.7 acres, paid $155,000; date: 1974; current appraised value: $525,000, overvalued; three children, ages eighteen, fifteen, three but she can't have any more"—he chuckled at this point—"last observed: sixteen May, skipped a day, it was raining yesterday morning; time: 7:50 A.M. . . ."

Following his excited voice by a few seconds, the CRT screen scrolled out, line by line, the same data, minus the asides. It was a weird demonstration. He had it so accurately you might have thought the computer was simply transcribing his voice, but what evidently delighted him was that his memory could "print" faster than the machine's. Meanwhile I realized, as Ruthven, Eleanor, disappeared around a curve in the road and the CRT screen finished displaying her file, why the scenery had looked so familiar. The camera that watched her had to be mounted either in or next to Bashard's gates.

"Do you keep a file on all your neighbors?" I asked.

"Of course I do," he retorted. "What would be the point of having some but not all?"

"Then the ones to worry about are the ones where there's no file."

"I see you've a penchant for stating the obvious, Revere," he said icily. "That's right. And wrong. The ones with a file could be just as dangerous." He straightened then and stared at me full face. The eyes were hard, dark, penetrating. They reminded me of cat's eyes, except that unlike the cat's his had a way of reflecting no light. We were standing close enough for me to smell his toothpaste faintly. It was hard not to back off.

"What do you know about the fans, Revere? Never mind, you will. You'll read the mail. Love, hate, resentment, adulation, slavishness, rage . . . every human emotion. Noble, ignoble. Dangerous, benign. But now more dangerous than ever. There are fans who write me every week, have for years. There was a woman who wrote me every day for four months, intimate letters, letters that made you blush. Then she stopped. I never heard from her again. When I had the kidney operation, they were lined up in the street to offer me transplants. Now you'll ask yourself: what did he ever do to deserve it? I'm a journeyman writer, Revere; that means I write books for a living. I've made a lot of money at it—that's thanks to them, they buy the books— but does that mean they have to move in with me? That's what they used to do. Camp out, hang out. It damn near killed my wife. When I still went to their conventions, it got so I had to sneak out of the hotels through the kitchen. So I stopped going. Heinlein, Herbert, Latham, Clarke, it's been no different for them. Heinlein lives in a place like this, except in the West. Behind barbed wire. Herbert, before he died, moved around all the time. Ollie Latham lives on a farm. Arthur's in Sri Lanka. I guess they don't read novels in Sri Lanka."

He laughed, red in the face, laughed a little too long, I thought, at his own joke. The laugh became a cough. He turned his head away, covered his mouth, and then I saw one of the signs: his hands developed a tremor when they had nothing to do, nothing to push against or grab. It was slight until he noticed it, or saw you noticing it. Then it got severe until he controlled it or, more often, distracted you with something else. Probably that was one reason he never shook hands with people.

"Do you know what happened here last week?" he went on. He'd turned back to the television screen, talking now as he watched two cars outside the gates. The cars slowed to negotiate the curve and the camera picked up their license plates. The computer, I learned later, had a file by license plates, too, but Bashard chose not to demonstrate. "Eight May; nine-thirty in the morning. There was a terrific commotion down at the gates. Somebody who wouldn't take no for an answer. He refused to go away until I talked to him. Do you think it was a fan? Hell no! It was an IRS agent! I was writing, damn it! I told him over the intercom to identify himself. He held his credentials up for the camera. Do you know what he wanted? He said he'd come to check the 'so-called' office space I deducted on my return! I told him he had no appointment, that he could write for an appointment, better yet that he could write my accountant for an appointment and the two of them could inspect the premises together. At *my* convenience, not his. I told him if he didn't cease and desist I'd get him transferred to Point Barrow, Alaska, and if he didn't believe me, he should just keep at it. Do you know what he did? He tried to stone the camera! Literally, he picked up a rock and threw it at the camera. It wasn't till we turned the dogs loose at the gate that he went away."

He was staring at me again, grinning.

"Science-fiction fans, IRS agents, who else? Women," he added. "Now do you understand why I live like this, Revere?"

I was a little at a loss for an answer.

"You should call me Phil," I said.

"Philip," he said. Then he repeated: "Science-fiction fans, IRS agents, women. And one of them wants to kill me."

He paused for a second, and I could've sworn I saw a gleam of pleasure in those cat eyes.

"But what's wrong with Pablo?" he asked. "That's a good name."

It stung me all right. That he should know the name, for one thing, and also that he would use it.

He saw that it stung, I guess. At least he pulled one of those little self-defense numbers, meaning his body seemed to sag, he said he was tired, that if he stood up too long in one place it hurt his back, etc. When I reached for his chair, though, he straightened abruptly, and his palms went forward onto the glass tabletop in the posture I'd first seen him in, his gaze now fixed on a new image on the television screen.

It was like I wasn't there.

"Look," he said after a while. "There are the only three creatures I trust. In this galaxy anyway."

There must have been another camera—not the only other one, as it turned out—mounted at the rear of the house. It covered gardens first, then a swimming pool and patio, then a wide sloping lawn that ended in woods.

Bashard himself controlled the shot. By working switches on his table, he could shift the camera angle and close in on his subject.

Two of the "trusted creatures" were four-legged. The third had two legs, and bare feet, straight blonde hair to the shoulders which coiled and uncoiled when she ran, and a body such as you don't see much anymore, large and voluptuous. She wore bright green shorts which matched the lawn and a forest-green sweatshirt, and she darted, swerved, ducked from the two dogs who lunged at her, biting for the object in her hands.

The dogs were a pair of king-sized, brown-skinned Dobermans, pointy-eared and sharp-muzzled. They hurled themselves at the object, she impervious and laughing as she twisted away from them, until she sailed it, discus-style—a white Frisbee—far out over the sun-swept lawn. Even as it landed, the dogs were on top of it, brown streaks, snarling and fighting. Then one trotted back toward her proudly, the Frisbee clamped in its jaws, while the other Doberman snapped at him. Then the three of them were rolling on the grass in a thrashing of limbs and bodies, the blonde girl and the two dogs, until she broke free again with the Frisbee. She stood up and came running bare-legged across the lawn, leapt at by the dogs, triumphant and laughing, toward the watching camera.

"Herbert and Jules," Bashard said, manipulating the camera. "Jules always wins. Do you know who they're named after?"

I shook my head.

"Wells and Verne," he said with enjoyment. "Herbert G. Wells, Jules Verne. They started it all. Without them, I wouldn't be here. None of us would."

I didn't quite get this last. I mean, neither H. G. Wells, nor Jules Verne, so far as I knew, had had anything to do with my forebears, and I assume I'd have been here even if they'd both been carpenters. But Bashard had his own vision of things.

"She's beautiful," I said, watching the girl wave toward the camera. "Who is she?"

"Grace Bashard," he answered. "My only child and heir."

He said this tonelessly, and without further explanation, but I couldn't help a double take. He was easily old enough to be her grandfather, and this calculation led to a more startling second one. Bashard's wife, who'd died some ten years before, had been a lot younger than he, this much I knew, but *that* much younger? To have had a baby—when? In her mid-forties, if not later?

The youngster on the lawn, as I found out shortly, was all of eighteen.

There was, of course, another explanation, and the Counselor had known it. But the Counselor has a bad habit of keeping his counsel when it comes to giving me my marching orders.

"You'll have breakfast with her at the pool in fifteen minutes," Bashard said. He turned off the television set. "She'll have her swim first. She'll tell you everything you need to know, show you everything you need to see."

"Won't you be joining us?" I said.

"I've had mine already. I work from eight-thirty to one-thirty, seven days a week. Luncheon is at two, dinner at seven-thirty. We go to bed early here. But we'll have ample time to review our preparations. If we don't get to it today, we'll get to it tomorrow or the next day. Meanwhile, meet the staff. Trust no one. Develop your own opinions. When you decide who's going to kill me, inform me."

He turned away. The audience was over.

I went out into the hall, down the curving stone steps to the main floor, and out back through rose gardens to poolside. The cook, who doubled as waiter, was carrying a tray out to the pool. A gardener in white coveralls and heavy gloves stooped among the rosebushes, working with clippers.

The cook, the gardener, the driver, Bashard himself . . . all male. In fact, the only female in the place, two-legged or four, was Grace Bashard, just taking a shallow dive off the springboard when I walked onto the patio.

CHAPTER
2

CONFIDENTIAL

To: Charles Camelot   Date: 20 May
From: Revere
Subject: R. R. Bashard visit (file *Bashard*)

There was no need for me to stay any longer. It would have been a waste of my time, Bashard's money.

The security is the most sophisticated I've ever inspected. By the way, he designed the system himself. Maybe helicopters could get in there, otherwise it looks like overkill to me. He's a lot more vulnerable to stepping on a cake of soap than to a crazy.

He says he trusts nobody except the daughter and his dogs. I interviewed the employees, reviewed their files (see *Bashard, staff*), found no basis for any suspicion.

One exception. (See *Bashard, Grace.*)

He seems like a lonely old man, probably paranoid.

I found no basis, at least as far as the physical
premises are concerned, for his life to be in danger.

If he's to go to the BashCon next week, I should
check out the facilities. The question, though, is
moot. I left against his will, even after he phoned
you. He said I wouldn't do. He said he had no place
for quitters. Etc., etc.

He is clearly not a man used to being thwarted.
What next?

For you to decide.

CONFIDENTIAL

To: Charles Camelot   Date: 20 May
From: Revere
Subject: Grace Bashard (new file: *Bashard, Grace*)

Bashard's daughter, Grace, is a screwed-up little
rich girl, right out of the movies. She is beautiful,
knows it, thinks she is sexually irresistible. She gets
extra sexy when she knows Daddy's watching.

According to our abstract (see *Bashard, will*),
Grace Bashard inherits the works. She knows it,
makes sure you know it, too. To judge from the way
she acts toward him, I'd guess she's in it for the
money.

It was too bad. I mean, after a day and a night and part of
another day of fending off Daddy's Little Girl, I was just
warming up. Writing a memo to the Counselor might sound
like small revenge, but it was all I had going for me at the
time.

Anyway, I was just getting into the subject of Grace that
afternoon in my office when the red button on my console
started blinking.

I pressed the intercom.

"Erase everything about Grace Bashard," the familiar
voice said.

So the Counselor was reading on his screen, even as I typed.

I started to protest.

"I said: Erase everything about Grace Bashard, Phil," the Counselor's deep voice interrupted. "There's no Grace Bashard file. Then get your ass up here."

The intercom went dead; the red button stopped blinking. I did what the Boss said.

A word about our setup.

We work, as I've mentioned, in a five-story town house in Manhattan's East Seventies. In the bottom two stories, to be exact. It's a lovely tree-lined block with mostly town houses on either side, a couple of sturdy redbrick apartment buildings, and one garage where the locals stable their chariots, at, the last time I okayed a bill, a measly three hundred dollars per car per month. You can still buy your way into the neighborhood, I guess, if you've got a few million dollars lying around. The last house to be sold on our block was advertised in the *Times* at a round $4 million, and it was snapped up inside of two months by a partnership of ob-gyns. There are, to judge, enough ob-gyns in the few blocks around us to leave an overflow even if the entire female population of the Upper East Side decides to get pregnant at the same time. And a heavy dosage of other medical specialties of the more expensive variety, including a goodly sprinkling of shrinks, surgeons, an orthodontist or two, one ophthalmologist. And only one attorney-at-law. In other words, although the Counselor might land on me for saying it, the professionals in the neighborhood are of either sufficient specialty or sufficient reputation to be able to pass on their costs to their clients.

Our building, good-sized in the neighborhood, would be considered small by Bashard standards, and it would be too small for any normal law offices (much less a combination law office and city residence). But it fits our professional needs, for particular reasons, and also fits the living requirements of the Counselor and his wife. Although if the Counselor's Wife ever lives up to her threat to bring a Baby

Camelot into the household, it's hard to know where we'd fit it in. As is, it's a handsome brick edifice from the double white half-columns and white lintel framing the doorway to the polished brass announcing: CHARLES CAMELOT, ATTORNEY-AT-LAW.

The first person you meet when you come in is the receptionist, Mr.—or Monsieur—Roger LeClerc, of New York and the Ivory Coast. To your left is a small reception room and a still smaller computer room. To the right is my office: PHILIP REVERE in brass on the door, a comfortable room with two windows giving out onto the street and a fold-out couch where I've been known to sleep when the Counselor has the pressure on. If you have to wait to see someone, chances are Roger will offer you coffee and tea; there's a small kitchen substation behind him, also a half-bathroom. The decor is subtle, the lighting mostly indirect—all such touches chosen, I should say, by the Counselor's Wife.

Upstairs on the second floor are the Counselor's chambers, the office of his secretary, Ms. Shapiro, and also the office of our "secret weapon," Ms. Charlotte McCullough, who's been with us since the Firm. She's a CPA and also a pure genius, if I may say so, at both financial and data-processing matters.

And that, except for the elevator and the main staircase, which ends in a closed door above the second floor, is the sum and total of the professional part.

What makes it livable (and an oddity compared to most legal offices) is the almost total absence of paper. Consider these two factors: for one, we are now well into the Computer Age and the Counselor has us computerized within an inch of our sometimes unwilling lives. Everyone who works for us, Roger included, must take at least an introductory course. Secondly, when he left the Firm to "go private," the Counselor didn't cut all his ties. Instead he negotiated an arrangement which, though unique in its time, is now becoming more and more commonplace in the New York profession: we are cabled into the Firm's main-frame, which houses our own data base and files. Thus, we have full access to the Firm's law library, which is now largely an electronic library, and other aspects of the Firm's services that no small law office could either afford or house. Those basic documents we have to hold on to—wills, contracts, leases and the like—are kept for the most part in water-proofed, fireproofed steel cabinets in the basement.

Our relationship to the Firm goes deeper, of course. In exchange for its services, the Firm gets to print a discreet "Charles Camelot, of Counsel" on its letterhead, a small but significant item any New York law firm would readily recognize and pay for. In addition, we use the Firm regularly for certain kinds of legal matters, including litigation, for Charles Camelot would, I suppose, cut his own throat sooner than appear in a courtroom. And the Firm, in exchange, refers certain matters to us, especially those of a sensitive, sometimes unsavory, nature that might besmirch its largely corporate practice. It is, in sum, a mutually useful connection—more hands-off than I've made it sound, but more hands-on than the outside world might suppose.

Above the offices begins the very separate world of the Camelot residence. The third floor of the building is their suite: living room and bedroom. The fourth contains the kitchen and dining room, and is where Althea and Gorgeous live. Althea is the housekeeper and sometime cook; Gorgeous is Althea's calico cat.

But what makes the house special, even in that gilt-edged neighborhood, is the top floor: an entire solarium glassed in on all sides and above, with awnings and plantings, a hot tub room, and a wraparound terrace on the outside. Its the Counselor's Wife's creation, and perfect for the parties she loves to give and which the Counselor puts up with. But if you're a reader of *Architectural Digest* and similar magazines, you will already have ooh-ed and aah-ed over it.

And there you have it. The two sections, home and office, are, as I've said, entirely separate. Except, that is, for the Counselor's Wife's cocker spaniel, Muffin. The cocker bitch has the run of the place, both sections.

Except for my office.

Oh yes, the Counselor's Wife has her own profession. She's a shrink, and she specializes in sex therapy. Her office is a few blocks north on Park Avenue. She practices under her maiden name: Nora Saroff. You've probably seen her on TV.

* * *

The Counselor was sitting at his desk, smoking a pipe and holding a set of documents. Whether he was actually reading them or not makes no difference. I've watched people from all walks of life, all kinds of experience, all sizes of bank accounts, sit on the client's side of the Counselor's desk and wait. To a man, and woman, they all learn to wait.

I sat down and waited. The CRT.screen behind him was blank.

He's a big man, with a craggy head and a shock of hair that was gray when I first met him and is now almost pure white. He reads with horn-rimmed glasses. He puffs nonstop at a pipe when he's working, a tobacco mixture made specially for him by Peterson's, and the atmosphere in his office is a constant struggle between pipe smoke and the air conditioner. Usually the smoke wins. Even in shirtsleeves, with the white French cuffs rolled back twice on themselves and the pipe smoke curling around his head, he has a well-dressed air. This wasn't always so. The bow ties, the matching suspenders, the silk socks and handkerchiefs—these are the Counselor's Wife's touches. His suits are now tailor-made, from fabric she chooses. Ditto his shirts. All in all, you'd have to admit there's been an improvement, but the Counselor affects not to notice. The only place she's failed totally is with the pipes. The hundred-dollar Dunhills, the Charentons, the Petersons, the Lullehammers from Scandinavia, all these get smoked once or twice and then put aside. The Counselor prefers the seconds he picks out himself, at a tobacconist downtown.

His office decor reflects a similar tug-of-war. It is all her doing—the carpeting, plantings, lighting, drapery, the signed Trova lithographs—but for the desk and chair. These are massive mahogany constructions that came with us from the Firm. One time, when he was out of town, she had them replaced with chrome and glass creations from Knoll. What went on between them I can't report, but the day after he came home the Knoll was gone and the originals were back in place, and the only improvement she's managed since was to get the chair reupholstered in a taupe-colored, brass-studded leather.

The chair still creaks when he tilts back.

The Counselor, I've long since realized, *likes* a cluttered desk, likes papers, memorabilia, pens, pencils, ashtrays, pipes, in a jumble. He would rather rummage for matches or his reading glasses than look for them in a set place, would rather twist a paper clip out of shape to scrape at his pipe bowls than use a tool. His desktop has defeated a run of secretaries. No matter how orderly they've made it when he comes down for the start of the working day, it looks like it's been totaled by the time he heads off for lunch at the French bistro he patronizes on Lexington near Seventieth.

I think the mess helps him think. I mean, the act of rummaging through the rubble gives him time to think. Time, too, on occasion, to hold his patience and his temper.

"You're the best thing that's happened to him since Pearl Harbor, Phil," the Counselor said without looking up. "That's what Raul Bashard told me."

"What happened to him at Pearl Harbor?" I asked.

He didn't answer. He continued to flip through the papers in his hands.

"What's with the daughter?" I went on. "Grace Bashard. Why no file? She exists, doesn't she?"

There was, of course, no rushing him.

"I'm surprised you didn't like her better," he said at length, glancing momentarily at me over the reading glasses, then down again. "Isn't she your type?"

"My *type*?" I said, irritated. "Have you met her?"

"Not recently . . . " he answered, distracted.

I realized after the fact that he was only teasing me. My alleged confirmed bachelorhood is a standing office joke. But I wasn't in the mood.

"In the first place," I went on, "I'm old enough, just about, to be her father. Second, I'm not used to teenage girls offering me their bodies before breakfast."

"Hmmm . . . " he said. "Did she really do that?"

"Yes," I said.

Finally he put down the documents, also the reading glasses. His chair creaked, and he locked his hands behind his neck.

"All right, Phil," he said, "let me tell you the story."

The Counselor, I should add, relishes being a raconteur. Like most lawyers, he wants you to think he could have made a career on Broadway, which means that he has a tendency to long-windedness.

"Raul Bashard's always said Pearl Harbor changed his life. It's true enough, in more ways than one. I imagine you found him a fairly exotic character, didn't you? Well, do you know what he did before the war? He was an accountant. Not a CPA, the distinction didn't mean much at the time, but an accountant. He worked for a pretzel company in Reading, Pennsylvania, where he grew up. He'd started as a junior bookkeeper and worked his way up to chief accountant, where he might have stayed the rest of his life.

"The week after Pearl Harbor—he would have been what then? Thirty-five? Thirty-six?—he enlisted in the Navy. He also married his childhood sweetheart, like thousands of other young men did when their lives suddenly changed. He went to Officer Candidate School, determined to go from that to pilot training. Of course the Navy had other plans for him. He was too old to fly planes. He ended up junior supply officer on a carrier—a bookkeeper, in other words. He spent most of the war bobbing around the Pacific while others got the medals and lost their lives. That was when he started to write stories. He says he did it to keep his sanity. He also discovered he could make money at it, not a great deal of money but enough to encourage him. He started out writing war stories for pulp magazines, then went on into science fiction.

"The war ended. His wife, meanwhile, had given him a baby. Six months later he quit the pretzel factory, divorced the childhood sweetheart and moved to the West Coast—San Francisco—took up writing full-time. About a year after that, the childhood sweetheart committed suicide."

He paused for effect. He knocked the dottle out of his pipe, then put the pipe aside and reached for another.

You didn't have to be a genius at arithmetic to figure that the baby in question wasn't Grace.

"It was a boy, anyway," the Counselor went on, seeming to read my mind, "not a girl. And it fell to him to bring the kid up.

"This he did, more or less. They banged around the country a lot during the fifties. They were up in the Northwest, then back here for a while, then in Europe for a year. Then the ranch out in Arizona. I guess it didn't do the kid much good, all the bouncing around, though Nora says that doesn't necessarily matter. Nora says it's love that matters. Love, and belonging. John Jacob Bashard was the kid's name. Maybe he didn't feel loved enough. At any rate, he was in and out of a number of schools. When it came to college, he just couldn't cut it. I don't think he ever got his degree. Hell, I don't think he ever got through freshman year."

It made me think of Grace, presumably John Jacob Bashard's kid sister. Or step-kid sister. She was eighteen and not going to school either. Her daddy, she'd told me, was her mentor. Her daddy was all the mentor she needed.

"Along the way," the Counselor said, "Raul started making money. A living first. Then more than a living. Then a hell of a lot of money. It's one of the great ironies of his life, he likes to say, that having wanted to be a hero in the war, he only got to be one through writing science fiction." I thought of the pictures I'd seen of Bashard shaking hands with astronauts. "Along the way, too, he met the 'woman of his dreams.'"

"And little Grace's mother?" I put in.

He shook his head.

"I'm disappointed in you, Phil," he said, a glint of humor in his eyes. "I'd have thought you'd have guessed it on your own."

His pleasure annoyed and confused me at the same time. I *had* guessed it, or something like it, when I first saw her frolicking with Bashard's Dobermans over the TV screen.

The scene was innocent enough, but Bashard hadn't looked at her like a father, then or later. Plus the numbers hadn't added up, and for a girl of eighteen she came on like she'd already forgotten things about sex you and I never thought of.

"Who is she, then? His *whore*?"

The Counselor laughed, his head thrown back.

"Wrong again," he said. "I must say, Phil, for a womanizer, you certainly can be a prude."

He waved off my retort, then went on with Bashard's story.

"The woman of his dreams," he repeated. "That's what he called her. Madge, Margaret. He met her in Arizona and married her a week later. Maybe this is what finally made Johnny crack. Nora says it was the final proof that he could never belong. Madge was only a few years older than he was, they could have passed for sister and brother. But now she was his stepmother. Anyway, Johnny took off. He went back to San Francisco where, in very short order, he got married, sired a child—a daughter, of course—and divorced, came out of the closet, and changed his name legally from Bashard to Jameson. I believe Jameson was his mother's name. Anyway, that's where I came into the picture, as you'll see here—helping Raul sort out the mess."

He handed me some of the documents he'd been looking at when I came in. I leafed through them: adoption papers, waivers, financial agreements, all—as I discovered when I read them later—neatly tied together by the Counselor.

"Grace is Bashard's granddaughter by blood," he said, "but his daughter and heir by law. It's all there in the papers."

"I didn't know you could legally adopt your own granddaughter," I said.

"You can do virtually anything legally," the Counselor answered, "if you're willing to pay the price." A remark he relished.

"What happened to Grace's real mother?"

"Money," he said. "Major money, as you'll see. She was a

so-called flower child, in the Haight-Ashbury district. She had more use for money than for a baby."

"And Johnny?"

"Cut out. Disinherited. Raul Bashard doesn't have much use for homosexuals."

I thought about that for a moment.

"Could be Johnny'd want to get even," I said.

"Could be. But the last I heard he was living in Sydney, Australia. That's the gay capital of the Southern Hemisphere, I'm told."

And a long way away, I thought.

"What about Grace?" I asked.

"What about her?"

"Well, in the first place, I could imagine her cutting somebody's throat. Particularly somebody who keeps her a virtual prisoner. And if she stands to inherit everything, then—"

But the Counselor shook his head at the idea.

"I know," I said, irritated, "he trusts her more than anything in the world, he—"

"It's not that," the Counselor interrupted. "Maybe he trusts her, maybe he doesn't. But if it's money she's after, she stands to lose a lot more than she'd gain."

I didn't understand what he was talking about.

"It's in his will," he said, handing a folder over. "Read the last section."

I found the last section. In the event of Raul Bashard's death by other than natural causes, Grace would inherit a vastly reduced amount, and it would remain in trust even after her twenty-first birthday. The rest would go to a variety of foundations and charitable organizations. Grace wouldn't be exactly destitute, but she might have to trade the silver spoon in for stainless steel.

So much for trust, I thought. Maybe the Dobermans fared better, but there was no reference to them in the last section.

I wondered if the proviso would stand up in court. Then I noticed that the will's sole executor was Charles Camelot, and I figured it would.

"You're wrong about the paranoia, Phil," the Counselor

said. "He may seem so, but we all might seem a little paranoid in his position. If he believes someone's out to kill him, then I think there's a good chance someone's out to kill him."

I disagreed. We argued the point. I'd ruled out everybody inside the castle except Grace, and Bashard's will tended to rule out Grace. Assuming money counted with her. A reasonable assumption, I thought.

The Counselor wanted to know about the hate mail. I'd sampled a lot of it the day before, more than I'd wanted to. The Dean of Science Fiction got mail by the sackful; a certain percentage of it could be (and was) classified as hate mail, and some of it was unprintable. People wanted money. People wanted (as he'd pointed out) to give him their organs and/or to acquire his organs. People (more female than male, but far from a hundred percent) were enraged that he hadn't answered their intimate invitations. And so on. Nobody so far as I know has ever made a study of it, but I'd still bet the percentage of hate in Raul Bashard's hate mail was no higher, no lower, than that in any celebrity's. There are crazies all over the place, some of whom write letters, and if Bashard had a would-be killer among them it would take a track team to find him.

In that case, the Counselor said, I should hire a track team.

"If you want my opinion," I said, "he's as safe inside that castle as anyone could be. The real problem is that he's planning to leave it—for the first time in God knows how long. If you want my opinion, that's what's got him scared: the BashCon. But when I suggested he cancel, he said, 'Once I undertake to do something, once I give my word, then it will require more than the threat of death to keep me from it.'"

If I say so myself, my imitation of Bashard wasn't half bad.

"It doesn't matter whether you think he's safe, Phil," the Counselor said. "It's whether he *is* safe. Hire the track team."

You win some, you lose some.

I shrugged and put the call through from the Counselor's desk. Bud Fincher was a private detective we sometimes used. He has his own agency and plugs into a network of other agencies across the country. I arranged for a meeting the next morning. Bud was no genius, but he could provide the track team, even though I was pretty sure nothing would come of it except a bill. Which the computer would charge back to Raul Bashard.

I'd just hung up and was starting to explain the BashCon to the Counselor when the door behind me opened. There was a commotion and a rush and a beige-colored whir bounded across the room and onto my lap. It was Muffin, the Counselor's Wife's cocker bitch, her stub tail going a thousand beats a minute.

I stood up.

"I'm sorry, darling," the Counselor's Wife's voice rang behind me. "I didn't know you were in the midst. Do you realize what time it is?"

The Counselor stood up, too, and the dog thrashed and rolled on the carpet, and Nora Saroff Camelot surged between us. *Surge* is the key word. I mean, when the Counselor's Wife comes into a room, nothing's ever the same as it was before.

She's a tall and some say beautiful woman, striking certainly, with ash-blonde hair and salient, highly photogenic features, plus a loud voice that takes over a conversation the minute she gets into it. I've always had a hard time imagining her a shrink, somebody who has to listen to people's troubles for hours on end.

"Oh hi, Phil, I didn't know you were back. How'd you like the Great Writer? If you two aren't finished, why don't you come upstairs for a drink, Phil? I want to hear all about the dread Bashard—you're more than welcome to stay for dinner, too. We're eating in, aren't we, darling? Yes, you're eating in, too, Muffie McTuffie . . ."

While she talked she was in constant motion around the office. The Counselor stood like an eye in the sudden storm, beaming, and I, for the umpteenth time, was struck by how he, who usually and easily dominates a scene, stepped aside and let her take control.

Maybe that's love.

I turned down her invitation. I said I had another engagement, but I thanked her anyway.

"Who is she tonight, Phil?"

This was part of the ritual. The Counselor's Wife is as insistent on trying to fix me up as she pretends to be convinced I'm a hopeless philanderer. I've sometimes wondered what would happen if I ever took her up on the first, or agreed with her on the second. As is, I mostly duck.

I did, as it turned out, have another engagement. Even if I hadn't, though, I'd have pleaded one. To simplify, say that I prefer West Side cooking to East Side.

Her name is Laura Hugger, a fitting name. We've been between-people people for each other, off and on, for a very long time. I guess we each think we could do better, and sometimes we try, and then when things fall apart for one or the other of us, we start off again. We go to the movies together, now and then to a Broadway show, once in a blue moon for a weekend in the mountains. But mostly we eat dinner together, Thai or Chinese, and then go to her place or mine and screw each other's brains out. And few questions asked. Only recently the questions have gotten more numerous again, which makes me think—Laura, too, probably— that we've been here before and maybe could do better elsewhere.

We were just getting started, chopsticks at the ready, on some General Ching's Chicken and Beef With Four Flavors on the upstairs floor of a Hunan joint we like. We'd dawdled over a couple of drinks. The coziness was setting in. It must have been around ten. Then the beeper went off in my pocket.

We use the system sparingly. I mean, we're not doctors and we don't make house calls. But the Counselor insists I carry one, and once or twice it's come in handy.

I excused myself and went to the phone.

I didn't get the Counselor himself, only his voice on the answering tape.

"Grace Bashard wants you, Phil. She called you. She claims an emergency. Call her immediately."

He gave me the phone number, then the tape went dead. No explanation.

I had one of those uh-oh premonitions. I saw Ms. Laura Hugger eyeing me across the restaurant.

I punched 0, then the number, then my credit-card number. "Thank you-u-u," droned the recorded operator. The number hadn't rung once before Grace answered.

"Oh Phil," she said breathily, "I'm glad you called. Thank God it's you. Oh Phil, it's terrible . . ."

She started to sob then.

"Grace," I interrupted, "pull yourself together now. I can't understand—"

". . . Jules! It's Jules, Phil! Jules is dead!"

I started to say: Who's Jules? Then I caught myself. Jules Verne, one of Bashard's Dobermans.

"Tell me what happened, Grace."

"I can't. Daddy's beside himself. Jules is dead, and Daddy won't talk to anybody. He told me to get you, then he shut himself up. Oh Phil, you've got to come, I . . ."

Then she was sobbing again.

There was no stopping her except to say I'd come. I told her I'd be there in forty-five minutes.

I hung up and went back between the tables. The joint was full, people talking, people eating, people making plans—all except Laura Hugger, who was still eyeing me as I came her way.

I hadn't told her about Bashard.

"I'm sorry, Laura, I've got to go," I said. It may have sounded stupid to say: "A dog is dead, a dog called Jules Verne," but I said that, too.

"Fine," said Laura, "it's fine, Phil," in a shorthand that told me that it wasn't fine at all but what the hell did I expect her to do about it?

I paid the check and took Laura home. No, she didn't want to finish dinner without me. Ten minutes later I had the Fiero out of the garage and was on my way.

CHAPTER
3

It was cooler in the suburbs by a good ten degrees, and pitch-dark in the estate area till I got to Bashard's. All the floodlights were on, lighting up the grounds like a baseball diamond, but there wasn't a living soul in sight.

Weird.

Price controlled me in through the front gates, and he was waiting for me at the portico entrance. Price was the button-down chauffeur in the Mercedes, and doubled as Bashard's bodyguard. He was a product, I knew, of the United States Navy by way of the University of Southern California. Bashard had recruited him out of the service simply by tripling his salary.

According to Price, Mr. Bashard had gone on a tour of the grounds with the two Dobermans after dinner. He often did this. After that, things became unclear. The dogs sometimes sat with Mr. Bashard until he went to bed. Sometimes they slept in the pantry, sometimes outside in their kennel. Sometimes Jules slept upstairs with Grace but never the two dogs together. In any case, they had access to the main

house through a dog door in the pantry, and they came and
went pretty much as they pleased.

Mr. Bashard had retired after their walk. Grace had been in
her room. Price himself, he said, was talking to MacGregor,
the cook, while the cook cleaned up after dinner.

They'd heard a howling outside the house. They'd paid it
no attention at first. Dogs howl. When it persisted, they'd
gone outside and found the other Doberman, Herbert,
baying alone in the darkness. Mr. Bashard had joined them.
They couldn't shut Herbert up. They'd turned the floods on
and gone investigating, Herbert leading the way, and had
eventually found Jules lying at the back end of the property—an area beyond the eyes of the cameras where the road
curved and the vegetation, mostly rhododendrons, grew
thickly over the fence.

"We carried him back here," Price said. "The poor bugger
didn't have a mark on him. He had to have been poisoned.
We found some meat samples just to this side of the fence.
Mr. Bashard said some crazy son of a bitch must have
thrown them there. Then Grace herself, when she saw the
body, she went crazy. She was very attached to that dog."

I asked Price where everybody was now. He said Grace
had been given a sedative after she'd called me. He guessed
she was asleep. She'd gone crazy, he repeated, when she'd
seen the dead animal. She'd wanted them to call the police.
Mr. Bashard had refused. He wouldn't have the police in the
house. She'd wanted to call the vet, at least to check out
Herbert. Mr. Bashard had refused that, too. Then she had
called me. As for Mr. Bashard, he'd left instructions that he
wasn't to be disturbed, not even when I got there.

Then what was the rush? I started to ask, getting a fleeting
last glimpse of Laura Hugger. And why me? But Price wasn't
the person to answer.

"Do you want to see the corpse?" he asked me.

I didn't especially, but he wanted to show it to me.

I followed him through the living room, its emptiness
startling with the lights on, and down the back hall past the
dining room, through the empty kitchen, to the pantry. The
pantry itself was larger than most kitchens I'd seen, even so-

called country kitchens. The walls were lined with glass-fronted mahogany cabinets that held glassware and china. They looked like they'd come with the house. But in the center was one of those enormous, modern, aisle-type counters, with double stainless-steel sinks and dishwashers underneath and a butcher block top that looked long enough to play shuffleboard on. Sitting on the butcher block was a bundle, wrapped in a plaid steamer rug.

Price unwrapped the bundle.

Jules's body was on its side, the front legs stretched forward and the hind ones back toward the rear, giving the dog a strangely elongated look. The eye I could see was almost but not entirely shut, showing a reddish slit, and the upper lip lifted slightly over the gums. I've little enough experience with dead animals, but this one's coat already seemed to have lost its luster. It was mat-textured and dry, like worn velvet.

"Go ahead," Price said next to me. "Go ahead and touch him." Price chuckled a little. "He won't bite."

I touched the Doberman's flank. It still felt velvety. The bodyguard picked up the front paws together, swinging the torso as he lifted them, then let them drop with a clunk.

"Already stiff," he said matter-of-factly.

I could smell, faintly, a doggy odor; but nothing you'd associate with death.

"Are you going to have an autopsy done?" I said.

"I thought so," Price answered. "But Mr. Bashard said no. We've got the meat samples, though. They're on ice, in the refrigerator. We'll have them tested tomorrow morning. But you already know the answer. I'll give you a hundred to one, and then some. You can see, there's not a mark on him. Flip him over on the other side, same thing."

Either Price was a frustrated mortician or he was enjoying baiting me.

"Go ahead," he went on. "Flip him over and take a look."

I didn't.

"The one thing that makes no sense," I said, "is if it was poison, why is only one of the dogs dead? They did everything together, didn't they?"

Price shrugged.

"Well, not everything," he said. "They're different, once you've been around them a while. But," he confided, "I thought the same thing."

"Then why not have an autopsy and make sure?"

"That's what I thought. But . . ."

I felt him stiffen next to me even before he turned around. I turned with him.

Raul Bashard was standing in the doorway behind us, propping himself with a cane in his right hand. With his left he held the flaps of his bathrobe together. The bathrobe was navy blue with white piping, and a white monogram and the pajamas underneath were a pale blue. He wore sneakers on his feet, untied, and no socks.

"There'll be no autopsy on my dog, Revere," he said. "I fought the vivisectionists once, I'll fight them again. The dog is dead. He'll be buried in peace."

"Yes, sir," Price said beside me, standing at attention.

"I don't know if you heard my question, Mr. Bashard," I said, "but if it was poison, why would one dog be alive and the other dead? They were brothers, weren't they? Didn't they do everything together?"

"Half brothers," Bashard said. "They came from the same bitch but a different litter. As to why Herbert didn't eat the tainted meat, there are any number of possible explanations, but the simplest one is this: he didn't eat it because he was with me. Herbert came up with me in the elevator after my constitutional. Jules didn't. I assumed he was with my daughter, but he must have gone out again. After a while Herbert must have left me, too. I paid no attention until I heard him howling."

I don't know whether it was the late hour or the bathrobe or the cane, but Bashard looked older as he came toward us. His complexion shone waxy pale, his eyes were semiclosed, and his body seemed to lean forward onto the cane.

He came between us, stood there with a slight tremor and put his hand on the dog's shoulder.

"Poor beastie," he said. Then, turning to Price, peremptorily: "You should learn to treat the dead with more respect, Price, even if it's only an animal. Wrap him up now."

"Yes, sir," Price answered.

"We'll bury him tomorrow. Right now, every man jack of us can go to bed."

We did, but at least one of us not to sleep—not immediately, anyway. I was bothered by a number of things, among them the dislocation of having been yanked out of my routine. And Grace asleep, under "sedation." Like what sedative? And Raul Bashard (apparently confusing the dissection of the dead with that of the living) refusing an autopsy—when the dog's murder, coming after his stated fear for his own life, ought to have made him want to know everything. And finally, one Doberman dead and the other still alive, locked up, so Price had said, in the kennel. Before I fell asleep I heard him howl outside, the mournful sound curling through my window and around my bed.

The household was roused at six-fifteen, I by a phone call from MacGregor, the cook. Breakfast was served, inside, at seven; the ceremony began at seven-thirty.

Grace arrived late in the dining room after Bashard; Price and I had already begun. The buffet was set up on a long mahogany sideboard: scrambled eggs in a silver tureen, hashed browns in another, sizzling strips of bacon on a hot tray, a large crystal bowl of fresh fruit set in ice, diagonal slices of toast in little silver racks. But all Grace wanted was orange juice. She gulped two glasses while she stood at the buffet, poured and drank a third, then poured a fourth and brought it with her to the table.

Bashard sat at the end of the long table, Price and I facing each other at his sides. Grace slumped in a chair several places down from Price and stared fixedly at her orange juice, then at the coffee which the cook poured from a silver pot. Her face looked puffed—the eyelids, lips, the cheeks—the way children's faces look when they're awakened too early. Her blonde hair swirled across her face. Sometimes she flicked it out of the way; sometimes she didn't bother, as though she'd forgotten it. She wore a starched white shirt that looked designer, the ends knotted at the midriff, and tight-fitting faded jean shorts with strings hanging from the hems that had, I guessed, been cut from full-length. Her legs and feet were bare, her yawns uncovered, her conversation minimal.

Bashard contented himself with a small silver pot of yogurt, which he scraped at determinedly, and repeated cups of tea. Price and I helped ourselves amply but we hardly made a dent in the food. I couldn't help but wonder who would eat the rest of it. Or, for that matter, sit at all the vacant places at the table. Or sleep in all the empty rooms.

Precisely at seven-thirty, Bashard got up and led us onto the back lawn, cane in hand. He wore approximately the same costume I'd first met him in: tailored jacket, a starched white button-down shirt open at the neck, knife-sharp trousers, and the inevitable sockless sneakers. The cook, MacGregor, met us at the corner of the house, still in his apron, carrying the bundle containing the dead Doberman— now covered with a white shroud that looked like it had been cut and stitched from a sheet.

We stopped once, at the kennel, where Bashard opened the gate and fastened a choke chain to the waiting Doberman. Herbert seemed subdued like the rest of us. He walked docilely by his master, gracefully, in the forefront of the procession.

It was a gorgeous morning. There was still a crispness in the air, a sharp blue sky dotted with pillow clouds, and a breeze swept across the hillside into the green woods before us.

At the edge of the woods the gardener waited, a short, stocky, balding man called Kohl. He'd served in the Navy, too, a twenty-year vet. He leaned on his shovel now. Next to the first of a stand of oak trees he'd dug a short narrow grave.

Bashard halted; so did the rest of the household. Again I was struck by how few they were. Gardener, cook, chauffeur, daughter, dog. Bashard. Somehow there should have been more. Goats, sheep, housekeepers. Instead of housekeepers, a professional cleaning service worked the house from top to bottom twice a week. Ditto a landscaping service for the grounds. Laundry and cleaning went in and out on a truck. Provisions were delivered. An outside secretarial service sent in temps, and a security service came monthly to verify their installations. Daily tasks were divided mostly by MacGregor and Kohl.

Bashard handed Herbert's choke chain to Price and his cane to me. He took the bundle from MacGregor and, kneeling, placed it in the shallow grave. Then he stood erect and started to speak.

It wasn't a sermon exactly, and certainly not a prayer. More of a statement. Some funeral music would have livened it up. Anyway, the part I remember went something like this: "This material that covers you, beast, will rot and crumble. Your flesh, your eyes, will be eaten away. Your bones will last longest, your skull, but these, too, will be pulverized. Your dust will seep into the ground, the earth and the sea will rise over you, and you will be part of the planet to whatever creatures then live on it. Until the planet itself dies. Only then will the continuity break on Earth."

Heavy stuff, but not a shred of emotion in the voice.

That was the last line: "Only then will the continuity break on Earth." Then Bashard beckoned to Kohl for the shovel and dug one, then a second shovelful of dirt from the mound beside the grave and emptied them into the hole. Then he stood back, breathing deeply, and turned to hand the shovel to Grace.

I wasn't paying full attention and missed her initial reaction. I felt her start back, though, like she was reacting to being struck. When I looked at her, her face was screwed into a grimace. Then she caught herself, glared at Bashard, big-eyed and breasts heaving, and screamed at him: "You lousy filthy *creep!*"

With that she swerved, stumbled almost to the ground, pushed off with her hand and, catching her balance, took off full tilt toward the house.

It all happened, and ended, in a couple of seconds.

I looked at the others for explanation, at Bashard holding the shovel, at Price pulling on Herbert's choke chain. But there was no explanation. Bashard just stared after Grace, head stiff into the breeze, expression impervious.

And Grace kept running.

Bashard broke the mood himself. He glanced down at his watch.

"Well," he said, surveying us evenly, "it's time I went to work. Here. You boys finish the job, will you?"

He handed me the shovel in exchange for his cane, then, pushing off, strode back across the lawn after his daughter at a pace so vigorous that us plain mortals would have had trouble keeping up.

I couldn't get anything out of them, not even with Bashard and Grace gone. If they were covering up, well, then they were covering up.

"She's like that," MacGregor, the cook, said while we filled the grave back in with dirt. "Up and down, that's just the way she is."

"Okay," I said, "but why'd she call him a creep? Does she think he did it? That he'd poison his own dog?"

"You'll have to ask her," Kohl, the gardener, answered with a half-laugh and a shrug. "She's some handful all right. You never know with her."

"A real pistol," MacGregor said. "Always has been, since she was in pigtails."

Price, I guessed, knew more, but if he had an opinion as to what had made her crazy, he wasn't telling.

During my first visit, I'd set up shop in one of the outbuildings, and that's where I went now. It was a sort of combination storeroom and office where there was access to the computer—limited access, as I found out—and a telephone.

First I called the Counselor and reported what had happened. Then I dialed Fincher and Associates, the private detective agency. Bud Fincher wasn't in yet, so I left a message calling off the meeting scheduled for that morning and putting him on standby for later that day. Then I called Muffin's vet. Muffin's vet was in all right, but he was in surgery. The place, his receptionist told me, was a madhouse, and I could hear barking in the background. I asked the receptionist about dog-training schools.

"*Dog*-training schools!" she answered. "But Muffin's too old."

"It's not for Muffin."

"Oh, don't tell me, Phil. You haven't gone and gotten one of your own? We've made you a convert at last. I bet you got a mutt."

I told her the information was for a friend, not for me. She sounded disappointed. She told me to hold on and left me listening to the barking. Then she came back and gave me a list of three. But the best, she said, was run by a group of monks out in the Poconos. She gave me the number.

I dialed Pennsylvania and got a Brother Alexander on the phone. When I told him I'd just bought a male Doberman pinscher pup, I learned more than I wanted to know about the Brothers' program. I managed to get my questions in here and there, and answers, but Brother Alexander was not to be deterred.

Then I started talking to the computer. I didn't have a lot of confidence in its capacity to solve the death of Jules Verne, and in this I was right. There was no "Animal" category in the file, no "Hate, Animal," no "Dog," no "Canine," no "Doberman," no "Jules," nor "Herbert," nor "Verne," nor "Wells." Maybe some specially gifted shrink, sifting through the crazy mail, could have detected the Bashard-hater who would have chosen the writer's dogs as the target in lieu of the writer himself. More likely, I thought, was that some secret dog-hater lurking in that placid neighborhood had planted the bait. But the computer couldn't help me there, Bashard had ruled out the local constabulary, and besides, something Brother Alexander mentioned had left me doubtful on that score, too.

I put the question of Jules aside. *Hire the track team*, the Counselor had ordered, so I set out to give the track team something to do.

There was plenty. Too much, in fact. If you'd tried to check out the authors of every piece of threat mail Bashard had received, you could still be looking long after he'd checked out himself, either by natural or unnatural means. I therefore had to apply some fairly arbitrary criteria. For instance, I ruled out all correspondents who hadn't written in the past two years. And I ruled out correspondents from places other than North America. With the single exception of Australia, Sydney. But there was no entry for Australia, Sydney.

The common wisdom has it that computers are stupid machines. Very fast, but fundamentally stupid. Bashard's programs, though, had a level of sophistication that made you wonder. For one thing, I'd had the idea that some poor human slob had had to key in every word of every piece of correspondence, a numbing task. Wrong. The computer did it itself. With the exception of the very worst handwriting samples, it deciphered human script, and when I ran across some apparent howlers and accessed the original documents, I found that it had done a better job of transcribing than most live secretaries could have.

In addition to sorting by correspondent, date, postmark, place (state and zip code), etc., the computer categorized by type—Dangerous, Moderate, Mild—and also by theme. There were five theme categories in all: Sex, Money, Race, Politics, and Miscellaneous. Strangely enough, Miscellaneous was the smallest. So much for the predilections of Americans, or at least science-fiction fans.

Sex was largely the "unrequited lover" group Bashard had mentioned, and some of the letters, as he'd said, were too steamy to print.

Money was the biggest category, mostly people dunning him, some with incredible persistence and vituperation.

Race and Politics were the most peculiar. I'd read somewhere that science-fiction writers in general, and Raul Bashard in particuliar, were racist and right wing, but the vast majority of correspondence in these categories accused him of not being racist and right wing enough. There were, for example, a number of mailgrams from a group calling itself The White Army, obsessed by Bashard's alleged promoting of miscegenation, that invited him to book burnings of his own works.

I mentioned that the computer limited my access to its

files. I came across two such instances that day, both linked, both in the Money category. The author of one was named Leo Mackes, who'd written a series of dunning letters more pitiful than threatening in tone, and the last of them just made my two-year cutoff so I paid it little attention. The second, more current, was from a Viola T. Harmel, who sometimes signed her name Viola and sometimes V.T.H. Viola's prose was pretty purple, and intimate enough at times to convince you Bashard had to have been more than a pen pal. I wondered why the computer had classified her under Money. But the latest received, a postcard, read:

> The charade between us has to stop. Frankly I need the money; you don't. I'm ready to talk about an equitable division, but if you won't negotiate, then you'll have to face the consequences. You'd better take my call the next time. Yrs. Viola.

The computer had classified both Viola T. Harmel and Leo Mackes under Moderate—fair enough, I thought. In both cases it gave the same cross-reference: see S.O.W. I tried to see S.O.W. The only trouble was that every time I asked for S.O.W., the computer asked back for the access code. I didn't have the access code, and I couldn't find a way in without it. I brought back the originals of the Mackes/Harmel correspondence but couldn't spot a resemblance between the two, either in style or handwriting. In the end, I made a mental note to get the access code later, then instructed the computer to print out by the criteria I'd selected, in state, city and zip code order.

It set about its tedious work.

At some point while I waited, I guess I sensed her coming into the office. I think she even said something, but I didn't focus—at least, that is, till her arms went around my neck from behind, then down my chest, and her hair brushed my cheek as she leaned over me. Then it was hard not to focus.

Grace giggled softly, nuzzling into my ear, and tried to pin me to the chair. I pulled her wrists apart and stood up. She had changed outfits, tight jeans now with baggy pockets and leather trim, and a bulky jeans jacket that was zipped about halfway up and gave you a glimpse of bright pink underneath.

"Well, Pablo," she said, "did you figure it out yet?"

"Figure out what?" I asked, ignoring the name.

"Well, whatever you're trying to figure out. Like who wants to kill Daddy? Like who poisoned Jules?"

"What makes you so sure he was poisoned?"

"C'mon, Pablo, give me a break. You don't suppose he died of a heart attack, do you?"

"I don't know," I answered. "I'd like to know why you called your father a creep this morning."

"The Big O won't tell you that, will it?"

"The Big O?"

"The computer. O is for Oscar. That's its name."

She was standing very close to me, her head down, her fingers twiddling her hair. She came up to about my shoulders. I could smell the hair.

"I could tell you, Pablo," she said softly, her head still down. She giggled a little. "Everything you wanted to know. A lot more than Oscar. If you knew how to ask me, Pablo."

"What's Sow?" I asked.

"Sow," she repeated, half-hearing.

"Or S.O.W.? Or Leo Mackes? Viola T. Harmel? Did you ever hear of them?"

She shook her head.

"You ask pretty weird questions, Pablo," she said.

"I don't like being called that," I said.

"I know," she said, giggling again. "Daddy said you didn't like to be called Pablo. Why's that? What's wrong with Pablo?"

I reached up, lifted her chin firmly with the palm of my hand.

"Where'd you learn about that? The Pablo part?" I said.

She ducked away from my hand and, leaning past me, tapped at the computer keyboard.

I turned to watch my own file come up on the screen, the lines scrolling up successively. It was accurate in every detail, and plenty detailed. Like:

NAME: Revere, Philip (Phil) white male (Born:
   Rivera, Pablo Evaristo Maria)
Age: 37
Health: good (quit smoking)
Sign: Gemini
Function: see Camelot
Marital status: single
Earnings: not kn.
Net worth: neglig.
Born: Salamanca, Spain
Resides: NYC
Education: Brooklyn Coll., NY; J. D. Brooklyn
   Law (never passed Bar)
Sexual preference: promiscuous

I wondered again where Bashard had gotten it all. The
name part in particular. Few enough people knew. It would
have been public information, sure, for anyone who wanted
to go digging. But who'd want to go digging that far back?
"What is it?" Grace said. "A spic name? Puerto Rican? Is
that why you changed it?"
I thought, but didn't say: *Ask my mother.* I said nothing.
Besides, she couldn't have asked my mother.
"You don't *look* Puerto Rican," she went on. "And why
Phil? Pablo is Paul, isn't it? Daddy said it was because
everybody would have laughed at you if you were called
Paul Revere."
The truth, in fact, isn't worth much space. Probably my
mother was right in that, to an American, anybody with the
name of Rivera had to be either Puerto Rican or Mexican.
And who wants to explain each time that you come from a
place called Salamanca, in western Spain? So when she got
here, a single mother with a single baby and some relatives
in Brooklyn, U.S.A., she'd changed it. And had picked
Philip over Paul for the reason Grace had said. As to why I
don't like being called Pablo, well, I guess it's nothing five
years or so on some shrink's couch couldn't explain. Only
I've never had the inclination.
   End of explanation.

"You're lucky," said Grace, swiveling to face me again and looking up into my eyes. "I hate Grace Bashard. I'd give anything to change my name. Why don't you marry me?"

Her face was all of two inches from mine, uptilted, unblinking, her eyes very wide. Maybe she was joking but I also had the unsettling feeling that if I said "Why not?" I could have found myself standing in front of a justice of the peace before dark.

"Why'd you call him a creep, Grace?" I asked again, a little unsteadily. "I mean, last night when you called me, you were worried, frightened. He was beside himself, you said. But this morning he's a creep. Is it because of that speech he made?"

I think she might have told me a lot of things then and maybe saved a lot of trouble. But she didn't, presumably because she knew we weren't alone. Instead, she threw her arms around my neck and kissed me flush on the mouth, her lips parted, even as Raul Bashard's cane pushed open the door of the outbuilding.

"Excuse me if I'm interrupting," he said, his head ducking forward a little in the doorway, that ceramic smile on his face. "Luncheon is about to be served on the terrace."

CHAPTER
4

"Item," said Raul Bashard crisply. "Jules was killed by cyanide poison. The lab will send us a written report. Item: Both dogs were sent to the same training school. Item: Both were taught not to accept food from strangers. Conclusion: Either the training broke down or the person or persons who left the poisoned meat was no stranger. Any one, or more, of the people who live here could have done the job, alone or in tandem. I prefer to think the dog's training broke down."

(According to Brother Alexander, this would have been impossible for a dog schooled by the Brothers. But Bashard's Dobermans hadn't been.)

We were sitting alone, in white wrought-iron chairs with throne backs and oversize cushions, by the long, glass-topped, wrought-iron table on the rear terrace. A pair of striped parasol umbrellas mounted on stanchions shaded us from the afternoon sun, but it was strong enough to throw dazzles of light off the shimmering surface of the swimming pool. I wore sunglasses, and Bashard a white cap with black beak.

The luncheon dishes had been cleared. Lunch had consisted of light salads, iced tea, and minimal conversation. Over dessert—fresh fruit in scooped-out melon halves—Bashard asked his daughter what she was going to do that afternoon. Grace shrugged, then said she was going shopping. Who was going to take her shopping? She didn't know, she thought she'd ask Price. Price couldn't, Bashard said, he had other duties. Then me, she said, she'd ask me. I couldn't, Bashard said, he needed to talk to me. Then silence. All this time, she'd had her head down. She'd taken off the jeans jacket and flung it over a chair. The jacket had a multicolored GUESS? printed in large capitals across its lining. She wore a bright pink tank top underneath, which showed off her breasts sensationally. Well, Bashard had said, he guessed she couldn't go shopping, was there anything she particularly needed? She shook her head. In that case, he said, he would ask her to excuse herself, he had business to attend to. To my surprise, she got up quietly and wandered into the house, trailing her jeans jacket over her shoulder.

"Item," Bashard said. "My daughter made that scene at the burial this morning because she believes I poisoned the dog myself."

"Why would she believe a thing like that?"

"My daughter often thinks the worst of me. And Jules Verne, she will tell you, was *her* dog."

He went on with another "item." At first, I thought, weirdly, that he was reading my mind, until, with a jolt, the truth occurred to me. Clearly he'd been listening in on my phone calls all morning and monitoring my work with the computer.

"Item," he said. "Sow, or S.O.W., is a defunct code. It should have been edited out of the system a long time ago. It identified members of a group who played chess by computer hookup. Leo Mackes and Viola T. Harmel belonged to the group, so did I. There were others. I never met either one of them. Viola Harmel was the best woman chess player I ever ran into. Well, the second best. Dasha was the best, of course, but that's another story. Viola could have held her own in the U.S. Open."

"You said you never met them?"

"That's right. We all subscribed to the same chess magazine. It had a section called Chess by Mail, a kind of clearinghouse for players looking for partners. Little by little, a group of us who had computers found each other. But I stopped playing years ago. Chess is an obsession. A writer can't afford obsessions. Other than writing, that is."

"But they haven't stopped writing you," I said. "At least Harmel hasn't."

He waved his hand in the air, a dismissing gesture. A very steady hand, I noticed.

"People fall on hard times," he said. "Even chess players. Particularly chess players."

"Have you ever sent her any money?" I asked.

He shook his head.

"It sounds like she thinks you owe her some."

"I don't," he replied. "What's she classed as now? A Moderate?"

His grin was genuine enough, not the perpetual ceramic one. He seemed to enjoy my realization that every phone call in the place was recorded, every computer inquiry monitored. For all I know, a camera had recorded Grace's kissing me.

"Item," he said. "Don't let my daughter's advances bother you. She tries the same thing on everyone who comes here. Ask Price. Hell, you can ask the cook and the gardener. It stops after a while. Teenage stuff. It's like a rite of passage into the household."

One rite, I thought, I didn't much want to pass.

"Unless," he added, "you'd *like* to marry her? That would be a different story."

The grin again, glinting even in the shadow of his capbill.

"Why do you keep her a prisoner?" I asked.

"A *prisoner*?" he replied, either surprised by the question or doing a good job of feigning surprise. "Is that what she said? Hell, she's no more a prisoner here than I am. She has everything she wants. Except a car, that's true. Do you think

I'm wrong not to give her a car? She has friends, plenty of friends." All of whom, I thought, would be in Oscar's file. "She can have them over anytime she wants."

"What about school?" I said.

"What about it?" he retorted.

"Well, why doesn't she go? I think it may even be against the law."

His face tightened, his teeth seeming to clench.

"And I think you're overstepping yourself a little," he said abruptly. "It isn't against the law, not anymore. She's eighteen now. And I've been through it with schools. The ones I've seen, they're not worth the cost of the heads." This was his only reference that I can recall, if it was one, to his son and Grace's blood father. "Besides, anything I haven't been able to teach her we've had tutors for. Do you want to know something, with your *schools*? She took the SAT's this year. That's Scholastic Aptitude Tests, if you didn't know. Do you know how she did? Well, I'll tell you. Well enough to get into any college in the country, that's how."

"If you'll let her go," I said quietly.

"*Let her go!*" he shouted hoarsely back at me. "What makes you think *I'll* have anything to say about it! *I'm* not going to be here, it'll be *her* decision!"

His hand had started shaking, and he had to lean it on the tabletop to stop it. Veins stood out on his neck. I half stood, reached forward, saw Price start forward from the French doors of the house. But Bashard waved me off, waved us both off, and by plain force of will—I can think of no other way to describe it—caught hold of himself. Then he sat back, breathing deeply, slowly. He took his cap off and wiped his forehead with a handkerchief taken from the breast pocket of his jacket.

Bashard's anger, I thought, was like another rite of passage. It built up fast, edged with scorn; it blasted at you; then it stopped.

"Excuse me," he said. "Don't you have work to do now, anyway?"

I nodded.

"Yes," I said, "I've work to do." I hesitated, hearing the

Counselor's voice in my head—*Hire the track team*—but I went ahead and said it anyway: "If you want to know what I think, though, the work won't add up to anything. Sure, there may be someone who wants to kill you out there, maybe more than one, and if there are, maybe we'll find them. But I see no evidence of it. *Wanting* to kill someone isn't a crime. *Trying* to kill someone is. Killing a dog, for instance, is, but you don't seem to want to pursue that one. As it stands, the odds of someone trying to kill you don't look very good to me."

"I wish I could share your confidence," Bashard replied.

"If you really feel yourself in danger," I went on, "then you should stay here. The only way you're going to die here is by stepping on a cake of soap."

"What do you mean?"

I'd already brought up the subject once and been shot down, but there was no harm trying again.

"I mean: if you feel the way you do, then cancel the BashCon."

He thought about that a moment. Then he drew himself up in his chair, very erect.

"There's no way I will do that," he said, gazing out firmly over the pool. "I'm only going to be eighty once—next week—and never again. My professional colleagues—fellow writers, critics, publishers, editors, booksellers, readers—have seen fit to honor the date. It may well be their last chance. There is no way I am going to let them down." He paused, as though to let the statement sink in. Then, leaning forward in a more confidential tone: "But I agree with you, Revere. Most likely, that is where the attempt will be made. At BashCon. That is how I see your assignment. Throw all your resources into it. Identify the suspects, observe them, track them."

He might be a little paranoid, the Counselor had said, *but we all might be a little paranoid in his position*. Yes. What he wanted, in any case, seemed do-able. With the help of Bud Fincher's track team, we could put an arm on the crazy correspondents I'd singled out, could observe and track them, could, if any of them showed at the BashCon, probably deter them. I could also get a line on the "professional colleagues" who would be in attendance.

It seemed a waste of time, though. From all I'd seen so far, the only one with murder in the eye was the eighteen-year-old bombshell, Grace. *You lousy filthy creep.* At that particular moment, she'd been capable of anything.

I wondered if Grace knew about that proviso in his will. I had an idea she did.

I tried to review the BashCon preparations, but Bashard plainly wasn't interested. He waved them away. It was all up to me, he said. He'd do whatever I wanted him to do.

He pleaded fatigue then. He glanced at his watch, said he wanted a nap before dinner. An old man, he said with a chuckle, needed his sack time when he could get it, particularly when he spent most of his nights with his eyes wide open.

He stood up unsteadily. I handed him his cane and walked slowly with him to the house. There Price took over. I watched the two of them rise up in the small elevator cage, then climbed the stairs, got my things and went back out to the garage where my Fiero was parked among the great foreign machines of Bashard's fleet.

No sign of Grace, meanwhile.

I drove down the driveway, flickered the gates with my headlights in the sequence Price had taught me, then down the winding road through the estates to the tree-lined streets of the town. It was good to be back to where normal people led presumably normal lives. I slugged a tape into the cassette player. It was good, too, a little later, to see the friendly skyline of Manhattan when the Fiero and I got hung up in the pre-rush-hour traffic on the Lincoln Tunnel ramp.

Bud Fincher was waiting for me in my office when I got there, a cadaverously tall man with a balding dome and rimless glasses that give him a professorial look. He's no genius, like I said, but thorough and well-organized. We worked through the lists I'd brought back, and he made some phone calls from my desk. It was only after he'd left, when I was emptying out my briefcase, that I discovered Grace's note.

I guess she'd intended it that way.

It read:

> "My Dearest,
> "You'll be away and safe when you read this. I'm very glad, even though it breaks my heart not to have you close. He would destroy you if you stayed. He destroys everything I care about. He killed Jules or had Jules killed, I know that. He knows I know that.
> "I have so many things to tell you, my heart is bursting, but I have to find a way to get this to you without him finding about it.
> "Love and XXXXXXXXXXXXXXXXXX"

The X's wound their way around her signature, which wasn't her name but a cartoon figure of a little girl. Then they continued down to an afterthought scrawled across the bottom of the page:

> "You must stay away from here, Pablo love. Don't try to come to me either. I'll find a way of coming to you."

"What do you make of it, Nora?" the Counselor asked, handing Grace Bashard's letter to his wife.

"I think the electric chair should be brought back for anyone who murders an animal."

"I mean the letter. Grace's letter."

We were upstairs in the fifth-floor solarium, watching night fall on the neighborhood. The Counselor sipped his usual drink, pure malt Scotch with a touch of water. The Counselor's Wife had changed clothes, I guessed. She wore a gauzy, big-sleeved lounging outfit of a color which matched her hair, and she drank some Campari concoction. Her hair, which she mostly wore piled on her head, hung loose and long. Muffin, the cocker bitch, panted quietly in the corner where their love seats met, her curled tongue protruding slightly from her mouth.

"Oh, it's about sex," the Counselor's Wife said blithely when she'd finished reading, handing him back the letter. "I don't mean Phil and Grace, darling. I mean Grace and Raul Bashard. From everything Phil's said, it's clear the idea of getting into her pants drives Bashard absolutely crazy. And she, knowing it, plays it for all it's worth. Writes love notes to other men, et cetera. Bored teenagers, even eighteen-year-old ones, are like that."

I usually avoided such moments—when the Counselor's Wife held forth—like the plague. As for the Counselor, he'd managed to get his pipe stuffed, meanwhile sprinkling some tobacco into his lap, and now he fumbled absent-mindedly for matches.

"I thought the Oedipus complex," he said, "tried to explain what happens between parents and children, not grandparents and granddaughters. Aren't they both a little old for that?"

"Not if it's unresolved," the Counselor's Wife said. "If it's unresolved, it can last forever. Where do you think most of my patients come from? Besides, Raul Bashard passes himself off as her father, not her grandfather. Do you think that's an accident?"

"But he's seventy-nine years old, almost eighty. And his health is atrocious."

"Sex is much more about mind than body. Men are capable of staying virile far longer than they think they are, darling. Into their eighties, even beyond. Look at the Georgians, they're still making babies when they're a hundred. From what Phil says about his life-style, Raul Bashard has had few opportunities for sex in recent years. Imagine that such a man is both virile and frustrated, put him into daily contact with an eighteen-year-old who may also be starved for sex, or at least wants to be, and knows how to tell men she is, including, I would guess, her father, or grandfather . . . and you have a very powerful combination."

Standing up, she handed the Counselor the silver match-box from the coffee table. Then she took his glass and hers and strode to the bar. Muffin got up, too, wagging her tail, and followed her.

"Another beer, Phil?"

I passed.

"Unless . . . " she said musingly, still at the bar. Then: "Tell us what you really think, Phil. Do they sleep together?"

"That's absurd and unwarranted!" the Counselor exclaimed.

"Is it? Hardly. You should see the current incest statistics, darling. They'd shock even you. Why do you think you have to pass laws against it? Besides, you haven't seen them together in a long time. Phil has."

She came back with the two glasses and, tossing her hair, sat down again. The dog followed her back and sat down, too. The Counselor looked for something else to fidget with.

"I don't pass the laws, Nora," he said.

"Never mind, you know what I mean," she said. Then she eyed me above her glass. "What do you think, Phil? You've seen them. Are they sleeping together?"

"I saw nothing that says they are," I answered.

This was true enough, but untrue too. Maybe the idea had occurred to me and I'd put it aside. "Suppressed" it, the Counselor's Wife would have said. Or else her theorizing about Bashard and Grace brought certain things to mind that hadn't quite registered at the time.

On the other hand, the Counselor's Wife's stock-in-trade is to explain the world in terms of sex.

"Either way," she went on. "Either way. If they're having sex, it can be a cause of terrible tension and not just because of the incest taboo. A seventy-nine-year-old man, even a virile one, is probably satisfied by doing it once a week. An eighteen-year-old woman isn't. Love letters like this"—pointing at Grace's missive on the coffee table—"could either be expressing a teenage fantasy, and teenage fantasies can be terribly real, or else a very real frustration. On the other hand, if they're *not* having sex but only thinking about it—and at the least it has to be latent in their situation—then the tension would be all the greater."

"In other words," the Counselor said, puffing away now at

his pipe, "you're damned if you do, damned if you don't. But the fact is, my client's convinced somebody's going to try to kill him. It's our role to try to prevent that, not to speculate on his sex life."

"You're the one who asked, darling," the Counselor's Wife said. "But all I'm suggesting is that perhaps you needn't look so far afield."

She turned to me, head tilted, eyebrows raised, mouth a little open.

"What do you think, Phil?"

My first thought was that I didn't want to get caught in the middle between them. Second, if Grace was what Bashard was really afraid of, there wasn't a hell of a lot I could do to help him.

"Besides," the Counselor's Wife went on, "doesn't she inherit all the money?"

I glanced at the Counselor.

"I'm afraid," he said to her, "that that's privileged information."

Which, needless to say, was about the last thing Nora Saroff could tolerate hearing.

She got up abruptly.

"In that case," she retorted, swirling, "you boys stay here and solve your little crime-to-be. I'm going to walk Muffin."

The Counselor stood up, too. So did the spaniel bitch, who, recognizing the buzzword *walk*, beat her owner to the elevator.

"It all sounds fascinating, Phil," the Counselor's Wife called back to me from the elevator, "being in on a murder before it happens. I can't wait to go to the BashCon."

"*What?*" I heard the Counselor shout. "What did you say, Nora?"

But the elevator door had already slid shut.

I knew, though, what would happen next. The Counselor would say they weren't going. Nora would accuse him of antisocial behavior, and the Counselor would say he didn't give a damn what kind of behavior it was, he'd be damned if he was going to spend a weekend in the Catskills with a couple of hundred science-fiction lunatics.

Etc. Etc.

In other words, they'd fight over it till one of them gave in, and in the end they'd show up at the BashCon.

As it turned out, I was right about the second, and I didn't stick around to witness the first. After a few more words with the Counselor, I went down in the elevator myself and out into the night. I guessed which way she and the dog had walked and headed in the other.

My beeper was busy those next days. Even after I disconnected it, Grace managed to get through a couple of times, including one awkward occasion when Laura Hugger and I were otherwise occupied. My home number is unlisted, mind you, and I only give it out to friends, but I suppose if Bashard and his computer had found out about Pablo they could find an unlisted number. So the next night I spent at Laura's, who has a listed number but not one presumably in Big O's file.

What got me was that most of the calls came from Bashard's. This meant that, despite her secretive and lowered voice, they were recorded and probably listened to. Either Grace knew and didn't care, or there was something in what the Counselor's Wife had said after all.

As for me, I ducked and dodged. I tried to reassure her that nothing awful was going to happen to me—or to her, or to anyone. I don't think she ever heard me. She talked in a fog, and as long as somebody was listening somewhere in the fog, that made it okay. Maybe she was stoned some of the time, but a lot of teenagers nowadays sound like they're stoned, and while Grace certainly talked enough about doing drugs, I'd never seen her under the influence.

Would Raul Bashard have tolerated her using them?

That was another question.

The last and wildest conversation we had came one afternoon when she caught me at my desk. Sometimes I pick up the phone myself when Roger LeClerc is too slow. This time it was Grace again.

Did I know where she was?

No, I didn't.

Then I should guess.

I couldn't guess. I really had no idea.

In a shopping mall, the one in Short Hills. I knew where Short Hills was, didn't I? In New Jersey? It was a super mall, she said. She wished I was there. Oh God. It was a bummer that I wasn't, one great big humungous bummer. If I hurried, if I left right away, she'd manage to stall till I got there. Why didn't I come?

I couldn't, I said.

Price had driven her, she said, but there were places in a shopping mall (with a giggle) not even Price could follow her. In fact, she'd already finished her shopping, wait till I saw what she'd bought. It was a teddy. Pause. She'd bought it for me only, she was going to wear it at BashCon. Pause. For me only . . .

She went on in that vein, about how she loved me, missed me, longed for me, and I didn't have anybody else, did I? And so on.

I remember thinking about what Bashard had said, something to the effect that it would wear off, that it was like a rite of passage she put everybody through. And wondering when, and what, it would take for it to stop.

Then suddenly, in one of her quicksilver jumps, it did stop.

I heard it in her tone first. The heavy breathing gone, in its place a harsh, pent-up voice, like she was holding the air in her diaphragm.

"I didn't buy it for you, Phil," she was saying, "I bought it for him. He *makes* me wear things like that." A gasping-for-air sound, short, like a sob. "Hey, that's a *lie*! He'll pretend not to notice, he won't even *care*! He thinks I want the money, that's why I'm there. Somebody ought to kill him. If nobody does, maybe I'll kill him myself. But at least I'll *cry* when I kill him!"

Then she was sobbing for real, and shouting at the same time.

"*You* don't know what it's like! He killed Jules. You've got to help me. If you won't help me, then maybe Price . . . Price isn't such a bad—"

"Stop it, Grace!" I shouted into the phone. Or something like that. "Stop talking like that!"

She went still for a minute. I could hear a hiccuping sound, then quiet. I think she said something like: "Price likes me. . . ."

"Okay, Grace," I said. "I like you, too. Calm down. Just pull yourself together."

Silence.

Then I tried: "Grace? Grace?" a few times, even though the last pause had come and gone and I realized I was talking to a dead phone.

CHAPTER
5

"**H**nnga Hnnga Hnnga."

"Hnnn Hnnn Hnnn."

"Hnnga Hnnga Hnnga."

"Hnnn Hnnn Hnnn.

The Hnngas wore horned helmets, Viking-style. They looked like giant long-haired humans with antlers. I didn't see one that weighed under two hundred ten, and they had big hearty voices to match. The Hnnns, on the other hand, were wiry little people who wore brown leather jackets and those close-fitting brown leather caps with earflaps hanging down, like old-time football players or World War I aviators. The Hnnns had a girl or two among them. The Hnngas were all male. Both groups wandered around the BashCon like rival gangs in some science-fiction novel where size and uniforms divided people into clans. What the purpose of their getups was, or their chants, I never did figure out, but the question didn't seem to bother them. They were harmless enough.

Or so the editor had said, at the publishing company that put out Bashard's works. She was a wispy, curly-headed thing, this Helga Hewitt, pretty in a prim sort of way, about my age but trying to look younger, and she'd come on very literary when I'd gone to see her. She *loathed* the "cons," she confessed to me in her office. The maimed, the unloved, and the crippled, she'd said, that's what they attracted. "Cons" was science-fiction shorthand for "conventions," and there was probably a "con" a week, she guessed, somewhere in the world. They were mostly money-making affairs, for the organizers, but she personally was tired of overweight fans wearing antlers who drank too much beer and thought they had the right to paw all over her. She didn't see why the celebration of Raul's eightieth birthday had had to be turned into another con.

Why had it been? I asked her.

Oh, I'd have to ask Ron that.

Ron was her boss, the publisher himself. Ron—Randall Whitefield was his full name—was a gruff, tall gent with a bald spot and a weight problem who seemed intent on proving to me and/or Helga Hewitt how profit-conscious he was. The answer was simple, Ron said, when I put the same question to him. He didn't have the budget for the kind of party that befitted Raul's eightieth birthday. He'd already told Raul that. If I wanted to see the letter, he'd show it to me. Besides, the fans would come anyway. There was no way anyone could keep them away. That was the bottom line. What the organizers had done, at his suggestion, was to set a registration fee high enough to discourage the unwashed.

What about security? I asked Ron.

Well, what about security? Ron asked back.

It turned out neither he, nor the organizers, had thought much about security. People, after all, didn't show up at science-fiction conventions carrying laser guns. Not real ones anyway. Maybe so, I said, but Mr. Bashard was concerned about security; therefore I was. Was I authorized to represent Raul? Ron asked. Yes I was, with regard to security at the BashCon. At which point, he pleaded another meeting and ushered Helga Hewitt and me out, telling Helga it was up to her to work out the details with me.

Helga Hewitt (I should call her Helga, please) was happy
to defer to me on such questions, only there was no budget
for security, who was going to pay? Did they want Mr.
Bashard (Raul) to pick up the tab? I asked. No, of course not.
Several phone calls later, I learned, that, yes, Ron and the
organizers would split the bill. Several more phone calls and,
yes, I should have the bill sent to the organizers. And no, it
didn't occur to me till later that I should have asked
Whitefield (Ron) why he'd pay Bashard (Raul) two million
dollars for the rights to a single novel but would duck the
cost of a birthday party.

I guess, in hindsight, this is what made him a publisher of
literary works and left me masterminding security at a
science-fiction convention.

The BashCon—WELCOME TO BASHCON HAPPY BIRTHDAY R. R.
BASHARD read the wide banner over the front gateway—was
held in an old rambling place by a lake in the Catskills. It had
been built as a private mansion, then converted into a resort
hotel, then most recently into a center for business meetings,
or "corporate campus." It had its own nine-hole golf course,
a boathouse, tennis courts, an Olympic pool, and three new
fully air-conditioned and sound-equipped buildings—two of
which broke up into meeting and seminar rooms and the
third containing an auditorium and/or banquet facility.
Guests stayed either in the old hotel or in cottages closer to
the lake, or (at least at the BashCon) in sleeping bags and
tents that dotted the grounds. For, as Ron, the publisher, had
predicted, there was just no way to keep people out, not
even with the help of the local police. There were too many
of them, they were too determined, and to judge from some
of the license plates on their cars, vans, and campers, they
had come too far.

There were about a dozen of us for security, including
several of Bud Fincher's people who'd been tracking Bashard's correspondents, and not counting the organizer's staff
or the center's staff, whom we looked to for auxiliary help.
Too many and too few you could say, but we had people in
every important building as well as scattered on the
grounds, and a walkie-talkie communications setup that was

less conspicuous than you might think in that gadget-oriented gathering. We even managed to recruit a Hnnga to our side. As it turned out, he managed a specialty store in Minneapolis, Minnesota, which sold comic books and *Dungeons and Dragons* paraphernalia as well as science fiction; he was happy enough to have his trip turned into an all-expenses-paid affair. We monitored as many individuals as we could against our lists, including the few on Bud Fincher's hot list who turned up, but there were just too many. There were on the one hand professionals of all sorts: editors and writers, book publishing people, magazine publishing people, movie people, journalists, photographers, literary agents, booksellers (some of whom rented booths in the meeting rooms and sold autographed copies signed by the writers present), science-fiction artists (similarly selling their own work), comic book collectors, and what I can only call the trinket dealers (peddling a whole range of paraphernalia from Mr. Spock ear sets to little cast-iron figurines of space people and dragons and wizards with wands and pointed hats). There were food concessions in umbrellaed outdoor stands, beer-and-soft-drink concessions, portable outdoor toilet facilities, and computer and electronic-game facilities. All of them at the service of (and making money off) the fans.

How many fans were there, all in all? The registration roster, fee-paid, ran to some fifteen hundred names. It seemed like they all showed up. How many gate-crashers there might have been is anybody's guess. With a crowd that size you were bound to find every type and age of humanity—ranging from babies on the breast to octogenarians—and we had both extremes. But it was a predominantly young scene, average age probably in the twenties. The sexes were about evenly mixed. They were all white, mostly scruffy, long-haired, overweight, and pasty in complexion—like this was the first time in months most of them had been out-of-doors. Not a drinking crowd, just a noisy one, and people who didn't mind jamming together.

"The maimed, the unloved, and the crippled," Helga Hewitt repeated to me Saturday morning on the porch of the main building, as we surveyed the incoming throng. "It's every guy who never made the team, every girl who never had a date in high school."

"That seems a strange observation," I said, "from somebody's whose career depends on them."

"*Career*?" she asked. "Oh, I see what you mean. Yes, the readers. Well, I may like the literature well enough, some of it, but I don't have to love the people who read it, do I?"

I guessed not.

"Do you think any of them are dangerous?" I asked her.

"*Dangerous*? Oh, you mean from a security point of view? I'd think not. There might be some who'd tear Raul's jacket off his back for a souvenir, but I can't imagine that they'd do him bodily harm."

The BashCon was scheduled over the two weekend days. Bashard himself was set to arrive early Saturday afternoon. He would lead a panel discussion that afternoon on the subject of "Science Future/Science-Fiction Future," then would be guest of honor at the Saturday night black-tie birthday banquet. I had wanted him to leave immediately after the banquet and be driven home. I'd even gotten the Counselor to intercede. But Bashard wouldn't be pinned down. This was his event. People would be coming from far and near because of him. He wasn't going to let them down. He would wait and see. If the Sunday program appeared to "require his presence," then of course he would stay over for it, provided, that is, that the accommodations suited him.

I myself had arrived the night before. I'd arranged for Bashard and his immediate entourage, myself included, to be quartered in one of the annexes to the main hotel building. The annex was a two-story affair. The upper floor could only be reached from the inside by two staircases and an elevator, and you'd have needed a ladder to get to it from outside. At one end was a two-bedroom suite where I put Bashard and Grace. I was in a single next to them, and Price across the hall. Behind us, down the corridor, were to be an assortment of science-fiction dignitaries, all chosen with Bashard's approval. Among them were the Counselor and his Wife, and Ron Whitefield the publisher (but not, I noted,

Helga Hewitt). Of the Science-Fiction Greats Bashard had wanted invited, Bradbury and Heinlein had regretfully declined their invitations, Latham was coming, and Clarke hadn't replied. A room had been reserved for him anyway, at Bashard's instructions. From the security angle, it couldn't have been better. Two of Bud Fincher's people could and did control the stairways and elevator from the lobby floor, and there was no other way in, or out.

By Saturday noon, though, surveying the scene with Helga Hewitt from the hotel buildings, I had a case of the green chills. This didn't, in fact, have so much to do with Bashard's arrival. Noon was when I figured Mr. and Mrs. Charles Camelot would show up. The Counselor's Wife would be behind the wheel and the Counselor, to judge from history, would be in one of his foulest moods.

I don't mean to give the wrong impression. The Counselor's not a misanthrope really. He is invariably gracious in social situations, can even be charming when he wants to be. But only, really, on his own turf. Take him against his will from the East Seventies or the house in the Hamptons, add hundreds of people like the BashCon crowd, and he can become a holy terror.

I expected them, as I say, around noon. I'd organized things as well as I could. Before I left the office the day before, I'd typed out the route instructions and left them with a marked New York State road map in Ms. Shapiro's capable hands. That morning I'd given the traffic control at the BashCon entrance their license plate number and arranged that they be waved right on through, and I had a busboy and the valet parking attendant lined up for duty at noon.

Twelve came and went, and twelve-thirty. No sign of them. I called the front gate. No, the car hadn't showed yet.

At one, I started calling the various numbers at the town house. No one answered, not even Althea the housekeeper (who's supposed to guard the fort on weekends), and I couldn't think of a message to leave on the machines that would make any sense. I tried the house in the Hamptons and Ms. Shapiro at home, with equal luck, and went through the cycle again for good measure. It seemed as though the entire city had been evacuated. I began to imagine the car breaking down on the thruway, or the Counselor's Wife (who I knew was a technically skillful but emotionally incompetent driver) having smashed it against a tree at seventy miles an hour. I saw the hood up and smoking and the Counselor in his shirtsleeves trying to make sense of the engine, about which he understood zero. Alternatively, I saw him trying to thumb a ride at the side of the road, his shirtsleeved arms flailing in the air, his voice bellowing words I couldn't hear at his wife, who now sat cheerfully on a tree stump next to the BMW.

By two, I was totally convinced one or the other had happened and alerted the state police.

At 2:12, Bashard's limousine arrived at the BashCon entrance. Bud Fincher and I got the call on the front steps of the main building, and by one of those peculiar kinds of osmosis I've never understood, the crowd seemed to know it at the same moment we did. They pushed forward toward the building and lined the driveway on either side, waving hands, hankerchiefs, banners, breaking into cheers and applause as the limo rolled between them.

The limo was a gray stretch, one of those city-block affairs with black windows they use mostly for mafiosi and politicians. It stopped a few feet away from me and Bud. I saw Price emerge from the front passenger's seat and move to open the rear door. Somebody somewhere started to sing "Happy Birthday" and suddenly a thousand voices were singing "Happy Birthday." I remember getting one of those hot-and-cold sweaty feelings that if there really was a determined maniac among them singing "Happy Birthday to You," maybe there wasn't a hell of a lot Bud Fincher and I and our little army could do to stop him.

The first thing to emerge from the rear of the limo was Muffin, the Counselor's Wife's cocker bitch, dragging her owner behind her, the two of them followed by the Counselor himself.

He wasn't in shirtsleeves after all. He was wearing a navy blue silk suit and a blue broadcloth shirt with a white collar, from which his tie had been pulled loose. His massive head swiveled in a kind of daze for a second, as though he was surprised to see all these people, not one of whom he recognized.

Then he recognized me.

"Phil!" he shouted. "You've got to find a *typist*!"

"A . . . ?" I started to say, confused and relieved at the same time. "God! Where have you been?"

"Where have I been? Where the hell do you think I've been? Where does it look like I've been?"

I heard the foul mood in his voice, saw it on his craggy face—in living color, as they say—but by then Grace Bashard had swished her way out of the limo, wearing something pastel and clinging. Before I could react, she flung her arms around my neck, her body into mine, and planted a long and wordless "Hi Phil" special on my mouth.

Somebody had started to cheer, but it wasn't for us.

Raul Bashard, ducking his head, had emerged from the limo. Extricating myself, I saw him push away the cane Price offered him. Then he stood erect and turned to the crowd, his face shining in the sun and now breaking, creasing, into a very full and genuine smile. He lifted his arms, clasped his hands together and shook them above his head, victory-style, and people started singing "Happy Birthday" all over again.

"Phil!" The Counselor was shouting at me, pulling me vigorously by the arm. "Phil! You've got to find a typist!"

I couldn't imagine what he was talking about. Where was I supposed to find a typist at the BashCon, and what on God's green earth did he want one for?

I said something to this effect, or started to.

"I don't give a good damn *where* you find one," he raged at me, "but *find* one. In all these people there's got to be one who can type and keep her mouth shut. But if you can't find a typist, then goddammit, find us a typewriter! *You* can type, can't you?"

He knew goddammit-well I could.

The foul mood syndrome, like I said.

It wouldn't have done any good, either, to point out that I

was supposed to be in charge of a twelve-man security force which was supposed to be saving his client from the threat of imminent death, and not a typist pecking out the latest amendments of R. R. Bashard's Last Will and Testament.

Because that was what was involved, as I learned once the Counselor had calmed down. Bashard had "summoned" him early that same morning. He and Nora had driven out there. He'd thought it was only because Bashard wanted company on the trip, but no, he really had wanted the will redrafted. They'd worked on it all morning, until it was time to leave.

So that was how I got to spend the first afternoon of the BashCon, and how come I missed the Dean of Science Fiction's seminar on "Science Future/Science-Fiction Future." I was typing on a typewriter and paper borrowed from the hotel on the desk in the Counselor's room on the second floor of the hotel annex, while the Counselor, in shirtsleeves now and suspenders and stockinged feet, dictated to me from a sheaf of notes in one large fist and a copy of the previous will in the other.

When we were done and, later on, the signatures affixed, I was also the one who notarized the documents. Yes, I'm a notary public, too, and yes, I always carry the seal and stamp pad with me when I travel.

You never know when they'll come in handy.

Account for anxiety if you can.

I'm not talking about the one-cause kind, like when your landlord is knocking on the door for the rent and your bank account is zeroed out. That's not anxiety. Trouble, maybe, but not anxiety. That's reality time.

No, I'm talking about the free-floating kind, which has no cause and a million causes, when everything you do, see, hear, think, has foreboding at the edges, and maybe it's rational and maybe it's not. Like the sound you hear in the night: is it a "natural" sound or is somebody inside the house? Or the smoke you think you smell: is it from your own last cigarette or could something be burning?

Let me put it Bashard's way.

Item: that the Counselor and his wife hadn't shown up as planned.

Item: that flash I'd had, on Bashard's arrival, that nothing I could do could save him from a maniac.

Item: that Bashard spent the afternoon outside my surveillance.

Item: the amendments to Bashard's will, and Bashard's arguing about getting the will changed.

Item: the Counselor's attitude toward same.

If I haven't made it clear already, the Counselor is a cool and unruffle-able bird, ninety-nine percent of the time. That afternoon at the BashCon, when I blew his dictation a couple of times, or when proofreading the documents he discovered an error, he was the other one percent. Which, I understood, had nothing to do with my secretarial skills. It simply proved—didn't it?—that the amendments made him as jumpy as they did me.

Item: the results of Bud Fincher's investigations, or lack of.

We'd had a chance to review these that morning. They were skimpy enough, but they had to be, didn't they—so Bud and I told each other—given the size of the list and the short time we'd had? For every suspect he'd located, there was an Address Unknown or a No Contact Made. (Both Leo Mackes and Viola T. Harmel, for example, Bashard's one-time chess partners, were Address Unknowns.) Only two on the list had been traced to the BashCon. We had people watching them. But suppose, in the categories I'd chosen with the computer that day at Bashard's, suppose I myself had missed somebody?

The point is simply this. Rational or not, important or petty, each of the above "items" contributed.

Conclusion: by banquet time, I was a nervous wreck.

Further conclusion (from the benefit of hindsight): by banquet time, I had become convinced that

1) I alone, no matter what help I had, was responsible for Raul Bashard's well-being, and 2) that somebody at the BashCon was actually going to make an attempt on his life.

Bashard came back from the afternoon's seminar triumphant and exhausted. According to Bud Fincher, who'd stood in for me, there'd been heavy discussions, with rapid-fire questions from the audience and lengthy answers from Bashard. Bud, though, hadn't understood two words of it.

The Counselor and I were waiting for the guest of honor in his suite. When he saw us, Bashard dismissed the entourage that accompanied him, dismissed even Grace, shut the door behind him and slumped in a comfortable chair by the fireplace. He took off his jacket, tie and his shoes. He wasn't, by the way, wearing his habitual sneakers but half-boots in a cordovan leather, highly polished.

At his request, I brought him a bottle of Perrier from the bar but he didn't touch it. The Counselor had a Scotch on the rocks and lit a pipe, and I nursed a beer.

"To work, gentlemen," Bashard said.

The Counselor tried to show him the changed provisions, but Bashard wasn't interested. He made some testy remark to the effect that if the Counselor wasn't competent to do his bidding, he (Bashard) would have to find another attorney. He asked where he was supposed to sign and what he had to initial. The Counselor showed him, in triplicate. Bashard signed, and initialed.

The Counselor served as witness and I, as I've said, notarized the documents. But with his pen poised above the papers, the Counselor paused.

"Are you sure this is what you want, Raul?" he asked.

It was rare, I knew, for the Counselor to question a client's intent.

"If what you're asking . . . " Bashard retorted, "What's the legal phrase? Mental competence? Are you asking if I'm mentally competent at this moment? Of sane and sound mind? Then if something happens to me and my will is contested, it will be up to you two gentlemen to testify, won't it? What do you think, Revere," he said, turning to me with that cracked, half-smiling expression, "am I of sane and sound mind?"

"That's not what I meant, Raul," the Counselor interrupted, leaning back in his chair and fumbling for matches.

"I see. But in that case, if this *wasn't* what I wanted, why in hell do you think I'd have put you to all this trouble?"

The Counselor found his matches, relit his pipe.

"One other question, Raul," he said imperturbably through a cloud of smoke. "Phil's question, really. Who knows of these changes?"

I hadn't, I should point out, so much as mentioned the question. But the Counselor could have been reading my mind.

"I do," Bashard replied, his eyes narrowing slightly. "And you do, Charles. And you, Revere. But as to anybody else? No, I don't think that's any of your business."

I looked at the Counselor.

"So be it," he said.

The Counselor then signed the documents. He passed each set to me. I stamped each, signed, and dated my signature.

The moment I'd finished, Bashard stood—a little unsteadily, I noticed.

"Do you think anyone would mind," he asked us in a strangely plaintive voice, "if I skipped the cocktail party? It's all been a little much for me, I'm afraid."

"Of course not," the Counselor answered. "It's your day, Raul, you do what you want to do."

"In that case, gentlemen," he said, glancing at his watch, "I'm going to have a shower and shave and catch me forty winks. If one of you would make sure I'm on my feet by seven-thirty . . ."

I promised him I'd see to it. Then the Counselor and I left him. I made sure the door to the suite was locked behind me. I'd had the lock replaced the day before, over the management's objections. Only Bashard and Grace, Price and myself, had keys. Even the maid service had to apply to one of us to get in.

The Counselor went back to his room to dress for the party, and I, after checking that Bud Fincher's people were in place downstairs, to mine. I had a beer from the minibar. Not long afterward there was a knock at my door, a soft one at first, then louder, then a voice—Grace Bashard's—saying: "I know you're in there, Phil. I've been looking all over for you. Why are you avoiding me?" I didn't answer. A few moments after that, I heard the door to the suite open and slam shut. Then my phone rang.

At first I let it ring, thinking it was Grace. Then, Grace or no Grace, I picked it up.

No Grace.

"Phil," the Counselor's Wife said, "you've got to do us a favor. It's taking me longer than I thought to get dressed, Charles, too, and Muffin has to be walked. I hate to ask you—you know that—but she wouldn't walk with a stranger. Would you walk her for us?"

I thought of a dozen different excuses why I couldn't, all in the space of two seconds, and the dozen different rebuttals she'd give me. No matter. Raul Bashard's suite could have been being attacked by hand grenades and submachine guns, and the mortars zeroing in—Muffin would still have to be walked. So I passed on the prebanquet cocktail hour, or much of it, being tugged all over the BashCon in my dress shirt and striped black trousers by a cocker bitch in a state of semiecstasy.

The Catskills are usually much cooler than the city, but the clear sunny sky of the afternoon had gone whitish gray. The air, still warm, had grown still and humid; you could feel the thunderstorms coming hours ahead of time. The gnats came out at twilight, and I heard the zing and whine of mosquitos. It wasn't my lookout, but I found myself wondering, as Muffin zigged and zagged across the terrain, what would happen if the storm did break. There wasn't shelter for half the people.

Most of them, of course, wouldn't be at the banquet. They didn't seem to care. There were parties already in progress all over the grounds. I saw paper cups and beer cans in people's hands, smelled the acrid smell of grass, heard guitars playing, even ran into a group of horned Hnngas clustered around a long-haired blonde in an ankle-length gown who was bent over and plucking a stringed musical instrument. I heard someone call it a dulcimer. Maybe it was. A peaceable-enough throng, in sum, at least for the moment.

One of Bud Fincher's people pointed out his particular stakeout to me. I knew the name from the hate-mail file but not what he looked like. I was surprised how young he was, and how small. He had a crew cut and a thin goatee beard. He wore Trotsky glasses, those small rimless affairs that I thought had gone out with the sixties, and he was holding forth in a small group. I heard him rattle off some names of science-fiction writers—Sheckley, Oakes, Sturgeon, Herbert, Latham—to what purpose I didn't know. He was a self-styled science-fiction writer called Malakowski, who belonged to a group of writers that called itself the Philadelphia Scribblers. Two of the Scribblers, in fact, had novels out in paperback from Raul Bashard's publisher. But not Malakowski. Helga Hewitt knew him vaguely, knew his work. He'd tried to write satire, she'd told me, but either satire and science fiction didn't mix or his efforts weren't very funny, because she'd sent back every manuscript he'd submitted. Maybe this failure was what had prompted the personalized attacks I'd read, which seemed to escalate in scorn every time Bashard published a new novel. But even if his letters were violent he didn't in the flesh look like much of a threat to me, and besides, we had him monitored. This should have reassured me.

It didn't.

Walking the dog should have reassured me, too, because it gave me something to do. It didn't. Then, handing the dog back to the Counselor's Wife in our hallway should have (she looking her striking self now with her makeup on and her hair upswept) because I was rid of the dog. But it didn't. Or finishing getting dressed in my own room, or calling Bashard's number at seven-thirty sharp, and after fencing with Grace, who was in the midst of her own toilette and was, she said, going to pop my eyes out, and getting

Bashard on the phone, he was up, no problem, he'd be ready at eight o'clock, thank you, Revere . . .

But no. Nothing did. Not even walking out of the air-conditioned hotel annex into the still, prestormy dusk of the Catskills, and down the path that linked us to the auditorium building where the banquet was being held. Bashard walked to my left in impeccable black tuxedo, and Grace between us in a black sequined number cut to the coccyx in the back and with sparkling combs in her hair, her arms linking the three of us. Price walked point in front of us and Fincher brought up the rear. Others of the combined staffs cleared the well-wishing crowds from our way . . .

No. No reassurance.

It was then that Grace pulled me down to her so she could whisper in my ear.

"I brought it," she said. "Just for you."

"Brought what?" I asked.

"Have you forgotten? Never mind, Pablo," she answered back in a husky whisper. "You'll find out tonight."

My experience with banquets is limited. May it stay that way. They say banquet food is as bad as the speeches are long. I don't remember what the food was like, if I ate any, and I only half heard the speeches.

I remember hearing the music of the dance band without registering the tunes.

I remember drinking some, then more than some. But I didn't feel a thing.

Nervous time.

Seating at the banquet was by table number and place card, over three hundred invitees in all at some twenty-five tables, plus the dais, plus the dance floor oval. I had all the angles covered, I thought. Bud Fincher's people were stationed at every exit, and there was another out of sight in each of the side wings behind the dais. Bud himself was strategically placed at a table at one corner nearest the dais, and Price at the other. I sat at the centermost table, right under the speakers and special guests. I had the Counselor's Wife on one side of me and Mrs. Richard Brinckerhoff on the other. Mrs. Richard Brinckerhoff was the wife of a retired shipping magnate and science-fiction buff and collector who, as a guest speaker, sat on the dais. Across from me was the Counselor, flanked by Grace Bashard and Helga Hewitt. He was still in a foul mood, I could see, and so (in one of her quick changes) was Grace. Helga Hewitt managed to prod the Counselor into conversation, but nothing would prod Grace. Pouty-faced, she kept her head down, ate little, and once or twice when her eyes met mine across the table she sharply averted her gaze.

Meanwhile the Counselor's Wife was in her best party form. Once between courses she asked me to dance with her, and I did, but my mind was elsewhere. Back at the table she chattered away, undaunted by my being distracted, until she discovered that she and Mrs. Richard Brinckerhoff had something in common. Mrs. Richard Brinckerhoff, a sturdy dowager-type with blue hair and a massive, heavily perfumed bust, confided across my plate that she thought science fiction was a pastime for boys. No more stupid and silly than sports, maybe, but she couldn't understand why grown men (like her husband) spent so much time over it. Nora Saroff seemed to think this one of the most hilarious things she'd ever heard, as well as apt, and soon enough she was holding forth about repressed male adolescence.

I made several patrols of the premises during dinner. Then, when the lights dimmed for the speeches, presentations, and the slide show, I stood permanently at the rear where I could catch the stage and the audience in one scan. They seemed to me a generally happy and well-oiled crowd of eaters and drinkers, if on the geriatric side compared to the younger throngs outside. Wine of both colors flowed with this dinner, this on top of the cocktail party, and the champagne came out later with the birthday cake. By the time the emcee called people to attention, or tried to, the atmosphere had gone from sedate to raucous.

Except for Grace Bashard. She caught me in the lobby on one of my rounds. Only Bud Fincher's minions were there. Maybe she was headed for the ladies' room, or maybe she was headed for me.

"You *bastard*!" she began. "Why didn't you *tell* me?"

"Tell you what?"

"*Tell me what*! Didn't I ask you if there was somebody else? Didn't I?"

"Grace, I don't know what you're talking a—"

"*He doesn't know what I'm talking about*!" she repeated, the decibels rising, "As if you're not in love with her. It's written all over your face, you crumb. Do you think everybody in there doesn't see it?"

I could feel the anger now vibrating in her voice. I'd heard, seen it once before. Only this time, strange to say, it made her something to behold.

The woman-in-the-child, something like that.

Suffice to say that if nothing else happened that night, she still gave Bud Fincher's three stakeouts in the lobby something to talk about.

"Nora Camelot," she went on scornfully. "Nora Saroff. TV star. I can see what she sees in you all right, look at that disgusting old creep she's married to. But you, Pablo. Only why did you have to make a fool of me? Why humiliate me? What have I ever done to you except fall in love with you? Why didn't you tell me? Why did you have to sit across the table from me with that . . . with that TV star . . . and make me watch? You even *danced* with her!"

I tried to shut her up. Her hair had come loose from one of the combs, and I reached for her, and she swung at me, knocking my arm away with her evening bag, then ran away, in a swaying, sobbing dazzle of sequins, like I'd watched her run away from Bashard a few days before, and disappeared into the ladies' room.

I watched her disappear.

Bud Fincher's men were playing the three see-no-evils.

I started to explain to them, but how to explain?

"Never mind, guys," I told them. "It's not what it looks like. She's a crazy kid, that's all. Bashard's daughter. It doesn't have anything to do with why we're here."

They pretended to understand.

By the time I got back into the banquet room, the lights were dimming and the emcee was trying to quiet people down. This in itself was a compromise. The organizers had wanted nothing but candles on the table and the speaker's light on the lectern in the center of the dais. I'd vetoed that, but because of the slide show had accepted the dims.

The emcee was none other than Ron—Randall Whitefield, Raul Bashard's book publisher. He spoke with fairly heavy-handed wit but with surprising economy of words. His first task as cosponsor of the BashCon, he said, and the happiest, was to welcome one and all to the eightieth birthday celebration of one of the great literary figures of our time. Applause followed, and the audience rose in unison for Raul Bashard. His second task, the publisher said, was to introduce the six other honored guests and speakers on the podium.

These were, in the order he gave them:

George Varga, publisher and editor of *The World of Science Fiction* ("the most influential magazine in the field");

Samuel Elliott Wright, "Mr. S. F. Con," organizer and cosponsor of the BashCon and a noted collector and author in his own "right";

Cyn Morgan, the most "awarded" and best-loved science-fiction artist in America and the remarkable illustrator of all Raul Bashard's covers;

Richard Brinckerhoff, eminent bon vivant, collector and "the most generous friend and benefactor science fiction has ever had";

Norman L. Hermatius, noted film producer and director, and the first to translate Raul Bashard's work to the screen;

Oliver "Ollie" Latham, Raul Bashard's old friend and accomplice, the "writer's writer," or the "science-fiction writer's science-fiction writer" and one of the last of the legendary greats.

The speakers came and went, relieved finally by the slide show (a kind of *This Is Your Life* of Raul Bashard's career) that Sam Wright, the organizer of the BashCon, had put together, and which showed on a large screen behind and above the dais. There were stills and film clips of Bashard at various times and places, including meeting with the astronauts I'd seen shots of before and sequences from the films that had been made of his books. There were interesting shots of him as a much younger man—an extraordinarily good-looking one, I'd have to say, but with that same determined, cold expression I knew—and a last one, a group photo, from the 1950s, that brought people to their feet once again because it was used to introduce Oliver Latham.

"Back in the fifties," Ron Whitefield said into the microphone, "when science fiction was a little-respected genre read mostly in the pulp magazines and paperbacks, these six writers, obscure and hard-pressed to make a living, turned out many of the seminal works that are considered mainstream science-fiction classics today." He named four of the writers. "Unfortunately these Titans are no longer among us, except through their works. But two of them remain, and to help us celebrate Raul's birthday, it is a special treat for all of us to welcome Ollie . . ."

Whatever he went on to say was lost in the clamor. Latham stood, a tall figure with a mop of curly white hair—in his seventies, I learned later, but a man whose looks belied his years. He was the only one on the dais who didn't wear conventional evening getup. He had on what used to be called a smoking jacket, a maroon affair with wide curving lapels, and a black string tie on a white shirt.

I knew him by name, but I realized a bit ruefully that I couldn't name the title of any of his books.

It was around when Latham started to speak that the Counselor's Wife showed up at my side. I'd been aware of her threading her way through the tables (headed for the ladies' room, I'd thought) and now, hair tossing, there she was.

"I don't know what you're so tense about, Phil," she said, linking her arm through mine and taking my hand. "Nothing's going to happen tonight. It's all Bashard's fantasy. Can you imagine anybody up there killing him, or attempting to? They're all too *old!*" She laughed, and I could smell wine on her breath, and I thought probably she was right. Then she said, teasingly: "But Phil, typical Phil, you never told me how *gorgeous* she is!"

I knew who she meant, but I said it anyway: "Who's gorgeous?"

"Why, the daughter!" the Counselor's Wife said. "And does she ever have a case for you!"

The Counselor's Wife squeezed my hand.

"Does she?" I said, smiling a little. "You should've heard her just now. She thinks I'm in love with you."

"Well . . . ?" She stared at me. "And what's so funny about that?"

"I didn't say—"

I didn't get to finish the sentence, though, because just then the one untoward incident of the banquet took place. Latham had been saying something about money, about the money Bashard had made, and the audience was laughing. Then suddenly, while I sparred with the Counselor's Wife, there was a commotion on the dais. Bashard was standing. Latham seemed to teeter away from the speaker's lectern. He looked bewildered. His arms flailed in the air, like he was drunk and off-balance, and I saw Bashard reach out for him. Latham, either because he was drunk or off-balance or angry, swept Bashard away from him with an outthrust of his arm.

Latham was shouting something that sounded like "Burro."

The Counselor's Wife had heard it, too.

"What's Burro?" she said.

I didn't know. I started forward, but by the time I got down to the dais it was all over. People had helped Latham back to his seat. He sat there docilely enough. Maybe he *was* drunk, I remembered thinking. I heard people saying it. Maybe Bashard was, too, to judge from his wandering speech afterward. But in between Randall Whitefield took matters in hand.

I saw him signal to the wing behind him. The lights went back on. The band struck up the tune and in wheeled about the largest birthday cake I've ever seen, with a full eighty candles burning. Ron, the publisher, led the audience in "Happy Birthday Dear Raul."

* * *

Nothing happened.

Like the Counselor's Wife said, nothing would happen at the banquet. Nothing did.

Chalk it up to my excellent organization. Not that anybody congratulated me for it, least of all Raul Bashard. After all, that was what I'd been paid to do, see to it that nothing happened.

His speech, I thought, was surprisingly short, given the sheaf of papers in his hand. He thanked everybody, he read for a minute, then he got off into some slurred speculations about "continuity" and "breaks in the continuity"—things I'd heard before. It didn't matter much, though, what he said. The audience interrupted with applause at every other word, and the special BashCon issue of *The World of Science Fiction* later printed the written version of it.

The World of Science Fiction, though, had a special motive by that time.

It took a while for Price, Bud Fincher and me to get him back to his suite after the banquet. The dignitaries had mostly left, and Grace, and the Counselor and the Counselor's Wife, but Bashard stayed on, like he wanted to shake hands with everybody down to the waiters. Finally we got him outside. The air was thick with humidity and gnats, but the storm hadn't broken yet and the BashCon complex seemed largely settled down for the night.

Bashard wobbled between us. Another one, I thought, who'd had too much to drink. He was also mad as hell about something, but it wasn't clear what. The minute we were inside the suite, he turned on me, teeth clenched.

"Go ahead and ask it, Revere," he said. "You can ask it till you're blue in the face. The answer is no. I'm *not* going home tonight. I'm going to spend the night here and as much of tomorrow as I damn well feel like. Hell, maybe I'll stay here forever. You're still on duty, Revere, is that clear?"

I didn't answer. In fact, given the lateness, I'd already assumed he was staying. But I didn't like being treated like a servant either.

"Somebody . . . where's Price? . . . make me another

drink. And where's my daughter? I'm surprised she's not with you, Revere. Go find her."

On this score I didn't have to do anything. Just then Grace Bashard came into the suite. Her hair combs were gone, her face flushed, and something had gone awry in her makeup. She stalked between us without a word, eyes averted, and into her room, slamming the door behind her.

All present and accounted for.

Bashard looked like he wanted to talk some more, but I'd had enough. I took Bud Fincher with me, and together we toured the premises, upstairs and down, into the hotel lobby and once around for good measure. All present and accounted for, from the security standpoint. We checked the second-shift arrangements which would take place at three in the morning. Then Bud sent him to bed, putting him on call for seven.

When I got back to my end of the upstairs corridor Price was just coming out of the suite. Bashard, he said, was going to bed. I reviewed the security setup with him. Together we checked the suite double doors. Locked.

Then Price went to bed.

Then I went to bed.

But not to sleep.

Maybe it was the nothing-happened part. Maybe I'd been keyed up too long for nothing to happen. Maybe I'd had too much to drink myself. Or too much of Grace Bashard. Or the Counselor's Wife. Or the Counselor. Or Bashard.

Or combinations of same.

I had the paperback of an old Elmore Leonard with me, my own answer to science fiction. I tried reading it in the king-size bed, but I couldn't stay with it. I worked my way through the minibar's supply of beers and played the TV dials by remote control till I found a rerun of *Baretta*. I always liked *Baretta*, particularly the parts with the cockatoo and Tom Ewell, but the commercials drove me away. For a while I lay there in the dark, listening for sounds I couldn't hear.

I sleep, by the way—or don't sleep—in the raw. I don't own pajamas. I don't even own a bathrobe.

At some point I got up and opened my door. I left it open. I hung up the rented tuxedo that I'd left sprawled on a chair. I turned off the air conditioner and opened the windows. Night sounds in the countryside, nothing untoward. Thunder was rumbling distantly across the mountains. I got back into bed and watched the rectangular shaft of light from the corridor through my narrow entrance. I watched the curtains begin to stir and listened to the thunder.

All right, say I was *restless*. Nothing happened.

A little after three I got up again, put on a pair of pants and went barefoot down the carpeted corridor to the ground floor. The members of the second shift were already in place. I told them—some joke—not to fall asleep. Then back upstairs to my room. All quiet, like a mouse without shoes.

I had the beginnings of a hangover. I took two aspirins. I left my lights on this time. The door still open.

Sometime later, the big guns opened up on the battlefield. Tremendous bolts of lightning, like the flashes of giant cameras, lit up the sky, followed by explosions of thunder. Gales of wind blew the curtains to the ceiling and rain gusted through the windows. The temperature must have dropped ten degrees in seconds. I remember thinking about the hundreds camped out on the BashCon grounds. I remember thinking they at least weren't my worry.

The big rain put me to sleep finally, with my lights on.

I dreamed a thousand and one dreams. I dreamed I woke up like a shot, knowing I'd be late for the office even if I ran all the way. I dreamed I saw the Counselor's Wife and Muffin, the cocker bitch, being blown down a rainswept city street by a hundred-mile-an-hour hurricane. I dreamed one or more horny dreams. I dreamed I was in bed with some unbelievably luscious woman. God knows who the unbelievably luscious woman was, but I dreamed she was begging me to enter her. She kept saying she was sorry. I didn't know what she was sorry about, but it excited me. I dreamed somebody turned out the lights and got into bed behind me and snuggled up against my back.

Only that part wasn't a dream.

* * *

I awoke in a blur. I think my lights had just gone on. I had a terrific headache the minute I sat up. I saw everything through a colored filter.

The filter was red.

Raul Bashard was leaning forward against the wall of my narrow entrance hall. His face still had that weird ceramic grin, but it looked bashed, mashed, like his head had gone lopsided. He was wearing splattered pajamas. He was croaking something. It took a split second to register that he was calling my name.

Raul Bashard leaned, or slid, farther forward against the wall. His hand went up to his head. When he ran out of wall he simply fell forward on his face, on the carpet.

My feet were tangled in the covers. Somehow the covers had squeezed down to the bottom of the bed. I twisted to free myself and glimpsed her behind me.

Grace was lying on her side, facing where I'd just been. Her knees were up; her head lay in the pillow of her right hand.

She was wearing, I guess, what she said she'd brought for me, and there wasn't much of it: a red and black lace teddy that looked like the next-to-last costume in a striptease.

She slept through it all though, in the bright light, while her grandfather died.

PART TWO

PART TWO

CHAPTER
6

"**W**hy *should* I believe you?" Squilletti said. "How do I know?"

Squilletti was your quintessence of Catskill cop. All right, ask the question: What's the quintessence of Catskill cop? Also: How many Catskill cops do I know? The answer to the second is: more now than I did before. The answer to the first is: Squilletti.

He was a sawed-off, chunky Italian-American, with black eyes, a black mustache, and a strutty way of walking. When we got to be buddies, I learned that his family owned a roadhouse-and-package-store combination where the local constabulary dined and boozed, on the cuff mostly. The family business wasn't big enough to support all the Squillettis of Al's generation, so one brother became a cop and another worked for a funeral parlor owned by a cousin. When we got to be bigger buddies, I learned that Al Squilletti had a great-uncle who was in garbage collection in the city and had done time for extortion.

The great-uncle's name wasn't Squilletti.

My Squilletti wore plainclothes and had worked his way

up to Detective Sergeant. You can find cops like him all
around the metropolitan area where Italian-Americans have
settled in—New Jersey, Brooklyn, Long Island, and so on.
The more Italians in the community, the more you'll find on
the police force. They tend to be smart on their own turf, also
smartass, also racist and sexist, also unhappy when out-
siders come in and disturb the peace and the boat starts
rocking.

Like the BashCon.

The BashCon itself may have been a nuisance to the
Catskill constables, but except for traffic control on the local
roads, they could pretty much look the other way and hope
there weren't too many complaints till the foreigners packed
up and went home.

But the BashCon Murder, so-called, while it got Al
Squilletti on the TV news and would make him a hero if he
solved it, also put him on the line. To a degree he could hide
behind his chief and the county sheriff's office, even the state
police (whom he summoned—too late—to try to seal off the
"corporate campus"), not to mention the local district
attorney. But he had to call in favors every step of the way,
and he'd spend the rest of his Catskills career paying them
back. Furthermore, with the media chasing his every move
and enemies and obstacles popping up unexpectedly like
targets on a firing range, there was no way he could keep the
boat from rocking.

For instance, the minute the ambulance carried Raul
Bashard's body away that Sunday morning, siren wailing,
and people realized that the BashCon was over, it would
have taken the National Guard to hold those who wanted to
leave on the premises. As it happened, a lot of people did
hang around. But it didn't prevent the media from claiming
that the police might have let the murderer, or murderers,
walk away scot-free without so much as questioning them or
examining their belongings.

Then Squilletti had the center's management to contend
with. They had two corporate meetings scheduled to begin
the next day with advance parties arriving that same Sunday
evening, and there was no way they were going to call them

off even after the threat of a court order. Yes, they would appeal a court order. Apparently they had as many connections as Squilletti did. This led to protracted negotiations and to Squilletti's retreat. By Sunday evening, all he could seal off was the hotel annex and subsequently just the second floor of the annex.

And then there was the Counselor.

I gave the Counselor a hurried report moments after Bashard died and before I called the police.

The Counselor, as it turned out, didn't wear pajamas either. He had on a blue terry-cloth bathrobe and his white hair was matted, like he'd washed it the night before or had sweated during the night.

He asked me three questions: Did I know who'd done it? Did I know how it had happened? Where was Grace? To the first I answered no, to the second that I thought Bashard had been beaten to death, to the third that she was asleep in my bed.

Then at the Counselor's instructions, I carried Grace back into her room. The door to the suite was wide open but the lights were out. She may have moaned once or twice but she didn't wake up. I put her into bed, covered her with a sheet, then closed the door, then closed the suite door. From the glimpse I had of the suite, there'd been some minor skirmishing in the living room, but nothing to suggest mayhem. The blood, it turned out, was mostly in Bashard's bedroom.

I woke Price up, explained what had happened. Then I got a doctor's name from the hotel and called him and explained why I'd roused him out of his sleep. He said he was on his way.

Then I called the police. Then I called Bud Fincher.

The whole of it, from the moment Raul Bashard collapsed on my rug and I satisfied myself that nobody was going to bring him back to life, until I called the police, couldn't have taken more than twenty minutes, half an hour maximum. But there was a gap. And Squilletti eventually spotted it.

"Why didn't you call the police right away?" he asked. "How do I know you weren't covering up evidence?"

"You don't," I answered. "But I wasn't."

"Oh no? Then why did you take the girl back to her room?"

"I was told to. By Mr. Camelot."

"And why was that?"

"You'll have to ask him."

"I already have. If you ask me, Revere, you're going to need a lawyer. Unless you want to defend yourself."

This was a Squilletti habit, to change subjects in midstream, in the hope, presumably, of catching someone off-guard.

"I'm not a lawyer," I said. "I already told you that. I only work for one."

"Then maybe you'd better get one."

"Why? Are you charging me?"

"Not yet. But you could well be an accessory. Just taking the girl back to her room could make you an accessory if nothing else does."

This, too, was a Squilletti tactic. He worked us like a running back cruising the line on Monday Night Football, looking for a weak spot. To Squilletti the Counselor, Grace, Price and I were the front four of the defense, and by Sunday afternoon (when this conversation took place), he was still short of a first down.

The truth was that he might have blown his chance earlier, and I think he knew it. According to the Counselor's instructions that morning, I was to cooperate with the police but at the same time protect the confidentiality of attorney and client. The ticklish thing about that was that it wasn't clear at first who the Counselor represented, other than the corpse. By the time Squilletti figured this out though, the Counselor had had a chance to talk to Grace, and yes, Ms. Bashard was represented by counsel, Mr. Charles Camelot by name, and no, the police couldn't interview her, she was suffering from shock, by physician's order she needed rest, etc. It wasn't until Sunday afternoon that Squilletti got his first, abbreviated chance to interview Grace, by which time the Counselor was in full attendance.

Score one for the Counselor. Score another for the Counselor when Squilletti tried to get a court order to have Grace undergo a semen test. But score one for Squilletti when the Counselor tried to block an autopsy on Raul Bashard.

So it went. As for me, I went in a few hours from the man in charge to a suspect. Get a lawyer, Squilletti said, but the Counselor was otherwise occupied. Along the way, I'd failed in my duty, however you look at it. And the way Squilletti looked at it, there was Bud Fincher's and my list of suspects culled from the Big O's files, but no evidence of a break-in from outside the building. Plus there was the testimony of Bud Fincher's people that nobody had gotten up from the ground floor; that left the other guests on the annex's second floor; and that left me with the door open and the victim on my rug and the victim's granddaughter in my bed.

Unless Grace Bashard had done it all herself.

In other words, you look for the weak point in the defense and you bang away at it.

Granddaughter, I notice I said. Somehow, once Raul Bashard was dead, I couldn't think of her as his daughter anymore.

Here's what I knew, augmented by what Squilletti found out:

Sometime after 3:30 A.M., the time when the local weather service estimated the storm had broken over the immediate area, I'd fallen asleep. I'd left my door open.

Sometime between 3:30 and 6:40 A.M.—the precise time had not been determined—Grace Bashard had left the suite and, finding my door open, had crawled into bed with me and gone to sleep. To the best of my knowledge, I had not had sex with Grace Bashard.

Sometime between 3:30 and 6:40 A.M.—presumably closer to 6:40 but how close could not be determined—someone had entered the suite and, using a brass-handled poker from the set of fireplace tools in the living room, had set about to beating the victim to death in his bed. He, or she, had not succeeded at first. There were signs that Bashard had tried to defend himself with a pillow, signs that he had fallen near the doorway from his bedroom and had lain there. The poker had been abandoned in the living room. No forensic evidence could be developed that specifically related to the killer, not even fingerprints, nor was there a way to show definitively whether Grace Bashard had left the suite before or after the event.

At or near 6:40 A.M., Bashard had gotten up and reached my room, where he collapsed and died.

I awoke at 6:40 A.M. I checked the victim, determined that he was dead. His pulse ws nonexistent, his heart had stopped beating. I went to Charles Camelot's room and, after receiving his instructions, carried Grace Bashard back to her bedroom. I didn't have to use my key to the suite, the door was open. Then I woke up Price. It took a somewhat long time for Price to answer, and I had to knock more than once. I instructed Price to get dressed and stand guard at the suite. Then I called the doctor, the police, and Bud Fincher, whom I asked to inform the hotel management.

I was talking again to the Counselor, who was up and dressed when the doctor arrived. I took him first to inspect Raul Bashard's body. Then I let him and the Counselor into the suite.

The police came almost immediately after, followed in the course of the morning by more police, in waves, including a twosome armed with a vacuum cleaner.

Squilletti arrived in the second wave. He wore a white short-sleeved shirt with no tie and the collar out wide over the lapels of a camel-colored blazer. The blazer had brass buttons, patch pockets, and a center vent in the back that spread apart over his backside. He took the blazer off shortly after he got to work, but then he had it on again later that day when he interviewed Grace Bashard. I noticed he carried one of those plastic pen holders in his shirt pocket, the kind you associate with construction bosses, but he took no notes. Sometimes he had a partner along for note taking, but Squilletti himself watched people when he asked them questions, watched them when he listened, and kept his hands mostly in his pants pockets.

All right, so I paid a lot of attention to him.

Why?

Because he paid a lot of attention to me.

He also paid a lot of attention to the doors to the suite. It figured. As I've said, I'd had the locks changed. I'd hired a local locksmith to do it over the hotel's objections, a fact which Squilletti corroborated, also that the locksmith was due to restore the original later that day. I'd had four keys made: one for myself, one for Price, one for Grace, one for Bashard. Mine was in my pocket, Price's was in his. Bashard's was found in his room; Grace later produced hers.

There was no evidence of tampering with the lock.

If the doors to the suite (which I affirmed had been locked when I went to sleep) had remained locked, then either Price, Grace, or myself, alone or in combination, had at least participated in the crime. But if the door had been left open, possibly by Grace when she left her bedroom for mine, then the field of suspects would have to be enlarged to include at least everybody staying on the floor.

Unless—third possibility—somebody had knocked on the closed door and had it opened from the inside?

Possible, but unlikely. I'm not normally an insomniac. On the other hand, I'm not a deep sleeper. I knew I'd "dreamed"—that is, *heard*—Grace get into my bed. I hadn't woken up, but I'd *heard* her. I hadn't heard anybody at the suite door.

There were blood smears on the interior doorknob— Bashard's as it turned out—but that didn't prove anything either way. Bashard could have opened the door or he could have reached out for support. By that time he'd needed all the support he could get.

I myself believed Grace had left the door open behind her. Squilletti, though, wanted it the other way. It simplified things.

"Let me see if I got it straight," he said. "The way you say it happened, sometime after three-thirty in the morning, Grace Bashard came out of the suite, leaving the door open, found your door open, got into bed with you and innocently went to sleep. Leaving your door open, too. Is that your version?"

"It could have been that way."

"Sure. And she could have carried a megaphone into the

hall, said: 'Hey look, everybody, I'm shacking up with Revere here. Anybody who wants to kill my old man, come ahead. The door's wide open.' Is that it?"

I didn't answer.

"Had you been shacking up with her before this?"

"No."

"Did you want to?"

"Not particularly."

"Well, she must have wanted to. One of you must have wanted to. Else why did she climb into bed with you?"

"You'll have to ask her that."

"I'm going to," Squilletti said, "but I figure you've got an opinion."

I shrugged.

"Maybe she was cold," I said. "Maybe she wanted a warm body."

His eyes narrowed at me. I guess he thought I was pulling his leg.

"It sure sounds like she wanted to be found out," Squilletti said.

Maybe so, I thought.

"So who do you think did it?" he asked, not for the first time.

"I don't know."

"All you know is that she didn't?"

"I didn't say that. But I don't think so, no."

"But couldn't it also have been that she got up in the middle of the night, clubbed her old man to death, then came in here and went to sleep, leaving the doors wide open? I mean, if she wanted to be found out about the one thing, then why not the other?"

I started to say something about evidence, that there'd have to be evidence of it, like on her clothes, but then I remembered what Grace had been wearing when I woke up and I kept my mouth shut.

"Stranger things have happened," Squilletti said. "We had a case like that a couple of years ago. Teenage kid went on a rampage, murdered his whole family, then went to sleep in his own bed. When he woke up, he called the cops. The first thing he did when we got there was confess to the whole thing.

"But it could also have been," he went on in the same flat tone, "that you've invented this whole crock-of-shit story by way of protecting the girl. Or who knows? Protecting the both of you."

"Sure," I said. "And if pigs had wings . . ."

His eyes squinted again.

"I don't get that," he said.

"It's just an expression. If pigs had wings, they could fly."

"Oh," he said. I guess he thought I'd been using pigs for cops. "Then tell me this: who stands to gain from it?"

"To gain from what?"

"Well, Bashard's a rich man, isn't he? Or was? You make a lot of money writing books these days. I imagine she gets it, doesn't she?"

I didn't answer.

"I guess you'd know, wouldn't you? You work for the lawyer, the lawyer draws up the will. What's in the will?"

It was going to come out eventually, but right then I was still following the Counselor's instructions.

"That's privileged information," I said.

"What do you mean, privileged information? You're not a lawyer yourself, are you?"

"No, I'm not. But the confidentiality between client and counsel applies to me, too."

"Is that right?" Squilletti said, tilting his head at me. "Well, that's one I never heard of before. There's also the question of obstructing a police investigation into a homicide. Did you ever hear about that one?"

"Yes I have."

"So?"

"It's still privileged information."

This wasn't my first conversation with Squilletti, and it was far from my last, but along the way he managed to unnerve me. Not that he didn't have help. There were the circumstances, for one thing. It wasn't just that Bashard had been murdered; he'd been horribly, painfully murdered. And like I said, I'd gone from being the man-in-charge to somebody under suspicion. I could recognize the fact of it in people's faces, in what they said or didn't. For instance, the police asked everybody who'd spent the night on the second floor of the annex to stay in or near the hotel until the police had interviewed and released them. This included the Brinckerhoffs, Latham, Cyn Morgan, Sidney Frankaman and his wife, Norman Hermatius, Varga, Sam Wright and his wife, as well as the Counselor and his wife, Price and myself. For the most part they—that is, the science-fiction crowd— sat around a large round, rustic table in the hotel bar, where Ron Whitefield, Helga Hewitt and some others joined them. Some drank booze, some drank coffee, some didn't drink anything. A couple of times I joined them. The first time I thought I might learn something, by getting people to talk. But nobody was talking. They sat like people in shock, together but separate, each well inside him or herself. The second time, maybe I was in search of company myself and the conversation around the table had grown animated. But the minute I sat down, it dropped to the proverbial pin drop. And stayed there. Ping. Until Sidney Frankaman turned to me.

Mr. Frankaman was a balding, round-faced man from Los Angeles with goggle glasses that magnified his eyes in concentric rings. I'd met him the night before at the banquet when he'd boasted to me, in figures, that he owned and ran "the largest chain of pure science-fiction stores in the world."

Now Mr. Frankaman said to me, goggle eyes staring: "Who invited you?"

"Nobody," I answered. "I didn't know you needed an invitation."

"Then why are you here?" Frankaman said, still staring at me.

I thought of a retort, but it stuck in my throat. Some of the others had averted their eyes, but those who were looking my way, including my former friend, Helga Hewitt, wore the same expression.

Call it their "Man from Mars" look.

I excused myself, beer in hand, and heard the conversation start up again behind me.

I ran into the Counselor's Wife and Muffin in the lobby. They were on their way for a walk. To judge from the way she wriggled and pulled toward me, Muffin was the only one on the premises who still believed I was innocent till proven otherwise. While normally I'd have invented any excuse to avoid joining them, this time I welcomed the Counselor's Wife's asking. The hotel had become claustrophobia city.

The outside wasn't much better.

The police, by then, had sealed off the hotel building to all who didn't belong there. Outside, television crews with portable cameras ringed the walk from the main entrance to the driveway. Their motors idling, so to speak. Presumably they'd already exhausted the outside interview possibilities, for the minute they saw us, they went into action.

"How do you fit into the case?" a pushy young blond woman asked me, pushing a microphone in the general direction of my mouth.

I made the mistake of answering: "No comment."

This brought a crowd.

Then I heard someone shout: "Isn't that Nora Saroff? Sure it is. Hey, Nora, what're you doing here?"

"She's the lawyer's wife!" somebody answered.

"That's right! She's Camelot's wife!" said another.

"Did she do it, Nora?"

"Did the daughter do it?"

"What was the cause of death, Nora? It's murder, isn't it?"

"Sure it's murder! They beat him to a pulp. Where's your husband, Nora?"

"Is Charles Camelot defending the girl?"

And the persistent microphone in my face: "What's *your* name, sir? How do *you* fit into the case?"

Hit 'em high and hit 'em low, as they say. Muffin growled, snarled, bared teeth. Between us, the dog and I drove a wedge, pulling the Counselor's Wife behind us. Even so, we could still be there if the Counselor's Wife hadn't freaked.

"Fuck off!" I heard her shout behind me. "Just fuck off!" Then spinning angrily on them: "And if a single one of you runs so much as a second of this, you'll be featured on my show next week for media harassment. Just try me! Name, picture *and* channel!"

Whether she'd have actually done it or not, I've no idea, but it worked. The ring parted, the Counselor's Wife tossed her hair angrily for emphasis, and with Muffin leading the way and me bringing up the rear, we headed across the driveway and onto the grounds.

You'd never have known there'd been a storm during the night. It was afternoon by then, the sun bright and hot, and a fresh wind scudded puff clouds across the blue Catskills sky. Still there was a feeling of mourning across the grounds, like a pall, like a vigil. The people were sparser than they'd been on Saturday, but plenty had stayed around. Some of the Hnngas and the Hnnns were still there—at least I saw the one Bud Fincher and I had recruited—but their horns and the leather helmets had been packed away and they looked just like regular people: pale, solemn-faced, silent. I spotted Malakowski and his Scribblers hunkered together in a quiet circle on the grass, as other groups were, lounging or sitting or kneeling, but quiet, like waiting for something to happen. No music. Some of the stands and booths from the day before were still up, here and there, but their display shelves were mostly empty, as though their owners had already packed up.

Still, they hung around. Why, I don't know. Bud Fincher (I knew) had gone over our key list with Squilletti's people, and the police (I learned later) had checked out those they could find—but by that time nobody outside the hotel was being held against his will. And the ambulance carrying Bashard's body had long since left, and it wasn't coming back. Nor was anybody going to come out of the hotel and make an announcement. The event was over. The BashCon was over.

Muffin pulled us down through pine trees to the lake. A picture-postcard affair. A boathouse, canoes and rowboats neatly racked at the open end. On the lake itself, a pair of sailboats making good time in the wind. The Counselor's

Wife said to me: "You really got yourself into it this time, didn't you, Phil?"

"What do you mean by that?"

"Poor Phil. Well, I guess you couldn't be expected to resist her forever, could you?"

The words were familiar enough. I mean, it was part of her routine that I was fair game and prey to anything that moved, provided it had two legs and a skirt on. True, I'd had my share of encounters with the fairer sex, and even if the Counselor's Wife didn't know the details, she enjoyed prying. And failing at that, making the details up herself.

Only this time, the bantering tone wasn't there.

"Men are such dodos," she went on, shaking her head. "Really. She could've been fourteen or forty. Or eighty. No difference. It's what defeats you every time. It's all in the boobs. And if the truth be known, not even the boobs matter that much."

Or words to that effect.

"Maybe so," I answered. "Only this time you've got it wrong. I can't help it if she got into bed with me. I was asleep. I didn't lay a hand on her."

She laughed a little, and shook her head slowly in that men-are-such-dodos way, and it irritated the hell out of me.

"At least you're consistent," she said.

"What does *that* mean?"

"That's what Charles said you said: that you didn't lay a hand on her."

"And what else did he say?"

"He said that Raul had been murdered and that Grace was in bed with you and that the shit was about to hit the fan."

"And what else?"

"He said you said you'd had trouble sleeping but that you said you'd slept through the killing."

We'd gotten down to the land side of a narrow wooden dock, or pier, that extended out into the lake. Muffin, excited by the water, wanted to head out to the end of the dock, but we stopped at the land end. We sat down on the dock, and the dog mucked around in the weeds by the water's edge, sniffing for scents.

"And what else?" I said.

"That's it. I've hardly seen him since this morning."

Me, too, I started to say. Instead I said: "What do *you* think happened?"

"Me? I think she killed him. I bet you think so, too."

"It so happens I don't," I said. "But why would she do that? What was the motive?"

"Rage," she answered. "I'd call it sexual rage, but most people would find that too esoteric. I don't know if they were screwing or not, but something was going on between them, some kind of sexual activity, and I think it drove her crazy."

"Crazy enough to kill him?"

"That's right."

"And then come get into bed with me?"

"That's right. And why not? For some of us, rage is the most powerful aphrodisiac there is."

"I don't get that," I said. I could, in fact, think of a better motive without hardly trying. I wondered if the Counselor's Wife knew about the changes in Bashard's will, decided she didn't.

"Maybe you don't," she said, "but if you heard what I hear every day, you would. You'd be surprised how many couples there are who hate each other's guts, who fight like animals, and who have model sex lives at the same time. Rage, anger, whatever you want to call it, but it's tempting to say that's the ingredient that keeps them together."

At some point, I stood up and started to pace the dock. The fact is, the Counselor's Wife often had that effect on me. But the cocker took this as a signal that it was water time, meaning she started tugging at the leash, trying to head up the dock. So I sat down again.

"Yes, I think she killed him," the Counselor's Wife went on. "Patricide. Or grand-patricide. But I also think Charles and you will get her off. You'll have the police running around in circles, looking for somebody else, and by the time you're finished, they won't be able to prove anything about anyone."

A real conversation-stopper, in sum. Maybe it was then that I got up and paced around. I remember seeing her legs dangling off the edge of the wooden dock. She had on a white dress with a full skirt that ended below the knees, and white sandals that strapped over her bare feet. She swung her legs back and forth, her feet crossing each other a few inches from the water.

She asked me how long I thought we'd be stuck there. She had appointments in the city the next morning. I said I didn't know. I was between Squilletti conversations. As to what the Counselor had in mind, I had no idea.

"Let me ask you something," I said to the Counselor's Wife. "Not that it makes any difference, but what makes you so sure I had sex with her? Aside from the fact that men are such dodos?"

She laughed, her legs swinging, then leaned back, propping herself on her elbows.

"She's gorgeous for one thing. The boobs. For another, you couldn't sleep. There are statistics that show that insomnia and sexual deprivation have a very high correlation."

I asked myself, in passing, if there weren't statistics to show that *anything* and sex (or sexual deprivation) had a high correlation.

"Besides," she was saying, staring at me coolly now, "I saw you last night. Remember?" She paused, waiting for me to say something. Then, when I didn't: "C'mon, Phil. At the banquet, remember? You were ready enough. Maybe we'd all had too much to drink, but if circumstances had been different, couldn't you and I have ended up in bed?"

Maybe I blushed, maybe I didn't. I didn't say anything.

"It's okay, Phil," she said cheerfully. "You don't have to be such a prude. There's nothing so terrible in *thinking* about it. Come on"—starting to get up—"we probably both could use a beer. I'll let you buy me one." The cocker led us back the way we'd come. We went up the slope under the pines, the dog first, the Counselor's Wife second, I in the rear, wondering in spite of myself what the Counselor and his wife did in their spare time (or didn't do) and realizing—also in spite of myself—that it wasn't really the first time I'd wondered it. I ended up mostly disconcerted. Which was par for the course whenever I spent time alone with the Counselor's Wife.

Probably there had to be a correlation there, too.

I didn't get to buy her the beer.

When we got back to the hotel, the Counselor was waiting for me. Squilletti's first interview with Grace Bashard, the short one, had already taken place. The second and longer one, in which I participated, didn't happen till that evening.

The Counselor was back in charge but kept me dangling for a while. All he told me was that at the police's request he, myself, and Grace Bashard would be spending the night. Meanwhile, his wife had to get back to the city. I was either to rent her a car or lend her mine.

The exchange I'd been waiting for didn't come till later in the afternoon, but here's how it went:

> The Counselor: "Do you know who did it, Phil?"
> Revere: "No, I don't."
> The Counselor: "Do you suspect anyone?"
> Revere: "Everyone. And no one."
> The Counselor: "Do you think Grace could have done it?"
> Revere: "*Could* have, certainly."
> The Counselor: "Could have, yes. But I'm inclined to think she didn't. I also think Sergeant Squilletti disagrees. And I think he's going to disagree more before he disagrees less."
> Revere: "When he finds out about the changes in Bashard's will?"
> The Counselor: "Exactly. He also suspects that you're involved, that at the very least you're covering up for her."
> Revere: "That's not true."
> The Counselor: "If it's not true, then you were goddamned stupid. And there's only one way you're going to convince Squilletti of it."
> Revere: "How's that?"
> The Counselor: "By finding out who killed Bashard for him."

* * *

Try renting a car in the Catskills, on a Sunday afternoon, in high tourist season. In the end, however much against my will, I saw the Counselor's Wife off behind the wheel of my Fiero, with Muffin beside her in the passenger seat.

I tried telling her about some of the vehicle's quirks, but she wouldn't hear me.

"For God's sake, Phil, I've driven a car before!" she shouted through the driver's window. That was precisely my worry. Then, with a screeching of rubber and Muffin hanging out the window on the passenger side, nose into the wind, she was off.

I went back to the hotel to await developments.

There were two, both of a revelatory kind. At least to me. One came out that Sunday. The other didn't until the next day, after the autopsy results were in.

Cranial X-rays taken in the course of the examination of Raul Bashard's body disclosed that the victim had been suffering from a brain tumor. The tumor was the kind for which there's no treatment, surgical or otherwise, because its cancerous tissue was inseparable from the normal tissue of the brain.

And oh yes, the Sunday revelation: According to Grace Bashard, oh yes, she and I had had sexual relations the night—or really morning—before.

CHAPTER
7

The Counselor, I've said, was in control. Nothing demonstrated this as much as the bargain he struck with Squilletti and the district attorney that Sunday night.

"If you're not ready to charge my client with a crime," he told them, "then you gentlemen have a choice to make. You can hold her under suspicion, or even as a material witness, but not for very long, and doing so will only increase the pressure on you to bring an indictment. For that matter, you can attempt to try her in the media, but with the same effect: pressure for an indictment. Either way, you will have me as a determined adversary, for I am convinced of her innocence, and I will vigorously oppose every move you make.

"Alternatively, if you will agree to certain conditions, you will have my full cooperation. Mr. Revere here, and Mr. Fincher, his associate, who know far more about the circumstances leading up to the Bashard murder than anyone else, will assist you in every way possible in your investigation. And if, at any time, you produce evidence warranting that

Ms. Bashard be charged, I will deliver her to you immediately. You have my personal guarantee on it."

In other words, the Counselor was setting himself up as a sort of intermediate judge and jury. I doubt he'd have gotten away with it in the city, but here he was playing on their insecurity: small-town officials dealing with a big-time crime, a big-time attorney and the bright lights of the media. He was also betting that they had no hard evidence linking Grace to the murder and that their forensic studies would turn up none.

(He won that bet. A dozen people or more had left their fingerprints in Bashard's suite, myself included. The vacuum cleaners sucked up similarly inconclusive evidence. The blood traces were Bashard's only.)

"What are these conditions of yours?" the district attorney asked when the Counselor had finished.

The Counselor waved the question aside.

"Let's call Ms. Bashard in first. Ask all the questions you want. Then we'll discuss it further."

We were meeting in a small private conference room off the hotel lobby. The Counselor, Squilletti, the district attorney and myself. The district attorney's name was Harmon Waller. He was a small, spare, neat man with rimless glasses and a bony skull, close-cropped graying hair that had receded from the temples, and a high-pitched voice that sometimes squeaked. I learned later from Squilletti that the Wallers had made their pile in Catskill real estate, that Harmon Waller had once had higher political ambitions, but that he'd never gotten past the primaries.

The Counselor went to the door and ushered in Grace Bashard. How much he had prepped her I can only guess at, and it had less to do with what she said than how she said it. If I didn't know better, though, I'd have sworn he'd gone out and bought the outfit she was wearing.

It was a two-piece affair, soft white, of a kind of T-shirt material, with long sleeves pushed up her forearms and a loose-fitting white skirt. It was clean and fresh-looking, as if it had just been laundered, and it made her look even younger than she was. She wore a pale pink scarf in her hair, and no makeup that I could see. Her complexion was pale, her eyes tired and a little puffy, as though she might have been crying. Her manner was composed, subdued.

She only looked at me once the whole time.

Squilletti led her back through the events as she'd experienced them, starting with the night before. She'd gone to bed while other people were still in the living room of the suite, her father included. She'd fallen asleep almost immediately, but she'd woken up in the middle of the night.

Did she know what time it was when she woke up?

No, she didn't.

Had something specific woken her up? A sound? A movement?

Yes, it was the storm. There'd been terrific thunder and lightning, she'd thought. She'd tried to go back to sleep but the storm frightened her. She'd always been afraid of thunder and lightning.

And then what happened?

She'd gotten up and gone into the living room.

Was there any sign of disturbance in the living room?

She didn't remember exactly. She didn't think so.

Were the lights on in the living room?

She didn't think so. She didn't remember.

Had she turned them on?

She might have. She didn't remember.

Where was her father?

She didn't know. She assumed he was asleep in his room.

Then what happened?

Then she'd gone out into the hallway and into Phil Revere's room.

Was the door from the suite to the hallway open?

She didn't think so.

So she'd opened it, and had she closed it behind her?

She didn't remember.

Why had she gone into Revere's room?

Because the door was open.

Was that the only reason? Because the door was open?

No. Because she was lonely. And a little scared.

So she went into Revere's room. Was Revere awake?

No, he was asleep in the bed. She'd gotten into bed with him and cuddled. A little later he'd woken up and then he'd made love to her.

Had this happened against her will?

No, not really.

Was it the first time they'd had sex together?

Yes, it was.

Progressively, during the questioning, her head dropped and her voice lowered. From time to time, she looked at the Counselor, as though asking whether she had to answer. The Counselor would nod reassuringly.

"Are you in love with Revere?" Squilletti asked.

"Yes," she answered softly, head down. "At least I was. At least I thought I was."

"Was this the first time you had had sex with anybody?" Squilletti asked.

At this point the Counselor intervened. He didn't think the question appropriate or in any way relevant to the investigation. He advised Grace not to answer.

Squilletti acquiesced.

And after they'd had sex, what had happened?

They'd fallen asleep.

Did she know that Revere had fallen asleep, too?

She wasn't sure. She assumed so.

And then what happened?

The next thing she knew, she'd woken up in her own bed, in the suite. The doctor was there, and Mr. Camelot. She hadn't even known her father was dead until Mr. Camelot told her.

They had other questions for her. The district attorney asked about her father, about his enemies, about who might have wanted to kill him. The crime had been an unusually violent one; who would have hated him that much? She answered that there were a lot of people who had sounded jealous of him, mostly because of all the money he'd made, but no, she didn't know of any one person specifically. And who would get all the money? She didn't know. But she'd get it, wouldn't she? A lot of it? She supposed she would.

And who else? She didn't know. And she shed no tears, she didn't get hysterical, she spoke in low, measured tones.

It was, all in all, a terrific performance, the more so because it seemed unplanned. I mean, you couldn't find the seams unless you knew exactly where to look. The only trouble was that part of it, at least, was a crock.

I could see, though, why the Counselor let it happen, whatever he really believed. It was practically impossible, listening to her, to imagine that she'd gotten into bed with a man she thought she was in love with, had made love with him for the first time, and either before or after had beaten her father to a pulp with a fire poker.

The girlish outfit helped, too. I wonder what she'd have said if Squilletti had asked her what she'd been wearing when she visited me.

Then it was my turn. Al Squilletti stood up, his hands in his pockets, and said to me: "You've got a different version of it, Revere. According to what you told me, you and the girl didn't make love. Do you still stick by that?"

I remember glancing at the Counselor, looking, I guess, for a cue as to how he wanted me to answer. But there was none.

"That's right," I said.

"You're *sure*?"

"Sure I'm sure."

"Well, it's possible you don't remember, isn't it? You said you'd had a lot to drink. Or could you have thought you dreamed it when it actually happened?"

I thought about it a minute. I had had a lot to drink, but that was earlier. I also remembered having sexy dreams.

"Anything's possible," I said. "But it'd be a first for me. I'll stand by what I said."

"Well," Squilletti said, "you've got two different accounts. One of you's gotta be lying. Or else remembering wrong. Why would she lie about it, Revere?"

"I can't imagine why. Maybe wishful thinking?"

Nasty words. But I wasn't feeling very kindly toward Grace right then.

"Or flip it over: Why would you lie?"

"I've no idea."

"Well, it'd be pretty embarrassing to you, wouldn't it?"

"Not to that point," I said.

"Well, let me put the same question to you, Revere. Are you in love with this girl?"

This was the point where I felt Grace look up at me—the one time.

"No," I said, looking back at her. Her eyes, I noticed, had turned big and watery blue. But no tears.

"Well, is she in love with you, do you think?"

"I don't think so, no," I answered.

Squilletti shrugged his shoulders and sat down again, his hands on the table.

"Look," I said, "I don't see why it's that important, one way or the other, but if it is, there're ways of finding these things out."

"That's exactly what I've been trying to tell your boss," Squilletti answered.

"Enough," the Counselor interrupted. "If there's going to be any further debate on that subject, I see no reason why my client has to listen to it. She's answered all your questions. If you've any more, now's the time for her to answer them. If not, I suggest we excuse her."

Neither Squilletti nor Waller had anything more. The Counselor got up and escorted Grace from the room. While he was gone, Squilletti told me he'd already tried to get a judge to order that Grace be tested for semen, but that the Counselor had outargued him. He tried to pump me further on Grace, but the Counselor (the last I'd heard) was still my boss, and Grace Bashard our client.

The Counselor returned. The buddy-buddy atmosphere Squilletti had tried to foster between himself and me evaporated.

"You surprise me, Sergeant," the Counselor said sharply, glowering down. "Neither I nor Judge Conlan saw any reason for my client to be tested for the presence of semen, but you persist in bringing it up. If you want our cooperation, that's a damned stupid thing to do. My client and my colleague here have different versions of what took place, or didn't, in Revere's bed last night. So? Neither of them is testifying under oath. Maybe if the subject is ever brought up in a courtroom, one of them will change the story. But as my colleague points out, it's of no importance whatsoever. And Conlan agrees."

Squilletti had nothing to say. He clearly didn't like being slapped, verbally or otherwise. Waller, the district attorney, simply sat there, his hands in his lap, his thin face expressionless.

The Counselor sat down again.

"To business, gentlemen," he said, staring directly at them. "My offer still stands. I'm ready to offer you full cooperation, including certain information you don't now have and which may prove hard to get if I choose to oppose you. Revere and Fincher will work with your investigation in any and every way, until it is finished."

"You mentioned conditions," Waller said. "What are the conditions?"

"Very simple. Nothing, not a word, is to get into the media. As far as the media are concerned, the investigation is proceeding. Period. Nothing about this sexual incident, which Revere says didn't happen. Nothing about some of the things I'm going to tell you."

"That kind of thing's pretty hard to control," Squilletti said.

"No it isn't. You two will know certain things. Whether people who work for you need to know is up to you. It's also up to you to shut them up."

"And if we don't? If something leaks out?"

"Then you'll wish to hell you never heard of me. I know the press and the media, gentlemen, know them much better than you do. Any leaks will rebound on you, rest assured, and once that happens, you'll have cameras and reporters on you every step of the way."

"Is that all?" the district attorney asked.

"No, it isn't. Ms. Bashard will be allowed to leave here tomorrow morning. She will be made available to you, as needed, through me."

Squilletti hesitated, glanced at Waller, then back at the Counselor. You could tell Squilletti wasn't happy about it, but making him happy wasn't the Counselor's top priority.

Squilletti started to say something, but the district attorney interrupted him.

"Please excuse us for a minute," he said.

They got up and left the room. The Counselor stoked a pipe. He lit it and puffed silent clouds of tobacco smoke toward the ceiling. I watched the square air-conditioning ducts suck them in.

They were gone long enough for an argument to have taken place, and when they came back they didn't sit down.

"We have your offer, Mr. Camelot," the district attorney said. "We'll give you an answer by tomorrow at one."

Buying time, I figured, to evaluate the physical evidence.

But the Counselor wasn't to be denied. He pressed home.

"No you won't," he said. "You'll give me your answer right now, or you can consider the offer withdrawn."

I thought Squilletti was going to explode, but the district attorney said: "All right, Mr. Camelot. You have a deal."

"Good," the Counselor replied. "Then please bear with me for a few more minutes. Sit down. There are some things you ought to know."

It was then, and only then, that he told them about the changes in Bashard's will. Grace, he told them, was going to inherit everything. Bashard has originally put in restrictions in the event of violent, or unnatural, death, but these had been removed the day before.

Squilletti knew he'd been had. He glared at the district attorney and started forward in his chair, then just as quickly slumped back. The Counselor had trapped him. Bashard's will was hardly enough of a basis, in and of itself, for him to charge Grace with murder. Which meant that all he could do with it, for the moment anyway, was chew on it.

I watched him chew.

A few days later Bashard's ashes, at his request, were scattered over the grounds of his estate. It was the second funeral I'd gone to there. By comparison to Jules Verne's, Bashard's was even shorter in ceremony. Those present included Grace, Bashard's three full-time employees (Price, MacGregor, and Kohl), the Counselor, myself, Bud Fincher, and Al Squilletti. There were two absentees, one named in Bashard's instructions and one by implication.

I'd called Oliver Latham the day before. He couldn't come, he said. His health was poor, he said; he was too tired to make another trip so soon. He said something to the effect that the next funeral he attended would probably be his own.

Bashard's instructions, which were typically detailed, had called for the immediate family to be present. His immediate family consisted, at most, of two people: Grace and her by-blood father, John Jameson, born John Jacob Bashard. I sent a cable to the last address we had for him, in Sydney, Australia. I also tried calling. I did get a number out of Sydney Directory Assistance but when I dialed it a recorded voice interrupted, saying the number was no longer in service and that I should call Directory Assistance. I gave Directory Assistance one last try and got nowhere.

Squilletti noticed the small turnout, too.

"Jesus," he said to me, "for a guy that famous, you'd think there'd be more of an affair."

"That was his doing," I said. "No media, no flowers, no announcements in the papers, no donations. No speeches over his grave. No grave."

The media was there, of course, but outside the gates.

"That's a lot of nos," Squilletti said.

"That's the way he was. He shut himself off."

"Weird," Squilletti said.

"Weird," I agreed.

We stood in a small clump on the back lawn of the estate. We were all appropriately dressed, more or less, except for Squilletti. Grace wore black. Even Price, MacGregor, and Kohl had on dark suits. Squilletti wore brown slacks and a cord jacket. The man from the undertaker's wore a morning suit and gray gloves.

Nobody wept. Who mourned I can't say.

We stood in the clump while the man from the undertaker's walked the grounds, sprinkling ashes from a handled
brass pot he cradled in his left arm. It wasn't strictly legal,
but who was there to challenge him? He did a thorough job,
too, dipping his gray gloves into the pot. I guess he was paid
to. I thought about how weird it was, even though the
body's supposed to be ninety-eight percent water, that a man
Bashard's size could be reduced to the contents of a brass
pot. I thought about the speech I'd heard Bashard give a
couple of times, at the dog's funeral and again at the
BashCon, the one about continuity. Maybe birds would peck
at the ashes, or squirrels, bugs, worms, get some kind of
nourishment out of them. Ashes were supposed to be good
for trees, plants. Still, the idea of it depressed me. I guess I
was still thinking about the number the Counselor had done
on me.

Suffice it to say that, when he's roused, Charles Camelot
has a tongue that stings like a hornet. He'd landed on me for
two things mainly: one, I'd fallen asleep on the job; two,
I'd encouraged Grace Bashard. I'd tried to defend myself on both counts, but the Counselor wasn't interested.
I wasn't paid, he'd said—highly paid—to defend myself. I
wasn't paid, he'd said—highly paid—to be unprofessional in
my performance. Nor was I paid—highly paid—to have
seduced the client's eighteen-year-old daughter.

"You may not want to hear it," the Counselor had said,
"but I'm holding you responsible, Phil. I'm going to be
sitting on your neck from now on. Together we're going to
find out who killed Raul. It's damned important to me. And
do you know why that is?"

He'd looked at me, waiting for an answer.

"No, I don't know why that is," I'd said, hot under the
collar.

"Because I don't like people getting murdered, and I don't
like somebody making assholes of us. And that's exactly
what happened."

If his aim had been to light a firecracker under me, I guess
it worked. But right then (and the morning of Bashard's
funeral, or nonfuneral) I was in one of those who-said-life-

was-meant-to-be-fair moods, which made me think of the years I'd spent, or wasted, as a working stiff in the Counselor's office, which made me think of the bar exams I'd never passed and why that was, and so forth, all the way back to Rivera, Pablo Evaristo Maria (whoever he was), while the man from the undertaker's finished sprinkling Bashard's remains over the hillside in New Jersey.

Nothing like a funeral to lift your spirits.

The man from the undertaker's finished his work. I remember that he dusted off his gloves by clapping his palms together. Then he took off his right glove—a delicate touch—and for some reason went to shake hands with everybody present. Then he left, in a black sedan with a driver.

The Counselor escorted Grace to the limo that had brought them out from the city. That was the only shot they showed on the evening news: the limo bearing Grace Bashard and her attorney, picking up speed as it emerged from the gates—because that was as close as the mobile units parked on the road outside had gotten to the funeral.

If you assume that neither Grace nor I, together or separately, had murdered Bashard, then Squilletti had blown it on the Sunday of the crime. He as much as admitted this to Bud Fincher and me. Yes, either he or one of his men had interviewed everyone who'd been staying on the second floor of the hotel annex. Yes, either he or one of his men had been inside every room on the floor while the guests were convened downstairs. But none of the people had heard a thing. All had claimed to have been asleep between the hours of 3:30 and 6:40 A.M., athough some stated they'd been awakened briefly by the storm. And the forensic investigation, Squilletti said, had focused on Bashard's suite and on my room because the body had been found there. If there'd been evidence in any of the other rooms—on somebody's clothes, in somebody's suitcase—then there was a good chance "it had walked out the door."

"Look at it this way," Squilletti said. "I focused on you and the daughter, that is true. Maybe I still do. But otherwise, there were hundreds of people there. What was I supposed to do? Hold them all? Impossible. A physical impossibility."

"Wrong," I said.

"What do you mean, wrong?"

"There weren't hundreds. There were only fifteen by my count, sixteen if you include Grace. You yourself found no evidence of a break-in from outside. And you've got Bud's testimony that nobody came up from downstairs the whole night. That leaves the people on the second floor, twelve rooms not counting the suite, eleven of which were occupied. Fifteen people in eleven rooms, any one of whom could have done it."

"If the suite door was open," Squilletti said, "or they had a key."

"If the suite door was open or they had a key," I repeated.

"Shit on a stick," Squilletti said, twisting one end of his mustache. "I still couldn't've held them. I'd've had every high-priced lawyer in America sitting on my head."

"Maybe so," I said. "But let's look at them now."

We'd set up shop in the outbuilding I'd worked in that time before, where Grace, I remembered, had asked me why I didn't marry her. I had an idea the computer, the Big *O*, might help us; and in any case I wanted it to walk Bud and Squilletti backward through where I'd been myself. We had Bashard's three staff members on tap for Squilletti to interrogate, and meanwhile the cook, MacGregor, supplied us with a platter of sandwiches and a pot of coffee.

Bud Fincher produced his floor plan of the annex's second floor, the same one we'd used setting up the BashCon, with the names of the guests written in the places. He also had a typed alphabetized list of the names, with brief captions of who they were. It read as follows:

Brinckerhoff, Mr. and Mrs. Richard, collector.
Camelot, Mr. and Mrs. Charles, Bashard attorney.
Frankaman, Mr. and Mrs. Sidney, store owner.
Hermatius, Norman, filmmaker.
Latham, Oliver, writer.
Morgan, Cyn, illustrator.

Price, Robert, Bashard security.
Revere, Philip.
Varga, George, magazine publisher.
Whitefield, Randall, book publisher.
Wright, Mr. and Mrs. Samuel, BashCon organizer.

The floor plan included the twelfth room, the one reserved for Arthur Clarke, the writer. But Arthur Clarke had never shown up, and the room had remained vacant.

"There're two we can eliminate," I said, drawing a line through the Counselor's line and my own. "That leaves nine. Twelve people in nine rooms."

"Not so fast," Squilletti said. "Who said you could eliminate anybody?"

"I did," I said. I looked at him and grinned. Maybe I couldn't pull a number on him like the Counselor had, but I had my own version of it. "Look, Al," I said, "Mr. Camelot already said it. You want to play games with us, go right ahead, but you'll do it without Bud and me. The way I see it, though, you've already made your choice."

He stared at me, then at Bud, then back, like he was trying to make up his mind. Then his face broke into one of those broad, pizza smiles, with the creases cut out to the edges of his face.

"You're right, Phil," he said. "But that doesn't mean you're not a suspect. Or your boss and his wife either."

"Suspect all you want," I said. "Only do it on your own time."

"Fair enough." Then, pointing at Price's name on Bud Fincher's list: "We'll start with the one closest to hand."

"Right," I said. "But let's see what the computer's got on them first."

I should have known better, I guess. I mean, if the Big O's memory bank contained detailed files on the neighbors who lived down the road, it would—logically—be encyclopedic on people Bashard had known well. But it didn't turn out that way. The computer had entries for them, and they were detailed enough, but nowhere near what it had on the neighbors. Maybe Bashard carried his friends in his head and hadn't bothered to enter all their dirty laundry. Squilletti asked me who had done the entering. I didn't know for a fact—I knew Grace and Price had had access to the computer, and that Price had taken care of a lot of the sorting and entering of correspondence—but I thought Bashard himself had done most of it. I remembered him hovering over the keyboard that first morning, bringing up the jogger's file, the pleasure he'd gotten out of it. It was a hobby with him, like a kid collecting nature specimens.

Still, it took us a long time to wade through them, with their cross references to correspondence and telephone conversations. And even though (assuming the data was accurate) it represented a hell of a shortcut, particularly for Bud Fincher and me, there was something numbing about the exercise.

About the correspondence in particular.

Squilletti noticed it, too.

"Jesus," he said at one point. "What a cold fish the son of a bitch was!"

We were looking through the letters Bashard and Latham had exchanged. Latham, mind you, was supposed to be his oldest friend, and certainly they'd known each other since way back. Apparently whenever Latham finished writing a book, he sent Bashard a copy of the manuscript. They also wrote from time to time (Latham more than Bashard), but any personal stuff the letters contained was so formal, so dry and deadpan, it was like reading the obituaries in a newspaper—or a letter from the IRS.

And the same with the other people, at least from Bashard's side. Cyn Morgan, the artist, wrote short little notes that at least gave a sense of personality. And there were one or two gossipy letters about Hollywood from Hermatius. But Bashard always answered—and he always did answer—in the same deadly writing, invariably polite, sometimes short, sometimes long, but always so formal, so impersonal!

The only possible exception we came across involved Bashard and—at various times—three of the people on our list: Brinckerhoff, Frankaman, and Wright. Bashard, I knew, was himself a collector of science fiction, as were the other three, and Sidney Frankaman was also a dealer. But what Bashard collected most seriously was his own work. There were letters from him to the others asking about prices in the market, questioning fluctuations, particularly downward fluctuations. Sometimes he bought; there was also evidence that he'd sold off duplicate copies of some of his first editions. But there were a few items of his own that he didn't have, in particular an issue of a magazine from the 1940s called *Twenty-fifth Century Tales* that had printed one of his early stories. A relatively recent series of letters extending over a year or more traced the complicated affair.

It started apparently with a letter from Sidney Frankaman, informing Bashard that he had heard of someone who had an entire set of *Twenty-fifth Century Tales* in mint condition, which he might be persuaded to sell at the right price. Bashard replied that he wasn't interested in the entire set, which included some two years' issues, but only in those that had published his own work—all of which he already owned but the one issue. Frankaman answered that he thought only the entire set might be available, because to break one issue out of it would considerably lower the value of what was left. However, if Bashard insisted on making an offer on the single issue, he would be glad to transmit it. Bashard offered $1,800 for the single issue. At the same time, he wrote Sam Wright asking his opinion on what a complete set of *Twenty-fifth Century Tales* might be worth in the open market. Wright replied that there were few mint sets known to be in existence, the magazine in its day having been unsuccessful and unrecognized until years later, that the last set to be offered in open auction had sold for $6,200, that he'd heard rumors of one private sale since but not of the price. It was, Sam Wright thought, a seller's market. One month later, to the day, Bashard wrote Frankaman:

My dear Sidney Frankaman:
    As of this date, I have had no answer to my last letter to you (photocopy enclosed).

In consideration of our long association, I am
surprised, at the least, by the absence of courtesy.
In the expectation of a prompt reply, I am,
Very truly yours,
R. R. Bashard

At this point Brinckerhoff entered the story through, it
looked like, a telephone call or series of calls followed by
more letters. Brinckerhoff knew of the set in question. In
fact, if he had known Raul Bashard was the prospective
buyer, they might have circumvented Sidney Frankaman. It
was too late for that now, but possibly he, Brinckerhoff,
could facilitate matters. Of course, only the full set would be
for sale. Bashard answered that he saw no reason why
Frankaman couldn't be circumvented. For obvious reasons,
he would prefer not to deal with someone of Frankaman's
"type." What was the seller's asking price? The seller would
not set a price, according to Brinckerhoff, but wanted
Bashard to make an offer. Bashard offered $5,250. The offer
was refused. Why wouldn't Brinckerhoff put Bashard in
direct touch with the seller and let them negotiate? The seller
didn't want that.

Little by little Bashard raised his offer to $6,750.

At this point Sidney Frankaman came back into the
picture. Sidney Frankaman was outraged to have learned
that Bashard had tried to deal behind his back. If Bashard
still wanted to buy the set, he would have to deal with
Frankaman. Bashard replied that he hadn't tried to deal
behind Frankaman's back, but that he'd assumed, in the
absence of an answer to his last letter (photocopies enclosed
of original letter and reminder letter), that Frankaman had
lost interest. He was still prepared to pay $6,500 for the
entire set. Frankaman countered that he knew Bashard's last
offer had been $6,750, accused Bashard of dealing in bad
faith, and said that even $6,750 was unacceptable and
embarrassingly low. The seller's asking price, he said, was
$11,000, and it was nonnegotiable. In fact, the set would be
withdrawn from sale within seven days if Bashard declined
to meet the price.

A flurry of phone calls and telegrams followed. Bashard wanted to know what percentage Frankaman's commission was. Frankaman refused to tell him. Bashard called Brinckerhoff; Brinckerhoff was no help. Bashard accused Frankaman of gouging. Frankaman replied that the price was $11,000.

In the end, Bashard wrote one last letter:

> Dear Frankaman:
>   Enclosed you will find my check in the amount of $11,000 (eleven thousand dollars) as payment in full for one complete set of *Twenty-fifth Century Tales*, mint condition, as per our discussions.
>   You will note that the check is postdated by one week. This is to allow you to send me the above-mentioned set by courier for my inspection. If I find its condition satisfactory, you may submit my check for deposit. If I do not, the set will be returned to you by courier and payment stopped.
>   I must warn you, sir, that the last thing on earth I will tolerate is to have appeared the fool within the science-fiction community. If this appears to be the case, and/or if this transaction is publicized, then I will look to you for satisfaction in full.
>   Very truly yours,
>   R. R. Bashard

Bashard's warning notwithstanding, we found two further letters—one from Brinckerhoff, one from Sam Wright, both congratulating Bashard on his acquisition.

For once, Bashard didn't seem to have answered.

"It sure looks like they fleeced him," Squilletti said.

"Who?" I asked.

"All three of them probably. Frankaman anyway."

"Maybe so."

"What do you mean, 'maybe so'? The stuff's garbage. My old man used to read magazines like that. They called them pulps. They're garbage."

"Anyway," I said, "I guess he could afford it."

"Yeah," Squilletti said. "Besides, it doesn't add up to murder."

No, it didn't add up to murder. Maybe they'd fleeced Bashard, but Bashard was the one who was dead. Hard as we looked though, it was as close as we came to anything out of the ordinary that afternoon. What were the motives for murder? the three of us asked each other. And for a particularly bloody murder? Money and passion. Most of the people on the list were well off, if the computer was right. A couple weren't, but no one was what you'd call destitute, and how could they profit from Bashard's death anyway? And passion, whether hate, jealousy, revenge, or what-ever—maybe it was there, hidden somewhere, but it sure wasn't evident to us on the green screen.

By the time we got through hashing and rehashing the twelve people on Bud's list, it was well into the afternoon. Bud Fincher and I divided them up. At first Squilletti wanted to assign a man to go with each of us, but we talked him out of it.

We still had Price to do, and Squilletti wanted to talk to MacGregor and Kohl.

"Phil," Bud Fincher reminded me, "didn't you want to run Al through the hate stuff?"

I remember sighing.

"That's right, I did." Maybe it wasn't important, but I wanted to walk Squilletti back to where we'd been before the BashCon and through what now seemed, I admitted in hindsight, to have led us off the track.

"Are any of these people in there?" Squilletti asked, pointing at the list.

"No," I answered.

"Then I don't see why—never mind," he interrupted himself, reaching for a cigarette. "Go ahead."

We ran through some samples. He saw some Sex Danger-ous and Money Dangerous. He even saw those correspon-dents whom Bud's people had never succeeded in tracing. A couple of times he whistled low—there were, as I've said before, some pretty steamy examples. But his mind wasn't really on it, and you could hardly blame him. Because if the answer was in the hate mail, then we were wasting our time with the people who'd been on the second floor of the hotel annex. We'd have to start all over again, where Bud Fincher and I had started, going through the whole wide world, practically, to look for a murderer angry enough to beat a man to death with a fire poker.

Maybe that explains why I missed it. Or rather missed seeing what wasn't there anymore.

Or even saw and registered what wasn't there, but simply didn't pay attention.

S.O.W.

CHAPTER
8

NAME: Price, Robert   white Caucasian male
Age: 31
Health: excellent   Physical condition: excellent
Sign: Taurus   IQ test: 119
Function: Security Officer   Earnings:
     $35,000 annum
Employer: R. R. Bashard
Marital status: single   Children: none
Net worth: Est: $41,000 (see Bashard, financ.)
Education: B.S. U of So. Calif., OCS, USN, grad-
     uated 51 in class
Military Service: six years USN, San Diego, Ca.,
     Pensacola, Fla., Canal Zone, Washington D.C.;
     last rank: Lt. j.g.; reason for separation: resign.
     w/o prej.

"Why'd you leave the Navy?" Squilletti asked.
"Ask the Navy," Price, Robert replied.
"C'mon, c'mon, you can do better than that," Squilletti

said sharply. We were sitting on the back terrace near the swimming pool, otherwise deserted, and though it was late in the afternoon we were into the longest days of the year and the sun was still hot over the hilltop.

Price shrugged slightly. He had changed out of his funeral garb. He wore buck shoes with red soles and white socks, sharply pressed chinos and a red-and-blue-striped polo shirt that looked like it, too, had just come from the laundry. Ditto his crew cut and the clean-shaven lantern jaw.

"The peacetime Navy's no place to get ahead. I was passed over once for promotion. I was told I was going to be passed over again."

"So you got out."

"I resigned, yes."

"How'd you come to work for Bashard?"

"I was recommended to him."

"Who recommended you?"

"It worked through Navy channels."

"Why'd you take the job?"

"Why? Because the pay was good, better than I could've gotten elsewhere. He told me if I'd give him two years, he'd stake me to whatever I wanted to do."

"How long have you worked for him?"

"Two years and four months."

"Oh? What made you stay on?"

"I almost didn't. He promised me a bonus if I gave him another six months."

"How come you almost didn't?"

"Because of his daughter."

Squilletti paused, as though to give Price room to elaborate. But Price didn't elaborate. He held his head stiffly, chin in, eyes straight ahead.

"You mean you didn't like her?" Squilletti asked.

"I didn't say that. But I was hired to take charge of Bashard's security, not to be his daughter's chauffeur."

"Hmmm," Squilletti said. "So you ended up driving Grace around a lot. You must've gotten to know her pretty well. What do you think about her?"

"Spoiled," Price said. "Otherwise okay."

"Did you screw her?"

That was vintage Squilletti, but Price didn't blink.

"No," he said.

"No?" Squilletti repeated, raising his eyebrows. "How come? You must've had plenty of opportunities."

But Price didn't rise to the bait. All he said was: "I worked for him."

Squilletti took him away to other background subjects— dead end, I thought—then tried to get him to talk about the relationship between Grace and Bashard. But he didn't get very far. Yes, Price said, they fought sometimes, mostly about Grace's freedom to come and go, to do whatever she wanted. Mostly Bashard won. But if Price had anything to add to what we already knew, he wasn't putting it on the table.

"Do you think she killed him?" Squilletti asked.

"I don't know."

"Well, come on, you were there, you knew the people. You've got to have an opinion."

"Why don't you ask Revere?"

"I'm not asking Revere," Squilletti persisted. "I'm asking you."

"Revere was the one in charge."

"What does that have to do with it?"

"It has everything to do with it. Revere was the one in charge, and he blew it."

I started to butt in, but Squilletti waved me off.

"What do you mean, he blew it?"

Then it came out, a little of it anyway. Maybe the strongest feeling a guy like Price has is resentment at being passed over. He'd been in charge of security, he said, and he'd always gotten the job done. But then Bashard hired this hotshot from New York (me), without so much as asking Price's advice, and this hotshot had blown it. He had fallen asleep on the job.

What would Price have done in my place?

He wouldn't have fallen asleep on the job. He wouldn't have gone to bed with the boss's daughter. If anybody had wanted to get to Bashard, they'd have had to climb over Price's dead body.

"He was some kind of man," Price said. "Great. He treated me like a . . . like a . . ."

His face had gone all stiff, muscles on bone. For a split second, I thought he was going to blubber. Instead, he did a strange thing. His neck arched, his chin tucked into his collarbone. Then, with an upward heave of his chest, his chin lifted and at the same time he seemed to gain a couple of inches in height.

Ramrod straight.

Squilletti glanced at me, I glanced at Bud Fincher, Bud Fincher looked back. None of us could read it. Whether Price was covering up or literally pulling himself together, it was strictly name-rank-and-serial-number time.

Squilletti led him through the night of the murder. He didn't add anything to what we already knew. He'd been the last one out of the suite. Bashard was going to bed. Grace was already in her room. He'd shut the suite door behind him, and he and I had made sure it was locked. Then he'd taken a shower and gone to sleep; the next thing he knew I was knocking on his door.

He'd opened the door in his undershorts, I remembered. I remembered seeing one of those portable pants pressers behind him, with his pants in it.

Squilletti then took him back to Jules Verne, the poisoned Doberman. According to Price, someone had thrown poisoned meat through the fence and they'd never found who'd done it.

"But Grace thought her father did it, didn't she?" Squilletti asked.

"I heard her say something like that."

"Why would she have said something like that if it wasn't so?"

"She was very attached to the dog."

"If that's what she thought, though," Squilletti persisted, "mightn't it have made her want to kill him?"

But all Price said was: "She wanted to do a lot of things she didn't do."

"Like what things?" Squilletti asked, but he couldn't make Price be more specific.

Squilletti then showed him Bud Fincher's list. Price either knew them all, or knew of them. The only ones he'd met at the house, he thought, were Morgan, Varga and Whitefield. Cyn Morgan had been out on different occasions, Varga and Whitefield maybe once or twice. Several times he'd driven Cyn Morgan to the local bus stop, once into the city. He thought he'd talked to all the others on the list on the telephone, except maybe Oliver Latham.

Did any of them have any grudge against Bashard? Not that he was aware of. Were there ever any arguments, or signs of enmity? Not that he was aware of.

"What's going to happen to you now, Price?" Squilletti asked.

Price shrugged.

"Mr. Camelot asked me to stay on," he said, "but it won't last long. I'll have to find another job."

"Why do you say that?"

"Because it's over," Price said. "He's dead."

We made as if to get up from the table, but Squilletti had an afterthought or two.

"Did you know Bashard was dying?" he asked. "That he had a brain tumor? I mean, before last weekend?"

"I didn't," Price answered. "But it stood to reason."

"What does that mean?"

"I used to drive him to a clinic in New York."

"And he told you he was sick?"

"He never told me anything," Price said. "He always said he'd gotten a clean bill of health. But you don't go to the doctor that often and get a clean bill of health. And when my two years were up and he renewed me . . ." He paused. Then: "It'd have been for more than six months otherwise."

True to form, Bud Fincher and I got hung up in Lincoln Tunnel traffic. At that time of day, they've got four lanes coming out of the tunnel and only two going in, and the inbound traffic was backed up almost all the way to the New

Jersey Turnpike. We inched along in the exhaust fumes, hashed and rehashed our material, and got nowhere.

By the time I got uptown the office was closed, but a message from the Counselor told me to come up to the fifth floor. I could hear the hum of conversation, the tinkling of glasses, even before I got off the elevator. Party time. People thronged on the terraces in the pleasant dusk and overflowed inside around the bar, and I saw the Counselor's Wife, in yellow chiffon, moving animatedly from cluster to cluster.

The Counselor spotted me and took me into the hot tub room, where we sat in deck chairs while I gave my report on Price.

"Ultra U.S. Navy," I concluded. "The ramrod kind. To hear him tell it, Bashard was his hero of heroes. He also claims he knew Bashard was dying."

The only thing I'd thought of that Squilletti had left out of his questioning was to ask Price how he came out in Bashard's will. The answer was zero. Ditto for MacGregor and Kohl. I wondered if that would change Price's opinion of his boss.

"Do you think he's covering anything up?" the Couselor asked me.

I thought about it for a second.

"Could be," I said, "but the chances are good we won't get at it unless we find it somewhere else."

"Then go find it," the Counselor said.

Aye aye, sir, I thought. Instead: "Is it true you asked him to stay on at Bashard's?"

"That's right," he answered. "Somebody has to keep the souvenir hunters away."

"It's also a way of keeping him on tap."

"Exactly."

"And what about Grace?"

"I've taken care of Grace myself," he said pointedly.

We were interrupted then, and it wasn't till the next morning that I learned he had Grace sequestered in a fancy hotel, one a little off the beaten track, under an assumed name.

Right then, though, the Counselor's Wife sailed into the hot tub room.

"Well, here you are, Charles! You can't just duck . . . oh," spotting me, "hi, Phil. I didn't even know you were here. Welcome to the party. Don't you want a drink? Leave it to my husband to forget to offer you one. So how's the crime solving going? Haven't you two figured out who did it yet?"

She leaned back against the hot tub, perching herself on her hands, and gazed at me with head tilted and a twinkle in her eye.

"We're working on it, dear," the Counselor answered.

"Puh-lease. Don't give me that don't-worry-your-pretty-little-head-about-it line, Charles. I was there, too, remember?"

"We're working on it," the Counselor repeated. He may have said it to bait her, but it also confirmed what Bud Fincher and I had told each other on the way into the city: that we were going on a fishing expedition, with no evidence, no motive. No suspect either.

Other than Grace.

And that was the point.

"If you have any shortcuts for us, Nora," the Counselor said, "let's hear them."

"Both of you know what I think," she answered.

"Do we?" the Counselor said, looking at me.

"It's very simple," she said, "and I bet I could prove it, too, if you'd let me. Grace did it. You don't have to look further than a classic case of patricide."

"Oh?" the Counselor said.

"But what I don't understand," she went on, "and this is the interesting part, is why the two of you are so intent on protecting her."

"Is that what we're doing, Phil?"

"Don't ask Phil," she retorted. "All he wants to do is get into her pants, and that much I get. But what about you? What do you want?"

Uh-oh, I thought, feeling my own gorge rising.

But the Counselor just stared back at her calmly, as though considering his words.

"The truth," he said at length. "And I promise you this, love. If we find out we're wrong about Grace, you'll be the first to know."

NAME: Morgan, Cynthis Ewer   white Caucasian
  female
Age: 44
Health: good (corrected vision, complete hyster-
  ectomy)
Sign: Pisces
Function: Artist/illustrator
Marital status: divorced (1978, Morgan, John H.)
Children: none
Employment: self-employed
Earnings: $50,000 per annum
Net worth: $200,000 (divorce settlement: $20,000
  cash plus apartment, current valuation:
  $100,000)
Born: Keene, New Hampshire   Resides: New
  York City
Education: B.A., U of New Hampshire
  Art Students League (New York)
Sexual preference: Males (young), chronic pro-
  miscuity

She lived in the basement apartment of a brownstone in the South Village, near the old printing district, where giant trucks rumble through the streets on their way to the Holland Tunnel and the inhabitants are sandwiched in like an accident between Soho and the Hudson River. The apartment was small, dark, low-ceilinged, and crammed with objects—furniture that had seen better days, bric-a-brac, pictures on every inch of wall space, and cats everywhere you turned. Artists are supposed to need light and space, but Cyn Morgan's place looked more like a squirrel's nest, one where any normal-size human would have to keep his head ducked all the time.

Cyn Morgan herself, though, was a miniature of a woman, somewhere short of "petite" in stature, with bare feet, a voluminous skirt down to her ankles, a tight-fitting white shirt, a lot of antique-looking jewelry. She had an intuitive and sharp-featured face with Irish blue eyes, and curly jet-black hair that didn't look real but somehow belonged. Pretty, in sum, and she didn't look anything close to the forty-four years the printout claimed.

"I was glad you called," she said over her shoulder, leading the way. "I've never met a real live detective before."

She took me through a small cluttered bedroom and a narrow kitchen where pots and pans hung on nails, then up a few steps to a postage-stamp backyard, which barely had room for a small wrought-iron table and two chairs, a cracked stone tub bursting with roses, and a spindly-trunked ailanthus tree.

"I know," she said, hugging herself while I sat down at the table, "it's tiny. It's just too *small* a place. Even for one person. That's what everyone says. If you told me when I moved in that I'd still be living here fifteen years later, I'd've laughed at you. But I like it. And how could I do that to the cats? I mean, cats can't stand moving. Well," she said, still standing, "tell me everything you want to know. But first, tell me how you like your coffee."

I told her I liked my coffee black. I also repeated what I'd said over the phone, that I wasn't a detective, but that didn't seem to matter. She served the coffee on a small round metal tray, in one of these flip-over European pots with a miniature creamer and sugar bowl on the side, even though she drank it black, too.

"All right," she said, sitting close to me at that wrought-iron table. Her bare feet, I noticed, didn't quite reach the ground. "Tell me who *did* kill Raul."

"If I knew that," I said, "I guess I wouldn't be sitting here drinking coffee with you."

"Well, in that case I'm glad you don't," she said. "Don't know, I mean. But wait a minute," she said, her eyes going round and blue, "you don't think *I* did it, do you?" She laughed, throwing her head back, a busy, musical sound. "*That* would be a switch. Why, I'm the most *timid* person in the world! Ask anybody. I have trouble swatting flies. Not that there weren't times when I didn't *feel* like killing him."

"What times were those?" I asked.

She was one of those people who dawdle over their coffee, then drink it all at a gulp. She was in the dawdling stage now, stirring the dark liquid with a miniature spoon while she talked.

"All right," she said, "let me try to guess the questions, and I'll answer everything. First off, when did I first meet him? Oh, Lord, longer ago than I like to think about. I was just starting out. I'd done a few book jackets, exhibited at some of the cons, but I was a long way from . . . what did Ron say? . . . The best-loved science-fiction artist in America. Now there's a joke for you. What does that *mean*, The best-loved science-fiction artist in America? Who? *Me*? Anyway . . . where was I?"

"You were just starting out," I reminded her.

"That's right. And I couldn't afford to turn any work down, I had to take my assignments where I got them. Anyway, one day the phone rang, and this voice said"—here her own voice dropped down to a masculine register—"'Mr. Bashard wants to see you, at ten o'clock tomorrow.'

"So I went, what would you expect?" she went on in her normal voice. "Even though I don't like being *summoned*, you know what I mean? It turned out he'd seen some of my art, wanted me to do some sketches for the jacket of his next novel. Mind you, I wasn't exactly a beginner; I thought I was past the audition stage. But it was R. R. Bashard; you didn't say no to him. At least I didn't. He said he'd pay me for my work, even if the sketches weren't accepted. Anyway, they were accepted, pending revisions—there were always revisions with him—and I've done all his jackets ever since. Or did . . ."

She drank the coffee at a swallow and wrinkled her nose.

"It's gone cold," she said. "Do you want me to heat up the rest?"

Before I could answer she was gone, the flip-over pot in hand, talking at me from the kitchen door while she waited.

"I *hated* going out there. Awful. That dark, lugubrious

place, like a morgue, everybody over sixty. Why did he lock himself up there? You should talk to the secretaries, they'd have things to tell you, but they're all dead, I think. He had a bunch of them before he put in the stupid computer. All retired-professor types." Then, in the same deep male voice: "'Mr. Bashard wants to see you, at ten o'clock tomorrow morning.'"

A shiver shook her shoulders as she stood in the kitchen doorway.

"So why did I do it? Well, the money, first off. We always had the same deal: whatever the publisher paid me, he'd match it on the side. My fee's gone up over the years—it's six thousand dollars now for sketches and finished art. Does that sound like too much? The trouble is, I work very slowly. I'm too much of a perfectionist. But whatever it was, Raul would match it. He got his money's worth, too."

I started to ask her what she meant by that, but she did it for me.

"We fought like cats and dogs," she said. "He was a perfectionist, too, knew exactly what he wanted. The breasts, for instance. I like to paint big boobs, I can't help myself. And make no mistake, the fans like it, too. Ask anybody in science fiction—the covers with big boobs outsell everything else. But they gave Raul grief. He had trouble coming right out and saying it. He'd criticize this or that other detail, sometimes I'd do sketches for him on the spot, but in the end there was nothing for him to do but come out with it."

She cleared her throat.

"'The chest,'" she began in a weirdly familiar voice, then cleared her throat again. "'The chest is too prominent.' Can you beat that? 'Cyn, I think you've made her *chest* too prominent.'"

She had mimicked Bashard's voice right down to the intonations. I laughed, and she laughed with me. She'd come back to the table, pot in hand. She refilled our cups and perched again on the chair next to me, giggling.

"In the end, I'd have to reduce 'the chest.' Or else bring the hair down further over the boobs, so you couldn't see.

Probably the next year—or the next time I worked for him—I made them even bigger."

She dawdled with the coffee again, stirring, not drinking. She was thinking about something, I thought, and something told me to give her room.

"Did I tell you he tried to buy me?" she said finally. "That's right. He was always after me to find out what my annual income was. He told me he'd double it if I worked for him exclusively, did no other covers but his. Once I was almost tempted. It was when I got divorced. I had the shorts. Not just money; I'd lost my confidence generally. But it's a good thing I didn't, a damn good thing. I mean, where would I be now, at thirty-eight? The Best-Loved Science-Fiction Artist in America Who Nobody's Ever Heard Of?"

She'd fudged her age by a good six years, I noticed. Unless the computer was wrong. I figured it wasn't, but she looked a lot closer to thirty-eight than forty-four, even close up.

She was staring at me over the rim of her small cup, the blue eyes large, the forehead wrinkled. Then it crinkled a little, and her nose, too, in a half-smile.

"All right," she said, putting the little cup down. "Something makes me trust you, trust your discretion. Besides, if I don't, somebody else is sure to tell you."

She seemed to draw herself up to full size in her chair, as though getting her act together, and the crinkle went away.

"I once had an affair with him," she said. "I know it was stupid, *knew* it was stupid. But I told you I'm timid. Too timid. I guess I don't know how to say no easily. Anyway, it was more embarrassing than anything else. It didn't last long. You could almost say it *didn't* happen."

She looked away, at the wall of the neighboring building which protruded past her own and formed one boundary to her backyard.

"What do you mean, 'embarrassing'?" I asked.

"What do I mean, 'embarrassing'?" she repeated, her chin jutting in profile. "He couldn't *do* anything, that's what I mean. He was too old, or too something. But do you know what he said afterward? Try to guess. He said it was *my* fault.

He said he thought I was too *aggressive*! Can you beat that? Me? Too *aggressive*?"

She laughed abruptly—a harsh sound—then turned back to me.

"I don't mean to insult you," she said, "but sometimes men are such assholes. Most men. Some men anyway."

"When did this happen?" I asked.

"When? Five or six years ago. Six, I think. But that's not the point. Do you know what happened after that?"

"What?" I said.

"He asked me to *marry* him, that's what! You'd have thought it was a joke, but he didn't have much of a sense of humor. It *was* a joke, really, only he took it seriously. *Very* seriously. He offered to sign a premarital contract, giving me half his estate when he died. He even went so far as to have one drawn up."

I made a mental note to check our files. I didn't remember ever seeing such a document, which meant that Bashard had drafted it himself, that he'd gotten someone other than the Counselor to do it, or that Cyn Morgan was lying.

"The last time I saw him," she went on, "before last weekend, I mean—it was a couple of months ago. I went out to discuss the jacket for his new book—he brought it up again. Poor bastard. He told me I was stupid, that he didn't have much longer to live, that if I'd marry him, I'd be set up for life. What did I tell him? I told him to stop being morbid, that if he'd lasted this long he'd last forever. In other words, I told him no. I tried to make light of it, but he wasn't much of one for . . ."

Her voice trailed off. Then, as if interrupting herself: "Lord, do you think I made a *mistake*?"

I didn't know what she meant at first. A mistake in not marrying him?

My confusion showed, it seemed.

"All the money!" she said gaily. "Why, I'd be rich now, if I'd married him. Set up for life."

She looked at me, blue-eyed, and burst out laughing.

"Never mind," she said. "It's a pretty sick joke. Besides, if I'd done it, I'd be your prime suspect now, wouldn't I?"

She waited for me to answer.

"I guess so," I said. "But I take it you're telling me you didn't kill him."

"You're right. I didn't."

"Well, who do you think did?"

"Everybody thinks Grace did, Raul's daughter, and that you helped her cover it up."

"What makes you so sure?" I said.

"I didn't say I agreed with them," she answered. "For what it's worth, I think Grace is too young to murder anybody. Maybe not too young to *think* it, but too young to do it. Like I was too young to murder my ex-husband."

I thought, irrelevantly, that Cyn Morgan was also too small to murder anyone, unless she stood on a chair. But maybe I was wrong about that.

"If it happened now, though," she said fiercely, narrowing her eyes, "I'd slit his throat with a straight razor."

"What happened?" I asked.

"Oh, never mind," she answered. "It was too long ago, and too boring. He found somebody sexier than I was. When he got tired of her, he tried to come back. That's when I would have slit his throat. Or should have. I didn't. End of story."

Whoever Mr. Morgan was, I don't think I envied him.

"If you don't think Grace killed Bashard," I said, "who do you think did?"

"I don't know. You're the detective." Then, before I could say anything: "I know, you're *not* the detective, you only work for Camelot. Well, who does Camelot think did it?"

A good question, and one I couldn't answer.

I took out my list then, Bud Fincher's list, with the floor plan of the second-floor annex clipped to it. She'd seen the floor plan before, had been over it with one of Squilletti's people, had gone over the details of what she had done that night and early morning. She couldn't add anything to it. She'd seen nothing, heard nothing.

Then I led her through the list of names, one by one. She knew them all, commented freely on them. She said she'd slept with about half of the men, and half the men would tell me they'd slept with her, and that it would be up to me to guess which ones were telling the truth. Still, as she chatted on, you could feel a curtain being drawn inside her, not the who-invited-you kind that Sidney Frankaman had thrown up that Sunday in the hotel bar, but a curtain that said: we all know each other, everyone on your list, and maybe one of us did murder Bashard for reasons good or bad, but I'm not going to finger anyone for you—at least not inadvertently.

It wasn't that she turned hostile either. There was something appealingly brash and no-nonsense about her, and I think she liked me, too. In fact when it came time for me to leave, it was all I could do to get out the door without staying for lunch.

Still. Not, I guessed, that she was covering up something she knew, but she wanted to keep her suspicions to herself.

I thought I might be imagining it.

I found out I wasn't.

The Brinckerhoffs, she'd always thought, were assholes of the first degree. Actually, Richard wasn't so bad, but maybe the only reason she said it was that he'd bought several of her paintings, including the original artwork to three of Bashard's jackets. Actually, he'd called her the day before. He wanted to buy the art for the last Bashard, the one that would be published posthumously. He was putting a check in the mail. She didn't know if she'd accept it or not. She'd always heard it said that he'd helped Bashard financially, years ago.

Sidney Frankaman, she said, was an ass-pincher, so was George Varga, but she took it from George while she couldn't stand it from Sidney. She'd done business with them both. Frankaman, who owned a chain of stores specializing in science-fiction books and regalia, had started a line of greeting cards several years before with her art. She'd always guessed, though had never been able to prove, that he'd cheated her on royalties. George, on the other hand, knew exactly what he wanted, bought art for his magazine at fixed prices, and you either took it or you didn't. You also got your bottom pinched in the bargain, but he paid on time. Both went back a long way with Bashard. Varga had printed lots of Bashard, including serializations of all Bashard's novels up until some ten years ago. She'd heard it said that after then, Bashard wanted too much money for the rights.

Ollie Latham was a gentleman of the first order, she said, which made him the more dangerous. Also an extraordinarily gifted writer. She'd always heard it said that he was Raul's oldest friend, at least living friend, although she'd hardly ever seen them together. Probably he could tell me more than any of the others, if I could get to him. He lived a reclusive life. She had talked to Ollie, too, since the weekend. He had invited her to create the cover art for his own next novel, when it was finished. She was pretty sure she'd do it, even though the money wouldn't be as good as for a Bashard.

Norman Hermatius she knew the least. She'd always found him something of a windbag in person, but he made good films. Or hired people who made good films, she didn't know which. He and Bashard collaborated only the one time, and she'd heard they'd had terrible fights—presumably because Raul thought he knew more about movie scripts than anyone else, including Norman.

Ron Whitefield was okay, a good businessman and a fairly decent person. She thought he resented her because her fee was so high, yet he had to pay it because of Bashard. He paid slowly; most book publishers did. He screamed to high heaven over what he had to pay Bashard, but he always paid, she supposed. She thought he didn't give a fig for science fiction, or what was between the covers of any book as long as it sold. Between the covers was Helga Hewitt's department. Had I met Helga Hewitt? She'd heard Helga and Ron spent time between the covers themselves, but you heard a lot of that in publishing. Ron Whitefield had called her, too, to make sure she'd be on time with her last Bashard jacket.

Sam Wright, finally. Sam Wright was a pure gem, married to one of the world's greatest bitches. If Sam Wright could get rid of the bitch, she—Cyn Morgan—would marry him in a minute, and she'd told him that. But the bitch had the money and the money, she guessed, had Sam. Of all of them, with the possible exception of Latham, Sam had the most genuine love for science fiction. For most of them—herself, too, she thought—it was a way of making a living, but Sam really cared. He'd called her as well, but just to say hello.

"I don't know," she said when we'd finished the list. "Seriously, I mean. Maybe somebody there did have a reason to murder Raul, but it escapes me. That was a terrible way to die. A lot of people didn't *like* him, but a lot of people don't like any of us and we don't get ourselves beaten to death. I guess you'd have to eliminate the married couples, wouldn't you?"

"Why is that?" I asked.

"Well, unless you think two people bashed his head in *together*? Well, maybe they did. Come to think of it, in case you didn't know, Richard's wife, and Sidney's, take mega-sleeping pills."

"How do you know that?"

"I heard them talking about it. The night before at the banquet. In—please pardon the expression—the 'little girl's room.' Charlotte Frankaman said she'd have to take an extra pill or she wouldn't sleep a wink. Frau Brinckerhoff . . . what's her name? Serena . . . Serena said she was going to do the same. Come to think of it, I think I like the idea of that: Sidney tiptoeing through the hall with a poker in his hand while Charlotte snored in the bed. And—

"But it's not so funny," she interrupted herself, slowing down, "is it?"

"Did you know Bashard was going to die anyway?" I asked in turn, taking a leaf from Squilletti. He, Bud, and I had agreed that we could use this information, at the right moment.

"What do you mean, die anyway?"

"It came out in the autopsy examination."

"What came out?"

"That he had a brain tumor. They think he had maybe a year to live at the outside. I think he knew it, too."

"Lord," Cyn Morgan said. "That's heavy stuff."

She stared at me, bewildered. Clearly she hadn't known. Equally clearly, she was thinking something but not sharing it.

"Right there, Cyn," I said. "What're you thinking?"

"What do you mean?"

"You're thinking something, I can tell. What is it?"

"Nothing," she said, recovering. "I was just wondering if he knew that when he proposed to me the last time. I guess he must have, huh?"

I wouldn't swear to it, but I had the impression that wasn't what she'd been thinking at all. Much as I tried, though, I couldn't pry it loose. She went on talking, covering up the moment, about Bashard's money and the will—she supposed I knew about the will, didn't I? and was it true Grace would get everything?—about how maybe the murder involved something that had happened a long time ago, before her time, and maybe one of the others could throw some light on it. I was going to talk to them all anyway, wasn't I?

Yes I was, either myself or someone else.

Good.

It was around in there that she invited me to stay for lunch. A part of me might have liked to, but I had other things to do, so I declined. She pushed, but not too hard.

"I'm sorry I haven't been much help," she said over her shoulder, leading me back through the cluttered little apartment. "If I think of anything else, I'll call you. Or if you think of any other questions . . . You have my number, don't you?"

"Yes, I do."

"Well I'll be here," she said, laughing throatily. "Until I move, that is."

The door to the street opened right from her living room. She held it open for me. She held out her hand, and when I took it, she said something that threw me altogether off balance. I turned and stumbled up into the street, feeling small in a suddenly giant world.

When I turned around, she'd closed the door behind me.

What she'd said was: "I think I like you, Phil. I also think you're going to find out who murdered Raul. But a part of me hopes you fail."

CHAPTER
9

There's nothing wrong with a beeper that couldn't be cured by putting it in a bag of cement and dropping the bag off the Brooklyn Bridge. The way Bud Fincher and I had divvied up the list, I was supposed to catch a plane for Los Angleles the next morning. In between I had an appointment with Oliver Latham, about a two-hour drive each way I figured. On the assumption that I'd be back in the city not long after nightfall, I'd made a late dinner date with Ms. Laura Hugger.

A few minutes after I left Cyn Morgan, though, the beeper went off in my pocket. I stopped at a booth on Sixth Avenue and called the office and got Roger on the phone.

"Mr. Camelo', Philippe, he wants you at three o'clock," said the mellifluous, vaguely foreign voice of our receptionist. "In the office."

Monsieur Roger—or Ro-jay—LeClerc, could, I knew, handle English as well as he wanted to, but he liked calling me Philippe, French-style, and dropping the *t* from Camelot. Particularly when he was passing orders along.

"You'd better put me through to him, Rodge," I said. "I can't make it at three o'clock."

"I'm zo sorry, Philippe, he is out to lunch."

"Where did he go? To La Gonzesse?" I asked, thinking of the bistro on Lexington the Counselor favored.

"How should I know that?"

"Well, give me Ms. Shapiro."

"Sorry, Philippe, Ms. Shapiro has also gone to lunch."

"Charlotte, then."

"She also. To lunch."

"*All* gone? Well who's there beside yourself?"

"Muffin's here," he answered. "Do you want to speak to Muffin?"

I was in no mood for his humor. I stood there on the avenue while the diesel trucks roared by, figuring out the pros and cons. I wouldn't give Roger the benefit of asking him how important it was that I be there. I thought of trying the restaurant, but God knows what emergency it would take for the Counselor to tolerate having his luncheon interrupted. I also knew the Counselor knew my schedule.

"*Allo*? Philippe? Are you there?"

"Yes, I'm here," I said, still thinking.

"Do you want me to tell him you can't make it?" asked Roger, enjoying the idea.

"No. Never mind."

I hung up on him.

I called Latham twice, both times a poor connection. No, he said, I couldn't come the next morning. He said something to the effect that it was too bad I had to cancel, he'd been looking forward to my visit. Finally I made a new appointment with him two days away, and told him I'd call to confirm before then.

I thought of taking Cyn Morgan up on her lunch invitation, but in the end I settled for a hot dog and soda from a Sabrett's wagon on Sixth Avenue.

I was back in my office by two-thirty. The Counselor still hadn't shown up. Ms. Shapiro had, but when I went upstairs to ask, she said she didn't know what the Counselor wanted me for, only that he did. I ran into the cocker bitch on my way back downstairs, but for once she gave me a wide berth. I sat at my desk and stared at the English hunting prints, which had once hung in the Counselor's office, and the glassed-in mahogany cases which held what was left of our law library. Then I started my report on the Cyn Morgan interview. I hadn't gotten very far, though, when the Counselor came in the front door accompanied by Harmon Waller, the small, spare district attorney from the Catskills.

I joined them in the Counselor's office.

I sat by the massive desk, across from Waller, while behind it the Counselor started his stuffing and lighting routine with a pipe.

"How far along are you in your investigation, Phil?" the Counselor asked through a cloud of smoke, shaking out a match and rummaging for an ashtray to drop it into.

He knew full well how far along I was. I assumed he was asking for the district attorney's benefit.

"We're working on the list," I answered, "Bud Fincher and me."

"Any progress?"

"Some," I said, knowing that with the exception of the info picked up in the Cyn Morgan interview, he knew we were nowhere.

"Any new suspects?" Harmon Waller asked in his dry, high-pitched voice.

"We've plenty of suspects," I answered. "But no, no new ones."

"What about facts?" Waller said.

"Some facts, too," I answered.

"Relevant facts?"

"It's still too early to say which ones are relevant and which ones aren't."

"In short," the district attorney said, the light glinting off his rimless glasses, "you haven't gotten anywhere, isn't that right?"

"Wait a minute!" I started to retort. "Squilletti . . ." but the Counselor waved me off with his pipe hand.

"Easy does it, Phil," he said. "Mr. Waller here has come down to New York because he wants to talk to Grace

Bashard. I believe he even has a subpoena in his pocket. He's close to bringing an indictment against Grace, and naming you as an accessory."

"That's *not* what I said!" Waller protested, his voice escalating a note up the scale.

"I know that's not what you said," the Counselor rumbled on, "but it's clearly in the logic of what you did say." The Counselor had a habit—a conscious one I knew—of talking to someone while looking at someone else. He was doing it now, gazing at me while talking to the district attorney, and I thought I could feel Waller's irritation. "You seem to forget, Harmon," he went on, "that we made an agreement. We agreed to cooperate with you to the fullest, and Phil and his people are working 'round the clock to that end."

"Yes," Waller snapped, "and you agreed to make the daughter available to us, as needed."

The Counselor's pipe had gone out already, or so he pretended. He pushed papers around on his desk, apparently looking for matches. Such gestures had a way of distracting people's attention, and I was conscious of the district attorney watching them.

The Counselor found matches, lit one, but then held it in the air.

"The problem, Harmon," he said, shifting his gaze and now firing it on Waller, "is that you haven't really convinced me of your need." Then, when Waller didn't answer: "In fact, if you're *not* close to bringing an indictment against her, then I can only conclude that what brings you to our city is a mere fishing expedition."

The Counselor brought the match to his pipe and puffed, sucking the flame up and down into the bowl. He shook out the match and puffed some more, while smoke swirled upward in front of his face.

"I don't understand something," I said. "Yesterday, after the funeral, we sat down with Al Squilletti and—"

Waller started to answer but the Counselor talked through him.

"From what Harmon's been telling me, Phil," the Counselor said, looking back at me, "your friend Squilletti is on the verge of being removed from the case. In all fairness to Harmon, the pressure on him has been intense. The media have begun to bay at the moon—as we all knew would happen. For whatever reason, Bashard's murder has attracted international attention. There are journalists in town from all over the world. They haven't been able to locate Grace, which was our intention, and the police aren't telling them anything. Harmon may be forced to give them Squilletti. There have been suggestions of everything ranging from incompetence to cover-up and collusion."

"Collusion?" I asked. "Between who and who?"

"Between us and the police," the Counselor answered. "I had a reporter this morning who said that if I didn't talk to him, he was going to print that I'd made a deal with the police to keep Grace out of it. I told him to go ahead and print it."

"You *what*?" the district attorney said, the rimless glasses bobbling on his nose.

"Don't worry, Harmon," the Counselor said, chuckling. "His paper won't print it. Remember, they have lawyers, too. The last thing they want is another libel action from me."

I remembered the incident he referred to. The case in question had never gone to court, but the settlement had cost the newspaper big money, as well as an embarrassing retraction.

"There is time pressure though, Phil," the Counselor went on. "Tell us, how long do you expect your investigation to go on?"

He knew, probably Waller did, too, that there was no good answer. But the Counselor stared at me, clearly expecting one.

"This phase?" I said as blithely as I could. "About a week maybe. A week at the outside."

"In which you may or may not turn something up?" Waller interjected.

"That's right."

"It's too long," he said sharply. "A week's too long."

I started to object, but the Counselor interrupted: "He's

right, Phil. A week's too long. If we're still in the same place a week from today, all hell will have broken loose. The media just aren't going to let this one die, short of a new war or a hostage crisis."

I started to object. He cut me off.

"What's your schedule, Phil? Give us your plan."

He already knew it, but I gave it to him, for Waller's benefit, including that the present meeting had prevented me from getting to Latham.

"When are you going to Los Angeles?" the Counselor asked.

"Tomorrow morning."

"That's too late. Why don't you get out there today? You can still catch a plane this afternoon."

I glanced at my watch. It was three-twenty.

"Don't worry about the time. Get Myrna to help you." The Counselor was the only one in the office who called Ms. Shapiro by her first name.

"But I've already got appointments sched—"

"Never mind," he said, pressing the intercom on his phone console. "Ms. Shapiro? Phil is going to need your help. He'll be out in a minute."

"Yes, Mr. Camelot," the voice answered. "You should know that Mr. Trout's waiting."

"Arthur Trout?"

Arthur Trout, I knew, was, or had been, Bashard's personal accountant.

"Yes sir."

"Well, tell him to wait. I need five more minutes." This sudden display of busy-ness was, I guessed, at least partly for the district attorney's benefit. The Counselor cut off the intercom, then looked at me, then at Waller. "Three days, Harmon," he said firmly. "We're going to give Phil three days."

"And then what?" the district attorney asked.

"Then?" the Counselor repeated, his bushy brows lifting. He glanced at me. "Well, if he's got nothing after three days, then we'll give you Grace. And Philip, too."

On this note of confidence I left them arguing, knowing

the Counselor would win, if at my expense. Ms. Shapiro got me on a flight after all (not that anything she could manage ought to have surprised me), and I left her with the phone numbers of the people I had to see in L.A.

I ran into Arthur Trout downstairs but had no time to talk to him. No time to go home either. I grabbed my briefcase from my office, and a toiletry case I always keep there for emergencies. As it was, I had to hustle to make the flight.

I remember sweating up a storm in the taxi. Three days. The pressure on Waller had passed to the Counselor, who'd lateraled it right into my lap. Three days. Maybe I shouldn't stop when I got to L.A. It only later occurred to me that had the Counselor left me out of that meeting, or had I deep-sixed the beeper, we might have kept somebody else from getting killed.

Might have.

I had time for only one hurried phone call at the airport.

No, Ms. Hugger wasn't at her desk.

I left a message.

> NAME: Hermatius, Norman Leon (born: Hermanski) white Jewish male
> Age: 54
> Health: fair (heart bypass operation, 1980)
> Sign: Taurus
> Function: Film producer
> Marital status: twice divorced (1968, 1973) Children: two
> Employment: contract employee (independent contractor)
> Earnings: circa $600,000 annum
> Net worth: unclear (Hermatius Assoc., Chapter 11 bankruptcy proceedings 1976, annual IRS penalty payment: circa $150,000) Tax shelter investigations pending.
> Current val. residence: $1,200,000; dbl. mtge.
> Born: New York City
> Resides: Brentwood, California

Education: Columbia College
              Columbia Law School (no degree)
Sexual preference: promiscuous (susp. bisexual)

Get somebody else to tell you about L.A. The few times I've been there I've done mostly driving. The street signs are good but the streets go on forever, and the houses sometimes get up into the five-digit numbers. Everything looks kind of temporary, even the hillside homes and the skyscrapers, but that may be because the people I've run into tend to talk a lot about natural disasters: fires, mudslides, earthquakes. The hilly parts have the best air. I've never had a chance to swim in the Pacific.

The best Ms. Shapiro had been able to do for me with Norman Hermatius was a prebreakfast meeting. Even that, I gathered, had been hard to arrange. Hermatius, according to his secretary, had already talked to the police about Bashard. Besides, he was a busy man. Finally, his secretary had said that he had a breakfast at eight-thirty but that if I could be there at eight, he'd give me a half hour.

But a half hour only.

"There" was one of those swank hotels in Beverly Hills where the fast trackers stay in detached bungalows half hidden by flowers and palms, the most expensive of which have their own swimming pools. I met Norman Hermatius in the hotel dining room, promptly at eight. He was sitting alone, at a rear table for four, with a telephone plugged into a wall outlet behind him. Apparently he'd had a preprebreakfast meeting because the place next to him hadn't been cleared, but all Hermatius was having was black coffee.

He was a ruddy-cheeked, heavy-browed type with curly salt-and-pepper hair, the kind who looks like he started exercising only in middle age. He wore a navy blazer, a blue-striped shirt with a white collar open at the neck (chest hair curling out of it), gold cuff links, a Rolex. He seemed to know half the people in the dining room. A number of them waved at him while I was there, and he waved back, and a few came up to shake his hand. But we almost didn't get that far.

"Where's Camelot?" he said when I introduced myself.

"In New York," I answered.

"In *New York*?" he exclaimed. "Then how the fuck did *you* get in here?" I started to say I'd walked in, but he cut me off. "I agreed to talk to Camelot. I'm not wasting my time with a *pisher*." He glanced at the Rolex. "You've got half an hour, less two minutes. Up to you. Either get Camelot on the phone or stop wasting my time. Want to order something first?"

I hesitated. As little as I liked it, the Counselor would like it less, but I reached for the phone. Instead Hermatius pulled it away and, barking at a waiter and holding the phone up in the air, gestured for another one.

I guess being a two-phone table counts for something in L.A.

While I was getting through Ms. Shapiro to the Counselor, Hermatius talked to somebody else, his broker presumably. It was hard not to overhear him, and maybe that was the point. He seemed especially interested in the film-studio stocks. I heard him ask for MCA, Fox, and Gulf and Western, but if he was buying or selling it didn't happen then.

In any case I was explaining the situation to the Counselor when Hermatius, glancing again at the Rolex, broke in on us.

"Charles? Is that you, Charles? This is Norman. I thought you were going to be here yourself, babe, there must have been—"

"Never mind," the Counselor's voice interrupted. "I understand you're a busy man, Mr. Hermatius. I am, too. Why—"

"Norman," Hermatius cut in. "Call me Norman. Anyway, you want to know if I could have killed Raul? Sure I could have. I could've killed him a thousand times, if I'd thought of it. It would have saved me a fortune. How?" Hermatius held his coffee cup up to a passing waiter and gestured at me. "He all but wrecked my company, that's how. He practically put me out of business! If you don't know about it, I'm not going to waste my time telling you what you ought to know. 'How Success Wrecked Norman Hermatius

Associates.' It's all true, too, most of it. Do you guys know what cost overruns are?"

I knew, the Counselor did, too, and we also knew the Hermatius Associates story. But that didn't seem to matter.

"It's when you commit to bringing a picture in at a figure"—he went on, while the waiter refilled his cup and filled mine from a silver pot—"and when the accountants are finished, you're at two, three times the number. Usually you can stick the studio for it; if they want the picture, they ante up. But this was *my* picture, *my* money, and the son of a bitch all but ruined me. I cut a stupid deal, a mega-stupid deal. Monumental. I gave the son of a bitch *approvals*. Crazy. For years everybody out here wanted to make that picture, but Raul insisted on approvals and nobody would put up ten mill to make a picture and give the writer approvals. Nobody except me. I thought I could manage him, can you beat that? Ego. Let me tell you something, boys, if you ever go into the motion-picture business, keep your egos out of it. If you can't, don't."

I watched him talk in staccato, rapid-fire style, his face flushed, and thought about the bypass operation listed in his printout.

"But what am I telling you this for?" Hermatius shouted. "*You* were his fucking lawyer!"

"So I was," the Counselor said. I could imagine him enjoying the moment. While he hadn't negotiated Bashard's contract with Hermatius directly, he had masterminded the negotiations from long range. "But that's not why I sent Mr. Revere out to talk to you."

"I know that, I know that," Hermatius said. "And it was a hell of a picture, too, six Academy nominations and strong enough at the box office till *Star Wars* ran everything else out of the theaters. Shit, people still go to see it. So sure, I could have killed him once. Only I didn't. Poor bastard."

"But you had a motive, didn't you?" I heard the Counselor say.

"A motive?" Hermatius's eyebrows shot up. "For *killing* him?"

"That's right," the Counselor said. "Alive, he all but

ruined you. But you stand to make a fortune with him dead."

The Counselor had set him up nicely, without the producer so much as realizing it. It shut him up for a minute, and when he reached for his coffee cup, I could see the china shiver.

"You own the sequel rights to Bashard's book," the Counselor went on. "As long as Raul Bashard was alive no studio out there would touch the property, because of the approval problem you mentioned. But now? With him dead? And a clever filmmaker who could pull two, three, four more pictures out of the material . . . ?"

The Counselor paused. I imagined him creaking his chair.

"Sure," Hermatius said, staring out across the dining room. "So I'd pick up a poker and beat him to death. Is that it?"

"That's not for me to decide," the Counselor replied. "But according to my information, you're pretty close to a deal already."

"Your information . . ." Hermatius started to retort. Then, deflating: "Your information's pretty good."

He looked across at me, as if in search of corroboration.

"Look, Charles," he said. "For Christ's sake, I'm not your murderer. I may come on strong, but I'm a peaceful man at heart. Ask anybody. Hell, ask my shrink, I'll give you his number. When I lived in New York I couldn't even kill the cockroaches—that's why I had to move out here."

He started to laugh but stopped when nobody laughed with him.

"As I said," the Counselor answered, "that's not for me to decide. But I wish you'd cooperate with Mr. Revere."

"Cooperate? Who says I'm not cooperating?"

"Good," the Counselor said. "I'm sorry, but I have another appointment now. Phil will put the rest of our questions to you."

So help me, Norman Hermatius started to say he had another appointment, too, but the phone was already dead in our ears.

We hung up. Hermatius sighed, then drained his cup and wiped his mouth with his cloth napkin.

"That's one tough son of a bitch," he said, subdued. "How much does he pull down a year?"

"I don't know," I answered. At this point I pulled out our list and put it on the tablecloth next to him. He glanced at the names, handled the paper briefly like somebody looking at a menu and deciding there's nothing he wants.

"Sure I know them," he said. "None of them well. They're all nice people. But science-fiction people—they're a separate world unto themselves. I don't understand them. Hard to talk to. If you want to know the truth, I can't read the stuff. Spielberg, Lucas, they're different; they grew up in the midst of it, they feel it in their bones. Not me. All I ever wanted to put on film was Raul's story. And I did it. If you ask me, though, most science fiction's a crock of shit."

He was looking at the list, though, while he talked. Then he pointed at one of the names with his finger.

"Jesus," he said, "you've just given me an idea. What do you think of Latham?"

"Oliver Latham?" I said.

"Oliver Latham, the last of the greats. Jesus Christ. The fans love him. Did you see them at Raul's party? If I could get Latham, that would complete the package. He wouldn't even have to script it, I could get somebody else. Cheaper. But Latham would give it credibility. Credibility? Shit, *stature*! Screenplay by Oliver Latham, based on a novel by R. R. Bashard. *Humungous* stature! And I'll tell you something else: I bet I can get him. Do you know who his agent is? I bet he needs the money. Do you think he needs the money?"

His recovery, I'd have to say, was nothing short of amazing. His face flushed again, and the words came rapid-fire.

"I wouldn't know," I started to say, but he wasn't listening.

"Of course he needs the money!" Hermatius said with a guffaw. "Who doesn't need the money?"

He was laughing then, his whole torso joining in. But then his eyes caught something, or someone, behind my head.

"I'm sorry, babe," he said, glancing at the Rolex one last

time and standing. "Time's up, my meeting's here. I meant what I told your boss, though: I wouldn't kill a fucking cockroach. If you need anything more, though, call my office." To my surprise, he not only shook hands but patted me on the cheek with his left hand. "And remember, what we just talked about, that's a secret. Understood? For your ears only."

As it turned out, we'd run twenty minutes over.

His two guests, both wearing dark blue suits and carrying briefcases, were easily close enough to see the cheek patting and hear the last part. But who they were I've no idea. We weren't introduced.

Nor was there much of a secret. A few days later the gossip columns ran several items about the Bashard sequels, and one of them even mentioned Oliver Latham.

Come to think of it, I never did get to ask Norman how he'd gotten to Hermatius from Hermanski.

> NAME: Frankaman, Sidney   white Jewish
>   male
> Age: 57
> Health: good (poor vision)
> Sign: Capricorn
> Function: retailer, rare-book dealer
> Marital status: Married (Edna Samuelson, 1953)
>   Children: 3
> Employment: self (owns eleven Dark Star Stores)
> Earnings: salary: $150,000
>   est int & div: $175,000 (possibly low)
> Net worth: circa $1.7 million
> Born: Brooklyn, New York   Resides: Tar-
>   zana, Calif.
> Education: Erasmus Hall High School
>   no college
> Sexual preference: promiscuous

For some reason, Sidney Frankaman was the only one I hadn't gotten in touch with from New York. I'm not sure why. Maybe it was the cold-shoulder treatment he'd given me in the hotel bar, that Sunday at the BashCon. Maybe I assumed I'd find him at the Dark Star. Maybe I hoped I wouldn't.

I was finished with Hermatius, or he with me, at eight-fifty. I drove down to Westwood, getting there in time to join the rush-hour snarl and making a few wrong turns before giving up and parking the car in a garage that took up, weirdly enough, the first few stories of an office building. The Westwood I remembered from years ago was, because of the proximity of the UCLA campus, something of a college town: movie theaters and head shops, little boutiques, book and record stores, cutesy restaurants tending toward vegetarian food. *Quaint* would have been the descriptive word. It still had some of its quaint, and probably the younger set still took over at night, but office towers had encroached and at that time of day you could have thought you were in the downtown of some middle-sized mid-American city. The Dark Star's main store was still closed, so I bought a newspaper out of a sidewalk machine and had my own breakfast—ham and eggs and hashed browns—in a local cafeteria. By the time I'd finished, the Dark Star had opened for business.

The Dark Star—at least that main, three-storied affair in Westwood (because there are some ten more up and down the West Coast)—is supposed to be the largest store anywhere devoted to science fiction and fantasy, and I'd never seen anything like it. It sold books, hardcover and soft, and magazines you never heard of. It sold video and games, adult games and kiddie games and those role-playing games some teenagers devote their lives to. It sold toys: transformer robots, laser swords, space helmets, miniature figurines, transformer watches, T-shirts, junk jewelry and a lot of miscellaneous stuff you could only classify as accessories. It had an enormous section devoted to comic books, old and new. It also had, up on the mezzanine floor, a Collector's Corner, which I gathered was where the serious bucks came and which was where I headed, once I got past the sleepy-eyed staff of T-shirted youths, reminiscent of the Hnngas and Hnnns of the BashCon. At that hour, they far outnumbered the clientele.

A young woman very out of character with the prevailing atmosphere was just coming out of an office when I got to the top of the ladderlike stairs and onto the mezzanine. She was tall, with long reddish hair, horn-rimmed glasses, a white shirt with a bow at the neck, and a mid-calf navy skirt. High heels, too.

"May I help you?" she said.

"I hope so," I answered. "I'm interested in *The Twenty-fifth Century.*" I expected the line to draw a laugh, or at least a smile.

It didn't, though.

"Magazine facsimiles are on the main floor," she answered matter-of-factly, pointing a red-nailed finger behind me.

"Oh? I didn't know there was a facsimile edition."

"I'm not sure there is," she answered. "But if there is, you'll find it downstairs."

"But I'm not interested in a facsimile edition," I persisted. "It's the originals I'm after."

"Oh?" She sounded surprised. I guess I didn't look like a collector was supposed to, but whether this meant I was overdressed or under, I couldn't say. "Which numbers?"

"Numbers? You mean issues?"

"Yes."

"All of them," I said. "I'm looking for a complete set."

She stared at me, as though registering the details for the first time. Apparently what she saw made her suspicious. I decided I didn't look freaky enough.

"Complete sets are quite rare," she said.

"I know," I said. "That's why I'm here."

"Well? You'd have to see Mr. Frankaman himself about that."

"Then I'd like to see Mr. Frankaman himself."

"Mr. Frankaman only sees customers by appointment," she answered tersely.

"Is he here now?"

"No, he's not." Clearly I'd begun to annoy her.

"Then I'll wait."

"You'll have to make . . ."

Something going on behind me, though, distracted her for

an instant. She looked surprised. I glanced around, down over the main floor, and saw that "Mr. Frankaman himself" had just arrived. I recognized him by the bald pate and the goggle glasses, also by his short-bodied strut. He stopped briefly at the cash register on a raised platform near the entrance, exchanged words with the security guard, then marched through the aisles and up the stairs.

Halfway up the stairs he spotted me, and stopped.

"Oh Sidney," Ms. Petulant called out beside me, suddenly all smiles. "This gentleman's looking for a complete set of *Twenty-fifth Century Tales.* He—"

"No he isn't, Virginia," Frankaman interrupted. Then, to me: "Good morning, Revere."

He came up the rest of the stairs.

"I knew you were a phony," Virginia said, glaring at me. "What are you, an insurance salesman?"

"Wrong again," I said.

"Never mind, honey," said Frankaman, "I'll take care of him."

She hesitated, then swerved on her heels and stalked back into the offices. The heels made her hips swivel.

Sidney Frankaman watched her go, his eyes on the hips. Cyn Morgan had called him an ass-pincher, but you couldn't tell from his concentration whether he had already pinched Virginia's or was just thinking about it.

"Eat your heart out, buddy," he said, shaking his head as she disappeared. "There goes some piece."

Sidney Frankaman wore black tasseled shoes, a gray nubby silk suit, a white shirt open at the neck and a pinkie ring shiny enough to hurt your eyes, the more so when he jabbed it at you, which he did often. His office was an interior room with a long picture window overlooking the main floor, and he sat in a high-backed stuffed swivel chair near the window, where he could keep an eye on things. There was a lot of chair left over the top of his head.

"Let's cut out the bullshit," he said, once we were seated. "You're here because you want to pin the murder on me. It's the dumbest thing I ever heard of. You haven't got *bupkis.* I haven't been convicted of a crime in my whole life. I

wouldn't hurt a fly. But you want to pin it on me. Well, go
ahead. Try. But cut the bullshit, I'm a busy man."

"Why do you think I want to pin it on you?" I asked,
thinking that whereas Norman Hermatius wouldn't hurt a
cockroach, Frankaman wouldn't hurt a fly.

"How do I know?" he shot back. "Maybe you and Camelot
don't like Jews. Maybe you and Camelot got nobody else." I
didn't say anything right away, but he wasn't one to put up
with silence. "Look," he said, jabbing the pinkie, "how
dumb do you think I am? I know I'm on your list. Never
mind how I know, I know. And what do you do? You call up
everybody else on the list, you make nice, you go to see
them, you ask lots of questions, you ask lots of questions
about me, and so on. But do you call me up, too? No. Do you
make an appointment? No. What do you do instead? You
come snooping one morning when I'm not around, trying to
dig something up, asking lots of stupid questions. *Twenty-
fifth Century Tales* my ass. How dumb do you think I am?"

I started to laugh part way through but squelched it. If
Sidney Frankaman was sensitive about the slight, not to say
paranoid, maybe I could make some use of it. I didn't get
very far, though.

"About *Twenty-fifth Century*—" I began.

"Who told you about that?" he said, his glance darting out
the picture window.

"Told me about what?"

"Come on, come on," he retorted. "I said let's cut out the
bullshit. All right, so maybe we took Bashard to the cleaners
a little, so what? He could afford it." He laughed briefly, a
braying sound. "Is that a crime? If that's a crime, then put the
handcuffs on." Then, more subdued: "*Gevalt*, that's what
you get for trying to do somebody a favor. You end up taking
gas."

I didn't quite get what he was talking about.

"Who's *we*?" I asked. "You and Brinckerhoff?"

His eyes darted again, then fixed on me.

"Is that what Brinckerhoff said?"

"I haven't seen him yet."

"You haven't seen him yet? Then who told you about *Twenty-fifth Century Tales*?"

"Nobody. I read the correspondence."

"Ahhh," he said. "Then ask Brinckerhoff."

I pushed him on the point, but he clammed up. It was all "ask Brinckerhoff." I pushed him on other points, his version of things I already knew. He'd visibly relaxed by then, and I looked for something to jolt him with again.

"All right, Mr. Frankaman—"

"Sidney," he corrected.

"Sidney," I said. "Who do *you* think killed him?"

"You don't want to know," he answered.

"Maybe I do."

"Really?"

"Yes, really."

"Okay," he said, his small eyes suddenly large and ringed through the magnifying lenses. "You and I both know it, and I doubt we're alone. The cunt did it. His so-called 'daughter.'"

"Why would she have done it?"

Frankaman rubbed his thumb and first two fingers together.

"The money," he said, "what else? Once he changed his will, what did she have to lose as long as she could get away with it?"

That he, too, knew about the revised will, and the matter-of-fact, almost accidental, way he said it, jolted me in turn.

"Excuse me," I said, "but how did you know he'd changed his will?"

"How did I know? Because he said so. He told everybody at the banquet, the night before he died."

"Everybody?" I asked.

"Sure he did. Everybody up on the dais anyway. During dinner. He said he'd made a mistake, never trusting his own daughter. Some mistake, huh?"

"But you weren't on the dais. How did you find out?"

"Of course I wasn't on the dais. I should have been, but that was the bastard's way of punishing me."

"Then how did you find out?"

"I don't remember. Everybody knew it. Somebody must have told me, maybe the next day. What difference does it make?"

"Did Grace know it, too?"

"Come on," he said, staring at me. "How dumb do you take me for? Would she have murdered him if she didn't?"

Before I knew it, he was off on a weird kind of diatribe. It was about the young people of today. The young people stank, he said. No morals, no learning. All they cared about was money. Money and garbage. Given half the chance, they stole it.

"Look at what I've got to sell to make a living today!" he shouted, jabbing toward the main floor of the Dark Star. "Garbage! Do you think I like selling garbage? It was better in the old days. We didn't make so much money, but I was never greedy. That was when science fiction meant something. Oakes, Heinlein, Bradbury, Latham, Sturgeon . . . even Bashard. All right, Bashard, too. They were *real writers*! I read them when I was a young man. Can you imagine what it was like to *meet* them? But today? A bunch of hacks, typists. That's all the new ones are, typists. Gimme a break. But that's what the kids want, that's what you sell 'em. I'll tell you what; you want to buy a business? The whole chain is yours. I've already turned down six mill, but make me a decent offer, I'll give you the keys today. Enough is enough. I've made mine, I'm not greedy."

From what I knew of him, six million dollars was probably double the price he would take, and for all I knew, the Dark Star was worth it. But I didn't have a handy six million or half of it lying around. I tried instead to bring the conversation back to Bashard's will, but that set him off in a new direction.

"He was a mean and stingy goy, I'll tell you that. Sure, he could write, but even when he made a fortune and others didn't, do you think he'd share any of it? All right, Herbert did all right, one or two others, but take Oakes. Did you ever read Clem Oakes? A *terrific* talent, let me tell you. As good as Latham. He never made much money at it. He didn't write enough, for one thing. He was sick half the time. He smoked like a chimney, drank like a fish, and died of emphysema. Not so long ago. A couple of years. Drugs, too, so they say. He tried to get money out of Bashard, used to say he was entitled to it, but the bastard never gave him a nickel. When Clem died, we had to pass the hat to get him buried. Even Latham kicked in, who couldn't afford it either. But Bashard? *Bupkis*. Do you know what he said? 'I've already given enough.' The lying son of a bitch. I even kicked in myself, can you believe that?"

He was puffed up enough about it that you had to believe him, and he underlined the point by taking out a bandanna-size handkerchief and blowing his nose emphatically into it. Then he folded the handkerchief over and dabbed his forehead.

"Poor bastard," he said.

At this point the phone on his desk buzzed. A moment later Ms. Petulant stuck her head in the door, glancing first at me and then at Frankaman through the horn-rims before she announced that someone was waiting to see him.

"Tell 'em to wait, honey," he said, then to me: "Bunch of sales reps. Garbage peddlers."

He stood up, though. He came up to my shoulders.

"Did I convince you, Revere?"

"Convince me of what?"

"Of the futility of trying to pin it on me?" He laughed heartily, then put a hand on my shoulder, the one with the pinkie ring. People in L.A., it seemed, like to touch. "Let me give you a piece of advice, though. You seem like a nice-enough young man. Stop trying to pin it on somebody else. The cunt did it, we all know that. A terrible thing. I know, it's money. Camelot's in for a piece if you get her off. A big piece, I'd guess. You don't have to tell me. But money isn't everything. You'll sleep better nights."

He'd steered me into the outer office by then, where Ms. Petulant was standing by and the two sales reps were just getting up from a couch. The gesture was so swift I almost missed it, but I'm pretty sure he patted her on the ass as we walked by. Or, given what he said next, he may have wanted me to notice.

He came with me to the top of the stairs. He offered to answer any other questions I had, any time, then stopped and took my arm.

"One other thing," he said in a confidential voice. "Are you going to see Charlotte?" It took me a second to remember that Charlotte was Mrs. Sidney Frankaman. "A waste of your time, she was out like a light that whole night for one thing. But if you do, do me a favor, honh? Don't tell her about that one." He pointed with the ringed pinkie in the direction of his office. I gathered he was talking about his secretary. "It doesn't mean anything, but I'm in trouble enough as it is."

> Name: Brinckerhoff, Richard   white Caucasian male
> Age: 68
> Health: good
> Sign: Gemini
> Function: retired
> Marital status: married (Serena Baker, 1945)
> Children: 4   Grandchildren: 3
> Employment: former chairman, mbr board, Baker Ocean Transport Corporation
> Income: circa $2 million annum
> Net worth: circa $25 million
> Born: Riverside, Conn.   Resides: Pasadena, California
> Education: B.A., Yale
> Sexual preference: faithful spouse

I've heard it said that Pasadena was once a haven for the rich, which in California means very rich, but that it's lately gone to seed, which in California means an influx of blacks and Hispanics. I didn't find out that day, because my route took me off the freeway outside Pasadena and until I got up into the hills a brown haze of smog hid the horizon. To tell the truth, I didn't much care either. I was focused more on the dense traffic, the length of time it took me to get there, and my own very recent lapse of memory.

Before I left Westwood I'd made two calls. The first was to the office. The Counselor wasn't available, but he had a question for me.

"What's the S.O.W. Account?" the Counselor wanted to know, via Ms. Shapiro. "*S*, period, *O*, period, *W*, period. Is it some kind of writers' club?"

I didn't know what the S.O.W Account was, or anything about a writers' club. I didn't know if S.O.W. stood for "sow" or if the initials meant something else. But I knew immediately that I'd seen it before, and where, and I remembered Raul Bashard's explanation. I was also willing to bet my last buck it had been missing, or erased, when Bud Fincher, Squilletti, and I reviewed the computer hate-mail files two days before.

I told Ms. Shapiro as much.

Only the names escaped me. A man and a woman, I thought.

I hung up and called Bud Fincher. Mr. Fincher was out, his secretary said, "in the field." Where precisely, I asked her. She said he'd had an appointment with a Mr. Varga, did I want Mr. Varga's number? I decided I didn't, but told her that if Bud wasn't going to be in his office later, he should leave me his whereabouts for the rest of that day and evening on my home phone. I'd be calling in.

Then I drove out to Pasadena in the smog, wrestling with the traffic and my memory, or lack of memory.

The Brinckerhoffs, Richard and Serena, were a hearty, open couple, visibly satisfied with each other and their circumstances. He was East Coast money; she was more money from the West. She had inherited the Baker Ocean Transport Corporation and he had made it what it was, or is, today. They lived in Pasadena because she'd grown up there and loved it. So did Richard. They loved their home, a Spanish-style manse in the Pasadena hills. I found it remarkable for its spaciousness and lightness, given that style of architecture. It was all chintz and light walls and red-tiled floors. The tiles, Serena Brinckerhoff told me, had been imported from Spain. Interior and exterior. The wrought iron, too. They loved swimming and had their own pool, a long, kidney-shaped affair of pale, shimmering water implanted in tile and surrounded by flower beds of Serena's own planting. They loved tennis and had a pair of courts, clay, with lighting for night play. They loved travel and were gone now three to four months every year, but the best part of travel was always coming home, to their home. The portrait of them which hung in their living room had been painted twenty-four years ago in that very same living room. They loved that portrait. It showed her as beautiful and him as handsome. For a couple in their sixties, they still looked pretty good.

I suppose that if they loved golf, they'd have laid out eighteen holes somewhere on the grounds.

And Richard loved science fiction, and his extensive collection (which I toured), because he had read H. G. Wells as a boy. Serena didn't, not at all. It was one of the few things they disagreed about, but that maybe added spice to their harmony.

The first question I asked Richard Brinckerhoff, once the niceties were over, was what kind of chess player Bashard had been.

"I never knew that he played chess," Richard Brinckerhoff told me. We were sitting, finally, in what they called their indoor-outdoor room, a plant-filled, screened-in terrace really, which was covered by a single striped awning that rolled out from the side of the house. "Not that it would surprise me. Back when Madge was still alive, he did a million and one things."

"Did you know him well then?" I asked.

"Yes, we did," Brinckerhoff said. "He was a different man when Madge was alive."

"Well," Serena Brinckerhoff put in, "he was never exactly what you'd call the life of the party."

"I don't know, dear. Maybe he wasn't the life of the party, but he *went* to parties. And talked, was interesting to listen to . . ."

"And always wore those awful sneakers," Serena said.

"Yes, he did."

"I don't know," she said. "I always found him dour." She

pronounced the word *dower*. "Do you know what *dour* means, Phil?"

I nodded.

"Stiff, more," Brinckerhoff corrected. "And I always felt he was stiff because he was shy, inside."

"*Shy*?" Serena exclaimed, laughing.

"All writers are shy."

"Well, he wasn't so shy that he couldn't make a pass at me."

"He made a pass at you?" Brinckerhoff asked cheerfully. "You never told me that."

"Oh yes I did. You just don't remember. He was very correct about it. I mean, he waited till Madge was out of the room. He said he'd like to see me sometime, if I was free. I told him I wasn't free, and that was that. I gather he tried elsewhere, too."

"You don't know that for a fact, darling," Brinckerhoff said.

"Oh, no?" she retorted gaily, patting her husband on the knee. "Do you still believe women don't tell each other things?"

They sat side by side on a wrought-iron couch with flowered cushions. I noticed that they touched each other frequently.

"It's hard to believe he's dead," Richard Brinckerhoff said. "I mean, he had more things wrong with him than a dozen men have, but he always pulled through. He had the constitution of an ox, isn't that right, darling? But now he *is* dead, murdered. Brutally murdered. It's hard to believe."

This was as close, I realized, as any of these people came to expressing regret over Bashard's death.

"Did you know he was going to die anyway?" I asked Brinckerhoff.

"Aren't we all?" he answered.

"No, I mean that the doctors had given him only a few months to live?"

"I think I read something to that effect," Brinckerhoff replied.

"But did you know it *before* he was murdered?"

"No. But we wouldn't have paid much attention if we had. He was always being given up for dead, or dying."

"Anyway," Serena Brinckerhoff said, "have you found the murderer yet?"

"If we had," I answered, "I probably wouldn't be here. But we're working on it."

"Well in that case," she said brightly, "I'm glad you haven't, because you wouldn't be here otherwise. But I suppose you want to know who we think did it, don't you?"

"Yes," I said.

"I'm not sure he does, darling," Brinckerhoff put in.

"Of course he does!" Then, to me: "We think Grace did it. It's obvious, isn't it? And that you're trying to cover up for her. You and that lawyer you work for."

"Camelot," her husband said.

"Camelot," she repeated.

They made the accusation so conversationally, like it fitted into a general chitchat, that I couldn't summon up any indignation. Or maybe that was because, by then, I'd gotten too used to hearing it.

"Why do you think she did it?" I asked. "For his money?"

"No, not the money," Brinckerhoff said. "She had that anyway."

"Because of what he'd done to her father," Serena said. "We've talked it over, and we think that was the motive. She killed him because of how he'd treated her real father. You know all about that part, don't you?"

"Some," I said. John Jameson, last known address: Sydney, Australia. "Did you know him? The son, I mean?"

"Hardly," Brinckerhoff said. "You'd have to ask—"

"When we first met Raul," Serena interrupted, "we didn't even know there was a son. Raul was with Madge then."

"The first we knew about it," Brinckerhoff said, "was when they showed up with a baby."

"That would have been Grace?" I asked.

"That's right."

"And Madge hadn't even been preggers," Serena added. "If I remember right, she couldn't have children. At least that's what Raul said. So he'd done the next best thing, he'd gone out and gotten her one. That's what he always said."

I tried to push them on the subject, but they didn't tell me anything I didn't already know. Like why had Johnny— Bashard's son—given up the baby? Money, they said. Bashard had paid him off. Besides, they said, the son was gay, a homosexual. How did they know that? They couldn't remember exactly. It was common knowledge. It was also common knowledge that Raul Bashard hated homosexuals.

"Why did he hate homosexuals?" I asked.

Brinckerhoff shrugged, but his wife said: "Most men do. At least those who're worried about their own sexuality."

This was as close as they came to what you could call marital discord. Brinckerhoff said she was talking psychological hogwash. Serena said if Bashard was as much in love with Madge as everybody said, why did he make passes at everything in skirts? And why, more recently, had he locked himself up with his own daughter? Or granddaughter? Or whatever she was?

Brinckerhoff went red in the face. All that incest stuff, he said angrily, was dirty talk, disgusting gossip. He didn't want to hear it—not from her, not from anybody else.

I wondered who else he might have heard it from, but it didn't seem like an opportune question. It was Serena herself who saved the moment.

"Honey, you don't understand these things," she said, reaching over and patting him again. "And how could you? You've never had the problem, and praise the Good Lord, you never will."

At this she burst out laughing, a guffawing sound, and he, once he got the point, joined in. By the time tea was served, they were holding hands.

By the time tea was served, I also realized I'd blown the last daytime flight out of LAX. This meant either the red-eye or spending another night, but since I had an appointment the next morning, the red-eye would be it. And since it was the red-eye, Serena Brinckerhoff pointed out, there was no reason for me not to stay for tea.

As for the beverage, I never touch the stuff. I had a beer

instead, and Brinckerhoff joined me. But along with tea came varieties of little sandwiches on decrusted breads cut into triangles, miniature stuffed croissants, and mounds of those one-bite Danish where one bite leads to half a dozen more. To watch the Brinckerhoffs put them away, you'd have to figure they needed all the tennis they could get. I reminded myself that I was a long way, in distance and days, from the reservoir in Central Park.

During tea, I asked Richard Brinckerhoff about the *Twenty-fifth Century Tales* affair. He seemed surprised I knew about it, then a little annoyed by what Sidney Frankaman had told me, then finally amused as he remembered how furious Bashard had gotten.

"How much was the set really worth?" I asked him.

He shrugged.

"Whatever somebody was fool enough to pay, I guess," he said. "When you're a collector of scarce things, it all depends on how badly you want the item."

"But eleven thousand dollars was a high price?" I asked.

"Exorbitant, I'd say," he answered with a chuckle. "But Raul could afford it."

"And you were the owner, weren't you?"

"Me?" A look of surprise. "No, not at all. I only acted as an honest broker."

"Then who was?"

"What did Sidney say?" he asked suspiciously.

"He said to ask you."

"Oh, come on, Richard"—Serena put it, popping another miniature croissant into her mouth and dabbing her hands on a linen napkin—"tell him. It doesn't make any difference anymore, does it?"

"I guess not," he said. "Well, the set belonged to Ollie Latham."

"Latham?" I said. "But wouldn't he have sold it directly to Bashard?"

"You'll have to ask him that," Brinckerhoff said guardedly.

"C'mon, honey," Serena interrupted, "Raul never would have paid that much money if he'd known it was Ollie, because Ollie's too much of a gentleman to have asked for it. You know that. That's why he needed a heavy like you."

"He made out like it was a joke on Raul," Brinckerhoff said, "but I think it was really because he needed the money. Not that he'd ever admit it. You know Ollie."

I explained that I didn't, not really, although I was going to see him the next morning.

"A beautiful man," Serena said.

"Something of a hermit, too," Brinckerhoff said. "At least I've never been invited to his place when I've been East. It always struck me as ironic that Raul made all the money because a lot of people will tell you—at least people who know science fiction—that Latham's better."

"What do you think?" I asked.

Brinckerhoff hesitated, and his wife echoed a remark I'd heard her make once before, at the BashCon banquet: "It's all boys' stuff," she said, "like a bunch of grown men watching another bunch of grown men chase a pointed ball around a football field. That's all science fiction is. I've been trying to get my husband to admit it for years."

"Never mind, darling," Richard Brinckerhoff said, taking his wife's hand in his. They were still holding hands later, standing before the entrance to their Pasadena hacienda, when I finally managed to get back behind the wheel of my rented car.

I got to LAX in the trough between the last daytime flights and the red-eye. Airports are among my least favorite hangouts, next to California freeways, but you can only kill so much time handing in your rented car. I was the only one on the Avis shuttle bus, and I had my choice of phones when I got inside the terminal building.

I chose one of the ones where you slide your credit card through the slot. I punched my home number, then broke into my own recorded voice by punching the beeper into the receiver and got my messages.

There were three.

The first was from the Counselor, asking me some more

questions about S.O.W. and telling me he wanted to see me first thing in the morning.

The second was from Bud Fincher, giving me a couple of numbers where he could be reached.

I'll get to the third.

I hung up and found Bud Fincher.

The Counselor had been on to Bud Fincher, too, about S.O.W. Bud didn't know what it meant either, but he'd given the Counselor the two names I'd been trying to remember all afternoon from the Big O's hate-mail file: Viola Harmel and Leo Mackes, and he'd already reactivated his search team on the Counselor's instructions. Maybe, we decided, Viola Harmel was someone Bashard had had an affair with, who'd been trying to shake him down. Bud didn't hold out much hope, though. Most of the Harmel correspondence had been postmarked from the Philadelphia area, most of the Mackes from Northern California, but that hadn't led anywhere in his previous search. He, too, had the same recollection I did: that the S.O.W. references hadn't shown on the computer screen when he, Squilletti, and I reviewed it the day of Bashard's funeral. At the Counselor's request, he and Charlotte McCullough, our resident guru in accounting (and particularly computer accounting), were going out to Bashard's the next morning. Unless it was a glitch, the only two people we could imagine who might have tampered with the computer were Grace Bashard and Price. Grace was the Counselor's responsibility. Bud wanted us to question Price the next day, and I told him I'd join him at Bashard's on my way back to the city from the Latham meeting.

Between us, Bud and I had covered all but one of the list of interviewees. He had done Varga, Whitefield, and Wright. I was finished on the West Coast, had done Cyn Morgan, had Latham to go. We compared notes at length. In a factual, evidentiary sense, we were nowhere further than we'd been two days before. If either of us had sat in the presence of a brutal murderer, it was a very well-guarded brutal murderer. Nobody who'd spent the night at the BashCon on the second-floor annex had heard a thing between the storm and the morning. Nobody had cast the least suspicion on anyone other than Grace. They were all good friends, more or less: friends of science fiction, friends of each other.

I'd drawn several general conclusions, and I tried them out on Bud. The most important ones, or so I thought, were:

1) The group had decided as a whole that Grace was the murderess. Explanations for her motive varied: money; sex; revenge. Furthermore, I had either helped her or was trying to cover up for her, or both.

2) Nobody much regretted Raul Bashard's death. No mourning, no keening, no flags at half-mast. It was almost as if they'd expected it. Even as if he'd deserved it.

3) Everybody, although I couldn't begin to put my finger on it, was covering up something they knew, or suspected. No, I couldn't put my finger on it, but the impression had come and gone for two days.

4) Therefore, whatever the group had decided as a whole, the individuals in it thought Grace Bashard might *not* be the murderess.

5) I felt—continued to feel—the same way. Don't ask me why.

Bud Fincher agreed with the second point. Only with the second. The only regrets he'd heard he'd judged to be skin-deep. The "Grand Old Man of Science Fiction" kind of regrets, except for Ron Whitefield, the book publisher, who had business reasons for caring. George Varga had said that Bashard's writing had deteriorated badly, best-seller lists or not. Sam Wright had called him a mean, coldhearted son of a bitch. Ron Whitefield had run black-bordered in-memoriam ads in papers across the country.

But Bud *hadn't* felt people were covering up, at least things to do with the murder. It was more like: Bashard was dead, however it had happened, and life went on. Maybe, he said, a little apologetically, he hadn't asked the same questions I did.

"Come on, Bud," I heard myself say over three thousand miles of cabling, "is that the best you can do?"

"That's the best I can do, Phil," he answered back.

I felt myself going hot and a little prickly under the skin.

"Well, why the hell don't you ever tell me what *you* think?"

"You never asked."

"All right, I'll ask. Do *you* think Grace did it and that all we're doing is covering up for her? Or trying to?"

There was a long pause on the line. I thought I could see Bud's face and the jaw muscles working a little under the skin.

"I'd rather not answer that one, Phil," he said quietly.

"Why not?"

"I don't see the point."

So be it.

I made two other calls, at least for form's sake. Sidney Frankaman wasn't home. He wasn't expected till later. Was this Mrs. Frankaman? Yes, it was. I explained who I was. I asked her if she'd ever heard of a Viola Harmel or a Leo Mackes. No, she hadn't. Were they science-fiction people? Yes, in a way. Well, she didn't know much about science-fiction people, but she'd ask her husband when she saw him.

I thanked Mrs. Frankaman. Then I tried Norman Hermatius, but his office didn't answer, and his home number was unlisted. I called the Brinckerhoffs. Serena was delighted to hear from me again, so soon. No, I wasn't disturbing them. She'd put Richard on.

Richard Brinckerhoff hadn't heard of them either. As for S.O.W., what was that? He didn't know anything about it.

I hung up, still sitting in the partitioned booth, the plastic credit card still in my hand, while the hot and prickly came over me again.

All right, ask me why.

The third message on my answering machine. Like a voice from another life. Now breathy, whispery, like trying to avoid being overheard. Now shrill, angry, and punctuated by the high-pitched buzz when she'd have had to redial to continue the message.

Phil, my darling, where are you? Why haven't you come? Why haven't you called? I need you, I've never needed you more. I thought you'd get me out of here long before now. I hate these hotels, I hate being cooped up. I'm frightened, worried, I want—(*buzz*) . . . "Phil, it's me again. I *hate* your Mr. Charles Camelot! I want to go home, Phil. I want you to come take me home. Phil, I'll make it worth your while. I mean, I know how to make it worth your while, remember, darling? . . . (giggle)— (*buzz*) . . . God *damn* your machine! Where *are* you when I need you? About the murder, Phil. I didn't kill him, I *swear* it. I swear it to you, my baby. Everybody thinks I did except you, even Mr. Camelot does, but I'm ready to talk about it, Phil. I couldn't before. But only to you. I'll only talk about it while you— (*buzz*) . . . I hate this. I'm so frightened. Something terrible's going to happen, I can't tell you what, but I'm so scared. I can feel it. I'm all alone. I hate it. Please come get me. I'll do all the things you like, anything, I'll run away with— (*buzz*) . . . All right, Phil, it's me again. Remember me? If you don't come, if you don't call, I'm going to . . . (starting to sob) . . . I'm going to tell them everything we did that night . . . (sobbing, accusing) . . . I'm going to tell them . . . every thing you did for . . .

At this point, though, the machine must have run out of tape.

PART THREE

PART THREE

CHAPTER
10

Creature of habit.

I could have gotten on any number of flights out of LAX, and maybe I should have. United States and foreign, Alaska, Japan, Europe, Mexico, Hawaii, New Zealand, Singapore, South America, and points north, east, south and west. Fly the Friendly Skies. Per my own vital statistics in Bashard's computer I was as footloose as the next guy, with enough plastic credit to get started and, actuarially speaking, good years in front of me.

Why not? Start a new life from scratch, bury the old one. Let the Counselor solve the crime.

He'd collect the fee anyway.

But I had a ticket that said New York, a boarding pass with a gate number and a seat number, a pillow and a blanket waiting for me, and an empty seat next to mine that I took over for my knees. I told the stewardess not to wake me up for earphones, drinks, dinner, movies, seat belts, hot towels or anything she had on her schedule. She actually wished me "sweet dreams."

Creature of habit.

As it was I sat up most of the night, in the darkness. I watched a movie off and on, without earphones. Somewhere in the dark cabin a baby cried, as fretful as I was, and every so often I heard its mother shouting at it in Spanish to shut up, which didn't work. I had one of those weird obsessive feelings, the stronger because of the night, that all the answers were there in my head if I could only put the pieces together in the right order. I kept running them through, like the rewind and fast forward on a VCR machine: Grace sneaking out of the suite in the middle of that stormy night to get into my bed, and, key question, did she leave the suite door open or shut? Because if she shut it, then she or I or Price or Bashard himself was either the murderer or the murderer's accomplice. But wouldn't it stand to reason that, if she was sneaking out on Raul Bashard, she'd have shut the door behind her? Yes, it would stand to reason, but was Grace Bashard a creature of reason? Maybe she'd wanted him to discover her in my bed, and had left the suite door open, the lights on, the tom-toms beating, looka Daddy, come looka what your baby's doing now, while the murderer, he or she, had stolen down the corridor and, selecting the poker from the arsenal of fire tools, had methodically beaten Raul Bashard to his death while Grace tucked her body behind my sleeping, dream-besotted self. Only why methodically? It had been a brutal crime; an overkill. Why not madly? But I couldn't get near the image of him or her, the murderer in the corridor, even though I knew it was there. Grace was in the way, holding me to her, and I knew at the same time I was in the position of having to defend this poor little screwed-up rich teenager against the accusation that was only twenty-four hours and change away, because if I didn't she was sure as hell going to drag me down with her.

There was more to it than that, sure enough. What was it the Counselor's Wife had said about sexual deprivation?

I remember straightening myself out of the cramped position I'd gotten into on the two seats. I remember sitting up in the darkness, and the baby crying, and the black sky finally turning gray and then red under the wing, then over the wing, and light coming into the cabin from outside. And my fellow passengers, those who'd been lucky enough to sleep, stretching in their seats, in the aisles, and clustering at the lavatories, and somebody announcing that we were beginning our descent into the New York area, and only then did I drop off for the few minutes till the wheels bumping against earth woke me up again along with the surge of the power of the engines breaking against their own momentum and the people standing to get at the overhead compartments who had to be told to sit back down.

Home.

Home is wherever you are, maybe.

I rode a taxi into the hazy city. The streets looked foreign to me, even after we came through the park at Seventy-ninth and headed south on Columbus. The people looked foreign too: the dogwalkers, the joggers jogging, the truckers unloading at the food stores, and the business males and females heading for their subways with their briefcases. It was going to be one hot son of a bitch of a day, you could tell that already.

I went upstairs to my place. It was silent, empty, neutral. Unslept-in. It even smelled unslept-in. I plugged in the coffeemaker. I showered, hot followed by cold, and shaved away the twenty-four-hour beard. I got dressed again, leaving the clothes I'd taken off in clumps on the bedroom floor. I swigged a couple of swallows of coffee. It wasn't good, wasn't bad. Neutral. I didn't listen to the message tape again, didn't stick in a new one, didn't turn on the radio, didn't call the office, and when I left I stepped over the newspaper that had been dropped outside my door in the interim.

I felt like an interloper in my own place, like I was doing everything in reverse.

I walked to the garage and woke up the Fiero. First I had the Latham interview, and afterward I wanted to talk to Price again. I headed down Columbus, then Ninth Avenue, and ducked into the tunnel through the jumble of traffic near the Port Authority Bus Terminal. Traffic came against us into the city, backed up from the ramp all the way into the Meadowlands. Even the buses in the special lane were immobilized, bumper to bumper in a diesel fog. Shadow Traffic would be calling it a thirty-minute delay, or worse, but I didn't turn that on either. Instead I triggered up the windows, put the air-conditioning on, and stuck an old Stevie Wonder tape into the dashboard. We fingertipped west against the flow, Stevie and me, with the cruise control at sixty-five.

Name: Latham, Oliver   white Caucasian male
Age: 72
Health: good
Sign: Leo
Function: novelist
Marital status: divorced (1968)
Children: none
Employment: self-employed
Income: $35,000 annum (est)
Net worth: minimal (farm: 2nd mtge; copyrights: negligible mkt value)
Born: San Mateo, Calif.   Resides: Monkton, Penna.
Education: B.A. Stanford,
Sexual preference: unknown

His directions had been good, up to a point. Route 80 West to the Delaware Water Gap, over the bridge into Pennsylvania, then south. I knew the way that far because Route 80 keeps going into the Poconos, where I'd spent some weekends in my time. The countryside is beautiful even before you get to the river, rolling hills and brown-earthed farms in the valleys and, every so often, real-live horses and cows nibbling at the ground. By the time we reached the Gap, Stevie had quit, having sung his bit twice through, and I had the windows open and my sleeves rolled up and was inhaling what even a city boy knows the world is supposed to smell like.

But somewhere south on the Pennsylvania side, I lost first the river and then my way. I never did find the town of Monkton. Maybe there wasn't one. Instead I stopped at one of those combination general store, diner, and gas stations at a country crossroads and asked for directions. No, the proprietor had never heard of a Latham, nor had the beefy blonde (his daughter?) working the diner section. Oliver Latham? Never heard of 'im. I noticed a fresh-looking cherry pie, uncut, on the counter and, sitting down, ordered a piece with coffee. This seemed to thaw the atmosphere to a small degree. The pie dough, at the bottom, resisted even strong measures but the filling was fresh, delicious. A neighboring customer, in coveralls and T-shirt and with a toothpick in his mouth, took an interest in my situation.

"Maybe it's the old Gorman place," he suggested, looking over my shoulder at the sheet of instructions I'd written down.

"The name's Latham," I corrected over a forkful of pie.

"Isn't that the one Tiny Babbidge's workin'?" asked the owner, ignoring me.

"That's right," said my neighbor. "The old Gorman place."

"If it's Tiny Babbidge," the blonde said, "he's a fat pig." She was rinsing dishes behind the counter and drying them with a grayish towel.

"The man I'm looking for, Latham, is a writer," I said. "I know it's a farm."

"I wouldn't know about that," the owner said.

"Tiny's got somebody else livin' up there," my neighbor put in, "but I wouldn't know what he does."

"Raises sheep," the blonde said, making a face.

"If it's Tiny Babbidge," the owner said, "you've come too far."

"The old Gorman place," my neighbor said, "that's all it could be."

If they were so sure of it, I'd give it a try. I finished the pie, minus the crust, paid up, and headed back for the Fiero accompanied by the man with the toothpick who seemed to want to give me last-minute instructions.

"The old Gorman place," he repeated one last time.

And, as it turned out, he was right. Two miles back on the road I found the turnoff I'd missed before because of the

overhanging trees. A half mile or so, after climbing to the top
of a ridge, the macadam gave way to dirt, and soon enough,
through the hedgerows to my left and below the level of the
road, I glimpsed the gray farmhouse and the larger gray
barn. There was no sign, no mailbox, like he'd said, just a
narrower dirt lane (really two furrows cut through the
meadow) that led to the farmhouse.

I parked the Fiero in the wide place between the barn and
the farmhouse, next to a pickup truck and a Buick Riviera.
An elderly but robust woman in an apron came through a
screen door at the side of the farmhouse and eyed me as I got
out of the car.

"Mrs. Babbidge?" I tried.

"Who wants to know?" she called back in a flat voice.

"I'm looking for Oliver Latham."

"He's not here."

"But I've got an appointment," I called back.

I'd misunderstood her meaning, though. She was pointing farther down the slope where, I could now see, there
was a second smaller house half hidden behind a stand of
trees.

"Can I drive down there?" I asked. "Or should I walk?"

"Suit yourself," she said. Then she went back inside, the
screen door slamming behind her.

I walked down the ruts. When I got closer I saw a dusty
VW Beetle baking in the sun and, standing in the doorway of
the small house, seeming to duck his head, the writer
himself.

He appeared to have been waiting for me.

I'd met Latham but the one time before, at the BashCon. I
remember thinking then that he looked a lot younger than
his years, a tall lanky figure with a shock of gray-white curly
hair and wearing an old-fashioned string-tie costume. But
now he looked his age. He seemed to have shrunk some. He
moved a little stiffly, as though his joints hurt him. He wore
gray dungaree pants and a matching jacket over a faded blue
denim shirt. Dusty sandals with thick rubber soles. He had
blue eyes, pale blue, overhung by gray-white eyebrows, and
his face up close was deeply lined and crisscrossed.

"Come on in," he said without, I noticed, offering his hand.

I followed him inside, ducking, too, and almost immediately bumping into something. It took a moment for my eyes to adjust to the sudden dark. Then I realized I'd bumped into the back of a couch, the seat of which was piled with books and papers and cartons with more papers spilling out of them. The inside of the house was smaller than you'd have guessed, made smaller still by the clutter and the crush of furniture. You could see cones of dust in the rays of light coming through the dirt-streaked windows. I learned later that he used to live in the farmhouse himself, then had switched houses with his tenant farmers. It looked like he'd never gotten around to unpacking.

I followed Latham into the kitchen, the largest room I saw. Apparently it was where he spent most of his time. He had his desk in there, a wood-burning fireplace, twin sinks with worn porcelain set in wood and those old-style curved iron faucets, and one of those mammoth ceramic stoves people now pay a fortune for in antique stores. Oak chairs. A dropleaf oak table. A 1940s style Frigidaire. The remnants of a meal in pots on the stovetop and dishes in one of the sinks, and a kind of musty smell that was hard to identify but seemed to grow out of the linoleum itself.

Latham made no apology for the condition of the place. In fact, once he settled himself at his kitchen desk, in a creaking leather swivel chair, it was like pulling teeth to get him talking about anything. Had he lived on the farm a long time? Yes. Did he enjoy it? Enjoy it? The isolation of it, the country life? It was where he lived. Was it a good place for a writer to work, the quiet of it, no interruptions? He wrote every day, wherever he was. Etc., etc., broken by silences. Broken by my efforts to get comfortable on the straight-backed wooden chair he'd offered me.

"All right," he said at length, in his quiet voice. "You didn't come all the way out here because you're writing a master's thesis on the living habits of writers. If you have questions to ask, ask them. Otherwise, I've work to do."

The voice was quiet, the tone sharp, direct. The pale blue eyes unblinking. A trifle watery. Bloodshot in the corners.

"You're right," I said. "I'm trying to find out who killed Raul Bashard."

"What makes you think I might have?"

"Anyone who stayed on the second floor of the hotel annex the night of the BashCon might have."

"I see," he said. "That includes myself."

"Yes."

"And who else was there?"

I ran off the names for him. I no longer needed Bud Fincher's list.

"Have you talked to all of them?"

"That's right. You're the last one."

"And who do the others think killed him?"

I hesitated a moment. In an odd way, he'd managed to become the one asking the questions. Then I said: "Most people tend to think Grace Bashard did."

For the first and only time that day I heard his laugh. It made a dry and scornful sound, like crumpled paper. The lines in his face cracked and crisscrossed even more. Then abruptly the laugh changed into a cough, and he coughed so violently, his face reddening, that I thought he might choke. He excused himself with a wave, stumbled from the kitchen head bent over and still coughing, and a few moments later I heard a toilet flush. Then he was back and in his chair, recovered.

"Why did you think that was so funny?" I asked him.

"Why? Because people never fail to amaze me. They're so true to themselves. All they can think about is the money."

"But Grace was going to inherit everything anyway, wasn't she?"

"You'd know that better than I would," he answered. "But I would have assumed so. Once he died."

"Did you know he was going to die anyway?"

"Aren't we all?"

"I mean, that doctors had told him he had only a limited time left to live?"

"I've heard that since," he said with a shrug, "but I don't give it much credence. It wouldn't have changed anything.

He was always dying, only he never did. You could argue that he'd lived too long as it was."

The remark registered, acid in content if not in delivery, but I had something else on my mind.

"About his money," I said. "I understand that you got some of it, too. Is that right?"

"What do you mean by that?" he answered sharply.

"The *Twenty-fifth Century Tales* set?"

"Who told you about that?"

"A couple of people. They also told me you took him for about twice what it was worth."

"I see. And why did they say I did it?"

"One of them said you needed the money. In fact several people I've talked to seem to feel you need money."

I watched him closely for a reaction, but there was none. Actually, although it didn't altogether register at the time, he was a man of remarkably few gestures, few physical tics or movements. He simply sat in his chair, gazing either at me or at the clutter of papers on his desk, which seemed to have been pushed to either side to make room for the Smith-Corona electric that occupied the center. Half the time, he seemed far off. It wasn't that his face was without expression, but that I had trouble reading the changes.

"It's as I told you. People like Richard, Sidney, whoever it was you talked to, that's the only way they can interpret other people's motives. The money. Do you realize how long it took Raul to earn what he paid for the set? Two days' work. Less."

"But that's not true for people like you and me," I said.

"No," he said reflectively. "No, it isn't." Then: "Us mere mortals," but without any bitter sound to it.

The conversation lagged again. He shifted in his chair as though he supposed, or hoped, I was finished.

"There's one thing I don't understand," I said. "I've talked now to a lot of people who knew him, in one degree or another. Some who knew him well. But not a single one of them seems to *mourn* him."

"Does that surprise you?"

"Well, yes," I said. "Some."

"Why should they?" Latham said matter-of-factly, leaning back. "He was a son of a whore. A real one. Particularly to people close to him."

"But you were close to him," I answered. "How was he one to you?"

"Close to him? Who told you that?"

"Practically everybody I've talked to. They say you were his oldest and closest friend."

He fell silent, apparently reflecting on it, as though his mind was far off. Then he looked back at me.

"Oldest?" he asked. "Yes, I guess that's true. Oldest living one, anyway. But closest? That would have been a long time ago. If ever."

"When did you break with him?"

"Break with him? I don't know that I broke with him. Better that you ask him that, if you could."

"Did you know his son?" I asked, trying a shot in the dark, some way to get a reaction out of him.

The question did seem to startle him momentarily.

"Who, Johnny? Of course I did. I was the boy's godfather, a long time ago."

"I didn't know that."

"Well, I was."

"You must have been around, then, when Bashard disowned him."

"Around? Of course I was around."

"Well?" I said.

"Well what?" He seemed, at last, a bit irritated.

"Were you involved?"

"Involved? Involved in what, the disowning? Fathers and sons, that's the most complicated of themes. I've used it myself on occasion, in books, or tried to. John was homosexual, and his father detested homosexuals. He loathed them. Now that you mention it, I was involved in a way."

"How's that?"

"John came to me for advice at the time."

"And . . . ?"

"And nothing. I told him that if he didn't care about the baby—he had a new baby then and he admitted finally that he didn't care—he should take the money and run. Which is what he did. He changed his name and went to Australia."

"Why did he change his name?"

"I guess because he was Bashard's son."

"And have you been in touch with him since?"

"With John? For a time, we corresponded. He used to ask me for money. Once I think I sent him some."

"Why only once?" I asked.

A slight chuckle.

"Probably because I didn't have it the other times."

"And since? Have you heard from him since?"

But Latham didn't seem to hear the question. He was leaning back in the tall leather chair and for a moment he closed his eyes, as though resting. His body, though, was rigidly held and his hands, I noticed, were splayed out stiffly and down the faded denim of his trousers. Long fingers. Then he revived and stared at me, as though waiting for me to go on.

"You said before," I said, "something to the effect that maybe Bashard had lived too long. What exactly did you mean by that?"

"It's neither here nor there," he said. "A literary observation. It so happens I think the craft of writing is a very serious one . . . to writers anyway. What the rest of the world makes of it, that's something else."

"Do you think Bashard didn't take writing seriously?"

"I didn't say that."

I pushed him on the point. Finally he said: "What he cared about was being the acknowledged master. But he should have quit years ago. He didn't have anything more to say, except to repeat himself."

"Did he know that?"

He glanced at me testily.

"Why do you care?" he said. "What difference does it make?"

"Maybe it does, maybe it doesn't," I answered. "But it's interesting."

"Interesting?" he asked, his eyebrows arching briefly. "Well, maybe it is at that. The fact is, though nobody knew it, we used to exchange manuscripts. One of us would finish a book and, before showing it to anyone else, send it to the other. I was a better reader for him than he was for me. Not that he ever acknowledged it publicly, but some of his books, including the more famous ones, were heavily rewritten before they were published.

"Rewritten by you?"

"By me?" He laughed briefly. "Of course not. But I'd tell him what to do. I even gave him some of his titles. He had a terrible sense of titles."

"Then why did it stop?" I asked. "I mean, exchanging manuscripts?"

"Stop? I don't know," he said, shrugging. Then, correcting himself: "That's not true. It doesn't matter anymore anyway. Did you read a book of his—some six, seven years ago—called *The Second Vale of Tears*? His title, mind you."

I shook my head.

"It's just as well," he went on. "It was a terrible book. I told him so. I even advised him to put it on the shelf and get on with something else. He didn't listen. He went ahead and published it, word for word, as written. Same title. If money's what counts, he was right, too: it was a big best-seller. I don't know if anybody read it, much less his publishers, but people bought it. By that time, I guess he could have published books with blank pages and people would have bought them. Only after that one, he stopped sending me his manuscripts."

"Did you stop sending him yours?"

"Mine? No. I kept on sending them, but whether he read them or not, I couldn't say. I never heard from him about them."

He patted his pockets, rummaged briefly among the papers on his desk, then leaned forward toward me.

"Say," he said conspiratorially, "you wouldn't happen to have any cigarettes on you, would you?" I told him I didn't. "No? Nobody smokes anymore. I'm trying to quit, I'm a great expert on quitting. Never mind, I think I know where I might find some. Excuse me a minute."

He got up. I heard his bones crack. Ducking his head, he

went into the living room. I listened to him moving around, thinking—again—that though the content of what he said was cynical he said it without affect, like it was past history, done. Stiffly.

He came back, holding a wrinkled pack of Camel Lights. I watched him fish one out, straighten it carefully between his fingers, then light it. The hand holding the match trembled a little. He inhaled deeply, like a man who knows and relishes his poison.

The smoke made him cough.

"Filthy habit," he said when he'd stopped coughing. "Do you have any other questions?"

"Yes," I said, "in fact I do."

I asked him about S.O.W. He said he'd never heard of it, didn't know what it referred to. I asked him about Viola Harmel and Leo Mackes. He said they sounded like the names of characters in a private-eye novel. I told him they were people who'd written Bashard threatening letters. He expressed surprise that the Grand Old Man of Science Fiction had gotten threatening letters. I asked him if he didn't get any himself. He said he got some fan letters from time to time, but that was all. I asked him if he was still writing, and he said of course he was. In fact, he and his agent were thinking of changing publishers. Helga Hewitt— I knew her, didn't I?—wanted a chance to bid when his new book was done.

It occurred to me that with Bashard dead, Latham might become the Grand Old Man himself.

As much to keep the conversation going as anything, I asked him about the old days. There'd been a photograph shown at the BashCon banquet of Latham and Bashard when they were young, along with some others. Ron Whitefield had used it as a way of introducing Latham.

He remembered the photo, too. In fact he named the others in it, noting that he was the last one still on his feet.

"Times were different then," he said, "that's all. I wouldn't say better, that would be stupid nostalgia. Different. We were young, broke, not two nickels among the bunch of us. We wrote, we read each other's work, we drank a ton, we argued, fought; we also helped each other. We were going to change the world. I guess we didn't. Everybody had to make a living some other way. Do you know what Raul did? He was a free-lance typist. He'd take in typing, whenever he could get it. Ten cents a page, that was the going rate, then it went up to twenty-five cents. Plus a nickel for every carbon. There were years he made more typing other people's manuscripts than his own. Hard to imagine, isn't it?"

"You must have known his first wife," I said.

"I met her once," he answered.

"She committed suicide, didn't she?"

"That's right."

"Why was that?"

He shrugged slightly.

"I told you," he answered. "He was a son of a whore. A real one."

"To his second wife, too?"

"Who, Madge? No, I guess if there was an exception, she'd have been the one."

"But I've heard that didn't keep him from chasing other women."

"I wouldn't know," he said. "Maybe so."

There was another lull, during which he found the last cigarette in the pack and lit up. He looked inside the pack, as though hoping to find more inside, then crumpled it and dropped it among the desk papers.

"How well do you know Grace Bashard?" I asked.

"I knew her very well as a child. She was a beautiful little girl. Impulsive. Also utterly charming, when she wanted something."

"Is she still that way?"

"I wouldn't know. Still beautiful, at any rate."

"But let me ask you something; before, when I said most people thought she was the one who'd killed him, you found it funny. Why was that again?"

"I told you that. Not because of her but because of the people, the way people think."

"So you still think she might have done it?"

"I never said I thought she did," he corrected.

"But it was a particularly bloody crime. Do you think she'd have been capable of that?"

If I expected some reaction, I got none.

"I wouldn't know," he repeated imperturbably. "How people murder each other doesn't interest me that much."

This was, I thought in passing, a surprising statement for a writer to make. But it was virtually the last one he made.

"One other thing," I said. "At the BashCon, at the end of the banquet, did you and Bashard have an argument?"

"An argument? I don't remember one."

"You said something, shouted something . . . strange. It sounded like Burro."

"Did I?"

I remembered that I wasn't the only one who'd heard it.

"It sounded like Burro. What could that have meant?"

"I've no idea," he answered. "I'd had too much to drink, I think. I'm not so used to it anymore."

Abruptly, then, he ended the interview. Without fanfare. He'd already given me more time than he could spare, he said, and he had work to do. He hadn't slept well the night before, he was tired even before his day began.

He didn't apologize. That was simply, clearly, the way it was. Nor did he offer me his hand, nor stand up.

I left him sitting, a thin and bony figure, paper-thin, and made my way out through the clutter and the dusty shafts of light. I'd left my jacket in the car, and still squinting in the sunlight, the midday heat started me sweating. I stopped level with his dusty VW, listening to the insects buzzing, and it was there that he caught up with me.

"I know I asked you before," he said, patting at his pockets, "but are you sure you don't have any cigarettes?"

"I'm afraid not," I said. "I quit."

"I know, nobody smokes anymore. But goddammit it, it's hard to write anything without a cigarette."

I volunteered to go get him some if he wanted me to, but he said never mind, he was quitting, too, he thought he'd find some more in the house somewhere anyway. Then his voice trailed off and I noticed he was staring off through the trees, uphill, toward the farmhouse, his eyes squinting and unblinking.

"Sons of bitches," he said quietly, as if to nobody. "I used to live up there, did you know that? But I'm going to get it back, never mind."

He stood next to me for a moment, still staring, eyes squinting, then left me without another word. I watched him duck his head and disappear into the dark interior of the little house. I trudged back to the Fiero. If anybody was watching me from the farmhouse I couldn't see them, and the only sound I heard was the bugs.

I was back on the New Jersey side of the river, heading home, when, twiddling with the radio knob, I hit one of the twenty-four-hour all-news all-crime stations. I was half listening, I guess, to the rapes, muggings, robberies, because only the tail end of one of the stories broke into my consciousness. At that, it sent me off onto the Route 80 shoulder, and I stopped the car. I didn't believe what I'd heard, or thought I'd heard.

I was addled enough, I remember, to reach for the tape rewind, thinking I could call it back. Then, knowing the same news item would recycle in twenty minutes or so but not having twenty minutes I drove off again and swung the dial indicator over to the other all-news station. The sound kept yinging and yanging as I descended into the valleys, but when their version of the report came on I caught it on a yang, loud and clear.

Police were investigating the apparent homicide, the night before, of one John Jameson, whose body had been found this morning in a downtown hotel room. John Jameson was the assumed name of John Jacob Bashard, son of Raul Bashard, the famous science-fiction writer, whose own recent murder in the Catskills was still unsolved. Raul Bashard had been beaten to death. His son, John, had apparently been killed by two pistol shots, at close range, at or about twelve midnight. NYPD headquarters had no comment as to whether the two crimes were linked.

I had to drive some ten miles before I reached an exit, then another few of winding road till I found a gas station with a telephone.

"He's absolutely *screaming* for you, Philippe," said Roger LeClerc. "Where are you?"

"Never mind, put me through to him."

"I can't. The lines are tied up. Where are you, Philippe?"

"Then put me through to Shapiro!"

"I told you I can't, Philippe. Do you want to hold on?"

"Well, who else is there besides you?"

"Nobody but Monsieur Fanshare. Monsieur Fanshare is sitting in your office."

"Then for Christ's sake put him on!"

A moment later—which Roger, typically, made a long one—I had Bud Fincher on the line.

Had I heard the news? Yes, I'd just heard it. What in hell was Bashard's son doing in New York? Had anybody known it? He didn't have the answer. He himself had only just gotten back, with Charlotte McCullough, from Bashard's place in New Jersey. Why had he left? I was supposed to meet him there to talk to Price, wasn't I? Because the Counselor had called him back. The Counselor wanted us all there. All he knew was that the Counselor was enraged that I wasn't there, too, that the police wanted to talk to Grace Bashard and that the Counselor would be held in contempt if he didn't produce her by the end of the day.

Where was Grace? I asked him. He didn't know that. Was there reason to believe she'd done it? He didn't know that one either. He knew the name of the hotel where Jameson had been killed, a Village fleabag known to us both (by reputation anyway) as a gay hangout. Beyond that he could add nothing to the radio report. Also that it had, in fact, happened around midnight; there were witnesses to the time.

At this point there was a break in the line. Then the Counselor's voice broke in.

"Where in goddamn hell are you, Phil?" I could see the face behind that tone, brows descended.

I told him. I had about an hour and a half's drive.

"That's not good enough," he said. "Put wings on the car. I need you in less than an hour."

At that, the phone went dead in my ear.

I took him at his word. Fortunately the New Jersey state troopers were out to lunch. With my headlights on and the use of the horn, I made it to the tunnel and was parking next to the hydrant a couple of blocks from the office, which was the closest I could get, exactly fifty-seven minutes from the time he'd hung up.

And all the way in, in spite of myself, two thoughts kept bonging into my head. The first was that the Counselor had evidently missed his lunch at La Gonzesse. The second was that at least this crime, to judge from the timing, was one nobody could try to pin on yours truly.

Third thought: How in God's name did 1010 WINS know that John Jameson was Raul Bashard's son?

CHAPTER
—11—

$\mathbf{N}$YPD time.

This put the Counselor in his element, because he knew how they played the game. Personally I'd choose the simpler Catskills version, where there was Al Squilletti and Harmon Waller, and you could figure out pretty easily who called which shots and where one individual's power and responsibility stopped and another's took over. With the NYPD, you never know entirely. The further up the organization you go, the more you have to worry about an individual covering his own ass, and covering it not only from an immediate superior, which would be easy, but from a totally different branch or division that is always looking out for its own piece of the power pie. In other words, the New York Police Department may look like a monolith to the outside—self-protective, secretive, autonomous—but inside, particularly in the upper echelons, the power struggle never ends.

This creates a hell of a dangerous situation for somebody who doesn't know how the game is played. But for somebody who does, like the Counselor, there can be hidden opportunities.

Translate, please, into the murder of John Jameson.

All right. In a city where a major crime is committed every few minutes, ninety-nine out of a hundred times nobody gives a damn, and that nobody includes, obviously, the police. Blacks kill blacks, Hispanics Hispanics, etc., etc., and it'll make the radio, sometimes TV, headlines in the *Post* and the *News*, once in a while the *Times*, but twenty-four hours later it's gone and the police can forget about it. Sure, once in a blue moon you'll read about their unsolved-crime statistics, but statistics make lousy headlines, and whereas most crimes that aren't solved in the first hours stay that way, time works for the police. Which isn't to say, mind you, that they do a bad job or don't care, only that crime detection requires manpower—and short of putting the entire populace in uniform there just aren't enough cops to handle the caseload.

From the police's point of view, this is not their problem. They're right. And the citizenry, while they may not like it, accept it.

But what most people don't realize is that most cases that stay in the headlines are put there, and kept there, by the police and the media working hand in glove. One example ought to prove what I'm getting at:

Question: When you stop to think about it, is there anything intrinsically worse about a cop killing than any other murder?

Answer: Of course not. Dead is dead, murder is murder and punishable by the laws of the land and so on.

Question: Then what is it, *who* is it, that makes a cop killing *seem* worse?

Answer: The media and the police, themselves, and for obvious reasons. The police are motivated by self-preservation, also by the ongoing need to create public sympathy. (Nothing works for the police, at union contract time, like the public's sense of how thankless and dangerous their task is.) The media are motivated by their need for serial stories, ones that'll keep people buying papers day after day, or tuning in the six o'clock news to catch the latest episode,

complete with pictures of uniformed men in funeral proces-
sions.

What I'm getting at is simply this: the killing of John
Jameson would have been buried in small print and forgotten if somebody hadn't known about the connection. What
could be more humdrum in a city like New York than one
more crime of passion, in this case one gay shooting another,
particularly in a notorious joint like the Village "hotel" in
question? Only somebody did know the connection—a
reporter, as it turned out—and the police, once they learned
that the victim was Raul Bashard's son, went public in
spades.

By the time I got to the office, as I've said, there wasn't a
parking place for blocks around, not even an illegal one.
Mobile units from the local TV stations were parked up and
down our street and around on Park Avenue, and NYPD
plates were double-parked to Madison. A tangle of cables
and wires led the way up from the ground floor to the
Counselor's office where, it turned out, the Counselor
himself was holding an impromptu press conference for a
media mob. All designed, needless to say, to ingratiate us
with the neighborhood.

Roger LeClerc met me downstairs. He was a nervous
wreck, poor soul. His domain was in the process of being
trashed and trampled, and he'd had nothing to say about it.
Althea, the housekeeper, was standing guard over the
residential floors, but who knew how long she'd hold out?
Roger's instructions for me, if I arrived too late for the press
conference, was to go straight up to the fifth-floor solarium,
by elevator, but otherwise he was too busy to talk to me; no,
he didn't know where Bud Fincher had gone, and he ran off
in about four directions at once, accomplishing nothing
much that I could see.

As a result, I missed the press conference, though I caught
snatches of it that night on the late-night news.

I'll give you one guess who called it. Or to put it another
way: when in doubt, counterattack.

The Counselor had no information concerning the death of John Jameson, nor did his client, nor did he have any basis to link it to the murder of Raul Rogan Bashard, Jameson's father. For all he knew it was a tragic coincidence, though that was for the police to determine. Meanwhile his client, Grace Bashard, legal daughter of Raul Bashard and daughter by birth of John Jameson, was understandably in a state of shock and being kept in seclusion.

Was it true that Jameson had information about the Bashard case? The Counselor didn't know. Where was Grace Bashard? The Counselor was not at liberty to say.

When would the media be allowed to interview her? The Counselor couldn't say. Certainly not at present.

But she was the subject of considerable public interest. How long was Charles Camelot going to hide her?

At this question, the camera closed in on the Counselor behind his desk. He drew himself up, furrowed his brows dramatically, and pointing with the stem end of his pipe (a still-smoking pipe), said: "I know many of you individually, you ladies and gentlemen of the media. You're fine people, individually. Most of you take your jobs seriously. But all together, you're like a pack of hyenas. I'm not going to expose an eighteen-year-old girl, in a troubled and bereaved state of mind, to a pack of hyenas."

This response drew a new torrent of questions all at once (thereby, it should be said, tending to prove the Counselor's point). But he, now in command and still pointing with the pipe, took them one at a time.

Would the police be allowed to interview Grace? Yes.

When? That was currently being discussed with representatives of the police department.

Was Grace Bashard a suspect in the second Bashard murder? They would have to ask the police that. But he wouldn't be surprised if she were.

How long had John Jameson, Raul Bashard's son, been in New York? He had no idea.

Had he seen John Jameson? Not in many years.

Was it true that John Jameson was an avowed homosexual? If the word *avowed* meant a public declaration of some kind, he was unaware of one, but yes, he understood that John Bashard had been of the gay persuasion.

Was it true that John Jameson had been suffering from AIDS? The Counselor had no such knowledge.

Did he believe the Raul Bashard murder would ever be solved? The Counselor certainly hoped so, but that was a question that should be put to the appropriate authorities.

At this point, at least on the late news, a female reporter-in-the-street took over, mouthing some so-called irony about tragedy having struck the Bashard family twice. Then the image of our building, shot from the street, gave way to a commercial. I don't remember what the commercial was about. I was too busy by then drafting my letter of resignation.

Back to that afternoon, the elevator, the fifth-floor solarium. I've described the place before. What a great idea, you'd say, an indoor tropical garden all your own complete with hot tub and smack in the middle of New York City. Only try it in the New York summer heat—even with the shutters down over the skylights and the great striped awnings shielding the outer terrace as well as the glass walls—when the air-conditioning has to be kept low and the humidifying up because of the plantings. You'd say whoever designed it had to be crazy.

I never said the Counselor's Wife was crazy. Only a shrink.

Maybe it wasn't the temperature that brought little beads of sweat onto my forearms that afternoon. Maybe it was the sight, totally unexpected, of Grace Bashard, the troubled and bereaved eighteen-year-old, standing as I came off the elevator and walking toward me, barefooted, arms outstretched.

She was wearing a black linen summer dress, with short sleeves and, so help me, white lace trim around the neckline. Bare legs, bare feet (though she put her shoes on later). No makeup that I could detect. Blond hair swept back and held in place by a black ribbon. Pale of complexion, younger-looking even than her years, and yes, to borrow from the Counselor again, a generally troubled and bereaved look.

"Phil," she said. "My God. Mr. Camelot said you'd be coming but I didn't know whether to believe him. Oh Phil, it's been so long and I've been so frightened."

All this in the same breathy tones. Call it her telephone voice, her made-for-television voice. Her Phil Revere voice.

By this time she was against me, reaching up, her hand burrowing into my shoulder, her arms tight around my neck. The smell of some perfumed shampoo lingered in her hair. It took a while for me to disengage her. There were tear streaks on her pale cheeks, and they looked real enough.

"Oh, Phil. Promise me you'll never leave me again."

She clutched at my arm, clung, as I walked her to where she'd been sitting.

"Never say never, Grace. But there's no reason for you to be frightened."

"Oh no? That's easy for you to say. You haven't been shipped around like a suitcase from hotel room to hotel room, and left alone, nobody to talk to. And nobody answering your calls. Did you know I'd been calling you, Phil?"

"Yes," I said. "I got your messages."

I started to say I didn't know where she was, but that wasn't altogether the truth. I didn't know, but I could have found out. Instead, thinking that the Counselor was taking a hell of a risk when the New York media was just three floors below us: "When did you get here?"

"A couple of hours ago. More. Less. I've lost track of time. They brought me here this morning."

"Who's they?"

"My bodyguards. The watchdogs. I hate them."

I knew about this, too. Bud Fincher had hired the teams the Counselor had wanted to keep an eye on her.

I sat her down where she'd been sitting, then made the mistake of sitting across from her, in a two-seater. A moment later she was next to me, under a spreading palm tree, sitting sideways on the floral print of the couch, legs tucked up so that the skirt of her dress was taut above the knees, hair splayed against the cushion and her free hand reaching out to hold mine.

"Have you found him yet, Phil?"

"Found who?"

"Whoever it was that killed my father?"

"Which one?" I asked, immediately regretting it, because after a moment's incomprehension it started her crying in earnest. "Which father, I mean."

"I only had one," she said, squeezing my hand hard. "Raul Bashard was my father. This other man . . . this . . ."

"John Jameson," I prompted.

". . . whoever he was. He wasn't my father. I never knew him. I never even talked to him."

"But he was your real father, Raul was—"

"No he *wasn't*! He walked out on me the day I was born. Raul brought me up, Raul took care of me, Raul . . ."

I never was much for tears. Like most men, a woman in tears makes me fidget, wish I was somewhere else.

". . . Raul loved me," she managed in a small voice.

I handed her a handkerchief, watched her wipe at her eyes. I told her to blow her nose. She did. Then quickly she seized my hand again. I thought distractedly that she'd come quite a ways, on the subject of Bashard, from *you lousy filthy creep*. I also thought, in spite of myself, that she might have been coached. But if so, she needed no further rehearsals.

"Where were you last night?" I asked her.

"What difference does that make?" she answered.

"It doesn't particularly to me," I said. "But the police are going to want to know."

"I was in my room."

"In the hotel?"

"In the hotel."

"You didn't go out?"

"No. If you want to know the truth, Phil, I was waiting for you to call. Why didn't you call?"

"I couldn't," I said, half lying. "I was in an airplane. It wasn't one of the ones that has a phone."

"In an airplane? What were you doing in an airplane?"

"I spent yesterday in sunny California, talking to people about your gr . . . about Raul Bashard's murder."

"Oh?" she said. "Who did you talk to?"

I gave her the list, adding Cyn Morgan and Oliver Latham for good measure, plus the ones Bud Fincher had covered.

Her mouth made an *O*, but no sound came out. Then, letting my hand go: "Do you think one of them did it?"

"Either one of them, or you, or Price."

"Price," she said, giggling, "he's such an asshole. Have you talked to Price?" Then, before I could answer: "So? Which one do you think?"

"I don't know," I said, shrugging. "Most of them say you did."

If I expected a strong reaction from her, she disappointed me.

"I'm not surprised," she said matter-of-factly. "They all hate my guts."

"Hate your guts? Why is that?"

"Because I was so close to him, silly. Didn't you see it? They're all like leeches, you know. Every one of them. He was such a big man, don't you see? Didn't you see it at the party? He was a star . . . you know . . . famous, the *celebrity*. Center of attention. Without him, nobody else was anything, except—"

"Except who?"

"I don't know. Except Ollie, maybe."

"Ollie Latham?"

"A sweet man."

"How well do you know him?"

"I used to know him very well, when I was little. He brought me presents, little things. Not so much anymore. I've only seen him a few times in . . ."

Her voice trailed off, and then she put some kind of barrette in her mouth, temporarily. She'd pulled the ribbon free of her hair and shook her head, with the barrette in her mouth, so that the blonde hair swirled and unswirled. It reminded me fleetingly of the first time I'd seen her, on the television screen, standing next to Bashard. Then she reached behind her head with both hands and swept her hair up, the gesture lifting her breasts into the black fabric of her dress. She took the barrette out of her mouth and repinned it to her hair, then retied the ribbon. Then reached again for my hand.

I stood up.

She was pretty, very. She might grow up to be a great beauty, or maybe not, I wasn't good at guessing such things. But you couldn't help wishing you could freeze her looks right where they were, and her age, with the body too luscious for eighteen years, and the pale, perfect complexion totally free of makeup, and the fresh swirling hair. Too young for an adult, too old for a child. Too young to kill anybody, you'd almost have to say.

Okay, and I was feeling sweat, too, inside my shirt.

"There's one thing I don't understand, Grace," I said. "Why did you tell everyone we made love that night? At the BashCon?"

I stood waiting. There was no answer, but I thought I could hear her breathing. Maybe she was debating whether she could make it stand up with me, too. Then, with a soft giggle: "You can't blame a person for wishing, can you?"

I turned on her. She was facing me now, her legs off the couch, and half smiling up at me. Then, maybe because she saw something in my face, she bit at her upper lip.

"Is it that?" I said angrily. "Or is it that you were covering up?"

"Covering up what? I don't know what you're talking about!"

"Because you thought nobody would believe you could have murdered you own gr . . . all right, your own father . . . and then gone and had sex with a man in the room next door. Because you thought nobody would believe you could be that cold-blooded. Because you believed it would get you off!"

I watched her cover herself up. Her arms went across her breasts to hug her lace-collared shoulders, and she rocked her body forward and back and the tears came again.

"But Phil, that's not true! . . . I *didn't* say it to cover up!"

I took her back through it then, in detail. I started her with the banquet, when she'd been furious, enraged at me she said, and she'd gone off drinking and how, when she'd seen me later in the suite, she was still furious and had gone to bed. Yes, and she'd gone to sleep. Passed out was more like it. And how she'd woken up in the middle of the night, awakened by the storm probably she thought, and was still kind of drunk but felt terrible about what she'd said to me, the way she'd acted. She'd wanted to tell me that, at least that, apologize. So she'd gotten up and left her room, yes, everything was quiet in the suite, and she'd gone outside, intending to knock on my door and wake me up but, finding my door open and me lying in bed sound asleep, so sweetly she said, looking so innocent she said (giggling a little), she'd just gotten into my bed and passed out again. The next she knew, she woke up back in her own room and the doctor was there and Mr. Camelot and they were telling her that her father was dead.

But when she'd left the suite, had she left the door open or not? She didn't remember. What about the lights? She didn't remember that either. Had she seen anybody in the hall? No, she hadn't. She hadn't heard a sound either, not from Price's room or anywhere else. But why hadn't she closed the door behind her? She didn't know she hadn't. She thought she might have, but she wasn't sure. She'd been groggy, like hung over, all she'd wanted to do was talk to me. Apologize.

"If all you wanted to do was to talk to me," I said, "why were you wearing that getup?"

"What getup?"

The next-to-last costume in the striptease, I thought. Red and black lace. I described it, more or less. She giggled.

"Do you normally go to bed wearing outfits like that?" I asked.

"No," she said.

"But had you that night?"

"I don't think so," she said. "I probably wasn't wearing anything. I don't usually . . . to bed, I mean."

"So when you woke up in the middle of the night, naked, you said, and groggy, *that's* what you put on?"

She giggled again, softly.

"When all you wanted to do was *talk* to me?"

And again. Then she adjusted the hem of the skirt, continuing to gaze up at me, her eyes wide and steady.

"I told you, Phil," she said. "You can't blame a person for wishing."

The feeling came over me, not for the first time, that I was being set up. And not only by her. In this, as it turned out, I was both right and wrong. I walked over to the glass terrace doors and stared out at the nearby rooftops. I realized this was the first time since Bashard's murder that I'd been alone with Grace. I wondered if that was just a coincidence. Why else had the Counselor made me rush from New Jersey? Downstairs he was meeting with the media, and sooner or later he was going to have to expose his client. Sooner, probably.

"There's something I want you to know, Phil," Grace said behind me. "It's important. I mean, it's important to me. I mean, that you know it."

I turned to her. She was sitting in the same spot, her hands now propped on the couch cushions, her arms stiff-elbowed and her teeth biting at the upper lip.

"Nobody's ever had me," she said, smiling a little over her lace collar. "I'm a virgin." Then, when I didn't react: "Does that surprise you?"

I don't know that I'd thought about it, either way.

"It's not that I didn't want to," she went on. "They just never gave me the chance. No way." A giggle. "I'll prove it to you if you want."

"Who's they?" I asked.

She shrugged. "My father certainly. And everybody who worked for him. God," she said, sighing, "I'm so tired of bodyguards."

I thought of Price, Robert, OCS, USN. According to Bashard, she'd tried Price. According to what she'd just said, she'd failed.

"Are you going to tell the police this?" I asked.

"That's up to you, Phil," she answered, lowering her eyes. "I'll tell them whatever you want me to."

The setup grew clearer.

"Did you tell this to anyone else?"

"Yes. To Mr. Camelot. He asked me if I was a virgin and I told him the truth."

"And what did he say?"

"He said I'd better talk to you about it."

So there it was, the fine hand of Charles Camelot, Esq., Attorney-at-Law. The Counselor was leaving the choice up to me. Either I could make our client reverse her story, in which case, quite clearly, anyone investigating the murder would start to doubt and question every other element in it. Or I could reverse my own story which, on a scale of one to ten, would be but a small sin. And it would go down, too. Us practiced seducers, you could say, don't like to brag about our teenaged conquests.

"I didn't do it, Phil," Grace said, as though to help decide me. "I won't say I never thought it. I mean, not to kill him but to wish him dead. I did that. But I didn't kill him."

She gave me the tearstains and the quivering lip to go with it, but I, at least, didn't need them. I believed her anyway.

The dress rehearsal was over. In other words, the last changes had been made to the script, and the show could go on.

The script called for the elevator to open right then. As it happened, the Counselor missed his cue by a little, and I had the chance to question Grace further.

She claimed not to know anything about S.O.W. or a Sow Account. Raul Bashard, I said, had told me S.O.W. referred to a group of people who played chess by mail. She said she'd never seen him play chess, but she didn't know that he hadn't either. The names Leo Mackes and Viola Harmel meant nothing to her, she said.

"Well here's the funny part," I said. "To get to the S.O.W. file in the computer, you apparently needed some kind of access code. For all we know now, the file's gone. At least somebody deleted the references to it in the Mackes and Harmel correspondence. Now why would somebody have done that?"

She had no idea what I was talking about.

"Then who else could have done it?"

She shrugged. Maybe her father had done it himself. He was always tinkering with the Big *O*.

If he had, I thought, it would have had to be in the last day or two before he died. In which case, why?

She had no idea.

And if not Bashard, who else had: one, access to the machine, and two, enough knowledge of programming to make a change like that?

"Price," she said. "Price probably did."

Bud Fincher and I, I thought, would have been talking to Price right then if Johnny Jameson hadn't gotten himself killed.

"And who else?" I said. "Who else besides Price had the access and the knowledge?"

She thought a minute, then grinned.

"Only me," she said.

At this point the elevator door slid open and, ever the gentleman, the Counselor ushered out three people. I knew the two men by sight, but not the woman. Harmon Waller wore a cord suit and tie, Al Squilletti a cord jacket, brown slacks and a Windsor-knotted tie pulled down from the collar. The woman wore the uniform, city-executive-style, of blue summer suit and white blouse with the attached white cravat knotted in a bow. She turned out to be Anne Garvey of the New York District Attorney's Office. Ms. Garvey's name, at least, was familiar to me. The Counselor had always described her as an "up-and-comer," a skilled attorney with political ambitions well above her current job. She was a thin nervous creature about my age, with an aquiline face and brown hair a little too big and bushy for her face.

It took me a little while to figure out the Counselor's orchestration. Harmon Waller and Al Squilletti were there because Anne Garvey was. Anne Garvey was there because the Counselor, given the range of possibilities open to him, had chosen her. He had furthermore brought the two murders and their investigations together, not only because if he didn't the media clearly would, but because by demonstrating Grace's innocence in the one, he could encourage the belief in her innocence in the other.

He'd also moved fast. Like I said: When in doubt, counterattack.

He made sure everyone was seated, myself included. He even offered drinks all around and got two takers, Squilletti first and then Harmon Waller, for sodas. Then, still standing, an imposing shaggy-haired figure in double-breasted summer blue blazer, tan twill slacks, blue oxford shirt and repp bow tie, he said: "Given the stress my client has been under, I've requested that this meeting be informal and off-the-record. If, when we're finished, any of you want to take it further to sworn depositions, then I'm open to that. Now Grace," he said, turning to his client, sitting alone now on the floral couch, "I want you to answer these people's questions as freely as if you were talking to me alone. You and I have gone over everything. Don't be afraid to tell them anything you've told me. Don't be afraid to say you don't know when you don't."

"I understand," Grace said in a small voice, her hands now clasped in her lap.

"All right, Counselor," he said, turning and with a flourish extending his hand toward Anne Garvey, "why don't you begin?"

Anne Garvey's questions were sharp and to the point. So were Grace's answers. No, she didn't know John Jameson. She hadn't seen him since she was a baby, had no memory of him, had had no contact with him. She didn't even think she knew he'd changed his name from Bashard to Jameson. He may have been her father by blood, but she wouldn't have recognized him if she'd bumped into him. She had no knowledge of his having been in New York. As to her whereabouts the night before, yes, it might have been theoretically possible for her to have sneaked out of her hotel without having been seen, even by her watchdogs (a possibility Bud Fincher's men themselves later denied). But she hadn't gone out. She'd ordered room service for dinner.

She hadn't eaten much of it. She watched some TV. She'd made a few phone calls. Whom had she called? Well (with a glance in my direction), me. But as it turned out, I wasn't home. Finally, with the help of a sleeping pill, she'd gone to sleep.

Did John Jameson, Ms. Garvey wanted to know, stand to benefit from Raul Bashard's will?

Grace looked up at the Counselor. The Counselor, still standing, looked down at Ms. Garvey.

"That's still privileged information," he said. "But if it doesn't leave this room, I've no objection to telling you." Ms. Garvey had been taking notes in one of those leatherbound, executive-looking affairs. The Counselor waited for her to close the notebook before he went on. "The answer is no. Not one penny. His name isn't even mentioned."

"But that wouldn't prevent him from bringing an action against the estate, would it?" Anne Garvey said.

"No," the Counselor agreed. "People bring suit against estates all the time, whether they've cause or not. But in this case, he wouldn't have stood a chance. He signed off on any interest in Raul Bashard's estate years ago. We can document that for you."

"I see. I wonder why else he would have been in New York?"

The Counselor shook his head. "People come to New York for all kinds of reasons. We can't help you there."

At this point Anne Garvey yielded to Harmon Waller. With occasional help from Squilletti, Waller questioned Grace on the chronology of that night, and morning, at the BashCon. Item by item, detail by detail.

Grace stood up to it. What Waller and Squilletti didn't know, of course, was that I'd just taken her over the same terrain. Only when she got near the place in the script where our accounts diverged did she hesitate slightly. She glanced at me, her pale skin flushing.

The Counselor, I noticed, didn't so much as bat an eyelash. He didn't have to.

Maybe I flushed, too.

"I want to set the record straight on one point, Mr. Waller,"

I heard myself say. "Ms. Bashard . . . Grace . . . and I did in fact have sex that night."

"You *what*?" Harmon Waller exlaimed, coming halfway out of his seat.

"Just like I said," I answered as calmly as I could. "We had sex. We made love."

Squilletti, I noticed out of the corner of my eye, had broken into an ear-to-ear grin. But Harmon Waller wasn't the kind of man who liked surprises.

"Then why in Hades didn't you tell us that before?" he asked.

"It doesn't make much difference, does it?" I said with a shrug. "I guess I was embarrassed, kind of."

"*Embarrassed*?"

"Well, the man I was supposed to be guarding was about to be murdered. And there I was in bed with his daughter."

"Had you had . . . ?" Waller caught himself, on the verge of the three-letter word. "Had you had relations with her before then?"

"No."

"And since?"

"No."

"But just that one night. Why that one night?"

"I guess I'd had too much to drink. Also . . ."

"Also *what*?"

"Well," I said, probably flushing again, "Grace is a very seductive young woman."

The idea seemed to make Waller nervous.

"And what happened after that?" he persisted. "What else do you want to change in your story?"

"Nothing," I said. "I fell asleep. Sound asleep. I usually do," I added for good measure, "after lovemaking."

"And you still claim you woke up with the victim dying in your room?"

"That's right."

"And slept through the rest of it?"

"That's right."

Waller was sore all right, like I'd offended him personally, but there wasn't much more he could make of it. A small sin, like I said. My version now lined up with Grace's, and either we were both telling the truth or both lying, Waller could take his choice.

As to what I'd say if I were ever asked the same question on a witness stand, well, I'd worry about that then.

Or let the Counselor do the worrying.

At that particular moment, the Counselor didn't look worried at all. Or approving either. I was aware of him listening to my exchange with Waller impassively, like nothing he heard about people's private lives would surprise him. But the minute Waller was finished with Grace, having taken her into that morning-after at the BashCon, he stepped in again. He thought his client had had enough. If anyone had any more questions, she could answer them. If not . . . ?

There were no more questions.

"All right, then, Phil," the Counselor said. "Would you show our visitors out? Thank you for coming, Anne, and thank you, gentlemen. We're at your disposal." With handshakes all around, he shepherded us toward the elevator. Grace Bashard waited behind him, in that black dress with lace trim.

Then, while the four of us stood inside the elevator: "Oh Phil"—as an afterthought—"when you're finished I'd like to see you in my office."

The elevator door slid shut on him.

The resignation part, then.

It's probably misleading for me to make such a big deal of it, because the Counselor was full of revelations that afternoon in his office—at least one of which showed what thin ice he'd been skating on during the press conference. But that's where my head was. I mean, I'd just lied for his client—all right, *our* client—and I didn't much like it. I'd done it because the Counselor as much as instructed me to. *Mr. Camelot said I'd better talk to you about it*, Grace had said. So I'd gone ahead and lied, partly, I admit, because I myself believed she was innocent of the murder. I assumed the Counselor felt the same way.

All right, the revelations part.

As I mentioned, and verified later that night on TV, the Counselor had only been asked at the press conference if he'd *seen* John Jameson. No, he'd answered. Fortunately nobody thought to ask him if he'd *heard* from him. In any case he had, and sitting in the clouds of pipe smoke at his desk that afternoon, he played the tape of their phone conversation for us.

The call had been logged in the morning before. That is, the morning before Johnny was murdered in the Village hotel. The caller had announced himself as John Jameson but then, in case the Counselor's memory needed jogging, said he was Johnny Bashard. He'd refused to say where he was calling from, but the connection had been clear. His purpose, he said, was to find out where he stood in his father's will.

The Counselor replied that he was under no obligation to answer the question, but after an exchange he said there was no provision for John in Raul Bashard's will, that in fact he wasn't mentioned at all.

You could almost hear Johnny suck air and hold it on the tape.

"Then my daughter gets it all, is that it?" he asked after a long pause.

"I'm not at liberty to divulge that information," the Counselor answered.

"Not at liberty to divulge that information," Johnny mimicked. "Well, suppose I make you divulge that information? What then?"

"You can try," the Counselor said imperturbably, "but I doubt you'll succeed."

"We'll see about that, Camelot. But I'll tell you this. If that's what the will says, if she gets it all, then it's not worth the paper it's printed on. I'll fight it all the way. I'm his son, and I can prove that. There's no way you're going to cut me out, you can bet on it."

And words to that effect, more and less printable. John Jameson, it seemed, had been one of those people whose voice went higher and nastier the more he got worked up. He'd started in a flat monotone, ended in a near shriek.

"I'm sorry, Mr. Jameson," the Counselor said. "I doubt

you will succeed, but I can't prevent you from pursuing any possible legal remedies you may choose."

"You're damn right you can't!" Johnny shouted back excitedly. "You'll hear from my lawyer, you can bet on that!" Then a pause, a long one, like the connection had been broken. Then, loud and clear: "What about the Sow money?"

"What about it?" the Counselor asked, fishing.

"I bet you're going to try to stop that, too. Well, rots o' ruck. He outsmarted himself on that one, the bastard. It's locked up tight. There's no way you can touch it."

"And you can?" the Counselor asked, fishing again.

Only it didn't work this time.

There was another silence, then a sound like a laugh or a snicker, then: "I bet you don't even know about the Sow money, Camelot. He never told you, did he? He was such a secretive bastard. It must've driven him crazy, but there wasn't a goddamn thing he could do about it."

The Counselor had tried to keep the conversation alive. He asked Johnny how he'd learned about Bashard's death. Johnny had seen it on Australian TV. It had been a big story Down Under, where there weren't enough good murders to go around and the best ones came from the United States. When he'd seen it, Johnny said his first thought had been that there was some justice in the world after all. And so he'd come to New York? Exactly. He thought the plane ticket was the best investment he'd made in years. He was going to fight the will all the way to the Supreme Court, if that's what it took.

But try as he did, the Counselor couldn't budge him on what the Sow money was. If Johnny knew, and it sounded like he did, he wasn't telling.

The Counselor leaned forward, pressed the stop button on the tape recorder, then the rewind.

"What do you make of it?" he said.

I shrugged. It was weird, kind of, hearing the voice of somebody you never met and knowing it was one of his last conversations. Weird, too, hearing a grown man use a teenage expression like "rots o' ruck."

If Johnny had lived to attack the will, I thought, it might have made an interesting legal case—the whole question of whether you can actually disown a son. But the man was dead, there wasn't much he could contest from a city morgue.

The Counselor also had a pretty good idea why Johnny had been shot, if not by whom. It turned out Johnny had made at least one other phone call the evening before. He'd called a newspaper columnist we both knew, one of those self-styled dese-dem-and-dose journalists who had (or so I always thought) an inflated reputation as an investigator of local crime and corruption and actually did it by playing the NYPD game about as well as anybody in his business. According to the columnist, Jameson, who'd identified himself as Bashard's son, had had information to sell—information that would solve the Bashard case. He'd wanted ten thousand dollars for it. The columnist had wanted documentation but had agreed to meet Johnny the next morning.

Too late as it turned out. But it explained the source of all the media hoopla.

"Sounds like Johnny might have been blackmailing somebody," I said.

"It does," the Counselor said.

"Who?"

"I don't know," the Counselor said. "The police don't either."

"Well, what about the Sow money?" I asked.

The Counselor leaned back in his chair.

"Sow," he said. "S.O.W. The Sow Account. What have you found out about it?"

"Nothing," I said.

He was running one hand through his white hair from front to back. Then he stopped to scratch behind an ear. Obviously he enjoyed the moment. At such times, when the Counselor comes on like he's got all the answers, I wonder why he bothers employing me.

Sometimes the only reason I can think of is that he likes an audience.

Only this time, as it turned out, he didn't have the answers.

He had asked Arthur Trout, the accountant, and Charlotte McCullough, our resident genius in numbers, to dig for any peculiarities in Bashard's finances, and uncovered the S.O.W. Account.

Well, not uncovered really. Arthur had known about it all along. Bashard had had a number of similar arrangements. The difference was that the Counselor had set up all the others himself, but this one predated us.

Anyway, for as long as Trout had worked for Bashard, ten percent of all Bashard's royalty income had been paid, by bank transfer, to an account in another New York bank. On the one of two occasions when he'd asked Bashard about it, Trout had been told to mind his own business.

Twice a year Trout received a statement from one of those downtown fiduciary outfits, the ones which watch over trusts and estates for a fee or a percentage, outlining the activity in the S.O.W. Account in the previous six months: deposits, securities bought and sold, etc. Trout forwarded these on to Bashard but, like any good accountant, he'd always kept copies for his files.

"As you'll see," the Counselor said, handing me a file, "the amount of money involved is not to be sneezed at."

To say the least.

I let out a low whistle.

The market value of the account, summarized in printout form on the top page, was in the seven figures. S.O.W., whatever it was, owned shares in a number of blue-chip companies and enough Treasury bonds and triple-A securities to keep, say, the Revere household in Chivas Regal for years to come. The last page in the file was a written summary of the account's activity, complete with "investment philosophy" and the market outlook for the next period. It was signed by one Gwendolyn Graw, who called herself Account Executive.

"I've talked to Ms. Graw," the Counselor said. "Ms. Graw

is a very testy lady, at least over the phone. She said she'd never heard of Raul Bashard. Hard to believe, but you never know. She said she had no idea he was making deposits into *her* account. She sounded doubtful about it, whatever proof I had. In no event was she going to reveal anything about the account to a total stranger."

I didn't say anything at first. One thing at least was clear though: why, when I was in Los Angeles, the Counselor had suddenly "discovered" S.O.W. First Charlotte and Arthur Trout's discovery, then Johnny Jameson's call, and, in the background, the deletions in Bashard's computer files.

Leo Mackes, I thought. Viola Harmel. I said the names aloud.

"Exactly," the Counselor said, holding up the memo pad he kept next to his tobacco jar. I saw the names written on the top sheet and underlined. "Why haven't you found them yet?"

That was Bud's assignment I started to say, but didn't. Instead: "I guess we had better things to do."

Lame enough, from the sound of it.

"Well, now you don't," the Counselor said. Then, when I started to get up, "Never mind, I've already put Fincher on it. I've got another assignment for you. But what do you make of it? S.O.W.? A pool of some kind? A shakedown?" Then, gesturing with the stem of his pipe, "Look at the last deposit sheet there."

I found it. There were several entries covering the six-months period. One of them, for a comparatively small amount, had been circled in red.

"Charlotte found that," the Counselor said. "All the others she could correlate to Bashard's own deposits, but the one she circled was from another source. If you ask me, it's a shakedown of some kind, something Raul was embarrassed enough about to hide from me. It's not in his will, not part of the estate. It predates Arthur, and Johnny Jameson clearly knew about it. If Johnny knew, somebody else must have, too. Who?"

I shook my head. Bud Fincher and I had put the question to everybody we'd interviewed. I ran down the list for him.

"Maybe you didn't ask hard enough," the Counselor said, reaching toward the tobacco jar.

This wasn't the kind of statement designed to improve employee relations, but I was used to it. What followed, though, caught me short.

"Anyway," he went on, "I want you down there tomorrow morning to call on Ms. Graw. Maybe you'll have better luck in person that I did over the phone. If not, then we'll have to resort to stronger measures, though I'd rather keep the law out of it till we know more.

"Meanwhile . . . I hope you don't have anything planned for tonight?"

Actually I did have something planned for that night.

"I want you to take Grace home," the Counselor said.

"Grace?" I think I said. Or maybe, "Home?"

"That's right," he answered.

At some point the Counselor said: "Seems to me you protesteth too much, Phil," and in view of what happened later . . .

But at the time, well, I'd had enough of Grace Bashard for one day, and maybe one lifetime. Ever since I'd started on the case, people had been pushing her on me. It had begun with Bashard, who, I figured, liked to play games with other people's lives. The Counselor's Wife had joined in, for fun. And, of course, there was Grace herself. In the beginning, I'd figured that was the bored little rich girl in her, all dressed up and no place to go. But *after* Bashard's murder? Well, she was still bored, still cooped up, and now a little scared in the bargain, with nobody to turn to.

Okay, from Grace's point of view maybe it was more than that. And okay, from mine, yes, she was by anybody's standards a delicious physical creation. It was like whoever had made her had had sex in mind from day one.

But for Christ's sake, I was old enough to be her father! Plus I was, and am, old enough to choose my own sexual partners.

And now, finally, there was the Counselor himself. Like they say in the military, I'd already saluted and charged up the hill once that day, in the client's interest, by lying to Waller, Garvey, and Squilletti. Wasn't enough enough?

Or did he really think that, in lying, I was actually admitting the truth?

"Seems to me you protesteth too much," said the Counselor.

I think that's what set me shouting.

He had his reasons, of course. He didn't want Grace in a hotel anymore, didn't want her left alone either. For all we knew it was open season on Bashards, and as long as the killer or killers hadn't been identified, Grace was our responsibility. She wasn't going home, in any case, to stay. The house was going on the market. Price had already been dismissed. Kohl and MacGregor would be once the house was sold. Grace was going to rent an apartment in the city, she wanted to go home just to collect some belongings, if I'd take her out there and just spend the night, I'd be relieved in the morning. Etc., etc.

Of course, none of the above was his real reason.

Grace wanted me to take her. She'd specifically asked.

"Is this an order?" I remember saying.

"Phil, come on," the Counselor answered, conciliating, "We've worked together too long. I don't give you orders. That's not how we relate to each other."

Relate was a Nora Saroff word.

"Then maybe it's how we should," I answered.

"I wouldn't want that. I doubt you would either."

I took a deep breath and shook my head.

"I don't care," I said. "Is it an order?"

He sighed, creaked his chair, and stared at me quizzically.

"If you insist then. Yes, it's an order."

No job's worth that much, etc., etc.

In hindsight you could say, Quit the bitching, and given what happened, I'd have to agree with you. But that was how I found myself, again, in Bashard's ghostly mansion, in the same room I'd stayed in that first time, having driven Grace down in the Fiero through the summer evening heat because suddenly I couldn't stand the windows closed and air-conditioning in the car. And how I found myself watching the Counselor on TV, doing his number expertly, I thought, not even blinking during the thin-ice part when, with the camera on his craggy face, he was asked if he'd seen John Jameson. And how I found myself insomniac, dictating my letter of resignation to myself because maybe he was right, maybe we *had* worked together too long, maybe it wasn't too late for me to go back and pass the stupid bar exam and . . .

Etc., etc.

And found myself, meanwhile, waiting for the proverbial other shoe to drop.

I watched parts of the *Tonight* show, and *David Letterman*, but I couldn't tell you what I saw. At some point, I took a shower. At another, I carried the remnants of the sandwich tray MacGregor had made up for me all the way down to the kitchen, just to help tidy up, but I couldn't tell you if the house lights were on or if I made my way down and up in darkness. I do remember stopping on the second-floor landing, looking, listening. Not a sound. That was where she'd left me earlier. She'd kissed me good night, on the cheek, saying she was really glad I was there, repeating that, for the first time in her life, she was scared to be in the house. She wasn't going to stay there another night if she could help it. Then she'd gone off down the hall, carrying her own tray, and I'd continued on up with mine.

We'd talked a while before that. She said the house weirded her out now. She'd never been scared of it before. It had been more like a prison, sometimes. Now it scared her, being there. Still, she was glad Price was gone from the estate. She would have felt awkward around Price, she said. She'd talked to Mr. Camelot about it. Mr. Camelot had said he'd take care of it, and she'd asked him to be generous with Price. She'd asked him to give Price a special bonus. She thought Price would be happier that way, because his loyalty had been to her father, not to her. And Kohl and MacGregor could take care of the place till the new owners decided what they wanted.

Still, she was awfully glad I'd come with her. She didn't know if she could have stayed in the house alone.

She was excited about having an apartment of her own.

That was a little scary, too, because everything had happened so suddenly, but she was getting used to the idea. What she really wanted now was for her father's murder to be solved so she could put everything behind her and start fresh. She wanted to be involved in the case, she said. She was ready and willing to help me any way she could, only she wanted to talk to me, and me only, not all those other people.

I asked her again about S.O.W., the Sow Account. She couldn't help me there. I told her what we now knew about it. The news that a percentage of Raul Bashard's wealth had gone somewhere else didn't seem to bother her. Maybe, I thought, with all the millions in his estate coming to her she didn't have to worry about the one or two that got away.

She asked me what I thought about the John Jameson murder. Were the two connected? I said I thought they had to be. She disagreed. She knew he was gay, she said. She thought it might be a gay crime. She thought it might be a crime of passion and have nothing to do with her father's murder.

Then she said she thought she'd like to take some sandwiches up to her room, if that was okay with me. It was. She got MacGregor to fix them. I asked MacGregor to wake me up at seven the next morning. She said she wanted to come with me the next morning, wherever I was going. I said I didn't think that would be practical. She didn't argue. Then MacGregor brought our trays, and she kissed me good night on the second-floor landing sweetly. On the cheek.

Her best behavior, in sum. Even ladylike.

Maybe it was Bashard's absence that kept me awake. The only time I'd stayed there before, he'd been very much in evidence. It was *his* place; Grace clearly felt the same way. She'd called it a prison. To me, it was more like a tomb, soon to be abandoned. With his ashes scattered outside.

Shiver city.

From the second-floor landing, where I stood in the middle of the night, I could make out the closed mahogany door of his study, where I'd met him for the first time. His bedroom suite, I knew, was farther down the hall, and

Grace's opposite. I remembered him standing over his control center, surrounded by his own books, watching her on the lawn. In his sneakers. She in bare feet. She'd been wearing a forest-green sweatshirt, and her blonde hair swirled and coiled around her head when she ran with the dogs. Later, one of them had been poisoned. Jules. In the rush of human murders, everybody had forgotten the dead dog. If she had poisoned the Doberman, would she have been able to call her father a filthy, dirty creep? If he had, why would he have gone through that charade of a funeral? If his murderer had . . . ?

But why? A warning? Maybe the dead pooch, too, was just a coincidence, like Johnny's murder?

Shiver city.

The last time I'd had insomnia, I'd fallen asleep with my lights on and the door open. I'd been trying to read a book. I'd been drunk, or hung over, or both. And Grace Bashard had slipped into bed with me while I slept. While somebody bashed in her father's head.

This time I was cold sober.

I jumped when I felt her hand slip into mine. The hall must have been dark at that, because I'd neither seen nor heard her coming. She was barefooted. I think I was too. She had on one of those little white nighties that ended mid-thigh and was held together by a lacy tie at the neck.

She tugged at my hand and led me soundlessly past Bashard's study. I could hear her breathing in the darkness, my own, and the Victorian pile didn't so much as creak.

His bedroom suite on the right side, hers on the left.

She led me in. Still holding my hand, she pulled the covers from her bed. Then, turning to me, hair swirling gently, she undid the nightie's tie.

There was a high correlation, the Counselor's Wife had said, between insomnia and sexual deprivation.

Maybe Bashard's ghost was snickering somewhere.

Hnnga Hnnga Hnnga.

Hnnn Hnnn Hnnn.

CHAPTER
12

I missed out on my jogging again the next morning, which was getting to be a habit. Grace hung on to me before, during and after breakfast. And when my "replacements" arrived (as the Counselor had promised they would) and it was time for me to leave for the city, she clung all the harder.

The main effect her first sex had had on her was to make her babble. She danced and hovered throughout breakfast. She served me plates from the buffet, snatching bites from my plate. She sent the impassive MacGregor out for more coffee, taking the pot from him when he came back and refilling my cup. And all the while she chattered away. About sex first. And her father a close second. Sex had at least liberated her in that sense, because she dumped the whole kitchen sink on him. How he hadn't touched her in years, not once, not since she was little. How he wouldn't let anybody else touch her either. It was like he was afraid somebody would break her. Nobody could touch him either, not even his best friends. But he didn't have any best friends, he didn't have any friends at all. He just exploited

218

people, that was all. And gave nothing back. And she was supposed to be *grateful* to him, was she, because he'd changed his will and left everything to her? If she felt anything, it was *sorry* for him. Whoever heard of somebody leaving somebody all his money only if they weren't murdered? Didn't he know anyway that she never *cared* about the money? Not really?

"Only I do now, Phil! Don't you see? I earned it, I *deserve* it! Oh Phil, I feel so *grown-up* all of a sudden. It's really *weird*. Don't I *seem* grown-up?"

Later, when Bud Fincher's people showed and it was time for me to go and we'd already said good-bye, she ran after me. I was standing at the door to the Fiero in my shirtsleeves and with my jacket thrown over the passenger's seat because you could tell already it was going to be another New York summer scorcher. She clung to me all right, and got her body between me and the car.

I couldn't leave her there. She had to come with me. She wouldn't even go in with me, if I didn't want her to. She'd wait for me in the car. Wouldn't it be helpful to me if I had her wait in the car? She could drive it around the block, and keep driving it around the block till I . . .

Then suddenly she blubbered. The tears flooded out of their ducts and her whole face crumpled, red like a little kid's.

"But I can't drive, Phil!" she wailed. "I don't even know how! *He* wouldn't let me . . . !"

I held her, felt her shaking, gave her my handkerchief, calmed her down as best I could.

Eventually the tears subsided.

She looked up at me, her cheeks stained.

"Can't you stay with me, Phil?" she said softly, staring into my eyes. "Don't you want to have me again? Wasn't I good?"

What's a guy supposed to answer? Instead I made her a proposition: If she'd stay there and do what she'd come to do and let Bud Fincher's men drive her into the city, then I'd hook up with her later. She said she didn't have anything to do there, there wasn't anything at the house she needed, nothing that money couldn't buy. Then she'd tricked me, I said. This made her grin. Still, I said, she couldn't go with me. I promised, again, to call her as soon as I was done. Where? she wanted to know. At my place, I said. I even gave her my keys. As soon as I was done? As soon as I was done.

She let me go then. As I swung around the driveway, I saw her standing there, waving. And when she saw me looking back, she blew me a kiss.

All right, call it a mistake.

Upton Fiduciary was located high enough up in the World Trade Center that you had to switch elevators. You took one of the big ones up to the seventieth-something floor and then transferred to a smaller local one. Up in that World Trade stratosphere, it was hard to tell the men from the women; everybody wore dark suits.

Upton Fiduciary's offices were cool, modern, and spacious, with panoramic views of New York Harbor. They were of modular design, meaning that the furnishings of your individual space formed your walls, shoulder-high, which could be shifted, stretched or shrunk, I guessed, depending on how many seven-figure accounts you'd brought in lately. Or hadn't. And quiet. A mortician's quiet. There didn't seem to be much action in the place. I supposed that when you're in the business of managing estates and trusts in the seven figures and beyond, and taking your comfortable piece off the top in good times and bad, there isn't a hell of a lot to do except sit back and contemplate the Statue of Liberty.

I had plenty of time, the way it happened, for these and other thoughts. I'd shown up unannounced, and that's apparently a no-no in the World Trade stratosphere. The receptionist expressed surprise when I told her I had no appointment. So, a little later, did Ms. Graw's assistant. As for Ms. Graw, maybe she was doing her nails, talking to her bookmaker, or (for all I knew) hadn't shown up for work yet. Whatever it was, she kept me cooling my heels for a good forty-five minutes. First in the reception area, then later in an interior miniconference room.

I was working on my second cup of coffee when Ms. Graw rumbled in behind a pair of steel-rimmed glasses. I use *rumbled* advisedly. She was a beefy-faced, no-nonsense type of woman. She wore a navy blue linen suit which fit over her body like a box, and a white shirt with navy cravat. She had blue eyes behind the glasses and iron-gray hair. I put her in her mid-fifties. She wasn't the type, I thought, to whom I'd entrust my fortune—unless I was dead. Maybe, come to think of it, that was the point.

We exchanged cards.

"I believe you spoke to Mr. Camelot—" I started.

"That's correct," Ms. Graw interrupted. "In fact, I don't know why you're here this morning. I have nothing to add to what I told him."

"Nothing?"

"Nothing."

"But it's true that you do manage something called the Sow Account, isn't it?"

"The S.O.W. Fund, yes."

"Fund, then," I said. "What do the initials stand for?"

"I'm sorry. We at Upton wouldn't be at liberty to tell you that."

"Or who the beneficiaries are?"

"Of course not."

Progress, I could see, was likely to be slow with Ms. Graw, and it was hard to see how to nudge things along.

"Ms. Graw," I said, "I don't know how much Mr. Camelot told you. The fact is that we represent the estate of Raul R. Bashard. Mr. Bashard was recently brutally murdered, and the authorities have yet to identify the killer or killers. I'm sure you've heard of the case?"

No response.

"We also have discovered," I went on, "that Mr. Bashard, before his death and for a very considerable time, was a substantial contributor to the S.O.W. Fund."

"I wouldn't know about that," Ms. Graw replied. "As far as Upton is concerned, contributions have been anonymously made."

"And the beneficiaries? Are they anonymous, too?"

"I didn't say that," she snapped.

"I know you didn't," I countered mildly. "But you must

also know that there's been a second murder, that of one John Jameson, Raul Bashard's son, also unsolved. Both cases are, you could say, very much in the public eye."

"That may be," she answered, "but I don't see what that has to do with Upton."

Slow progress, like I said. All I'd been able to accomplish so far was to get her from her feet into a chair across the conference table from me.

I decided to take the plunge.

"Well, I'll tell you, Ms. Graw," I said. "We have reason to believe the S.O.W. Fund is directly connected to at least one of the murders, and maybe both. Good reason. It may well have been a motive in the Raul Bashard killing. Maybe *the* motive."

"If that's so," she asked, "then why are you here and not the police?"

I smiled at her.

"Because we haven't told them yet," I said.

No response.

"Look at it this way, Ms. Graw," I said. "Of course we're going to tell the police. We have to, Mr. Camelot being an officer of the court and so forth. And once we tell them, the media are going to have the story, believe you me. But *how* we tell them can make a big difference. If we tell them Upton Fiduciary is withholding information in the Bashard case, you can bet the media will be swarming all over this office. You'll never have seen anything like it. You'll have TV cameras in the ladies' room and newspapers telling the world what you ate for breakfast. Under a picture of you with curlers in your hair, if you use curlers. And of course, all you'll have gained for your troubles is a little time. You'll have to reveal the information in the long run anyway. After a lot of bad publicity."

Silence. The only word I can think of to describe how she looked is *steel*. Steel eyes, steel jaw.

"Mr. Revere," she said, sucking a little air, "we at Upton aren't used to being threatened."

"Ms. Graw," I answered, "we at Camelot aren't used to threatening people either. And it's not a threat, furthermore. I'm only telling you what's going to happen."

Silence. Maybe the muscles tightened another notch in her jaws. Maybe they didn't.

"I'm sorry, Mr. Revere," she said, standing. "You're going to have to excuse me for a moment. You wait here, please."

She rumbled out of the conference room. She was gone a while, giving me time to refill my cup and study the market charts on the walls some more. I still couldn't make head or tail out of them. I figured she'd gone to talk to her boss and, given the time that elapsed, that her boss had had to talk to his boss. And maybe to Upton's attorneys on the way.

Progress, maybe.

She came back. A little less self-assured, I thought, like she was pushing a barge this time, and the current was pushing up against her.

She sat down, across from me again.

"Mr. Revere," she said, "I'm authorized to tell you that the S.O.W. Fund has been terminated."

"Terminated?" I said, feeling a jump in my stomach. "What does that mean?"

"Just what it says," she answered tartly. "Terminated. Once certain conditions pertaining to the fund have been fulfilled, the fund is dissolved and the proceeds paid over."

"Paid over?" I said. "Paid over to whom?"

"I'm not at liberty to tell you that."

"But has it actually been paid? The check written and cashed?"

"You don't have to shout at me," she said coldly.

I wasn't aware that I'd been shouting.

"I'm sorry," I said, pulling down on the decibels, "but don't you see? This makes it worse for Upton. If you've actually paid over the money, you may have—however innocently—aided and abetted a criminal."

Maybe I was overstating the case, but I thought I could feel her running out of oomph.

"The money hasn't actually been paid," she said. "Everything is ready, but there are certain closing formalities . . ."

"What kind of formalities?"

"Documents," she said.

"What documents?"

She took off her glasses as though she was going to wipe them, then seemed to think better of it and put them back on again. A pulling-herself-together gesture.

"What precisely is it you want to know, Mr. Revere?"

"Everything," I said, pushing the advantage. "What the S.O.W. Fund is, or was. When it got started. How it works. What those conditions are you mentioned. Most important, who gets the money."

She sighed, shook her head.

"I'll have to ask you to come with me," she said, standing up.

She said it in a way that suggested failure, or resignation, or both. She led me out of the conference room and out through some more of the modular affairs, where Upton Fiduciary employees were laboring at computer consoles. But quietly—you couldn't hear your own footsteps on the carpeting, and the telephones didn't ring. Gwendolyn Graw walked in front of me, her head down. Her stride was purposeful, but you could tell the barge was too heavy for her alone.

She led me to a large and permanent-looking office, where the walls went all the way up to the ceiling, in what must have been the northwest corner of the tower. It belonged to one Pierce Upton III. You could tell from the plaque on the door.

Ms. Graw knocked, then entered without waiting. After a brief introduction, she left me there. She shut the door behind me.

The view, you'd have to say, was spectacular, and the man behind the desk seemed to have been staring at it, his hands pursed in a steeple, when I came in. That must have been Hoboken across the river, and Jersey City behind it, and they didn't look half bad from that height and distance. Probably on a clear day you could see Bashard's, but it wasn't a clear day. A bank of summer haze blurred the horizon.

What Pierce Upton III was doing, surveying New Jersey, I've no idea. Maybe he owned it.

He swung around in his swivel chair when I entered and eyed me across his desk. He didn't stand up, didn't offer his hand, and the polished wood expanse of his desk was virtually empty. I spotted a small white oblong near him— my card, as it turned out.

I sat down, uninvited.

He was younger than you'd expect, about my age in fact, blond and blue-eyed. Unlike the rest of the World Trade employees I'd seen, he wore an olive-colored gabardine summer suit, a yellow oxford button-down, and a repp tie that probably signified some school or club, but I couldn't tell you which one. Not a strand of his blond hair was out of place, not a crease, not a drop of sweat. Wasp America, in sum, which his accent confirmed. Money, sure, but Old Money, and I'd have bet the house he drove a beat-up old Chevy when he could have afforded a string of stretch limos.

He picked up my card, looked at it, put it down.

"How can I help you, Philip Revere," he said.

I repeated substantially what I'd said to Gwendolyn Graw. I may have emphasized the bad-publicity part. My experience with the III's of this world is that the last thing they want is publicity, good or bad. TV lights make you sweat, after all.

"I see your point," he said when I'd finished. "You ought to realize, though, the problem this gives me. We at Upton Fiduciary have built our reputation on qualities like integrity, probity, confidentiality. Maybe they're old-fashioned and out of date, but that's what our clients seem to want. We're a very conservative company. However, in certain exceptional circumstances, maybe we have to learn to be a little more flexible. The decision I have to make now is whether this circumstance is sufficiently exceptional."

He paused. I guess he was deciding. Probably he was deciding what Pierce Upton I would have done.

"In addition," I put in to be helpful, "the S.O.W. Fund is being dissolved. Once it's gone, there's no more money you can make on it, is there? So why not?"

Clearly I should have kept my mouth shut. I should have remembered that Old Money doesn't like to be reminded of profits, at least not by the riffraff. Pierce Upton III's mouth tightened, and for a moment I thought I'd blown it. What I got instead—I kid you not—was a lecture on the meaning of the word *fiduciary*. It comes, I learned, from the Latin *fidus*, an adjective meaning "faithful" or "trustworthy." Pierce Upton III, I figured, must have endured the lecture himself from his forebears, and this was his revenge.

All it cost me in the end, though, was time.

"I didn't mean to cast aspersions on your firm," I said when he'd finished. "If that's what it sounded like, I apologize. But I still need the information."

"All right," he answered, clasping his hands on the bare wood surface in front of him. "The S.O.W. Fund, when we took it over some years ago, had only very modest capital. In fact, I doubt we would have touched it today. But under our investment management, and with growing contributions over the years, it now constitutes . . . well, quite a reasonable portfolio for the beneficiary."

"There's only one beneficiary then?" I asked.

"Yes, only one."

"But how does that work? I mean, did it name just one beneficiary?"

"No," he said. "It was constituted as a pool."

"And Raul R. Bashard was one of the contributors?"

"I wouldn't know," he answered. "As far as Upton Fiduciary was concerned, the contributions were anonymously made."

True enough, I knew, from what Arthur Trout had reported.

"But what about the beneficiary?" I persisted. "How was he, or she, to be chosen?"

"Originally there was a list. I believe there were six in all."

"But now there's only one, right?" I continued for him. "It was set up by six people and kept going until only one of them was still alive, wasn't it? Winner take all?"

"More or less." He nodded.

I was warm, all right. Hell, the griddle was sizzling.

"Then who's the survivor?" I asked, standing up.

"I can't tell you that," he answered.

"You don't have to," I told him. "All you've got to do, Mr. Upton, is nod your head when I give you the right name."

I ran them down for him then, Bud Fincher's list and mine, all our friends and neighbors from the second floor of the annex at the BashCon: Price, Brinckerhoff, Frankaman, Latham, Hermatius, Wright, Whitefield, Varga, Morgan.

But he didn't bat an eyelash.

"What about Raul Bashard himself? Wasn't he on the list of eligibles?"

"No," said Pierce Upton III, "he wasn't on the list."

I didn't get it then. Unless . . . ?

"What about Mackes? Leo Mackes?"

Stone time.

"Viola Harmel?"

Hands clasped.

And for me, caution to the winds.

"Look, Mr. Upton," I said, shouted maybe, jabbing the rarefied air at him, "don't tell me if you don't want to, don't tell Charles Camelot either, but it's going to be squeezed out of you—and the longer you wait, the more it's going to hurt!"

Plus a few dozen more ill-chosen words, to this effect.

He looked at me when I was done like I was a disagreeable smell, and he managed it without even wrinkling his nostrils.

"Sit down, Revere," he said. "I don't have to tell you the time of day, if I don't want to. You can stand here and read me the telephone book, and just because you tell me to nod my head at the right time, it doesn't mean I'm going to."

"We all make our choices," I said, still standing. "Sounds like you've just made yours."

"Sit down, Revere," he repeated.

Slow progress, like I said.

I sat down.

"It so happens," Upton went on, "that there's an outside trustee to the Fund. I'm not going to stand in the way if the outside trustee wants to identify the beneficiary for you."

Cover your ass, Pierce Upton, I thought.

"Then get him here," I pressed.

"I've already called him," he said. He leaned left and pushed a button on his telephone console. "Please put that call through now," he ordered to the unseen secretary.

Pierce Upton III didn't have a telephone receiver in sight, just one of those squawk boxes you can talk at while trimming your fingernails. The call went through fast, and a male voice said hello. Pierce Upton III introduced himself, then me, and asked me to repeat what I'd just told him.

"Who am I talking to?" I said in the general direction of the box.

"That doesn't matter now," the voice answered. "Let me hear what you've got to say, please."

I didn't recognize the voice, I thought. It had a rasp to it, or rale, like older people usually do, and it was male, but that still left about twenty-five percent of the population.

I ran through it one more time for my unknown listener. I said we hadn't taken what we knew to the police yet, but that we would have to shortly. I said that sooner or later the details of the S.O.W. Fund were going to have to come out.

There was a silence when I'd finished.

Pierce Upton III had swiveled in his chair and was gazing at New Jersey again.

"Revere, this is Sam Wright speaking. I think we've met. In view of what you've said, I think it's time I had a talk with Charles Camelot. I'll be at his office at two o'clock this afternoon. Can you arrange that?"

I glanced at my watch. The sooner the better, I thought, but then there was the Counselor's luncheon to worry about. At the same time I was trying to remember what I knew about Sam Wright. I'd met him at the BashCon. Bud Fincher had interviewed him; various people had mentioned him.

"Two o'clock, Revere," Sam Wright repeated. "Can you arrange that?"

I told him I would and heard him break the connection.

Pierce Upton III swung around in his chair, pushed a button on the console, and stood up, facing me. No hand extended.

"One other thing, Mr. Upton," I said. "If I were you, I'd put a freeze on the S.O.W. Fund. I wouldn't pay out a nickel right now."

"I don't need you to tell me how to run my affairs," he answered coldly.

"I'm sure you don't," I said. "Just a thought."

I left him with it. But before I took off from Upton Fiduciary, I put in a call to the Counselor. It gave me some small pleasure to use Pierce Upton's quarter.

By the time I drove uptown, parked the Fiero and got to the office, the Counselor had already left for La Gonzesse. I brown-bagged it at my desk. I had a Revere special— Muenster and tomato on a bagel, lightly toasted, mayo, a bottle of Moosehead, and two cups of Roger LeClerc's special-blend coffee. I found Bud Fincher and compared notes with him on Sam Wright. Bud Fincher wanted to know when we were going to reschedule Price. I told him it would have to wait. Then I listened to the tapes of two calls from Grace Bashard. The first was from New Jersey; she was about to leave; she still loved me. The second was from New York; she'd just gotten in. For some reason the calls made me think of the Counselor's Wife and what she would have to say about my dalliance with Grace. Or maybe it was Muffin who made me think of the Counselor's Wife. The cocker bitch hung out outside my door all during lunch. In case, I guess, I got tired of the sandwich.

I remembered Sam Wright as an elderly man, short and bald and jolly. He'd been introduced at the BashCon as "Mr. S. F. Con," meaning, I'd gathered, that some of the conventions were his doing and, probably, that when there was a deficit he picked it up. I'd more or less lumped him in the same category as Richard Brinckerhoff. Someone had told me Sam Wright had a rich bitch of a wife, and Bud Fincher had described a fancy penthouse in the Sutton Place area, with a view of the East River.

Shortly before two, the Counselor returned and summoned me to his office. I briefed him on what we knew of Wright and what I suspected. He listened, his chin down toward his chest. Then, looking at me sideways, he said he was glad I'd decided not to resign.

I didn't have time to find a retort. Ms. Shapiro buzzed. A Mr. Wright and a Ms. Morgan were there.

"Ms. Morgan?" the Counselor said to me, his eyebrows raised.

"*Cyn* Morgan?" I said. "He didn't mention anything about her."

But Cyn Morgan it was. The last time I'd seen her, she'd had a decidedly Bohemian, downtown look. Now she looked more like she was going to a funeral. Black skirt, black-figured shirt under a natural linen jacket. Her face seemed drawn, unanimated.

Sam Wright was sweating in a seersucker suit. Even in the Counselor's air-conditioning, he mopped often at his forehead. He was as round as I remembered him, and ruddy, and his bald head seemed to rise to a point which gave his face, head-on, a kind of teardrop effect.

"We'd prefer to talk to you alone, sir," he said to the Counselor when he saw me there.

The Counselor shook his head.

"Phil Revere here is privy to all our secrets," he said, "particularly insofar as Raul Bashard is concerned. If it's confidentiality you're concerned about, you can tell him everything you're willing to tell me. I, in turn, am curious as to why Ms. Morgan is here."

"There's a good reason," Sam Wright said.

"I'm sure there is," the Counselor agreed.

Wright and Cyn Morgan sat down facing the Counselor, I in my usual chair to his left.

The Counselor waited, head down, his eyes watching Sam Wright.

"All right," Sam Wright began. "Some years ago, I was asked to become trustee to a special fund, which, as you now know, is administered by a company called Upton. My role was to make sure certain conditions were fulfilled when the time came for the fund to be dissolved. It was left to me, if I felt it necessary, to appoint a replacement. That's why Cyn is here." Wright smiled, turning his already round face into a full moon. "I'm getting old. About a year ago, when I was in poor health, it seemed the fund might well outlast me. I asked Cyn to be ready to take over."

"I'm glad to see that hasn't proved necessary," the Counselor said.

"Yes," Sam Wright said. Then he added, cryptically: "And no."

"Let's go back a moment," the Counselor said. "I assume we're both talking about the so-called S.O.W., or Sow, Fund."

"That's correct."

"What does Sow stand for?"

Wright smiled again.

"I'm afraid I don't have the foggiest," he said.

"When exactly did you become involved with it, Mr. Wright?"

"About fifteen years ago. Almost to the day."

"But the fund predated your involvement, didn't it?"

"That's correct."

"Then why were you brought in?"

"I came in at the same time as Upton Fiduciary. I was asked to."

"Why?"

Wright shrugged, and mopped. "I never knew," he said. "I always supposed it was because the money in the fund began to take on significant proportions."

"Which coincided, didn't it, with the period when Raul Bashard began to make real money as a writer?"

"I guess that's right."

"But Raul was the one who brought you in, wasn't he?"

"No," Wright said. Then, "Not officially anyway. Officially, it was Upton."

"But you suspected, at least, didn't you?"

"Yes."

"But why?" the Counselor asked. "The contributions were made anonymously, I understand. If it was Upton, not Raul, who brought you in, how did you know?"

Sam Wright wasn't the squirming type, but you could tell from his silence that the Counselor had maneuvered him into a corner.

"All right," the Counselor said. "The Sow Fund existed, whatever Sow stands for, and through contributions and investments it was big enough to warrant bringing in a management firm. But why you? I assume it must have had to do with the beneficiaries, isn't that right?"

"More or less."

"With certifying the beneficiary, or beneficiaries?"

"Yes."

"Was Raul a beneficiary? I mean, a potential beneficiary before he died?"

Wright hesitated. I remembered putting the same question to good old Pierce Upton III.

"There was a list of beneficiaries," Wright said. "Or potential beneficiaries."

"Which you had?" the Counselor asked.

"Yes."

"Was Raul one of them?" Wright hesitated again. "Come on, Mr. Wright, you're not under oath here."

I saw Sam Wright glance at Cyn Morgan. I, too, looked at her, at her small and tired face. Now she did match her age, and I remembered suddenly her last words to me, that day outside her apartment, to the effect that she thought I'd find out who'd killed Bashard but she hoped I wouldn't. And now I began to see why.

"Mr. Camelot," Wright said stubbornly, "I'm prepared to give you the name of the surviving beneficiary, but nothing more. At least not without my attorney's advice. Is that clear?"

The Counselor didn't answer. He sat impassively, chin down in his listening pose.

"Viola Harmel," Sam Wright said. Then: "Viola T. Harmel, to be precise."

Goddamn! And, a moment later, *double* damn. Because the Counselor, reaching for a pipe and glancing at me, said gently: "Never mind, Sam. You don't have to tell us who that is. We already know."

CHAPTER
13

All right, I'd missed it. I'd missed it that day I sat at Bashard's computer and first saw the names, and I'd missed it ever since. It had blown right past me.

I don't know how many times I'd seen the names, thought them, written them down. Leo Mackes. Viola T. Harmel.

And Bud Fincher likewise, and Fincher's people, and Squilletti, and God knows who else. All of us had missed it.

Including, I should add, the Counselor.

Maybe the Counselor said to Sam Wright, *You don't have to tell us who it is, we already know,* like the poker player turning over the ace in the hole and reaching for the pot. But the truth was, as I found out, that the Counselor had missed it, too, had missed it right up till just before lunch that morning.

The truth, much as it pinches, is this: The person who figured it out was none other than the Counselor's Wife.

I guess it helps to be into word games and puzzles. Some people have that mind-set, others don't. The word around the household was that the Counselor's Wife polished off the

Sunday Times crossword puzzle in fifteen minutes or so. Without working up a sweat. In ink.

I guess the only reason she never held the solution over our heads was that she'd been wrong, too.

Anyway, she'd come home just before lunch that day to give the cocker her noontime walk, had stopped in on her husband and, in passing so to speak, had figured out why Bud Fincher and his people and I and everybody else had never been able to locate Leo Mackes and Viola T. Harmel. One of whom was dead in any case, but one very much alive.

All right, you do it. I'll give you the names, in block letters:

LEO MACKES

VIOLA T. HARMEL

By way of a hint, I'll give you a third name, though it didn't come out till later:

DASHA BURRAL

(*Burral* was what we'd heard at the BashCon banquet, *Burral*, not *Burro*.) I'd give you the other three, too, but they were long-since dead and unless you were a science-fiction fan, they wouldn't mean much to you. But all you need really is one, and if you've a mind-set like the Counselor's Wife or know that all you're supposed to do is push the letters around till they make new names, then it won't take you very long to come up with the real ones.

LEO MACKES. VIOLA T. HARMEL. DASHA BURRAL. CLEM OAKES. OLIVER LATHAM. RAUL BASHARD.

Once there had been six of them, six young hotshots out to write the history of the future. Only nobody was listening, at least not then, and there wasn't enough money in all six pockets to put potatoes in the stew. Raul Bashard took in typing to feed his family; God knows what the others did. There was even a photograph of the six of them together. I'd seen it myself, at the BashCon banquet. It had been part of Sam Wright's slide show. Sam Wright, it turned out, had taken the picture himself.

But I'm getting ahead of myself. Once there were six.

Three of them died young, and that left three. Then Clem Oakes died, and that left two. Oliver Latham. Raul Bashard.

Viola T. Harmel and Dasha Burral.

And the money in the Sow Fund, Sam Wright said, had reached significant proportions. And the sole surviving beneficiary?

Oliver Latham.

"This alone doesn't make a murderer," Sam Wright said, in the Counselor's office.

"I don't believe I claimed it did," the Counselor replied. "That's a question for the police to decide, and the courts."

"But you're going to tell them?"

"It's my obligation," the Counselor answered.

"Ollie Latham wouldn't kill a flea," Cyn Morgan blurted out.

She said it with her head down. I looked at her, trying to measure the degree of her conviction. She glanced up at me, then quickly away. I saw that her eyes were blurry, but whether that expressed conviction or something else was anybody's guess.

Nobody said anything for a minute. Then Sam Wright, after dabbing at his forehead again with an oversize handkerchief, said: "If you're going to call the police the minute we walk out this door, Mr. Camelot, then we're going to have to warn him."

"That could make you both accessories to a crime," the Counselor observed.

"We'll take our chances on that," Cyn Morgan snapped back.

"I'm sorry," the Counselor said to them, fussing with a pipe, "but I must be missing something. What do you propose we do?"

"He's a lonely old man," Sam Wright said by way of answering. "And dignified in his way. A lonely and dignified old man, and a great writer. We don't want anything to happen that'll rob him of his dignity." Then Wright turned to me, and I saw the light dancing off his ruddy pate. "You've met him, Revere. Does he strike you as a man capable of bashing in someone's head?"

I shrugged.

"Nobody strikes me as being capable of bashing in someone's head," I think I answered. Like a lot of things, it was true and not true. I could as well have said: Everybody strikes me as being capable.

"Let Phil go," Cyn Morgan put in, her eyes glistening. "After all, he's running your investigation, isn't he? He's met Ollie. Let him go out there. Let him confront him with what we know. Then . . ."

Her voice trailed off.

"Yes?" the Counselor said, pushing her.

"Then what will happen will happen," she said, her head down again.

"One question," the Counselor said to Sam Wright, meanwhile digging into the bowl of his pipe with a pipe tool, stuffing it with tobacco from the bowl, and tamping with his forefinger. "Has the claim been made on the Sow money?"

"Yes, it's been made," Wright answered.

"But the money hasn't been paid over yet? Or so I've been given to understand?"

"That's correct."

"And your role . . . ?"

"My role is to verify. Or was."

"To verify what?" the Counselor said. "That Harmel and Latham are one and the same person?"

"That's correct. I have documents to prove it. I did for all of them."

"When was this supposed to happen?"

"This afternoon," Sam Wright answered. "But I've put it off. After I talked to Revere this morning, I called Ollie."

"And told him what?"

"Nothing," Sam Wright said. "I made up an excuse, that's all. The meeting's been rescheduled for tomorrow morning."

"And so you've known all along?" the Counselor asked, reaching for his matches.

Sam Wright didn't answer at first. The Counselor filled the time, as usual, by lighting his pipe. It took him two tries.

"Raul Bashard," Sam Wright said, "was a cruel son of a bitch by any standard."

The observation hung out there, in midair, as though waiting for somebody to take a swipe at it. Nobody did.

Then Sam Wright said: "I wanted Ollie to get his money."

The Counselor puffed smoke. It wreathed around his head and floated toward the ceiling.

"Ms. Morgan said it, Phil," he said, looking at me through smoke. "It's your show, your decision. What do you want to do?"

Of course I didn't go alone. The Counselor wouldn't let me. The way he put it, if Latham had already killed at least once, he could do it again. The Counselor wanted to call Anne Garvey and Harmon Waller and send in an army with me, using the situation (incidentally if not coincidentally) to build up credit for the future. But I refused that, and we compromised.

I arranged to meet Al Squilletti on the Pennsylvania side of the Delaware Water Gap Bridge. Call it my own credit system. Squilletti had the shorter distance but I beat him by a good quarter of an hour. So did the deputy from the local sheriff's office that Squilletti had called. The deputy was Squilletti's idea, and there was a measure of cover-your-ass in it because Squilletti hadn't liked the idea of making an arrest, if that's what it came to, outside his own turf. The deputy was a tall gangly country boy whose name was Roman, and he got there first, so I filled him in on the case, and who I was. By the time Squilletti showed, this deputy Roman had realized that maybe he could be a hero, too, and get on TV, and you could see the light bulb shining inside his country skull.

The Fiero led the procession, followed by the two law officers in their unmarked cars, down the state road, then the country road, then the narrow turnoff between the overhanging trees and up onto the ridge where the macadam gave way to dirt. The time I'd been there before, it had been in the heat of the morning. Now it was in the heat of the late afternoon, the sun still well up in the sky at that time of year. The bugs and the birds were playing games, and I could feel

238 / PETER ISRAEL

the sweat starting to rivulet down my back the minute I stepped out of the car.

I'd had a lot of time to think along the way. I'd thought back over the details of Raul Bashard's murder, thought back over the blood, the mayhem, and the impression that whoever had killed him had had to have been out of his mind. Yes, everything fit all right; Latham could have done it. What was new was the motive. Money, impatience, greed. The Viola Harmel letters, as I remembered them, corroborated same. So had the Leo Mackes letters, but they'd stopped two years ago, when Clem Oakes died. Leaving Bashard and Latham. Burral and Harmel. Johnny Jameson's death, though, was something else. Two shots, that was all. Cold, calculated. All I knew about it for sure was that, yes, it would have been physically possible for Latham to have driven up to the city, kill Johnny, and return home long before I showed up that next morning. I thought back to our meeting. Had Latham shown any sign of being fresh from a killing? No. He'd looked tired, old. He'd seemed held back, held in, like I was an intrusion that would go away in a little while. The only time he'd expressed what you'd call emotions were over the cigarettes, for one, and about the house up the hill where the farmers lived. He was going to get that house back, he'd said.

Money. The Sow Fund. If he could get away with murder, he'd get the house back all right.

But the truth was—and it hit me again—that I didn't have any idea what a murderer looked like. I mean, sometimes you can look people in the eye and see emotion: fear, excitement, greed, sorrow, boredom, whatever. Often, with a woman, you know if she's had sex lately. But killing, murder? Either it's too foreign, or too commonplace. Ever walk down the street and try picking out the murderers?

I stood on top of the ridge with Squilletti and the deputy, gazing down on the farm. A rural scene in summer, warm, peaceable. No sign of life, human life anyway, all the way down the slope. Squilletti and the deputy wanted to come with me. I didn't want them to. We made a deal. They could follow me down, keeping out of sight, but they'd stay out of Latham's house unless there was good reason not to.

I slung my jacket over my shoulder and walked down the ruts, between the buzzing, growing grass, to the barn and the farmhouse. The pickup truck stood there, but the Buick Riviera I'd noticed the time before was gone. No sign of the Babbidges, but I spotted Latham's Beetle tucked behind the line of trees below. If I was thinking anything, it was what I'd been thinking all along: that if I were Latham and Phil Revere rode his white charger into my front yard, accusing me of murder, I'd tell him to go scratch. Yes, I was Viola T. Harmel, yes I was now the last surviving heir to the Sow Fund, but that was motive, that wasn't evidence. Where was the evidence?

The last thing I expected, I guess, was that he wouldn't be there. His front door was open. I walked in.

Evidence. In all that dust and clutter, what kind of evidence would you look for, and where? Murder weapons? Confessions? The poker that had bashed in Bashard's skull was somewhere in Squilletti's file of exhibits. The .22 pistol that had shot and killed Johnny Bashard was another question, although if Latham had shot his godson, there were a hundred miles of places between the scene of the crime and here where he could have dumped the gun.

I went up steps to the unfinished half-attic where he slept. A mattress on the floor, half covered by a sheet. Two lamps and an electric heater, all plugged into the same floorboard outlet. A clothes bar mounted on a wall served as his closet, and a pale blue dresser with the paint flecking off it held some clothes. There were storm windows piled in a corner under the eaves and hunks of that pink insulating material sticking out of the rafters where the Sheetrock that was supposed to hold it in place had given way.

"Rustic," you could say, meaning it was pretty much of a rural slum. With a lot of hard work, and a little money, it might have been improved, but Oliver Latham apparently didn't care. I guess he didn't do much entertaining.

I found nothing. No weapons, no incriminating papers.

Downstairs, the living room clutter looked undisturbed from my last visit. The kitchen, too, with its musty-smelling linoleum. He seemed to have been working on some kind of script, maybe a movie script. It had characters' names in capital letters and then lines of dialogue, but I scanned several pages of it and couldn't make much sense of what was going on.

I felt thirsty, searched for a clean glass, found none. I picked the likeliest candidate from one of the twin porcelain sinks and was rinsing it with my fingers when suddenly Latham spoke up behind me, "You're late," he said.

I jumped in spite of myself, put the glass down, turned the water off, turned my head.

He was standing in the doorway into the kitchen, head ducked, shoulders slumped, his hands in the pockets of his dungarees. He was wearing pretty much the same outfit as the other day, without the jacket. Shirt sleeves rolled up to the elbows. His forearms were skin and bones, the veins knotty. If anything, he'd lost weight in the few days since I'd seen him. Bare feet in the dusty rubber-soled sandals.

"Go ahead," he said. "Water's cheap. Help yourself."

"It doesn't matter," I answered.

We stared at each other for a minute. I saw an old man, with an old man's slump and bony, creased face.

"I expected you an hour ago," Latham said. "I got tired of waiting. I went out for a walk. It's a beautiful day."

"Hot," I said.

"Yes, hot," he said. "But you get used to it. It's worse in the city, isn't it?"

I shrugged. He didn't seem to be sweating, not at all.

"But you've got air-conditioning in the city," he went on. "No air-conditioning here. Just air. D'you want a beer? I think I've got some beer around somewhere."

He patted his pants pockets as he spoke, then his shirt pocket, and pulled out a pack of cigarettes. He lit up with a red disposable lighter, and inhaled deeply. Then the coughing took him, bending him, driving the smoke out of his chest. His complexion reddened, his eyes watered. Then he straightened, seeming to shake it off, and took a smaller puff, then stubbed the cigarette out in a dish on his desk.

"What about that beer," he said, moving past me, "and what about your friends outside? Don't you want to ask them in? I don't think they saw me but they look kind of stupid, sitting where they're sitting. What are they, cops?"

I accepted the beer. I told him who they were. I told him I wanted to talk to him first.

"Why'd you bring them then? Did you think I was going to shoot you?" This made him laugh—that dry sound—and the laughter led to more coughing. I watched him recover from it. Then he came back from the old refrigerator with two cans of a brand I'd never heard of. The label said it came from someplace in Pennsylvania. He motioned me to the chair I'd sat in that time before and he took the old leather job by the desk. We popped the cans, drank.

"When I didn't find you here," I said, "I figured you'd taken off."

"Why?" he answered. "I live here."

"I don't know," I said. "People who are suspected of murder sometimes do."

"Am I suspected of murder?" he said mildly.

There was something different about him, though. A kind of brittleness. The other time I'd been there he'd been composed, remote, gesture-free. I noticed it in his hands mostly. His fingers fiddled with the beer can, papers, pencils. They took the cigarette pack out, fished one out, lit it. One hand held it while he coughed and the other turned the lighter over from end to end when he stopped.

I told him I thought he'd quit smoking. He said he'd quit smoking a hundred times.

"We know about the Sow Fund," I said.

"I know you do," he said. "The good old Sow Fund. It's mine now. I guess I earned it. I waited a long time for it."

"What's it stand for?" I asked.

"What's what stand for?"

"The Sow Fund. S.O.W."

"S.O.W.," he answered. "It started out, officially, as Sons of Wells. H. G. Wells, get it? The so-called Father of Science

Fiction? It sounds pretty corny now. I always thought of it as the Sons of Whores anyway."

"Tell me about it," I said.

"What's to tell? You know all about it anyway."

He did tell me, though. They'd been six at the beginning, six hungry writers writing for nickels and dimes when they got published at all. He'd forgotten which one of them had thought it up, but the idea was that, if they pooled a piece of their earnings, maybe one of them would survive to enjoy it. They'd set it up legally, complete with the anagrammed code names. The joke was that none of them really thought he'd survive. It was a different time. All of them believed nuclear disaster was around the corner, and if one of them did live through the bombs to collect the money, there'd be no place to spend it. The worse joke was that three of them did live through—Oakes and Latham and Bashard—and that the Fund grew to proportions beyond anybody's expectations. And that two of them at least—Oakes and Latham—could have used the money. Maybe the contributions had been mostly Bashard's, but the Fund, one-third of it anyway, was rightfully theirs.

"When Mackes died," Latham said, ". . . I saw him just before he died. He'd literally wasted away. Every penny he got his hands on went for drugs, and there was never enough. I wrote Burral. I called, I begged. Can you imagine that? Me? I *begged*! Let's dissolve the goddamn fund, I said, get Mackes into a hospital, get him cured, give him a stake. But Burral wouldn't hear it. The fund was the fund, the bylaws the bylaws. 'Let's amend the fucking bylaws!' I said. Unh-unh. Wouldn't hear of it. D'you know what? Right then I vowed I'd outlive him. Whatever it took, Viola T. Harmel would outlive Burral."

He'd gone stiff in the telling, face carved out of stone and eyes staring straight at me.

What was weirdest was that he'd used their scrambled names in telling it.

"Even if it meant killing him?" I said.

But that was the wrong thing to say. Too soon, too something. He'd been holding his hands together, clasping them, but now they broke loose again. His face creased in laughter, and a new spell of coughing racked him.

"Are you accu—? Are you accu—?" The coughing again, and then a convulsion of coughing, and he had a handkerchief in his hand and hocked into it, wadding the handkerchief after. Sweat now popped out on his forehead.

I watched him mop at his forehead with his shirtsleeved upper arm. His complexion had gone pale again. He shook out another cigarette and lit it, his hand trembling a little so that the lighter shook.

The smoking, though, seemed to calm him this time. He sucked smoke in and exhaled it through his nostrils without coughing.

"What about Johnny?" I asked. "John Jameson?"

"There's scum for you," he answered.

I gave him room, time to explain, but he fell silent.

"He knew about the fund, didn't he?" I tried. "We know he knew about it. You used to send him money, you said, but then you stopped. Did he come to the United States to try to shake you down?"

No answer. I knew I was right, though, knew suddenly that that was what had happened.

"And so you had to kill him, too?" I said. "Either that, or pay him off? To keep him from telling?"

I knew I was right, sure, but I also saw I was losing him. He continued to smoke, the ash dropping off without his paying attention. He stared straight ahead, not at me, not at anything. It was like I knew he'd done it, both crimes, and he knew I knew. But also that beyond the Sow Fund there was no evidence, no proof, no witness. Maybe we'd turn some up; maybe we wouldn't. And maybe the Sow Fund itself was enough to win an indictment, but where was the jury that would convict?

"What about Grace?" I tried. "Suppose Grace was brought to trial for either crime? What would you do? Would you still be sitting there?"

No answer.

It was then that I heard a sound in the living room, followed by Squilletti's voice.

"Are you in there, Revere? Are you all right?"

I got up abruptly and went to the doorway. My shirt was sticking to my back. I saw Squilletti standing against the back of the couch near the door, looking bewildered in the sudden clutter and darkness. Maybe I looked a little weird, too, because the minute he saw me, his hand started toward his jacket where he wore the holster.

"Get out of here," I called to him.

"Are you okay, Revere? What's going on? Is he in there with you?"

"Yes I'm all right! But get the hell out!"

"But it's getting—"

"I don't care what it's getting. Go home if you have to, but get the hell out of here!"

I watched him back out of the house, shaking his head, shielding his eyes from the sun. He spoke to somebody, presumably the deputy, but I couldn't hear the words. Then he disappeared.

I went back into the kitchen. Latham was still sitting in the leather chair, leaning forward, his head propped up by the palm of his hand. His free hand was doodling with a pencil. I felt dry in the throat again. I shook my beer can. It was empty, even though I didn't remember drinking any past the first swallow. I put the can down on the side of his desk and stood there until he looked up at me. He stared at me with suddenly tired eyes. Old man's eyes, rheumy, with blood in the corners.

"You're a lousy excuse for a cop, Revere," he said matter-of-factly.

"I'm not a cop," I answered, but it was as though he didn't hear.

"You've got it all figured out," he went on, in a scornful, brittle tone, "but you can't prove a thing. Now you're stumbling all over yourself. Well, I can't help you, wouldn't help you if I could. All I want is the money, don't you know? I've earned it. Now I'm going to get it."

"I wouldn't be too sure," I said.

"Yes, sir," he said, without hearing. "I was going to get it this afternoon, don't you know? But you got in the way. Now it's tomorrow. You can arrest me if you want to. Go ahead, arrest me. I'll be out on bail next week. Today, tomorrow, next week, what difference does it make when I collect? I've waited years for it."

"You may not get it tomorrow, or next week, or in a month or six months," I said. "It may take years. In fact, you may never get it."

". . . tomorrow, next week, next month, don't you know?" he was saying. But then suddenly, what I'd said seemed to dawn on him.

He straightened up, sat back in his chair. His hands slipped back off the desk into his lap, then lifted to grip the arms of the chair. His gaze fixed on me.

"You can't stop it," he said, his mouth tight.

"That's not true," I answered. "If you're being held on suspicion of murder, any judge will issue a temporary restraining order against the money being paid out. Then there'll be injunction proceedings. If you have to stand trial, the money will be held in escrow till a verdict's been reached. If you're acquitted, of course, then it would be released to you. But if—"

"Suppose I'm convicted," he interrupted. "Then what?"

"Then you'll never see it," I said. "The courts nowadays take a dim view of criminals profiting from their crimes. There are laws on the books to protect the victims of such crimes."

"What victims?" he said animatedly. "Burral's dead, there's nobody else but me!"

"In that case," I said, "then I guess the money would eventually go to Grace. As the victim's—or the victims'—sole surviving heir."

I watched him closely for a reaction, any reaction. All he did, though, was reach for another cigarette and light it. This time his hand didn't waver. Then he shook his head slowly from side to side.

"The rich get richer," he said softly. Then, subsiding in his chair, smoking, his eyes seeming to follow the swirl of smoke upward toward the wall and the ceiling: "How much of what you're saying is true and how much bluff?"

Without looking up the finer legal points, I'd have guessed ninety percent certainty and ten percent hunch. Zero percent bluff. If Grace pressed it, I guessed she could get the Sow Fund. If Latham was convicted, he never would.

"It's no bluff," I said.

I watched him in the silent kitchen. His teeth clenched, and then I saw a strange thing. The last thing I would have expected. No sound, no sobbing, just tears, maybe one to each eye, rolling out onto the cheekbones and down, to end in stain.

We sat there.

Latham inhaled and coughed again, and wiped his face with the back of his forearm. Turned his head to me.

"I don't like you, Revere," he said, "but I want the money. I want it so badly that if I confess to your murders, will you guarantee me the money?"

"I can't do that," I answered.

"Then bring in your cops from outside," he said. "Let them guarantee it."

"They can't either."

"Well who can? Somebody's got to be able to."

I thought about it. Practically, I guessed it could be done. There were at least three people who'd have to give the kind of guarantee Latham wanted. One was Harmon Waller, the second was Anne Garvey. The third was Grace Bashard. In other words, if neither the State of New York nor Bashard's heir objected, who was there to contest the Sow Fund?

The route to all three went through the Counselor.

"Let me make sure I understand," I said. "If you can be guaranteed the Sow money, you'll confess to killing Raul Bashard and his son—a sworn confession, that is. Is that correct?"

"That's correct," Latham said.

"But why would you do a thing like that?" I blurted out without thinking.

"Because it's mine," he answered. "Because I earned it."

Because it's mine.

A seven-figure sum, I thought. How many people were there who would kill, even for seven figures?

Maybe more than you'd think.

"And if you don't get the money?" I asked.

"If I don't get the money?" he repeated. He grinned, and his face broke into sharp creases. "Then you'd better arrest me. Call your friends in from outside and arrest me. Prove your case. But let me ask you this: What do you think your chances will be of convicting me without my cooperation?"

I guessed he was bluffing then, and it turned out I was right, but in a way and for reasons I hadn't thought of. If so, though, he was bluffing from strength. Unless we found a murder weapon, or a witness who could put Latham at the gay hotel, the best any prosecutor could do with the Jameson case would be circumstantial bits and pieces, mostly having to do with the Sow Fund and Raul Bashard's own murder. And as far as that first crime went, Latham would produce a parade of character witnesses in court, those very people Bud Fincher and I had traipsed back and forth to interview, and Norman Hermatius would tell the court what a great writer Latham was, and Cyn Morgan would cry on the witness stand, and where was the prosecutor who could break their see-no-evil, hear-no-evil versions of the BashCon night?

The more I thought about it, the more I came to believe that they'd all known, all along. Or at least suspected. But not a one had admitted a thing to Bud and me.

What was it Sidney Frankaman had said to me when I sat down at his table, that Sunday of the BashCon?

Maybe Latham had read my mind.

"I've waited this long for it," he said in his kitchen. "I can wait that much longer if I have to."

Bluff?

Maybe.

"I've got a couple of calls to make," I said finally.

"Go ahead," he said, with a gesture. "There's the phone."

"I'd like to make them alone."

"That's all right," he said, standing up. I heard his joints crack. "I need to stretch my legs anyway. Go ahead."

He walked into the living room, and I came out of the kitchen behind him.

"What's the matter?" he said. "You're not afraid I'm going to make a run for it, are you?"

I was thinking just that in fact, but I said: "No. I just want to make sure the others know what's going on, when they see you walk out the door alone."

I accompanied him outside and called out to Squilletti and Roman. The light had begun to fade, even on one of the longest days of the year, but heat still hung in the air.

I watched the deputy and the Catskill cop walk toward us, one tall and gangly, the other sawed-off and looking out of place, his dark pants and shoes powdered with country dust.

I introduced them to Latham, then pulled Squilletti aside.

"What's going on?" Squilletti asked in low tones.

"I think we're close," I said.

"Close to what?"

"I think he's going to confess," I said. "I can't explain now. But the two of you should keep an eye on him."

Latham had walked toward his VW Beetle, then past it, but instead of heading up the path toward the big house he turned left beyond the stand of trees and into the meadow that stretched upward from the line of trees. A tall, stoop-shouldered figure. Skin and bones.

I watched Squilletti and Roman head after him. Then I went back into the house and called the Counselor.

In the end, we spent the night there.

Oliver Latham himself cooked us dinner—corned-beef hash out of cans with sunnyside-ups, salad with his own lemon dressing, and more of the Pennsylvania beer. The beer got better as it went, and it seemed to loosen him up. He was quite the raconteur when he got going. He talked and gestured all during the meal, his face flushed, not about murder but mostly about what it had been like to grow up in California a long time ago, when the big events were the war that had happened in Europe and the Black Sox scandal in 1919. Another world, in sum, but it made Latham seem almost human. Like the rest of us.

Roman went home after dinner. The Counselor had called

back. Squilletti drove his car down the slope from the road and slept in it. Latham went upstairs, after helping me unload one of the couches in the living room that became my bed.

I slept off and on, more off than on. The couch was one of those three-quarter jobs, and either you curled up in it or the arm caught you under the knees. The heat didn't go away that night. I missed air-conditioning. I missed the familiar sounds of my air conditioner and the trucks rumbling up Amsterdam Avenue. I missed my own city bed where, at least in theory, Grace Bashard was now curled up herself, waiting for me to come home. Instead of the sirens of police cars and ambulances, which you could learn to sleep through, I had the whine of a lone mosquito and other small sounds that grew in menace the more I tried to figure out what they were.

I was also waiting for one of two things to happen. That they hadn't didn't mean they wouldn't.

Once I walked outside. Squilletti was asleep in his backseat, in the moonlight.

Once I walked up the slatted stairs, in my socks. Latham had left one of his lamps on, a squat job that sat on the floor. He was lying on his back in the shadows, on the floor mattress, his face shadowy. He was wearing pajamas. Motionless. While I watched, though, he turned toward me, his gray face toward the light, and as though to tell me he was still alive, started to snore. Half snore, half whistle, and short breathing. I could hear a rattle in his chest. He coughed once, but it didn't wake him up. Then a pajama-sleeved arm lifted in the air and fell over his eyes, as though to shield them. He still didn't wake up.

This guy murdered two men, I thought while I stood there, one with a fire poker, one with a gun. This is what a murderer looks like. This is the guy you've got to watch like a hawk, for when he dives off the shallow end.

Squilletti woke me in the morning. The sun was already up. I could hear sounds in the bathroom, and a little later Oliver Latham emerged.

Neither of the two things I'd been expecting had happened. Yet. Instead, Oliver Latham was dressed up just like a commuter on a business day.

He wore an olive-colored poplin summer suit, a blue-and-white striped shirt, and a black string tie like the one he'd worn the night of the BashCon banquet. Maybe the same one, for all I knew. His shaven cheeks glistened from cologne. Put a briefcase in his hand (which, in fact, he produced before we left) and, but for the tie, he could have passed for any old-timer on his way to Wall Street.

After coffee we drove into the city, Latham with me in the Fiero and Squilletti trailing us. It was one of those steaming hot days, a haze of cloud and smog above, and I'd finally grasped that nothing was going to happen after all until Latham got the money.

Sam Wright met us high above the harbor, in the offices of Upton Fiduciary. Ms. Gwen Graw was waiting for us, too, with the relevant paperwork, but in a larger and fancier conference room than the one we'd sparred in the day before. This one had coffee and Danish and china cups and saucers and a large portrait painting of, I assumed, Pierce Upton I.

Whatever he knew or didn't, Sam Wright looked like he was attending a funeral. But Oliver Latham was in his element. He talked, joked, throughout the paper processing. He even made Ms. Graw smile. Then, finally, he took the check she held out to him, examined it, folded it, put it in his inside jacket pocket, patted his jacket to make sure, then thought better of it and took it out, stuck it in his briefcase, locked the briefcase. And put out his cigarette. And stood, a tall, papery figure, laughed out loud, coughed into a handkerchief, and, recovering, shook hands with Ms. Graw, with Sam Wright. Then he put a long arm around Sam Wright and hugged the short man awkwardly. And then turned to me, and I saw a defiant expression in his rheumy old eyes.

Because it's mine, I guessed he was saying. *Because I earned it.*

"Where're we going now, Revere?" he asked me.

"Uptown," I said.

We drove slowly. I kept braking in the traffic to make sure Squilletti was behind me but every time the Fiero slowed or stopped I thought now, now's the time if ever, now that he's got what he wanted.

But it didn't come. Not at the farm, no, nor during the night after the Counselor called back, and that much I understood. But not at the World Trade Center either, or coming down in the elevators from Upton Fiduciary, and not in the car, and not at the office, where the Counselor waited with Waller and Garvey and other representatives of the law, local and Catskills, complete with stenographers. And not during the long afternoon while Latham spilled it out for them, crime by crime, detail by detail, patiently.

I had it wrong, you see.

I'd thought one of two things: either he was going to make a run for it or he was going to try to kill himself. I'd expected it at the farm and he hadn't, but he didn't have the money yet. *It's mine*, he's said, *I earned it*, and in hindsight nothing was going to stop him from getting it.

But after . . . ?

Maybe he didn't run because he had no place to go. Maybe you get too old to run.

I thought he was wacko enough to do something drastic. He'd been wacko enough twice, why not a third time?

The point was, he didn't have to do anything drastic anymore. Drastic had already happened.

Putting it another way, which never occurred to me until we found it out: The reason he didn't kill himself—not that day and not in the days that followed—was, simply enough, that he knew he didn't have to.

CHAPTER
14

Oliver Latham, a.k.a. Viola T. Harmel, never stood trial.

Oliver Latham never so much as spent a night in jail.

With the proceeds of the Sow Fund, he had more than enough money to post a bond. And he enjoyed sufficient prestige and connection to convince two judges to let him out on bail—a rarity in murder cases. He also had enough money to pay attorneys who managed, one way and another, to get the trial dates postponed. It didn't hurt their endeavors either that he was a dying man.

Furthermore, the media mostly took his side. Somehow the fact that Raul Bashard had refused to permit the Sow Fund to be dissolved got translated into justification, sort of, for murder, while John Jameson, at the hands of the media, became a cheap homosexual blackmailer. At worst, Latham was portrayed as an embittered and possibly crazy old man, but also a great writer who'd never gotten his due. The literary press set about to rediscover him, and his publisher rushed through reprints of books that had been long forgotten.

252

And then there was Grace. Once the number-one suspect, now at eighteen the bereaved heiress, she gave interviews freely. She remembered the Latham of her childhood— "Uncle Ollie," she called him, as gentle and generous a man as she'd ever known. He had also been her father's closest friend. She had never understood what had driven them apart, and certainly, in spite of his confession, she couldn't begin to imagine what had led such a gentle man to commit murder. Even now with all the evidence in, and his confession, and even though she could never see him again, a part of her couldn't believe he'd done it.

Four months to the day after Raul Bashard's murder, Latham died in a Philadelphia hospital, of emphysema and allied complications, and taking certain secrets with him. He died alone, and his funeral was poorly attended. I know, because I went.

It was one of those gorgeous fall days in the country, the tree leaves yellowed and some of them red, a strong wind sweeping the meadows down the slope toward the little house Latham had lived in, where the old Beetle still stood, apparently unclaimed. I'd heard he'd bought back the farm, but whether the Babbidges were still in residence I couldn't tell. And more police, it seemed, than mourners, there and at the cemetery. I saw Deputy Roman at the cemetery, and he told me they'd expected quite a turnout, but only a dozen or so gathered at the graveside.

The only other person I recognized was Cyn Morgan, the artist. She wore a long, ankle-length velour coat and a little hat with a veil that made her look even shorter than she was. She avoided me like the plague.

As to why I went, well, you could say I'd developed a predilection for the funerals of the greats of science fiction and leave it at that.

There was more to it, of course.

There always is.

The weekend before, the auction had been held—a funeral of a different kind. . . .

But here, too, I'm ahead of the story.

* * *

Oliver Latham confessed on a Friday. The relationship between Grace Bashard and yours truly peaked that weekend.

As far as Grace was concerned, she was, she said, learning about love for the first time. I guess she was at that, but she was a quick study.

And as for me? Well, maybe I *was* old enough to be her father, but seventy-two hours in bed with Grace Bashard kind of reduced the age gap.

I must have said something to her about it.

I remember her calling me her dirty old man.

I remember that turning me on.

We went at it for a week or more. In between I gave my last depositions concerning the Bashard murders and tried to hold down my job. Grace thought that was stupid. We were going to have all the money in the world, she said. Enough to last us a lifetime. What did I have to work for? We could live in Florida, the Caribbean, Hawaii, anywhere we wanted to, so what did I have to work for? And why did I have to work for that dreary old crumb who did nothing but blow pipe smoke in your face and make you feel like you were two years old?

For a while—a week, more—she played housewife on the Upper West Side. She shopped, and tried to teach herself to cook. She cleaned up the mess she made in the kitchen and all the other messes. She rearranged the furniture, rearranged my clothes, and there were flowers in bottles on every available surface. Mostly we ordered in Hunan and fed each other in bed, out of cardboard containers.

Clearly it wasn't meant to last. But I helped things along. As follows:

I walked home from work that following Friday, across the park, on what must have been the hottest day of the summer. Even the sailboats in the pond were becalmed in the soggy sunlight, their sails wilted. People wore the scantiest of clothing the law would permit. The few joggers I saw, my onetime companions, had slowed to a walk. There was another drought warning, the fountains had been turned off, and you weren't supposed to use your air conditioners below seventy degrees, though nobody paid attention.

I bought cold beer at my local deli, iced white wine at the liquor store, the bottles sweating through the paper bags, and went upstairs out of the inferno. Grace met me at the door, wearing a bandanna in her hair and nothing else. She was bursting with excitement, among other things.

"Guess what I did today?" she bubbled at me. "You'll never guess! Guess what I did today?"

"All right," I said, shedding my clothes on the way to the shower, "I give up. What did you do today that I can't guess?"

"Never mind. If you can't guess, I'll tell you in bed."

We showered together, went to bed, and sometime later, she told me.

She'd bought an apartment was what she'd done. It was four rooms, in a building in the sixties, off Park Avenue, and we could move in as soon as the paperwork got done for the financing. The asking price had been a million dollars, but they'd accepted her bid of $825,000. Did I think she'd overpaid? It didn't matter. She'd have paid a million for it. Wait till I saw it. It was perfect. And I could walk to work, as long as I insisted on working for that crumb. And so on.

By the way, the crumb—the Counselor, that is—wasn't representing her anymore. She'd found another lawyer, one who understood what she wanted and didn't get in the way.

I guess I didn't react quickly enough. Or with the right enthusiasm. This was typical of me, typical of men. Whatever she did for herself, on her own, was no good, and I had to dump all over it. Well, she was tired of men who wanted to take care of her, tired of doing what she was told to. She didn't have to anymore. And if I was satisfied, satisfied with the shitty work I was doing, satisfied with the shitty way I lived, in this shitty apartment, in this shitty neighborhood, maybe that was okay for me, but did I think she had to be satisfied, too? Maybe I *was* too old for her, except for sex.

Even for sex. She hadn't thought so, she still didn't think so, but it was up to me. Strictly.

And so on, and so forth.

In hindsight, you could say she knew it wasn't going to happen between us beyond (so to speak) the first blush. In hindsight, you could say this buying the apartment was her way of telling me so. Of telling both of us so.

But there was more to it. Yes.

Turn to the middle of the night, one of those middle-of-summer nights when you hear the sirens even through the closed windows, and you wake up sticky in spite of the air-conditioning and, except for the stickiness, you're not sure whether you've been asleep or not.

She asked me if I was awake. Yes, I said, I was awake.

I lit up a cigarette in the darkness. I'd started smoking again.

"Why did you leave the door open for Latham?" I heard myself ask, in the darkness.

"Why did I *what*?" came her answer, from next to me in the bed.

"According to Latham's confession, the door to the suite was open. The only way it could have been open was for you to have left it open."

We'd been sleeping with a sheet over us. She'd been lying on her stomach. Now the sheet went off me and she was sitting up on her knees.

"Why are you bringing *that* up again?" she said, her voice startled. "What if I left the door open, how do I know? I was coming to you."

"Latham said he had a terrific argument with your father, about the Sow money. This was before the BashCon. He said that he'd planned to kill him then, if he got the chance. He got the chance all right." I reached over, turned the light on on the bedside table. "He came out into that corridor in the middle of the night, and he didn't have a key, and he didn't need one. The door was open. That's one hell of a coincidence."

I heard her intake of air. She brushed her hair away from her eyes, which had that puffy look from sleep.

"Why are you bringing this up *now*?" she repeated, punching the words out.

A good question, maybe.

"Because I've got to know," I said.

"Why don't you ask Ollie?"

"I did," I said.

"Well what did he say?"

"All he said was that the door was open."

"And that's not good enough for you?"

I stubbed out the cigarette, stood up.

"Not when your grandfather rewrote his will the day before, leaving it all to you no matter what happened to him."

"But I *told* you I didn't know about that."

"Did you?" I said. "Funny, I don't remember your telling me that."

"Well I *did*. I *know* I did!"

"Maybe you did. But that would be a hell of a coincidence, too, wouldn't it? A man rewrites his will the day before he dies, and *doesn't* tell his daughter, who stands to get all the benefit? Then he gets murdered in the night because his daughter just happened to leave the door open for his murderer?"

She didn't say anything, I gave her space, but I couldn't hear a thing. Like she was holding her breath.

"What're you getting at, Phil?" she said softly.

"What I'm getting at is that I think you helped him. I don't like thinking it, but I think you knew about Latham and the Sow Fund all along. It was on the computer: 'See Sow Fund.' It was you who erased the references to Viola T. Harmel, in the hate mail. You thought nobody would notice, and without it nobody would make the connection. I think that was part of your deal with him, that you'd set it up so that he could kill Raul. I think when you came out of the suite that night, you walked down the hall and woke him up before you got into bed with me. I was your alibi. And then you covered it up. If I didn't notice that the references to the Sow Fund had been erased, we'd never have linked him to it."

"Is that what Ollie said?"

It was my turn to suck air. Latham had already made his confession and signed it, and he'd confessed and signed because it didn't matter anymore to him. He'd gotten what he wanted. He had nothing to gain now by implicating anybody else. This I knew, and though it occurred to me to have another crack at him, the truth was that when I'd had the chance—the day and the night when we'd traded the Sow Fund for his confession—it simply hadn't occurred to me to ask.

And that was because Grace Bashard had gotten to me.

"It doesn't matter what he said, baby," I heard myself answer in the dim light. "I know what happened. What I can't finally figure out is why you did it. It wasn't just the money, was it?"

She seemed to shiver on the bed. She'd been holding herself together as tight as she could, but now, kneeling, the sheet flung back, her head down and hair down over her head, her body gleaming faintly, I saw her rock forward a little onto her fists, then back onto her toes and forward onto her fists, back and forth.

"You'll have to beat that out of me, Pablo," she said. "Come on, why don't you beat it out of me?"

Revelation time. She rocked forward onto her fists, and held the position. Her ass was up, her hair hanging, her breasts hanging.

And yes, it turned me on.

And yes, clearly, I wasn't the only one.

"Is that what *he* did to you?" I said hoarsely.

She turned her head back toward me, like an animal looking over its shoulder. Her face was red and puffy and stuck in a bitter grimace.

"What do *you* think?" was all she said.

It didn't end there, or neatly.

We went through withdrawal by messy stages, all the way down to the last messages she left on my machine after she'd moved out. I guess she'd realized I wasn't her answer. Maybe she'd known it all along. Maybe she strung it out so long just to make sure I wasn't going to tell anybody else what I knew but couldn't prove.

Maybe, maybe, and maybe.

Along the way I learned more about her life with her grandfather than there's a point in detailing. Suffice it to say that the way she told it she'd been a prisoner of a particular kind, and subject to particular punishments. The one that had finally triggered her, it seemed, had been the poisoning of the Doberman.

I'll leave it to the shrinks to state whether Latham had been her instrument of revenge, or liberation, or whatever.

What I was her instrument of is all too obvious. Call it Bashard's last laugh. Or next-to-last laugh.

As for me, I took off.

The summer's a quiet time in the legal profession. The courts close, the clients are mostly away, and attorneys with houses in the Hamptons are more there than here, leaving their staffs to man the phones. We open late on summer Mondays, close early on Fridays, and when I told the Counselor I wanted two consecutive weeks in August, he, for once, could think of no reason to turn me down. The way it worked out, I was gone only one week. I pointed the Fiero north, drove up the New England coast as far as the Canadian border, then turned around and came back. Along the way, I did what tourists do mostly. I went to the beach and went shopping. Give it another decade and that whole coast is going to be one long strip of outlet stores and ye olde gift shoppes, but even now there're more than enough to keep vacationing Americans consuming all summer long. When they're not baking in the sun or taking lobsters apart.

Come to think of it, I don't remember buying anything, and I didn't go into the water. What I did do was write out various versions of my report to the Counselor, in a string of motels all the way up past Bar Harbor, Maine. When I finally got it right, I turned the Fiero around and did the I-95 home. When I got to my apartment, the tape on my answering machine was empty.

* * *

"Erase it," the Counselor said. "Erase it, tear it up, do whatever you have to do. I want nothing in our files."

This was mid-week, in August. Ms. Shapiro and Roger LeClerc were gone, leaving Charlotte McCullough and me to mind the store. Plus Althea, the housekeeper, and Gorgeous, the cat. The Counselor's Wife was in the Hamptons, with the cocker bitch.

The Counselor sat at his desk in a short-sleeved shirt and bow tie, his jacket draped around the back of his chair. His desk was even more of a clutter than usual, but he seemed to be enjoying it. His gray hair was cut short for the summer, and he had a Hamptons tan that made him look about ten years younger.

"Why?" I said. "We at least should have a record of it, if nothing else. It's all true."

"And conjecture," he said.

"Some," I said. "But true conjecture."

That made him chuckle. He liked the sound of it, he said, repeating the words. A new legal concept, true conjecture.

I guess I wasn't in a funny mood, though. I guess he saw that.

"I thought I told you already, Phil," he said. "There's no Grace Bashard file. Besides, there's no way you could make any charges stick against her, you know that. Unless Latham wanted to, and as you point out, if he wanted to, he would already have done something about it."

"Maybe I could convince him," I said, though I was less than convinced myself.

"Do you really think so?"

I shook my head. But I couldn't let it go at that, not even then. And the business about the file caught me short. I remembered it from the beginning, from when I got back from Bashard's that first time.

"Why is there no Grace Bashard file?" I asked. "Why was there never supposed to be one?"

He shrugged.

"That's the way the client wanted it," he answered.

"*Bashard* wanted it?"

"That's right."

"But why?"

I guessed the answer, though, even as I asked the question. A horrible answer, and maybe if I'd lived inside Raul Bashard's skin all those years I'd have understood it. But not even then, I thought.

"I think he expected her to kill him," the Counselor said, "or try to. I think part of him wanted to make it hard for her. And part of him easy."

"But in either case, to protect her if she did?"

"That's right."

"Because of his guilt toward her, right? Because of what he'd done to her?"

The Counselor shook his head.

"I doubt that," he said. "Whatever he did or didn't do to her—and by the way, we'll never know how much of what she told you is truth and how much a disturbed young woman's fantasy—he wasn't a man to feel guilty about anything. No. All I know is that he was afraid of dying. Of dying slowly, that is."

"Then why in the hell did he want *me* there?" I said.

The Counselor smiled and ran his hand through his hair, front to back.

"A good question, Phil. Too bad we can't ask him now. I assume he panicked at the end, and flip-flopped back and forth. People do, you know, once they know they're going to die. Maybe he thought you'd deflect her. Or protect her, if you couldn't."

Which, I thought, is precisely what I'd done.

I didn't altogether buy his version. I felt like I had a dozen other questions to ask, more, and for once he gave me room. But the words wouldn't come, and we sat and stared at each other in the August quiet. I guess there was nothing more for him than to hand me back my report, in hard-copy form, and say: "Tear it up, Phil. Erase it from the file. The case is closed, let's be done with it."

Which he did, and which I did.

* * *

My last "official" act in the Bashard case was to represent the office at "the disposal at auction of the last worldly goods of Raul R. Bashard." So it was advertised, and the Counselor had acceded to the auction as the quickest way of moving Bashard's estate toward liquidation.

He offered to send someone else if I didn't want to go. Strangely, though, I wanted to.

The serious, big-bucks part took place in the main hall of the house, where folding chairs had been set up in rows and the auctioneer used a microphone to announce the lots. The hall was full. I recognized Varga, Sam Wright, Sidney Frankaman and Mr. and Mrs. Richard Brinckerhoff among the people I knew. There were bidders pointed out to me from university libraries and collections all over the country, and several from overseas. They sat sedately enough through the disposal of Bashard's cars, his works of art, furniture, furnishings and other memorabilia, which the auctioneer used as a kind of warm-up to the main event. But when the literary collections—the books, the magazines, the manuscripts—came under the gavel, a kind of crazy fever took them all. People stood on chairs so that their bids would be seen, and it was like a bull market bursting loose on Wall Street.

Big bucks, like I said.

The auction, all in all, brought in a seven-figure total. The damage wrought to the property in its aftermath ran allegedly into the hundreds of thousands, although the ultimate settlement figure reached between the new owners, the estate and the auction house's insurance company was in fact lower. I'd left before the worst of it, but even as I drove down the driveway toward the gates I could see people— kids mostly—running across the grounds in the fading light and more of them milling at the gates themselves, where the security guards had lost control and I had to keep the Fiero inching forward to get through.

A second, and posthumous, BashCon, I thought. But the extent of the carnage wasn't clear until the next day, after the police had shown up, made arrests and sealed off the grounds. In between, windows and doors had been smashed, the auctioned-off cars dismantled, pieces of fence, pieces of house, even clods of turf ripped up, dug out and carted away.

I watched it on the Sunday night news. The footage was extensive, taken largely after the fact, and the headline ran: BASHARD: THE CULT CONTINUES

Latham died the next week.

A month more passed, the leaves fell off the trees, the dark of late-November nights settled in on the city, and you could begin to smell traces of snow in the air.

I was leaving the office one Monday evening, and in a hurry, when a bundle of energy, force against counterforce, tackled me at the knees. It was Muffin, the cocker spaniel bitch, acting like I was the long lost friend she hadn't seen in a decade and dragging her leash as she jumped and pranced. I saw the Counselor's Wife rushing after her from the Park Avenue corner, yelling, and I grabbed at the dog's leash, caught it, then got pulled back toward her owner.

I hadn't seen the Counselor's Wife in some time.

"Hi, Phil!" She called, bending down to kiss the dog on the snout. She took the leash from me. "What do you think about it? I guess there's no stopping love, is there?"

For a second I thought she was teasing me about the dog, which she often did. But it wasn't that.

"Come on, Phil, tell me the truth," she said gaily, swirling her blonde hair. "What did you really think when you read it?"

"Read what?" I said.

"You did read the paper yesterday, didn't you? The society pages?"

No, I hadn't. In fact the society section was fairly low on my Sunday-paper priority list.

"Oh, God," the Counselor's Wife said. "You haven't heard, then?"

No, I guessed I hadn't.

She hesitated, as though trying to gauge what I'd make of it, whatever it was, then tossed her hair again.

264 / PETER ISRAEL

"Your girlfriend Grace, or ex-girlfriend . . . Grace Bashard? She's getting married. It was in the paper: '. . . of New
York and Palm Beach, daughter of the late Raul R. Bashard
. . .' I guess she bought something in Palm Beach, did you
know that? But guess who she's marrying!"

"I've no idea," I said.

"Robert Price!" she said. "Robert Price, wasn't that Bashard's bodyguard?"

"If it's the same one," I said.

"Well, of course it's the same one, silly!" Then, looking at
me closely: "God, Phil, you don't still care about her, do
you?"

I don't know what expression I had on. But inside I was
thinking: Price, too. Holy shit, we'd let Price walk away from
it, too. And in my mind's eye I saw that ceramic smile on the
dead writer's face.

"Come on, Phil," the Counselor's Wife was saying, "come
walk with us. I was both right and wrong about it, wasn't I?
We can talk about it."

"I can't," I said automatically, "I've got a date."

"A date?" She smiled prettily, then: "You never stop, do
you? Who's the lucky lady this time? What's her name?"

"Never mind," I said, but the dog by then was pulling her
in the other direction and I don't think she heard.

I stuck up my coat collar in the wind and headed west to
Laura Hugger's.